THE GATHERING STORM

COLIN SLATER

"The Gathering Storm," by Colin Slater. ISBN 1-58939-159-4 (softcover), 1-58939-160-8 (electronic).

Published 2002 by Virtualbookworm.com Publishing Inc., P.O. Box 9949, College Station, TX , 77842, US. ©2001, 2002 Wolf Tracer Studios Inc. All rights reserved. No part of this publication may be reproduced, stored in a retrieval system, or transmitted in any form or by any means, electronic, mechanical, recording or otherwise, without the prior written permission of Colin Slater.

TO TANSANTA

CHAPTER ONE

The forest of Fontainebleau was at its loveliest. The past winter had been exceptionally severe but now, towards the end of April, spring had come to northern France again. In the long rides the young grass made a carpet of emerald and the great trees were feathered, with tenderest green. The day was Sunday, the weather fine, the air balmy and the sky a palish blue.

No hunting, except by the King's packs, was ever permitted in the royal domain, and the only buildings in it were widely separated keepers' cottages. Once clear of the town, and the huge slate-gray Château with its many courts, gardens, promenades and lake, one might ride for miles without setting eyes on a human being. Only the occasional scurrying of an animal, and the faint, mysterious whispering of the branches overhead, broke the stillness.

Down one of the rides, deep in its solitude, a young man was riding his horse at a walking-pace. He was dressed with considerable elegance in the fashion of the year, 1789. His three-cornered hat was laced with gold, as were also his long-skirted dove-gray coat and embroidered waistcoat. His breeches and gauntlets were of the softest doeskin; his tall riding-boots polished to a mirror like brilliance. His brown hair was unpowdered, but elaborately dressed with side-curls above the ears and a neat queue tied with a ribbon at the back of his neck. He had a thinish, brown face, straight nose, mobile mouth and a good chin. He was twenty-one years of age, although he looked somewhat older.

At first sight a man might have put him down as a young gallant who had never fought outside a fencing school, but that impression was hardly in keeping with his sword-an old-fashioned weapon with a plain steel hilt entirely contradicting his otherwise foppish appearance.

Had anyone meeting him on his solitary ride spoken to him they would never have suspected from his reply that he was anything other than the young French nobleman that he appeared to be, because four years' residence in France while in his teens, and a natural flair for languages, had made him bilingual; ; but he was, in fact, the son of an English Admiral, and his name was Richard Blane.

However, he was not using his own name at the moment. On his return to France, after an absence of close on two years, he had again assumed the soubriquet that he had earlier adopted-that of M. le Chevalier de Cavasuto. So doing not only saved him the annoyance of being cheated by innkeepers and others as presumably a rich English milord', but for his present purpose it served him better to be thought a Frenchman.

For the past four days he had been living at the Auberge du Cadran Bleu in the little town of Fontainebleau, and he had spent the greater part of his time wondering how he could manage to get himself admitted to the private apartments of the Château.

It was in a further attempt to find a solution to that extremely knotty problem that he had hired a horse and was riding slowly through the forest on this April, afternoon ; for he had felt that two or three hours of complete solitude and concentration might produce the inspiration of which he stood so badly in need.

Like all the royal Palaces at that date anyone was at liberty to saunter about its grounds or walk through its great halls and galleries, even when the King and Queen were in residence-as Louis XVI and Marie Antoinette were now. They lived for most of the day in public and there was no bar to the curious coming to stare at them as they went from one part of the Palace to another, or even while they ate their food at State dinners. But it was quite a different matter to acquire the entrée to the royal circle, with the privilege of attending levees and mingling freely with the members of the Court.

To do so was Richard Blane's object in coming to Fontainebleau; in fact it was one of the main reasons for his return to France, and unless he could find some way to get on intimate terms with the Royal Family itself, or at least some of its most trusted advisers, the mission upon which he had been sent was doomed to failure. '

Two years earlier he had, partly by chance but also largely owing to his own wit and courage, been able to render a signal service to his country in providing the key to the successful outcome of some extremely delicate diplomatic negotiations.' It was then that Britain's twenty-nine-year-old Prime Minister, brilliant Billy Pitt, had realized the possibilities that lay in a young man who possessed his qualities of good birth, education and manners, coupled with a certain innocence of expression which covered considerable shrewdness and determination.

The Government of the day was dependent for its information about affairs at foreign Courts on its diplomatic representatives abroad and the spies they employed. But the former, while having the entrée to society in the capitals in which they served, were naturally greatly handicapped in obtaining particulars of secret policy through the very fact that they were Britain's representatives; and the latter, while valuable for securing purely military information, were not of the social status to penetrate the cabinets of Kings and the boudoirs of their mistresses.

Richard Blane, on the other hand, could both pass as a Frenchman and be received as an equal by the aristocracy of any country. So Mr. Pitt had decided to employ him as his personal secret agent and, in the previous year, had sent him to the Courts of Denmark, Sweden and Russia`. Now, after a short but hectic sojourn in England, the Prime Minister had charged him with further work in France.

His new mission was a delicate and nebulous one. It presented no apparent dangers or call for heroic measures, but needed considerable tact and the ability to form cool, unbiased judgments as to the real value of statements made by a great variety of people, most of whom were bitterly prejudiced. It was, in fact, to assess the probable outcome of the political ferment which was now agitating the whole French nation.

That drastic changes were about to take place no one could doubt. The centuries-old feudal system, of which the monarchy was the apex, had worked reasonably well in its day; but Cardinal Richelieu had destroyed the power of the great nobles and a generation later Louis XIV had turned them into little more than bejeweled lackeys by insisting that they should leave their estates permanently to add to the luster of his own setting at Versailles; so the monarchy had become absolute, with no restraint of any kind on the power that the Kings exercised over the whole nation.

The so-called Parliaments of Paris, Bordeaux and other great cities were no more than judicial assemblies, without power to make or alter laws, their function being only to register the royal edicts and conduct trials of special importance. The Monarch ruled through a number of Governors and attendants who again had no power to legislate but were high Civil Servants charged with administering the royal decrees in their respective provinces and collecting taxes. So the people had no legitimate outlet of any kind for their grievances, and had become entirely subject to the good or evil influences that a handful of men and women near the King, but incredibly remote from them, exerted on him.

Thus a situation had gradually developed in which new taxes were levied, restrictions placed on commerce, treaties made, armies conscripted and wars declared, all without nobles, clergy or people having the least say in these matters which concerned them so vitally.

Richard Blane had had an unusually good opportunity of absorbing the background of the situation, owing to the variety of his experiences during his four years in France as a youth. He had for over a year occupied a privileged position in the household of a great nobleman in Paris but he had for still longer lived with a middle-class family in a provincial city. He had for some months enjoyed the comfort of a luxurious château buried in the heart of the country, but he had also spent many weeks tramping. from village to village through northwestern France as the assistant of a poor quack doctor. So he knew that discontent at the present state of things was far from being confined to one class.

He had seen the miserable mud-walled, windowless hovels of the peasantry and knew the many impositions, which made their lives so hard. There was the forced labor, often at seasons most inconvenient to themselves, that they were compelled to give on the King's highways; the Government's control of grain, which forced them to sell at a fixed price, so that they were debarred from making a good profit; the petty dues that they had to pay on going through toll-gates whenever they moved a mile or so from their homes, and a great variety of small but irksome taxes which provided the main incomes of the local nobility and clergy.

Yet he also knew that many of them were by no means so abjectly poverty-stricken as they appeared. The fact that few of even the better farmhouses had glass in their windows was not because their owners could not afford to pay for it; the reason was that their taxes were assessed quite arbitrarily on their apparent capacity to pay, and this evil system drove them to conceal every sou they made above their bare living expenses instead of using the money for the betterment of their own condition.

Deplorable as was the state of the peasantry, the great bulk of the nobility felt that they had equally good grounds for complaint.

By tradition only the profession of arms was open to them, and that was so ill-paid that during the past two centuries they had gradually become impoverished through having to sell much of their property to equip themselves to fight in France's wars. The thrifty peasants had already acquired over a third of all the cultivatable land in France, and hundreds of noble families now had nothing left but a dilapidated château and a few acres of grazing ground.

Yet neither class had any sympathy for the woes of the other. The nobles-some of whom eked out a miserable existence on as little as twenty-five Louis a year-knew that their tenants cheated them whenever they could. The peasants bitterly resented the freedom of the nobility from all forms of taxation, and grudged every sou they had to surrender in that variety of petty dues, which made up the sole source of income of their masters. Neither the uncouth, ragged tillers of the soil, nor the proud, out-at-elbows country gentry, had collectively any animus against the Court; but both were sullen, discontented, and ready to welcome any change which might lead to a betterment of their lot.

It was in the cities and towns that the real trouble was brewing. The growth of industry had produced in all of them a slum population that recognized no individual master. Their poverty was appalling and in times of scarcity they died by the thousand

so they were inflammable material for the fiery words of any agitator.

In the towns, too, the greatest change had occurred since the breakdown of the feudal system. With it had passed the mediaeval thralldom of the Church, leading to freer thought and the spread of secular education. An extremely numerous middle-class, including thousands of respectable artisans as well as professional men and wealthy merchants, had grown up in them. It was they who most bitterly resented the privileged position of the idle, arrogant nobility. Moreover, for half a century past, many of them had been reading the controversial works of the political philosophers, and this had led to an almost universal demand among them that they should be given some share in the government of their country.

Finally, it was the deplorable state into which the finances of France had fallen in recent years, coupled with a succession of bad harvests that had inflicted grievous hardship on the poor. both in town and country, which had led to a nation-wide agitation for a complete overhaul of the machinery of State.

Even when Richard had fled from France twenty months earlier,

as the result of a duel, the popular clamor for reform had reached such a pitch that the government was seriously concerned by it.

That spring of 1787, so desperate had the financial situation become that the King had resorted to an expedient which none of his predecessors had been forced to adopt for over a hundred and fifty years-the summoning of an Assembly of Notables at Versailles to discuss ways and means of re-establishing the nation's credit. But instead of accepting their advice his Ministers had endeavored to use them as support for a new patchwork of ineffective measures. The nobles and the higher clergy, of which the Notables were almost entirely composed, had become openly resentful, and the Parliament of Paris had refused to register the new edicts. Thereupon the King had temporarily exiled the Parliament to Troyes and dissolved the Assembly; so, far from any good having come out of this meeting, the grievances of the nation had received the widest possible publicity, which led to still more violent agitation against the incompetent Government.

For a further year the ancien régime had been bolstered up by one expedient after another, but by the summer of '88, faced with an empty treasury, the King had been driven to dismiss his principal Minister, the vain and ineffectual Lomenie de Brienne, Archbishop of Toulouse, and recall the Swiss banker, Monsieur Necker, who, since he held the most liberal views, had the confidence of the public. It had then been decided to give way to the insistent demand for the calling of an Etats General-the- nearest thing France could be said to have to an assembly truly representative of the nation.

As a States General had not been convened since 1614 many months had elapsed since the decision to call one, while innumerable questions of procedure were argued by a second Assembly of Notables, and arrangements made for the election of clergy, nobles and commoners to the Three Estates which it comprised; but at last all these matters had been settled and the deputies were to meet at Versailles in the coming month.

The hopes placed in the outcome of this meeting were many and varied. The King hoped it would find him a . way out of his financial difficulties without loss of his authority, the people that it would lead to a reduction of their taxes, Monsieur Necker that it would result in his increased prestige, and both the bourgeoisie and the majority of the nobles and clergy that out of it would emerge some form of constitutional government.

But until it actually met one man's guess was as good as another's. It might -become a permanent institution on the lines of the British Parliament, or it might be summarily dismissed after a few ineffectual sessions, as had been the Assembly of Notables. It was to assess the most likely possibility that Richard Blane had been sent to France, and, further, to form a well-grounded opinion as to what would follow in either case.

If the Estates were abruptly dismissed, would that lead to open rebellion-or even civil war? If so was it likely or unlikely that Louis XVI would succeed in holding down his rebellious subjects? Was there any likelihood of him granting his people a Constitution? If that occurred and the Estates became a permanent body with legislative powers, who would dominate it Necker or some other? And would whoever it might be incline to friendship or enmity with Britain? All this and much more Mr. Pitt was most anxious to know, so that as the situation developed he might adjust his policy accordingly.

Richard had just spent a fortnight in Paris. He had looked up a number of old acquaintances and made many new ones; he had talked with innumerable people in cafés, shops and places of entertainment. Having lived for `so long in France he already knew that the average Englishman's belief, that the French were a nation of bloodthirsty cut-throats dominated by a leaven of fastidious but decadent and unscrupulous aristocrats, was far from the mark; and that in reality the individuals of the two races were inspired in their private lives by very similar thoughts and feelings. But on his return to the French capital he was very soon conscious of two things.

Firstly, although he had thought himself so well informed at the age of nineteen, how abysmally ignorant he had really been upon a great variety of matters. Secondly, that a quite staggering change had taken place in the mentality of the French people.

Previously, with the exception of one in a thousand, they had given their whole minds to business and pleasure, regarding politics as a thing apart that concerned only the King and his Ministers: so that however much they might deplore the state into which their country had fallen it was futile for them to think about it, since it was quite impossible for them to influence the future course of events. But now, with the extraordinary innovation of being given the opportunity to elect representatives who would voice their opinions, politics had entered like a virus into the blood of the whole race. They were like a child with a new toy, and wherever he went people were discussing in a most heated fashion the forthcoming meeting of the States General, the excellencies of Monsieur Necker or the iniquities of the `Austrian Woman', as they now called the Queen. It was therefore easy for him to gather a consensus of opinion and his unobtrusive activities had soon led him to three definite conclusions

That the people of Paris were not in the main antagonistic towards the King or the monarchy, as such ; but they were towards the Queen and a continuance of absolutism. That there would be serious trouble if the King dismissed the States with nothing accomplished. And that His Highness the Duc d'Orléans was sailing very near treason in some of his measures to gain popularity for himself at the expense of the Court and his cousin the King.

From the provincials he met he gathered that the elections had set the whole country in a ferment, and that opinion in the big cities, particularly Marseilles and Lyons, was running nearly as strongly in favor of forcing some definite concession from the King as it was in Paris; but a tour of the provincial cities to verify these possibly biased statements would have been a lengthy undertaking, and he had felt that in any case feeling in them could have little influence on events during the opening sessions of the States. On the other hand the much-abused Court might yet have some strong cards up its sleeve to play in an emergency, so he had decided that his next step must be an attempt to ascertain its real strength and disposition.

He needed no telling that it was one thing to lounge about Paris listening to any idler who cared to air his views and quite another to become acquainted with those of the King and his advisers; so on his arrival at Fontainebleau, five nights before, he had been very conscious that only then had his real mission begun, and from the first he had been extremely perplexed how to set about it.

Short of some unforeseen stroke of fortune, or the exercise of an ingenuity which seemed to have entirely deserted him in these past few days, the only means of securing the entrée to the royal circle was the normal one of being formally presented at the French Court; and during his previous stay in France his only visits to Versailles had been in the guise of a confidential secretary bringing papers to his master, the Marquis de Rochambeau, when that nobleman occupied his apartment in the Palace overnight.

Any traveling Englishman of good family could easily arrange for the British Ambassador to present him, but it was obviously impossible for Richard to do so and at the same time preserve his incognito. To abandon it would, he felt, be to throw away his best card for finding out the true situation at the very opening of the game: although to maintain it at Court would entail a certain risk. as the de Rochambeau family knew him to be English.

However, he had made careful inquiries before leaving Paris and learned that the old Marquis had for the past year or more retired to his estates in Brittany, his son, Count Lucien, was with his regiment in Artois, and the beautiful Athénais, whom he had loved so desperately, was also living in Brittany with her husband, the Vicomte de la Tour d'Auvergne. There remained the factor that a number of the Marquis's friends would also almost certainly remember him, but he doubted if any of them had chapter and verse about his antecedents and felt reasonably confident that he would be able to fob off any inconvenient questions concerning his past with a convincing story.

So, having weighed the pros and cons of the matter, he had decided to continue using his soubriquet of M. le Chevalier de Cavasuto, thus allowing everyone to assume that he was a Frenchman, but to leave himself an open door in case of trouble by refraining from any definite statement that he was one. He was still far from happy in his mind about this uneasy compromise, but felt that it was the best at which he could arrive for the moment, and that it would be time enough to develop a more definite policy, according to events, if, and when, he could devise a way to be received behind those golden doors.

To walk in to a reception without knowing anyone there to whom he could address a single word would be to invite discovery and expulsion if not actual arrest. So he had felt that his best hope lay in making the acquaintance at his fashionable inn of some well-placed courtier who would in due course invite his company to a levee or entertainment, on the assumption that he had already been presented; for, once inside, it was a hundred to one against the King remembering if he was one of the thousands of young nobles who had been presented to him in their teens or not.

But the trouble was that he had found no stool-pigeon suitable for such a maneuver staying at the inn ; neither had one appeared since his arrival, and it looked as if he might kick his heels there for weeks before one did. Moreover, frequent walks in the grounds of the Château and many hours spent lounging about its long, lofty corridors had equally failed to produce the type of chance acquaintance that he was seeking.

The factor that he had failed to take into his calculations when making this somewhat vague plan on his way from Paris was the election of Deputies to the States General. It was not only the People who were electing candidates to represent them in the Third Estate, but the First and Second-clergy and nobles-were

not to sit by right of their Episcopal ranks and hereditary titles ; they too were to elect representatives from their own Orders. In consequence, for the first time in generations, nearly the whole nobility of France had gone to the provinces, where they were either intriguing to get themselves sent to Versailles as Deputies or supporting the candidates they favored in their districts; so the Court and Fontainebleau were practically deserted.

Richard had been riding for well over an hour and, cudgel his wits as he would, could still see no way out of his difficulty, when up the long ride through the greenwood he saw a horseman coming towards him at a gentle canter. As the approaching figure drew nearer he could see it to be that of a lanky gentleman with narrow shoulders and a long, lean face, who appeared to be in his middle thirties. He was well mounted on a powerful bay but his dress, although of rich materials, was too flashy to be in good taste.

As the two horsemen came abreast both gave the casual nod which is habitual to strangers passing one another in the country, and as they did so each looked straight into the other's eyes for a moment without either showing any sign of recognition. Richard was still deeply absorbed by his own problem, and it was only after the lanky man had cantered on for a hundred yards or so that he began to wonder vaguely where he had seen that lantern jawed countenance before. ·

Having gazed at it only a few moments since from less than a dozen feet away it was easy to recall the man's quick, intelligent brown eyes, his full, sensual mouth, slightly receding chin, and the small scar on his left cheek that ran up to the corner of his eye, pulling the lower lid down a little and giving him a faintly humorous expression.

For a good five minutes Richard's mind, now fully distracted from its task, strove to link up those features with some memory of the past. His thoughts naturally reverted to the time when he had lived at the Hôtel de Rochambeau in Paris, and the many nobles who used to throw him a nod or a smile when they came there to see his master, but he did not think, somehow, that the lean-faced man was a noble, in spite of his fine horse and expensive clothes. After a little he tried to thrust the matter from his mind as of no importance; but the lean face would persist in coming back, so he began to range over the public dance-places and the inns that he had frequented while in Paris.

Suddenly something clicked in Richard's brain. Upon the instant he tightened his rein, turned his surprised mount right about and set off up the glade at a furious gallop. The fellow's name was Etienne de Roubec and he styled himself M. de Chevalier, but Richard thought his right to the title extremely dubious. He had met de Roubec at an inn in Le Havre on the very first night he had spent in France; but that was now nearly six years ago, and the Chevalier had then been a seedy-looking, down-at-heel individual in a threadbare red velvet coat.

As Richard urged his mare on over the soft, springy turf he was cursing himself for the time he had taken to identify his old acquaintance. He had a score to settle with de Roubec and the angry determination to call the fellow to account that now surged up in him seemed to have lost nothing of its violence during the five years and nine months since they had last met. His only fear was that as they had passed one another going in opposite directions and de Roubec had been moving at a canter he might, in the past seven or eight minutes, have turned down a side glade and ridden along it so far that it would prove impossible to find and overtake him.

Breasting the slight rise with a spurt, Richard peered anxiously forward along the downward slope. It stretched for nearly a mile but de Roubec was not to be seen. He might easily have ridden that far in the time and passed out of sight round the distant bend, so Richard rode on at full tilt. On reaching the bend he found that the ride continued for only a short way then ended in a wide clearing where four other rides met. Hastily he cast about from one to another; of de Roubec there was no sign, but up one of the rides a carriage was approaching.

While he was still frantically wondering which ride de Roubec had taken the vehicle entered the clearing. It was a closed carriage drawn by four fine grays which were moving at a small trot. Evidently it was the equipage of some wealthy person, but there was no coat of arms decorating the panels of its doors and the coachman, as well as the footman who stood on the boot clinging to straps at its back, were both dressed in plain, sober liveries.

As it passed Richard caught a brief glimpse of its interior through the open window. Two women were seated inside; both wore their hair dressed high in the fashion of the day and upon the coiffure of each reposed an absurd little be flowered straw hat tilted rakishly forward; and both of them were masked.

In Paris, or any other city, there was at that time nothing at all unusual about a lady unaccompanied by a cavalier wearing a black silk mask while she drove through the streets, either by night or day. The custom had originated as a form of protection for young and attractive gentlewomen from the unwelcome attentions of street gallants, but it had proved such a boon to ladies wishing to make their way unrecognized to secret rendezvous with their lovers that, in this century, when illicit love affairs were the fashion, the practice had continued to flourish. But it struck Richard as most surprising that two ladies should wear masks while taking a drive through the almost deserted forest of Fontainebleau in the middle of the afternoon.

As he stared after them with swiftly awakened curiosity, his glance fell upon some fresh hoof-marks plainly outlined on a muddy patch to one side of the track that the carriage had taken. Unless some other solitary horseman had recently passed that way they could only have been made by de Roubec's bay. With fresh hope of catching his quarry. Richard set spurs to his mount and cantered on in the wake of the mysterious ladies.

Some three hundred yards from the glade the ride curved sharply. The carriage was just about to round the bend as Richard came up behind it. Guiding his mare a little to the left, he made to pass. As he did so he saw that a quarter of a mile ahead there was apparently another clearing. A giant oak rose in solitary splendor from the place where the center of the track would otherwise have been, and immediately beneath it, quietly sitting on his horse, was de Roubec.

The second Richard caught sight of the Chevalier he dropped back behind the carriage. The fact that de Roubec had halted under the giant oak suggested that he had come there to keep a secret rendezvous with the masked ladies. From the outset Richard had realized that de Roubec's mount was much faster than his own hired hack, and had feared that if the Chevalier thought himself pursued he might easily use the superior speed of his bay to escape an unwelcome encounter. Therefore it seemed to him now that his best hope of getting within speaking distance of his quarry unseen lay in continuing on in the wake of the carriage.

As he trotted along, crouched low over his mare's neck so that his hat should not be visible to de Roubec above the line of the carriage roof, he feared every moment that the footman perched on the boot would turn and see him. But the hoof-beats of his mare were lost in those of the four grays, and, even when they pulled up under the great oak, the man did not glance behind him. Like a well-trained servant he instantly leapt from his stand and ran round to the side of the carriage to open its door for his mistress.

As he did so Richard slipped from his saddle to the ground. For a moment he stood there, holding his mare by the bridle; but she was a quiet old nag and, seeing that she at once started to nibble the grass of the track, he let her go, then stepped forward and peered cautiously from his hiding-place.

De Roubec, hat in hand, was bowing low over his horse's neck. One of the ladies was leaning out of the carriage door. In her hand she was holding out to him a fat packet. Richard had himself once entrusted a fat packet to Roubec, with dire results. At the sight of the present scene the memory of all that he had suffered in consequence by placing his trust in the Chevalier smarted like an open wound. On the instant he decided that he would not stand by and see this unknown lady tricked as he had been. But if he was to prevent it immediate action was called for; the second de Roubec saw him he might snatch the packet, gallop off with it and be lost for good.

With one swift, well-practiced movement Richard drew his long sword. At the same instant he sprang forward. De Roubec was just taking the packet from the masked lady and each still held a corner of it. Simultaneously both let out a gasp of amazement at Richard's totally unexpected appearance. As they stared at him, transfixed by surprise, his sword gashed in an unerring lunge and the tip of the bright blade passed through the center of the flat parcel.

He gave one upward jerk of his strong wrist and the packet slipped from between their fingers. Holding it on high he cried to de Roubec: 'You have forgotten me, Chevalier, but I have not forgotten you and I mean to slice off your ears in payment for what you owe me.'

'Who . . . who are you, Monsieur?' gasped de Roubec.

During their swift exchange the lady had emerged from the carriage. She was standing now upon the lowest of the folding steps that had been let down outside its doors. Richard saw at a glance that she was tallish with a mature but slim figure. As she drew herself up the additional height lent her by the step, coupled with her high headdress, gave her the appearance of towering over him. Next second he caught the angry flash of bright blue eyes through the slits in her mask, as she exclaimed impetuously

'Monsieur How dare you interfere in my affairs! And do you not know that it is a criminal offence to draw a sword in-....................

She never finished her sentence, breaking it off abruptly as a quick warning cry of 'Madame I pray you have a care' came in French, but with a strong foreign accent, from her companion who was still inside the vehicle.

But the lady on the step had already said too much to preserve her incognito. On several occasions in the past Richard had seen the determined chin, slightly protruding lower lip, and delicate but imperial nose. Her uncompleted sentence, pronounced with such icy dignity, had given him the clue to her identity, and he knew that she had meant to end it with the words `in my presence'.

Within a second his stupefaction was overcome by a wave of glowing elation. Where his wits had failed him it seemed that the goddess Fortune had dealt him a hand of her highest cards, and that he had now only to play them properly to be received at Court on the most favorable terms.

By preventing the packet from being delivered to the scoundrel de Roubec, he had every reason to believe that he had rendered a most valuable service to no less a person than Marie Antoinette, Queen of France.

CHAPTER TWO
THE MASKED LADIES

Richard still held the packet high above his head spitted on the point of his sword, so he was in no situation to make a graceful obeisance; but he could, and did, sweep off his hat with his free hand, lower his sword to the ground and go down on one knee before the Queen.

`I see you know me, Monsieur,' she said coldly. That makes your conduct even more inexcusable!

'I did not recognize Your Majesty until you spoke,' he replied in quick protest.

`Then I excuse your having drawn your sword, but not your interference.' She spoke more calmly now. `Rise, Monsieur, and give that packet to the gentleman to whom I was handing it, instantly.'

Richard stood up, removed the packet from the point of the sword, and sheathed his blade; but he made no movement to obey her last command. Instead, he said: `At the risk of incurring a further degree of Your Majesty's displeasure I was about to

add that had I recognized you when first I came up 1 would still leave acted as I did.'

`What mean you by this fresh impertinence, Monsieur?' Her voice was high and sharp again.

It was not the first time that Richard had been called upon to talk with royalty. In the preceding year he had held several long conversations with King Gustavus III of Sweden, and others of a far more intimate character with that bold, cultured, licentious woman Catherine the Great of Russia; so he knew very well that :t was regarded as a most scandalous breach of etiquette to ask any sovereign a direct question. But his experience had taught him that, although crowned heads showed themselves to their subjects only as beings moving in an almost god-like aura of pomp and splendor, they were, behind it all, just as human as other people; and that provided they were treated with the respect which was their due, they responded much more readily when talked to naturally than with slavish obsequiousness. So with a wave of his hand towards de Roubec, who, still sitting his horse, was staring at him with an expression of puzzled anxiety, he said

`Madame, I pray you pardon my temerity, but what do you know of this man? I'd take a big wager that you know little or nothing.'

To put such a question to the Queen of France was a bold gamble, but it came off. She was so taken by surprise that she overlooked the impertinence and replied with her usual impetuosity: `Then you would win your wager, Monsieur; for I have never seen him before. I know only that he was recommended as a trustworthy courier to carry a letter of some importance for me.'

`Then I beg Your Majesty to excuse me from obeying your last command,' cried Richard, swiftly following up his advantage. 'I know the fellow for a rogue. He is unfitted to be entrusted with the scrapings of a poor-box, let alone a weighty dispatch from your own august hand. Though, when I first came on the scene, I thought 'twas a package of jewels that you were handing him.'

`Why so?' asked the Queen, in fresh astonishment.

'Madame, in your own interests I crave your indulgence to relate an episode from my past, which is highly relevant to this present matter'

'Do so, Monsieur. But be brief.'

Richard bowed. `I thank Your Majesty, and in advance swear to the truth of what I am about to say. I am of noble birth upon my mother's side, but when I was a lad I decided to go out into the world and pick up a living as best I could, rather than be sent to sea. When I ran away from home my purse was lined with near r twenty . . ' He had been about to say guineas, but swiftly substituted the word 'Louis' and continued: 'But various expenses had reduced that sum to no more than a handful of silver by the time I entered the city of Le Havre.'

At the naming of the city de Roubec started so violently that he unintentionally rowel led his horse. Throwing up its head the mettlesome bay started to stamp its hoofs in a restless dance, and for the next few moments its rider had all he could do to control it.

Richard had been watching for the effect of his words and now pointed an accusing finger at him, exclaiming: `See, Madame! He has recognized me at last, though, 'tis small wonder that he took so long to do so after all these years; or that I, after passing him a mile back in the forest this afternoon, took several minutes to identify the ill-favored countenance of this gaudily clad popinjay, for those of the outcast-elbows rogue who cheated me so long ago.'

'Keep to your story, Monsieur,' interjected the Queen.

Again Richard bowed. 'On arriving in Le Havre, Your Majesty, I went to a poor inn on the quays. There, this Chevalier de Roubec scraped acquaintance with me. He accounted for the shoddiness of his attire by telling me that he had had his pocket picked of a considerable sum, and that the landlord of the inn had seized his wardrobe as security for the payment of his reckoning; but that he was the son of a Marquis who had great estates in Languedoc and a position of importance near the person of the King, so he would soon be in funds again. But that is by the way. Suffice it that, being but a boy and entirely lacking in experience of the ways of such rogues, I believed him and thought him my friend.'

'He lies!' broke in de Roubec hotly. He had now quieted his horse, and leaning forward across its neck was glaring down with mingled fear and anger at Richard. 'I give Your Majesty my word that 'tis ail a tissue of falsehoods. He has mistaken me for some other.'

'Be silent!' Marie Antoinette rebuked the interruption sharply, and signed to Richard to continue.

Obediently he took up his tale. 'I have told you, Madame, that I was by then near out of funds myself, bud. I had as asset, which I counted on to protect me from the pinch of poverty for a year at least. Before I left home a dear friend-one in fact whom I looked on as closer than a sister-knowing my intention, forced upon me a collection of gold trinkets. They were old-fashioned things and she had better jewels; but they were of considerable value and would, I think, have fetched some four hundred Louis.

This villain took advantage of my trust in him to persuade me to let him help me dispose of them. Then, Madame, he disappeared with the entire collection, leaving me, a boy of fifteen and a half, near destitute in a strange city where I knew not a soul.'

"Tis a lie ! A vile calumny!' de Roubec broke out again.

'It is the truth!' snapped Richard. `And I thank God that seeing you again today enabled me to come on the scene in time to prevent Her Majesty from placing her faith in so treacherous a viper. I doubt not that you meant to ride to Paris and sell her letter for the highest price you could get for it from her enemies.'

The Queen paled under her rouge, but her voice was firm as she addressed de Roubec. 'Old as the charge is that is brought against you, Monsieur, it still calls for full investigation. If in due course 'tis proven, 'twas a most despicable act to so despoil a child, leaving him a prey to every ill that infests the gutters of our great cities; and for it I promise that you shall see the inside of a prison for longer than you have enjoyed your ill-gotten gains. But His Majesty is the best judge of all such matters and he shall hear the case. I am now about to return to the Château. 'Tis my will that you should follow behind my carriage.'

She then turned to Richard and asked

`What is your name, Monsieur?'

'Cavasuto, may it please Your Majesty,' he replied with a bow.

'Then you, too, Monsieur Cavasuto, will follow us back to Fontainebleau. If your story proves false you will have cause to rue it, but if it is true you will not find me ungrateful for the service you have rendered me. In the meantime I charge you to say naught of the encounter to anyone.'

Marie Antoinette had scarcely finished speaking when de Roubec's horse threw up its head with a whinny and began to prance again. Richard guessed immediately that this time the false Chevalier had spurred his mount with deliberate intent, and he sprang forward to catch the bridle. But he was a second too late. De Roubec swung the bay round and let it have its head. In an instant it was thundering away across the turf.

'Stop!' cried the Queen. 'Stop! If you disobey me it will be at your peril,"
But de Roubec only waved his left arm in a vague gesture, which might have
signified that he had lost control of his animal, and galloped away down one of
the rides.

With a swift movement the Queen thrust a little. silver whistle between
her lips and blew a high, piercing blast upon it.

Richard, meanwhile, had run to his mare and thrown himself into the
saddle; but, even as he did so, he knew perfectly well that she had no chance
of overtaking de Roubec's powerful bay. Nevertheless, he was just about to set
spurs to her when the Queen motioned him to desist, and said: `Remain here,
Monsieur. I have better mounts than yours to send in pursuit of that rogue.'

Her words gave Richard the clue to her use of the whistle. She must, he
now guessed, have had an escort following her carriage at a distance. The next
moment his guess was confirmed, as he dismounted from his horse, and the
footman took it from him, two gentlemen came galloping into the clearing.

`Messieurs!' the Queen hailed them, pointing in the direction de Roubec
had taken: `I pray you pursue and bring back to me the man in a coat of purple
satin who has just disappeared down yonder ride.'

As-they dashed after the fugitive she turned back to Richard. For the first
time since they had met her voice was gracious and she smiled. as she said

'Monsieur Cavasuto, the flight of him whom you accuse is a sure sign of
guilt. In my youth I was a passable horsewoman myself, although my
preceptors, Madame de Noailles, would not allow me to ride as much as I
wished from the absurd notion that it would make me fat. Yet I know enough
of the art to be certain that the rascal incited his mount to bolt and even then
could have checked it had he so wished.'

Richard gave her smile for smile and seized upon the personal note. `I
have heard it said that Your Majesty nicknamed that old lady Madame
L'Etiquette ; and that once when you had a fall from a donkey you declared
laughingly to your companions that you would not rise from the ground until
Madame de Noailles could be brought to demonstrate the correct procedure for
assisting a Dauphine of France to her feet.'

Marie Antoinette gave a little laugh, then the smile faded from her lips:
but she regarded Richard kindly as she shook her head. 'I know not where you
heard the story, but in the main 'tis true, Monsieur; and it recalls memories of
happier times than these. I was then but the carefree girl-wife of the heir to
France, whereas I am now its Queen, with many troubles. By your knowing
that man for a rogue today, and acting as you did, it seems that you have saved
me from yet another matter for grievous worry. In what way can I reward
you?'

Taking his three-cornered hat from under his arm, Richard swept it
almost to the ground; then, drawing himself up, he replied

`This meeting with your gracious Majesty is in itself reward enough, and
if I have been of some small service I count that an additional privilege. But if,
Madame, your generosity prompts you to honor me further, then 'tis simply

done:

`Tell me your wish, Monsieur:

`It is to have some further opportunity of distracting Your Majesty's mind for a little from these troubles of which you speak. You listened with sympathy and interest to my tale of being robbed and left near penniless in Le Havre as a boy. Since then I have traveled in England, Holland, Denmark, Sweden and Russia, and in those countries it has been my lot to meet with many adventures both grave and gay. I am of independent means and crave no pension; but if you would grant me the privilege of unobtrusive attendance at your Court, and send for me from time to time when affairs of State weigh heavily upon your mind, I believe that I could dispel your gloom and make you laugh again as I did just now by mentioning the episode of the donkey. And if I could do that I should count myself happy indeed.'

'Oh, please, Madame!' The soft foreign voice came again from inside the carriage. `I pray you accede to his request. I am agog to know how he fared after he had been robbed of the jewels which were his only fortune.'

The Queen half turned towards her lady-in-waiting as she said

`And so you shall, child.' Then she smiled again at Richard, and added: 'Monsieur, your request is truly a modest and unselfish one. I grant it willingly.'

As Richard bowed his thanks he felt that he had every reason to congratulate himself, for his quick wits had enabled him to turn his stroke of luck to the best possible advantage. More, it seemed that Fortune had granted him yet another favor in his tale having caught the interest of the still barely glimpsed lady inside the carriage ; so that not only had he secured the permission to present himself at Court, but had also secured an unknown ally who would remind the Queen about him, and ensure his being sent for in order to hear more of his story.

His only serious concern now was as to what lies he might be forced to tell if he meant to keep up the pretence of being a Frenchman, as he knew only too well that one lie had a horrid way of leading to another until one found oneself enmeshed in a highly dangerous net of falsehood. Loath as he was to disclose the fact that he was a foreigner, he was beginning to wonder if the game of continuing in his incognito would, in the long run, prove worth the candle.

After a brief silence the Queen remarked: 'My gentlemen seem a long time in bringing back that rogue.'

'He was exceptionally well mounted, Madame; Richard gave a little shrug. 'And he had several minutes' start. So I fear it might well be an hour before they succeed in riding him down.'

'In that case, since the afternoon is fine, and it is pleasant here, let us sit for a while on the grass.'

As the Queen stepped down on to the ground her footman sprang to life, and running round to the boot got from it some thick rugs which he spread out at the foot of the giant oak. While he was doing so the lady-in-waiting descended from the carriage and, seeing her mistress now remove her mask, followed suit.

She proved to be a young woman of about twenty-two with lustrous black hair and an olive complexion. Her eyes were a velvety brown, her nose aquiline, her cheeks thin and her chin long. Her arms were well modeled and her hands were small with sensitive, tapering fingers. She was medium tall but on the thin side for her height. So considered on all counts by the standards of the day she would have been considered passably good-looking, but no great beauty. She had, however. one feature which made her face, once seen. unforgettable. To either side of the space above her arched nose dark eyebrows grew to nearly half an-inch in depth, then gradually turning upwards they tapered away to vanishing points at her temples.

Richard put her down at once as of Latin blood. and thought that he had never before seen hair of such exceptional blackness. But perhaps that was partly to be accounted for by its intense contrast with that of the Queen; for when Marie Antoinette first came to Court her hair had been so like spun gold that. long after her death, silks of an exquisite golden hue were still described as cheveux de la Reine.

As the olive-skinned young woman removed her mask, the Queen said to Richard: 'Monsieur Cavasuto, I present you to the Señorita d'Tansanta. When the Señorita's father was recalled to Madrid after having represented his country for many years at our Court, he was kind enough to let me retain her among my ladies for a while. It is not the least of my sorrows that she too will now soon be leaving me.'

'You are indeed unfortunate, Madame, to lose so charming a companion,' Richard murmured, making a gallant leg in response to the Señorita's grave curtsy. As he did so he wondered if she had inherited the intelligence and temper of her celebrated father. Don Pedro d' Tansanta had been a brilliantly successful General and the Prime Minister of his country for seven years before being sent as Ambassador to France, and no one would have denied his great abilities; but he had the reputation of being extremely haughty and violently intolerant.

While the two younger people were exchanging courtesies, the Queen called out to her coachman in German: 'Weber! You had better walk the horses, as we may remain here for some time.' Then she seated herself on a cushion that had been placed for her and, as the carriage moved off, motioned to Richard and the Spanish girl to sit down one on either side.

This was the first opportunity Richard had had to see her at close quarters without her mask, and he thought that apart from some tiny wrinkles round her tender blue eyes and a slight darkening of her golden hair she showed few signs of approaching middle-age. She was, at that time, thirty-three years old and had had four children. It was common knowledge that for the first eight years of her wedded life she had, to her bitter grief, remained childless, because her husband had proved incapable of consummating the marriage; but her daughter, Madame Royale, was now ten years old; the Dauphin, a child whose sickliness gave her much anxiety. Severin; her second son, the little Duc de Normandie, a lusty boy of four; and there had been a second daughter, who had died at the age of eleven months. Yet despite the strain and cares of motherhood, she had retained her beautiful figure. She had exquisite hands and arms; and her oval face, with its delicately arched nose and noble forehead, was so splendidly set on her fine shoulders that no woman could have better looked, as she was, a true daughter of the Caesars.

Richard had seen her in the past only from a distance, but even so he had been struck by her resemblance to his lovely Athénais, and now, at close quarters, he thought her far more beautiful than her dark-browed young companion. But he was not left in silent contemplation of their respective attractions for long, as the Queen said to him

'Monsieur; the Señorita d'Tansanta is, I know, positively dying to hear what befell you after you were robbed of your jewels in Le Havre, and I too have a great love for listening to such stories; pray continue your adventures.'

So, much sooner than he had expected, Richard found himself launched in his self-sought role of troubadour; and, as his blessings included ample self -confidence, coupled with the ability to express himself easily, the task presented no difficulties. Fortunately, too, he had abundant material in the months that he had spent with old Dr. Aristotle Fdnelon peddling quack medicines, so he was not called on to invent any particulars that he might have later regretted, and for over half an hour he kept the Queen and her lady pleasantly amused.

From their comments and laughter he had good reason to suppose that they would have been quite content to listen to him much longer ; but at the end of that time the sound of approaching hoof-beats interrupted his discourse, bringing them all to their feet, and next moment the Queen's two gentlemen cantered into the clearing.

'I feared as much,' murmured Richard. `That fine bay de Roubec was riding enabled him to get clean away.' But, even as he spoke, he had good cause to forget the pseudo-Chevalier in swift concern for a new development which threatened to jeopardize the favor he had so skillfully acquired with the Queen. As the two richly clad riders pulled up their foam-flecked mounts he recognized them both as friends of the Marquis de Rochambeau.

One was the handsome Duc de Coigny, whose name malignant slander had coupled with that of the Queen on the birth of her first child, and the other was the Comte de Vaudreuil, whom the scurrilous pamphlets of the day had also accused her of having taken for her lover.

Richard did not believe a word of such stories, as everyone at all well informed knew that, at the time of the Queen's first pregnancy, the one had been the lover of the Princess de Guéménee and the other of the Duchess de Polignac, and that Marie Antoinette herself was a model of wifely fidelity. The two noblemen were, however, her old and cherished friends, and were so devoted to her that when two years earlier the King had abolished the Duc's post as First Equerry and the Comte's as Grand Falconer, on grounds of economy, both had remained on at Court for the pleasure of serving her.

Seeing that she had gone out that afternoon to dispatch a letter at a secret rendezvous, it was not the least surprising that she should have chosen two such trusted friends to act as her escort; but their arrival on the scene brought Richard face to face with a situation which he had hoped would not arise until he had had a chance to secure a firm footing at Fontainebleau.

'Alas, Madame,' cried de Coigny, on pulling up. 'We lost our man some two miles distant heading in the direction of Courances.'

'We kept him in sight that far,' added de Vaudreuil, 'but had gained little on him. I fear he used his lead to double back on reaching a point where several rides converge. After casting about

for quite a while and finding no trace of him, we thought it best to return and confess our discomfiture to Your Majesty.'

"Tis a pity.' the Queen shrugged, 'but of no vital import. And as we can give a good description of the fellow, the police may yet lay him by the heels for us. I thank you, gentlemen, for your exertions.'

Turning to Richard, she said: 'Monsieur, 'tis my wish that Mon sieur le Duc de Coigny and Monsieur le Comte de Vaudreuil should number you among their acquaintances.' Then to them she added: 'My friends, this gentleman has today rendered me a considerable service. His name is Cavasuto, and I recommend him to you.'

The three men exchanged polite bows. Then de Vaudreuil said with a little frown: 'Cavasuto? Your name is familiar to me" Monsieur, but I cannot recall where I have heard it before.'

'I remember not only this gentleman's name, but also his face,' put in de Coigny. 'Surely, Monsieur, we have met upon some previous occasion?'

Richard saw that there was nothing for it but to take the plunge, so he bowed again, and said: 'Messieurs. In any other circumstances I would not have had the forwardness to claim the honor of your previous acquaintance. But in the past both of you have spoken to me with some kindness on numerous occasions. I was for some time confidential secretary to Monsieur de Rochambeau.'

'Mort Dieu!' exclaimed de Vaudreuil, so far forgetting himself as to swear in front of the Queen. 'I know you now! You are that young devil of an Englishman.'

'Monsieur!' cried the Queen in sharp reprimand.

"Tis true that I was born in England,' Richard admitted ; then added with a smooth disregard for the strict truth: 'But as I was educated in France I have long regarded myself as more than half a Frenchman.'

De Vaudreuil ignored the skilful evasion, which Richard had prepared in advance in case he should find himself in just such a situation, and hastily excused himself to the Queen.

'Your pardon, Madame. In my amazement at finding such a person in your company my tongue ran away with me.'

Marie Antoinette's blue eyes widened. 'I fail to see. Monsieur, why you should be so shocked. What matters it where Monsieur Cavasuto was born? I have always had a liking for the English, and count many of them among my friends.'

De Coigny came to his companion's rescue, and said quickly

'I too recognize him now, and know what Monsieur le Comte had
in mind. We can scarce believe Your Majesty to be aware that this fellow
is he who seduced Mademoiselle de Rochambeau.'

It had never occurred to Richard that such a charge would be brought
against him. His deep-blue eyes suddenly began to smolder beneath their dark
lashes, and before the Queen could reply he burst out

`Monsieur le Duc! Were it not for Her Majesty's presence I would call
you out for that. I know not what vile slanders were invented about me after I
left France; but 'tis a lie. I was no more than Mademoiselle de Rochambeau's
devoted servant, and aided her to escape an unwelcome marriage, in order that
she might wed Monsieur de la Tour d'Auvergne, with whom she was in love.'

The Queen gave a little gasp and turned to stare at him. 'Enough,
Monsieur!' she exclaimed imperiously. `The whole of that horrid scandal now
comes back to me. And on your own confession you must be the villain who
murdered M. le Comte de Caylus.'

`Nay, Madame I protest!' cried Richard firmly. 'I killed Monsieur de
Caylus in a fair fight. M. l'Abbe de Périgord witnessed the affair and can
vouch for the truth of what I say.'

'That unworthy priest!' exclaimed the Queen. 'I would not credit one
word his perjured mouth could utter. 'Twas reported on incontestable evidence
that you ambushed Monsieur de Caylus in the forest of Melun, and there did
him to death.'

'Madame; 'tis true that I waylaid him, for in my situation it was the only
way to make him fight. But I gave him ample opportunity to defend himself,
and he proved no mean antagonist.'

'At the least then you admit to having challenged him to fight, and
having forced a duel upon him?'

'I do, Your Majesty.'

'Yet you must have been aware that there are edicts forbidding dueling,
and that the breaking of them makes the offender liable to punishment by
death?'

'I was, Your Majesty; but-'

'Silence, Monsieur!' The Queen cut him short. 'I was too easily taken in
by your fair appearance and glib tongue; but now you are unmasked I have
heard enough I Mademoiselle de Rochambeau's father chose Monsieur de
Caylus for her. What others thought of that choice is neither here nor there; for
in such a matter the right of the head of a family is sacred. Yet you, while
acting as a servant in the house, took it on yourself to overrule his judgment,
and decided to assassinate the Count. Since you have had the temerity to return
to France I should be failing in my duty were I not to ensure that justice takes
its course, and that you pay the penalty for your abominable crime.'

She then turned to her gentlemen. `Monsieur le Duc, be pleased to call
my horses, for I would now return to Fontainebleau. And you. Monsieur le
Comte, I charge with the arrest and escorting back to the Château of Monsieur
Cavasuto.'

De Vaudreuil dismounted, and a moment later Richard was surrendering his long sword. Less than five minutes before he had been in a fair way to being accepted into Madame Marie Antoinette's intimate circle; now he was to be taken to Fontainebleau as a dangerous criminal charged with murder.

CHAPTER THREE
THE FAMILY COMPACT

As Richard climbed into his saddle the thought of attempting to escape entered his mind, but he dismissed it almost at once. His hired hack was good enough for an afternoon's ride but possessed of little stamina; whereas the mounts of de Vaudreuil and de Coigny were both fine animals and still comparatively fresh, in spite of their recent gallop. His mare might have kept the lead for some distance, but he felt certain that his pursuers would ultimately wear her down and that, with no initial start, he would never be able to get far enough ahead to conceal himself among the trees and rocks while the others passed, as de Roubec had evidently done.

If anything could have added to his bitter sense of grievance at the scurvy trick fate had played him, it was that had the Queen's two gentlemen not chanced to be close friends of Monsieur de Rochambeau, and had they been a little nearer to hand when she summoned them, it would have been de Roubec who would have ridden back to Fontainebleau as a prisoner, instead of himself.

That he was a prisoner was brought home to him in no uncertain manner by the way in which the two nobles closed in on either side of him immediately the carriage set off. His temper had subsided as quickly as it had arisen, and he was not normally given to fits of depression, but with every yard they covered in the wake of the carriage he became more fully conscious of the seriousness of his plight.

He had had perfectly adequate reasons for believing the affair of de Caylus to be done with and forgotten ; yet it seemed that the dead Count's hand was now stretching up out of the grave to draw him down into it, and that even evasion of the grisly clutch might be bought only at the price of a long term of imprisonment.

It was not until they had covered over half a mile that Richard's gloomy thoughts were broken in upon by de Coigny saying

'Monsieur; the fact that Her Majesty has placed you under arrest does not obliterate the memory of a certain exchange that recently passed between us. I refer to your threat to call me out.'

'Indeed it does not, Monsieur le Duc,' Richard replied icily. He was far from pleased that in addition to his other troubles he had brought a duel upon himself, but it did not even occur to him that there was any alternative to going through with it, so he added

`When last our paths crossed I was employed by Monsieur de Rochambeau as a secretary, so it may be that you do not consider me of sufficient rank to meet you; but let me at least assure you that I am fully entitled to that of Chevalier, as my grandfather was the Earl of Kildonan, and my uncle is the present holder of that title. So, if and when I become free of my present embarrassment, I shall be happy to give Your Grace satisfaction with such weapons and at any time and place you may choose.'

`In view of what you tell me of your birth I, too, should be willing to meet you, if it is your wish to press the matter,' said the Duke quite mildly. `But I am prepared to admit that I spoke without due thought. As you escaped to England shortly after you killed de Caylus, you are doubtless unaware that your duel, and the elopement of Mademoiselle de Rochambeau which immediately succeeded it, caused a positive furor. All Paris was buzzing with accounts of the matter. And as you clearly fought on the young lady's behalf the most generously accepted version of it was that you had abused your position as secretary to her father to become her lover. Like many other people I accepted the order of the day and on such few occasions as I have thought of you since it has always been as her seducer. But I have no evidence that it was so ; and had I not been surprised out of my sense of fitness by your sudden reappearance in the company of Her Majesty, I should certainly not have accused you of it:

Richard looked at the handsome middle-aged man at his side with new respect. For nearly two centuries the Kings of France had issued edict after edict threatening increasingly severe punishments in their efforts to suppress dueling, but that had had little effect on their nobility's attitude towards affairs of honor. No gentleman could afford to be subjected to a public slight and fail to demand satisfaction for it, for to do so was to invite certain ostracization by his fellows. Moreover, whenever such affairs took place with adequate reason and according to the established rules even the King's Ministers entered into a silent conspiracy to hush them up, and save the participants from the penalties of the law. It therefore required much more courage to apologize than to fight, and Richard rightly regarded M. le Coigny's retraction a most handsome one.

`Monsignor,' he said. `The honesty of your admission touches me deeply, and nothing would please me better than to forget the passage between us that gave occasion for it. May I add that I am all the more sensible of the generosity of your conduct from the sad plight in which I find myself ; for 'tis when in such straits as I am at this moment that a chivalrous gesture from another is most warming to the heart.'

He paused for a moment, then went on: `For my part, I can well appreciate that an evil construction could have been put upon my championship of Mademoiselle de Rochambeau. But, if you recall the facts, Monsieur de la Tour d'Auvergne had already challenged de Caylus, fought and been wounded by him; so naught but my sword stood between her and the hateful marriage that had been arranged by her father without her consent. Monsieur de la Tour d'Auvergne was at that time my closest friend, and it was on his account that, rather than see the lady he loved given to another, I fought and killed de Caylus.'

'If that is so, your conduct appears to have been most honorable, Monsieur,' remarked de Vaudreuil politely. `And had the affair been conducted according to the accepted code you would be in danger now of no more than a severe reprimand from His Majesty coupled with a period of banishment to some country estate. But since you waylaid de Caylus, furred a duel on him and fought without the presence of seconds to bear witness to fair play, that is accounted assassination, and I fear it may go hard with you.'

`Monsieur le Comte, I give you my word that I took no unfair advantage of my adversary, and that I was, in fact, several times in acute danger of receiving a mortal wound from him myself.'

`And we accept it, Monsieur,' put in de Coigny. `De Caylus had fought at least a score of times before and was accounted one of the finest swordsmen in all France. It was a remarkable feat to slay so notable a duelist, and if you will indulge us we should find it mightily interesting to hear what actually took place at the encounter.'

For all his natural self-confidence Richard was by habit diffident when speaking of his own abilities and achievements; so, while he willingly did as he had been requested, he confined himself mainly to the technicalities of the fight and made his final victory appear more a stroke of fortune than a brilliantly delivered coup de grâce. His modesty won him the respect of the two older men, and for the last few miles of their ride all three of them talked in the most friendly fashion of sword-play as an art, with its innumerable varieties of tierce, feint and thrust.

It was not until the small cortege was trotting down the cobbled main street of Fontainebleau that de Vaudreuil said with some hesitation to Richard: 'I pray you forgive me, Monsieur, but one thing has been troubling me for some moments past. When you fled after the duel I recall that a big reward was offered for your capture. In it I seem to remember some mention of a State paper with which you had made off. Was there any truth in that?'

It was the one accusation that Richard had been dreading for the past hour or more; but the form in which the question was put reassured him for the moment. Evidently the Marquis de Rochambeau had not disclosed to his friends the nature of the document of which he had been robbed, or its importance. In the circumstances, Richard felt considerable repugnance to telling a lie, but there was clearly no alternative if he was to stand any chance at all of saving his neck; and when a lie was necessary few people could tell one more convincingly than Richard. Without hesitation he replied.

' 'Tis true, Monsieur le Comte, that in the hurry of my departure I inadvertently took one of Monsieur le Rochambeau's documents with me. I came upon it many days later in one of my pockets. As I considered it of a highly confidential nature I did not like to risk returning it through the post, so I destroyed it.'

To Richard's relief de Vaudreuil seemed perfectly satisfied with this explanation and a moment later, as they turned into the broad carriageway between the Coeur Henri Quatre and the Coeur des Princes, the Count addressed him again.

'Monsieur de Blane after having enjoyed the pleasure of your conversation, I now find the duty with which I have been charged by Her Majesty a most distasteful one ; but I can at least offer you a choice of prisons. Normally you would be conducted to the dungeon and placed under guard there, but If you prefer to give me your parole d'honneur that you will not attempt to escape, I should be happy to offer you a room in my apartment.'

Richard barely hesitated. Apart from the discomfort that would certainly be his lot if he elected to be confined in a cell his chances of escaping from it would be obviously small; and even if he succeeded, that would put a definite end to all prospects of his succeeding in his mission, for he could never hope afterwards to be received at Court. Whereas the friendliness and sympathy displayed by his two companions during their long ride had buoyed him up afresh, and encouraged him to believe that he might yet make his peace with the Queen if only she could be induced to give him a fair hearing. With a bow he replied:

'I am indeed grateful to you, Monsieur le Comte. I willingly give you my parole for the privilege of accepting your hospitality.'

They had now turned right, through the Porte Dauphine into the Coeur Ovale, and the carriage drew up at an entrance to the right just inside it. De Coigny handed the Queen out and escorted her up to her apartments; de Vaudreuil followed them into the entrance with Richard but conducted him along a ground floor corridor and up a staircase at its far end in the oldest, central block of the Palace, where, just round the corner from the Galerie Francois 1, he had his own quarters.

Having shown Richard the small but pleasant bedroom he was to occupy the Count told him that dinner would shortly be served for him in the sitting-room next door, and that in the meantime he would send someone to take his horse back to the inn and fetch his clothes. Then he left him.

As Richard gazed out of the tall window, which overlooked the Cour de la Fontaine with its statue of Ulysses and the carp pond beyond it, he began to wonder again how he could possibly bluff his way out of the mess he was in. But he was not given long to brood over his ill-fortune as the Count's servant came in to lay the table, and he proved to be an extremely garrulous Bordelaise who seemed to consider it part of his duty to entertain his master's guest with an endless flow of small-talk.

Neither was Richard given any opportunity to grow gloomy over his prospects that evening, for he had scarcely finished his dinner when de Vaudreuil returned, bringing with him a number of other gentlemen. it transpired that Her Majesty had a slight migraine, so had decided against holding a small musical which had been planned for that night, and it being de Coigny's turn to remain

in immediate attendance on her, he was the only member of her intimate circle not left free by her decision.

Among the newcomers to whom Richard was presented were the Due de Polignac, the husband of the beautiful Gabrielle who was the Queen's closest friend and the governess of the royal children, the Due de Biron and the Baron de Breteuil, all of whom recalled having at times transacted business with him when he was M. de Rochambeau's secretary; while several of the others were known to him by sight and reputation. They included the Prince de Ligne, a soldier-poet and renowned horticulturist, whose talents and charm had made him persona grata at half the courts in Europe; the Comte Valentin d'Esterhazy, a wealthy Hungarian noble who had been specially recommended to the Queen by her mother, the Empress Maria Theresa; the Baron de Besenval, an elderly but robust Swiss who commanded the King's Swiss Guards; and August-Marie, Prince d'Arenberg, who was known in France as the Comte de la Marck, and was the son of Maria Theresa's most brilliant general.

They were a gallant and handsome company, fully representative of the gay and intelligent men whom Madame Marie Antoinette had delighted to gather about her in her happier days'; and now as her old and best friends, having only the true interests of the monarchy at heart, they remained at her side, while the hundreds of time-serving courtiers who usually frequented the Palace had gone off to the provinces for the elections.

All of them remembered the affair of de Caylus's death and Athénals de Rochambeau's run-away marriage, and were eager to hear a firsthand account of it; so while the daylight died the curtains were drawn, candles lit, fresh bottles of wine uncorked, and as they settled down round the big table Richard found himself called on to tell again the story of his famous duel.

Again he endeavored to belittle the part he had played, but when he had done the whole company was both loud in its praise of his conduct and most sympathetic about his present position ; so he was still further heartened in his hope that the Queen's friends would use their influence to secure her clemency on his behalf.

The talk then became general and naturally many references were made to the unsettled state of France ; thus Richard was provided with the opportunity, which had seemed so distant that morning. of hearing the views of these very men who stood so near the throne.

Somewhat to his surprise, he did not find them in the least reactionary; on the contrary, most of them appeared very liberal minded. De Ligne and de Vaudreuil were particularly so, and the latter, after inveighing against the artificiality of life at Court, declared that he would have long since left it had it not been for his attachment to the Queen.

As they talked the wine was kept in constant circulation. It was not the habit to drink so heavily in France as in England, and the wine, although a rich Anjou, was considerably lighter than the Port to which Richard was accustomed. Nevertheless, by the time de Vaudreuil's friends retired, Richard was carrying a good load, so on going to bed he thought no more of his worries and, within a ,few minutes of his head touching the pillow, was sound asleep.

However, when he awoke in the morning, the danger in which he lay recurred to him with full force, and over a breakfast of chocolate and crisp rolls, which was brought to him in bed, he tried to assess his chances of escaping the Queen's anger.

He felt now that he had been extremely rash to return to France without having made certain that the old charges against him in connection with de Caylus's death had been quashed, as he had believed them to be. Soon after his escape to England, in the late summer of '97, his dear friend, the Lady Melissa Etheridge. had offered to arrange the matter. The ravishing Melissa had, at that time, numbered amongst her beaux the recently appointed French Ambassador, Monsieur le Comte d'Adhémar ; and she had said that, having regard to the true facts, it should be easy for her to get the murder charge withdrawn, which would then reduce the affair to the much less heinous one of duelling.

Richard had gladly accepted her offer, and written out a long statement for her to hand to the Ambassador. As he knew that such personal matters were always subject to long delays before being dealt with, he had not pressed for an answer. He had been content to accept, via Melissa, d'Adhémar assurance after reading the statement that, if it was substantially true, the King would inflict on the culprit no more than a sentence of a year's banishment; and as nearly two years had elapsed since his deed he had had good reason to suppose that he need fear no repercussion from it.

On thinking matters over, he assumed that the Queen would now have him handed over to the police for indictment before a magistrate. If that occurred he could demand that the papers relevant to the original affair should be produced, and with any luck d'Adhémar recommendation would be found among them, or, ii Fortune really decided to smile on him again, a pardon by the King might come to light. On the other hand there was the unpleasant possibility that the Ambassador's report had never got as far as His Majesty, and in that case only the Queen's clemency could save him from being tried for murder.

His thoughts shifted to a murder trial that was still vivid in his memory. Barely six weeks before he and Melissa had been very near paying for their year-old love affair by finding nooses round their necks. The odious publicity of the trial had sent her hastily abroad, and she was now with her clever, indulgent father in Vienna.

He wondered how she was faring there, but had little doubt her splendid health and amazing vitality were carrying her triumphantly through an endless succession of parties. He felt certain, too, that being the wanton hussy that her hot half-gypsy blood had made her, she would have added another lover to the long list of handsome gallants she had taken since she had first been seduced by a good-looking highwayman. Whoever she was allowing to caress her dark beauty in the city on the Danube now-be he Austrian, German, Hungarian or Czech Richard had good cause to think him a monstrous lucky fellow, for he had laid seige to and won quite a number of lovely ladies himself, yet not one of them could offer Melissa's rare and varied attractions as a mistress.

But she meant far more to him than that. They were both only children, and it was she who had filled the place of almost a brother, as well as a sister, to him in their early teens. Then, in a moment when he needed self-confidence above all else, she had led him to think that he was initiating her into the mysteries of love, although in reality she was initiating him, for he was the younger, and not yet sixteen. It was she who had given him the jewels that de Roubec had stolen, and whatever love affairs they might have when apart they always returned to one another as confidants and friends.

Again his thoughts shifted, this time to his last interview with Mr. Pitt, and in his mind he began to live through the scene once more.

As on two previous occasions the Prime Minister had asked him down to Holwood, his country residence near Bromley, for a Sunday, in order to give him his instructions at leisure and in private. Two old patrons of Richard had been there, whom he had first known as Sir James Harris and the Marquis of Carmarthen; but the former had been raised to the peerage the preceding year as Baron Malmesbury, and the latter -from whom, as Foreign Secretary, Richard always received the funds for his secret activities had, only that week, succeeded his father as Duke of Leeds. Pitt's shadow, the cold, unbending but upright and indefatigable William Grenville, had also been there, providing by his unapproachable hauteur a strong contrast to the gracious charm of the new Duke and jovial warmth of the recently created peer.

Mr. Pitt never concealed from such close friends as these the object of the missions upon which he sent Richard, so after they had dined the talk turned to the state of France, and European affairs in general.

All of those present felt convinced that in its absolute form the French monarchy could trot survive much longer, but not one of them believed that the political unrest in France would culminate in the type of Great Rebellion that had cost King Charles I his head, and led a hundred and forty years earlier to Britain for a time becoming a Republic.

They argued that whereas in England the commercial classes had been supported by a large section of a free and powerful nobility against the King, the nobility of France had become too decadent to weigh the scales either way; that even the bourgeoisie although determined to insist on political representation, were monarchist at heart, and would never take up arms against their Sovereign ; and that the peasantry were so lacking in unity and leadership, that they were capable of little more than the local facqueries which had been agitating certain parts of the country for some time past on account of the corn shortage.

The general opinion, too, was that France must continue to be regarded as a menace to Britain. They had all lived through the Seven Years' War, in which Pitt's father, the great Chatham, had led Britain from victory to victory, so that at its end France lay beaten and humbled, her hopes of Empire in Canada and India forever shattered, her fleets destroyed and her commerce ruined. But they had also witnessed her remarkable recovery, and lived through the desperate years in which, while Britain was endeavoring to suppress the risings of her rebellious Colonists in the Americas, she had been threatened with a French invasion at home and had stood alone against a world in arms under French leadership.

They were all Englishmen who had been brought up in the hard, practical school that had been forced to regard the interests of other nations as of secondary importance provided that their country could continue to hold her own. Pitt alone among them had the vision to see that a new age was dawning in which the

prosperity of Britain would depend on the welfare of her neighbours across the narrow seas.

As they talked of those grim days when half Britain's immensely valuable possessions in the West Indies were lost to France, and the long drawn-out siege of Gibraltar had been raised only at the price of withdrawing the main Fleet from American waters, so that from lack of supplies and reinforcements a British army had been compelled to surrender at York Town, Grenville said:

'Whatever the late war with France may have cost us it cost her more; for 'twas finding so many millions to support the Americans which has resulted in her present state of near bankruptcy.'

'I have always heard, sir,' put in Richard with some diffidence, 'that her embarrassment is due to the vast sums spent on building by King Louis XIV and the almost equally great treasure that King Louis XV squandered on his mistresses, the Pompadour and the du Barri.'

'Nay,' Grenville replied ponderously, with a shake of his heavy head. 'You are wrong there, Mr. Blane. 'Tis true that for generations the Kings of France have dissipated a great part of the nation's income on their own pleasures or aggrandizement; but none the less the financial situation was by no means beyond repair when Louis XVI ascended the throne, some quarter of a century ago:

"Tis true,' Pitt agreed, 'and although the King is in many ways a weakling, he has ever displayed a most earnest desire to economize. His progressive cutting down of his Household, and the disbandment of two entire regiments of Royal Guards; are ample evidence of that. I judge Mr. Grenville right in his contention that the Royal Treasury might again be in ample funds, were it not that it has never had a chance to recover from the huge drain upon it caused by France going to the assistance of the Americans.'

'Their interference in our business cost us dear at the time,' remarked the Duke of Leeds smoothly, 'but now we should benefit from their folly ; for whatever changes they may bring about in their system of government, poverty will continue to reduce their ability to challenge us again for a considerable time to come.'

Malmesbury had spent half a lifetime as a British diplomat in Madrid, Berlin, St. Petersburg and The Hague, often unsupported from home, yet by his skill; forcefulness and personal popularity at foreign Courts again and again thwarting French designs. He saw France as Britain's only serious rival to world power, and did not believe that his country could enjoy permanent safety until her

great rival had been entirely isolated and reduced to impotence. Richard remembered this, as the diplomat said quickly.

'Your Grace's wishes are the father to your thoughts. The emptiness of the French treasury does not affect the fact that the population of France is more than twice our own, or that the pride of the whole nation is involved in regaining its lost hold on India and North America. King Louis having been fool enough to disband his Musketeers is no evidence whatsoever of his pacific intentions. He still retains the biggest standing army in Europe, builds men of-war with every sou that he can raise by depriving his nobles of their pensions-yes, even to denying his wife a diamond necklace so that he might build another-and he has spent a greater sum than his father squandered on the du Barri in creating a vast new naval base of Cherbourg, which can have no other purpose than the domination of the Channel and our shores. I would stake my last farthing on it that whatever new form of government may emerge in France out of her present troubles she will find the money somehow, whenever the opportunity seems favourable, to launch another attempt to destroy us root and branch.'

' The Duke laughed lightly. 'You overstress the danger, my lord But should you prove correct we are, largely thanks to your own efforts, now far better situated than we were a few years back to put a check upon any new French aggression. When we emerged from the last conflict in '83 it was only by skilful diplomacy at the Peace of Paris that we saved the shirts on our backs, and after it we were still left entirely friendless. Whereas now that we have formed the Triple Alliance, should we be compelled to march against the French, Prussia and the Dutch Netherlands will march with us.'

Malmesbury thrust his leonine head forward, his fine blue, eyes flashed and he banged his clenched fist on the table. ' 'Tis not enough, Your Grace! Britain can never enjoy full and permanent security, until the Family Compact has been broken.'

'In that I think your lordship right,' Pitt agreed. 'All of you know that I have no animus against France. On the contrary, one of my dearest ambitions was achieved when we succeeded in negotiating our Commercial Treaty with the French two autumns back ; for 'tis working most satisfactorily and may well bear out my hopes of forming a bridge over which the centuries-old enmity of the two countries may be forgotten. Again, you know that I am averse to the formation of new military alliances except when they are necessary for our own protection. Had I my way I would see us friends with all but committed to none; but that is impossible

as long as there exist foreign combinations which may take up arms against us.'

He paused to pour himself another glass of port, then went on

'It is just such alliances that breed wars, and no better example of their potentialities in that direction could be cited than the Family Compact just mentioned by my lord Malmesbury. Our recent treaties with the Prussians and the Dutch will secure us their aid in the event of direct aggression by France, and that being so, coupled with her present internal difficulties, I do not believe that we have anything to fear from a renewal of her desire for aggrandizement at our expense. But unfortunately, the Bourbon Family Compact still ties her to Spain.

`For a long time past our relations with that country have been far from good, and I do not see how they can be permanently bettered as long as present conditions maintain in South American waters. Spain has ever sought to keep her rich possessions overseas as a closed province from all other nations, whereas being ourselves a race of traders we have striven by fair means and foul to get a footing on the southern continent. Despite numerous formal prohibitions we have winked the eye at many illegal acts by enterprising ship-owners in the West Indies. The smuggling carried on from the Spanish main to our islands there has assumed enormous proportions, and skirmishes between our people and the Spanish guarda Costa vessels have long occurred with considerable frequency. That naturally gives great cause for offence to the haughty D=ups. and scarcely a month passes without our receiving heated remonstrance's from Madrid, or bitter complaints from the governors of our islands that British seamen have been seized, maltreated and falsely imprisoned while going about their lawful business.'

The handsome Duke of Leeds made a wry grimace. 'I know it well, and have an entire drawer stuffed with such papers at the Foreign Office. But Spain will never bring herself to the point of fighting on that account.'

'I would not wager upon it,' contended Pitt. 'There is always the last straw that breaks the camel's back.'

"Nay The Doges may bluster but the days of greatness are gone; and without the succor that she draws from her Empire in the Americas she would face total ruin. Did she declare openly against Britain our fleets would swiftly cut her off from that Eldorado, and she would even risk its permanent loss.'

'There I agree, should she have the temerity to challenge us alone,' Pitt replied. 'But Your Grace has left out of your calculations the Family Compact. In '79, when we were fully engaged against France, the Court of Versailles called upon the Court of Madrid to honor that treaty and King Carlos III entered the war against us. What guarantee have we that his successor, should he consider himself provoked beyond endurance, will not also invoke the treaty and King Louis, however reluctantly, in turn feel obliged to abide by his obligations? I regard all wars as regrettable, and although we could look to the outcome of one against Spain alone with reasonable equanimity, if we were called on again to face France and Spain in combination it might well go exceeding hard with Britain.'

The Duke shrugged. 'I regard the chances of Spain pushing her grievances about the depredations of our privateers to the point of war as exceeding slender; so I think such a situation most unlikely to arise.'

`Yet, should it do so,' Malmesbury put in persistently, `Your Grace must admit that we would find ourselves in a pretty pickle; for it should not be forgotten that the French Queen is a Hapsburg. The influence she exerts has enabled her to draw the Courts of Versailles and Vienna much closer together than they were formerly, and in the event of war she might well succeed in inducing her brothers to come to the assistance of France. Then we would find Spain, France, Austria, Tuscany and the Two Sicily's all leagued in arms simultaneously for the purpose of our destruction.'

'Indeed, my Lord Malmesbury is right,' declared Pitt. 'The nightmare spectacle he calls up could only too easily become a terrible reality did Spain ever invoke, that damnable Family Com- pact. The danger at the moment fortunately appears remote; but it is the one possibility that above all others we should spare no pains to render still more unlikely, or, far better, impossible.'

He had turned, then, to Richard, and said: 'I trust you will bear this conversation in mind, Mr. Blane. Previous to it your new mission called for no more than that you should act as a general observer; but in addition I now request that, should you succeed in becoming persona grata at the French Court, You will pay

special regard to all that concerns Franco-Spanish relations ; and, should opportunity offer, use your utmost exertions to weaken the goodwill that at present exists between the two nations. 'Tis too much to expect that any personal endeavor on your part could lead to the annulling of this long-standing treaty, but you

have shown considerable shrewdness in the past, and you could render no greater service to your country than by suggesting to me some line of policy that would later enable me to bring about the breaking of it.'

That night, when Richard had got back to Amesbury House in Arlington Street-where he had a standing invitation to stay when in London with the Marquess of Amesbury's younger son, Lord Edward Fitz-Deverel he and his tall foppish friend, who, from his perpetual stoop, was known to his intimates as 'Droopy Ned', had spent an hour in the fine library, delving into a score of leather-bound volumes to find out all they could, about the Family Compact.

Both of them knew well that it was one of the major instruments that had governed European relations for several generations, but Richard was anxious to secure details of its origin and very man to help him. In due course their researches produced the following information.

King Carlos II of Spain, who had died in the year 1700, was the last male descendant in the direct line of the Houses of Castile and Aragon ; so the succession had reverted to the descendants of his eldest aunt. This princess - known to the world owing to her Imperial descent as Anne of Austria, but nevertheless of Spanish blood-had married the head of the House of Bourbon, Louis XIII of France. In consequence, theoretically, the Spanish throne devolved upon her son Louis XIV. But as the two countries were not prepared to unite and the Spaniards were determined to have a King of their own, the immediate heirs to France were ruled out, and Louis XIV's, second grandson, the Duke of Anjou, had been selected. The choice had been strongly opposed by the late King Carlos's close relatives in Bavaria and Austria, which had resulted in the War of the Spanish Succession, but France had emerged triumphant and the Duke D'Anjou had ascended the Spanish throne as Philip V. Since then a branch of the Bourbon family had ruled in Spain; and more

recently relatives of the Spanish Kings had also reigned in both Naples and
Parma.

In 1733 the first Family Compact had been signed at the Escurial ; and it
was shortly after this that Don Carlos, Philip V's son by his second marriage,
had conquered Naples from the Austrians. Thereafter the interests of France
and Spain had tended to diverge somewhat, but in 1743 they had renewed the
treaty at Fontainebleau and, moreover, entered into a secret agreement to use
their best endeavors to restore the Stuart Pretender to the British throne.
Having failed in this their friendship cooled a little but Don Carlos was
fervidly pro-French, and soon after coming to the Spanish throne as King
Carlos III he engaged his time as a bookworm, in 1761, in a third treaty which
committed its signatories more deeply than ever before. This last Family
Compact had been confirmed in 1765, had been put into active operation by
Spain coming to the assistance of France in her war against Britain, in 1779,
and was still valid.

The earlier treaties had contained the statement in their preambles that
the alliance was `eternal and irrevocable' and the last, in addition, declared
specifically that `any country that should become the enemy of the one or the
other of the two Crowns would be regarded as the enemy of both'. It further
contained a clause that the two contracting parties should also afford full
protection to the dominions of the two Bourbon princes who ruled the Two
Sicily's and the Duchy of Parma, who were at that date Carlos III's younger
son, as King of Naples, and his younger brother.

Having got so far Richard and Droopy looked up the House of
Habsburg-Lorraine to find out the ramifications of Madame Marie Antoinette's
family. It emerged chat she had been one of the sixteen children of the
Empress-Queen Maria Theresa, and that her surviving brothers and sisters
included Joseph II, Emperor of Austria, the Grand Duke Leopold of Tuscany,
the Elector of Cologne and the Queen of Naples. It was therefore clear that
Lord Malmesbury had not been overstating the case when he had said that if
the powers concerned in the Family Compact together with Marie Antoinette's
relatives combined against Britain she would be in a `pretty pickle'.

As Richard recalled these scenes he felt that there was now very little
hope of his being allowed to remain at Court, and so having even a chance of
being able to furnish Mr. Pitt with data which might help him to put a spoke in
the wheel of the Family Compact. But he did feel that owing to his having had
the luck to meet so many of the Queen's gentlemen the previous evening, he
could count on several of them speaking to her on his behalf ; so there was a
fair prospect that instead of sending him for trial she might give him his
freedom, and that would at least allow him to continue with the less intricate
part of his general mission.

It would be bitterly disappointing to have got so near the Queen only to
be banished from her presence, but he could make a tour of the provincial
cities or develop the acquaintance of men such as the Comte de Mirabeau, La.
Mounier, the Abbe Sieyes and the Comte de Lilly Tollendal, who were in the
forefront of the agitation for reform, and thus still procure a certain amount of

quite useful information for his Government. The thing that mattered

above all else was to regain his freedom; with some anxiety, but a reasonable hope of doing so, he got up and dressed.

Finding that M. de Vaudreuil had already gone out, he spent the morning browsing through his host's books until, shortly after midday, the Count returned. As soon as they had exchanged greetings Richard said

`Comfortable as you have made me here, Monsieur le Comte, I must confess to being on tenterhooks to learn my fate. If you have seen Her Majesty this morning, pray tell me if aught was said about my affair and if she persists in her determination to send me before a magistrate.'

`Why do you suppose she ever intended to do that, Monsieur?' asked the Count in some surprise.

Richard's face showed even greater astonishment. `But you were present, Monsieur le Comte, when she declared her intention in no uncertain terms of seeing to it that justice took its course.'

'I was indeed, but that did not imply that the services of a magistrate are called for.'

`Sacre nom!' Richard exclaimed in swift dismay. `Surely you do not infer that I am to be condemned without a trial?'

De Vaudreuil shrugged. `Her Majesty will no doubt discuss your affair with the King, and His Majesty being the chief magistrate in France, no other is required. A lettre de cachet will be issued and His Majesty's Lieutenant General of Police will carry out whatever order it may contain.'

Richard endeavored to hide his sudden panic. It had never occurred to him that he might be thrown into prison for an unspecified period and perhaps forgotten there, or even executed, without a trial; although he was well aware that judicial procedure was very different in France from what it was in England.

In France there had never been any equivalent of Magna Carta or the Bill of Rights. There was no law of Habeas Corpus to protect people from being detained in prison without ever having been brought before a court; and even in the courts there was no such thing as trial by jury. The old feudal system of dispensing justice remained unaltered. The nobles still possessed powers little short of life and death over the peasants on their estates, and had the right of appointing anyone they chose to act for them in their absence.

In the towns, courts of all kinds had grown up in higgledy-piggledy confusion. There were those of the King's Intendants in the provincial capitals and of the Sub-Intendants in lesser places ; those of the clergy, who had special jurisdiction over certain matters; those for cases in which the nobility were concerned; those of the merchants, who could be tried by their own Guilds; and others which dealt with petty crime and the litigation of the common people. In addition there were the Parliaments which still functioned in some of the great cities, dealing with appeals and matters of outstanding moment, such as accusations against highly placed persons that the King might choose to refer to them. And above all these there remained the absolute power of the King to pronounce sentences of death, imprisonment, mutilation and banishment by lettres de cachet, against which there was no appeal.

During the past century the lettre de cachet had become mainly an instrument for disciplining the younger nobility. If a young man defied the parental will and was on the point of making an unsatisfactory marriage, got heavily in debt, or was leading a glaringly immoral life, it had become customary for his father to apply to the King for a lettre de cachet and get the recalcitrant youth sent to cool his heels in prison until he thought better of his insubordination. Lettres de cachet were also used quite arbitrarily by the greater nobility to imprison servants who they believed had robbed them and writers who had libeled them by publishing accounts of their extravagances and follies. So widespread had this practice become under Louis XV that his mistresses and Ministers regularly secured from him sheaves of signed blanks, which they gave to any of their friends who asked for them, so that the King no longer had the faintest idea who or for what people were being imprisoned in his name.

The mild and conscientious Louis XVI had endeavored to check this glaring abuse, and it was no longer easy to secure a lettre de cachet without providing a good reason for its use; but the King continued to use them freely himself in his capacity of Supreme Magistrate, and Richard had good cause to feel extremely perturbed by de Vaudreuil's pronouncement.

`Monsieur le Comte,' he said hurriedly, `if I am to have no opportunity of defending myself, I beg you most earnestly to entreat Her Majesty to grant me an audience before she speaks to the King. Or at least that you and your friends will take the first possible opportunity of recounting my story to her as I told it to you last night, and beseeching her clemency towards me.'

`Alas, my poor Chevalier,' replied de Vaudreuil, with a sad shake of his head. `De Coigny, de Ligne and myself have already done our best for you with Her Majesty this morning; but she would not listen to us. Indeed, she berated us soundly on the score that we were seeking to protect you because, contrary to the King's will, we nobles continue to regard duelling as the only recourse of a man of honour who considers himself aggrieved. I am distressed beyond words to dash your hopes, but she proved unshakable in her opinion that you had committed a very serious crime and must be suitably punished for it.

CHAPTER FOUR
THE LADY FROM SPAIN

As a further means of showing sympathy for his prisoner, de Vaudreuil suggested that a little fresh air and exercise might serve to distract Richard's thoughts; and told him that, since he had his parole, he had no objection to his going out unaccompanied, provided that he remained within the precincts of the Palace. Then he picked, up a riding-crop he had come to fetch and went out himself.

Richard, now as pessimistic about his prospects as he had previously been sanguine, felt no inclination for a walk, so remained where he was, plunged in gloomy speculations.

If he were not to be given any form of trial it now seemed improbable that the original documents referring to the case would be produced; and if they were not the recommendation to mercy that the Comte d'Adhémar had promised to send in would never come to light. Presumably the Queen regarded his own confession, that he had been the man who had forced a duel without provocation on the Count de Caylus, and killed him, amply sufficient for the King to sentence him to anything that, in their mood of the moment, they considered to be his deserts. He thought it very unlikely that they would impose the death sentence, but in his vivid imagination he already saw the black bulk of the Bastille yawning to engulf him ; and once inside that vast stone fortress it would prove exceedingly difficult to get out again.

The only line of escape which now seemed to offer was an appeal to the British Ambassador, the Duke of Dorset. It was part of His Grace's function to protect the interests of all British subjects resident or traveling in France. He could take the matter up with the King, through his Foreign Minister, soliciting a cancellation of the lettre de cachet, or at least a further investigation of the case, if there were reasonable grounds for supposing that there had been a miscarriage of justice.

But Richard realized with most distressing clarity that although he might plead a miscarriage of justice in the event of his being condemned for murder, he certainly could not do so if he were imprisoned for duelling; and it was entirely outside any Ambassador's sphere to seek to protect any of his nationals who had admittedly broken the laws of the country to which he was accredited.

There was still one way out. Via the Ambassador, he could send a letter to Mr. Pitt, begging his intervention. If the Prime Minister chose to do so he could instruct the Ambassador to use his own discretion as to the means he should employ to secure the prisoner's release. The Duke of Dorset, and his extremely able First Secretary, Mr. Daniel Hailes, both knew that Richard was a secret agent, and they would then resort to extreme measures. Dorset could declare that Richard was a new member of his staff who had just been sent out to him, and had not yet been officially presented owing to his recent arrival in France. He would then claim for him diplomatic status with its accompanying immunities. These did not cover arrest for felony, but duelling had never been regarded in the same light as other crimes. There was little doubt that the King would surrender Richard to the Ambassador rather than give umbrage to the Court of St. James; but at the same time it was certain that Dorset would be-informed that this new member of his staff was non persona grata at Versailles and must be sent back to England forthwith.

The thought of the humiliation entailed made Richard's bronzed face flush. How would he ever be able to face Mr. Pitt after having bungled matters so badly? That his arrest was not altogether his own fault would prove no excuse, for lie had laid himself open to it originally; and the Prime Minister had every right to expect that any agent he employed should have wit enough to get out of trouble without raising an annoying diplomatic issue. He would be sent on no more missions, never again be let into the fascinating secrets of high policy, or enjoy the traveling as a rich English milord' that he had so come to love. Instead he would be, as his father, Admiral Blane. would have put it, 'on the beach' at twenty-one, with an income quite inadequate to support the habits he had acquired and entirely untrained for any profession or profitable occupation.

Promptly he resolved that nothing short of actually finding his

life in jeopardy would induce him to squeal to Mr. Pitt for help. If there was no escape it would be better to endure a spell of prison, and leave it to Dorset or Hailes to ask for his release when they felt that sufficient time had elapsed for King Louis to be mollified enough to grant him a pardon on normal grounds. But the thought that it was unlikely that the King would be inclined to do so for at least a year was anything but a rosy one. better part of two hours Richard strove to interest himself again in de Vaudreuil's books, but he found that his mind was not registering the words he read, and that on their pages horrid visions of thick stone walls with iron grilles set high in them kept intruding themselves, so he decided he would take advantage of the Count's permission to go out.

At first he wandered disconsolately for a little while through some of the lofty public rooms and corridors, but their rich furnishings and intricately woven tapestries made no appeal to him today; and he dial not even raise or lower his eyes as he passed through the Galerie Henri ll, to admire again the exquisite workmanship by which long-dead craftsmen had mirrored the elaborate design of the ceiling-the royal arms of France entwined with the moon centered cipher of the King's mistress, the beautiful Diane de Poitiers by an inlay of rare, richly colored woods which formed the parquet of the floor.

After a while he turned back, stood gloomily for a few minutes on the balcony where Madame de Maintenon had induced Louis XIV to sign the Revocation of the Edict of Nantes, which had outlawed all the Protestants in France, then went down the main staircase and out into the garden.

Still unheeding his surroundings his footsteps carried him round to the Fountain Court, and he noticed idly that a group of ladies at its open end were gathered at the edge of the pond amusing themselves feeding the carp. As he approached one of them turned, caught sight of him and, leaving her companions, began to walk in his direction. Even at that distance he needed no second glance to recognize the lady's intensely black hair and striking eyebrows as those of the Señorita d'Aranda.

When they arrived within a few yards of one another she rippled her full skirts of lilac silk in a graceful curtsy and he swept his tricorn hat past the ground in an arc that paralleled his forward-thrust leg. From the instant he had recognized her his quick brain had been speculating on whether she might have good or ill news for him, and how he might gain some advantage from this chance meeting in view of her closeness to the Queen; so it was only on lifting his head from his bow that he noticed a strange little figure that had come to a halt a few feet in her rear.

It was a boy of about ten, but a boy the like of which Richard had never seen. The child's eyes and hair were as black as those of the Señorita, his nose was considerably more hooked, and they both had high cheekbones; but there the resemblance ended; his lips were thick and his skin a deep red-brown. He was clad in a kilt and mantle beautifully embroidered with an assortment of strange intricate symbols in rich colours wore a headdress of bright feathers and carried a thin-bladed dangerous-looking little hatchet stuck in his gilded leather girdle. Although Richard had never set eyes on one before he knew from pictures he had seen that the little fellow must be some kind of Indian from the Americas.

`Good day, Monsieur de Cavasuto,' said the Señorita, regarding him with an amused smile. 'You seem quite taken aback at the sight of my page. Do you not think him a handsome poppet?'

It was true enough that the boy had distinction in every line of his thin, eagle-beaked face and proud bearing. Quickly recovering his manners, Richard replied hastily: `Indeed he is, Señorita. I trust you will forgive me for having stared at him, but 'tis the first time I have ever seen one of his race, and it took me by surprise to see a lady like yourself accompanied by such an unusual attendant.'

She shrugged. `Madame du Barri had her Blackamoor, so why should not I have my Indian? Though fittingly, I feel, her Zamora was a vulgar little imp, whereas my Quetzal is an admirably behaved child and the son of an Aztec Prince. Turning, she spoke in Spanish to the boy, telling him to make his bow to the handsome gentleman.

Instead of returning the bow Richard held out his hand English fashion.

After a slight hesitation Quetzal placed his small red hand in Richard's long one, and said something in Spanish to his mistress.

`What did he say?' Richard asked.

The Spanish girl gave a low, rich laugh. 'He says that he admires your blue eyes Monsieur and wishes he had jewels of their colour to put into his head-dress.'

`Tell him then, please, that I find the velvet blackness of his own surpassed only by your brown ones, Señorita.'

Her olive complexion colored a little as she translated. Then she said to Richard: `our meeting is a happy chance, Monsieur, for but ten minutes back I asked Monsieur de Vaudreuil to seek you out and bring you to me'

Richard caught his breath. 'Señorita. Spare my suspense, I beg.

Can it be that Her Majesty has relented towards me, and that you are the bearer of these happy tidings?'

She shook her head. `I am sorry to disappoint you, Monsieur; but I bear no message from Her Majesty. I wished to see you again only from the interest that you inspired in me yesterday.'

To cover his disappointment he bowed; but he had difficulty in keeping it out of his voice as he replied. `I am fortunate indeed, Señorita, in having aroused the interest of a lady so charming as yourself.'

Fluttering her lace fan to hide another blush, she said with slight hauteur: `I fear that my command of the French language is still far from perfect, and that I expressed myself badly. I refer to my interest in your story. Monsieur.'

He suppressed a smile, for experience had taught him that where women were concerned interest in such stories of his past as he chose to tell, and in himself, amounted to much the same thing. Again, with a critic's eye, he took in her features and decided that she was by no means beautiful. Her soft, dark eyes were as large as, but lacked the sparkle of, Melissa's; her hair was no more lustrous, and in all other points she was by a long way inferior. The malicious might have described her complexion as sallow; her mouth, though full, was not a very good shape, her teeth were slightly uneven and the heavy brows were a mixed blessing. for though they gave her face great character they were somewhat overawing when seen close to.

`I had not flattered myself that your interest was in any way personal,' Richard declared, to spare her further embarrassment, `but I am entirely at your disposal, Señorita.' Then, offering his arm, he added. `While we converse shall we promenade for a little?'

She laid her fingers lightly on it and allowed him to lead her away from the group of other young women-who, since their meeting, had covertly been taking more interest in them than in the carp-and round the corner of the Palace theatre into the parterre designed for Louis XIV by his famous gardener, Le Notre.

After a short silence she said: `The principal reason that the story of your running away from home intrigued me so much, Monsieur, is because it would be quite impossible for such a thing to occur in Spain. I mean, of course, for a boy of good family to do such a thing. There children are made much more of by their parents than they are in France, but all the same they are brought up very strictly, and kept under constant supervision until the young men are of an age to go out into the world, and the girls to marry. I think things must be very different in England, but I know little of your customs there. Pray tell me of them.'

It was a subject that presented no pitfalls, so Richard willingly launched out on an account of the Public School system and the type of life led by boys of the upper classes when they were living at their homes during the holidays.

The Señorita showed the most intelligent interest in all he had to say and led him on to speak of his own home and his family; then, when she learned that he had an allowance of only £300 a year from his father, she enquired why he had not entered the service of his King to carve out a career for himself.

Not wishing to give the impression that he was altogether an idle good-for-nothing or, worse, an adventurer, he said that he had a passion for seeing new places and new faces, so traveled for the love of it as far as his means permitted; but that to eke them out and at the same time indulge his taste he had, on occasion, acted for his Government as a special courier, carrying dispatches to the Baltic countries and Russia.

At that her interest quickened still further and she asked if his coming to France had arisen from some commission of that kind.

He told her that it had not, and that but for his arrest he would have remained entirely his own master for some time; adding the easy lie that, an aunt having left him a nice legacy, he had decided to spend some months making a leisurely tour of the great cities of France with the object of inspecting the historic monuments they contained.

They had, by this time, walked right round the eastern end of the great Palace and entered the Garden of Diana to its north. Richard knew that the Queen's apartments looked out on it and the little town that lay immediately beyond its wall. He had wondered at her choice until he had been told that all the apartments facing south and west had at one time or another been lived in by the mistresses of past Kings, and that she was so proud that she preferred the comparatively sunless aspect to making use of rooms in which immoral women had received their royal lovers. Now, Richard glanced up at the first-floor windows and added bitterly:

'However, it seems that Her Majesty has other plans for me.'

His companion slightly increased the light pressure of her fingers on his arm. 'Be not too despondent, Monsieur. Did I believe that you had committed the heinous crime of which you were at first accused, you may be sure that I would not be talking to you now; and I can vouch for it that, although Madame Marie Antoinette allows her impulses to make her appear harsh at times, she is in reality one of the tenderest-hearted women alive. When she has had time for reflection I cannot think she will prove over-severe towards you.'

'I pray you may be right,' Richard said somewhat doubtfully. 'Yet I understand that several of her gentlemen approached her on my behalf this morning, and she refused to listen to them.'

"Tis true, and I was the witness of it. But at the time she was much occupied with other matters; for tomorrow the Court leaves Fontainebleau to return to Versailles. On that account, too, I fear I must leave you now, as I still have many matters to attend to:

Richard accompanied her to the staircase leading to the Queen's apartments, thanked her for having distracted him from his anxieties for a while, received her good wishes for a better turn in his fortunes, and then made his way back to de Vaudreuil's rooms.

This unsought interview had put him in a slightly more cheerful frame of mind. He felt that he had gained another friend near the Queen, who would do what she could on his behalf ; but he now feared that the imminent departure of the Court might prejudice the issue against him. In the bustle preparatory to the move the Queen would have little time for quiet consideration of his case, and her impulsive nature might easily lead her to not even discuss it with the King, but simply scribble a line to the Lieutenant of Police, instructing him to fill in a blank lettre de cachet to the effect that M. de Cavasuto was to be imprisoned during His Majesty's pleasure.

Such a procedure was often adopted instead of ordering imprisonment for a definite period, and it was one of the bitterest complaints of the bourgeoisie that such sentences sometimes led to people who had been incarcerated for quite minor misdemeanors, and had no influence at Court, being forgotten and left for years to rot in a dungeon.

The later afternoon was rendered no more pleasant for Richard from the fact that de Vaudreuil's garrulous servant was dismantling the sitting-room and packing up his master's things; then, after dinner, instead of enjoying the gay society that had borne him company the evening before, he found himself left alone with his worries, owing to it being the night of the Queen's weekly card party.

The jeu de la Reine had long been an institution at the Court of France, and the Queens were provided with a special allowance to support it. In addition to play the occasion was used by them to show special flavor to distinguished visitors, one or more of the Ambassadors, or others that they wished to honour, by inviting them to sit near them. Maria Leczinska, the Queen of Louis XV, had always insisted on keeping the games down to modest stakes in order to protect the players from heavy losses ; but a few years after Louis XVI ascended the throne Marie Antoinette had developed a taste for gambling, partly perhaps to distract her mind from her unhappiness at being unable to produce an heir for France.

Once bitten with the fever she had played nightly and for increasingly high stakes, so that at the end of 1777 she had lost £21,000 in excess of her income, and had been obliged to ask her husband to pay her debts. The sum was insignificant compared with those that the royal mistresses had thrown away at the tables in the past; but her gambling losses had been made much of by her enemies. It was this which, when the French Treasury had become near bankrupt, had caused the people to accuse her of having emptied it and christen her with the opprobrious name of `Madame Deficit'.

Since the birth of her children her character had changed. She had longed for them for so many years in vain that when at last they came they absorbed her interest to the exclusion of all other pleasures. She had given up frequenting the lavish, entertainments given by the younger set at her Court, reduced her even lavish expenditure on clothes, and both her stakes at the gambling tables and the frequency with which she played.

But she still enjoyed a game and naturally continued to hold her official card-parties as a part of the Court ceremonial; so that on this evening Richard, finding himself deserted and knowing that her reception was unlikely to be over before ten o'clock, decided to .go early to bed.

He hoped that sleep would soon banish his anxieties, but in that he was disappointed, and he found his wakeful mind playing round the Spanish girl with whom he bad talked that afternoon. Although she was not strictly beautiful he admitted to himself that she possessed a certain subtle attraction, and after some thought he decided that it lay largely in her voice. It was peculiarly soft and melodious, and her slightly broken French with its Spanish accent added to its fascination. Perhaps too her nationality played a part, for Spain, shut away as it was from the rest of Europe by the barrier of the Pyrenees, was still almost unknown territory, which endowed it with a glamour all its own. Very few foreigners ever visited it, but travelers' tales described it as a land of dazzling sunshine where great sterile deserts were interspersed with areas of vines, olives and orange blossom, and in which the most degrading poverty existed cheek by jowl with fabulous riches. He hoped that one day his travels would take him there, so that he would be able to witness the fiestas and bullfights for which the country was renowned.

Having got so far in his musings, he made another effort to get to sleep, but again it was not to be. A heavy knocking came on the sitting room door. It was followed by footsteps inside the room, then a sharp knock on the door of his bedroom. He had hardly called out 'Entrez' when it was opened, and by the light from outside he recognized one of his previous night's visitors. It was M. de Besenval, the Commander of the King's Swiss Guards.

'I regret to disturb you, Chevalier,' said de Besenval, in his heavy Germanic voice, `but I bear orders from Her Majesty. I must ask you to get up, dress, and accompany me:

The fact that it was de Besenval who had come to fetch him immediately confirmed Richard's fears that he might be condemned unheard and sent to eat his heart out in a fortress. He felt certain that had the Queen decided to give him a chance to justify himself she would not have used the Colonel of the Guards, but de Vaudreuil, or some other of her gentlemen, to bring him to her.

With a low-voiced assent he got out of bed; and, as he began to dress, determined to put as good a face as he could on his misfortune. De Besenval went back into the sitting-room and Richard rejoined him there some seven minutes later. On entering the room he saw that the Colonel was accompanied by two stolid looking German-Swiss privates, who were standing rigidly to attention, facing inwards on either side of the door. At the sight of them

Richard's last faint hope vanished, but he smiled at de Besenval and made him a graceful bow before placing himself between the two soldiers.

The Colonel gave an order, on which the little party left the room and began to march with measured tread down the corridor. De Besenval brought up the rear, and he had evidently given his men their instructions beforehand as they continued in silence past the first stairway, round the inner curve of the Oval court and along a gallery that gave on to the royal reception-rooms.

As the Queen's card-party was just breaking up a number of ladies and. gentlemen were leaving them to return to their own apartments. All of them looked at Richard as he passed with sympathy, and here and there among them one of the men he had met bowed to him with respect.

Having been brought round to this side of the Palace have Richard a sudden flicker of new hope that he was, after all, to be taken before the Queen; but almost as soon as it had arisen, it was quenched. His escort turned away from the tall gilded double doors and led him down the staircase opposite to them. Outside the entrance a two-horse carriage stood waiting; one of the soldiers got on the box beside the coachman, the other scrambled on to the boot; de Besenval ushered Richard into the carriage, got in beside him and pulled down the blinds. Then they set off.

After they had proceeded for a few minutes in silence, Richard said: 'is it permitted to ask, Monsieur le Baron, whither you are conducting me?'

'I regret, Monsieur,' the elderly Swiss replied, `but except in so far as my duty requires I am under orders not to talk with you.'

Left to his own speculations Richard considered all the odds were that he was being taken to Paris, and that as prisoners of gentle birth there were nearly always confined in the Bastille, that was his most probable destination. If so, they had a journey of some forty miles before them, so would not arrive in the capital until the small hours of the morning.

Now that he was under guard again the parole he had given to de Vaudreuil was no longer valid, so he took swift stock of his chances of escape. His only opportunity would be when they changed horses, as it was certain they would do a number of times on the road. Since de Besenval had not locked either of the carriage doors, should he get out of one to stretch his legs when they halted there would be nothing to stop his prisoner slipping out of the other. But from the second the prisoner pest his foot to the ground he would be in acute danger-as the two Swiss on the box and the boot were both armed with muskets, and it was a hundred to one that they would shoot if he attempted to make a bolt for it.

Having weighed the pros and cons Richard decided that, even if the opportunity occurred, to present himself as a target for two musket-balls fired at close range was too great a risk to take, so he had better resign himself to captivity, at least for the time being.

After he had settled himself more comfortably in his corner of the carriage the rhythm of its wheels and the horses' hoofs began to make him drowsy. For the better part of two days he had been subject to acute anxiety and the sudden, if temporary, cessation of wondering what was about to happen to himself had its reaction. The sleep that he had sought in vain an hour before now kindly enveloped him.

He awoke with a start. The carriage had stopped and he felt certain that he had not been asleep for long. De Besenval was getting out and said over his shoulder: 'Be pleased to follow me, Monsieur.'

As Richard stumbled from the carriage he saw, they had not drawn up before a post-house; and no ostler was at work unbuckling the traces of the horses. The carriage had halted in a broad, tree-lined avenue and, to Richard's amazement, to one end of it he caught a glimpse of the south facade of the Palace of Fontainebleau outlined by the rising moon. Suddenly it impinged upon his still drowsy brain that for the past half-hour they must have been driving away from the Palace only to return to its immediate vicinity in secret by a circuitous route.

To one side of the avenue the trees opened to disclose a path and at its entrance stood the cloaked and hooded figure of a woman. De Besenval saluted her and, beckoning Richard forward, said gutturally: 'Chevalier, my instructions carry me no further than this point. Here I hand you over into the keeping of this lady. My compliments to you:

Richard returned his bow and stepped forward. The female figure stretched out a hand and took one of his. Then she said in a low, melodious voice, which he recognized as that of the Señorita d'Aranda : 'You are late, Monsieur; please to come with me and quickly.'

For a moment, as Richard hurried with her along a narrow, twisting path bordered on both sides by thick shrubberies, he thought that she must have engineered his escape; but he could scarcely believe that the Colonel of the Swiss Guards would have lent himself to such a plot.

Before he had time for further speculation they emerged into a clearing, in the center of which stood a small pavilion. Chinks of light between its drawn curtains showed that it was lit within. Ascending the three steps that led up to its verandah the Señorita drew him after her, knocked on the door and, opening it, pushed him inside.

Momentarily he was dazzled by the light; then almost overcome with stupefaction, he realized that he was standing within a few paces of the Queen. She was wearing an ermine cape over her décolleté and diamonds sparkled in her high-dressed, powdered hair. Beside her on a small table lay a sword, and he recognized it as his own.

As he sank upon one knee before her she took up the sword; and, still bewildered by this swift, unexpected turn of events, he heard her say:,

'Chevalier, I have ever been most averse to dueling, and I cannot find it in myself to condone that method of settling differences as a general principle. Yet I now know that in your affair with the Count de Caylus you were inspired by no base motive but a selfless devotion, which does you, honor. I therefore return to you your sword.'

`Madame! Madame! I . . .'.stammered Richard.

The Queen went on evenly: 'On the evening of your arrest I sent to Paris for your papers. They arrived this morning and soon after midday I found an opportunity to look through them. Among them I found a recommendation for the reconsideration of your case from my good friend M. le Comte d'Adhémar. That alone would not have been sufficient to exculpate you, but I also found a statement made by M. le Vicomte de la Tour d'Auvergne. After his flight to Brittany His Majesty dispatched an order requiring him to justify himself for his part in the affair. In doing so he takes the blame upon himself for your meeting with de Caylus ; and Monsieur le Vicomte is one of our nobles whose word everyone must respect. In the circumstances, I would think myself ungenerous were I to condemn you for the part you played.'

As she finished speaking Richard took back his sword and murmured: 'It has ever been my desire to be of service to Your Majesty, and I am now so overcome by your clemency that there is naught I would not do to prove my gratitude.'

Her blue eyes regarded him thoughtfully for a moment, then she said: 'Do you really mean that, Monsieur, or is it just one more of the empty phrases that I hear only too often at my Court? Seeing the treatment you have received at my hands, it would be more natural in you did you bear me a grudge; and I now found that my impulse to see justice done had earned me yet one more enemy.'

'Indeed, Madame!' he protested, his overwhelming relief at having escaped scot free filling his mind to the exclusion of all else. 'Your enemy I could never be. I pray you only to command me and I will prove my words; even if it means the risking of my life-'tis little less that I owe you.'

A faint smile came to her pale lips. 'Then if you have spoken rashly the fault is yours; for I have a mind to seize this opportunity and request a service of you.'

'Speak Madame. I am all attention.'

She hesitated a second before saying: 'this afternoon I sent the Señorita d'Aranda to find out what she could about you. She reported to me that you have a great love of travel and no commitments for the next six months. Is that correct?'

'It is, Your Majesty!"

'The Senorita also repeated to me all that you had told her of your youth and upbringing in England. What you said confirmed the statement of M. de la Tour d'Auvergne, that you are no common adventurer but an honorable gentleman in whom trust can be placed without fear of betrayal. At this moment I am in urgent need of such a friend.'

At the inference that she was now prepared to regard him as a trusted friend Richard could hardly believe his ears, but he said boldly

`Madame. I cannot credit that Your Majesty has not about your person a score of gentlemen who would willingly sacrifice their lives rather than betray you ; but if you need another I am your man.'

'I like your forthrightness, Monsieur,' she remarked, now smiling full upon him, 'and you are right ; but I will make myself more plain. I am indeed fortunate in having a number of gentlemen who, I feel confident, would serve me to the peril of their lives, but every one of them is known by my enemies to be my friend. They are marked men, Monsieur, whereas you are not.'

Richard now saw the way her mind had been running, and the intuition, which had often served him so well on previous occasions, told him in advance what was coming next.

From the drawer of the table she drew the thick packet that he had spitted on his sword-point as she was handing it to de Roubec two afternoons before, and said

'You will recognize this packet with which I propose to entrust you, but first I request you to listen carefully to what I am about to say ; for I do not wish to engage you in this matter without informing you of its importance to me and possible danger to yourself.'

She went on with the frankness that characterized her when speaking to people that she liked, and which was only too often abused. 'You cannot fail to be aware of the present troubled state of France. Many of the ills of which the people complain are, alas, attributed to myself. It is true that in my early years as Queen I was sometimes thoughtless and extravagant, but I cannot believe that I ever did any great harm to anyone; and in more recent years I have done everything in my power to atone, and to help the King in his projects to economize. Yet the people hate me and call me the "Austrian woman". And a certain section of the nobility bear me a hatred yet greater still'

The tears came to her blue eyes, but she brushed them aside and continued: 'These last would stop at nothing to bring about my ruin, and even in the Palace I know there to be spies who endeavor to report my every action. That is why I dare not send this packet by the hand of anyone who is known to be my friend. Should its contents be suspected they would be set upon and robbed of it before they had traversed a score of miles.

'It was in this dilemma that I thought to send it by a stranger, the man de Roubec. The Marquis de St. Hurugb, whom I now judge to be one of the many traitors that infest the Court, recommended him to me. It is yourself I have to thank for having saved me from that, and I now feel that I should have sent last night to let you know that I had not forgotten it. For I do assure you, Monsieur, that even had I not learned the truth I should have counted your service to me as going a long way to mitigate any sentence that His Majesty proposed to inflict upon you.'

Richard smiled. 'I thank you, Madame; although, knowing de Roubec, it was an act I would have performed to protect the interests of any lady.'

'Nevertheless, Monsieur, I happened to be that lady, and you served me well. But now about yourself. I sent Monsieur de Besenval for you with his guards deliberately tonight, and gave him orders to march you through the gallery outside my anteroom, then downstairs to a closed carriage, just as my reception was breaking up. Having witnessed your departure in such circumstances the whole Court will now believe you to be in the Bastille, and even if you are seen at liberty later my enemies will never believe you to be any friend of mine. In this way I have sought to give you immunity from their attentions, and I trust you will be able to convey this dispatch to its destination without encountering any opposition.'

As she handed the packet to him he saw that it bore no superscription, so he asked: 'To whom am I to bear it, Madame?'

'To my younger brother, the Grand Duke of Tuscany,' she replied. 'For some time past reports from Vienna have informed me that my elder brother, the Emperor, has been seriously ill, so he has no longer been in a state to take his former interests in my affairs. It is on that account that Grand Duke Leopold is showing additional concern for me. He wrote recently asking that I should furnish him with full particulars of the crisis with which we are faced, and my own personal views as to what course events are likely to take. This dispatch contains all the information he has requested of me, including my private opinions of Monsieur Necker and the other Ministers in whose hands His Majesty has now placed himself. Some of those opinions are by no means favourable, so I need hardly stress how vital it is that this document should not fall into the hands of my enemies. If it did it would certainly prove my ruin.'

`Have no fear, Madame; Richard said firmly. `No one shall take it from me while I live, and His Highness the Grand Duke shall know your views as swiftly as strong horses can carry me to Florence.'

`I thank you from my heart, Monsieur,' sighed the Queen, and once more there were tears in her eyes. Then she drew a fine diamond ring from her finger and added: `Take this and sell it to cover the expenses of your journey ; or, if you prefer, keep it as a souvenir of an unhappy woman.'

Richard took the ring and, kneeling, kissed the beautiful white hand that she extended to him.

As he rose and backed towards the door, she raised her voice and called: 'Tansanta! Tansanta, my child I Pray conduct Monsieur le Chevalier back to the carriage.

At her call the Señorita opened the door behind him and led the way out down the steps of the little pavilion into the semidarkness of the shrubbery.

`You have accepted Her Majesty's mission, Monsieur?' she asked in her soft voice.

`Willingly, Señorita,' he replied. `And it would not surprise me overmuch if it was yourself who proposed me for this honor.'

`Her Majesty was at her wits' end for a messenger who would not be suspected by her enemies,' murmured the Señorita, `and I had the happy thought that you did not seem the type of man to bear a grudge, so might be willing to serve her in this emergency.' Then she added quickly.

`The carriage will take you the first stage of your journey south during the night. In it you will find your valise with all your things. Monsieur de Vaudreuil packed them for you and brought them here himself. It remains, Monsieur, only for me to wish you a safe and pleasant journey.'

They had traversed the, short path while they were speaking, and already come out into the open, where the carriage waited some ten yards away. As they halted he turned to face her for a moment in the moonlight. In it her olive complexion no longer looked near sallow, and her black eyebrows no longer seemed to overpower her long oval face. It suddenly came to Richard that in her own strange way she was beautiful.

He said in a low voice: 'Directly my mission is accomplished I shall return to Versailles. May I hope, Señorita, that you will permit me to wait upon you there; for I should much like to develop our acquaintance.'

She shook her head. 'I fear that is not to be, Monsieur; and that our . . . yes, let us say friendship, in view of the secret that we share, must end here. When the Court moves tomorrow I leave it to quit France and return to my parents, so 'tis most unlikely that we shall ever meet again:

But the Fates had interwoven the destinies of these two, and while they thought they were making a final parting it was decreed that they were to cross one another's paths again quite soon. And, by the weaving of those same fates, Queen Marie Antoinette, who believed that she might yet enjoy many happy years with her husband and children, was never to witness the setting of another sun at Fontainebleau.

CHAPTER FIVE
THE UNWORTHY PRIEST

Richard's tentative bid to start an affaire with the Señorita Tansanta d'Aranda was no more than a momentary impulse, brought about through the additional attraction lent her by the moonlight. No sooner was the carriage bowling down the avenue than she had passed entirely from his thoughts and his whole mind became occupied with the Queen.

He was already aware that during the past twenty minutes he had been very far from his normal self. That was partly due to the stunning suddenness with which his despair of escaping a long spell of imprisonment had been dissipated. But he felt that it must be something more than that which had caused him to use expressions of such extravagant devotion to Madame Marie Antoinette, and declare himself so instantly ready to undertake a mission for her.

He had got only so far in his musings when the carriage, having reached the entrance of the park, drew to a halt. The coachman lifted the little panel in its roof and, out of the darkness, his voice came down to Richard

`Where do you wish me to drive you, Monsieur?'

It was a pleasant surprise that the man had no definite instructions; as Richard had vaguely anticipated being set down some ten miles south of Fontainebleau, then, for his own purposes, having to drive all the way back to Paris the following day.

`Can you take me as far as Paris?' he asked.

`Certainly, Monsieur,' replied the coachman. The little trap flipped to and they set off again.

Richard's mind at once reverted to Madame Marie Antoinette; and, while he admitted to himself that the extraordinary fascination she exerted had been the cause of his pledging himself so wholeheartedly, he was relieved to think that he had nevertheless kept his head sufficiently well not to forget the interests of Mr. Pitt.

The Prime Minister was not dependent on him for information as to what happened when the States General met, the issue of fresh edicts by the Court, a change of Ministers, or renewed resistance by the parliaments to the Royal Authority. All that and much more, he would learn from the official dispatches that the Duke of Dorset sent at least once a week to the Duke of Leeds at the Foreign Office. Richard's province was to collect special information, particularly about the private lives and intentions of the principal protagonists in the coming struggle. Of these the King and Queen were clearly by far the most important; so if by undertaking a secret journey for the latter he could return from it with the prospect of being given her full confidence, his absence for some weeks from the storm-center should more than repay him later for the loss of any smaller fish that might have swum into his net had he remained in Paris.

All the same, he wondered now if he would have been able to resist acceding to her request had it involved him in doing something contrary to the interests of his own mission. He thought he would, but was by no means certain, for he was conscious that he had been near bewitched while in her presence. Her beauty was incontestable; and, from the time of his first sight of her at quite a distance several years before, he had always thought of her as one of the most beautiful women he had ever set eyes on. But it was not that alone. He recalled an occasion when Mr. Horace Walpole had dined at Amesbury House, and how lie had raved about her, saying that she had the power of inspiring passionate and almost uncontrollable adoration. Richard understood now what the distinguished wit and man of letters had meant; for he too had come under her spell and experienced the strange effortless way in which she could move and trouble a man's spirit.

In view of her extraordinary charm, integrity and kindness, it seemed difficult to understand how it was that she had become so hated by her people. On her arrival in France, in 1770, as a young girl of fourteen to marry the Dauphin who was some fifteen months older than herself, the populace had gone wild with excitement and admiration of her beauty. Cities and towns had rivaled each other in sending her rich gifts, and at every public appearance she made she received the most enthusiastic ovations. Yet gradually her popularity had waned until she had now become the most hated woman in all Europe.

Such youthful follies and extravagances as those of which she had been guilty had not cost the country one hundredth' part of the sums Louis XV had squandered on his mistresses; and it was not until quite recently, when the dilatoriness and indecision of her husband had threatened to bring ruin to the State, that she had played any part in politics. Nevertheless, all classes, with the exception of her little circle of friends, held her responsible for the evil condition into which France had fallen.

Richard could put it down only to deliberate misrepresentation of her character and acts by those secret enemies of whom she had spoken, and he knew that they were no figment of her imagination. During his stay in Paris he had traced numerous vile calumnies, against her back to the Duc d'Orléans, and he felt certain that this cousin of the King would stop at nothing to bring about her ruin.

It occurred to him then that the Duke probably knew that the Queen had written the highly confidential letter he was carrying to her brother. She had said that the Marquis de St. Huruge had recommended de Roubec to her as a messenger, and it seemed unlikely that he would have set about finding one for her without first ascertaining where she wanted the man to go. So the odds were that de St. Huruge had known de Roubec's destination to be Florence, and that would be quite enough for him to make a shrewd guess at the general contents of the dispatch. It was just possible that he had not been aware of de Roubec's true character, but Richard doubted that; and, if the Marquis had known, it proved him to be a traitor. Knowledge of what the Queen had written to her brother could be of no value to an ordinary nobleman, but in the hands of His Highness of Orléans it might prove a trump card for her undoing; so if de St. Huruge had planned to secure the dispatch it could only be because he intended to pass it on to someone else, and, in the circumstances, everything pointed to that person being His Highness.

Assuming that there had been a plot to get hold of the letter, Richard argued, as it bad miscarried, by this time de Roubec would have reported his discomfiture to de St Huruge, and the Marquis would have told the Duke; but there was no reason to suppose that they would be prepared to accept their failure as final, any more than that the Queen should have abandoned her intention of sending her dispatch. She had said that she was surrounded by spies, so although she might no longer trust de St. Huruge, others about her person who were secretly in the pay of d'Orléans might have been primed to do all in their power to find out whom she would next select as her courier to Tuscany. Evidently she feared something of the kind or she would not have taken such elaborate precautions to conceal her choice of a new messenger, and his departure.

Richard felt that in that she had shown considerable skill; for after having seen him marched away between guards it was highly unlikely that any member of her Court would suspect her of having entrusted him with anything. Nevertheless, to give him the letter she had had to slip out of the Palace late at night; and, if there was an Orleanist spy among her women, it was quite possible that she had been followed. If so he might have been seen leaving or entering the carriage when it was drawn up near the little pavilion, and recognized; in which case her stratagem had by now

been rendered entirely worthless news would soon reach the Duke.

Even if such were the case, and the Queen's enemies knew the direction he had taken, it seemed unlikely that they would have time to arrange to lay an ambush for him before he reached Paris, but he felt that from then on he ought to regard himself as in constant danger from attack, and take every precaution against being caught by surprise.

Had he been entirely his own master, he would not have returned to Paris at all, but there were several matters in connection with his work for Mr. Pitt that required his attention in the capital before he could take the road to Italy with a clear conscience. All the same, he decided that he would lie very low while in Paris, both to prevent as far as possible such people as believed him to be in the Bastille becoming disabused about that, and in case the Orleanists were on his track.

It was with this in mind that, soon after four in the morning, when the carriage reached the village of Villejuif, just outside Paris, Richard told the coachman not to drive into the city but to take him to some quiet respectable inn in its south western suburbs.

Although dawn had not yet come, and only a faint grayness in the eastern sky heralded its approach, the barrier was already open to let through a string of carts and wagons carrying produce to the markets. The coachman was evidently familiar with the quarter as, having passed the gate, he drove without hesitation through several streets into the Faubourg St. Marcel and there set Richard down at a hostelry opposite the royal factory where the Gobelins tapestries were made. Having thanked the man Richard knocked up the innkeeper, had himself shown to a room and went straight to bed.

When he awoke it was nearly midday. His first act was to take the packet entrusted to him by the Queen from beneath his pillow and stare at it. Already. the night before, he had been considerably worried on the score of a fine point of ethics in which the possession of it involved him, but he had put off taking any decision until he had slept upon the matter. Now, sleep on it he had, and he knew that he must delay no longer in facing up to this very unpleasant dilemma. -

As an agent of the British Government who had been specially charged, among other matters, to endeavor to ascertain the Queen's views on the course that events might take and the personalities most likely to influence that course, it was clearly his duty to open the dispatch and make himself acquainted with its contents. In fact, had he prayed for a miracle to aid him in that respect, and his prayer had been granted, Heaven could hardly have done more than cast the packet down with a bump at his feet.

On the other hand he felt the strongest possible repugnance to opening the packet, in view of the fact that the Queen herself had given it into his hands, believing him to be entirely worthy of her trust.

For over a quarter-of-an-hour he turned the packet this way and that, agonizingly torn between two loyalties; then at length, his ideas began to clarify. His paramount loyalty was to his own country and had this beautiful foreign Queen asked him to do anything to the prejudice of Britain he knew that he would have refused her. More, in undertaking to act as her messenger he had been influenced, at least to some extent, by the thought that by doing so he would win her confidence. But why did he wish   to win her confidence? Solely that he might report how her mind was working to Mr. Pitt. And here, in the letter he held, he had, not just stray thoughts that she might later have confided to hum, but her carefully considered opinion, under his hand already. Surely it was to strain at a gnat and swallow a camel, to deliver the letter unopened then return to Versailles with the deliberate intention of spying on her afterwards.

There remained the fact that he had given her his word that he would protect the letter with his life from falling into the hands of her enemies. But Mr. Pitt was excellently disposed towards her and would certainly not allow the contents of her letter to be known to anyone who wished her harm. As an additional safeguard he could write to Mr. Pitt, relating the circumstances in which the letter had come into his possession, and requesting that the copy of it should be for his eye alone. The Prime Minister was too honorable a man not to appreciate the delicacy of the matter and strictly observe such a request.

Getting out of bed Richard took his traveling knife from his breeches pocket, lit the bedside candle with his tinder box, and, having heated the blade of the knife in the flame, began gently to pries up one of the heavy seals on the letter. After twenty minutes' cautious work he had raised three of the seals without breaking any of them, so was able to lift the flap of the envelope and draw out the twenty or more sheets covered with writing that it contained. One glance at the document was enough to show him that it was in code.

He was not at all surprised at that, and had half expected it, as he knew that the members of all royal families habitually conducted their private correspondence with one another in cipher. But such ciphers could be broken with comparative ease, and although the circumstances deprived him of learning the Queen's outlook he knew that it would not long prevent Mr. Pitt-from doing so.

Returning the papers to their envelope, he put the whole in a deep pocket in the lining of his coat, then he proceeded to dress, and go downstairs to the coffee-room. There he ordered an extremely hearty breakfast, which he ate with scarcely a thought as to its constituents but considerable relish. Having done he Wormed the landlord that he would be requiring his room for at least one, and perhaps two, nights, after which he went out and, knowing that he would have difficulty in finding a hackney coach in that unfashionable district, took the first omnibus he saw that was going in the direction of central Paris.

At the Pont Neuf he got out, walked across the point of the Isle de la Cite and on reaching the north bank of the Seine turned left along it, all the while keeping a sharp look-out to avoid any chance encounter with some acquaintance who might recognize him. Having passed under the southern facade of the Louvre he entered the gardens of the Palais des Tuileries. There, he picked eleven leaves and a single twig from a low branch of one of the plane trees and inserted them in an envelope he had brought for the purpose.

Continuing his walk he traversed the gardens, came out in the Rue St. Honoré and turned west along it. He had not proceeded far when he encountered a mob of some thirty rough-looking men who formed a ragged little procession, moving in the opposite direction. A foxy-faced fellow somewhat better dressed than the others led the group, carrying a placard on which had been scrawled: `Help us to choke him with his fifteen sous`. Down with the oppressors of the poor: Beside him a woman with matted black hair was beating a tattoo on a small drum, and several of their comrades were calling on the passers-by to join them.

Throughout most of the country the elections had now been completed but Paris was far behind and the contests were still being fought with considerable high feeling; so Richard assumed that the little band of roughs were on their way to a political meeting. Soon after passing them he went into a barber's shop and asked for Monsieur Aubert.

The proprietor came out of a back room and greeted Richard civilly as an old acquaintance; upon which he produced the envelope containing the eleven leaves and the single twig from his pocket and said:

`I pray you, Monsieur Aubert, to give this to you-know-who, when he comes in tomorrow morning.'

The barber gave him an understanding smile, pocketed the envelope and bowed him out of the shop.

Having no desire to linger in a quarter where he might run into other people whom he knew, Richard hailed a passing hackney coach, and told the driver to take him out to Passy, but to stop on the way at the first stationer's they passed.

At the stationer's he purchased some sheets of fine parchment, some tracing paper, and several quill pens, all of which had been sharpened to very fine points; then he continued on his way.

The coach took him along the north bank of the Seine and round its great bend to the south-west, where the narrow streets gave way to houses standing in their own gardens and then the open country. After proceeding some way through fields it entered the pleasant village of Passy, where Richard directed the coachman to a charming little house. Getting out he told the man that he might be there only a few minutes or for a couple of hours but in the latter case he would pay him well for waiting; then he walked up the neat garden path and pulled the bell.

The door was opened by a man-servant in dark livery, of whom Richard enquired if his master had yet returned from the country. To his great satisfaction the answer was in the affirmative and the owner of the house at home; so he gave his name to the servant, and was shown into a handsomely furnished parlor on the ground floor, that he had come to know well when he had been living in Paris two years earlier.

While he waited there for a few moments he congratulated himself on having run his old friend to earth. He had been bitterly disappointed at his failure to do so a fortnight before, owing to his belief that the man he had come to see could, if he would, give him a shrewder forecast of what was likely to happen when the States General met than anyone else in the whole of France. Had it not been for that he would never have come out to Passy today; but he had felt that he must make a final effort to secure this interview, even at the price of the news getting about that he was again a free man; as before leaving for Italy he had to make out a final report for Mr. Pitt.

The door opened to disclose a slim, youngish man of middle height, richly dressed in violet silk and leaning on a malacca cane. His face was thin and aristocratic, its haughty expression being redeemed by a dryly humorous mouth, lively blue eyes and a slightly retroussé nose. He had, until quite recently, been known as Monsieur l'Abbe de Périgord, he was now Bishop of Autun, and in time to come was to bear the titles of Due de Bénévent, Prince de Talleyrand, Arch-Chancellor of Europe.

Richard's engaging smile lit up his bronzed face, as he bowed. 'I trust that you have not forgotten me, Monseigneur l'Evéque?'

'Mon ami ; how could I ever do that?' replied the Bishop with his accustomed charm. Then limping into the room he waved Richard to a chair, sat down himself, and added in his unusually deep and sonorous voice: 'But tell me, where have you sprung from? Have you but just crossed from England, or have you been for some time in France?'

'I have only this morning been let out of the Bastille,' lied Richard glibly.

'Ho! Ho!' exclaimed the prelate. 'And in what way did you incur His Majesty's displeasure to the point of his affording you such an unwelcome hospitality?'

' Twas that old affair of de Caylus. I thought the charges against me long-since withdrawn and the whole matter forgotten; but I proved mistaken. On going for a change of air to Fontainebleau I was recognized by some members of the Court and found myself clapped into prison.'

'Were you there long?'

'Nay; though I experienced all the distress of mind occasioned by believing that I might be. Evidently it was felt that after such a lapse of time a single night's imprisonment would be sufficient to impress upon me how unpleasant a much longer stay would be should I err again. When I had breakfasted the Governor came to tell me that simultaneously with receiving the order for my incarceration he had had instructions to let me out in the morning.'

'You were lucky to get off so lightly; and most ill-advised to return to France without first making certain that the order for your arrest had been cancelled. Monsieur de Crosne's people have a long memory for cases such as yours:

Richard made a wry grimace. 'I did not find it in the least light to spend a night in a cell imagining that I was to be kept there, perhaps for years. And 'twas not the Lieutenant of Police sent me there. The people I saw at Fontainebleau, with one exception, proved most sympathetic; so I would, I think, have escaped this extremely unpleasant experience had it not been for the malice of the Queen.'

'Ah I ' murmured de Périgord with a sudden frown. 'So you fell foul of that interfering woman, eh?'

Richard was well aware of the strong animosity that his host, not altogether without cause, bore the Queen, and he had deliberately played upon it. Only three days before, too, he had had ample confirmation that the dislike was mutual from the Queen stigmatizing his friend as 'that unworthy priest'. With a cynical little smile he remarked:

'I well remember you telling me how Her Majesty intervened to prevent your receiving the Cardinal's Hat that His Holiness had promised you on the recommendation of King Gustavus of Sweden. but I had thought your animus against her might have softened somewhat since they have given you a Bishopric.'

'Given!' echoed de Périgord with a sneer 'Save the mark." And what a miserable Bishopric at that! I want not if Their Majesties resented it most having to appoint me to it or myself receiving such a mess of pottage. They did so only because my father when on his deathbed eighteen months ago made it a last request, so it was one, which they could scarce, refuse. As for myself, I am now thirty-four, and have had better claims than most to a mitre for these ten years past. On the King belatedly agreeing to my preferment he might at least have given me the Archbishopric of Bourges, which was vacant at the time. But no, he fobs me off with Autun, a see that brings me in only a beggarly twenty-two thousand livres a year.'

At that moment the man-servant entered carrying a tray with a bottle in an ice-bucket and two tall glasses.

'You will join me in a glass of wine, will you not?' said the Bishop.' At this hour one's palate is still fresh enough to appreciate une tête de cuvée, and I believe you will find this quite passable.'

It was in fact a Grand Montrachet of the year '72, and in its golden depths lay all the garnered sunshine of a long-past summer. Having sipped it, Richard thanked his host for the joy of sharing such a bottle. Then, when the servant had withdrawn, he reverted to their previous conversation by remarking with a smile:

"Tis indeed sad that Their Majesties' narrow-mindedness should have deprived Your Grace of enjoying the best of both worlds.' It was as tactful a reference as could be made to the fait that de Périgord had only himself to blame for being passed over, since, even in this age of profligacy, his immoralities had scandalized all Paris, whereas the King and Queen 'were notoriously devout. But the Bishop took him seriously, and protested.

'Mon ami, to mix up one world with the other is to ignore reality. Like hundreds of other ordained priests-yes, and many of them high dignitaries like myself-I was not consulted when put into the Church, and felt no calling whatever for it. Women, scripture tells us, were created for the joy of man, and to deny us our right to the enjoyment of them is, therefore, clearly against the will of God, let alone Nature. Since we are forbidden to marry we resort to other measures, and where is the harm in that? From time immemorial the Kings of France have known and condoned it. And I count it most unfair that the fact that I have been more fortunate than many in securing those enjoyments should be held against me.

'On the other hand, in my role of Agent General to the Clergy of the Province of Tours I was zealous in my duties and proved myself a capable administrator. So much so that when the subject of my nomination to a see came before the King I had the full support of the leading Churchmen in France, who made strong

representations to His Majesty in my favor, and urged that my love affairs should be overlooked as no more than youthful peccadilloes.'

'Am I to take it, then, that you have now become a model of rectitude?' Richard grinned.

De Périgord grinned back. 'Far from it, I fear. And I have no more liking for playing the Churchman than I had of old. But you may have noticed the suit I am wearing. I found the violet robes of a Bishop most becoming to me, so as a graceful concession to the Church I had some lay garments made of the same colour.'

'How did your flock take that?' asked Richard. 'For I sought you out when I first arrived in Paris, some three weeks back, only to learn that you were absent on a visit to your see.'

'Ah,' sighed the Bishop. 'That was a serious business, and I could afford to take no chances of giving offence by my preference for lay attire. Believe it or not, for a whole month I played the dignified Churchman. But unfortunately I was so out of practice that at one High Mass I forgot the ritual.' He laughed, and went on: 'I had never visited my see before, feeling that it was quite sufficient to send them from time to time a pastoral letter that positively stank of piety ; and I pray God that I may never have to go there again. But this visit was essential, as I wished to get myself elected to represent the clergy of the diocese at the forthcoming meeting of the States General.'

'From the news-sheets I gather that you succeeded, and I offer Your Grace my felicitations.'

'A thousand thanks: De Périgord gracefully inclined his head. 'The result, though, was a foregone conclusion. I gave the poor wretches of clergy dinners the like of which they had never seen, and flattered every woman of influence into the belief that I wanted to sleep with her. But once elected I cared not a fig for what any of them thought of me. In, fact, so little did I care that, being near desperate to get back to the civilized air of Paris, I shook the dust of Autun off my feet and drove off in my coach at nine o'clock on the morning of Easter Sunday.'

The conversation having got round to the States General, Richard had no intention of letting it wander away again, so he said:

'There have been so many postponements of the meeting of the State. that one begins to doubt if it will ever assemble.'

'You need have no fear on that score,' de Périgord assured him quickly. 'And the postponements were quite unavoidable. As an Englishman. you can have little idea of what this meeting means to France, and the innumerable questions which have had to be decided before it could be brought about at all. Not only have the States not been convened for seven generations, but when last called together they were by no means representative of the nation; and in the present crisis to summon any assembly that was not would have been completely futile. In consequence nearly all-ancient precedent was found to be worse than useless. It is in fact the first general election that France has ever had, so we had to work out the principles upon which it was to be held from the very beginning. I spent several months last year assisting Monsieur Necker to do so, and the problem positively bristled with difficulties:

'What is your opinion of Monsieur Necker?" interjected Richard.

'He is an extremely capable financier but a most incapable statesman,' replied de Périgord succinctly. 'No one short of a financial genius could have kept the Treasury solvent during these many months it has taken to arrange the elections; but in all other respects he is a mediocre man. His mind is not big enough to grasp the magnitude of the issues at stake, and his Liberal leanings are inspired by sentiment rather than any true understanding of the needs of the nation. A year ago I placed considerable hopes in him ; but I have come to know him better since, and soon perceived that vanity governs nine-tenths of his actions. Were it not that when faced with a crisis he often takes the shrewd advice of his daughter I am convinced that' long before this the public would have recognized him for what he is-a man of straw.'

'By "his daughter" I take it you refer to Madame de Staël?'

'Yes. He has but one; and I count her far his superior in intelligence. She is a brilliant woman and should have done better for herself than to marry the Swedish Minister here. 'Tis a thousand pities that matters between her and your Mr. Pitt came to naught.'

'Mr. Pitt!' exclaimed Richard. 'I had never thought of him as a marrying man.'

'No doubt he has found himself too fully occupied in recent years to concern himself with matrimony. But when he paid his only visit to this country, in '83, I can assure you that the project of his espousing Mademoiselle Necker was broached, for he told me so himself. Monsieur Necker, although very rich, was no more than Sub-Controller of the Finances at the time, and an alliance with Lord Chatham's brilliant younger son would have been a strong card for his advancement; so both he and his wife were eager for the match. Mr. Pitt, too, was by no means disinclined to it. But I believe the young lady had other views, and it was on that account that matters got no further:

`You amaze me. But please continue with what you were telling me of Monsieur Necker's character. It seems from what you say that there is little likelihood of his being able to dominate the States General.'

De Périgord shook his head. 'Far from it. And his task will be rendered no easier from the fact that both the King and Queen distrust him. In that, for once, they are right. His popularity with the masses has gone to his head, and to retain the favor of the mob himself he is capable of advising them to commit any folly.'

`Then unless the King makes a change of Ministers it looks as if the deputies will be given free rein. Which among them do you consider are likely to prove the leading spirits:

'It is impossible to say. 'Tis clear too that you do not yet appreciate the complete novelty of the situation. As I was remarking a while back, no election even remotely similar to this has ever been held in France before. Only the very poorest persons, who pay no taxes at all, have been excluded from the franchise, so the total number of voters is nearly six million. But they do not vote directly for the deputies who will represent them in the States. The electoral machinery is of an incredible complexity, and final agreement on it was reached only after months of bitter wrangling. Many cities stood out for making their own arrangements and the system in some provinces differs from that in others. But, in the main, groups of people, varying widely in numbers, vote for somebody to represent them in a local assembly, and it is these assemblies, which in turn elect the deputies.

'Such a loose arrangement means that all sorts of strange characters will arrive at Versailles next month. One thing is certain; not even the names of most of them will be known to any of the others. Yet any one of them may prove a man of destiny whose name will soon be known throughout all Europe.'

Richard nodded. 'You are, of course, speaking of the Third Estate; but what of the first two Orders? Surely they will also include many able men, and men of far wider experience; so is it not highly probable that some among them are likely to become the new leaders of the nation?'

'Their assemblies will prove almost as chaotic. It is estimated that there are some one hundred and fifty thousand clergy in France, and that the nobles total about the same number; for the latter include all the lesser nobility, which in England you term

your gentry. Yet only three hundred-odd deputies will represent each of these great bodies of electors. In the elections of the clergy many high dignitaries have been passed over and a considerable number of cure who have never before left their villages have been returned. The same applies to the nobles. More than half of those so far elected are poor country dwellers whose fortune consists of little but a few acres of land and a coat of arms. And the Nobility of the Robe, which you might term the law-lords, who are undoubtedly the class most fitted to give an opinion on the matters we shall be called on to consider, are hardly represented at all.'

The Bishop offered his snuff-box ; took a pinch himself, held it for a moment under the slightly retroussé nose that gave his face such piquancy, made a graceful gesture of flicking away the grains with a lace handkerchief, then went on

'Moreover, I greatly doubt if either of the first two Orders will be in any situation to influence the Third. On ancient precedent all three should have had an equal number of representatives; and had I been the King I would have stood out for that, even had it meant calling out my troops. But the weak fool gave way to popular clamor, as usual, and assented to the agitators' demands that the Third Estate should be allowed to send deputies to Versailles that equaled in numbers the other two together. Since it is certain that many of the poorer clergy and nobility will side with the Third Estate, and few, if any, of them with the other Orders, it seems to me inevitable that the natural defenders of the royal prerogative are doomed to defeat from the very outset.!

'But I thought the three Orders were to deliberate separately,' Richard demurred. 'If so, you will still be two to one.'

'That is the present arrangement; but how long will it hold well when put into practice?' asked de Périgord darkly.

After a moment's silence, Richard said: 'From what you tell me, when the States do meet they will add up to a fine penn'orth of all sorts, so out of it should come some original ideas of-merit.' - 'Later, perhaps; but not to begin with, as all the deputies must, in theory, voice only the views expressed in their cahiers. The King has not convened the States to deliberate upon certain measures that his Ministers will put before them. He has been idiotic enough to ask everyone in the country to advise him how to get it out of the mess that it is in. So hundreds of thousands of know-ails have taken upon themselves the role of acting as his Ministers-designate overnight. For the past six months every group of voters has become a heated debating society, and the most determined members of each have drawn up programmes which their elected representatives took with them to the local assemblies. In the assemblies, once more, each separate cahier has been the subject of violent dispute, and at length the salient points in all have been combined in still stronger cahiers for each deputy. The deputies will bring these cahiers to Versailles as their instructions from their constituents, and they have no legal right to depart from them.'

Richard nodded. `Of that I was aware; but surely the cahiers, being the consensus of opinion of every thinking man in France, must contain many new proposals of value?'

'From those I have so far seen, they contain far fewer than one would expect. Most of the originals emanating from the peasantry were completely valueless. Naturally, such people are utterly lacking in every kind of knowledge outside their local affairs. Apart from the childish demand that all taxes should be abolished, and the two senior Orders deprived of their manorial rights, they contain little other than such requests as that His Majesty should be graciously pleased to order the cleaning out of the village ditch. As to the others, they are almost universally of a pattern, modelled upon prototypes which were widely circulated in pamphlet form, having first been drafted by men such as Monsieur L'Abbe Sieyès.'

`What do you think of Sieyès?' Richard enquired.

`I have no personal liking for him. He is a dry, withered little man 'to whom nature gave a cold, calculating brain instead of a heart. Beyond self-interest he has few passions, except for his bitter hatred of aristocracy in all its forms. As a Churchman he is no better than myself, and his own Order passed him over in the elections. But I understand that in view of his great services to the opponents of absolutism he is being permitted to offer himself for election as one of the deputies for Paris; so no doubt he will secure a seat in the Third Estate.'

The Bishop paused to refill the wineglasses, then went on. 'As an Englishman you may not have seen his pamphlet which began:

" What is the Third Estate? . What has it been until now in the political order? Nothing. What does it ask? To be something." Its circulation ran into many thousands and instantly placed him in the forefront of the struggle for reform. I would not trust him an inch, and do not believe that he has the courage required to become a great leader ; but if we achieve a Constitution he may go far. His specimen cahier has certainly exerted an immense influence on the drafting of a high proportion of those which will be brought to Versailles.!

'And what of your own?' smiled Richard.

De Périgord laughed. `I have no worries on that score, for I drafted it myself.'

`It would interest me greatly to hear its contents.'

Von ami, I would not dream of boring you with it. 'Tis full of the sort of clap-trap that fools swallow readily, and I have no intention of giving it another thought.!

'Tell me what other men besides Monsieur L'Abbe Sieyès you think likely to make their mark.'

'Malouet should stand out from the integrity of his character, if men of moderate views are listened to. Mounier also, for he is the best known politician in France, and esteemed an oracle on all questions of parliamentary procedure. Then there are Dupont de Nemours, the economist, Bailly, the much-respected astronomer, Louis de Narbonne and Clermont-Tonnerre, all of whom you will recall having met here when you used to frequent my breakfast parties, and all men of considerable ability. But, as I have already, told you, the potentialities of the great majority of the deputies-elect are still entirely unknown to us here in Paris.!

'You make no mention of the Comte de Mirabeau:

`I thought it unnecessary. Honore Gabriel Riquetti stands head and shoulders above all the others I have mentioned, not only physically but mentally. As his cantankerous old father, the Marquis, refused to give him even the small fief required for him to qualify for election to the Second Estate, he stood for the Third at both Marseilles and Aix. Both cities elected him and he has chosen to sit for the latter. Whatever may be the fate of other deputies, in an assembly resembling the Tower of Babel from everyone wanting to air his opinions at once, you may be certain that de Mirabeau will not allow himself to be howled down.!

'Think you he has the qualities to make himself a great leader?'

For once de Périgord hesitated, his smooth forehead wrinkling into a frown; then he said : - "Tis difficult to say. All the world knows that the fellow is a born scamp. That he has spent several years of his life in a variety of prisons is not altogether his own fault, as his father pursued him with the utmost malice, and consigned him to them on a number of lettres de cachet. But whenever he was out of prison he lived in a most shady fashion, resorting to many a degrading shift in order to get money to gratify his passions. I doubt if his immoralities have actually been greater than my own but he has certainly conducted them with greater folly. He deserted his wife and abducted that of a Noble of the Robe. Then he deserted her and ran away with a young woman from a Convent who was near becoming a nun.

`I believe him to be honest and a true patriot. He is certainly a man of great intellectual gifts and fierce determination. I am sure that he would shrink from saying, writing or doing nothing, which he believed to be- in the interests of his cause. But the Riquetti are of Italian origin, and his hot southern blood goes to that great head of his at times, and I fear that the violence of his passions may prove his undoing.'

'Great as is his popularity with the masses,' Richard remarked, `one can hardly imagine that, should the King grant a Constitution, he would be inclined to entrust a man having such a history with the formation of a Government:

A cynical smile twitched the corners of the Bishop's lips, as he asked: `Who can tell, mon ami, how much say the King will be allowed in the choice of his. future Ministers?'

`You feel convinced then that the States will not only succeed in forcing him to grant a Constitution, but reduce him to a cipher into the bargain?'

De Périgord nodded. 'I do. I think the monarchy, decadent as it has become, rests upon too secure a foundation to be overthrown, and none but a handful of extremists would wish it. But once the States meet you may be certain that they will not rest content with any half measures.'

`I agree with what you say about the monarchy, but what of the present occupant of the throne? Is there not a possibility that the Duc d'Orléans may attempt to supplant him; or at least get himself made Lieutenant-General of the Kingdom, with the powers of a Regent?'

The expressive eyes of the wily Churchman suddenly became quite vacant, then in a casual tone he replied: `His Highness of Orleans undoubtedly has ambitions to play a greater part in affairs of State, but I can scarce believe that he could carry them so far as to become guilty of treason to the King.'

Richard felt certain that his clever friend was now lying, and so, almost certainly, involved to some extent in the Orleanist plot himself. He therefore refrained from pressing the point and asked:

'Do you perchance know Monsieur de St. Huruge?'

Not intimately He frequents the royal circle, I believe, and for a long time past I have not been persona grata at Court. But why do you ask?'

'Because I was given a letter of introduction to him before I left England,' Richard lied; `and I have so far failed to discover his present address.'

`You might try the Palais Royale,' suggested de Périgord `I do not go there often these days, but it chanced that I was there last week, and as I was on my way in to His Highness's cabinet I passed de St. Huruge on his way out. Possibly one of the secretaries may be able to tell you where he lives:

The fact that the villainous de Roubec's sponsor had been seen coming from an interview with the Duc d'Orléans in his Paris home was no proof that he was necessarily an Orleanist himself; but it certainly lent considerable support to Richard's theory that he might be. And in view of de Périgord evident reluctance to discuss d'Orléans he felt that he had been lucky to pick up this little piece. of information. Having thanked the Bishop for his suggestion, he added:

`However, since I should still have to enquire of his whereabouts from a third party, I fear I shall not have time to find and wait upon him; as I am leaving Paris quite shortly.'

`Indeed!' De Périgord raised his eyebrows. `I am most sorry to hear it. You have been absent from Paris for so long; I was particularly looking forward t® the renewed enjoyment of your society.'

As Richard bowed his acknowledgment of the graceful compliment, the Bishop went on: 'Really; you should at least remain to witness the opening of the States. It will be vastly interesting; and I should be happy to introduce you to all the deputies of my acquaintance.'

`I thank Your Grace for your kindness, and most tempting offer.' Richard's voice held genuine regret. `But, alas, I must decline it. Her Majesty's disapproval of duelling did not manifest itself in my case only by her causing me to spend a night in the Bastille. When I was released this morning the Governor informed me of her further order, that within forty-eight hours I was to leave Paris:

'What childish tyranny!' exclaimed the Bishop with some petulance. 'Whither are you going?'

To Provence. I have never seen your great cities there or the Mediterranean; and I am told that the coast in those regions is particularly lovely at this time of year:

De Périgord took snuff again. 'You are no doubt wise to keep out of the way for the next few weeks. But I should not let any fear of that order deter you from returning by June if you wish to do so. The royal authority has already become so weakened

that it has almost ceased to count. And once the States have been sitting for a little the Court will be plaguey careful not to irritate them unnecessarily by forcing the observance of such arbitrary commands,'

'You feel confident, then, that the States will still be sitting; and that the King will not dismiss them after a few abortive sessions, as he did the Assembly of Notables?'

'He dare not, if he wishes to keep his crown.' A sudden note of hauteur had crept into the Bishop's deep voice. 'At present the King is still respected by the whole nation, and even beloved by the greater part of it. But the States will represent the very blood, brains, bone and muscle of France; and if he attempted to dismiss them he would become the enemy of the whole kingdom overnight. By his decision to call the States he has delivered himself bound into the hands of his subjects; for once they are assembled they will never dissolve except by their own will. I am positive of that.'

CHAPTER SIX
THE AFFAIRE RÉVEILLON

As Richard drove himself back to Paris he felt that he had good reason to be pleased with himself. Much that the Bishop of Autun had told him-he had known before, but he had also learnt a lot, and on no previous occasion had he heard a forecast of coming events from anyone approaching de Périgord for knowledge of affairs, political acumen and subtlety of mind. In addition, he had succeeded in putting over such a skillfully distorted account of the Queen's treatment of him, that it would be all to the good if it did get about; as it was likely to do, seeing that de Périgord was an inveterate gossip. No one but the Governor of the Bastille was in a position to deny that he had been imprisoned for most of the night there, and his imminent departure to Italy would confirm the story that he had been banished. In future, therefore, he would be counted among those who bore the Queen a grudge, but no one would be surprised to see him free again; and de Périgord had himself advised him to return to Paris in a few week's time.

Half an hour's amiable converse about mutual friends, and the general state of Europe, had succeeded Richard's political talk with the Bishop; and he had left the charming little house at Passy with the firm conviction that if there was one man in France who would succeed in fishing to his own benefit in the troubled waters of the States General, he was its wily owner.

On re-entering his hackney-coach Richard had told its driver to take him to the inn where he had slept and breakfasted, as it was then nearly five o'clock, and he had decided to sup there rather than at a restaurant in central Paris, where he might run into some acquaintance and feel obliged to give again his fictitious account of the outcome of his recent arrest. Moreover, he was still a little uneasy about the possibility of an Orleanist spy knowing that he had the Queen's letter; and he did not want to be recognized and followed.

He had much to do that night, and his thoughts were already occupied with his projected labours. By the time the coach reached the Tuileries Gardens he barely took in the fact that a column of infantry was issuing from them and heading east at an unusually rapid gait; and he gave little more attention to the sight of another regiment hastily forming up outside the Louvre. But when the coach turned south to cross the Seine the sound of distant shots, coming across the river from the eastern quarter of the city, suddenly impinged upon his consciousness. The shooting was mainly spasmodic, but now and then punctuated by fusillades of musketry, so it seemed evident that something serious was afoot.

As the coach was temporarily brought to a halt by a block at the entrance of a narrow street on the far side of the river, Richard thrust his head out of the window and shouted to a group of loungers on the corner: 'What is the cause of that shooting? What is going on over there in the Faubourg St. Antoine?'

Seeing the gold lace on his hat most of the group gave him only dumb, surly looks; but a big fellow, bolder than the rest, shouted back: 'They have unearthed an agent of the Queen--one of the pigs she pays to force down the workers' wages-and are burning his house about his ears. May the flames consume him!'

The suggestion that the Queen employed agents to force down wages was, to Richard, palpably absurd; but he felt quite sickened by the episode because the big fellow had an open, honest face, and obviously believed what he had said.

On arriving at his inn he enquired again what had caused the trouble, but could get no coherent account from anyone.

Apparently it had started the previous night as a factory dispute and had flared up again early that afternoon into a major riot, to quell which it had proved necessary to call out the troops. None of the people he spoke to could tell him why the Queen should be involved in such a matter, but most of them were convinced that she was at the bottom of it.

Irritated and disgusted by their ready acccptance of these evil, unsupported rumours about her, he ordered supper, ate it in morose silence, then went up to his room.

Having unpacked the things that he had bought at the stationer's that afternoon, he spread them out on the table and sat down to it. Then he took the Queen's letter from the capacious pocket of his coat and got to work.

The task he had set himself was no easy one, as his object was to form a cipher within a cipher: so that should the dispatch fall into the hands of anyone who already knew Madame Marie Antoinette's private code, or be given to someone as clever as Mr. Pitt's cipher expert, they would still not be able to decipher it in the first case, or break it without extreme difficulty in the other. Yet the process must be accomplished according to a set of rules simple enough for him to carry in his own mind; so that on delivering the re-coded copy to the Grand Duke he would be able to tell him how to turn it back into the Queen's cipher. A further complication was that he dared not make any drastic alteration in the symbols or formation of the letter, as if he did and the recoded copy was stolen from him by someone who knew her cipher at sight, they would immediately recognize it as a fake.

For over an hour he tried out various transpositions, until he had formulated one which he felt was as good as any he could devise ; then he began to write on his parchment, forming each letter with great care. so that when he had done the re-coded copy had a superficial resemblance to the original. Having finished, he uncorked a bottle of wine he had brought up with him, had a drink, and attended to certain other matters he had in mind ; after which he inserted his copy in the thick envelope that had previously contained the Queen's letter, warmed the underside of the wax seals that he had lifted and carefully resealed it.

The job had taken him the best part of five hours, so it was now well after midnight; but he had no thought of bed. Instead, he sat down to the table again and commenced a letter to Mr. Pitt. He had already sent one dispatch, before leaving Paris for Fontainebleau, making a general report on the situation as far as he could then assess it. But since that he had had his invaluable interview with de Périgord spoken personally with the Queen, and spent a whole evening listening to the views of a group of noblemen who were among her most intimate friends; in addition he had to explain the reason why he was temporarily abandoning the work he had been given to undertake a mission to Italy; so there was much to say.

Fortunately he possessed the gift of expressing himself as fluently on paper as in speech, so his pen moved without hesitation while filling page after page with fine writing; but, nevertheless, it was close on three in the morning before he finally rose from the table and began to undress.

In consequence he slept late, but even when he woke he did not hurry to get up; and, having rung for his breakfast to be brought to him, he found his mind turning to the Señorita d'Aranda.

He had not given her a thought since they had parted two nights before. but now her long, oval face and striking black eyebrows reappeared in his mental vision with extraordinary vividness. Idly, he wondered what would have transpired if she-had been remaining on at Court, and on his return from Italy he had followed his impulse to develop her acquaintance. Although that acquaintance had been very brief, from the beginning she had made no effort to disguise her interest in and liking for him. She was clearly no coquette but a straightforward person, so if he had laid seige to her it seemed highly likely that an affaire would have developed between them.

Richard had no desire to marry, but even had he felt that way inclined. he knew that there could be no question of making Tansanta d'Aranda his wife. For him it would have been a brilliant match, as she was the daughter of the greatest man in Spain after King Carlos. and her family were immensely wealthy. But for that very reason they would never have countenanced her marrying a simple gentleman of modest means such as himself. Moreover, as a Spaniard she would certainly be a Catholic, while he was a Protestant, and mixed marriages at that date were still regarded by both sides with abhorrence.

He knew well enough that no platonic affaire would have kept him interested for long, and wondered if he could have made her his mistress. As she had been so long in France, and high society there indulged in perpetual immoralities covered only with a graceful cloak of elaborately observed conventions, it was quite possible that she had been the mistress of one or more men already ; and, if so, her seduction would not prove very difficult. On the other hand she was unmarried, and so by convention still forbidden fruit to the more scrupulous courtiers ; and the Queen was known to regard any immorality on the part of her ladies with great severity. All things considered, Richard thought it unlikely that Tansanta had as yet taken a lover.

But she would, of course, as soon as she was married. All women of her rank married whoever their parents chose for them, so love did not enter into such alliances; and it would have been considered unnatural in them had they failed to take a succession of lovers afterwards. Somehow, though, Richard did not see Tansanta going to bed with one man after another. She was too intense to become promiscuous. He thought it much more likely that she would become desperately enamored of some man who possessed brains as well as looks, probably someone considerably older than herself, and remain faithful to him, perhaps for life, or at all events as long as he remained faithful to her. Then, after he died or left her, she would be heartbroken for a while, but eventually get over it and find solace in her children.

If that were so, it would have proved no easy matter to make her his mistress, had he had the chance, and he knew that he would not have attempted to do so had he found her to be still a virgin. All the same, her very intensity was a sign that once aroused she would be capable of great passion; and Richard, having known Melissa, greatly preferred really passionate women who met a man half-way, to the kind that pretended to faint, then suffered an attack of conscience and wept copiously afterwards.

Still, the question of whether Tansanta's hidden fires had yet led her to indulge herself in gallantry, or not, was of no moment now. If she had left Fontainebleau the day before, as she had said she intended to do, she would by now have accomplished the first stage of her long journey to Spain. At a rough calculation he estimated that she would have spent the night at Pethiviers, or even perhaps have got as far as Orleans. In any case when he took the road to Italy their ways would diverge further apart each day, so it teas waste of time to speculate further about her.

Dismissing her from his mind he finished his breakfast, then made a leisurely toilette. At a quarter past ten he left the inn and, as on the previous day, finding no hackney-coach in the vicinity took an omnibus down to the Pont Neuf. Then he once more walked along the Quai de Louvre and crossed the Jardin des Tuileries. On its far side he entered a small cafe, sat down at a table and ordered a glass of Jerez wine. It was now close on eleven o'clock and he had come there to keep a rendezvous he had made the previous day.

If, while posing as a Frenchman, he had been noticed going into the British Embassy on several occasions by any of his acquaintances, or a police-agent stationed in the quarter, that might have aroused most unwelcome suspicions; but he had to keep in touch with it, both for drawing funds from time to time and to send in his reports, so that they might be dispatched to London in the security of the Embassy bag.

To get over the difficulty, he had arranged with Mr. Daniel Hailes. who, apart from the Ambassador, was the only member of the Embassy Staff who knew of his secret activities, a simple code. They had selected a number of quiet cafes, each near one of the public gardens. If Richard sent an envelope to

Mr. Hailes containing chestnut leaves it meant: `meet me at the café in the Palais Royal'; if oak leaves, the cafe on the edge of the Bois de Vincennes; if plane tree leaves the cafe opposite the Tuileries, and so on. The number of leaves, designated the hour; the addition of one twig, `tomorrow', of two twigs `the day after tomorrow', etc. As Mr. Hailes went every morning to Monsieur Aubert to be shaved, it was simple for Richard to leave an envelope there any time during the day with the certainty that, even if the next day was a Sunday, Mr. Hailes would be given it first thing in the morning.

In this way .they could meet without the necessity of Richard having to put anything at all on paper; and in the event of somebody at Monsieur Aubert's opening the envelopes they would not have the faintest idea what the leaves and twigs meant; so no spy could be sent to the meeting place with orders to try to overhear something of the highly secret conversations which took place at them.

Richard had not been seated for many minutes in the café when the portly, middle-aged Mr. Hailes appeared and, giving him a friendly nod, sat down at his table. The diplomat had the rather prim appearance of a wealthy merchant and he was dressed more soberly than was customary with foreigners of his status who were attached to the Court. But he and his chief, the Duke of Dorset, formed a long-standing partnership that accounted for the particular efficiency of the British Embassy in Paris at that date. The Ambassador was a man of wit, wealth and fashion; he was extremely popular in French society and even the Queen frequently attended this dansant, which had become a regular feature of the Paris winter season. The First Secretary, on the other hand, kept in the background, but little escaped him, as he was both intelligent and extremely shrewd. So while His Grace stayed up all night, winning good will, Mr. Hailes worked all day, providing the brains and direction of policy.

Richard and Mr. Hailes greeted one another in French, and as though they had met purely by chance; then when the latter had ordered himself a drink, he said with a sly smile:

`Well, my dashing Chevalier? What is it you wish of me now? Not more money, I trust; for I furnished you with five hundred écus no longer ago than last week.'

`You have guessed it in one,' Richard replied with a grin. `To console you a little I will confess that I still have most of that five hundred. but I shall require at least a further thousand, and I would prefer it in bills of exchange to coin, as I am about to set out for Italy.!

'And why, may I ask?'

`The matter concerns a lady, and one of the most beautiful I have ever met.'

`I congratulate you,' said Mr. Hailes dryly. `But in such a case I fear you must look elsewhere for your expenses!

'On the contrary. Indirectly, this is very much the King's business, so I consider myself fully entitled to ask you, as His Majesty's representative, to supply me with funds:

`May one enquire the lady's name?'

Richard lent forward and lowered his voice. "Tis Marie Antoinette!

Mr. Hailes did not blink an eyelid; he simply said: `Pray continue, I am all attention.'

Without further ado Richard launched out into an account of his recent experiences. Then, producing his report and the Queen's letter, he handed them over.

For a moment Mr. Hailes remained silent, but having stuffed the two packets away in his pockets, he remarked with his dry smile: 'I think Mr. Pitt does well to employ you. Will a thousand écus be enough? You can have more if you wish.'

`I thank you,' Richard replied. `But I should be able to manage comfortably on that, as I have no intention of staying in Italy longer than I need; arid I have reserve funds of my own which I could use in an emergency.'

Mr. Hailes nodded. `That is settled then. Where shall I send the money?'

`Do you know a horse-dealer who is something less of a rogue than most?'

`His Grace recently bought a pair of greys for his new barouche

from a man next the sign of the Three Flagons in the Rue Beauberg, and I thought their price not excessive.

'Then send it by one of the Embassy messengers to meet me there at three o'clock this afternoon. I have to buy a mount for my journey and may as well patronize His Grace's man as any other:

After a moment Mr. Hailes said: `I approve your decision to undertake this mission ; but all the same 'tis a thousand pities that you should be leaving Paris just at a time when such momentous events are in the offing.'

`I, too, regret it on that score; Richard agreed. `But tell me, what was the cause of the riot yesterday? You are the first person to whom I have spoken this morning, and I could obtain naught but obviously spurious accounts of it last night.'

"'Twas by far the most serious disturbance that has yet taken place in Paris, although from what I hear the riots which occurred in Marseilles some weeks back were of an even more extensive nature. Yet this was in all conscience bad enough; for a number of the troops as well as of the mob were killed in the affair, and 'tis said that the wounded who have been accommodated at the Hotel Dieu total several hundred.'

Richard looked at his companion in considerable surprise. ` "Twas then virtually a battle l But whence came the spark that ignited this powder magazine?' .

`It seems that a certain Monsieur Réveillon, who is a manufacturer of paper in quite a large way, had been asked by his workmen f or a rise in wages on account of the increased price of bread ; and that he refused it to them. The story goes that he declared in public that fifteen sols a day was ample for any workman to live upon, and that incensed by this they met before his house on Monday night to burn his effigy. The appearance of some French and Swiss guards on the scene deterred them from any material outrage at the time, but they gathered again by midday yesterday in a most evil temper.

`The Faubourg St. Antoine, where Réveillon has his factory and also lives, contains the worst slums in the city; so his workmen were soon joined by rift-raff'' of all kinds and the mob was further swollen by bands of sympathizers marching from all quarters of it. In view of the disturbances the previous night detachments of troops had been posted at all the approaches to Rdveillons house, so the mob could not get at the object of their fury, but by early afternoon the streets round about had become blocked by a crowd of several thousand malcontents:

Mr. Hailes paused to sip his drink, then went on: `As you will be aware, the road to the Bois de Vincennes passes through that quarter. Yesterday it so happened that His Highness of Orléans was racing his horses against those of Monsieur le Comte d'Artois in the Bois, so many persons of rank and fashion were on their way thither. The sight of their handsome equipages inflamed the mob further, in spite of the efforts of additional bodies of troops that were now being hurried to the scene, many of the carriages were forced to turn back, and serious fighting broke out between the troops and the people.

`It continued for some hours and the military succeeded in maintaining a cordon round Rveillon's premises until about five o'clock. Then the Duchess d'Orléans drove up to one of the barriers they had formed, on her way back from the races. She asked permission for her carriage to pass, and apparently the officer did not feel that he could refuse such an important person. Immediately the barrier was opened the mob surged through with the carriage and a general melee ensued.

`Apparently the troops managed to prevent the rabble from getting into Rdveillon's house and he escaped with the aid of his neighbours, but they forced their way into that next door, stripped it of its contents and burnt them in the street. Many of the rioters were shot down, but others got up on to the roofs and tearing the slates from them hurled these missiles at the troops below, severely injuring considerable numbers. Eventually order was restored, but not before the whole garrison of Paris had been placed under arms, so you can judge the magnitude of the disturbance.'

`What sort of a person is this Réveillon?' Richard asked. `Is he in fact a bad employer?'

`On the contrary. And that is what makes the affair so mysterious. He is a good, honest man, who started life as a poor workman himself, and has risen to his present affluence solely by hard work and ability. Having known poverty in his early days he looks after the well-being of his workpeople far better than the average employer, and pays none of them less than twenty-four sols a day. Moreover, when trade was so bad last winter he kept them all on out of charity, although for some months his factory was standing idle. Tis that which makes it impossible to believe that he ever said that fifteen sols a day was enough for any labourer to live on.'

`Have you any theory why he should have been singled out for such unwelcome attention?'

'Possibly it was because he is standing for election to the Tiersbat in opposition to a firebrand; and has brought the hatred of

the rabble on himself as a result of his moderate opinions. But I cannot help believing that there is more behind it than that. The .probability is that whatever he did say was seized upon and deliberately distorted with the view to provoking a riot.'

Richard nodded. `Is there the least truth in the rumours running round last night that Réveillon is in some way in the service of the Queen?'

`Not an iota! 'Tis just another calumny against that poor woman. No opportunity is ever lost by her, enemies to besmirch her with fresh mire.'

`And what of His Highness of Orleans? Do you regard it as no more than a coincidence that it should have been his wife who enabled the mob to penetrate the barrier the troops had erected?'

Mr. Hailes's eyes narrowed. `There is the further coincidence that the riot should have occurred on a day that His Highness was racing his horses at Vincennes; otherwise it would have been remarked upon as strange that his wife should be driving through the poorest quarter of the city. Moreover, the fact that bands of marchers came from so many different parts of it to join the original demonstrators definitely points to the whole affair having been organized beforehand. For a long time past His Highness has gone out of his way to gain popularity for himself at the expense of his Sovereigns, and one can hardly escape the conclusion that he is secretly working for the overthrow of his cousin the King. Yet there is little proof that is so, unless we regard his connection with the Freemasons as such.'

`He is Grand Master of the Order in France, is he not?'

`He is.' Mr. Hailes drummed with his finger-tips gently on the table. `That in itself is no treason; for the Masons are an offshoot of the German Rosicrucian's and Illuminati, and are supposed to do no more than concern themselves with mystical matters. But I know for a fact that under cover of these activities they pursue political aims. Nearly every leading figure in the troubles that have afflicted France in the past few years has been a Mason; and 'tis my belief -that His Highness is using the widespread ramifications of this secret society to bring about a revolution.'

'I too have gathered that the Masonic clubs are hotbeds of sedition. But is there not a risk that by whistling for the wind His Highness may raise a whirlwind in which he will himself be destroyed?'

`No doubt he flatters himself that his great popularity with the masses will enable him to ride out the storm; and there are fair grounds for believing that it might be so. All classes are united in their demand for a Constitution, but not one per cent of the nation has yet reached the point at which it would even listen to any suggestion of abolishing the monarchy.'

For a moment they were silent, then Richard said: `Think you that the present state of Paris is an exception, or indicative of feeling throughout the greater part of the country?'

`The unrest is very widespread,' replied Mr. Hailes gravely. `And that is hardly to be wondered at. The elections have thrown the whole population into an unnatural fever, and in addition the great scarcity of corn in many parts gives real grounds for anger against the Government. There have been serious bread riots recently at Caen, Orleans, Cette and many other places; and the accounts from Marseilles are still very alarming. The troops were besieged in their barracks there until Monsieur de Mirabeau used his great popularity with the mob to call them off ; but street fighting has continued, and hardly a day passes without the loss of some lives:

"Tis said by many that the high price of bread is caused by the Government deliberately withholding supplies of grain, in order t to make more money. But I can scarce credit that there is any i truth in that."

`There is none. On the contrary, the King has done everything he can to bring relief to the people, even to buying corn from abroad. Such rumours nearly always become current at times of great shortage, and the present one is mainly due to the exceptionally poor harvest last year. You may not recall hearing mention of it but a storm of the first magnitude swept France and destroyed a great part of the standing crops. The ensuing floods were of such severity that houses and cattle were washed away and many people drowned. Then the situation was further aggravated by the wickedness of the winter. All the great rivers of France were frozen and even the port of Marseilles was covered with ice. In such conditions prices were bound to rise and many localities find themselves actually faced with famine. Unfortunately, apart from the better weather, the poor can hope for little amelioration of their hard lot until the next harvest has been gathered: so I fear we must anticipate a continuance of these outbreaks of violence all through the coming summer.'

`I note that you qualify your remarks by saying that the corn shortage is "mainly due" to these misfortunes,' Richard commented. `That infers that you have in mind some other cause which has made the situation even worse than it need have been.'

Mr. Hailes gave him an appraising glance. `You are very quick young man; and since we are talking in the strictest confidence I will name it. Having no proof of this I would certainly not do so in other circumstances, but I believe you were not far from the mark when you suggested that large quantities of grain are deliberately being withheld from the markets. Not by the King, of course, but by a ring of wealthy private individuals. Moreover, I suspect that their object is not so much gain as to ferment further outcry against the Government.'

`Then, in view of our conversation a while back, I think I could .make a good guess at the name of one of the ring, if not its leader.'

`And you would be right,' said Mr. Hailes with equal quickness. `His Highness is one of the richest men in France, and it is as certain as such a thing can be that he has been using a part of his millions for this nefarious purpose; for the names of those who made the biggest purchase of grain last spring were those of men I know to be his agents.!

'Would that of the Marquis de St. Huruge be among them?'

'No. But I think you right in believing him to be secretly an Orleanist, in spite of his position at Court. And he is by no means the only noble there whom I judge capable of biting the hand that has so far fed him. If my informants know their business the Duc de Laincourt is another; and I suspect that even the Duc de Biron is trimming his sails, so that should the wind from Orleans blow its argosy to a rich port his barque will be among it.'

`De Biron!' !' exclaimed Richard. `Surely you are wrong in that. In the days when he was Monsieur de Lazun the Queen showed him so much kindness that he was freely spoken of as her lover.'

`I know it; and he has never forgiven her for not being quite kind enough,' replied Hailes, cynically. `God forbid that I should appear to criticize Her Majesty's rectitude, or that of King Louis either ; but the present troubles of these two are in part, at least, the outcome of their own integrity. Neither have great brains nor he is cursed more than any man I ever knew with the incapacity to make up his mind. But both are reasonably intelligent and absolutely honest. Their tragedy is that they are too honest for this degenerate era, and refuse to pander to the greed and lusts of the frailer beings with whom they are constantly brought into contact. That is why, in their hour of need, I fear that they will find themselves entirely isolated.'

Mr. Hailes gave a sigh, then slapped the table with his hand and stood up. `I fear I must leave you now, Chevalier. I have a dispatch for London on the Réveillon affair that I must complete, so that His Grace shall sign it on a safe hand shall send his arising the money as you have directed. It remains only for me to you good fortune.'

Richard thanked him, and watched the portly but unobtrusive figure move away. Then he ordered himself another drink at spent an hour scanning the newssheets. None, other than Government publications, were then issued in France; but there vv: scores of pamphlets produced by private people holding eve, variety of opinion. Some were obviously inspired by the Cow but most of these struck Richard as weak and lacking in conviction. The great majorities were anti-Government and many of them wore both so treasonable and so scurrilous that even a year ear Ii they would have landed their authors behind bars. In one; the Dauphin's illness was asserted to have been caused by the Queen, habitually making him drunk for her amusement; in another she was accused of unnatural vice with her favorite, the Duchess Polignac.

It seemed extraordinary to Richard that the police permitted such filth to be left lying about openly in the public cafes; and he could only suppose that the output was now so great that it had become beyond their powers to deal with it; or that they too were league with the Queen's enemies. One thing was certain: it w:, a clear indication that the forces of law and order had already lost all power of initiative.

Feeling slightly sick from what he had read he left the cafe and employed himself for the next hour or so buying various things 1 might need on his journey. At two o'clock he sat down to a belated; dinner-as the French then termed their midday meal-and by three o'clock he was at the horse-dealer in the Rue Beauberg.

Mr. Hailes's man was there with the money; and after trying out several mounts in the riding school that formed part of the premises; Richard chose a well-set-up black mare. He then went in search of suitable saddler, and having found what he wants! had it carried back to the horse-dealer. The mare was saddled up, and he rode her across Paris to his inn. As it was now too late to start that day he spent a quiet evening and went to bed early but he was up by six and soon after seven o'clock on the 29th of April he set out for Italy.

As he passed through the open fields surrounding the little town: of Mongeron, just outside Paris, he noticed again, as he had t!; week before when riding post to Fontainebleau, the extraordinary number of partridges. He estimated that there must be a covey to every two acres, and in some places more.

il England with a gun had he had the luck to see such a sight. But he knew that in France not only was the game most strictly preserved for the nobles, but many of them never bothered to shoot it, and the depredations of the young birds on the corn was one of the major aggravations of the peasantry.

Soon afterwards he entered the royal oak forest of Senár from which much of the timber was cut to build France's fleets; then he came out of it at Melun, halting there to have a meal and give his mare a good rest

As he knew the Queen's letter to be a general resume of the situation, requiring no immediate answer, he did not feel called on to force his pace. Had he done so he would have traveled post, changing horses every five miles; but he knew from experience that such frequent changes were extremely tiring, so a means of traveling to be avoided unless one's journey was of considerable urgency. Nevertheless, having ridden through the forest of Fontainebleau most of the afternoon, by early evening he reached Nemours, which was some sixty miles from Paris, so he felt that he had had an uneventful but satisfactory day.

At that date, owing to the fact that all the wealthiest people in France lived in the shadow of the Court, and rarely visited their estates, there was far less travel than in England. In consequence except in the cities the inns were far inferior. Like most of the farmhouses, they lacked glass in their windows; they had no coffee-room, earthen floors, and could offer only the most primitive accommodation.

The Ecu de France, where Richard lay that night, was no exception; so when, in the morning, he was presented with a bill for close on ten livres, he naturally found it a matter for angry amazement. As he had supped very simply off soup, a roast partridge, fricassee of chicken, cauliflower, celery, biscuits and dessert, washed down by a single bottle of wine, he considered the sum-which was equivalent to eight shillings and seven pence--positively exorbitant, and told the landlord so in no uncertain terms.

To his further surprise the landlord refused to reduce the account, except to the extent of knocking off the odd sous, and on being threatened with a beating he called up his stable hands, declaring that it was Richard who would get the beating if he did not pay in full.

Rather than enter on an undignified scrimmage against odds, in which he might easily have got the worst of it, Richard threw the money on the ground and, mounting his mare, rode out of Nemours. His disgust at being so flagrantly cheated was forgotten in his humiliation at having to ride off with his tail between his legs. But when the fresh morning air had soothed his pride a little, he realized that the episode was simply one more example of the rapidly changing state of France. When he had lived there two years earlier no innkeeper would have dared to cheat and threaten to have his ostlers lay hands on a gentleman; yet now, it seemed, the dishonest sort could do so with impunity.

At midday he reached Montages, a smaller place where the people at the inn were both civil and moderate in their charges. Late that afternoon, after another uneventful day, he came to Briare, where for the first time he saw the great sweep of the river Loire; and, having cautiously enquired the tariff at the inn, he decided to stay there for the night.

Next day his road lay along the river bank ; and the country was so pleasant, with its green meadows and many white chateaux set among groups of trees, that, after taking his midday meal at Pouilly, he lingered there much longer than he had previously allowed for such halts.

It was nearly three o'clock when he reluctantly left the grassy knoll on which he had stretched himself near the edge of the river, to collect his mare. Then as the town clock chimed, he suddenly realized how the time had slipped away and began to press his pace, as he intended to sleep at Nevers that night, so still had some thirty miles to cover.

Having made good time to Pougues, he gave his mount half an hour's rest there while refreshing himself with a pint of wine; then set off on the last ten miles of his third day's journey. The road now left the river and rose to steeper ground where wild heath was interspersed with patches of woodland. The best of the day had gone by the time he was half-way to Nevers and twilight was beginning to fall. It was still quite light in the open spaces but among the trees there was a suggestion of gathering darkness,

Suddenly a woman's scream rent the evening quiet. He had just entered a belt of woodland through which the road curved away a little to the' east. Pulling one of his pistols from its holster he set spurs to his mare and galloped round the corner.

As he rounded the bend he saw that the road descended into a hollow. To one side of it the trees fell back in a glade leading to the open heath; in its center stood a coach drawn by four horses, The coach had been going in the same direction as himself. It was now surrounded by a group of masked men. Two were still mounted; one, in front of the horses, was holding up the coachman; the other, with his back to Richard was covering the footman on the boot. Two more were dragging an old lady out of the coach.

To tackle four highwaymen single-handed was a dangerous business. Richard cursed the ill-fortune that had brought him on this scene; but he would have been ashamed to ride off without making an attempt to succor the old woman. His decision to intervene was practically instantaneous. He knew that his only chance of driving off such odds lay in his sudden appearance having taken the rogues by surprise. Reining in his mare, he took aim at the nearest highwayman and fired.

The others, facing Richard, had given shouts of warning the instant they saw him. But the man in the rear of the coach was caught unawares. He half-turned to look over his shoulder, suddenly realized his danger, and ducked his head. Next second he jerked in his saddle, gave a cry and slumped forward with one arm hanging limp at his side. His pistol fell from his nerveless hand, clattered on the road and exploded with a loud report. Startled by the pistol going off almost under its belly, his horse reared, then cantered away with him lurching from side to side as he strove to keep his seat.

At the sight of their comrade's discomfiture the two men who were rough-handling the old lady let her go. Running to their horses they hoisted themselves into their saddles. Both drew pistols and came charging up the little rise. Richard wondered grimly how he would come out of the affair; but he was ready for them.

Before the smoke drifted from the barrel of his first pistol he had thrust it back in his holster and drawn his second. As the two came galloping towards him he took careful aim at the one on the right. He was within an ace of pulling the trigger when there came a bang like that of a small cannon. Now that aid had come the footman on the boot of the coach had recovered his courage. Pulling out a blunderbuss, and aiming at the backs of the two highwaymen, he had let it off.

With a horrid swish and whistle slugs and old nails sang through the air. The buttocks of the horse ridden by the man on the left got the worst of the discharge. With a pitiful neigh it swerved, nearly throwing its rider, and bolted with him, carrying him off into the woods. But a fragment of the charge grazed Richard's black, causing her to rear at the very second he fired.

His bullet went harmlessly over the head of the man at whom he had aimed, but the mare rearing at that moment probably saved his life. The highwayman had fired almost simultaneously with himself, and the bullet, instead of striking him, buried itself in the fleshy part of his mare's neck.

The impetus of the man's charge carried him past Richard. Both swerved their mounts in a half-circle and drew their swords. The blades met with a clash, parted, and came together again. From the feel of his opponent's steel Richard knew that he was pitted against a strong swordsman. Once more he cursed his luck for having landed him in this unsought fracas.

For a minute or more the two of them exchanged furious cut and thrust, neither gaining any advantage. Richard was now fighting with his back towards the coach. Owing to the noise made by the stamping of the horses' hoofs he did not hear the fourth highway man come galloping up the slope to his friend's assistance.

Suddenly another pistol-shot rang out. The newcomer had fired at Richard's back. Fortunately, as he was riding full tilt, his aim was bad, and low. The bullet struck the rear projection of the mare's saddle with a loud thud, ricocheted off and whistled through the sleeve of Richard's coat, tearing the flesh of his left arm above the elbow. The pain was as though he had been seared with a red-hot iron, and a sudden warm wetness below the wound told him that he was bleeding badly. But his fingers still clutched the mare's reins and answered to his pressure.

He knew that his situation was now near desperate. For help to arrive within a few moments on that lonely road, at such an hour, would be little short of a miracle. He still held his sword, and at the price of savage pain could control his mount. But at any moment one of the two unwounded men might wound him again, and this time fatally.

Hastily disengaging his blade he pulled his mare back on her haunches, and half-turned her to meet his new attacker. As he did so he caught a glimpse of the coach. Now that it had been freed from its hold-up the old lady had got back into it and was seizing the chance to escape. The vehicle was already in movement, and the coachman lashing his horses wildly. At a lumbering gallop it careered off down the road.

The man who had fired the pistol drew his sword. He came at Richard in the same instant that the other renewed his attack. Richard was now between them, so at a grave disadvantage. His peril made him gasp; but his wits did not desert him. In a desperate attempt to get out of his dangerous situation he parried one thrust, ducked the other, and spurred his mare forward. Then, as she shot past his latest antagonist, he delivered a swift sideways cut at the man's head.

The sudden move took the fellow off his guard. The point of Richard's sword caught the corner of his eye and slashed his face down to the chin. His mask fell off and blood spurted from the ugly wound. With a howl of rage and pain, he clapped his free hand to his face. Half blinded by blood, he reeled in his saddle and his horse ambled off with him to the side of the road.

Richard had barely time to realize that he had put one of his opponents out of the fight before the other was on him again. Once more their swords clashed and slithered. Weak now from loss of blood, he knew that unless he could end matters quickly he would be done. Exerting all his remaining strength in a fierce downward sweep, he followed it with a swift lunge.

His first movement beat down his antagonist's blade, the second pierced his right side. But the force of the man's own thrust had not been fully spent. His sword entered Richard's boot above the ankle, tore through the tendons on the inner side of his foot, came out at the back of the boot and buried its point in the flank of his mare.

As she whinnied with pain, and reared in an attempt to throw him, Richard caught a glimpse of his enemy. His face had suddenly gone deathly white beneath his mask and his sword had fallen from his hand. Next second Richard's mare lowered her head, dragging rely at the reins, lifted it again, and plunged wildly forward down the hill.

Richard still held his drawn sword in one hand; his other was weakened from the first wound he had received. His instep, too, was now paining him so severely that he could no longer exert the full grip of his right knee on the saddle. As the mare dashed down the slope it was all he could do to keep his balance.

In an effort to check her wild career he hauled on the reins, but all he succeeded in doing was to pull her head round slightly to the left. Leaving the road, she galloped through the clearing among the trees out on to the open heath.

For over a quarter of a mile he fought to regain control of her, while she avoided ditches and foxholes only by a miracle. His efforts gradually became weaker and he realized he was powerless to do anything until she slowed down of her own accord. Suddenly she stumbled, recovered, shivered violently; then, without warning, fell to her knees, pitching him forward over her head.

He let go the reins and flung out both hands in an attempt to save himself. His left arm doubled under him, his forehead struck the hilt of his out-thrusts sword, and the blow knocked him unconscious.

It was some time before he came to; but when he did the pain from his wounds swiftly brought back to him the events, which had led to his having been flung there, face downward in the young bracken. After a moment he raised himself on his good elbow and turned over. As he moved his injured foot the stab of pain from it was so acute that he gasped and shut his eyes. When he opened them he realized that it was now nearly dark.

Gingerly settling himself a trifle more comfortably he looked about him. He was lying in a shallow-bottomed gully, so he could not see more than half a dozen yards in any direction; but a faint, pinkish-orange glow breaking the dark night sky over his right shoulder told him that he was facing south-east, so the road must be somewhere in his rear.

From that he judged that his pull on the left-hand rein of the mare must have brought her round nearly in a half-circle before she threw him. Anxiously he looked to right and left in search of her; then screwed his head round as far as it would go. There she was, immediately behind him, about three yards away on the slope of the gully. She was lying quite still on her side, with her near hind leg sticking stiffly out at an angle. The light was still just sufficient for him to see a dark pool on the ground in front of her where the blood had poured from the wound in her neck. One glance was enough to tell him that she was dead.

He wondered what the devil he was going to do now. Night was fast approaching and he doubted very much if he could stagger even as far as the road. His head, foot and arm were all hurting him abominably. From the latter he had lost quite a lot of blood. and it was still bleeding. If he could not get his wounds attended to he might quite well die of weakness and cold before morning.

The coach had driven off; but even had he believed it to be still in the vicinity he would not have dared to shout for help. He thought that he had rendered three of the rogues hors de combat, but he was by no means certain. The wound of the man he had run through the side might be only superficial. Then there was the fellow whose horse had bolted with him after being shot in the buttocks by the footman. Either or both might still be quite close by. They would b' furious with anger at the wrecking of their plan, and thirsting for vengeance. If they found him in his present helpless state it was a certainty that they would murder him.

Nevertheless he knew that he must get help somehow. All over France wolves still abounded. In winter they often invaded villages and, made fierce by hunger; attacked men as well as women and children. Even now, when they had retired to their lairs in the higher ground, they still came down to roam the more desolate areas at night in search of stray cattle. Weakened as he was he knew with a horrid sinking feeling that he might easily fall a prey to them.

He felt that whatever pain it cost him he must somehow manage to crawl back to the roadside, as only there would he have any chance to attract the attention of some late passer-by. To do that was to risk an encounter with one of the highwaymen, but it was a gamble that had to be taken. To remain lying where he had fallen was to invite death, and perhaps a horrible death, in a ditch.

Turning over on his stomach he got slowly to his knees. Then he began to crawl forward, dragging his wounded foot behind him. He had not covered more than four feet when it knocked against a stone. The spasm of agony that went through him was so acute that he nearly fainted.

For a moment he lay there dizzy and helpless. As he did so the monstrous ill-luck of which he had been the victim came to his mind again. But for that chance encounter he would by now be dining in the warmth and comfort of the inn at Nevers. By interfering in someone else's quarrel, he had had his mare killed, was grievously wounded and likely to die himself.

Suddenly he began to curse, loud, long and fluently, in English, French and German. Then, as he paused at last from lack of breath, a soft voice just behind him said:

`Hush, Monsieur, I pray! That is no language to use in the presence of a lady.'

Jerking round his head he stared up at the cloaked and hooded figure of a woman. It was now too dark to see her face, but he would have known that voice anywhere. It was that of Tansanta d'Aranda.

CHAPTER SEVEN
THE ROAD TO THE SOUTH

Richard drew a hand wearily across his eyes. He could only suppose that the state to which he had been reduced had sent him temporarily off his head, and that he was suffering from an hallucination. But the cloaked figure ran down the bank, sank in a flurry of skirts beside him, and grasped his hands. He caught a heady whiff of the scent of gardenias, and the soft voice came again.

'Mon brave Chevalier! Thank God that I have found you! Are you gravely hurt? Oh, I pray that your wounds be not serious!'

`I have no vital injury,' Richard croaked, `though I am in some pain and weak from toss of blood. But by what miracle can it be you who have come to my assistance, Senorita?'

"Twas my coach that you protected from those villains. I leant out of the window and recognized you, but you were much too heavily engaged to see me. When we drove off and you failed to follow I felt sure you must be wounded. Pedro, my footman, confirmed my fears. He said your horse on to the heath was carrying the last glimpse he had of you away. So we returned to search for you.'

Still greatly puzzled, Richard murmured: `I thought you on your way to Spain.'

But she was no longer listening to him; she had stood up and was calling to her servants. There came an answering shout and from the gathering shadows Pedro emerged. He was accompanied by a buxom, fat-faced maid, whom Tansanta addressed as Maria, and in addition to his blunderbuss he carried a lantern. By its light the two young women examined Richard's wounds, exclaiming in sympathy and gabbling away to one another in Spanish while they attended to his arm and head. Both had bled copiously, making him a horrid sight, but his arm had been no more than laid open by the bullet and the skin of his forehead only torn where it had struck the rim of his sword-hilt. He was much more worried about his instep, which they had not so far noticed. When he pointed it out to the Senorita, she. exclaimed:

`Alas, yet another wound! And to get at it your boot will have to be cut off. But there is little blood and that about the slits where the sword passed through is dry already. I think we had best get you to the coach now, and so to Nevers, where you can receive proper treatment.'

Taking the lantern from Pedro she told him what she wished done. With the assistance of the two women the big Spaniard hoisted Richard across his shoulders; Tansanta then led the way with the light and Maria, supporting Richard's bad foot to prevent it from bumping, brought up the rear. Fortunately it was no great distance to the road and after five minutes' puffing and grunting Pedro lowered his heavy burden on to the back seat of the coach.

It was a huge vehicle and could have held eight people comfortably. In the other back-seat corner sat the old woman he had seen hauled out of it, and next to her was Quetzal. Although the roof of the coach was piled high with luggage, most of its front seat was also occupied with packages of all sorts and sizes; so Maria, still supporting Richard's foot, squatted on the floor, while Tansanta sat down between him and her Indian.

Having sent Pedro to fetch Richard's sword, saddler, valise and bedroll from the back of his dead mare, Tansanta said: `Monsieur de Cavasuto, I wish to present you to the Senora Poeblar. The Señora was my governess until I entered the service of Madame Marie Antoinette, and recently undertook the long journey from Spain in order to act as my companion when I left the Court of France.'

Richard was in no state to make graceful compliments, but the Señora made up for the brevity of his greeting by breaking into a spate of Spanish, and when she had done Quetzal added a few phrases.

`The Senora thanks you for having rescued us, Monsieur; Tansanta interrupted. `She is desolated at not being able to do so in a language you understand; but during her previous sojourn in France she hardly ever left our Embassy, so she knows only a few words of French. Quetzal also thanks you. He calls you Monsieur Blue-Eyes, and says that later he will give you a red feather to wear in your hair, because that is a mark given to especially brave men in his country to distinguish them from others.'

With an effort Richard murmured his appreciation; but to speak at all made worse the throbbing of his head, so he was much relieved when Pedro had fetched his things, and the coach set off.

Fortunately, Nevers being a place of some size, the inn there was a good one, and before the hold-up Tansanta had already sent her outrider ahead to secure the best accommodation at it. Richard was carried in, made as comfortable as possible on Tansanta's own traveling mattress, and a chirurgeon was sent for.

Even when the boot had been slit down, getting the injured foot out of it proved a most painful business, but the result of the chirurgeon's examination was reassuring. He said that all use of the foot would greatly retard its healing, so he meant to encase it in plaster in the morning; but that if it was kept rigid for from two to three weeks he thought the patient would be able to walk again without developing a permanent limp.

Tansanta, the plump, fat-faced Maria and the old Señora were all present at the conference and all three of them assisted the chirurgeon to wash and bandage their hero's wounds. Flattered as Richard might have been had he felt more his normal self, he now wished fervently that they would go away with the doctor and leave him in peace; but he knew there was no hope of that. He had been carried up to the largest room in the hostelry, which Tansanta's outrider had reserved for her and her women, and clearly they had no thought of going to another. Maria began to lay the table for supper with her mistress's traveling cutlery, and an inn servant brought up two screens for them to undress behind afterwards.

When the meal arrived the two ladies and Quetzal sat down to it while Maria waited upon them. They conversed only in hushed voices but every ten minutes or so Tansanta could not resist asking him how he was feeling and if she could get anything for him. At length he took refuge in pretending to be asleep. But he had now become feverish and his restless tossing brought their further ministrations upon him before they retired for the night.

Evidently having decided that his foot was the seat of the trouble, they undid the bandage. The Señora then produced a small package of oiled silk and a square of cardboard from her medicine chest. The oiled silk contained some tacky grayish stuff that looked like dirty cobwebs, and Richard began to protest vigorously when he saw that she was about to put it on the red gash across his inflamed and swollen instep.

He gave in only because he dared not struggle for fear of restarting the bleeding, and on receiving Tansanta's assurance that this old-wives' salve was a sovereign remedy for reducing fever in angry flesh wounds; but his apprehension was hardly lessened when he saw that the piece of cardboard, which the Senora had placed immediately over the salve, was a picture of St. Sebastian.

While Tansanta re-bandaged his foot the Señora took a glass phial from her chest, poured some of the liquid it held into a glass and, after adding a little water, brought it over to Richard. Thinking `in for a penny in for a pound', he drank it down; but this time no further qualms assailed him, as he recognized it to be Cordial Poppy Water; and ten minutes later he dropped off to sleep.

When he woke in the morning he felt decidedly better; and, whether he owed it to the cobwebs or the intervention of St. Sebastian, there was no doubt that the inflammation of his instep had subsided. Nevertheless, the Senora Poeblar evidently had no wish to flaunt her triumph over the chirurgeon, as she removed both before his arrival and, having done so, put her finger to her lips to enjoin secrecy on Richard.

It was the first opportunity he had had to regard her with any attention, and as he smiled his understanding and thanks, he thought she looked rather a nice old lady. She was very swarthy and fat, but big-built and strong-limbed. Her age might have 'peen anything between fifty and seventy, since her face was much wrinkled, but her beady eyes showed liveliness and humor. Had it not been for their smallness Richard thought that when young she would probably have passed as a beauty, for she still had good features. She was dressed entirely in black and in addition to a rosary of ebony beads her ample bosom was hung all over with a variety of sacred emblems.

When the chirurgeon arrived he expressed himself as both surprised and gratified at the improvement in the patient's foot, but, all the same, maintained his view that it should be set in plaster. Richard had been hoping that he might now escape so crippling a treatment, but both Tansanta and her duenna backed up this opinion, and as he had no wish to risk being lame for life he submitted with the best grace he could muster.

As the day happened to be Sunday, Tansanta and her entire entourage would normally have attended High Mass, but she excused herself on the plea that someone must stay with Richard. In view of the invalid's still weak condition, and the unlikelihood of his committing an amorous assault on her charge with a heavy plaster cast round his foot, the Señora agreed that the conventions would not be outraged by her leaving the two young people; so at a quarter to ten she set off, taking Quetzal and all the servants with her.

Directly they had gone Tansanta made a pile of the traveling cushions near the head of Richard's bed and settled herself comfortably upon them. Taking her hand he kissed it, then smiled up into her dark eyes and said

'Señorita, this is the chance I have been waiting for, to thank you for coming back to search for me last night. Had you not done so I might have suffered a most horrid fate.'

She returned his smile. 'Knowing that, how could I have abandoned so brave a gentleman?'

'Yet you ran a grave risk. You could not have known that I succeeded in wounding the last two of those cut-throats ; and, had I not, they might have set upon you again.'

'True, but forewarned is forearmed. They would not have found us such easy game as at the first encounter, for then they took us by surprise. On our return both Pedro and my coachman, Manuel, had their blunderbusses out ready, and I had my pistol on my lap.'

'Then, Senorita, I count you braver still, since you returned anticipating a fight and were prepared to enter it yourself:

`Monsieur, I am a General's daughter,' she said lightly, 'so reared to have no fear of arms. But a truce to compliments. Pleased as I am that we should meet again, I am nonetheless surprised at it; and somewhat concerned by your apparent dilatoriness in Her Majesty's service. How comes it that having been five days on the road you are got no further?'

Richard cocked an eyebrow. °I was under the impression that Her Majesty attached more importance to the safe than the speedy delivery of her letter:

"Tis true; and, in view of the injuries you have sustained, now most fortunate that should be so. I meant only that such a leisurely progress, seemed most unlike the opinion I had formed of you. Moreover I am still at a loss to understand how I, who have traveled but a grandmother's pace of twenty-five miles a day, should have passed you ; as I must have done, seeing that you left Fontainebleau a night ahead of me.'

'That is easy to explain. Before setting out for Italy I had certain private business that required my attention in Paris ; so I directed the royal carriage in which you left me, thither, and did not leave again till Tuesday morning. Therefore 'twas you who had two days plus near forty miles start of me; and although I was covering some sixty miles a day it was only last night that I caught up with you.'

She gave a not very convincing laugh and remarked: °I might have guessed that any gentleman of so dashing an appearance as Monsieur would have had tender adieux to make before departing on so long a journey.'

The way she said it, and the way her dark eyebrows drew together afterwards in a little frown, revealed more clearly than anything had yet done her feelings towards him. For an instant he was tempted to let her think her supposition correct, but his natural kindness overcame the impulse, and he said

'Nay, Señorita; ; but there were numerous invitations I had accepted, and in common politeness I could not leave without making suitable excuses to my friends; also I had to convert some of my English letters of Credit into Italian bills of Exchange, and these things are not done in a couple of hours. Yet, if you were surprised to see me again I was equally so to see you. I had thought of you as nearing Chateauroux by this time, on your way to Spain:

'You had not forgotten me then?' She could not keep the eagerness out of her voice, and her slightly uneven teeth showed in a smile.

'Far from it, Senorita. How could I, after the interest you displayed in-in my story? But how comes it that instead of taking the road to the Pyrenees you are on that to Marseilles? Is it that you have, after all, abandoned your plan of rejoining your family?'

'But no!' she exclaimed. 'You must have misunderstood me. 'Tis true that I am on my way to rejoin my parents, but for some time past they have been resident in the Kingdom of the Two Sicily's. I am proceeding to Marseilles with the object of taking a ship thence to Naples.'

"Twas stupid of me,' Richard murmured. 'I had temporarily forgotten that Naples is also a Spanish Court.'

'It is an easy mistake to make ; and my father retired there only after his differences with the old King.'

'Do you think you will enjoy life at the Neapolitan Court?'

She gave him a searching look. "Tis hard to say, Monsieur. The Two Sicily's have for so, long been under Spanish influence that I cannot think the life of the aristocracy there differs much from what it is in Spain. If so, despite any new distractions in my altered status, I fear I shall soon be sadly missing the witty and intelligent society which I enjoyed while with Madame Marie Antoinette.'

Richard frowned. 'Your mention of Her Majesty recalls me to my duty to her. By averaging sixty miles a day I had hoped to deliver her dispatch to the Grand Duke somewhere about the middle of the month, but my prospects of being able to do so now seem far from good.'

'As you infer that you would have ridden all the way, I take it you meant to go via Lyons, Chambery and Turin?'

'Yes, since 'tis May, and the passage of the Alps now open.'

'Yet had it been earlier in the year you would have had no choice but to go down to Marseilles, and take ship from there across the gulf of Leghorn. Now that it will prove impossible to ride, are you still set upon taking the Alpine route?'

'Why, yes; for it is normally the quicker at this time of year whether one goes on horseback or in a post-chaise. What now perturbs me is that it may be some days before the chirurgeon permits me to resume my journey; and that even when he does I may find the jolting of a fast post-chaise so painful to my leg that I shall be able to bear it only for short stages.'

Tansanta gave him a thoughtful look. 'It was just that of which I was thinking. If during your convalescence you are reduced to going in short stages anyway, you would travel far more comfortably in a well-sprung coach.'

Suddenly Richard saw the way her mind was working. If he went via the Alps, as he had intended, their ways would part at Moulins, only a good day's journey further south. She wanted him to change his route so that she could keep him with her all the way to Marseilles. Next moment she disclosed her thought:

'Even when the chirurgeon pronounces you fit to proceed, your wounds will require careful dressing for some days. Alone on the road to Italy you will be dependent for that on the unskilled ministration of slatternly inn servants; whereas if you come with me in my coach we can look after you properly.'

Richard's brain was now revolving at high speed. Crippled as he was there would probably be little difference in the time it took him to reach Florence whether he went by land or sea. But the latter involved certain highly perturbing possibilities. He now had little doubt that from their first meeting in the forest of Fontainebleau Tansanta d'Aranda had fallen in love with him. He was not in love with her, but he knew what propinquity could do to a man like himself who was easily attracted to pretty women. His heart was not made of the stuff to withstand for long the lure of being with her day after day for long hours in the close confinement of a coach. He knew that he would become more 'and more intrigued by her subtle charm until he gave way to the temptation to make love to her. And from that it might be but a short step to falling in love with her himself.

Such a development could end only in the misery of a painful parting at Marseilles, followed perhaps by months of hopeless longings. It would be far kinder to her to let her go on alone while her feeling for him had so little to feed upon that it could soon be forgotten. And the caution he had inherited from his Scottish mother warned him that to do so would also save him from putting himself in a situation that he might later bitterly regret.

'I thank you from the bottom of my heart for your thought for me, Senorita,' he said, after only a moment's hesitation. 'But I fear I must decline your offer. 'Tis true that when I set out again I may have to go carefully for the first few days, but after that I should be able to stand up to longer stages.'

Her dark brows drew together. 'Yet you said yourself that you counted the safe delivery of Her Majesty's letter of paramount importance, and speed only a secondary consideration.'

'Indeed I did. But what of it?'

'You seem to have forgotten that you are no longer in a state to defend yourself, and are unlikely to be so for some time to come:

`That is so, but now that I am well clear of Paris, why should I fear attack?'

Tansanta's brown eyes widened. `Surely, Monsieur, you realize that de Roubec, having seen you come to my rescue, may now think-'

`De Roubec !' exclaimed Richard, starting up, then falling back at the sudden twinge his foot and arm gave him. 'Do you mean that he was among the men who attacked your coach?'

`Why, yes. He was one of those who pulled the Senora Poeblar from it. I recognized him despite his, mask. Moreover, he got away unharmed by you, for 'twas his horse that Pedro shot in the buttocks.'

`I thought them ordinary highwaymen intent on robbery. But why, in Heaven's name, should de Roubec set upon you?'

She shrugged. `The Queen's enemies knew about that letter; they knew also that I am her friend and was about to proceed to Naples, from whence it would have been easy to send it by a safe hand up to Florence. What could be more natural than that she should entrust it to me?'

'I wonder, now, that she did not adopt that course:

'We talked 'of it, but decided that it was so obvious as to invite certain danger. In fact, at my suggestion we adopted the plan of using my departure as a red herring to cover your own. Her Majesty provided me with an escort of a half-troop of Monsieur d'Esterhazy's hussars, thus openly inferring that I was carrying something of special importance. They could not be spared to accompany me further than Pouilly, but their presence assured me against attack for the first four days of my journey. We hoped that by then the enemy would have abandoned any hope of securing the letter; and in the meantime, while his interest had been concentrated upon myself, you would be clear of all danger, a hundred or more miles to the south.'

'"Twas an admirable ruse,' Richard commented. `But I am much perturbed to learn-'

'Aye; yet it was brought to naught by de Roubec's following me further than we expected, and your arrival on the scene,' she interrupted. `For though you failed to recognize him he will certainly have recognized you.'

`Even so, as far as we know, he has never had any cause to suspect that I was bearer of the letter. On the contrary in fact, as otherwise instead of attacking your coach he would have attacked me.'

Tansanta made a gesture of impatience. `But do you not see that last night's affray has altered everything? Since de Roubec remained uninjured 'tis certain that he will now be spying on us. Should he see you leave me, and on reaching Moulins turn east, taking the direct route to Italy, he is sure to think that I, fearing another attack from him, have passed the dispatch on to you; and that you have agreed to take it to Florence for me:

`That certainly is a possibility,' Richard agreed, and even as he made the half-hearted attempt to temporize he knew that it was one that he could not afford to ignore. It was highly probable that de Roubec would reason that way; and if he were in the Duc d'Orléans' pay he would have plenty of money; so, although his original gang of bullies had been wounded and dispersed, he would be able to hire others in some low tavern of Nevers.

Leaning towards Richard, Tansanta swiftly followed up her advantage. `From Nevers onward I intend to hire two armed guards to accompany the coach to each further stage, so with my own three men and ourselves with our pistols we should form a party sufficiently formidable to frighten off attack. But if you set out alone in a post-chaise and are held up, once you have fired off your two pistols what hope would you have?'

`Plaguey little, I fear,' Richard was forced to admit.

`Then, Monsieur, I beg you to listen to reason. The safe conveyance of Her Majesty's letter is the thing that matters above all else, and you cannot deny that there will be less danger of its falling into her enemies' hands if you accept the protection I can offer you.'

Richard had done his best to evade a situation of which he feared the outcome both for her and for himself ; but he now felt that he was cornered, so he gave in gracefully, and replied.

`The last consideration certainly outweighs all others, Senorita. So I will gladly avail myself of your hospitality and protection as far as Marseilles.'

Tansanta's sigh of satisfaction was almost audible, but she made an attempt to hide her pleasure at having got her way by quickly beginning to speculate on how long it would be before they could resume their journey.

Now that the die was cast, and he appeared fated to spend a fortnight at the least as her constant companion, Richard felt that a few days more or less before they set out could make little difference to the outcome ; but since travel by slow stages had been forced upon him he thought that he owed it to the Queen to get on the road again as soon as possible, so he said

`Were I still set on going by post-chaise and alone, no doubt the chirurgeon would insist on my remaining here for some days; but seeing that my fever has abated, and I am to have the benefit of being accompanied by two excellent nurses in a well-sprung coach. I see no reason why he should not let us start tomorrow.'

She nodded. `Why not? And the gaining of those few days would, I am sure, ease any qualms you still may have at having forgone the more arduous and risky course in an attempt to get to Florence more quickly. But if we would avoid inviting a return of your fever we have talked enough for now. When the Señora Poeblar and the servants return from church I will send someone to ensure the chirurgeon coming to see you again this evening, and will make arrangements for the increase of our escort. Meanwhile try to sleep for a little; if you can it will do you good.'

Having had a good night, Richard did not feel like sleep, but ho made a pretence of obeying her while actually continuing to watch her covertly from under his long lashes.

Getting up she fetched a book from her valise and, sitting down again on the cushions close beside him, began to read it. Richard could see at a glance, that it was in Greek, which surprised him for two reasons-firstly because it was unusual for ladies of that day to receive a classical education, and secondly because, seeing that it was Sunday, he would have expected her to read only books of devotions. It occurred to him then that it might be a Greek Testament, but, being an excellent classical scholar himself, further surreptitious glances told him that, far from it being anything of the sort, it was a copy of the Poems of Sappho.

This small piece of information caused Richard to make a swift readjustment in his previous assessment of the Senorita d'Aranda. Intense, open and intelligent he already knew her to be, but an interest in Sappho indicated that she was by no means a prude. He began to think that however badly he might burn his fingers as a result of possible dalliance with this new flame, he was going to get more fun for his pains than he had at first supposed; and while considering that highly consoling assumption he quite unwittingly dropped off to sleep.

It was, no doubt, his still youthful capacity for almost unlimited sleep, when not otherwise engaged, that played a big part in the swift restoration of his vitality after he had sustained any serious hurt or strain. When the doctor came that evening he pronounced the patient's progress to be excellent, and agreed that provided his foot was kept up on a cushion no harm should come to his making a twenty-mile stage in a comfortable coach the following day.

Accordingly a leisurely start was made at nine o'clock next morning. Tansanta insisted on Richard having the same corner seat, next to the near window, as that in which she had brought him wounded from the field of honour; while, again she sat next to him with Quetzal on her other side and the Señora, Poeblar beyond the boy in the far corner. Room had been made for Maria on the front seat, opposite the Senora, and Richard's baggage was piled in with the rest. In addition to Pedro and Manuel with their blunderbusses on the boot and box, and Tansanta's armed outrider, Hernando, they now had two tough-looking hired men, both carrying pistols and cutlasses, riding one either side of the coach. So as they left Nevers behind, perched so romantically upon its hill above the confluence of the Loire and the Allier, they felt that de Roubec would be hard put to it to muster a sufficient number of mounted ruffians to attack them with any hope of success.

It was the 4th of May, the fateful day on which, provided there were no further postponements, the States General was to assemble for its first momentous meeting at Versailles; but Tansanta d'Aranda's party gave it no thought as they knew that, even by fast courier, it must be several days before news of what had occurred would catch up with them.

The weather was clement and the country through which they were passing mainly cultivated, as they were now on the, fringe of the Bourbonnais, which contained some of the finest farming land in France. Richard was no agricultural expert but, like every Englishman of his day, he knew enough of farming to realize that the rich soil was not producing crops at one half the value of that in his native Hampshire and the reason was not far to seek.

Even the poorest nobility of France considered it beneath them to farm their own properties. Instead, they- let it out in smallholdings to the ignorant peasants on the evil metayer system, by which the tenant surrendered half his produce to his landlord in lieu of rent; so economical tillage was impossible and such modern ideas as crop rotation entirely unknown. Whereas in England every big landowner for several generations past had taken the keenest interest in all new developments, and King George himself took pride in growing the biggest turnips in his realm.

But for the first hour of the journey Richard was given little leisure to study the countryside, as Tansanta had not yet heard a full account of his fight with de Roubec's men, and while he told her of it she had to translate the story bit by bit into Spanish for the benefit of the Señora Poeblar and little Quetzal.

When he had done, she mentioned for the first time that they would not normally have been on the road so late in the evening had not one of the horses cast a shoe in mid-afternoon. That had slowed their pace to a walk for several miles, and Geld them up when they reached a wayside village for the best part of an hour while the smith was fetched from his field to re-shoe the horse. She added that she blamed herself for having let Hernando ride on ahead to secure accommodation in Nevers, but it was a routine that they had adopted for the afternoon ever since leaving Fontainebleau, and she had not thought to alter it that morning after her escort of hussars had turned back.

All things considered they thought themselves lucky to have escaped as lightly as they had. But they agreed that with the protection they now enjoyed there was a very good chance that de Roubec would throw in his hand, return to Paris and report that the task he had been given was beyond his powers of fulfillment.

In the early afternoon they arrived at a little town called St. Pierre, where they meant to pass the night. The only inn there was the usual miserable place lacking both common rooms and glass windows; but it was one of the penalties of journeying by short stages that travelers who did so were forced to feed in their bedrooms. As Richard knew by experience, in such places single travelers often had to share a room with one or chore strangers, the landlord was also usually the cook and the chambermaids, almost invariably ugly, uncouth slatterns. There was never any garden to sit out in, the beds were bug-ridden and the other furniture either of the poorest quality or non-existent. The only point in which they were superior to their English counterparts was that they offered not more, but a greater variety of food.

However, persons of quality who traveled in France took every precaution to minimize such discomforts, carrying with them their own beds, window curtains, and even folding furniture, as though they were proceeding on a military campaign. And Tansanta was no exception to the rule. In half an hour the best of the three rooms in the place had been made tolerably comfortable, and Richard installed on his own bedroll to rest after his journey. He still felt weak from his loss of blood, so dozed for most of the rest of the day, while Tansanta whiled away the time playing chess
with her duenna.'

The following day they moved on to Moulins, and found it a surprisingly poor, ill-built town for the capital of the rich Bourbonnais and seat of the King's Intendants. The Belle Image, at which they put up, proved a more spacious but scarcely cleaner

hostelry than the pigsty in which they had passed the previous night, and on Richard sending out for news-sheets he was surprised to learn that none was available, even in the cafes. As with everywhere else in France, the town was agog with political speculations, but all were based on the wildest rumours and authentic news entirely lacking.

On the 6th they passed through pleasant country again, making a slightly. longer stage of thirty miles, to St. Pourcain. They arrived to find the place in a tumult, and it transpired that a foreigner had been arrested on suspicion of most nefarious designs. Further enquiry elicited the fact that he was a German who had been caught pacing out the measurements of some fields just outside the town and making notes of their acreage in a little book. Later, when his papers were examined, it emerged that he was a perfectly honest gentleman with large estates in Pomeranian, who, on traveling through the Bourbonnais, had been struck with the richness of its soil compared with his own semi sterile lands, and had formed the project of buying a property in the neighborhood. But it was several hours before the local authorities could persuade the angry, ignorant peasantry that he was not an agent of the Queen who had been sent to measure their land with a view to doubling the taxes upon it.

As Richard and Tansanta were discussing the matter that evening he asked her: `Why is it that so many people who have never even seen Madame Marie Antoinette believe her capable of the most abominable immoralities, and regard her as deserving of such universal hatred?'

Tansanta sadly shook her head. `It is a tragedy, and all the more so in that when she first came to France her beauty and graciousness instantly won for her the adoration of those very masses that now curse her. But she has since been the victim of many unfortunate circumstances over which she had no control.!

'I pray you tell me of them,' Richard said. `I know most of her story, but since, until quite recently, she has played no part in politics I find this long, gradual decline in her popularity quite inexplicable, and the problem fascinates me.' Settling herself more comfortably on her cushions, Tansanta replied: `She has been dogged by bad luck from the very moment that she arrived at Versailles as Dauphine. Then, she was a child of fourteen, lacking in all experience of intrigue; yet she found herself at once forced into the position of leader of the set that was striving to bring about the ruin of Madame du Barri. Her mother, the Empress-Queen Maria Theresa, had counseled her to re-conciliate her father-in-law's powerful mistress; but all her instincts revolted against making a friend of that rapacious, gutter bred courtesan.

'Instead, she quite naturally showed her liking for the du Barri's enemy, the Duc de Choiseul, who, as Prime Minister, had negotiated the Franco-Austrian alliance and her own marriage. He and his friends represented all that was best in France, but for years they had been fighting a losing battle against the greedy libertines with whom the bored, immoral old King surrounded himself ; and soon after Madame Marie Antoinette's appearance on the scene the struggle ended in the du Barri's favor. De Choiseul was sent into exile and the du Barri's protégé, the unscrupulous Duc d'Aiguillon, was made principal Minister in his place. Unfortunately the little Dauphine had already shown her colours too plainly to be forgiven her partisanship, and she had committed the unhappy error of backing the losing side. She could not be dismissed with de Choiseul and his friends, but with their departure she was left almost isolated. Within a few months of her coming to France most of the important places at Court were filled by people who knew that they would not have been there had she had her way, and whom she received only because she had to.'

Richard nodded. 'That was certainly a most unfortunate start for her.'

'It was more than that; it has influenced her whole reign. Four years later when she and her husband came to the throne they swept clean the Augean stable. But it was not only the du Barri who was sent packing. Out of greed a considerable section of the nobility of France had prostituted itself in order to grab the wealth and favors that it had been so easy for the du Barri to bestow. They too found themselves debarred the Court and all prospects of advancement under the new reign. In consequence, scores of powerful families have nurtured a grudge against the Queen ever since:

'But why the Queen and not the King?'

'Because they count him too lethargic to have bothered to deprive them of their sinecures unless she had pressed him to do so; and it was she, not he, who originally championed de Choiseul against them.'

Tansanta ticked off her little finger. 'So you see that is one set of unrelenting enemies who for fifteen years have lost no opportunity of blackening and maligning poor Madame Marie Antoinette. From the beginning too she had to contend against the spiteful animosity of the Royal Aunts, Louis XV's three elderly unmarried

sisters. Madame Adelaide was the leading spirit of those stupid, gossiping old women. She both hated the Austrian alliance and resented the fact that a lovely young princess had come to take precedence over her in doing the honours of the Court; so she egged on the other two, and between them they formed a fine breeding-ground for malicious tittle-tattle about their impetuous niece.

'Then,' Tansanta ticked off another finger, 'there were her husband's two brothers, the Comte de Provence and the Comte d'Artois; both of whom were much cleverer and wielded considerably more influence at Court than he did. Monsieur de Provence has pretences to learning, but he is a narrow pedantic man and possessed of the most poisonous tongue in the whole Court. From boyhood he has despised and hated his ungifted elder brother and even at times given vent to his rancor that the simple, awkward Louis barred his way to the throne. To a nature so warped by gall and jealousy the Dauphin's acquisition of a lovely wife could only mean the distillation of further venom, and Monsieur de Provence has never yet lost an opportunity of bespattering Madame Marie Antoinette with lies.'

'Well, at least Monsieur d'Artois has proved her friend,' Richard put in.

'In some ways, perhaps.' Tansanta shrugged. 'Yet he, too, helped to damage her reputation, even if unintentionally. He is certainly very different from his elder brother, for where Monsieur de Provence is fat and stolid he is slim and elegant; moreover he possesses wit and charm. But he is a shallow man and from his youth has indulged in flagrant immoralities. The Queen made a friend of him only from loneliness, and a young girl's natural craving for a little gaiety. As her brother-in-law she felt that she could go with him to parties that her husband was too mulish to attend, and yet remain untouched by scandal. But in that she proved wrong.

'Tis said that one cannot touch pitch without blackening one's fingers, and it proved true in this case. Her enemies seized upon Monsieur d'Artois' evil reputation to assert that since she was often in his company she must be tarred with the same brush.'

Tansanta held up four fingers. 'You see how these things add up; and we have not yet come to the end of the Royal Family. The Queen's ill luck persisted even to her sisters-in-law. As you may know, both Monsieur de Provence and Monsieur d'Artois married daughters of King Victor Amédeé of Sardinia, and the princesses of the House of Savoy have never been famed for their good

looks. One can perhaps forgive these two sallow, pimply creatures for being a little jealous of the beautiful golden-haired Dauphine; but, unfortunately, to their ugliness were added narrowness and spite. They hated her from the outset and combined with the Royal Aunts to invent malicious stories about her. Both of them gave birth to children several years before Madame Marie Antoinette was so blessed, and both took every chance that offered to mock her covertly with her barrenness. Then when she at last produced an heir, their rancor knew no bounds. And with the

second son born to the Queen it, if possible, became intensified, as each such birth has placed their own children further off in the line of succession.'

Richard smiled grimly `You have now more than a full hand.' - 'Yet I am far from finished. There was the affair of the Diamond Necklace, about which all the world knows. Personally I believe the Cardinal de Rohan to have been the innocent victim of a gang of rogues. But be that as It may, !:is prosecution by the royal command and later banishment damaged the Sovereigns as much as would have the loss of a province. The de Rohans, de Soubise, Guises and Loraine's are all one family, and that the most powerful in France. They stand united in holding the Queen responsible for their kinsman's disgrace, and have never forgiven her for it.'

' 'Twas the King's incredible stupidity in insisting on a public enquiry into the matter that did the damage.'

'Perhaps; but the public still does not believe her guiltless, and maintains that she sacrificed de Rohan to save herself. De Rohan, too, is far from being the only man who would have made love to her if she would have let him, and because she repulsed him has now become her enemy. That is the secret that lies behind His Highness of Orleans' vile and treasonable designs. If he could pull King Louis from the throne and seat himself upon it, he would, at one stroke, slake his vast ambitions and his thirst to be revenged on the woman who as a young girl slighted his advances:

Tansanta had given up counting, but she paused for a moment before adding: "Tis her still further misfortune that in this crisis in the affairs of France the King's First Minister should be a man that she can neither like nor trust. Both she and the King are devout Catholics, and the interests of Church and State have for so long been one in France that it is naturally offensive to their feelings that they should now have to rely for guidance on a member of the Reformed Religion. l `Moreover, Monsieur Necker's mental horizon is still that of a counting-house. They have every wish to aid him in his economies, but there are other matters of import quite as grave upon which, at times, he appears so vague they get the impression that they might almost be talking to him in a language that he does not understand. His reaction is to suspect them, and particularly the Queen, of endeavoring to deceive or make a fool of him; so he returns angry and disgruntled to his daughter's salon. Then that clever Madame de Stael makes bitter witticisms at the expense of Her Majesty, and one more place from which help should come has become instead a hotbed of slander and sedition.'

Richard sighed. `You have said more than enough, Señorita. I see now that almost from her childhood her enemies have been legion, so 'tis hardly to be wondered at that in the course of time they have succeeded in prejudicing the whole nation so violently against her.'

That was the last conversation in which Tansanta and Richard addressed one another formally as `Monsieur' and `Senorita'. On their first day together, at the inn in Nevers, she had asked his full name, and when he told her she had repeated Richard over two or three times as 'Riche', in the way that foreigners usually pronounced it, remarking that it was a pleasant name; but it was not until the morning after their talk about the Queen that she uttered it again.

They had barely cleared the last houses of St. Pourcain, on their way to Clermont, when some baggage that had been insecurely stacked on the front seat of the coach began to slip and threatened to come crashing down on Richard's injured foot. With a cry of:

`Quick, Riche! Quick! Guard your ankle!' Tansanta sprang from her seat and flinging out her hands managed to divert the landslide.

Half an hour later they got out the traveling chess set, with which they sometimes whiled away a few hours of their journey, and having set up the pieces Richard said quietly: `Which would you prefer, Tansanta? Will you be white or red today?'

`Thank you, Riche, I have no preference; since the white are nearest me I will play them,' she replied in an equally calm voice. But she quickly lowered her eyes and began to blush furiously.

In that formal age only the country people had retained their naturalness, and even they were not given to bandying about endearments lightly. In the upper classes only close relatives and friends of long standing called one another by their Christian names; so the first occasion which a young man and woman did so was a landmark in their intimacy surpassed only by their first kiss.

For the next hour or so both of them were too preoccupied with the step they had taken to play chess with even the moderate concentration which was all they usually gave the game, and they scarcely noticed the lovely vale of Riom through which they were passing.

They had now spent little short of five days and nights constantly in one another's company. For well over a hundred hours Tansanta had scarcely been out of Richard's sight, except when he was asleep, when she took off her outer garments night and morning behind a screen, and on such occasions as the ladies and Quetzal got out of the coach to lighten its burden when it came to an unusually steep hill. During that time her every feature and expression had become etched in his mind, and he had come to know her better than he of normal acquaintance.

could have done during several weeks.

As none of the party except themselves spoke French they had been able to converse with complete freedom on a great variety of subjects; and as she unfolded her mind to him he had more and more come to admire its breadth, intelligence and straightforwardness. He had already forgotten his first critical assessment of hers not strictly beautiful, coming instead to find an ethereal loveliness in her long thin face and an inexplicable attraction in her slightly uneven teeth; while he felt that he could have gone on for ever listening to her soft, melodious voice with its fascinating Spanish accent.

But he had never lost sight of the trouble and grief they would be laying up for themselves if they entered on an affaire; and he knew that even to start a light-hearted flirtation would be to step out on a slippery slope which might swiftly send him slithering headlong into passion. So he had watched himself like a hawk, and whenever their conversation had tended to grow sentimental he had gently guided it into other channels.

Now, after that morning's episode, he blamed himself for the rash impulse, which had led him to call her by her name, because she had inadvertently used his in a moment of excitement. Quite apart from any unhappy aftermath that an affaire with her might bring to himself, he was now more than ever convinced that it would be a wicked thing to arouse her passions.

He had loved a number of women, and one desperately, but even that he had got over comparatively quickly, whereas Tansanta was not of the type that having loved one man could soon find consolation in the arms of another. Richard was no moralist, but his innate decency made him acutely conscious that, since she could not hide the fact that she was strongly attracted to him, it was for him to protect her from herself. He had, so far, treated her with the courtesy due to a woman but the open friendliness he would have displayed to a man; and he knew that if the powder barrel created by their propinquity was to be kept damped down he must strive more rigorously than ever to preserve that attitude, despite the fact that there could now be no going back on their calling one another -by their Christian names.

At midday they passed through a plain as fiat as a lake with ranges of jagged mountains bounding it in the distance on either hand. Then, in the early afternoon, they came to the twin towns of Ferrand and Clermont, both perched picturesquely on volcanic hilltops. But the latter, despite its romantic situation, proved on closer acquaintance to be a stinking place of narrow streets and dirty hovels built of lava ; so that they were glad to leave it on the following morning for Issoire.

Their way now lay through fascinating country where conic mountains rose in every direction, some of which were crowned with villages and others with old Roman castles; but the steepness of the gradients necessitated the passengers in the coach frequently getting out to walk. The Señora Poeblar always got out with the others, as, in spite of her fat, she was a strongly built old lady, and she seemed to enjoy the exercise; so for several quite long intervals during the day Richard was left on his own.

Six days of complete rest with a plenitude of good food and wine had now built him up again, and he would have liked to stretch his legs from time to time with the rest, but the heavy block of plaster in which his foot was set ruled that out of the question. However, he put these periods of solitude to quite good purpose, as a few days earlier Tansanta had dug a Franco-Spanish dictionary out of her baggage and, with its aid, had started to teach him her language. She was giving him an hour's lesson each evening while their supper was being prepared, then at odd times during the day they ran through the phrases she had taught him; and now, while on his own, he passed the time in increasing his vocabulary by making lists of words from the dictionary.

Owing to the hilly nature of the country they covered only seventeen miles that day, yet were much more tired than usual when they reached the little town of Issoire. It was here they learned that the States General had actually met. The news had come with the passing through of the Marseilles Mail early that morning. It was said that Monsieur Necker had made a long speech that had pleased no one, that the Third Estate was disgruntled because it considered that it had been treated like a poor relation of the other two, but that all the same the meeting had passed off without any disturbances; otherwise there were no details.

The next day found Tansanta's party still wending its way slowly through the strange volcanic mountains of the Auvergne. As the strain on both horses and passengers was considerable they had decided to make another short stage of only eighteen miles to Brioud, and before the morning was far advanced they were all glad that they had not been more ambitious. It was now the 9th of May and with every day's journey further south it grew hotter, so that after ten o'clock even the Spaniards began to feel the heat, and Richard found the interior of the coach intolerably stuffy.

At the village of Lempdes they crossed a river spanned by a big single arch and a few hundred yards to the far side of it the way began to rise steeply again, so the coach made one of its periodic halts for the passengers to get out and walk. The Señora, Quetzal and Maria stepped down into the road, and Tansanta was just about to follow them when she stumbled and almost fell.

Richard put out a hand and caught hers in an effort to save her, but before she could regain her balance she was thrown back against him, and for a moment they were pressed against one another as she lay half-sitting in his lap.

With a little gasp she pushed herself upright again, then she laughed to cover her embarrassment and got out of the coach; but before Richard released her hand he could feel that it was trembling violently.

An hour later the coach halted at the bottom of another hill; again the Señora, Quetzal and Maria got out, but this time Tansanta made no move to follow them. Instead she said to her duenna: `I have a slight pain, so I shall not walk this time.'

The others commiserated with her, the door of the coach was shut and as it moved on they dropped behind.

She had spoken in Spanish but Richard now knew a few score words of that tongue, and he said:

`Did I gather that you are not feeling well?'

They were still seated side by side. She turned her head and looked full at him. Their faces were only a few inches apart and her eyes were dilated with excitement, as she whispered: `I told them so. But it was a lie. I, I had to be alone with you.'

Instinctively their mouths came together, and next moment they were locked in a wild embrace.

CHAPTER EIGHT
OF LOVE AND DEATH

A bout ten minutes elapsed before the coach breasted the hill and stopped to pick up its passengers. During that time neither Tansanta nor Richard uttered a word. For them the ten minutes seemed barely two as they clung together in the first surge of passion, It was not until she actually kissed him that he realized how great a strain he 'had put upon himself these past few days in resisting the temptation to kiss her; while again and again her mouth sought his with the avidity of one seeking to slake a thirst after having been lost in a desert.

As the coach halted they started apart and swiftly sat back in their normal positions. The seat was deep and, in spite of the bright sunlight outside, the interior of the vehicle was semi-dark, so when the Señora climbed in she did not notice their flushed faces; and as it moved on she took Tansanta's unaccustomed silence to be caused by the pain of which she had spoken.

The gradients were easier now and as the Senora had already walked some three miles that morning she was feeling tired, so none of them got out again until they reached Brioude.

The next day was a Sunday and normally Tansanta's party would not have traveled on it, but she agreed with Richard that they should do so in order to minimize the delay in the delivery of the Queen's letter. Nevertheless, instead of starting at eight thirty, as was their custom, they postponed their departure till eleven in order that they might first attend Mass. Having got herself ready for church, Tansanta suddenly declared that her pain had come on again and excused herself from going; so the Senora Poeblar went off with the rest, apparently quite unconcerned at leaving her with the still incapacitated Richard.

Normally, wherever he was, Richard followed the upper-class English practice of bathing two or three times a week, but on the Continent the custom was still regarded as eccentric and even dangerous. Instead, wealthy people of both sexes sprayed themselves lavishly with scent, bathing only with considerable ceremony three or four times a year, or when a doctor recommended a course of herb baths as a remedy for some illness.

During a journey people removed only their outer clothes at night and

Richard had been assisted in this by the footman, Pedro. That morning he had been dressed and shaved himself while the others were getting ready for church, but as he had to keep his foot up he was still lying propped up on his bedroll.

While the Señora and the others were going downstairs Tansanta sat looking at Richard, the blood draining from her face until it was as white as a sheet, her black eyebrows and full, crimson mouth standing out by contrast with startling vividness. As she heard them crossing the cobbled yard below the window she jumped to her feet and ran across to him. He opened his arms and with a little sob she fell into them.

After a few breathless kisses she drew back and cried: 'Say you love me! Say you love me! Please, Riche. I implore you to!'

'Indeed I do, my beautiful Tansanta he replied, kissing her afresh. And he meant it, for after the preceding day's scene in the coach he had known that further resistance was useless, and the violence of her passion had now communicated itself to him.

'You swear it?' she demanded.

'I swear it! Surely you must have seen that for days I have been fighting against the impulse to make love to you? Your sweetness has utterly overcome me; but I feared that to show my feelings openly could only bring you grief:

'Oh thank God I thank God!' she exclaimed, ignoring his last few words. 'Never have I felt so ashamed as after yesterday. What must you have thought of me? Yet I vow that far from being accustomed to behaving so I have always despised women who made advances to men:

'I know your mind too well ever to have thought otherwise,' he assured her quickly. 'How could anyone be constantly in your company for a week without realizing that your standards of conduct are as high as your person is beautiful?'

'But Riche, I have never felt for any man as I do for you,' she hurried on: 'The very touch of your hand makes me deliriously happy, yet terrifies me. How I shall bring myself to support Don Diego after this I cannot think.'

'Don Diego?' he repeated.

'Yes. I have said nothing of it because each time I have broached the question of love or marriage you have turned the conversation to some other topic. But I am going to Naples to be married.'

'Do you-do you regard your fiance with affection?'

'How could I? I do not even know him. He is my father's choice for me. I am twenty-two and should have been married long ere this, but Madame Marie Antoinette begged my father to let me remain with her until this spring ; then he insisted that I must return to take-my rightful place in Spanish society.'

'This Don Diego, I suppose, is a gentleman of ancient lineage?' Richard asked a little bitterly.

She nodded. 'He is El Conde Diego Sidonia y Ulloa. He has great estates in Castile and on his uncle's death he will inherit a dukedom. His father was one of the nobles who assisted Don Carlos to conquer Naples, so he also has estates there and in Sicily. He has lived in Naples most of his life and is one of

King Ferdinand's Chamberlains. Even my father considers that a better match could hardly be found for me.'

'What sort of a man is he?'

'He is just under thirty years of age, and said to be handsome.'

'Mayhap you will fall in love with him, then.' The second Richard had spoken he could have bitten off his tongue. The remark was not made cynically but it might easily be taken so, and in any case it suggested a lightness that was out of keeping with the moment. To his mingled relief and distress she took it literally, and confessed:

'I had hoped to. If I could have done that I might have .brought him some happiness, or at least derived some pleasure from being his Condesa. But how can I ever do so now?'

He took her hands and pressed them. 'Oh, Tansanta, my poor precious, I would not have brought this willingly upon you for the world.'

"Tis not your fault, Riche. Neither is it mine. And I would not have had things otherwise if I could.'

'I tremble with delight to hear you say it. Yet I know myself to be terribly unworthy of such love as yours'

'Why should you think that?' she asked seriously.

'Because I have loved much and-and been far from faithful,' lie replied with an effort.

She smiled. 'Men are rarely faithful! That at least I know about them, so I count it no crime in you. But in all other ways you are different from any man I have ever met. Perhaps that is partly because you are English. If so the women in England are monstrous fortunate. My own countrymen are deserving of admiration, for they are upright, kind and chivalrous; but they consider it beneath their dignity to talk to any female as an equal. Frenchmen are clever and amusing but they are rarely sincere and where a woman is concerned think only in terms of her seduction. But you combine gallantry with gentleness; you show no trace of condescension in discussing with me matters upon which a woman's opinion is supposed to be worthless, and treat me with the gay camaraderie that you would use towards another man. 'Tis that in you, more even than your handsome looks, that I have come to love.'

All too late Richard saw where he had erred. If he had displayed only an amused tolerance towards her intellectual leanings, or, better still, attempted to take liberties with her at the first opportunity, he would have repelled her and, most probably, nipped her embryo passion for him in the bud; but in the very method by which he had sought to do so he had defeated his own end.

Yet, now that his scruples had been willy-nilly overcome, he was much too human to allow his earlier misgivings to mar his delight in the love that she was pouring out so freely. Once more he took her in his arms, and for a while they mingled blissful sighs and kisses.

It was not until the time for the return of the church party drew near that he made one final effort to save them both from the slippery path they were treading. Putting her gently from him he said

`Listen. Tansanta, my love. I am but a gentleman of small fortune, and we both know that your father would not even consider a request from me for your hand:

`Alas,' she sighed. 'In that I fear you right beyond all question.'

`Then had we not best use the chirurgeon's knife upon our passion before it begets a lasting obsession? That we have seen not a sign of de Roubec these past eight days can be taken as a fair indication that he has abandoned his designs upon the Queen's letter: and I am now sufficiently recovered to travel on my own. If you tell the Senora Poeblar that I am carrying a Government dispatch that will be reason enough to excuse my leaving you here and hastening on to Marseilles. For both our sakes I urge you to let me take post-chaise this afternoon:

`Nay, Riche! Nay' she cried, flinging herself upon him again. `I beg you to do no such thing. We have but another week, or ten days at the most. My dear Senora is no fool and although she has said nothing of it I feel certain that she guesses what is in the wind. Yet she is too fond of me to prove difficult, provided we are circumspect. Between here and Marseilles we can snatch many stolen moments alone together. For me they will be memories beyond price to treasure in the years to come. I implore you not to rob me of them:

To that sweet appeal there could be but one answer, and Richard made it with a fervor equal to her own. `So be it then, my love.

When the time comes, part we must. But until then we will give no thought to the future.'

At eleven o'clock the party set off as planned, to sleep that night at the little town of Fix.. The country continued to be picturesque and hilly, so on half a dozen occasions the Señora Quetzal and Maria got out to walk; but Tansanta used her feigned indisposition as an excuse to remain with Richard. Whenever they were alone they seized the opportunity to nestle in an embrace in the warm semi-darkness of the coach, and even when the others were with them in it they now secretly held hands.

That evening at Fix they learned. fuller details of the momentous first meeting of the States General. The preceding Monday had been devoted to a solemn spectacle. The deputies had mustered at the Church of Notre Dame and, headed by the clergy of Versailles, marched to the Church of St. Louis to hear Mass and ask the blessing of God on their deliberations. The Third Estate, clad in humble black, had been placed in the van of the procession, while the King and Queen, surrounded by the Princes of the Blood, in gorgeous robes and ablaze with diamonds, had brought up its rear. The choice of so drab a uniform for the representatives of the people had been governed by ancient precedent, but it had been much resented. Many of them were men of substance who normally dressed with some richness, so they considered it a deliberate slight that they should be forced to appear like supplicants in contrast to the nobles and higher clergy, who followed them decked out in all the splendor of rainbow-hued silks, satins and velvets.

The entire population of Versailles, numbering 60,000, had turned out to see the procession, and the crowd had been swollen to more than twice that number by great contingents from Paris and visitors from every province in France. Although the ceremony took place in the royal city, where practically everyone owed their living to the Court, it was the Third Estate which had received by far the greatest ovation. The nobles and clergy had been allowed to pass almost in silence; the King had been cheered but even his presence had not prevented a few catcalls at the Queen, and it was said that by the time they reached the church she was in tears.

On the Tuesday the three Estates had met in the Salle des Menus Plaisirs, which had been chosen because It was an enormous room that was rarely used ; but it had been hastily fitted up and no arrangements made to separate the deputies from such members of the public as could press their way in. The deputies had been

summoned for eight o'clock but the proceedings did not begin till ten; and, during the long wait, while the clergy and nobles were allowed to wander about the big room the black-clad Third Estate had been herded into a narrow corridor.

Eventually, when everyone had taken their places, the King entered and formally declared the session open. The Keeper of the Seals delivered a lengthy oration outlining numerous reforms that should engage the attention of the Estates. Then Monsieur Necker started on an even longer speech, describing the state of the finances. On his voice giving out he had handed his script to a secretary, who read the rest of it, and between them they kept the deputies silently crowded on uncomfortable benches for four hours. So had ended the first session.

Two things of great moment emerged from it. Firstly that although the assembly was invited to discuss an immense range of subjects no definite proposals of any kind were put before it by the Crown. Secondly that the King and his Ministers had shirked the vital issue as to whether the three Orders should sit and vote jointly or separately. This was all-important, as the deputies totaled 1,214, of which 621 were representatives of the Third Estate. So if the assembly functioned as one house, seeing that many of the poorer clergy and a number of the nobles were in sympathy with the champions of radical reform, the Third Estate would be assured of a clear majority over the other two. But the irresolute King had left the three Orders to argue the matter out for themselves.

On the 11th of May Tansanta's party left Fix for Thuytz and soon after setting out they passed Polignac, where, even in that mountainous and romantic country, the castle from which the Queen's favorite took her title provided a feature of outstanding grandeur. It was very ancient, almost cubical in form, and itself perched upon a mountain that dominated the town.

As the coach crawled along the road a mile below it Richard asked Tansanta her opinion of Madame de Polignac, and if she was as bad an influence on the Queen as people said.

`She is certainly not an evil woman,' Tansanta replied, `but just light-minded and rather stupid. They are a very ancient family but were far from wealthy, so cannot be blamed for accepting the riches that Her Majesty has showered upon them. It was Gabrielle de Polignac's simplicity and straightforwardness on her being presented at Court that first attracted the Queen to her. Her Majesty asked her to become one of her ladies-in-waiting but she said frankly that she and her husband could not possibly afford to remain at Versailles, so the Queen made a generous arrangement for her.'

`Yet 'tis said that the Polignac's have had millions out of the royal coffers.'

`That is an exaggeration; but the Queen has certainly paid lavishly for her enjoyment of their society. She had Gabrielle's husband, Count Jules, made a Duke and secured for him the lucrative position of Intendants General de Postes. But it is his sister, the Comtesse Diane, who is the rapacious one of the family; she neglects no chance to abuse the Queen's generosity, and it is largely her extravagance, which has given them the ill-name of greedy sycophants:

"Tis a pity, though, that, having had so many undesirable relatives forced upon her, the Queen does not choose her own friends more carefully:

`They are as varied as her tastes, and some are well worthy of her friendship. But, unfortunately, she has little ability to see below the surface. Your own first meeting with her was an instance of that. She liked you well enough to start with, then on being informed that you were a murderer and seducer her sense of justice led her to the impetuous decision that you must be made to pay for your crimes; whereas anyone more discerning would have known from your own countenance that you could not possibly be capable of an unworthy action.!

'I thank you for your good opinion of me,' Richard laughed, but he wondered a little grimly what she would have thought of him if she knew that he now carried only a transcript of the Queen's letter and had sent the original to London. ,

On approaching Thuytz they entered a country of pinewoods, which in the strong sunshine smelt delicious, but the inn there proved one of the worst at which they had yet stayed.

From Fix to Thuytz was one of the longest stages that they had so far accomplished, and next day they planned to do another to Montelimar, but luck was against them. A few miles short of Villeneuve de Berg a more than usually bumpy piece of road caused the back axle of the coach to crack, and although it did not actually break in two Manuel declared that it would be dangerous for them to proceed further.

As they always carried ample provisions against such an emergency, while help was being sent for they were able to picnic -in the fringe of the beautiful chestnut woods that here spread for many miles covering all the lower slopes of granite mountains. In due course farm wagons arrived, to which the baggage was transferred and the coach, lightened of its .Load, was driven on at walking pace to the township. The rest of the day went in fitting a new axle to the coach, so it was not until the afternoon of Wednesday the 13th that they were ferried across the broad Rhone and reached Montelimar.

Here the post road from Lyons joined that upon which they had come from Paris, thereby doubling the traffic southward bound for the great port of Marseilles; so, for once, in the Hotel de Monsieur at which they put up, they enjoyed the comfort and good food of a first-class hostelry.

They enquired for news of the States General but no startling developments had occurred. After the first session the clergy and nobles had retired to deliberate in separate chambers, leaving the Third Estate in possession of the Salle des Menus Plaisirs ; which later proved to have been a tactical error, since that had been officially designated as the meeting-place of the whole assembly, and was the only one to which the public were allowed admittance.

The next step was the verification of credentials, at which each deputy had to produce to his colleagues the papers proving him to have been properly elected and the actual person nominated to represent his constituency. This was obviously a matter, which would occupy several days, but the manner of observing the formality .had provided the first bone of contention. The question at issue was, should these verifications be carried out in a combined assembly or by each Order separately?

As the decision would so obviously create a precedent it was not surprising that both the clergy and nobles had decided on separate verification, the former by 133 votes to 114 and the latter by 188 to 47. The Third Estate had therefore been left high and dry, as they had no powers to act on their own, and they had begun to protest more vigorously against the other two Orders' refusal to join them.

At Montelimar, in addition to the welcome change that the well-run inn provided, the travelers enjoyed the delicious newly made nougat for which the town is famous; although little Quetzal ate himself sick of it.

It was Quetzal, too, who provoked an episode the following day that showed Tansanta to Richard in quite a new light. After leaving Montelimar they had passed through still hilly but sterile, uninteresting country to the old Roman town of Orange, reaching it early in the afternoon. Had Richard been able to walk he would have set off to view the ruins of the great stone circus and the fine triumphal arch, but he had to be content with a distant view of them before being carried upstairs to the principal bedroom of the inn.

As the day was very hot he was made comfortable near the open window, and the inn being a comparatively new one on the outskirts of the town he could see some way down the road where it wound into the country. After a little while Tansanta and the Senora joined him there and embarked on his daily Spanish lesson. They had been thus employed for about three-quarters of an hour when a little party of excited people emerged from round the corner of a nearby hovel, and came hurrying along the road towards the inn. The group was led by Quetzal, who was being half pushed along by a tall, gaunt peasant; at their heels there tagged two slatternly women and several ragged children.

With a cry of angry excitement at seeing her Indian handled in such a fashion Tansanta jumped to her feet and ran downstairs. Richard, seeing that Quetzal had suffered no actual harm, did not unduly disturb himself, but watched out of the window with mild interest to learn the cause of the trouble.

He liked Quetzal. The boy was a droll-little fellow and could be very amusing at times; but generally he was inclined to be sedate, had charming manners and never obtruded himself, being apparently quite happy to play for hours with his toys or go off for walks on his own. His fearlessness was one of the things that Richard admired most about him. With his red-brown face, brilliantly embroidered clothes and feathered head-dress he presented an object calculated to arouse the amazement and possible hostility of the superstitious peasants in any village-as they might easily have taken him for a Satanic imp sprung from the underworld. But, although groups of villagers often followed him about, he had the superb self-confidence of a true aristocrat. Evidently he considered that an Aztec Prince who was in the service of one of the first ladies of Spain could afford to ignore such lesser beings, since he never paid the slightest attention to the unkempt children who sometimes shouted and pointed at him.

Running to the boy Tansanta tore him from the peasant's grasp, at the same time calling loudly to her servants. Hernando and Manuel came hurrying from the stable yard, upon which she screamed orders at them in Spanish. Instantly they seized the peasant and forced him to his knees in front of her. Then, snatching from Manuel a whip that he had been carrying, she raised it high in the air and brought it cracking down on the kneeling man's shoulders.

`Hi!' cried Richard from his dress-circle seat at the window. `One moment, Señorita, I pray! Before you belabour the fellow at least find out what is at the root of the matter.'

Turning, she scowled up at him, her black brows drawn together, her brown eyes blazing. `Why should I? This scum laid hands on Quetzal! How dare he lay his filthy paws on my little Indian!'

As she turned back to strike a second time, Richard shouted at her louder than before; begging her to desist until she had heard what the man had to say. It was only at his urgent plea that she lowered her arm, and by that time people were hurrying up from all directions. A number of scowling peasants had edged toward their kneeling fellow countryman but Pedro and the two hired guards arrived to reinforce Tansanta, and it was clear that the locals were too cowed to venture on attacking her armed retainers. Then the landlord of the inn appeared and with a scraping bow to Tansanta enquired what offence her victim had committed.

The lanky peasant and his women could speak no French but the landlord interpreted their patois, and it then emerged that Quetzal had had an argument with the man's nanny-goat. Whether Quetzal had teased the goat, or his unusual appearance had excited her to unprovoked anger, could not be satisfactorily determined. The fact was that she had charged him and, instead of taking to his heels as most grown-ups would have done, the courageous little fellow had dealt with the situation in precisely the same way as he had seen a matador deliver the quite in Spanish bull-fights. Drawing his tomahawk he had stood his ground till the last moment, then side-stepped and neatly driven the pointed end of his weapon through the skull of the goat, killing it instantly.

Tansanta and her Spanish servants were enraptured with Quetzal's feat, the Senora and Maria clapped loudly from the window, and Richard felt that whether the boy had first incited the goat or not he was deserving high commendation for his bravery; but, even so, his English sense of justice still urged him to ensure that the peasant had a fair deal.

'The miserable man pleaded that the dead nanny-goat had been his most treasured possession, as the milk and cheese she gave had formed the main items of food for his whole family ; and, knowing the abject poverty of the lowest strata of the French peasantry, Richard believed that he was telling the truth. In consequence he urged Tansanta to give the poor wretch a half a Louis to buy himself another goat, but she would not until Richard offered to pay, and even then she was swift to devise a judgment that tempered charity with harshness.

Hernando, in his capacity of their courier, always carried a supply of ready cash, so handing him Manuel's whip she told him to give the peasant eight lashes with it and a crown for each. As she had expected, Hernando gave the man eight lashes and threw him only four crowns, but his cries of pain were instantly silenced at the sight of money. The sum was sufficient to buy him several goats, so the bystanders applauded the foreign lady's generosity and he and his family shuffled off grinning from ear to ear.

That evening while they supped Richard argued the ethics of the episode with Tansanta, but he could not get her to see that her treatment of the peasant had been either unjust or brutal. She maintained that such creatures were for all practical purposes animals, and that if one failed to treat them as such they would in no time get out of hand and become a menace to all civilized society; that whatever Quetzal might have done the fellow had no right whatever to lay a finger on him, and had merited punishment just as much as if he had been a dog that had bitten the boy. She added by way of clinching the argument that had he been one of her father's serfs in Spain she could have had his hand cut off for such an act, and that he was extremely lucky to have had anyone so eccentric as Richard present to get him compensation for his beating.

Knowing her to be normally the gentlest of women Richard found it strange to hear her setting forth such views ; but he felt certain they were tenets that she had automatically absorbed in her upbringing, and no part of her personal nature. Cynically it crossed his mind that Louis XVI might not now be involved in such desperate trouble with his people if, earlier in his reign, he had had the firmness to give short shift to agitators and the dirty little scribblers who lived by producing scurrilous libels about his wife. But the thing that intrigued Richard most about the affair was the violence of the temper that Tansanta had unleashed. He had been right in supposing that her heavy eyebrows indicated that she could at times be carried away by intense anger, and that in addition to her father's intelligence she had inherited his well-known intolerance of all opposition to his will.

On the Saturday they temporarily left France to enter the Papal territory of Avignon, and soon afterwards arrived at the ancient walled city. It was here that early in the fourteenth century Pope Clement V had taken refuge on being driven from Rome. It had then become for the better part of a century the seat of Popes and Anti-Popes who were acknowledged by France, Spain and Naples in opposition to rival Pontiffs in Rome who were supported by northern Italy, central Europe, England and Portugal. The Great Schism of the Western Church had ended in the triumph of the Eternal City, but the domain of Avignon had been retained and was still ruled by a Papal legate.

As soon as they were settled in the Hotel Crillon Richard declared that even though his plaster-encased foot would not allow him to leave a carriage, they must not miss the- opportunity of driving round a town with so many monuments of historic interests. The Señora Poeblar replied that she felt far from well, but had no objection to Tansanta accompanying him provided they took Maria with them; so with Quetzal in the fourth seat of a fiacre they drove off in the strong afternoon sunshine to see the sights.

Even the hotel in which they were staying was of some interest, as it had once been the private mansion of King Henry III's famous Captain of the Guards, known for his indomitable courage as le brave Crillon ; but infinitely more so was the Church of the Cordeliers, as it contained the tomb of the fair Laura, whose beauty had been made immortal in the poems of her lover Petrarch.

From the church they drove down to the mighty Rhone to see the remnant of that outstanding feat of mediaeval engineering, the Pont d'Avignon. The river here was so wide and swift that even the Romans had failed to bridge it, yet St. Bénézet had succeeded in doing so in the twelfth century, and his bridge had withstood the torrent for 500 years. In 1680 the greater part of it had been washed away, but four arches still remained on the city side as a monument to his memory.

They then drove up the hill to the great fortress palace of the Popes, began by John XXII, which dominates the countryside for miles around; and it was here, while admiring the vast pile of stone, that Richard and Tansanta first touched upon the thorny subject of their respective religions.

She opened the matter by remarking that she thought that Avignon, being in the center of southern France, should form part of the French King's dominions instead of belonging to the Popes.

He replied: 'I entirely agree. But since the Roman Church needs revenues to support its dignitaries it would naturally be loath to give up territories such as this from which it derives them.'

She shook her head. 'Through the centuries the Cardinals and other great Prelates have acquired the habit of living in pomp and luxury, but I think it contrary to the true interests of their calling. Priests, whatever their rank, should be humble, clean-living men, and if they were so their simple wants could be amply provided for by donations of the faithful without their possessing any territories at all.'

Richard looked at her in some surprise. `Again I agree; but I must confess that I find it somewhat strange to hear such sentiments expressed by a Catholic.'

'That perhaps is because, not being one yourself, you are ill-informed regarding modern thought in the highest lay circles of the most Catholic countries. Did you not know that ii was my father who expelled the Jesuits from Spain?'

'Indeed I did not.'

'It was so, and for excellent reasons. The Order of St. Ignatius had become the most glaring example of all that true servants of Christ should not be. In all but lip-service they had abandoned their religious duties and, instead, devoted themselves to politics and intrigue. Worse still, in our South American Empire they had acquired vast territories which they ruled according to their own will and often in defiance of the King's commands. Their greed was such that they ground down the natives and treated them with the utmost barbarity to extract the last centimo from them. The tyranny they exercised would have shamed any King, and their arrogance was such that they even kept their own armies ; so that my father was compelled to dispossess them of their lands by force of arms.'

'You amaze me,' murmured Richard. 'I knew nothing of all this.'

Tansanta shrugged. `That is not surprising, as it occurred twenty years ago and in a distant land. But there are other Orders that are near as irreligious as the Jesuits, and many of the convents in Spain and Italy are sinks of immorality; so I hope the time will come when they too will be suppressed.'

'Such views might almost lead one to suppose that you incline to the Reformed Religion,' Richard remarked after a slight hesitation.

'Then I fear I have misled you ; for it stands to reason that all the Protestant Churches are founded on error. They owe their creation to men who have rebelled against Rome, either from pride or, like your Henry the Eighth, for the purpose of giving their own sinful ends a semblance of legality. Our Lord charged St. Peter with the founding of His Church and there has been no divine revelation since to justify any departure from the Apostolic Succession.'

`Yet certain of the Popes have been far worse than bluff King Hal of England:

`I do not deny it. Have I not just been deploring the type of life which has been led by many high dignitaries of the Church of Rome from mediaeval times onwards?'

`And how do you support your theory of the Apostolic Succession when we know that at one period the legally elected Pope lived here in Avignon while another in Rome wore the Triple Tiara? Half a century later, too, there were three of them each claiming to be God's Vicar on Earth, and all three were deposed in order to heal the schism by the elevation of a fourth who owed nothing to any of the others. In that upheaval of the Church the direct line from St. Peter was clearly broken.'

`Such unfortunate disruptions and the personalities of the Popes themselves have no bearing on the matter. It is the unbroken teaching of the Church which counts. That enshrines the tradition of near two thousand years, and all the interpretations of the sayings of our Lord by the truly pious early Fathers remain unaltered within it!

'As a Protestant, I would maintain that the interpretation arrived at by the great Divines, who led the Reformation, have as much right to be considered valid as those made, by monks and missionaries living in the third and fourth centuries of our era.'

Tansanta turned to smile at him. `Then 'tis fruitless for us to argue the matter. But this much I will admit. From what I have heard I believe the majority of your pastors do lead holier lives than those of our priests. And I cannot think that the Way to Heaven lies only in the slavish observance of ritual; for Christ could not be so unmerciful as to reject any who follow His teaching according to their honest convictions.'

As they drove back to their hotel Richard wondered what other surprises Tansanta might have in store for him. Of the many French Catholics he had met the great majority had either taken their religion lightly and so much as a matter of course as scarcely to think about it, or had been secretly Freethinkers. Tansanta's obvious faith coupled with broadmindedness was an entirely n •.•,r brand of Catholicism to him, but the basis of it was clearly derived from her strong-minded father's contempt for a decadent priesthood.

On reaching the Crillon they found other matters to concern them: In their absence the Senora had become markedly worse.

She was now feverish and complained of severe pains in her stomach. A doctor was sent for, who prescribed the almost universal remedy of the times and proceeded to bleed her. He was an elderly man and seemed sensible and competent, so when he was about to depart Richard waylaid him and raised the question of his foot.

The chirurgeon in Nevers had said that it should be kept in plaster for from two to three weeks, and now that a fortnight had elapsed Richard was anxious to get free of the heavy encumbrance that prevented him from walking. Moreover, he knew that even after the plaster had been removed it would take him a few days to regain the full use of his leg, and they were now only that distance by coach from Marseilles, where he would have to part from Tansanta and look after himself on his voyage to Leghorn.

The doctor agreed to do the job there and then, so a small hammer was sent for and the plaster broken away. It was then found that Richard's healthy flesh had healed perfectly; but when he put his foot to the ground he could not stand on it, so he had to be assisted as usual to the table for supper.

As the next day was again a Sunday they had already planned to allow time for church, then to set off at eleven o'clock for Orgon ; but before they retired that night Richard gave it as his opinion that the Senora would not be well enough to travel again till the Monday.

However, on the Sunday morning she seemed much better. She declared that the weakness she still felt was due only to the doctor having bled her the previous evening, and, although they urged her not to, she insisted on getting up to attend Mass.

Every day during the past week Richard and Tansanta had succeeded in snatching a few brief, blissful interludes alone together, but they had been looking forward to a full, uninterrupted hour on this Sunday morning with a longing by no means untinged with disturbing thoughts. Neither had again referred to the all too short duration that an arbitrary Fate seemed to have set upon their love-making, but both were very conscious that the hour of their parting was now imminent, and that the Senora's attendance at church might provide their last opportunity of any length to give free vent. to their feelings for one another.

Yet, in the circumstances, Tansanta felt she could hardly again pretend an indisposition, as she had planned to do; since her duenna was still so obviously not fully recovered it would have been callous in the extreme not to accompany her. Therefore,

reluctant as she was to do so, she got ready for church with the others, and after giving Richard a glance conveying her disappointment went off with them, leaving him to practice hobbling about on his game leg.

It was as well she did so, as half-way through the service the Señora was first overcome by a fainting fit, then, on their getting her outside, was taken with a violent vomiting. As soon as they got her back to the hotel she was put to bed and the doctor sent for again. He said he thought that she was suffering from some form of food poisoning and gave her an emetic, after which he bled her again, both of which processes weakened her still further.

That afternoon she became delirious and when the doctor called in the evening he could only shake his head. He told them that, the emetic and bleeding should have purged the ill-humors from her system, so everything now depended on the strength of her constitution. In view of the soundness of her vital organs he thought her condition far from desperate but could give no further opinion until it was seen how she got through the night.

Tansanta was terribly distressed and declared her intention of sitting up all night with her old gouvanante. Both Richard and Maria pressed her to let them take turns at watching by the sick woman, but she would not hear of it and insisted on their going to bed.

For a long time the delirious mutterings from the far end of the big room kept Richard awake, and even after they had ceased he found himself unable to do more than doze; so when Tansanta tiptoed over to him at about two o'clock in the morning he was instantly wide awake. Stooping over him, she whispered.

`My love; she has just woken and is fully conscious. Her fever seems to have abated and I think she is much better. But she has expressed a wish to speak to you, and alone. I pray you go to her while I wait out on the landing. Restrain her from talking as far as you can, dear one, for 'tis of the utmost importance that she should conserve her strength.

With a whispered word of endearment Richard got up, pulled on his robe de chambre, and as Tansanta left the room, limped over to the Señora's bed.

At the sight of him the old lady's eyes brightened perceptibly, and she began to speak slowly in Spanish. Knowing how little he as yet understood of that language she used simple phrases, choosing her words with great care, and where she found difficulty in expressing herself simply she here and there substituted a word or two of Church Latin.

'Señor Riche,' she began. `I am nearly seventy. I am very ill. Perhaps my time has come. Perhaps the Holy Virgin is calling me. Tomorrow I may not be able to speak to you.'

With a feeble gesture she waved aside his protest and went on

`You love the Señorita Tansanta. I know it. She loves you. It is a fire that burns in both. Without me she will be defenseless. She is very headstrong. If you lift your finger she will give all. Then she will wish to remain with you. But soon she will have bitter regret. Her whole life ruined. I beg you not to tempt her. To reject her even. Then her pride will make her leave you and go on to Naples. I beg you save her from herself, and let her go.'

Richard had failed to grasp a word here and there, but he understood her meaning perfectly. It had not previously even occurred to him that if the Señora died, Tansanta, finding herself free from restraint, might refuse to go through with her prospected marriage. Staring down at the big, once-handsome face on the rumpled pillows, that now, in the candlelight, appeared a frightening mask, he nodded assent.

The old duenna gathered her remaining strength and whispered

`You must be strong for both. You will not bring shame and regret upon her. I know you will not. If you are cold towards her the fire she feels for you will in time die down. Promise me . . . Promise me that you will not make the Señorita Tansanta your mistress.

Feeling that he could not possibly reject such a plea, Richard said firmly: `I promise.' Then Señora smiled at him, took one of his hands, in hers for a moment and pressed it gently, then closed her eyes.

Limping over to the door he beckoned Tansanta inside; and on her asking in a low voice what her duenna had wanted of him, he replied: `She is anxious that you should get some rest, so asked me to sit by her for the rest of the night'

At seven o'clock the doctor came. He thought the patient slightly better and hoped that the crisis would be passed by midday. But by ten o'clock the Señora had become delirious again, and Tansanta, now in tears, decided to send for a priest.

Half an hour later the tinkling of the mournful little bell, that announces the passing of the Host through the street, was wafted to them on the hot air coming through a window that Richard, in defiance of French medical practice, had insisted on opening.

For a while the priest sat with them. Then, as the sick woman seemed to be getting weaker and showed no sign of returning consciousness, he administered extreme unction. At a quarter past twelve the Señora Poeblar was dead.

Tansanta was utterly distraught, so Richard took charge of all arrangements. The muscles of his foot were getting back their life, so with the aid of a stick he was now able to hobble about fairly, rapidly. He had Maria put her mistress to bed in another room, and move all their things there; and-had his own moved by Pedro to a separate apartment. Quetzal he sent out to go fishing in the river with Hernando. Then he saw an undertaker, had the Señora laid out surrounded by tall candles, gave the priest money to send people to pray by her body, and settled the hour at which the funeral should take place on the following day.

He did not see Tansanta again until the funeral. At it she wore a mantilla of black lace so heavy that it was impossible to see the expression on her face, but it seemed that her calm was restored as she did not break down during the ordeal. As Richard gave her his arm to lead her to the coach she pressed it slightly, but she addressed no word to him, except to thank him formally in a low tone for the trouble he had been to on her behalf. On their return he escorted her up to her room, but as she did not invite him inside he left her at the door. He thought that she would probably send for him that evening, but she did not, so he supped on his own again and wondered with some anxiety what developments the next day would bring.

On the Tuesday at ten o'clock she sent Quetzal to him with a note, which simply said that she would like him to take her for a drive, so would he order a iacre and fetch her in half an hour's time.

When he went to her room he found her ready dressed to go out, but much to his surprise her costume displayed no trace of mourning. Catching his thought she said with a smile:

`I have decided that from today I will start a new life, so with the old one I have put off my mourning.'

Her declaration filled him with instant perturbation, but he tried to hide it by replying, somewhat inadequately: `I too have always felt that the dead would prefer us to think of them as happy, rather than have us wear the trappings of gloom to symbolize their memory: Then he offered her his arm to take her downstairs. '

As she left the room she remarked: `I am taking neither Maria nor Quetzal with me, since 'tis as well that they should recognize from the beginning my new freedom to be alone with you when I wish.'

Such an indication of the form she meant her new life to take redoubled his uneasiness, and with his promise to the Señora Poeblar only too present in his mind, he said seriously: `All the same, my dear one, I am very anxious not to compromise you.'

`I know you too well to believe otherwise,' she smiled. `But a carriage drive at midday will hardly do that ; and soon there will be no need for us to worry ourselves about such matters.'

At her words he felt at Once both reassured and miserable. Evidently the Señora had overestimated Tansanta's passion for him, or her sense of duty was so strong that she had no intention of allowing herself to be led into betraying Don Diego before their marriage. He had feared that to keep his promise he would be called on to exert his utmost strength of will, but it seemed clear now that while she meant to make the most of her last few days with him she had no thought of using her freedom to allow him to become her lover. Yet his relief at escaping the ordeal of having to refuse such a delectable temptation was now more than offset by his unhappiness at the thought that in a few days she would be on a ship bound for Naples, and lost to him for ever.

They drove out of the city by the Port Crillon and, turning left, along under the great castellated wall, until they reached the river. Some way along its bank they came to a low eminence from which there was a fine view of the broad, eddying torrent, and here Tansanta called on the driver to stop.

It was again a gloriously sunny day, and neither of them spoke for a few moments while they admired the view across the rippling water to the further shore.

Then Richard stole a glance at Tansanta. The thought that he was so soon to lose her now caused him an actual physical pain in the region of his solar plexus. Here in the strong sunshine of the south her skin no longer had even a suggestion of sallow ness but appeared a lovely golden brown. Her dark eyebrows seemed to blend naturally into it, her black ringlets shimmered with light where they caught the sun, her lips were a full, rich red and her profile delicate. And he knew her to be the most gentle. honest and lovable of companions.

Turning, she caught his glance and said: 'Well, you have not yet asked me what my new mode of life is to be.'

'Tell me,' he smiled. 'My only wish is that it will bring you happiness.'

'Then your wish is granted,' she smiled back. 'For it lies solely with you to ensure it. I have made up my mind not to go to Naples. Instead I intend to make you a most devoted wife.'

CHAPTER NINE
MEDITERRANEAN IDYLL

H ad the bottom fallen out of the carriage Richard could not have been more shaken. From the beginning the possibility of marrying Tansanta had appeared so fantastically remote that he had never given it a second thought. That she should secretly become his mistress for a brief season had always been by no means improbable, as, provided they were circumspect, she could have done so without sacrificing anything except, possibly, her virginity. But by marrying him she would at once lose her status as a great lady and the obvious highroad to a brilliant future, beside being repudiated by her family and excommunicated by her Church.

. Quite unsuccessfully he strove to hide his amazement and confusion; but as it had not even entered her mind that he might be unwilling to marry her, she took them as a charming compliment and was simply joking when she said: `Will you have me for a wife, Monsieur, or must I cast myself into the river and die a virgin?'

That settled one point for him, although for the past week or more he had had little doubt upon it. A little breathlessly he said: 'Tansanta, my beloved, I am so overcome at the joy and honour you propose for me that I can no longer find words to express my feelings. But what of your family? Are you indeed prepared to sacrifice all that they must mean to you for my sake? For I fear your father and mother will never forgive your making so poor a match.'

`Is it not said that a woman should leave all and cleave to the man she loves?'

'And what of the difference in our religions?'

`I will not pretend that I am not reluctant to place myself outside the rites of the Church. But as I told you on Saturday, I do not believe that the way to Heaven lies in the observance of rituals. If you are unwilling to be received into the Church of Rome I will marry you by a Protestant ceremony.'

Richard felt shamed and humbled in the presence of such a love, but he knew it to be his clear duty to point out to her the worst aspects of the marriage she contemplated, so he forced himself to say.

`Money is a sordid thing, yet happiness often hinges upon the possession of at least a near sufficiency of it by each person in accordance with their upbringing. From your childhood you have lived in great luxury, and I am far from rich. It would break my heart to see you pining for things to which you have been accustomed, and be unable to procure them for you.'

`I have no fear of that. I hate ostentation and my personal tastes are simple. From what you have told me you are in receipt of a regular allowance, and that, though small, should suffice to keep us from actual starvation. Then, seeing that you are an only son, and your father is a man of some substance, there seems good reason to suppose that he will increase it on your marriage. But, whether he does or no, however angry my own father may be at my marrying without his consent he is much too fond of me to allow me to want for the means to live respectably.'

`Think you then that after a time your parents will forgive you?' Richard asked in some surprise.

`My mother will not. She is deeply religious and so under the thumb of her confessor that I doubt her ever forgiving my marriage to a heretic. But my father is of a different mould. He is too old now and in his life has climbed too high to be any longer a slave to his ambitions. Naturally, for the sake of our house, he would like me to make a suitable alliance, but I am sure that my happiness means more to him than such second-hand aggrandizement. He will have no cause for shame in my marriage to an honorable gentleman who is an English Admiral's son, and he is too broadminded to allow the religious question to dominate his affections.'

From all she said it seemed that their prospects were far better than Richard would ever have imagined they could be in such circumstances. Every instinct urged him to have no further scruples about taking this lovely, rich, sweet-natured bride; yet the words of the dying Senora Poeblar persisted in ringing in his ears. True, it was no longer any question of making Tansanta his mistress, so that if she remained with him for any length of time their relationship must inevitably bring shame and unhappiness upon her; but the Senora had so clearly felt that if given time the fires of Tansanta's passion would die down. Ought he not to ensure a fair margin of time for that possibility to take effect, before allowing her to commit herself irrevocably to this drastic step which would revolutionize her whole life? With that in mind he said:

'Since there seems some prospect of your father eventually be-' coming reconciled to you, it would perhaps considerably increase it if you wrote first explaining our circumstances and asking his consent to our marriage; albeit making plain that in any case you could not be dissuaded from it. He would then have less cause for umbrage and might, at a pinch, become a willing party to the design.'

'Nay,' she cried swiftly. `That I will not do. I have too many relatives and he too many powerful friends for me to risk it. Some of them would surely get wind of our whereabouts and seek to take me from you. They would even use force if all else failed.'

He brought himself to adopt another line.

`All the same I am against any hole-in-the-corner marriage, as unworthy of you. Would you be willing to trust yourself to me until I can take you back to my mother in England? I vouch for it she could not fail to love you, and there we could be married with the solemnity and happy rejoicings which are beyond hope of attainment for a couple situated as we are, here in France.'

`My trust in you is absolute,' she smiled. `And now that we are pledged to one another I am not wild to marry you on the instant. I will gladly do so tomorrow if you wish; but if you prefer to wait a month or two the joyous anticipation I shall feel will amply compensate me for exercising patience.'

'Damme! I do not prefer to wait!' he blurted out. `How I will find the patience to support so long a delay in making you truly my own I cannot think. Yet my sense of fitness tells me there are good reasons for it:"

`I think you right. And the admirable restraint you put upon yourself makes me love you all the more. Yet the sooner we can get to England and be man and wife the better I will be pleased.'

`I fear I am committed to deliver Her Majesty's letter first,' he said with a genuine sigh.

She nodded. `I had not forgot it. And on account of your wound its delivery has been overlong delayed already. Let us set out for Florence tomorrow then, and as soon as you have completed your mission seek a ship in Leghorn which will carry us to England. But while we are in Florence we must have a care. The Grand Duchess is the daughter of the late King Carlos III of Spain. When she married she took an aunt of mine with her to Florence as one of her ladies- in-waiting. A year or two later my aunt married a Florentine nobleman named Count Frescobaldi, and. still lives there. Should she get wind of my presence in the city she will wonder why I have not sought the hospitality of her palazzo ; and if she learnt that I am lying at an inn in the company of a handsome Englishman instead of a duenna we might be hard put to it to get away.'

After pondering a moment, Richard said: `Perhaps then it would

be safest if I left you in Marseilles while I deliver the letter to His Highness ; although I would be very loath to do so, particularly seeing the unsettled state of France.'

`Nay!' she cried, grasping his hand in sudden panic. `I beg you never leave me from now on. I could not bear it. In spirit I am married to you already, and for the rest I am content to wait. But if I were parted from you even for a week I would die of anxiety that some frightful thing might prevent your returning to me. No! To Florence you must go, but I will go with you.'

'Then it had best be under an assumed name; and we will make all possible haste to be through with the business.'

`You are right on both counts,' she agreed swiftly. `And I shall not rest easy until we are on a ship bound for England. But tell me more now about the country that holds so sweet a future for me. I am anxious to hear every detail you can give me of It.

He laughed. "Tis the custom there that immediately upon a couple pledging their troth they should kiss. We have not done so yet and can scarce do so here in the open. Let us drive back to the hotel, in order that I may pay the tribute that I am so eager to give to my beautiful fiancée.'

When they got back he produced the fine ring that Madame Marie Antoinette had given him. It was a little large for Tansanta's engagement finger but she was enchanted with it; and it made him very happy to think that fortune had provided him with a jewel for her of much greater value than he could ever have afforded to buy.

That evening after supper she asked him to haul out from under her bed two heavy brass-bound coffers. He knew them well by sight, as when the coach was on the road they traveled concealed in a secret compartment under a false bottom to the coachman's box, but each evening they were carried up to her room, and it was for their protection as much as her own that either Hernando or Pedro slept rolled in a rug outside her door every night.

Kneeling down she selected three keys from the bunch at her girdle and opened the larger chest. Richard had naturally assumed that it contained money, but he was positively staggered by the amount and value of the coin in it. Apart from a few rouleaux of silver for immediate needs, it was three-quarters full of Spanish gold. Nearly all the coins were the equivalent of £5 pieces. as large as a crown and weighing an ounce. Most of them had been minted in America and bore the head of King Carlos III with the individual markings of Mexico or Peru. He had never before seen so much gold in his life and could not even form a rough estimate of its value.

But Tansanta laughed up at him and said: `This is the residue of the allowance that my father made me these last few years. As I lived at Court and mainly at Her Majesty's expense it was far more than I needed. There must be all of a thousand doubloons here, so you see we have ample funds to support us for some time to come.'

Turning to the smaller chest she picked out another group of keys and unlocked that. It contained her jewels ; ropes of pearls, gem encrusted crosses, rings by the score, ornaments for hair, nee'.,,, wrists and corsage. As she opened case after case the diamonds, emeralds, rubies and sapphires flashed and scintillated in the candlelight. Laughing up at him again she said.

`These are all mine. Most of them were left to me by my great-aunt, who was a Duchess of Alva. Were they sold they would fetch at least a hundred thousand $us ; so I do not come to you as quite a pauper. If need be we will sell some of them from time to time to provide ourselves with little luxuries.'

Richard was neither avaricious nor a spendthrift, and although he was normally generous by nature he had inherited from his Scottish mother's family a very sound appreciation of the value of money. So, soon afterwards, when he was undressing in his own room, he could not help it flitting through his mind that Tansanta's fortune in gold and jewels gave them a much better prospect of living in happiness and contentment than they would otherwise have had.

Some £30,000 was no mean sum on which to start married life, and it relieved his mind of the only real anxiety that he had felt on accepting Tansanta's proposal. He realized that in that he had had little choice, as without loss of honour he could have done nothing else; but for her character and beauty alone he had been fully willing to make her his wife, and now, as a fine bonus to all else, she was bringing him a handsome fortune. By postponing their actual marriage for a month or so he felt that he had observed more than fairly with the Senora Poeblar's dying concern for her charge. But he considered it most unlikely that Tansanta would now change her mind. So before he dropped off to sleep he decided that he was a monstrous lucky fellow.

Now that they were nearing the end of their journey by road there was no longer the same need to spare the horses, so on the Thursday and Friday they made two long stages, sleeping at Laforge Salon the night and arriving at Marseilles late on the evening of May the 22nd.

The following morning Richard went early to the harbor to find out about sailings to Leghorn, and learned that no ship was leaving for the Tuscan port until the 28th. However, the ship concerned was a fine, four-masted barque, which had been for sumo time in port undergoing repairs, and on learning that its Captain frequented the Cafe d'Acajon, Richard repaired there for breakfast in the hope of meeting him.

At the cafe he was informed that the Captain rarely came in before ten o'clock, so while waiting for him he seized the opportunity to acquaint himself with the latest news. Unlike must of the small towns in which he had stayed the night on his way from Paris an abundance of news-sheets and pamphlets was available, and as he ate he scanned a number of them.

The three Estates had got little further and were still bickering on the question of separate or joint verification. Le Chapelier, a Breton deputy to the Third Estate; had proposed to cut short the controversy by declaring that they would recognize as lawful representatives only those whose powers had been verified I n a joint assembly. But more moderate councils had prevailed and on the 18th of May commissioners had been appointed to confer with representatives of the nobles, while nominees of the clergy attended the debate acting as friendly neutrals.

After Richard had eaten he got in conversation with a man of fairly affluent appearance who introduced himself as a ship owner named Golard.

On Richard's remarking that he was pleasantly surprised to find the city so quiet after the ill-reports he had heard of it, Monsieur Golard shook his head gloomily,

`The sans-culottes are quiet enough for the moment. Now that the Estates have met they are expecting their representatives to secure the earth for them ; but since no one can do that they will soon be raging the streets again. You should have been here in April.'

It was the first time that Richard had heard the expression 'lacking trousers' applied . to the mob, but it was certainly descriptive enough of the miserable, ill-clad rabble that swarmed in the poorer quarters of France's great cities. Offering his snuff-box, he said: `The disturbances were, then, of a really serious nature?'

`There were times when many of us feared that the whole city would be burnt about our ears,' replied Monsieur Golard, after appreciatively sniffing up Richard's repose.

`The trouble started when the nobles met to elect their deputies for the States General. The mob surrounded their Assembly Rooms and became tumultuous past all hope of pacification. The meeting was broken up and the nobles, compelled to escape by the back doors, sought to regain their homes as privily as possible. But far from being appeased the sans-culottes then hunted out those most obnoxious to them, broke into their houses and pillaged everything. Among others the Bishop of Toulon was a marked object of their fury. He was fortunate to get away with his life disguised as a fishwife, but they entirely despoiled his palace and threw his horses and carriages into the sea.'

'And what were the military about all this time?' Richard enquired.

`They were mustered at various points, but the riots soon assumed such formidable proportions that it was judged unwise to disperse them further. The Mayor ordered one party of soldiers to fire upon the crowd, with the result that he was dragged from their protection and most brutally butchered. The Comte de Caraman was in command of the garrison and he did what he could, but the numbers opposed to him were so great that his men were swiftly overwhelmed. He succeeded in disengaging the remnant and taking refuge with them in the citadel. As many of the rioters were armed they proceeded to besiege him there, and he and his men would inevitably have perished had he not sent to Monsieur de Mirabeau and begged his intervention.'

`It is true, then,' said Richard, `that the Comte de Mirabeau succeeded in quelling the revolt solely by the use of his golden tongue?'

`Had it not been for him the citadel would certainly have been burnt and many human beings have suffered a horrible death within it. He was similarly successful in putting a check on the rioting at Aix when it had proved beyond the power of the troops to do so. But here, even his eloquence could not prevent a con. tinuance of more general anarchy and outrage. For days afterwards groups of sans-culottes went about burning houses, and robbing, maltreating, and even killing people whom they judged to be opposed to then horrid travesty of liberty; and it was highly dangerous for any well-dressed person to appear in the streets, or even show themselves at a window.'

`What think you of Monsieur de Mirabeau?' Richard asked.

`He is undoubtedly a politician of great ability and, while the idol of the mob, not, I think, himself an extremist. But the general opinion here is that he is not to be trusted. I think he owed his election to the fact that we Marseillais are ever hot for action, so most of us would rather be represented by an able rogue than an honest man of no talent.'

'Should the Third Estate succeed in their demand for one combined assembly, there seems a good chance of his becoming the new leader of the nation.'

`Let us pray that they do not,' said Monsieur Golard firmly. `Did that occur all moderate opinion would be overborne and the extremists gain control of the State with some semblance of legality. Within a year the mobs would rule the cities and the peasants the countryside, so the remedy for our ills would be infinitely worse than the disease.'

'What then is your own solution to the problem?'

`No man of sense can deny that sweeping reforms are necessary if the country is to be made healthy again. But 'tis an ill thing to let a starving man gorge himself with red meat. His hunger should be appeased gradually, and so with the nation. To my mind there should be neither one Chamber nor three, but two, as they have in England. Then, however drastic the measures proposed in the Lower, they will have their dangerous edges taken off and be rendered practical by the Upper, before they actually become law.'

It was by no means the first time that Richard had heard this solution propounded, as nearly all the leading French political reformers expressed a great admiration for the English system ; and a very high proportion of the French middle classes were entirely with Monsieur Golard in being anxious for sweeping reforms, but at the same time desirous that they should be carried out in carefully considered stages so as not to unbalance the economy of the nation.

As the ship owner ceased speaking a big black-bearded man came into the cafe and he proved to be the Captain of the barque. It then transpired that Richard's meeting with Monsieur Golard had been particularly fortunate, as he was the barque's owner. In consequence a fair bargain for the transport of Tansanta's party and her coach and horses to Leghorn was soon struck, and Richard returned to his hotel to report to his fiancée.

During the days they had to wait until the ship was ready to i sail they explored the city and enjoyed many pleasant excursions. Tansanta, who had come from Spain via Bordeaux, declared that its buildings, theatres and harbor were all much superior to those of Marseilles, but that the country round about offered more distraction.

They were now in the true south, a land of olives, vines, tamarisk, mimosa and flattish-roofed, lemon-washed houses. Tansanta seemed to blossom in it, and as they drove along the dusty roads beside the blue Mediterranean Richard never tired of looking at her. Yet, during the hot, sultry nights there were times when he could not help regretting that he had not taken her at her word and been married to her by the first Protestant pastor he could run to earth. She, too, he could tell, was feeling the strain of their unsatisfied passion, and as they spent every waking hour in one another's company there was at present no prospect of that strain lessening.

He had begun to speculate feverishly on how long it would take for them to get to Florence and from there back to England,, although he knew that such calculations could only be of the vaguest as so much would depend on the sailings of ships, Wind and weather. So, when the 27th arrived, he was much relieved by the thought that they would soon be on their way again.

Quetzal had spent most of his time in Marseilles exploring the city with Hernando, and had thoroughly enjoyed himself ; but the memories of the length, discomfort and squalor of his Atlantic crossing three years earlier now made him most averse to going aboard a ship. However, Tansanta gently overcame his fears and they slept aboard the barque that night; then early on the morning of the 28th she stood out from the harbor towards the famous prison island of Chateau d'If. Their passage proved uneventful; the sea was kind and the winds fairly favourable, so they dropped anchor under the picturesque Fortezza Vecchia, in the harbor of Leghorn, on the afternoon of the 30th. Neither Richard nor Tansanta had ever before visited Italy, and on landing they were immediately struck by the strong contrast made by both the buildings and the people with those of the port from which they had sailed. Marseilles boasted few ancient monuments or examples of fine architecture, having grown up higgledy-piggledy; whereas Leghorn owed its expansion into a city very largely to the wealth and admirable taste of the Medici, so many of its mansions and churches possessed the serene elegance of the great Florentine builders. And, where the great majority of the inhabitants of the French port had been slatternly, ill-clad and depressed-looking, those of the Tuscan were far cleaner, better clothed and going about their business with an air of cheerful contentment.

Richard took rooms for the party at a hostelry near the cathedral, the fine façade of which had been designed by Inigo Jones, while he was studying architecture in Italy before using his genius to incorporate many elegancies of the Florentine style into the innumerable buildings with which he later beautified England. As the lovers were anxious to see something of the city, but could not linger more than a night there, they left Maria and Pedro to unpack, and hired a carozza with a French-speaking cicerone to take them and Quetzal for a drive.

The old town was pentagonal in shape, being entirely surrounded by broad canals, and set in a fertile tract of land that rose gradually to a range of hills dotted with white villas and farmhouses. In the gentle light of the summer evening it provided a scene of peace and prosperity ; again in strong contrast to the barren poverty-ridden country outside Marseilles.

Richard remarked that many of the people they passed had a more oriental type of countenance than he had expected to find in Italians, and their guide told them the reason for this. In the sixteenth century Ferdinand de Medici had invited men of all nations to settle and trade in the city, and in addition to immigrants from all parts of Europe considerable numbers of Moorish, Hebrew, Turkish, Armenian and Persian families had established themselves there. Moreover, as for just on a century Leghorn had been a Free City, with its neutrality guaranteed by the leading European powers, these little minorities had never been oppressed but encouraged to intermarry. He also told them with pride that all citizens of Leghorn enjoyed complete religious toleration; then took them to see the two-hundred-year-old Jewish synagogue and the big Protestant cemetery, in which Tobias Smollett had been buried eighteen years earlier.

That night, while still breathing the perfume from Tansanta's last warm embrace, and with the knowledge that an English church and clergyman were within a stone's throw of his bedroom, Richard was sorely tempted to take advantage of her willingness for them to get married immediately. But it was that day only a fortnight since the Señora Poeblar's death, and with the memory of the old lady's plea that Tansanta should be given time for the possible cooling of her ardor he determined to restrain his impatience.

Nevertheless, he was up by dawn next morning and, soon after, down at the docks making enquiries about a ship to England. A British vessel was sailing in three days' time, but he knew that it would be impossible for him to get to Florence, execute his mission and return in less than five days at the least. No other ship

was sailing direct till the middle of the month, but a Genoese merchantman was leaving for India on the 7th, and would be calling at Gibraltar, from which it would be easy to pick up another ship en route for London; so he booked passages in her and hurried back to tell Tansanta.

When he had done so he added: `Loath as I should be to leave you even for an hour, do you not think it would be wisest if I proceeded to Florence on my own?'

`Why so?' she cried, her big eyes opening wide with sudden alarm.

'On account of your aunt, the Contessa Frescobaldi,' he replied. `You will recall, my love, that the day of our betrothal you spoke of her, and said that should she learn of your presence in Florence..

'Why should she learn of it?' Tansanta interrupted. `We disposed of that possibility by agreeing that I should change my name; and I can trust my servants not to give away that I have done so.'

`All the same,' Richard argued, `the very thought that you might be torn from me fills my heart with such sick dread that I am opposed to taking the smallest risk of it.'

She laughed, threw an arm round his neck and kissed him on the cheek. `Then you must love me very much. How wonderful. And how fortunate I am! But have no fear. I will remain within doors all the time we are in Firenze, or wear a mask when I go out. Such precautions will make my discovery next to impossible.'

He still looked dubious, and persisted. `I agree that the measures you propose should afford you full security, yet all the same I would be happier in my mind if you remained here. I could not have brought myself to, leave you in a place so prone to disturbances as Marseilles, but here in Leghorn all is quiet and orderly. Besides, I should not be absent long. Alone I could ride to Florence and back in two days, whereas by coach it would take us four. The Genoese ship sails on the 7th, so we have only seven clear days, and should I find difficulty in gaining access to His Highness' presence, those two days saved might make the difference between our getting our ship and missing it.'

'Ah!' she exclaimed. `You contradict yourself, my love. First you say you would not be absent long, and then that you may be detained in Florence some days before you can deliver the letter. No! No! If need be we will get a later ship; but I cannot bear to be separated from you. I insist that you take me with you.'

`Then I will do so gladly,' Richard smiled; but, although he gave in gracefully, he was still troubled by lingering doubts as to the wisdom of the decision.

Nine o'clock saw Tansanta's coach upon the road again; and, as the mountains behind Leghorn denied the port any direct route inland, it was carrying them north-west towards Pisa. They ate their midday meal in the ancient University city, under the vine covered pergola of a little restaurant hard by the famous leaning tower; then in the afternoon drove on to Pontailera, where they spent the night.

The inn in this little market town proved as primitive as many that they had lodged at in France; but it had a far more cheerful atmosphere, and they were served with willingness and dispatch. Richard had noticed, too, throughout the day, that the country-folk seemed not only of a different race but an altogether higher type than the French peasant. In France the round-shouldered, ageless creatures who worked in the fields were scarcely to be dignified by the name of women; but the olive-skinned Tuscans were sturdy, full-bosomed wenches wearing gaily colored scarves, many of them having lustrous, thick black hair, fine eyes and strong white teeth which gave them a Junoesque beauty.

Had it not been for his eagerness to get home as soon as possible in order to marry Tansanta, he would have been greatly tempted to prolong his visit to Italy. His love of travel was bound up with the fascination that history and art had always held for him, and he knew that Italy had more to offer in that way than any other country in Europe. Already, merely passing through two ancient cities had whetted his appetite for more and, added to that, he found the blue skies, smiling landscapes and cheerful people all most congenial to his sunny nature.

Next day they continued on their way through the plain of Tuscany. The roads in many places were avenues of pollarded trees, up which vines had been trained and gracefully festooned in garlands from one to another. Beyond them lay big plantations of olive trees, between which, strange as it seemed to English

eyes, wheat was growing; while along other stretches girls in large, floppy straw hats were tending flocks of sheep for the woolen industry that had made Tuscany rich long before fine cloth was woven in England.

Late that afternoon they entered Florence, and struck as Richard had been by the architectural gems of Leghorn and Pisa he marveled far more at those of the city on the Arno. Even on the outskirts hardly a new building was to be seen and most of the larger ones were from three to four hundred years old. On both sides of the river stood scores of noble mansions, their poems in carved stone vying with one another, and each possessed of an individual dignity; while a glance down every side street they passed provided a glimpse of new beauties in towers, churches and palazzos.

At length they came to the Ponta Della Santa Trinita, said to be the loveliest bridge in the world, and here they were met by arrangement by Hernando. They had sent him on ahead with careful instructions that he was not to get them accommodation at the Aquila Nera, Vanini's or Mr. Meggot's famous English-run hotel, but to seek out some smaller place where French was spoken, and there book rooms for them as Monsieur le Chevalier de Cavasuto and his sister-in-law, Madame Jules de Cavasuto. Hernando told them that he had taken lodgings for them with a Signor Pisani at the del Sarte Inglesi, in the via del Fossi ; and when they arrived there they found it to be just the sort of quiet, respectable place that they had had in mind.

An excellent meal was sent in for them from a cook-shop near by, and to Richard's surprise the charge, including a liter of sound Chianti, was only three pauls a head. As breakfasts and light suppers cost proportionately less and their rooms only two pauls each, it transpired that one could live well and comfortably in Florence for the modest sum of 3s. 6d. per person per day.

After they had dined Richard left Tansanta to amuse herself with Quetzal, went downstairs and got in conversation with the landlord. His habitual secrecy in everything to do with State affairs caused him to refrain from saying outright that he wished to secure an audience with the Grand Duke, so he opened the conversation by remarking on the beauty of Florence and the obviously happy state of the Tuscan people.

Signor Pisani was a fat elderly man with enormous ears and small, wrinkled-up, humorous eyes. 'The first, Monsieur, is incontestable,' he replied; 'the second an opinion expressed by the majority of our foreign visitors; yet comparatively few of my compatriots would agree with it.'

'Why so, Signor?' Richard enquired. 'I have heard it said that in His Highness the Grand Duke Leopold you have the most enlightened ruler in Europe, and the country through which I passed today showed every evidence of prosperity.'

The fat man nodded. 'I judge you right, Monsieur; but that is because when I was younger I traveled much. I have earned my living as an agent for Tuscan wines and olive oil, in France, England, the Austrian Netherlands, Cologne and Hanover; so I

know how the peoples of other countries live. But the average Tuscan is conservative by habit, and resents all innovations. During his twenty-four years as our sovereign His Highness has made many, and instead of being grateful to him, as they should be, nearly every class thinks it has some reason for complaint.'

Richard saw at once that his broad-minded landlord was a mail well worth cultivating, so he said: 'Having never before visited Italy I know nothing of Tuscan affairs, and would much like to learn of them. If you can spare the time to join me in a bottle of wine I should consider it a favor.'

'Willingly, Monsieur,' was the prompt reply, and five minutes later they were comfortably installed in Signor Pisani's parlor with a wicker covered bottle of Chianti between them.

'We are at least more fortunate than our neighbours in the Duchy of Milan,' began the fat Italian. 'As you must know, for many years most of northern Italy has been subject to Austria, but in 1765 we succeeded in inducing the Emperor to give us a sovereign of our own. So in that year, when Joseph 11 succeeded his father as Emperor, his younger brother, Peter Leopold, became our ruler; although he was only then eighteen. Both brothers are men of advanced ideas and great reformers; but whereas Joseph is a hothead whose innovations have brought only disaster to the Milanese and his other subject peoples., Leopold is possessed of a more balanced mind, and his have brought great benefits to Tuscany.'

`Why, then, these complaints you speak of?' Richard asked.

"Tis largely owing to the hatred borne him by the Church.'

`Yet I have heard that he was educated for it, and is a most religious man.'

`He was, and is. He became a sovereign only owing to the death of his elder brother, Charles ; but his views on religion are far from orthodox. He considers it his business not only to censure the morals of his priesthood but also to reform the rituals of the Church itself.'

`Does he incline to Protestantism, then?'

`By no means; although he expresses great repugnance, to all customs bordering on the superstitious and the habit of making religious ceremonies into gaudy parades. For instance, one edict of his which has given almost universal offence is that concerning burials. By it all corpses are removed the night following death in a plain shroud to the nearest church. There they receive simple benediction, after which they are taken to a common mortuary. No candles or singing are allowed. The following day the bodies are taken in a wooden cart to the cemetery outside the city, and there buried without further ceremony, as they come, two in a grave; and at that lacking coffins. The law applies to high and low alike, so a noble lady may find herself buried side by side with a scrofulous pauper, or a priest next to a harlot.'

`What an extraordinary idea!' Richard exclaimed. 'And 'tis harsh indeed that families should be debarred from ordering suitably the last rites for their loved ones. I wonder that such an outrageous interference with liberty is not openly defied, and His Highness forced to withdraw so monstrous an edict.'

The Tuscan shrugged. `We are by nature a law-abiding people, and have no means of forcing him to do anything. He is an absolute monarch, and does not even make a pretence of consulting a Senate, as did the Medici. 'Tis fortunate for us that he is, generally speaking, a beneficial autocrat; yet his absolutism is another factor which makes for his unpopularity, as the demand for popular government in France is not without its repercussions here.'

'In what other ways has he set Holy Church by the ears?'

`He and his principal adviser, Scipione Ricci, the Bishop of Pistoria and Prato, have encouraged the conducting of church services in Tuscan instead of Latin.'

`I see no great harm in that.'

`Nor I ; but the old-fashioned resent it. However, 'tis the priesthood that bears him the most bitter grudge, owing to his having despoiled it of the wealth and power that it has enjoyed for centuries. Twenty years ago Tuscany was entirely priest-ridden. Thousands of begging friars blackmailed their way from door to door, and many thousands of monks idled their lives away in monasteries battening on the labors of the peasants. Social custom, too, decreed that every girl lacking a dowry should take the veil; and you can imagine the state of things, which followed the unnatural segregation of so many healthy young women. The father confessors and visiting prelates had by long custom come to regard the convents as seraglios, and as a result infanticide in one or other of them had become a daily occurrence. But Peter Leopold put an end to all that. He raised the age for taking the veil and made it in many other ways more difficult to do so, thus greatly reducing the number of young nuns; and in order to give the others something to think about, apart from lechery, he turned all the convents into schools for the education of the local children.'

`That seems an admirable measure.'

`True ; but you cannot expect the priests to regard it in that light. Imagine, too, the wailing of the hosts of begging friars when a law was passed reducing their numbers by four-fifths, so that the majority of them were forced to return to the land and do an honest day's work upon it; and the outcry that was made by the monastic orders when certain of them were suppressed and their revenues taken from them.'

'Then the Grand Duke has followed the examples of other monarchs, and enriched himself at the expense of the Church.'

" On the contrary, Monsieur. He funded the money so obtained to abolish tithes, and provide better stipends for the poorer clergy.'

'In that case both his peasantry and village priests should be grateful to him.'

Signor Pisani shook his head. `Had the country folk any sense they would be, but they are ignorant and superstitious; so an easy prey to the multitude of monks and friars he has deprived of an easy living, who go about poisoning the people's minds against him.'

`Yet surely in these measures he has had the support of the better educated among the laity?'

'To some extent; but they have their own complaints against other reforms he has introduced. He has deprived the nobility of nearly all their old privileges. In Tuscany now no one is exempt from taxation. All must pay according to their means. In that His Highness does not even spare himself. He even has the value of his art collections assessed each year and pays revenue upon them.'

Richard raised his eyebrows. `That is indeed an altruistic gesture. Apart from his strange ordinance about burials he seems to me a model Monarch.'

`He is certainly far better than most, for in a score of years he has doubled the wealth of Tuscany. By making all classes subject to taxation he has reduced the average to eighteen pauls per annum per head, which must be considerably lighter than any. where else in Europe. I am told that even in England it is in the neighborhood of forty-five.'

By a swift calculation Richard arrived at 8s. as against f2, but Signor Pisani was continuing:

`In spite of that he has succeeded in extinguishing our National Debt, and by allowing free trade in corn he has brought its price down to a level which enables us to live cheaper here than in any other part of Italy. Moreover, he is always devising new ways to encourage trade and agriculture. Recently he has offered a gold medal every year for the proprietor who plants the greatest number of new olive trees, and the plantings of the winner this year exceeded forty thousand.'

With a shake of his head Richard took up the Chianti flagon to refill the glasses, and said: `Really, in view of all this, despite the antagonism he has aroused among the priesthood, I cannot conceive why he is not more generally regarded with affection by his people:

His informative host sank his deep voice to a lower note. `I feel sure, Monsieur, that you will not repeat me, but His Highness has one failing which would render him obnoxious to any race. He is the most furtive and suspicious man that ever was born. I am told that at times he even deceives his most intimate advisers, and 'tis certain that he sets spies upon them. Not content with that, he sets spies upon the spies. His secret police are legion, his curiosity unbounded, and he is for ever prying into the private affairs of every official or person of any consequence at all in the whole country:.

`When he learns that they have committed some fault does he act the tyrant?' Richard enquired.

`Nay! as a ruler he is remarkable for his humanity. He has much improved the dispensation of justice, abolishing the courts of the feudal lords, and securing for the meanest of his subjects the right of appeal to the highest tribunal. He has also done away with torture and reformed the prison system. But no one likes the thought that their every act is spied upon and reported.'

`What sort of man is he personally?' said Richard; now working round to the matter that particularly interested him. `Is he easy of access?'

`By no means,' came the prompt reply. `He works too hard to be able to give the time to appear in public except on State occasions. And his natural secretiveness provides a bar against his indulging freely in social intercourse with his nobility. He is most autocratic in temperament, believing that the people are quite incapable of reforming themselves, and that their condition can only be bettered by divine inspiration interpreted through their rulers. That, too, is the main-spring of all his religious reforms, as he regards himself as established by God to be the guardian and tutor of his people. Yet, pious as he is by nature, he does not deny himself mistresses.'

'That was also the case with the bigoted James II of England,'

Richard smiled, 'and of Louis XIV of France, even when he was in the toils of the Jesuits.'

`True!' laughed the fat Signor Pisani. `But did you set eyes on our Grand Duchess you would hardly blame His Highness for his infidelities. She is, as you may know, a Spaniard, and sister to the newly enthroned King Carlos IV. A plainer gawk of a woman 'twould be hard to find; she is as yellow as a lemon and pimply at that ; so 'tis not to be wondered at that her husband prefers the beds of other ladies, and in particular that of the beautiful Donna Livia.'

`Is this favorite mistress a noble lady or a courtesan?'

`She is an opera singer, and her voice, while good, is the least of her charms. She has Titian hair, green eyes and a figure . . . Ah!' Lacking words to describe it Signor Pisani could only break off and kiss the tips of his fingers with a loud smacking sound in an attempt to show his appreciation.

`Is she accepted by the Grand Duchess and given apartments in the palace, as was Madame du Barri at the Court of Louis XV?' Richard asked.

`His Highness's religious scruples do not permit him to acknowledge her openly,' Pisani grinned, `so she lives in a house of her own near the Palazzo Pitti, and he goes there to sup with her most nights of the week, except Fridays and Sundays. But the Grand Duchess is so tolerant of her husband's weakness that she often visits his favourite as an escape from her own loneliness. She is a great needlewoman and frequently takes her embroidery round to Donna Livia's house, to work upon it there in the afternoons.'

Richard regarded his fat landlord with new interest, and said

`You will, I trust, forgive me, Signor Pisani, if I remark that for an ordinary citizen you seem peculiarly well acquainted with the secrets of the Court.'

The Tuscan laughed again. `That is easily explained, Monsieur. It so happens that I have long enjoyed the friendship of Herr von Streinefberg, who is His Highness's confidential secretary:

`.I wonder, then,' said .Richard with appropriate diffidence, `if I might trespass on your good nature to arrange for me to meet Herr von Streinefberg berg? I have some business to transact while in Florence, in which I am certain his good offices could be of great assistance to me.'

`I would do so willingly, were it possible; but unfortunately my friend left here for Vienna only a few days since on urgent business connected with the Emperor Joseph's illness.'

`With whom then would you suggest my getting in touch with affairs?' the object of securing His Highness's interest in my business."

Signor Pisani considered for a moment, then he said: 'Monsignor Scipione Ricci enjoys his dubious confidence more than any other man. He has apartments in the Pitti, so I suggest that you should go there and secure an interview with him through one of his secretaries; or, better still, his major-domo, Signor Zucchino. The latter is not a particularly pleasant person, but he has his master's ear, and will, I am sure, pass you in if you grease his palm with a couple of sequins:

Richard thanked his new friend and, as the bottle was now empty, bade him good night; then went upstairs, well pleased with the information he had gained at so little cost, to spend an hour with Tansanta before going to bed.

The following morning by nine o'clock he was at the Pitti Palace, enquiring for Signor Zucchino. At first he had some difficulty in making himself understood, as be spoke no Italian, and French proving useless, he had to do his best with Latin and the smattering of Spanish he had picked up from Tansanta. But at length he was conducted through a maze of lofty corridors to a little room equipped as an office, where, behind a desk littered with bills, a small man clad in black velvet was sitting.

Having bowed to him Richard opened the conversation in French, and, to his relief, found that the major-domo spoke sufficient of that language to understand him. He gave his name as Monsieur le Chevalier de Cavasuto, and said that he had just arrived from the Court of France upon business which he wished to discuss with Monsignor Ricci.

Signor Zucchino's sharp black eyes appraised Richard quickly, then he enquired the nature of the business.

On Richard declaring that it was a strictly confidential matter, the major-domo showed signs of hauteur; but when his visitor gently clinked the gold in his breeches pocket and, producing two pieces, slid them under a paper on the corner of the desk, his manner changed at once.

In halting French he said that his master was, unfortunately, absent in Pisa, but would be back in Florence the following day, and he would do his best to arrange an audience.

Richard then handed him a slip of paper on which he had already written his name and address; and, on the major-domo promising to communicate with him, took his leave.

Now that he had a free day before him he was extremely anxious to take advantage of it to see the most outstanding of the many art treasures in Florence, so immediately he got back to his lodgings he consulted with Tansanta on this project. As they occupied separate rooms, and her servants now referred to her as Madame Jules, no one there had suggested by as much as the lift of an eyebrow that she was not his sister-in-law; and they decided that there could be no risk of her identity being discovered if she went out, provided she wore a mask.

By half-past ten Hernando had secured a carozza for them, and, leaving Quetzal in his care, they set off like a young honeymoon couple to see the sights of the city. First they paid tribute to the Venus de Medici, as the Venus de Milo was then called, and they agreed that no copies that either of them had ever seen did justice to the supreme beauty of Cleomenes' original. Then they devoted most of the rest of the day to the magnificent collection of pictures in the Grand Duke's residence, the Pitti Palace, which was always open to the public.

Richard had long been interested in paintings, but the Raphael's, Titians, Rubenses And Correggios aroused his enthusiasm for the art to a degree that it had never previously reached, and he declared that afternoon that when they had a home of their own they must certainly start a collection, however modest its beginnings might have to be.

It was this which made Tansanta insist on stopping at an art dealer's on their way back to Pisani's in order to buy him a picture as the foundation of his new hobby. By great good fortune they found a small head and shoulders of Saint Lucia, which was Tansanta's second name. It was a beautiful little thing of about nine inches by six ;the Saint was wearing a robe of brilliant blue, and behind her head there was portrayed a fairy-like scene of woods and a mountain with a tiny castle perched on top. The dealer swore that it was an original Andrea del Sarto, and wanted a hundred and twenty gold sequins for it. Richard demurred at such extravagance, and when Tansanta overruled his protests, he would at least have attempted to beat the man down; but she said she would not sully her gift by haggling about its price, and told the dealer to carry it to their lodging, where she would pay him what he asked.

On their second day in Florence they went out again early in the morning to see the famous sculpture of Niobe striving to protect her children from the murderous shafts of Apollo; and still more pictures. But at eleven o'clock they tore themselves away from a gallery containing some of the finest examples of Benvenuto Cellini's gem-encrusted goldsmith's work, and hurried back to Pisani's, in case a message had arrived for Richard giving him an appointment with Monsignor Ricci.

However, no word had yet come from Signor Zucchino, and to Richard's intense annoyance he had to waste the whole afternoon kicking his heels in their lodgings without hearing from the major-domo. It was not until he and Tansanta: were sitting down to supper that a messenger at last arrived, bearing a brief note which said:

Monsignor Ricci has been much engaged on affairs of State since his return at midday ; but he will grant you a few minutes if you attend upon him at half-past eleven tonight.

The script was in Italian but Tansanta understood enough of that language to translate it, and Richard sighed with relief when he learned its purport. After they had supped they ordered another bottle of wine, and sat up making fond plans for the future over it until it was time for him to set out for the palace. Then, having kissed Tansanta good night half a dozen times, he buckled on his sword, drew his cloak about him, and went out into the darkened streets of the ancient city.

A faint moonlight now lit the stone façades of the great mansions, making them even more impressive, and as Richard walked briskly along the narrow, cobbled streets he marveled once again that so small a country, with a bare million inhabitants, should have proved capable of producing such lasting memorials to the greatness of its rulers; when the Kings of France, with twenty times their resources, had failed to achieve one-tenth of the grandeur of the Medici's.

As he crossed the bridge over the Arno he was thinking of Tansanta, and the picture of her patron saint that she had bought him that morning. The thought occurred to him that at a not too distant date they must return to Florence for a delayed honeymoon. She seemed to derive as much pleasure from its unique treasures as himself, and in no country except his own had he found such congenial surroundings. Even if the people grumbled about the innovations introduced by their Austrian Grand Duke, they seemed remarkably carefree. There were no midnight beggars in the streets, or outcasts trying to snatch a few hours' uneasy slumber in the shadow of the doorways. The city now slept, its citizens serene, untroubled, secure within their homes. On the far side of the river he entered the street leading to the palace.

Suddenly a group of dark, swiftly moving figures emerged from the shadows. Richard glimpsed a patient mule being held by one as the others rushed upon him. Springing back he grasped his sword-hilt. His shout was drowned in the scamper of running feet. He had drawn his weapon no more than six inches from its scabbard before his arm was caught in a fierce grip. Next second he was overborne and hurled headlong into the gutter.

CHAPTER TEN
THE HOODED MEN

As Richard went down he kicked hard. His right foot caught one of his attackers in the crutch, drawing from him a screech of pain. But at' least three men had charged in simultaneously and two of them fell right on top of him. Clenching his fist he smashed it into the face of one and, with a heave of his body, threw off the other.

Since the age of eighteen he had been just over six feet in height, but in the past three years he had filled out; so although his slender-boned hips still gave him a fine figure he was now a fully-grown man with a broad chest and powerful shoulders. As he never lost an opportunity to practice fencing and often spent many hours a day in the saddle he had no superfluous fat and his muscles were as hard as whipcord. Moreover he had a cool head, great agility and, in a fight such as this, was never handicapped by the least scruples about using unorthodox methods to get the better of his enemies. So, had he not been taken completely by surprise, three or four underfed street roughs would have found that in attacking him they had caught a Tartar.

Even as it was, he had succeeded in inflicting grievous injury on two of them in as many seconds, and as he rolled over to get clear of the squirming body he had just thrown off he kicked out again backwards. His heel met solid flesh and elicited a spate of curses.

Thrusting one hand against the cobbles he gave a violent twist of his body and scrambled to his knees. To his dismay he realized that his attackers numbered five at least. Only one lay hors de combat, groaning in the middle of the narrow street. The two others who had knocked him down were staggering to their feet or either side of him; a fourth, who had been holding the mule, was running to their assistance, and the scraping of boots on stone behind him gave warning that one or more of the band were about to take him from the rear.

Once more his right hand grasped his sword hilt. If only he had time to draw it and get his back against the wall, he felt that he might yet succeed in beating off the gang of bravos until the sounds of the conflict brought the Watch to his assistance.

But in a moment his hopes were shattered. A man behind him threw a cloak over his head. Another seized his arms and wrenched them painfully together till his elbows met in the small of his back. Instantly a dozen hands were grasping him. Someone tied the cloak round his neck, so that his head was encased in a stuffy bag, and his shouts for help were muffled. His arms were tied together with a piece of cord. Still he kicked out, but he was borne to the ground, and while one man sat upon his legs another secured his ankles. Then he was rolled over and over sideways upon other cloaks that had been spread out on the ground, till he was encased like a mummy in a roll of carpet.

Next, he felt himself lifted up, carried a few yards and dumped face down across the back of the mule, with his head dangling on one side of the animal and his feet on the other. The cursing, panting and excited exclamations of his captors had now ceased, and in silence the party set off along the street.

The blood was running to Richard's head, and in addition he found it extremely difficult to breathe, so for him to think at all was by no means easy. But as he gasped for air in the stifling folds of the cloak, various half-formed thoughts came to him. He had been set upon by robbers! Yet they had made no attempt to take his jewels or money from him. If they were not robbers what possible motive could they have for attacking him? Perhaps they had mistaken him for someone else? Where was lie being taken? Perhaps they were robbers and meant to hold him to ransom? Anyhow it seemed clear that they intended him no bodily harm, as not one of them had drawn a sword or stiletto during the struggle. He had sustained no injury at all.

That at least was much to he thankful for.

At this point lack of air made him feel as though his head was going to burst, and with the steady jolting of the mule alone still impinging on his mind he lapsed into semi-unconsciousness.

When he came to someone was pouring Grappa down his throat. The fiery spirit jerked him back into full possession of his senses. He had been unwrapped and untied and was seated in a chair with his head lolling back, staring up at a low, vaulted ceiling of plain stone with Roman arches.

With a gasp he thrust aside the glass that was being held to his mouth and sat up. Two rough-looking fellows with close-cropped hair, who were dressed in leather jerkins and looked like men-at-arms, stepped away from him, and he saw at once that this stone. flagged cellar was no brigands' den. Yet, immediately opposite him, on the far side of a long table, was a sight calculated to make the boldest heart contract in swift alarm.

Beyond it sat nine silent figures. All were clad in loose black robes that entirely hid their ordinary clothes and individualities. From their shoulders the robes merged into high-pointed hoods, having in them only mouth and eye slits.

Richard's first thought was that he had fallen into the hands of the Inquisition; but he was quick to recall that in a further conversation with Signor Pisani the previous day his landlord had told him that the Grand Duke had deprived the Holy Office of much of its powers in Tuscany, and that it was now only permitted to act as an ecclesiastical court for the trial of priests who had disgraced their calling. It then occurred to him that the Grand Duke's measure had driven the Inquisition underground and that it still continued to function in secret. But, if so, what possible business could it have with him? Again, he could only suppose that he had been seized in mistake for someone else.

Swiftly, he was disabused of that idea. In the center of the line of figures, one whom Richard took to be the Grand Inquisitor, because he was seated on a larger and slightly higher chair than the others, had already signed to the two men-at-arms to withdraw: As a heavy, nail studded door closed behind them, he addressed Richard in good but stilted French.

'Monsieur. I regret the steps which have been necessary to bring you before us; but you have suffered no harm; and will suffer none, provided you obey me. It is known to us that you carry a letter from the Queen of France to her brother the Grand Duke. Be good enough to hand it to me, and a guide will be provided to escort you back to your lodging.'

Richard used his lashes to veil his eyes as he stumbled unsteadily to his feet. He could not even guess how the object of his visit to Florence had become known, or what possible reason the Holy Office could have for wanting to get possession of the Queen's letter; but he instantly made up his mind to admit nothing until it transpired how fully informed they really were about his activities.

For a moment he remained silent, so that when he spoke his voice should be as firm as possible. Then, in an attempt to bluff his way out of their clutches, he said

'Signor. I protest most strongly at your abduction of me. The only excuse there can be for it is that your bravos mistook me for some other person. I demand that you release me at once, or His Highness the Grand Duke shall hear of it; and I am told that he is swift to punish such of his subjects as molest foreign visitors in his capital:

'You use bold words, young man,' said the central figure quietly, 'but they will gain you nothing. Your threat is an empty one; and it seems that I must give you a word of caution. It would not be the first time that this tribunal has decreed death for those who oppose its will. There is an oubliette less than a hundred feet from where you stand and in the past few centuries many bodies have gone down it to be swept away by the undercurrents of the Arno. These old Florentine cellars keep their secrets well, and unless you wish to add to their number you will say no more of making complaint to His Highness. Now; give me the letter that you carry.'

Richard paled slightly under his tan. The cellar was lit only by two three-branched candlesticks, each placed near one end of the long table; the corners of the room were fall of shadows and the row of black, hooded figures in front of him had no resemblance to normal human beings. They sat unmoving, with their black-gloved hands folded before them on the table. Only the eyes, seen through the slits in their hoods, showed that they lived and were regarding him with cold, impassive curiosity.

in such surroundings it was difficult to make himself believe that their spokesman was trying only to frighten him; yet he strove to do so, by calling to mind that however horrible the fate to which the Inquisition had condemned its victims in the old days, it had never, as far as he knew, practiced secret murder. All the same, he found that his lips had suddenly gone dry, and he had to moisten them with the tip of his tongue before saying a trifle hoarsely.

`I repeat, Signor, you have made an error concerning me. I carry no letter from the Queen of France, and know nothing of one.'

`Yet you are the Chevalier de Cavasuto, are you not?'

Feeling that as they were aware of his identity it would prejudice his chances to deny it, Richard replied: `I am; and I am recently arrived from France. But my sole reason for coming here is to see the beauties and art treasures of your city.'

`Monsieur, it will go ill with you if you continue to trifle with us. At the time of your arrest tonight you were on your way to an audience with Monsieur Scipione Ricci, and your object in seeking an audience was to hand him this letter. You cannot deny that.'

`I do!' Richard answered with a modicum of truth; for he had had no intention of surrendering the letter to anyone other than the Grand Duke, and had meant only to approach the Minister as the most suitable person to secure him a private audience with the Sovereign.

`What, then, were you doing in the streets of Florence at an hour approaching midnight?' asked the spokesman of the nine.

Richard shrugged, and tried to look a little sheepish. 'I am young and have the natural inclination of my years towards gallantry. As I have not the acquaintance of any ladies in your city I thought I would go out, on the chance that on so fine a summer night I might come upon some fair one seated at her window or on a balcony, who would feel inclined to take compassion on me.'

It was a good, plausible lie; but nine pairs of eyes continued to regard him with cold, calculating suspicion, and. the spokesman said: 'upon the information we have received I cannot believe you. I should be reluctant to put you to the indignity of a forced search; but we intend to have that letter. For the last time, I bid you give it me.'

`Search me if you will, Signor.' Richard spread out his hands in a little foreign gesture that he had picked up in France during his youth. `But you will not find this letter you seek, for I have not got it.'

The principal Inquisitor spoke in Italian to the hooded figures at each extremity of the table. Obediently they stood up, came over to Richard, and spent some minutes searching him with considerable thoroughness. Raising his arms he submitted quietly, knowing that their labours would be in vain.

As they returned to the table empty-handed he felt a new confidence in his prospects. Now that their information had been proved to be incorrect he had a fair hope that they would accept his statement that he was not the man they were looking for, and release him.

But his hopes were doomed to disappointment. The spokesman picked up a small silver hand-bell that stood in front of him and rang it. The door opened and one of the men in leather jerkins appeared. An order was given and the door closed again. For a few minutes Richard remained facing the line of sinister, black-clad figures while complete silence reigned. He wondered anxiously what this last move foreboded. Did they mean to let him go; or would they consider it necessary to protect themselves from his reporting the manner in which he had been attacked to the authorities, and take measures to ensure that he should never have the chance to do so? Involuntarily a shiver ran down his spine.

The door opened once more. A new figure entered. It was that of a man in a long-skirted coat of bright-blue satin. He wore no mask and, having bowed in the doorway, advanced carrying his three-cornered hat under his arm. Even before the newcomer had emerged far enough from the shadows for his features to be seen

distinctly Richard recognized him. It was de Roubec.

Instantly now, Richard realized what had led to his being in his present plight. On finding Tansanta's reinforced escort too much for him the lantern-jawed Chevalier had not given up the game and returned to Paris, as they had supposed. Instead, he must have decided to take the direct overland route via Chambery, Turin and Milan to Florence, in order to await their arrival there; and only then, when they were off their guard, make another attempt to secure the Queen's letter before it could be delivered to her brother. The only thing that Richard could not understand was how the rapscallion adventurer had managed to inveigle the Holy Inquisition into pulling his chestnuts out of the fire for him.

De Roubec took a few more paces forward, bowed again to the sinister tribunal; then, with a mocking smile, to Richard.

Controlling his fury with an effort, Richard not only refrained from returning the bow, but met the Chevalier's glance with cold indifference as though he had never set eyes on him before.

The spokesman of the hooded men addressed de Roubec. `The prisoner admits that he is Monsieur le Chevalier de Cavasuto, but denies all knowledge of the letter. Are you quite certain that you have made no mistake, and that this is the man you required us to arrest?'

'It is indeed, Monseigneur. I know him too well to be mistaken.'

`He has been searched and the letter is not on him.'

De Roubec gave Richard a suspicious glance. `Perhaps, Monseigneur, he did not after all intend to deliver it tonight.'

`Our information that he had been bidden to wait upon Monsignor Ricci at a half hour after eleven came from an impeccable source.'

'Even so, Monseigneur,' de Roubec submitted deferentially, `he may have been prepared to deliver such a letter only into the hands of His Highness personally. If it was not found on him, he must have left it at his lodgings, in the care of the Señorita d'Aranda.'

`The Senorita d'Aranda!' exclaimed one of the hooded men halfway down the line on the spokesman's left. Then he asked in bad French: `did I hear aright? If so, how comes she into this?'

Richard felt his heart jump, and looked at de Roubec in fresh alarm, as the Chevalier replied to his new interlocutor.

`It is my belief, Signor, that Her Majesty originally handed her dispatch to the Senorita d'Aranda, when that lady left the Court of France to travel to Italy. In an attempt to secure it I organized a hold-up of her coach near Nevers, but Monsieur de Cavasuto's inopportune arrival on the scene caused the affair to miscarry. They continued on their way south in company, and hired additional coach-guards, -which would have rendered any further attempt of this kind too costly. I decided to ride on direct to Florence and enlist your help against their arrival. But as far as I know they have been together ever since. At all events, they have both been lying these last two nights at del Sartre Inglesi in the via deli Fossi, and unobserved by them I have seen them several times visiting the galleries together.'

'But what you tell me is extraordinary!' cried the hooded man who had challenged de Roubec about Tansanta. If the Senorita d'Aranda is in Florence, why has she not sought the hospitality of her aunt, the Contessa Frescobaldi?'

Richard's hands were trembling. He now felt that at all costs he must intervene.

`Signor ' he said quickly. `I can explain this matter. As you may know, the Senorita is proceeding to Naples in order to be married there. At Marseilles, no ship was due to sail for Naples under three weeks, but one was leaving for Leghorn almost immediately. Therefore, in order to get to Naples the quicker she decided to travel by this slightly longer route. Had she informed her aunt that she was passing through Florence, she thought that the Contessa would have insisted on her breaking her journey here for not less than a week. She felt that she could not deny herself two days in which to visit the galleries, but was most opposed to delaying longer; so she decided to risk her aunt's later displeasure by maintaining an incognito while in your city. She is resuming her journey to Naples tomorrow.'

The original spokesman rapped the table impatiently and said something in Italian to his colleagues. Richard just caught its sense, which was:

'Gentlemen! The time of the tribunal is being wasted. The fact that some young woman elected to stay in a lodging, rather than with her aunt, is no concern of ours.' He then looked again at Richard and resumed in his careful French:

`You admit, then, that although the document we require was not originally trusted to you, this lady with whom you traveled has it; and that you acted as her escort in order to prevent it being taken from her?'

`By no means,' Richard replied quickly. `I am certain that she knows no more of it than myself. As I have told you, it was not her intention to pass through Florence, and she would never have come here at all had it not been that there was no ship sailing from Marseilles under three weeks by which she could travel direct to Naples: Then he shot out an accusing finger at de Roubec, and went on:

`But this rogue here has already confessed to you how he and his bullies attacked the Señorita's coach. We thought it was her jewels on which they wished to lay their dirty fingers. It was to assist in frustrating any further such attempts that I offered her my escort:

De Roubec gave Richard an ugly look, and muttered: 'Put a guard upon your tongue, Chevalier, or I will make you pay dearly for such insults.'

Richard swung angrily upon him. "Tis you who are due to pay by the loss of your ears for the treacherous theft you long ago committed upon me. And as a bonus, for this present business, I will slice off your nose into the bargain.'

'Silence!' cried the spokesman, again rapping the table; then he once more addressed Richard: 'I am convinced that this young woman with whom you are traveling has the Queen's letter. Either you will obtain it from her and hand it over to a representative whom I shall send back with you to your lodging for that purpose, or I shall take steps to have her lured forth and brought here. In the latter case we shall soon find means to loosen her tongue, and when she has disclosed its hiding-place I will send someone to collect it, Now; which course do you prefer that I should adopt?'

Richard stared down at the silver buckles of his shoes while swiftly considering the dilemma with which he was now faced. He still had one good card up his sleeve, but did not wish to play it if that could possibly be avoided.

Seeing his hesitation the Chief of the tribunal said: 'If you force me to it I shall not hesitate to use torture. But I would much prefer that the matter should be cleared' up without harm to either the Señorita or yourself. Therefore, I will not press you for an immediate answer. In any case it would be preferable to avoid arousing comment by knocking up the people at your lodging in the middle of the night, and the tribunal has other business, which will occupy it for some hours to come. You may utilize those hours to make your decision, and I will send for you to learn it a little before dawn.'

He rang his silver bell and the two men-at-arms appeared again. Between them Richard was marched away down a gloomy corridor, a door near its end was opened, and, there being no alternative, he entered a narrow cell. One of the men set down a single candle on the stone floor, then the door was slammed to and the key grated in its lock.

The cell was quite bare, and windowless, its only inlet for air being a row of round holes in the upper part of the heavy door. Apart from a wide stone bench long enough to sleep on, which protruded from one wall, it contained nothing whatever. Richard sat down on the slab and began to think matters out.

One thing was clear: de Roubec had himself confirmed that it was his machinations which had led to the present situation, and that it was for him that the Holy Office were endeavoring to get hold of the Queen's letter. It also seemed evident that Signor Zucchino must be one of the Inquisitors' spies, and had reported Richard's visit; as in what other way could they have learnt that the major-domo had made an appointment for him to wait on Monsignor Ricci that night?

Richard was much comforted by the thought that he had it in his power to prevent Tansanta being drawn into the affair. All he had to do was to agree to return to his lodgings in the morning and hand over the letter. But he wondered if there was not some way in which he might secure his freedom without doing that. The Inquisitors' reluctance to arouse the inmates of Pisani's house showed that they were anxious to avoid drawing attention to their activities; so it seemed probable that they would now wait until the following evening, then send a messenger to inform Tansanta that he had met with an accident, and bring her to a place where

she could be overcome under cover of darkness with a minimum risk of disturbance.

If that proved to be their intention she would have the whole of the coming day in which to endeavor to find him. She must already be worried by his non-return. First thing in the morning she would go to the Pitti and insist on seeing Monsignor Ricci. The probability was that Zucchino had never made the appointment at all. In any case it would come out that his intending visitor had never arrived there. If the Minister showed indifference to the matter, however reluctant Tansanta might be to let her aunt know of her presence in Florence, the odds were that her acute anxiety would drive her to do so. There would be no necessity for her to disclose the fact that he was her affianced ; she could enlist her aunt's aid immediately by telling a part of the truth that he was the bearer of a dispatch from Queen Marie Antoinette to the Grand Duke, had saved her from attack upon the road, and given her his escort as far as Florence. The Contessa would at once go to the Grand Duchess, who, on account of the letter, if for no other reason, would report his disappearance without delay to the Grand Duke. Then the whole of His Highness's secret police would be put on the job of finding him.

Whether they would succeed in doing so before nightfall remained problematical. But even then, if Tansanta had secured the protection of either Monsignor Ricci or the Contessa, she would inform them of any message she received, and they would have her followed ; so instead of her falling into a trap, she would lead the forces of law and order to his prison.

The more Richard thought the matter over the more inclined he became to stand firm and put his trust in Tansanta's succeeding in rescuing him. But one thing remained a puzzle and defeated all his efforts to solve it. How had de Roubec managed to secure the assistance of the Holy Office?

De Roubec was the agent of the Duc d'Orléans, and His Highness was the supreme head of all the Freemasons in France. The Masons were freethinkers and revolutionaries, so regarded by the Church as its bitterest enemies. Yet the Chief Inquisitor had actually used the words when speaking of his prisoner to de Roubec: 'Are you quite certain that you have made no mistake, and that this is the man that you required us to arrest?' To 'require' signified to 'order', and inexplicable as it seemed that de Roubec should have persuaded the Holy Office to help him, the idea that he was in a position to give it orders appeared positively fantastic.

At length Richard gave up the conundrum as, for the time being, insoluble, and consoled himself with the thought that it was into the hands of the Holy Office, and not into those of the Masons, or their associates the Rosicrucian's, that he had fallen. He knew the latter to be quite capable of murder to protect their secrets or achieve their ends, whereas he felt convinced that even a branch of the Holy Office that had been driven underground would never lend itself to actual crime from political motives.

In the more backward Catholic countries the Inquisition was still permitted to carry out public witch- burnings-and for that matter witches were still burnt from time to time by Protestant congregations in Britain, Holland, Sweden and Germany-but the Holy Office had long since given up any attempt to adjudicate on cases other than those which involved a clear charge of sacrilege or heresy. It was such powers they were still striving to retain against the mounting wave of anti -clericalism; so it stood to reason that, even in secret, they would not risk torturing or killing anyone outside their province, from fear that it might come to light later and provoke a scandal most prejudicial to their whole position.

Richard admitted to himself that at the time, when the Chief Inquisitor had spoken to him of the oubliette and threatened to use torture, he had been badly scared ; but now he had had a chance to think things over quietly he felt certain that the hooded spokesman had been bluffing, and simply trying to frighten him into producing the letter without having to resort to further measures which might attract the attention of the police.

In spite of the warmth of the summer night outside it was cold in his cell, and as the chill of the place sent a slight shiver through him he leaned forward to warm his hands at the flame of the candle. While he was doing so they threw huge shadows on the walls and ceiling, and when his hands were warmer he began to amuse himself with the old children's game of making the shadows into animals' heads by contorting his thumbs and fingers. He had been occupied in this way for about five minutes when he noticed same writing scratched on the wall opposite him low down near the floor. Moving the candle closer he bent to examine it.

The inscription was not cut deeply enough to catch the casual glance, nor was it of the type that take prisoners many weeks of patient toil to carve. It was in German, many of the characters were so badly formed as to be almost illegible, and it had the appearance of having been done hurriedly-perhaps in a single night. Richard's German was good enough for him to understand such words as he could decipher; and it ran, clearly at first, then tailing off into illegibility when the writer had grown tired or weaker, as follows:

May God's vengeance be upon the Grand Orient. I have suffered horribly. Both my legs are broken. They have decreed death for me tonight. I am glad . . . my end. I . . . to escape them . . . Italy. Carlotta . . . betrayed . . . Milan . . . Florence . . .

The inscription ended with two lines in which Richard could not make out a single word, then a signature that looked like 'Johannes Kettner' and underneath it a plain cross with the date 10.XI.'88.

Another shiver ran through him, but this time it was not caused by the chill of the cell. The inscription had led him to a terrifying discovery. He was not, as he had supposed, a prisoner of the half moribund Holy Office, but of the vital and unscrupulous Society of the Grand Orient.

As the unnerving truth flashed upon him de Roubec's puzzling relations with the tribunal were instantly made plain. The Rosicrucians and their kindred secret societies had, in the past quarter of a century, spread from Germany all over the continent. The Duc d'Orléans was Grand Master of the Grand Orient in France, so his agent would know where to find its associated Lodge in Florence. A request from the agent of such a high dignitary in the Freemasonic hierarchy would be regarded as an order, so it was no wonder that the hooded men had arranged for the abduction of de Roubec's quarry-as, no doubt, they had acted on the request of some Masonic Master in Germany to abduct and take vengeance on the unfortunate Johannes Kettner.

At the thought of the wretched man lying there, his legs already broken by torture, on the last day of his life, painfully scratching out the inscription while waiting to be dragged to the oubliette, and thrown down into the dark waters below, Richard felt the perspiration break out on his forehead. And that foul murder had taken place only the previous November-less than six months ago-so everything pointed to the very same hooded men before whom he had stood that night being responsible for it.

As he bent again to verify the date, he found himself staring at the little cross. Had he needed further evidence that he was not in the hands of the Holy Office, there it was. He knew that in every cell of every Roman Catholic prison, however bare the cell, a crucifix was nailed to one of its walls, but there was not one here. Apart from what he had read of the Inquisition he knew that behind the tribunal of the inquisitors a much larger cross, bearing a great ivory figure of Christ, was always in evidence as though to sanctify their deliberations ; but there had been no such perverted use of the emblems of Christianity made by the hooded men. The only cross he had seen in this sinister Florentine dungeon was that scratched by the hand of their condemned prisoner and enemy.

Without a moment's further hesitation he set about readjusting his ideas. The threat to torture and perhaps kill him had not been bluff ; it had been made in all seriousness; so any chances he now took would be at his dire peril. Only one thing remained in his favor. Unlike France, where people were tending more and more to defy the law, Florence was ruled by a strong and capable sovereign with an efficient secret police at his disposal. Evidently, here, the members of the Grand Orient were frightened of drawing attention to themselves. Therefore they were averse to using strong measures unless forced to it; and, rather than risk an enquiry following his disappearance, were prepared to release him unharmed if he would hand over the Queen's letter.

If he stood out, Tansanta might succeed in tracing and rescuing him next day, but, on the other hand, there had always been the possibility that they might find means to lure her from her lodging and abduct her before she could succeed in doing so ; and in the light of his recent discovery that was a risk that lie was no longer prepared to take. Both for her safety and his own there could be no doubt that the wise thing to do would be to agree to surrender the letter, and so get out of the clutches of the Grand Orient as soon as he possibly could.

It took him no more than a few minutes to reach this new conclusion, and, having resigned himself to it, he endeavored to keep himself warm by pacing the narrow limits of his cell until he was sent for.

At last the summons came, and he was led back to the vaulted cellar where, behind the long table, the nine black-robed, hooded men sat inscrutable, but for the occasional flash of their cold, malignant eyes. De Roubec was no longer present.

Without preamble, their Chief asked Richard his decision.

Without embroidering matters he gave it.

The silver bell tinkled. Five men entered the room. Four of them were big bullies wearing leather jerkins ; the fifth was a little runt of a man with a cast in one eye. They closed round Richard and marched him out of the room in their midst. Outside in the corridor the little man drew a nine-inch stiletto from inside the wide cuff of his coat sleeve, and showing it to Richard, said in most atrocious but fluent French:

'My instructions are clear. I am to accompany you to your lodging and there you will , hand me a dispatch. Should you attempt to escape on the way, or cheat me when we get there, I am to stick you like a pig with this pretty toy. And do not imagine that I shall be caught after having done so. My men are well practiced in covering my escape after such transactions. They have assisted me before, and there have been times when my prisoner has paid with his life for trying to be too clever:

Richard gave a dour nod of understanding and his eyes were then bandaged. He was led up a flight of. steps and soon after felt the fresh morning air on his face. Next he was told to step up again and when he had done so was pushed down into the corner seat of a carriage. He could hear the others scrambling in after him, the door slammed and the carriage set off at a gentle trot. As far as he could judge their drive lasted about seven minutes, then the carriage halted and the bandage was removed from his eyes.

He saw that dawn had come but as yet only a few people were in the street or opening their shutters. They were in the via del Fossi and the carriage had drawn up a few doors away from Pisani's; all five of his captors were crowded into it with him.

The little horror with the wall eye grinned at him and said: 'Before we get out I should like to explain my method to you. Two of my men will accompany us inside and the other two will remain here. Should you be so ill advised as to try any tricks when we get upstairs I shall promptly deal with you as I promised. As is usual in the case of people who compel me to make them my victims you will give a scream of agony. The instant the men who are to remain below hear it, one of them will jump from the carriage and run down the street; the other will run after him shouting 'Stop Thief! Stop Thief !' The people in the del Sarte Inglesi will naturally run to their windows instead of to your room. Even should anyone come to your assistance the two men who are with us will prevent their laying hands upon me. I shall then walk quietly out of the house, and in the excitement of the street chase disappear without being noticed.'

During the drive Richard had been turning over in his mind the chances of securing help swiftly if, directly he got inside Pisani's house, he turned upon his captors and shouted loudly for assistance. But he now had secretly to admit that, had he been in the little man's shoes, he could not have thought out such an undertaking with a better potential chance of getting clean away.

Obviously it would' be the height of rashness to play fast and loose with this professional assassin. With a shrug of his shoulders, he got out and, accompanied by three of his captors, walked along to the porch of del Sarte Inglesi.

The door was already open and a bald-headed, baize-aproned porter was busily sweeping down the steps. He wished Richard good morning with barely a glance, and entering the hall the prisoner and his escort went upstairs.

After Tansanta had shown Richard her two brass-bound chests in Avignon he had given her the Queen's letter in order that she might keep it locked up in one of them for greater safety ; so he now led his captors to her room and knocked upon the door.

Although at this early hour she would normally still have been asleep, her voice came at once, asking who was there; and on his replying he heard her gasp out an exclamation of thankfulness before calling to him to enter.

As he opened the door a crack he saw that she and Maria were both already up and fully dressed. Pushing it wide he walked into the room, followed by the little man and the two bravos.

,At the sight of Richard, dirty, disheveled and in such undesirable company, Tansanta gave another gasp. Then, restraining an obvious impulse to run to him and fling her arms around his neck, she stammered

`Where-where have you been? I-I beg you reassure me that no harm has befallen you.'

He gave her a tired smile; then, wishing to say as little as possible in front of his unwelcome companions, replied: 'I passed a somewhat uncomfortable night, but I am otherwise quite well. May I trouble you to give me the letter you wrote of?'

She gave him a scared, uncertain glance, but on his adding:

,

`Please, Señorita ; I require it at once,' she turned, knelt down beside her bed, pulled out one of the chests with Maria's help, and unlocked it.

Richard had purposely remained standing just inside the door, so that he and the men at his back were some distance from the bed; and he now saw with relief that as Tansanta lifted the lid of the chest her body hid its contents from them, for he had feared that if they caught sight of the valuables inside it they might attempt to rob her.

Closing the chest and rollicking it she stood up with the packet in her hands. Again her voice faltered as she said: `Are you-are you sure that you wish me to give this to you now?'

`Yes,' he nodded, stepping forward and taking the packet from her. `I will explain later ; but I have to give it to these people.' Then he thrust it into the hand of the wall-eyed ghoul behind him.

The little man took a quick look at the big red seals bearing the arms of Queen Marie Antoinette, grinned at Richard, made a jerky bow to Tansanta, and, signing to his men to leave the room, closed the door gently behind him.

`Oh, what has happened?' Tansanta burst out, the second the door was shut. `Surely those evil-looking men were not in the service of the Grand Duke! Why did you make me surrender Her Majesty's letter to them?'

`I was forced to it,' Richard replied with a weary shrug. `I have been held captive all night, and escaped with my life only on promising to give up the letter.'

`No promise that is extracted under a threat is binding!' she cried, vehemently. `Why, having succeeded in getting back here, did you not shout for help and put up a fight?'

`That wall-eyed creature had sworn to kill me if I did.'

`That shrimp!' exclaimed Tansanta contemptuously.

`He was holding a poniard at my back, and at the first sign that I meant to trick him would have jammed it in my liver.'

Richard had temporarily forgotten that his sweet-natured Tansanta was a soldier's daughter, but he was swiftly reminded of it as her brown eyes flashed and she cried angrily: `You still wear your sword. Why did you not spring away, draw it and turn upon them? Maria and I would have helped you fight them off, and our shouts would soon have brought assistance.'

Suddenly the anger faded from her eyes and they showed only acute distress, as she added bitterly: `Oh, Riche, Riché, you have betrayed the Queen! How could you do so?'

He smiled a little wistfully. `Nay, my sweet; I had the last trump in the pack up my sleeve, and cheated those scoundrels with it at the finish. That was the original cover to the dispatch, with Her Majesty's seals upon it; but it contained a letter in her cipher so altered by myself that they will not be able to make head nor tail of it in a month of Sundays.'

A sigh of relief escaped her, and she began to stammer an apology for having cast doubt upon his wit and courage. But he begged her to desist ; then said unhurriedly:

`We'll have ample time to talk of all this anon. Another matter must engage our attention now. One man at least who is acquainted with your aunt has learnt that you are in Florence. He may not know her well enough to see her frequently, and if he is as fully engaged with his own affairs as I suspect, he may not think the matter of sufficient importance to make a special visit to her. But on the other hand 'tis possible that he may see and mention it to her before the day is out. I do not think we have any cause for immediate anxiety; but, to be on the safe side, the wise course would be for us to bestir .ourselves, and make ready to depart this morning.'

Tansanta showed no surprise, but her thin face was drawn with fear and distress as she listened to him. Then, when he had done, in a spate of words she suddenly shattered his complacency.

`Alas, our case is far worse than you know! De Roubec is in Florence and also knows that I am here. He knocked the house up an hour or so after midnight on pretence of bringing a message from you. Instead he demanded from me a thousand ducats as the price of refraining from telling my aunt that we are living together. When I attempted to fob him off by saying that I had no such sum, he told me to sell some of my jewels as soon as the goldsmiths opened in order to procure it. He left me with an ultimatum, that if I failed to meet him at nine o'clock this morning with the money, outside the west door of the Church of St. Lorenzo, he would go straight to the Palazzo Frescobaldi.'

CHAPTER ELEVEN
THE GRAND DUKE'S MISTRESS

After his sleepless night of acute anxiety, Richard was very tired, but this new and immediate danger spurred his brain to fresh activity.

`I might have guessed it!' he cried bitterly. `De Roubec was present when this other that I spoke of mentioned your relationship to the Frescobaldi; and 'twas too golden an opportunity to attempt blackmail for such a scoundrel to ignore. What answer did you make him?'

`To keep him quiet till nine o'clock, I said I would do my best to raise the money,'

Tansanta sighed. `Yet with so malicious a man, did we produce the gold, I greatly doubt if he would keep his bargain.'

`I judge you right in that. His animosity to myself is such that to give him the thousand ducats he demands would be as useless as to cast them down a drain. He will betray us In any case.'

She nodded, and choked back a sob. `Through this ill chance I fear our danger is extreme. Unless you would have me forcibly taken from you, we must fly instantly.'

`His avarice may save us yet!' Richard said in an attempt to reassure her. `It is not yet seven o'clock. He'll give you a quarter of an hour's grace at least, so 'tis unlikely that he will get to the Frescobaldi Palace before half-past nine. Even if the Contessa has him admitted to her presence without delay it will be ten o'clock by the time she takes any action. If we pack at once, we should get away with the best part of three hours' start.'

`We are packed already,' Tansanta replied. `I have been up all night, half crazy with anxiety about you. Maria did my packing soon after de Roubec left, and before dawn I sent her to rouse Pedro with orders to do yours. I will send her now to order the coach. That also is in readiness ; so we can leave as soon as it comes round and you have settled our reckoning.'

As Maria left the room Richard took Tansanta in his arms, kissed her fondly and murmured: 'Blessings upon you, my love, for keeping your beautiful head and showing such forethought. Your family shall not snatch you from me. Have no fear of that. I would rather die than lose you to them.'

`But whither shall we go?' she asked. 'And what of the Queen's letter? From what you tell me I take it you have the original concealed in your belongings somewhere. If so you are still pledged to deliver it.'

Richard had told Tansanta nothing of his secret activities on behalf of Mr. Pitt, and he loved her so much that he could not help blushing as he answered with swift prevarication: `I thought the original too difficult to hide on account of its bulk, so I disposed of it. But before doing so I made the transcript of which I have told you and took a tracing of that. The former was the same bulk as the original, and I made it as a precaution against just such an emergency as has occurred, the latter I have ever since carried sewn up in the buckram lining of my coat collar. I must, as you say, somehow contrive that it reaches its proper destination safely; and on that account I fear we must part company for a while.'

'No! No!' Tansanta protested.

`Nay, this time it is yes, my love,' he said firmly. "Twill not be for long, and our only chance of later securing a lifetime of happiness together. De Roubec's blackguardly attempt to blackmail you has no more than hastened by a few hours the steps we should have been compelled to take in any case, on its becoming known that you are in Florence. I thought the whole matter out in the night; but we have not long together, so listen carefully.'

He told her then, as briefly as he could, of the attack upon him and of his abduction; of the hooded men and of what had passed at their tribunal. When he came to the episode which concerned her personally he repeated the actual words, as far as he could remember them, that he had used in explaining why she had come with him to Florence instead of sailing direct to Naples; then he went on:

'So you see, if what I said is reported to the Contessa Frescobaldi she will have no grounds for supposing that you are running away with me. And if, as I said we intended to do, we part company this morning, it will further confirm her in the belief that there is nothing between us. There is even a fair chance that such lies as de Roubec may tell will be discounted; and should your aunt still fear that I may have seduced you, but is led to believe that I have left you for good, what action can she take that would in any way benefit you or your family? If she thinks that of your own free will you are proceeding on your way to Naples to get married, it would be pointless to send in pursuit of you and haul you back to Florence. More, if she is a woman of any sense, she will realize that the less attention that is drawn to your brief stay here and possible lapse from virtue, the better. So I have hopes that she will threaten de Roubec with the wrath of the Frescobaldi unless he holds his tongue, and as far as we are concerned let sleeping dogs lie:

Tansanta nodded. `There is much shrewdness in your reasoning, my clever one. Very well then; I will do as you wish. But when and where will you rejoin me?'

Much relieved by her acquiescence, Richard proceeded with the unfolding of his plan. `The road to Naples goes inland from Florence, and only

turns south when it has rounded the mountains to the east of the city. About
ten miles along it lies a small township called Pontassieve. Go thither at a
normal pace and take rooms there. I shall remain here for a few hours, as I
intend to buy riding horses on which we will later make our way back by
circuitous route to Leghorn. But I hope to rejoin you soon after midday, and
we will then discuss our further plans in detail.'

At the thought that he would be with her again so soon, she brightened,
Then, after a moment, she said.: `To purchase horses you will require money.'

He nodded. 'It would not come amiss; as to buy good ones, and the pack-
mules we shall require as well, the outlay will be considerable.'

Kneeling down she unlocked her money-chest again, and took from it a
hundred of the big gold pieces. He protested that it was far too much, and that
he still had considerable funds of his own. But she insisted on his taking the
full hundred in case, while separated from her, he needed a large sum for some
unforeseen emergency.

She had scarcely relocked the chest when Maria returned to say that the
coach was below, and a few moments later Pedro and Hernando came in to
carry down the baggage.

While they were about it Signor Pisani appeared on the scene, still in his
chamber-robe and much agitated by these signs of unannounced departure. But
Richard explaining matters soon pacified the fat landlord, on the grounds that
Madame Jules had had news by a messenger who had knocked her up in the
middle of the night that her husband was seriously ill in Naples, and she
naturally wished to get to his bedside at the earliest possible moment. He
added that as his own business in Florence was not yet completed he would be
staying on for another night or more; after which he would be returning to
France via Leghorn. Then he produced a few of Tansanta's Spanish gold
pieces and asked Pisani to change them for him, deduct the amount of the bill,
and let him have the balance in Tuscan money when he returned in the course
of an hour or so.

When Pisani left them to get the money changed, and the servants had
gone downstairs with the last of the baggage, Richard and Tansanta snatched a
quick embrace. He made her repeat the name of the township where she was to
wait for him, told her that to conform to his plan she should take rooms there
in her own name and swore that nothing should prevent him rejoining her at
latest by the afternoon. Then he accompanied her to her coach. In the presence
of Pisani's people he took leave of her in a manner suited to either a brother-in-
law or close friend, shook hands with Quetzal, and said good-bye to her
servants as though he did not expect to see them again.

As soon as the coach was out of sight he set off down the street. After a
few enquiries he found a man who understood him sufficiently to direct him to
a horse-dealer. There, after a short delay, an apothecary who could speak a
little French was fetched from a nearby shop to act as interpreter; and with his
aid Richard looked over the dealer's stock. For himself he settled on a gray
gelding with strong shoulders and an easy pace, for Tansanta a brown mare
that he felt confident would please her; and, feeling certain that she would

refuse to leave Quetzal behind with her servants, he bought a fat little pony for the boy. Having added two sleek mules to his string, he then got the apothecary to take him round to a saddler, where he purchased all the necessary equipment for his animals, including two pairs of panniers for the mules.

Not wishing to let the apothecary know too much of his business, after arranging for the saddlery to be sent round to the horse-dealer's, he thanked and left him; then he found his own way back to the Lungarno Corsini, where the best shops were situated.

There, he hired a porter with a barrow to follow him and collect his purchases as he made them. With Tansanta's slim figure and Quetzal's small one in his eye he bought two complete outfits of boys' clothing. Then he set about choosing a new hat, cloak and coat for himself. The first two were easy, his only requirement was that they should be a different shape and color from those he had been wearing ; but the selection of the last called for a certain niceness of judgment. It had to be a garment in which he would appear suitably dressed to pay a social call in the evening, yet at the same time one which was not too ornate for him to wear in the daytime. Fortunately the Italian sunshine lent itself far better to such a compromise than the uncertain weather of northern Europe would have done; and he settled on a long skirted coat of rich red brocade. When he had done, with the porter behind him, he made his way back to Pisani's.

It still lacked a few minutes to nine; but, all the same, he now approached del Sarte Inglesi with some trepidation. He had little fear that de Roubec had as yet set the Frescobaldi on to him, but felt that at any time he might be in fresh danger from the Grand Orient.

When he made the copy of Madame Marie Antoinette's letter with the jumbled cipher in Paris he had had in mind the possibility of its being stolen from him, and no attempt being made to decipher it until it reached His Highness of Orléans, perhaps many days later. But it seemed a fair assumption that any such secret society as that of the hooded men would be sufficiently curious to learn what the Queen had written to her brother to investigate the contents of the dispatch before handing it over to d'Orléans agent. And Richard felt there was an unpleasant possibility that, when they found they could not read it, they might endeavor to get him into their clutches again in the hope that he might know the cipher, and could be forced to interpret it for them. It was fear of this that had caused him to devote so much time during the night to a fruitless endeavor to devise a way of getting out of their hands without surrendering any document at all, instead of deciding right away to fob them off with the one in which he had altered the cipher.

While he thought it unlikely that he would be attacked in open daylight in the street, there was at least a possibility that the little wall-eyed assassin and his men had returned by now to del Sarte Inglesi, menaced Pisani into silence, and were waiting upstairs in their late captive's room ready to pounce on him when he got back. Therefore, instead of going into the house, he remained outside it and sent the porter to fetch Pisani. When the landlord appeared Richard said to him:

`This morning I have had a great stroke of good luck. Ten minutes ago I ran into the very man who can settle my business for me. I am to meet him again to conclude matters in half an hour's time, so I shall be able to set off at midday by post-chaise to Leghorn. I am going round to the post-house to order a conveyance now, and as I have this porter at my disposal he might as well wheel my baggage round there at once and be done with it. My things are already packed, as in the excitement this morning my sister-in-law's servants made the error of thinking that I should be going south with her. Would you be good enough to have them brought down to me?'

The Tuscan scratched one of his large ears, expressed regret that he was losing his lodger so soon, and went back into the house. A few minutes later Richard's things were carried out and piled on to the barrow, and Pisani returned with his bill and the change from the money that had been given him. Only then could Richard be sure that his fears of a second ambush already having been laid for him were groundless; but, all the same, he felt that he had been wise to take precautions.

After leaving a generous donation for the servants and bidding Pisani a warm farewell, Richard signed to his porter to follow him down the street; but instead of going to the post-house he led the way back to the horse-dealer's. There, he had his valise and purchases loaded into the panniers of one of his mules, mounted his gray, and taking the long rein on which he had had the other four animals strung together rode out of the dealer's yard. At a walking pace he led his string cautiously through the narrow and now crowded streets until he reached the Arno, then

he took the road that Tansanta's coach had followed earlier that morning, and by it left the city.

His way lay along the north bank of the river, and as he proceeded at a gentle trot he suddenly realized with delight where the early Florentine painters had found their landscapes. Florence now lay behind him set in her bowl of hills, and before his eyes were the very river, green meadows, occasional trees and castle-topped slopes that they had used for the backgrounds of their Madonna's.

At once his thoughts turned to the picture that Tansanta had bought for him, and from it to her. He had taken every precaution he could think of to cover their projected disappearance, but he knew that his measures had not been altogether watertight. Pisani and his servants could only inform an enquirer that she had left early that morning in her coach for Naples, and that he had departed a few hours later by post-chaise for Leghorn; but if the enquirer pursued his investigations at the post-house he would learn that no one whose description tallied with that of Richard had been booked out. It was also possible that the horse dealer, the apothecary or the porter might talk of the foreign gentleman with whom they had had dealings that morning,- but even if they did, he thought it unlikely that the sleuths of either the Grand Orient of the Frescobaldi would pick up and co-ordinate such scraps of casual gossip in so large a city as Florence.

One thing it had been impossible to cover up was the fact that Tansanta had lodged at del Sarte Inglesi as Madame Jules de Cavasuto, and he now realized that when the Frescobaldi learned that it would lend colour to de Roubec's allegation of her fall from virtue. Another was that Tansanta and he had left Florence within a few hours of one another, although ostensibly in different directions ; so her relatives might suspect the truth-that their separation was nothing but a ruse, and that later they meant to reunite at some prearranged rendezvous.

If they did suspect, it was possible that they might follow her, thinking that they would catch. her with her seducer. But Richard had already made allowances for such a pursuit and felt that ha had ample time to prevent it leading to disaster; as, once he had arranged matters with Tansanta, he meant to take adequate precautions against their being surprised together. And if the Frescobaldi found her alone he thought it highly improbable that they would prevent her going on to Naples.

So, although he was not altogether free from anxiety, he was, no longer seriously perturbed about the future, and considered his chances excellent of getting Tansanta safely to Leghorn and so to England.

Although, during their month together, he had told her a great deal about his home and country they had never gone into the actual details of the life they meant to live there. Somehow there had always seemed so many pleasant or urgent things to occupy his immediate attention that he had never given it serious thought.

As he began to do so now, he realized with a pang that marriage might mean his having to give up his work for Mr. Pitt. To forego the travel and excitement that had already become second nature to him would be a sad blow, but he could not see himself being content to leave Tansanta behind in England for many months at a stretch while he was abroad on secret missions. However, by marriage Tansanta would become an Englishwoman. She was intelligent, gifted, high-born and entirely trustworthy ; so, if given the opportunity, could be of the most valuable assistance to him in such work. But would the aloof, woman-shy Prime Minister agree to his engaging her in it? That was the rub. If he did they could have a marvelous life together. They would move in the best society of the European capitals and meet all the most interesting people; yet remain immune from becoming bored by the idle round owing to their fascinating task of uncovering State secrets.

But what if Mr. Pitt could not be persuaded to agree to such a programme? Well, there was the possibility of going into Parliament. Only a few months previously his father had suggested that he should do so, and had offered to put up the necessary funds out of the big prize money that had come to him as a result of the last war. Mr. Pitt would, he felt confident, find him a good constituency to contest at the next election, and having married the daughter of a Prime Minister and Grandee of Spain would add greatly to his social prestige.

The prospect now seemed rather a thrilling one. He knew himself to be a fluent speaker and began to make mental pictures of Mr. Richard Blane, M.P., swaying the House in some important debate, so that he saved a Government measure by a few votes, and in this new role earned the thanks of the master he so much admired. After such a triumph what fun it would be to come home and give Tansanta a designedly modest account of the matter, then witness her surprise and delight when she read eulogies of her husband's great performance in the news-sheets next   day.

They would live in London, of course, but they must have a house with a garden. In spite of his love of gaiety and city lights Richard was a countryman at heart. And a garden would be nice for the children to play in. He felt sure that Tansanta would want children, and although, having no young brothers, sisters, nephews or nieces, he had had little to do with children himself, he regarded them as the best means of ensuring a happy married life.

He wondered for how long he would be faithful to Tansanta, and judged that it would not be much over a year. In his day, age and station it was a great exception for a man to remain a 'Benedict' longer, and few wives expected more of their husbands. But such affairs could be conducted either with brutal openness or in the manner of the French, with courtesy and discretion. Tansanta, he knew, was very prone to jealousy, so he would take every possible precaution to protect her from unhappiness. There would probably be the very devil of a row when she first found out that he had been unfaithful to her, but if he was firm about it that should clear the air for good. And he certainly meant to be, as he had been brought up in the tradition that man is polygamous by nature and therefore enjoys special rights. Like other women she would soon come to accept that, and after a few trying weeks of tears and complaints they would settle down into enduring contentment together.

But why anticipate the inevitable reaction of satiated passion when the passion itself was still to come? They had only the two days' journey to Leghorn, then they would be out of all danger. With any luck they should reach England before the end of the month. No doubt Tansanta and his mother would insist on a week or two in which to make preparations for a proper wedding. Those extra weeks would be a sore trial, as he was already boiling over with suppression; but he would manage to get through. them somehow. Then at last would come the fulfillment of the rosy dreams, which had been tormenting him ever since Tansanta had kissed him in the coach. While still dwelling on the joys of being separated from his beloved neither by day nor night, he approached Pontassieve. But he did not enter it.

The fields in that part of Italy were not separated by hedges, as in England, but only low ditches, so it was easy for him to leave the road and lead his string of animals across the river. There, he let them have a drink, then when they had done led them along the bank, through the fields again, and so back to .he road some way beyond the town.

Continuing along it for a little, he examined such scattered buildings as came in view with a critical eye until, on rounding a bend in the road, he saw just the sort of place for which he was looking. It was a good-sized farmhouse with a yard and some big barns, set well off the highway. Riding up to the door, he shouted: `Hello there l' several times, until a middle-aged woman came round from the back of the house to him.

Dismounting, he smiled at her, and putting his hand in his fob pocket produced a gold half-sequin. He knew that neither of them would be able to understand one word the other said, but he also knew that his smiles and his money were worth a mint of talk. She returned his smile, and then her eyes swiftly focused on the small piece of gold in his palm.

Without more ado he gave it to her, hitched his gray to a post near the door, then beckoned her to follow him, and led the way with the rest of his string round to the yard. A man was working there and at a word from the woman he took over the animals. Richard watched him stable them, then he unloaded the panniers of the mule, and the two of them carried his various packages round to the house door for him.

Inside, it was, as he had expected, a poor place, but the beaten earth floor of the living room was moderately clean; and, undoing his sleeping-roll, he laid it out in one corner, indicating by gestures that he meant to sleep there. Next, he unpacked his new suit, and by the same means conveyed that he was about to change into it; upon which, with nods and smiles of understanding, the couple left him. .

When he had put on clean linen, he redressed his hair with the aid of his travelling -mirror, then wriggled into the red brocade coat, but before repacking his old one he slit the end of its stiff collar and drew out the tracing paper with the involved cipher into which he had transcribed the Queen's letter.

Calling the couple in he took out his watch, pointed to the figure ten upon it, shrugged his shoulders and moved his fingertip in a circle nearly twice round the dial to finish on seven. He meant to indicate that he would be back either that night or the following morning, but from their blank faces he concluded that they did not know how to tell the time by a watch. However, he thought it probable that they had made occasional visits to Florence, as the city lay within ten miles of the farm, so would have seen the clocks in the buildings there, and realize that he meant to return in the fairly near future. He then showed them two more half-sequins, put them back in his pocket, mounted his gray and, with a friendly wave of the hand, rode off towards Pontassieve.

He had told Tansanta not to expect him before midday, so that she should not be worried if his arrangements took him longer than he anticipated; but everything had gone so smoothly that when he dismounted in front of the solitary inn it was still a few minutes before eleven.

Tired as she was from her sleepless night, her anxiety had kept her from going to bed until he rejoined her, and she was sitting in a chair dozing at an upper window. The sound of his horse's hoofs roused her at once, and with a cry of delight she ran downstairs to welcome him.

After he had assured her that all had gone well, and handed his gray over to the ostler, he accompanied her inside, and said

`My love, you look sadly in need of sleep, but I fear I must keep you up for yet a while, as I have much to say, and much to do before the day is out; so it is best that we should settle on our final plans without delay:

'In spite of the fine new coat you are wearing, you too, look near exhausted,' she said solicitously. 'Have you yet eaten, or shall I order something to be prepared for you?'

'Nay. I pray you do not bother them to cook a roast for me; but I could do with a light repast if it be handy.'

She took his arm. 'Come up to my room then. There is a bowl of fresh fruit there and you can eat, some of it while we talk.'

When they reached her chamber Quetzal was playing there, but except for smiling at Richard he took no notice of them, and they settled themselves in chairs near the window.

'What is the meaning of your new suit and your hair being done differently?' she asked, as she handed him the bowl of fruit.

He smiled. 'The coat does not fit me as well as I could wish, but 'tis a fine, rich piece of stuff. With my old one I put off my French identity and have become again Mr. Richard Blane. When compelled to play such a game as we are at the moment, 'tis a considerable asset to be able to pass at will for a man of either nationality.'

'What do you hope to gain by this sudden metamorphosis?'

Richard sighed ; then on his old principle of taking the worst hurdle first, he said:

'Should I chance to come into view of any. one who knows me, I hope to escape recognition unless they see me at close quarters. You see, my love, within the hour I have to return to Florence.'

Tansanta dropped her reticule with a thud; her heavy eyebrows drew together and tears started to her big brown eyes, but he hurried on:

'You must surely realize that. as yet I have had no opportunity to deliver this letter of the Queen's that is proving such a millstone round our necks. And from your attitude this morning I know the last thing you would suggest is that I should abandon all attempt to do so.'

She nodded unhappily, and he continued:

'This, then, is what I propose to do. On our first arrival in Florence Pisani told me that the Grand Duke sups with the opera singer Donna Livia most nights of the week except Fridays and Sundays. As today is Thursday, and his religious scruples will cause him to observe tomorrow's fast in his amours, as well as other matters, the odds are all upon him seeking the embraces of his favourite mistress tonight. By hook or by crook I mean to gain admission to her presence, disclose to her the secret reason for my journey to Florence, and beg her aid in delivering the letter:

'How long, think you, will it be before you can get back?' Tansanta asked, with an effort to keep out of her voice her distress at the thought of him leaving her again.

'It depends upon the hour at which His Highness goes to Donna Livia's house. Now that we are in the long days of the year he may do so before sunset. If that proves the case I may be able to get back tonight. But I greatly doubt it. 'Tis hardly likely that he would sup with her till eight o'clock, and the gates of the city are closed at sundown; so 'tis much more probable that I shall be compelled to remain within its walls till morning. If so, I shall leave at dawn and should be back soon after seven. But either way my plan precludes, my seeing you again until tomorrow.'

`Why so, if you get back tonight?' she exclaimed in surprise.

`Because on my return I do not propose to come to the inn. I mean to go to the lemon-colored farmhouse with the red roof, which lies to the right of the road some half mile further on after having passed through Pontassieve. You may have noticed that I arrived from that direction.'

`I did; and wondered at it.'

`Well, I have already made certain arrangements with the owners of the place. If my business in Florence is concluded before sundown I shall sleep at the farm tonight. If not they will give me breakfast when I arrive in the morning. Then, at let us say half-past eight, I want you to join me there:

`I do not yet see the object of all this mystification.'

Richard bit into his second plum. `Believe me, dear one, our best chance of escaping further trouble lies in our playing out our piece in this way. I should not have come here at all today had you not had to leave Florence so hurriedly, thus denying us the opportunity for a full concerting of our plans. If de Roubec leas told his story to your aunt, by this time she will believe me to be your lover. The odds are that she is now enquiring about us in the city. We dare not ignore the possibility that she may send someone after you. 'Tis for that reason I must make myself scarce as soon as possible:

Tansanta gave him a scared glance. 'Think you then that she will have me pursued?'

He took her hand and pressed it reassuringly. `I am in hopes that, believing you to be on your way to Naples, she will think it pointless to do so ; but she may wish to assure herself that I have not rejoined you.'

`If she dispatches riders along the road to Naples, 'tis certain they wilt enquire here, learn that I am within, and also that you have been with me.'

' I know it, and am not unduly perturbed at such a possibility. For me to have snatched this apparently last chance of being with you for a few hours is quite understandable. The important thing is that if they do make enquiries here they should also learn that I have returned to Florence. If they find you alone they can have no excuse for making trouble, and I feel that we can count on them returning to your aunt with a report that she no longer has cause to be concerned for your reputation. But, lest some spy is left to loiter near this inn, I think it essential to the completion of the deception that you should give the appearance of resuming your journey to Naples tomorrow morning.'

'And what then?'

`I shall be awaiting you at the farmhouse. There I already have a horse for you, a pony for Quetzal and two baggage-mules to carry your treasure-chests and other most valuable possessions. I also bought a lad's clothes for you and a boy's for Quetzal. When you have changed into them, we will send your coach on its way and ourselves by a devious route so as to avoid Florence, ride to Leghorn.'

'But Riché!' she gasped. 'Do you mean that I must part with all my servants?'

He had overlooked the possibility that, never having been without several people to do her bidding, she might take the loss of her retinue hard ; but he restrained his impatience and said gently:

'My love. Your coach cannot go by bridle-paths or across fields as can mules and horses ; so since it must remain on the road there is no alternative to its going forward. Were it to turn back and any agent of either your aunt or the Grand Orient 'chance to see it and your liveried servants passing through Florence, that would give away the fact that you are not on the road to Naples after all; just as surely as it would if anyone who knows Quetzal to be your page saw him with us in his Indian costume. Besides, as I have told you, when we are married we shall not be able to afford to keep several men-servants, so it would be no bad thing if you begin to accustom yourself to doing without them now. I pray you, in order to make more certain our escape to happiness, to give them each a handsome present tomorrow morning and send them back to your father.'

'I'll do so with the men, since you desire it,' she said after a moment. 'But I must keep Maria. I could not even dress myself without her:

Again he had to restrain his impatience. But, having on numerous occasions indulged in the fascinating pastime of assisting young women to undress themselves, he knew quite a lot about the complicated systems of hooks and eyes that fastened their dresses at the back, and of the efforts required to tight-lace them again into their corsets. So he said:

'Take her if you must, then; but it will mean the sacrifice of a certain amount of your baggage, as she will have to ride on one of the mules.'

For a further twenty minutes they discussed details of their projected journey to Leghorn; then he went to the stairs and called for his horse. While it was being saddled they took another fond but temporary farewell of one another. After urging her to go to bed and get some of the sleep that she needed so badly, he went down to the street, mounted his gray and set off back to Florence.

In spite of his fatigue, now that he no longer had a string to lead he made better time than he had on the outward journey; and at a quarter past one he pulled up outside Meggot's English hotel.

The porter there said that he did not think they had a room vacant, but that if Richard would be pleased to wait for a moment he would find out from Mr. Meggot.

Having arrived unattended by a servant, Richard had expected some such reception, as he had learned in casual conversation with Pisani that Mr. Meggot always had rooms to spare, but was the greatest snob on earth, and kept them empty rather than admit to his hotel anyone who was not of the first quality. He had even been known to turn away a Countess, because she had been divorced. But Richard felt quite capable of dealing with such a situation ; so he threw the reins of his gray to a groom, told the porter to take his valise, and followed him inside.

The portly Mr. Meggot emerged from a small office, cast a swift eye over Richard, noted the imperfect fit of his coat, and said coldly: `I fear that we are very full just now, sir ; but my porter omitted to tell me your name.'

`My name is Blane,' replied Richard with extreme hauteur.

`Blane,' repeated Mr. Meggot a little dubiously; but, evidently impressed by Richard's manner, he added: `Would you by chance happen to be one of the Shropshire Blanes?'

'No,' said Richard, assuming a tone of bored indifference. `I am of the Hampshire branch. My father is Admiral Blane, and my mother, Lady Marie, is sister to the Earl of Kildonan. Since his lordship travels much in Italy it is possible that he has honored your establishment from time to time. But why do you ask?'

Immediately Mr. Meggot became all smiles and obsequiousness. `Only, sir, because I feel it my duty to have a care who mingles with my other guests. Our Ambassador, Lord Harvey, does me the honour to dine here quite frequently, and I should not like to put His Excellency in the position of having to meet anyone who-er-well, anyone who was not quite-you understand. At the moment we have with us the Earl Fitzwilliam. who is no doubt known to you, Lord Hume and his charming sister the Honorable Mrs. . . . . '

`Quite, quite l' Richard interrupted. `But have you a room for me?'

`Of course, Mr. Blane. of course. Come this way, if you please. I know your uncle well. He often spent a night here on his way to attend King James in Rome. He was not truly King, of course; but many of the Scots nobility like your uncle continued to regard him as such until his death last year. I always found Lord Kildonan a most gracious nobleman-most gracious. He once said to me----'

Again Richard cut the garrulous Mr. Meggot short. `In the last twenty-four hours I have ridden far, and I have to watt upon His Highness the Grand Duke this evening.

So I wish to go to bed at once and be called at five this afternoon. Kindly arrange for that.'

`Certainly, Mr. Blane, certainly. No doubt, then, you would like a bath. I will have the maids bring you up cans of hot water while you undress.'

For Richard that lovely English touch outweighed all Mr. Meggot's pomposity, and dropping his curt, supercilious manner he accepted the offer with alacrity. Half an hour later, still rosy from his warm ablutions, he slipped between a pair of Mr. Meggot's fine Irish linen sheets, and almost instantly was sound asleep.

When he was called he got up reluctantly, but nevertheless felt much refreshed. While he had slept one of the hotel valets had made some slight alterations to his new coat, so that it should fit better, and now came to assist him to dress. He put on white silk stockings and his best silk breeches, had his hair freshly dressed and powdered, scented himself lavishly, stuck a beauty patch on his cheek and hung his quizzing glass round his neck. So when he went downstairs at six o'clock with his hat under his arm he presented a sight guaranteed to gladden the heart of any young woman, and received a glance of deferential approval from Mr. Meggot.

Having asked that worthy for writing materials he then sat down and wrote the following note in careful copperplate, so that the English in which it was written should be easily legible to a foreigner who might know only a little of that language:

Mr. Gilbert Courtney, director of His Majesty's Opera House, Haymarket, London, presents his compliments to the Lady Livia Gallichini.

To Mr. Courtney's regret his present journey permits him to stay for only one night in Florence, but, even on passing through this illustrious city, he cannot deny himself the pleasure o f laying his homage at the feet of the talented lady who now, more than any other, perpetuates its ancient luster.

I f the Lady Livia would deign to receive Mr. Courtney for a few moments he would count that the most distinguished honor of his passage through Italy.

On his ten-mile ride back from Pontassieve earlier in the day Richard had given his whole mind to the problem of how he might most easily gain swift access to Donna Livia, and the note he had just written was the result of his cogitations. He thought

it very unlikely that the prima donna would refuse to receive a director of the London Opera, and that even if the Grand Duke were already with her she would ask his permission to have such a visitor sent up.

All the same, he was by no means happy about the identity he had decided to assume. For one thing, while it was not uncommon for men of his age to be Members of Parliament or hold field-officer's rank in the Army, he greatly doubted if anyone as young as himself had ever been the director of a Royal Opera Company. For another, although like every educated person of his time he spent a fair portion of his leisure listening to music, it had never been a passion with him, and lie knew practically nothing of its technicalities. If he found Donna Livia alone that would not matter, but if circumstances compelled him to rut up a bluff that he was conversant with the works of all the leading composers, it might prove extremely awkward. But, with his usual optimism, he thrust such misgivings into the back of his mind, had a carozza summoned, and drove in it to Donna Livia's house.

As he knew that one of the fashionable recreations of Florentine ladies was holding conversazioni, he thought it quite possible that he would find her so engaged. But, on enquiring, he learned that she was not receiving, so he gave his note and a silver ducat to the footman who had answered the door to him.

For a few minutes he waited in a hall floored with chequered squares of black and white marble; then the footman returned and ushered him through a pair of fine, wrought-iron gates, beyond which were heavily brocaded curtains, into a spacious salon.

There were five people in it, but there was no mistaking which one of them was Donna Livia. She was reclining on a lion headed day-bed in a loose white robe with a silver, key pattern border, and in the first glance Richard decided that he had rarely seen a more beautiful woman, Evidently she was proud of her luxuriant Titian hair, as she wore it unpowdered. Her checks and jowl were just a shade on the heavy side, but her green eyes were magnificent, her forehead broad, her nose straight, her mouth a full-lipped cupid's bow and her teeth, as she smiled a welcome at him, two perfectly even rows of dazzling whiteness.

Her companions were two middle-aged ladies of aristocratic mien, a very old one who sat dozing in a rocking-chair in a far corner of the room, and an elderly cherub-faced man. The latter was holding Richard's note and immediately addressed him in in. different English.

`The Lady Livia say verri much pleasure you come sir. But she no speek Inglish. She have only Italian an' German. You speek some per'aps?'

Richard was much relieved, as he spoke fairly fluent German; and, having kissed the plump hand that Donna Livia extended to him, he thanked her in that language for receiving him.

She then introduced the two ladies, whom he gathered were both Marchesas, although he did not catch their names, and the plump man as Signor Babaroni, master of the Grand Duke's ballet. The old woman she ignored. Having made his bows, Richard was given a chair and, as he had feared would be the case if he found Donna Livia with company, the conversation at once turned to opera.

Fortunately for him, Signor Babaroni spoke no German and only one of the ladies understood it; the other spoke some English, and asked him if he talked French; but he promptly denied all knowledge of it, so was able to confine himself to two languages and thus be open to his remarks being challenged by no more than two of them at one time.

On Donna Livia asking him what operas were now being per. formed in London, he said that at the time of his leaving they were giving Bianchi's La Villanella Rapita; as it so happened that he had taken Tansanta to see that piece while they were in Marseilles.

She then enquired his opinion of Bianchi and lie replied that he considered La Villanella Rapita by no means that composers best work.

It was a shot in the dark and, apparently, not a very good one, as Donna Livia gave him a slightly surprised look. Moreover, it immediately produced the question: `Then to which of his operas, Miester Courtney, would you give the palm?'

This completely bowled him out, as before his visit to Marseilles he had never heard of the composer. But for the moment he saved himself from exposure by his wits; although he flushed to the eyebrows as he said: `To whichever one you might lift from the rut by singing in it, gracious lady . . . .'

Pleased by the compliment she smilingly repeated it .to her, friends in Italian. Then she asked him where he had heard her sing, and in what part.

This was infinitely worse than anything he had expected, and he had all he could do to hide his dismay; but he punted for Milan, that being the safest bet he could think of, and for Scarlatti's Telemaco as a classic in which she must have played on many occasions.

Again he seemed to have saved his bacon, as she did not declare that he could never have done so; but remarked that he must have traveled in Italy when he was scarcely more than a boy, as His Highness had not allowed her to leave Tuscany since her first season in Florence.

To that he promptly, replied: `My, lady; people are often deceived at a first meeting by my youthful appearance; but I vow that I could give you two years for every year you are over twenty.'

As it seemed impossible that he could be anywhere near thirty the remark inferred that she could hardly be more than twenty-four, and as in fact she was twenty-eight, he had succeeded in paying her another pretty compliment.

Acutely anxious now to avoid further questions on the subject of music, he hardly gave her time to smile before rushing into a panegyric on the beauties of Florence and its art treasures.

Here he was on safer ground, but after he had been speaking with glowing enthusiasm for a few moments on the masterpieces in the Pitti, she said

`But I thought, Miester Courtney, that you were only passing through Florence? You speak as though you had been here several days, and if that is so, I take it ill of you that you should have waited almost till the moment of your departure before coming to see me.'

Hastily he bridged the pitfall he had inadvertently dug for himself, by assuring her that his sightseeing had been limited to a few hours during that afternoon. But the statement cut the safe ground from under his feet; as, after it, he dared not develop the conversation as he had intended, by talking of the Duomo, the Badia, the house in which Blanca Capella had lived, and other places of interest in the city.

Signor Babaroni seized Richard's pause to say in his halting English that as a young man he had visited London and heard the great Françesca de l'Epine sing at Drury Lane.

Richard showed suitable awe although he had never heard of this long-dead prima donna. The ballet master then revealed that his father had done much to ease the last years of her equally famous English rival, Mrs. Katherine Tofts, who had eventually gone mad and died in Venice. As he translated his remarks for the benefit of the ladies the conversation was soon back to opera and the individual triumphs of great artists past and present.

Gamely Richard strove to keep his end up, by putting in a remark here and there that he could only hope was suitable. He was now heartily cursing himself for his folly in having adopted his new role; but as one of the Marchesas spoke German he dared not tell Donna Livia that he had got in to her on false pretences and was anxious to talk to her on a private matter. Yet every moment he feared that he would make some hopeless gaffe that would reveal him beyond all question as an imposter.

At length his hostess provided him with a welcome respite, by saying: `No doubt, Miester Courtney, like so many Englishmen you are interested in gardens. Would you care to see mine?'

With almost indecent haste, he jumped at the proposal; so, languidly rising from her couch, she signed to the others to remain where they were, and led him to the far end of the room.

It gave on to a verandah of beautifully scrolled ironwork from which sprouted gilded lilies, the outer edge of its roof being supported by a row of slender rose-colored pillars of Verona marble, crowned with acanthus-leaf capitols carved in white stone. Beyond it lay the garden, which was actually no more than a big yard enclosed by high walls; but it contained a lovely fountain surrounded by small Cyprus trees, an arbor, stone seats of delicate design, camellia and magnolia bushes, and many delightful rock plants in the interstices of its stone paving.

As they were descending the steps from the verandah she said softly: `For the director of a Royal Opera Company you know singularly little about music, Meister Courtney; and I thought it best to take you away from them before you made some fatal slip.'

Her friendly, conspiratorial air made him sigh with relief, and he replied with a smile: `I will confess, my lady, that I was on tenterhooks, as I did not seek admittance to your presence to talk of opera, but of a very different subject:

In a glance her magnificent green eyes swept him from head to foot, then came to rest upon his deep-blue ones. She did not seek to conceal her appreciation of his handsome looks and fine bearing; and with a wicked little smile, she said

`Few women could fail to be flattered by the attentions of such a beau as yourself; but you are a very rash young man. ',;one of my Florentine admirers would dare to practice such an imposture. They would be much too frightened that discovery

of it would land them in prison, as the victims of His Highness's wrath:

Instantly Richard was seized with a new apprehension. He saw that he had jumped out of the frying-pan into the fire. Clearly the beautiful Donna Livia now thought that he was so desperately in love with her that he had risked imprisonment for the chance of pouring out his passion at her feet. How was she going to take it when he confessed that he had come to see her only on a matter of business? But without waiting for a reply, she turned back towards the house, and said

`Such audacious gallantry reminds one of an old romance, and is worthy of at least some reward. I am inclined to give it to you, so I will get rid of these people and you shall tell me about your real self.'

More worried than ever by the turn matters had taken, Richard followed her inside. There she spoke to her other guests in Italian, and as they took their leave Signor Babaroni said to him:

`I doubts verri much eef 'is 'ighness consent to a London season for 'is company. But I much like to veesit London again ; so I wish you most well:

Quick to realize the excuse Donna Livia had made to talk with him alone, Richard thanked the ballet master politely and said that he had good hopes of arranging matters, but had naturally felt it proper to ascertain the inclinations of the prima donna before proceeding further.

When they had gone the beautiful Tuscan resumed her indolent pose on the day-bed and beckoned Richard to a seat beside her. Knowing that, sooner or later, he must show himself in his true colours, he decided that he had better do so before she had any further opportunity to give proof of the favor with which she evidently regarded him, and so spare her an increased embarrassment when he disclosed that he was not in love with her. Approaching the thorny subject as tactfully as possible, he said:

`Gracious lady; first I must tell you that my real name is Richard Blane, and that I come not from England but from France. While there I had the honour to be entrusted with a commission by Queen Marie Antoinette, and it is that which

has brought me to Florence. I bear a secret dispatch from Her Majesty to His Highness, and certain of Her Majesty's enemies have resorted to most desperate measures in the hope of preventing its delivery. I beg that you will not think too harshly of me when I admit that it was to seek your aid in completing my mission that I resorted to my recent imposture.'

For a moment her green eyes narrowed and her arched brows drew together; then she laughed.

`After such a blow to my pride I suppose I ought to show a sad confusion, or by a cold detachment endeavor to pretend that the thoughts to which I so recently gave expression had never entered my head. But having admitted that your looks please me, why should I now deny it? Call me a bold, forward creature if you will, but whatever the reason for your coming, I am glad you came.'

On such a handsome admission Richard could do no less than his best to restore her amour propre, so he smiled at her and murmured: `I count it my misfortune now that my entry here was not inspired by sentiments more delicate than the delivering of a letter to another. For I have never seen a lady to gain whose favors I would more willingly risk a prison.'

`I thank you, Miester Blane. Your manners match your looks, But a truce to compliments. In what way can I serve you?'

` 'Tis' said that His Highness sups here several times a week. If he proposes to do so tonight, and you would do me the great kindness to present me to him on his coming, I could then deliver this letter to him personally.'

She nodded. `That I will do with pleasure, but he will not arrive before ten o'clock, and 'tis as yet not seven.'

`I am indeed grateful, Donna Livia. May I take it then that I have your permission to return at ten?'

For a moment she considered the matter, then her eyes became mischievous. `Why should you not remain here till he comes? You can have no idea what a pleasant change it is for me to talk with a personable man alone.'

`Is His Highness so jealous, then?' Richard asked with a smile.

`Jealous!' She threw up her hands, and the draperies of her robe fell away from her beautifully rounded arms. `He treats me like a nun. Whenever I appear in Opera I am escorted to the theatre and back by a posse of his servants who spy upon my every movement. At my conversazioni no man under fifty dare talk with me for more than two minutes together without incurring the royal displeasure. And even when in the company of ladies, as you found me tonight, I am allowed to receive only elderly pussycats like Babaroni. Had they not been here, and your excuse for asking an interview been both so good and so pressing, I would never have risked permitting you to enter:

`Then, will not His Highness be much annoyed at finding me here?'

`This secret letter that you carry should prove your passport to immunity from that. Moreover, as you have never before seen me and are leaving Florence at once he will have no grounds for suspecting that our being together is the result of an assignation. But at times he is unpredictable; so I guarantee nothing. The choice is yours, and you are free to go if your prefer not to risk it:

It was the sort of dare that Richard had never been able to resist, and he replied without hesitation: `Provided my remaining brings no trouble to yourself the prospect of angering all the crowned heads in Europe would not drive me from you:

The corners of her mouth twitched. `For that I like you better than ever, Meister Blane. And now I will set your mind at rest. Some little time before His Highness is due to arrive here I shall put you to wait in a room apart. So you need be in no apprehension that he will think naughty thoughts about us.'

`He is said to be an intelligent man,' Richard remarked. 'If so, no doubt you find his company a compensation for his monopoly of you.'

She pouted. `He is well enough, and would be a pleasant companion were he not so atrociously suspicious that everyone is for ever hiding something from him. Even his own brother, the Emperor Joseph, once wrote to him: "Let people deceive you sometimes rather than torment yourself constantly and vainly." Yet he will not take such advice, and undoes the effects of his natural kindness by his unremitting itch to pry into everything.'

`Far from putting a check upon deception, contact with such a nature usually irritates others into practicing it:

No sooner had Richard uttered the truism than he regretted having done so; as Donna Livia gave him a swift glance, and replied: `I can imagine circumstances in which I might well be tempted to amuse myself at his expense.'

Richard found her glance perturbing, but before he could turn the conversation she went on smoothly: 'At one time or another he has suspected me of wanting to have an attire with practically every presentable man in Florence; but there is not one of them who could keep a still tongue in his head afterwards, and I am not quite such a fool as to wish to be deprived of my jewels, and a secure old age on a handsome pension, for the sake of a few hours' pleasure. Yet were there a man I liked enough-and one whom I might regard as gone out of my life for good, tomorrow

-then, the very fact of deceiving my royal lover under his nose would lend zest to such an adventure.'

'I can well understand your feeling,' Richard nodded; but he hastily continued: 'I wonder if he ever suspects his Grand Duchess; though from what I hear the poor creature is so plain that he can have little cause to do so.'

`You are right in that,' Donna Livia smiled. 'And she is a model wife. She has had sixteen children by him-the same number as the brood of which he was one himself-and despite his infidelities she still dotes upon him. But even she and I in combination are not sufficient to hold his entire interest. He often lies to me about it, but I know quite well that whenever he fails to come here, apart from Fridays and Sundays, it is because he is supping with some young thing that has caught his eye:

For the best part of an hour they talked on in the same intimate vein. Donna Livia was making the most of this unforeseen opportunity to unburden herself to a sympathetic and attractive stranger; and Richard both intrigued by the extraordinary situation in which he found himself and fascinated by her beauty, had not given a single thought to Tansanta. Neither of them sought to disguise from themselves that they were physically attracted to the other.

Several times they got on to dangerous ground when one word too much would have proved the spark to ignite them; but some. how, one or the other always turned the conversation just in time, and the electric current that threatened to flash between them was checked by a transfer of the subject from the personal to the general.

At length she asked him if he would like a glass of wine. On his accepting she stood up, and he followed her to a low, curtained doorway at one side of the roof. The old woman who had been there when he arrived was still dozing in her corner. With a casual glance in her direction Donna Livia said:

`Do not concern yourself about old Pippa. She was His Highness's nurse, and is the one person he trusts; but I have long since bought her. Besides, she was once young herself, and knows that occasionally I must have a little recreation.'

As Richard passed through the curtains, he swallowed hard, for he saw that she had brought him into a small room that he presumed few people except the Grand Duke were permitted to enter. It was obviously a chambre d'amour. The whole of its ceiling was made of mirrors; the walls were decorated with frescoes depicting the metamorphosis of Jupiter into a Bull, a Swan, and a Shower of Gold, while in the act of seducing various ladies in these disguises. The only furniture in the room consisted of a huge divan with a small table to either side of it, and one cabinet having a bookcase for its upper part and a cupboard below.

From a cupboard Donna Livia produced a bottle of champagne and glasses. While Richard opened the bottle and poured the wine, she took a thin folio volume from one of the shelves and began idly to turn its pages.

`What have you there?' he asked, his voice coming a little unsteadily.'

"Tis one of His Highness's favorites,' she replied quietly. 'This folio contains a set of beautifully executed paintings to illustrate the works of Pietro Aretino the Divine. Since this is His Highness's room and you are in it, perhaps it would amuse you to look through them with me.'

Richard was already conversant with the writings of that extraordinary man who had been the boon companion of Titian and Sansovino three centuries earlier in Venice. With his heart pounding in his chest he took a pace forward and looked over her shoulder. The book was at that date the greatest treatise on the art of love that had ever been written, and the illustrations of the height of human rapture were the work of a great artist. Yet none of the women portrayed in them were more beautiful than Donna Livia.

Richard's arm slid round her waist. Beneath her flowing robe she wore no corsets. She turned and her big green eyes, now languorous with desire, met his. Suddenly she dropped the book, pressed her warm body against him and whispered.

'I would that I could prolong this moment. But we have little enough time. Let us make the most of it'

CHAPTER TWELVE
HOSTAGES TO FORTUNE

It was ten o'clock. Richard sat alone in a small library on the far side of the marble hall from Donna Livia's salon. It was very quiet. No one seemed to be moving in the big house and he could have heard a hairpin drop.

Instead of amusing himself by looking at some of the thousand or so calf-bound, gilt-backed volumes the little room contained he was sitting uncomfortably on the edge of an elbow less chair, staring at the mosaic of the floor. It was well worthy of inspection, as it had once known the tread of patrician Roman feet in a villa at Baie ; and, only after having lain buried there for many centuries, been removed and re-laid, piece by piece, in its present position at the order of a Medici.

But Richard was not even conscious of it. With a mental pain, that almost seemed a physical hurt, he was thinking of Tansanta, and wondering miserably what could have possessed him to spend the past two hours in the way he had.

He knew perfectly well that it was no question of his having fallen in love with Donna Livia at first sight. But for the subtly intoxicating urge to passion that had radiated from her, he would have continued to regard her with much the same detached pleasure that other supremely beautiful, but inanimate, objects had afforded him during his stay in Florence. And he felt no love for her now. One does not have to love the ripe peach taken from a sunny garden wall because one enjoys its luscious flavor. On the contrary he felt that he loved Tansanta more than he had ever done before.

The thought that he had been unfaithful to her troubled him greatly. It was one thing to recognize that time might cause passion to fade and lead to other loves; but quite another to betray love when it was still in its first blooming. He found it difficult to analyze his troubled mind, but the nearest he could get to doing so was the feeling that he had committed a kind of sacrilege.

His sense of guilt made him nervy and apprehensive. He now dreaded seeing Tansanta again, yet at the same time was more anxious than ever to get back to her, so that they could get away together as swiftly as possible. His uneasiness was further added to by the horrid lurking suspicion that in some way or other the gods would make him pay for his betrayal of love. He felt that he had given hostages to Fortune and would not feel secure again until he and Tansanta were safely out of Italy.

The sound of movement in the hall aroused him from his unhappy brooding. He hoped that it was caused by the Grand Duke's arrival, and that proved to be the case. A few minutes later a servant came to fetch him, and he was conducted back to the salon.

Donna Livia was again reclining on her day-bed. Not a hair of her head was out of place and the expression on her beautiful face was now so demure that she might have been a picture of 'Innocence' painted by Titian himself. The Grand Duke was standing beside her.

After three formal bows Richard permitted himself a good look at the ruler of Tuscany, while waiting to be addressed. Peter Leopold was then forty-two years of age. He was a tallish man with a slim figure. He had the same high forehead and blue eyes as his sister, but unlike her his nose was inclined to turn up at the tip. With a friendly smile at Richard, he said in German

'Herr Blane, I understand that you are the bearer of a dispatch to me from Her Majesty, my sister:

Altess!' Richard bowed again, and produced the sheets of tracing paper from his pocket. 'I have that honor. Here it is; though you will observe that it is not the original. I considered that too bulky to carry with safety, so I made this transcript which was more easily concealable.'

The Grand Duke took and glanced at the letter. 'This is in our family's private cipher, but so altered as to be unreadable.'

'May it please Your Highness, that was a further measure of my own for its greater security in transit. But the rules I devised for altering the original makes its re-transposition simple to anyone who knows the secret. With your permission I will write them out for you.'

'Be pleased to do so.' The Grand Duke motioned Richard towards Donna Livia's secretaire, on which pens and paper were laid out. Sitting down there Richard quickly wrote out the key, and with a bow handed it to the sovereign, who said

'I see the dispatch is of considerable length, so I will not read it now, but at my leisure. It is possible that I may wish to send a reply. If so, I assume you would be willing to take it for me?'

At this bolt from the blue Richard felt that Nemesis had caught up with him already. But he was determined not to allow his own plans to be upset if he could possibly avoid it. So after only a second's hesitation, he replied.

'Any command Your Highness may give me, I should naturally feel it my duty to execute. But I am not in the service of Her Majesty of France. I acted as Her Majesty's messenger only because any gentleman of her own nation would have been suspect by her enemies; and urgent family matters now call for my return as soon as possible to England.'

To his immense relief the Grand Duke did not press the matter, but said amiably: 'In that case I would not dream of detaining you. I trust that you have been well looked after during your short visit to my city. Meggot's hotel has a good reputation for making those who stay there comfortable.'

Richard was a little taken aback at this evidence that the secret police of Florence had thought it worth while to report his arrival, and done so with such swiftness-; but he at once gave an assurance that he had lacked for nothing.

'How long is it since you left Versailles?' the Grand Duke enquired.

'It is, alas, five weeks, Your Highness,' Richard confessed. 'And I humbly crave your pardon for not delivering Her Majesty's letter to you sooner. But I was attacked by her enemies on the road and sustained wounds which, though not of a serious nature, compelled me to do the greater part of my journey in a coach.'

'I am sorry to hear of it, and glad to see now that you appear fully recovered. It seems, though, that you can tell me nothing new of the state of affairs in France, as I have received much later intelligence from agents of my own who left long after you. But tell me, Herr Blane, why, on arriving in Florence, did you seek an audience of me through the Donna Livia, instead of waiting upon me at my palace?'

'I first attempted to do so, Altess, but Her Majesty's enemies had reached Florence ahead of me, and frustrated my attempt by a further attack upon me here last night.'

The Grand Duke frowned. `I was informed that you arrived at Meggot's only this afternoon.'

'That is correct. But I reached Florence on Monday last, the first of June ; and although the precaution against attack proved futile in the outcome, I sought to avoid it by taking lodgings under an assumed identity.'

`Tell me of this attack. I have succeeded :n making Florence a law-abiding city compared with many others; and the Watch shall be punished for their laxity in not having frustrated it. Give me, please, full particulars.'

Richard then described how he had been kidnapped and taken before the hooded men. As he spoke of the tribunal the Grand Duke began to walk uneasily up and down, and muttered angrily to himself.

`These accursed Freemasons! They will be the undoing of us all. The stupidity of the nobility is past all understanding. How can they be so blind as to allow their liberal leanings to make them the allies of anarchists'? They flatter themselves that they can control the movement, but in that they make a hideous error.

By using their wealth and influence to foster and conceal its activities the fools are weaving a halter that will one day be put round their own necks.'

In deference to this royal monologue, Richard had paused; but the Sovereign added impatiently in a louder tone: `Go on, Go on. I am listening to you.'

Richard had as yet made no mention of Tansanta and, as briefly as he could, he now concluded his account without any reference to her.

When he had done the Grand Duke stood silent for a moment, then lie continued his unhappy musing aloud. 'I wonder if Scipione Ricci is concerned in this? He may be. Or it may be only his major-domo who is a traitor. Oh, I wish I knew How can I find out? I must find out somehow and you What guarantee have I that you are not lying to me about these people for, some purpose of your own? Is there no one that I can trust? No one?'

For the first time Donna Livia spoke; addressing the Grand Duke in German, that being the language habitually used between them. With a wicked little smile at Richard from behind her royal lover's back, she said:

'At least, dear Prince, you know that I would never deceive you; and Herr Blane's account of this matter seems so circumstantial that it would be hard to doubt his veracity.'

The Grand Duke swung round upon her. 'I pray that you may be right in the first, grading frau, for you are certainly wrong in the second.'

Again Richard felt Nemesis rushing upon him as the suspicious ruler turned about, his slightly protuberant blue eyes now filled with a baleful light, and exclaimed:

`You have told but half the truth ! If that I For now that I know you to be the man called de Cavasuto, who lodged at del Sarte Inglesi, I can add much to your story. You concealed yourself there instead of going on to a larger place not from any fear of attack, but on account of a young woman who wished to hide the fact that she had come with you to Florence. Can you deny it?'

Since it was obvious that the Grand Duke knew about Tansanta it would have been senseless to enrage him further by a downright lie. But, drawing a deep breath, Richard joined issue with him as best he could.

`Your Highness. The truth of all that I have had the honor to tell you is in no way invalidated by my omission to mention that I arrived in Florence with a lady. I owe to her my recovery from the wounds I received in the service of Her Majesty, your sister ; and sought to repay something of my debt by giving her my escort on a part of her journey through Italy.'

`And made her your mistress into the bargain, eh?'

'Nay, Altess.' Richard could reply with perfect honesty. `She is unmarried, and I have treated her with every respect.'

The Grand Duke evidently did not believe him, as he retorted with a sneer: `I will ask you a riddle. "When is a Señorita not a Señorita?" And lest you lack the wit to find the answer I will give it. 'Tis: "When she is lying at a lodging with a young man of your name and calls herself Madame de Cavasuto."'

It is unthinkable to give a royal personage the lie, Richard was momentarily at a loss what to reply; but Donna Livia intervened on his behalf. Pretending to smother a yawn, she said:

`Forgive me, dear Prince, but I am hungry, and our supper waits. You must surely appreciate that if some young lady has granted her favors to Miester Blane, the elementary dictates of chivalry would restrain him from admitting it to you. In any case, his private affairs can be of no interest to a person of such exalted station as yourself.'

He shot her a swift glance. `The trouble is that his private affairs are also those of others; and I have myself been dragged into them this very afternoon.

'Tis a niece of the Frescobaldi that he has seduced, and they are clamoring for his blood.'

Richard endeavored to conceal his perturbation at this alarming intelligence; and, feeling it more essential than ever to attempt to establish Tansanta's innocence, he cried: `Your Highness,. I do beg leave to protest. The lady adopted the married style only because her duenna died on the journey ; and afterwards it provided a more circumspect appearance for our lodging at the same inns that she should pass as my sister-in-law.'

`Where is she now?' demanded the Grand Duke.

`On her way to Naples, Altess.'

"Tis well for you that she left when she did. Had the Frescobaldi caught you with her they would have killed you out of hand. And they may catch you yet. This afternoon they asked the assistance of my police to trace you, and if you are apprehended you will be brought before me.'

`Then vowing my innocence, I take this opportunity of throwing myself on Your Highness's mercy, and craving your protection.'

    ·   The Grand Duke gave Richard an unsmiling stare. `As to your innocence, I cannot bring myself to believe it. The circumstances against you are too strong. And if my judgment is at fault in that, you have still placed yourself in a position where you must pay the penalty for what you might have done, had you had a mind to it. You do not seem to appreciate the iniquity of your offence, and must, I think, have been crazy to compromise so great a lady:

`Altess, I am now deeply conscious of my folly,' Richard admitted, in consternation at the way in which matters were going. `But I beg to remind Your Highness that the lady is not yet compromised; nor will she be if 'her relatives have the sense to refrain from making the matter public.

'In that your hopes are vain, for 'tis already the talk of Florence. And should you be brought before me, I shall have no alternative but to deal severely with you. Were not proper safeguards maintained against young men ruining the reputations of unmarried girls of high station there would be an end to all society. The

Frescobaldi have incontestable grounds for demanding that I send you to cool your ardour in prison for a term of years; and they are too powerful a clan for me to go contrary to their wishes in any matter where a major policy of the State is not concerned. Besides, did I quash the case, on learning of the insult to his daughter, General Count d'Aranda would ask His Most Catholic Majesty to make representations on the matter to me. And I have no intention of allowing so trivial an affair to be magnified to the extent of creating bad feeling between Spain and Tuscany:

At the threat of a term of imprisonment Richard felt again all the dismay he had experienced while in de Vaudreuil's custody at Fontainebleau; and more, for now it would mean his losing his beloved Tansanta. Hastily he pleaded:

`Altess, since I sloughed off the identity of a Frenchman at midday, 'tis possible that I may escape the attentions of your police while lying at Meggot's tonight. As I have already informed Your Highness, now that I have fulfilled my mission, I am most anxious to return to England. If I remain un-captured I shall leave Florence first thing tomorrow morning. But it may be that by this time your police have already concluded that de Cavasuto and myself are one. If so, on my return to Meggot's, or in a few hours' time, I shall be arrested. May I not beg your clemency at least to the extend of affording me your protection for tonight?'

The Grand Duke shook his head. `Nay. That would entail my withdrawing the order for your arrest, and I am not prepared to compromise myself that far. I have no personal animus against you, so I will take no steps to prevent your leaving Florence if you can. But by your folly you have made a bed of nettles for yourself, and if you are caught must lie upon it:

Richard's mind began to revolve in swift, desperate plans for evading capture. He dared not now return to Meggot's. Would it be possible to get out of the city by dropping from one of its walls during the night? If not, he must hide himself somewhere till morning. But in either case he would now have no horse, and it would take him several hours to walk to Pontassieve. He was about to beg his permission to take his leave when, suddenly, Donna Livia came to his rescue.

`Dear Prince,' she said quietly. `I trust you will not take it amiss if I recall to you that you owe a debt to this gentleman. He has travelled far upon your business, and shown both wit and courage in executing his mission. Indeed, he has actually sustained wounds while bringing Her Majesty, your sister's letter to you. However incensed you may justly feel at his personal conduct, surely his , request for a night of grace is but a small reward for the service

he has rendered?'

'True, true!' muttered the Grand Duke. `With the complaints of the Frescobaldi still fresh in my ears I had forgotten about the letter.' Then, his expression changing to one of suspicion, he gave her a dark look, and added: `But what is he to you? Why should you take up the cudgels on his behalf? Tell me. What is he to you?'

Richard's heart missed a beat. For a moment it had seemed that Donna Livia's good nature had saved him. But now his hopes were in jeopardy once more. Would she dare to continue in the role of his champion? And if she did might she not further inflame to his disadvantage her royal lover's jealous mania?'

She shrugged her shoulders. `He is no more to me than a foreigner whose opinion may be redound to my dear Prince's credit or otherwise. Should he succeed in escaping unaided he will carry but a poor opinion of Your Highness to England and elsewhere. Therefore, for the honour of Tuscany, I pray you give him a pass so that he may leave the city tonight, and thus at least have a fair chance of eluding his enemies.'

In horrible suspense Richard waited for the Grand Duke's reply. At length Leopold nodded. `You are right. To let him be caught through having remained here on my business would ill become me. And if I do as you suggest it cannot afterwards be proved that I did so knowing that he was this

Monsieur de Breuc that the Frescobaldi are seeking.'

Fishing in his waistcoat pocket, he produced a small gold medal
lion that had his head on one side of it and a figure of Mercury upon the
other. Holding it out to Richard, he said.

'This is a talisman carried only by couriers bearing my most urgent
dispatches. Even should the police already be at Meggot's, on your producing
it they will not dare to detain you; and on your showing it at the guard-house
of the Pisa gate the gate will be opened for you.'

As he took the medallion Richard went down on one knee and murmured
his gratitude; then, his boldness returning, he begged permission to kiss Donna
Livia's hand, as that of his protectress.

Permission being granted she extended her hand to him and said
severely: 'I trust your narrow escape will be a lesson to you, Miester Blane.
And that should you return to Tuscany you will bear it well in mind that His
Highness's high moral rectitude is unlikely to permit him again to show
leniency, should you indulge in acts of seduction.'

Richard felt the laughter bubbling inside him, but he dared show his
appreciation of her witty sally only by the twinkling of his eyes. With renewed
thanks to the Grand Duke he bowed his way from the room, and two minutes
later was out of the house.

At Meggot's he learned to his relief that no one had enquired for him; so
he had his things packed, paid his bill, mounted his grey and rode off through
the almost deserted streets to the Pisa gate. There, after a short wait, an officer
was fetched who, at the sight of the medallion, at once had the gate opened.
The clocks of Florence were chiming eleven as he left the city.

He thought it almost certain that the courier's talisman would have
secured his exit at any other gate, and that the Grand Duke had specified the
one opening on to the Pisa road only because he had been led to suppose that
his visitor meant to head for Leghorn and England. But now, being aware of
his suspicious nature, Richard feared that he might check up the following
morning, so had followed his instructions to the letter. Doing so necessitated
riding in a great semi-circle round the outside of the city wall, but another
twenty minutes brought him on to the Pontassieve road. As he turned eastward
along it he felt that at last he had put Florence and its dangers behind him.

Yet, again he became oppressed by his sense of guilt as the thought of
the way in which he had spent the earlier part of the evening kept on recurring
to him. For a little he took refuge in the argument that if he had not pleasured
Donna Livia she might not later have come to his rescue, and that by this time,
instead of still being a free man, he might be on his way to one of the Grand
Duke's prisons. But he knew that the argument did not hold water, because he
had given way in the first situation, before he had the least idea that the second
might occur.

He then began to wonder if the episode had b,-en a great exception in
Donna Livia's life, and, flattering as it would have been to assume so, he
decided that it probably had not. Her remark that he need not concern himself
about the old nurse certainly suggested that it was not the first time she had

deceived her royal lover. No doubt she had to be extremely careful to whom she offered such opportunities, and confined her gallantries to men like himself, who came to her house by chance and it was unlikely that she would see again. He wondered if any such had ever refused her, and in view of her beauty decided that was most improbable. If so, the odds were that some of those others had also betrayed young wives or sweethearts at the temptation of her passionate embrace. That thought was a comfort in a way, but somehow it did not make him much less ashamed of himself.

Once more the idea came to him that a mocking Fate might yet make him pay for those two hours of blissful abandon that he had spent in Donna Livia's arms. But he had suffered such acute apprehension during the hour that followed that he hoped the god of Fidelity-if there was one-might consider he had been punished enough already.

At he rode through Pontassieve every house was dark and shuttered. On passing the inn he looked up at Tansanta's window, and he wished desperately that he had never been compelled to leave her that afternoon. But it was no good crying over spilt milk. The great thing was that he would be with her again the following morning, and the sooner he forgot the existence of the lovely, wanton Donna Livia the better.

Ten minutes later he was knocking up the people at the farm. The man had been sleeping in his day clothes and, shuffling out, led the gray round to the stable. Richard took off his outer things, pulled the blankets of his bedroll round him, and in a few minutes was sleeping the sleep of the unrighteous-which at times a merciful Providence permits to be as sound as that of the just.

When he woke in the morning he felt splendidly well. All the heaviness that he had been feeling for the past few weeks was gone. He decided that the night before he had been making mountains out of molehills, and could now view his brief aiffaire with Donna Livia in proper perspective. It had been a marvelous experience and one that he would not have misted for worlds. To take a Grand Duke's favorite mistress practically under his nose was no small triumph. No young man of courage and sense could possibly have resisted such an opportunity; and had he been fool enough to do so he would have regretted it ever afterwards. Just to think of lying on one's deathbed and remembering that one had had such a chance, yet acted the prude and not taken it! How his dear Melissa would have mocked him, had he confessed to her such a failure to play the man through silly scruples. Far from forgetting the passionate Tuscan, she would become one of his treasured memories, and that would not interfere in the very least with his genuine devotion to Tansanta.

Having washed himself and dressed he ate a simple but hearty breakfast, of four fresh eggs and a huge chunk of home-cured ham, with voracious appetite. Then, humming gaily to himself, he sought to kill time by wandering round the farm slashing the heads off weeds with the point of his sword. He felt that he could

have jumped a five-barred gate or taken on half a dozen of the Grand Duke's police single-handed.

At ten past eight he loaded his things into the panniers of one of the mules, and the farmer helped him to saddle up the other

animals; then, at a few minutes before the half-hour, now filled with happy anticipation at the thought of getting off, he strode with a buoyant step as far as the road to welcome Tansanta on her arrival.

Half past eight came but no Tansanta. For ten minutes he sauntered, up and down quite unperturbed, but by a quarter to nine he began to grow a little impatient. At ten minutes to the hour his exaltation had collapsed like a pricked balloon; five minutes later he had become the prey of desperate anxiety.

Suddenly it occurred to him that she might have thought that he had timed the rendezvous for nine o'clock. For a few minutes the idea brought him intense relief. But the hour still brought no sign of her. With an effort he compelled himself to give her a further five minutes' grace. Then he could bear it no longer. Running to his gray, he swung himself into the saddle and galloped off up the road to the inn.

Outside it there was no coach; none of her servants was visible. The place lay quiet in the morning sunshine; it showed no activity of any kind. White with dismay, and feeling as though the heavens were about to fall upon him, he flung himself from his horse and dashed inside.

In the kitchen he found the innkeeper, preparing a piece of raw meat. The man gave him a curious look, then with a greasy thumb and forefinger drew a letter from his apron pocket.

'I was expecting you, Signor,' he said in Italian. 'The Signorina left here late in the afternoon of yesterday, and her maid asked me to give you this.'

Snatching the letter Richard tore it open with trembling fingers. The writing was barely legible having run in places where it had been copiously watered with Tansanta's tears. Half-blinded with his own, and, in agony to know what had occurred, skipping from line to line, he gradually made it out. It ran:

O love of my life,

All our stratagems have proved in vain. My aunt and cousin arrived here this afternoon. They were half-mad with rage and mortification at the dishonor they say I have done our house. They treated both myself and my servants like criminals. Under their threats Pedro broke. down and confessed that he believed you to be my lover. It is due to your chivalry alone that I was able to prove to my aunt that I am still a virgin.

That mollified her somewhat. She considers that it will save me from repudiation by my fiancé. But she insisted that I should proceed at once to Naples under the escort of my horrid cousin and his men-at-arms. For two hours I withstood her while she prated of my duty. At length she confronted me with the terrible alternative. If I persisted in my refusal she would have you slain as the cause of it.

Something, I know not what, has made them suspect that you mean to rejoin me here. She threatened to carry me to Florence as a prisoner and leave men in ambush at the inn to kill you on your return.

I love you more than my life. To save yours I will face any future, however repugnant to me. I have now consented to do as she wishes. In a few minutes I set out again for Naples under my cousin's escort.

I begged my aunt for a brief respite before setting out to compose myself by prayer. I am using it to write this. Maria will see that the innkeeper has it to give to you.

I pray you by our love not to follow me. Gusippi Frescobaldi has with hint a dozen men, Any attempt to snatch me from them could result only in your death. That would render my sacrifice in vain. The thought that I had brought about your death would drive me insane. I would go mad and dash out my brains against a wall.

I am resigned. I assure you I am resigned. For a month I have lived in a sweet dream. To think of it will be my-consolation all my life long. But I am awake again. I must be brave and undertake the duties to which my birth has called me. But without the knowledge that you still live and sometimes still think of me I should lack the courage. .

I shall never love anyone else. Never! Never!

Good-bye, dear chivalrous English Knight. Good-bye, sweet companion of my soul.

While life doth last,

Your Tansanta.

His eyes blurred with tears, Richard thrust the letter into his pocket. His throat was tight with the agony of his loss and, as he stumbled from the kitchen, he shook with rage at this annihilation of all his plans. In spite of Tansanta's pleas he had already determined to follow her. Twelve men or a hundred might guard her, but somehow by wit and courage he would get her back.

He had hardly covered half the distance to the street when a side door in the passage opened. An officer came out and behind him Richard vaguely glimpsed a squad of soldiers. He made to push his way past, but the officer barred his passage and, thrusting another letter at him, said curtly in bad French:

`For you, Monsieur. By His Highness the Grand Duke's orders:

In a daze Richard tore the missive open, and read:

As we supposed would be the case, instead of proceeding to Leghorn you have attempted to rejoin the Señorita d'Aranda. Consider yourself fortunate that we have not ordered that you be brought back to Florence to face the accusations of the Frescobaldi. It is our pleasure that within three days you should have left Tuscany. You may proceed at your choice either towards Leghorn or Milan. The officer who delivers this letter will escort you to our frontier.

CHAPTER THIRTEEN
THE FIRST REVOLUTION

During the month of June 1789, an event took place some 10,000 miles from Florence that was to have serious repercussions in Europe and, eventually, decide the fate of Tansanta and Richard.

On the other side of the world, in the distant Pacific, Spanish and English seamen became involved in a local dispute that later threatened to develop into a world war.

Many years earlier the Spaniards had sent expeditions from their South American ports northward along the Pacific coast on voyages of exploration. Mexico was already one of their oldest colonies, and they further claimed sovereign rights over the western seaboard all the way up to Alaska. More recently, one of their captains, named Perez, had, in 1774, discovered the harbor of Nootka Sound on the island of Vancouver. But Britain's great explorer, Captain Cook, paid a lengthy visit to the place four years later; and, as the Spaniards apparently content with their rich possessions in Chile, Mexico and Peru showed no signs of developing this outpost in the far, cold north, it was assumed in Whitehall that it could now be regarded as British.

Owing to the wars that ensued during the next seven years the shipping of both nations was so fully occupied that the North American Pacific coast remained deserted. But from '85 numerous British vessels visited Nootka Sound to buy furs from the Indians. Then in '88, Catherine II's greed for territory led to the Russians pushing eastwards across the Behring Strait into Alaska. The Spaniards, alarmed for their theoretical sovereignty over lands first discovered by them, decided to bestir themselves. In the following summer, Flores, Viceroy of Mexico, sent the Captains Martinez and Haro north in the warships Princesa and San Carlos to occupy Nootka before a base could be established there by any other Power. On their arrival they found two English traders, the Iphigenia and Argonaut, in the Sound; upon which they seized the ships, imprisoned their British crews and sent them as captives to Mexico.

Nothing of this was known in Europe until many months later; but owing to it, had things taken only a slightly different turn, all history from that year might have entirely altered its course. The King and Queen of France might have escaped execution, the Revolution never culminated in a monstrous Terror, Napoleon Bonaparte never emerged to disrupt the lives of millions; and those two tiny pawns in the game, Richard and Tansanta, might have met with a fate far removed from that which actually fell to them.

But in those middle days of June neither believed that they would ever meet again. Miserable but resigned, she was travelling south in her coach to Naples; while, filled with bitter rage and frustration, he was riding as though possessed by devils northwestward back across the Alps into France.

On learning of her departure there had been nothing that he could do. Nothing. In his saner moments he realized that he was extremely lucky to have escaped being hauled back to Florence and thrown into prison. So, electing to return to France by the shortest route, he had allowed himself to be escorted to the Tuscan frontier; and from there on endeavored to allay his grief through the physical exertion of hard riding.

In any other circumstances he would have lingered among the treasures that Bologna, Modena, Parma, Piacenza and Turin had to show, and delighted in the landscapes of snow-capped mountains against blue skies as he wound his way through the Mont Cenis pass; but he dismounted only to eat and sleep; his eyes were blind and his heart numb from the belief that he had lost for good the love of a lifetime. On June 16th he arrived in Paris, half dead with fatigue, yet still consumed with unappeasable longings and such poignant grief that he felt he would never again be capable of taking a real interest in anything.

Next morning, although he woke early, he lay long abed; but eventually he felt that he could not stay there indefinitely and must sooner or later make an effort to pull himself together. It was a subconscious impulse to deaden the pain in his mind by employing himself with his original mission that had dictated his return to France; and he realized now that he must either go on to England with the object of resigning his task, or take it up again with such initiative as he could muster. If he adopted the first course he knew that it would lead to a brief interval of wild dissipation in London, followed by a long period of penniless brooding at his home in Leamington ; moreover, it would probably mean the untimely end of a career which, despite its occasional dangers, provided him with everything that he normally prized most highly. On the other hand, the second course, while seeming at the moment dreary, fatiguing and lacking in all interest, would at least prevent him making a fool of himself. So, being at rock bottom a sensible young man, he decided on the latter.

When he had lived in Paris as secretary to Monsieur de Rochambeau he had often dined at La Belle Etoile in the Rue de l'Abbe Sec, and had come to know well the patron and his wife, a couple from Cabourg in Normandy, named Blanchard. In consequence, on his return in the previous April he had taken a room there ; and, once more, the preceding evening, they had welcomed his reappearance. So, when he was dressed, he went downstairs and invited his old friend, the landlord, to join him in a midday draught.

Monsieur Blanchard was a fair-haired, blue-eyed man; honest according to his lights, intelligent and hardworking. He was also shrewd enough to realize that in these times of violent and diverse opinions it paid an innkeeper better to let his customers talk, and agree with them, than to air his own views. As mine host of a well-patronized hostelry in central Paris he missed very little of what was going on in the capital; and, knowing his deliberately cultivated impartiality, Richard felt that a talk with the cautious Norman would be the quickest way to bring himself up to date with the news.

The good Mère Blanchard, an apple-checked, motherly soul, had already solicitously remarked on Richard's haggard looks, and he had put them down to a slow summer fever contracted in the south of France; so he was not called on now to give further explanations to account for his sadly altered appearance. Without preamble he announced that, having been absent from Paris for seven weeks, he had heard little of what had been going on, except that the States General had met early in May, and was anxious to be acquainted with more recent events.

The landlord shrugged. `Really, Monsieur le Chevalier, there is little to tell. So far the States have disappointed us sadly. Their proceedings go on with zealous regularity but they have not yet got to the point of discussing the ills of the nation, let alone proposing remedies for them. The whole time of the Third Estate has been taken up with urging the other two to join it, but the nobles continue adamant in their refusal and meanwhile the clergy sit upon the fence.'

'Has , nothing whatever been accomplished, then?' asked Richard in some surprise.

`Nothing, Monsieur; although the events of the past week give slightly better promise. On the 10th the Abbé Sieyès moved that a last invitation be issued to the first two Orders to join the Third, and that if it was refused the Third should proceed on its own with the verification of credentials. No reply being forth coming verification was started on the 12th. Since then nine of the clergy have come over, and verification has been completed. What will be the next move remains to be seen.'

'And how have the people of Paris taken this inactivity?'

`With patience, Monsieur. There have been no major disturbances. But a new element seems to be percolating into the city which fills many of us with uneasiness. As you walk abroad you will now notice here and there little groups of foreigners idling on the street corners-rough, brutal-looking men who speak only a patois of the South. How or why they should have come here, and who supports them, nobody knows; but wherever there is an outcry they are to be seen participating in it, although it is no concern of theirs.'

`Is there no other news?'

'None of moment; other than the death of the Dauphin on the fourth of this month; but naturally, you will have heard of that.'

Richard shook his head. `I had not. As I told your wife and yourself last night, I have been ill for some weeks; and on my journey north I still felt too poorly to enter into conversation with strangers. Of what did the young prince die?'

'None of the doctors could put a name to his ailment, Monsieur; although it lasted for fifteen months. 'Tis said that all the poor little fellow's hair fell out and that his body was covered with pustules. And further, that since his corpse was embalmed it has shrunk to the size of a new-born infant's. His sufferings were great but I understand that he showed extraordinary fortitude for a child, and spent his last moments comforting his distraught parents.'

`His loss must have proved a tragic sorrow to the Queen.'

`Aye,' nodded the stolid Norman dispassionately. `Perhaps it was a judgment on her; but wicked as she is one cannot help feeling sorry for the poor woman in the loss of her eldest son.'

It was Richard's business to collect information; so he refrained from the impulse to prejudice his source by entering on a defense of Madame Marie Antoinette. For a moment he remained silent, then, feeling that nothing more was to be gathered from his landlord, he ordered his horse with the intention of riding out to Versailles.

While it was being saddled he pondered the mystery of the Dauphin's death. To him, the symptoms-loss of hair, suppurating sores and decayed bones-sounded suspiciously like hereditary syphilis. Yet the Queen came from healthy stock, and the King was said to have refrained from sexual intercourse until eight years after his marriage, owing to a slight malformation which was later rectified by the nick of a surgeon's knife. Perhaps the boy had been the innocent victim of the immoralities of his great-grandfather, Louis XV. On the other hand it was just possible that one of the lecherous old King's cronies had, when Louis XVI was only a lad, amused himself by initiating the young prince into vice. If so, such a terrible disease contracted in his youth might easily account for his later horror of women and continued celibacy even after his marriage. It was an interesting speculation.

When Richard arrived at Versailles he found to his annoyance that the Court was not in residence. On the previous Sunday, following the obsequies of the Dauphin, the King and Queen had retired with the barest minimum of attendants to the privacy of their little château not far distant at Marly. Nevertheless, owing to the sittings of the States General the royal town was a seething mass of people ; and the very first of his acquaintances that Richard ran into was the suave and subtle Monsieur de Périgord.

Limping up to him, the elegant but unworthy Bishop first congratulated him on his return, then expressed concern at his woebegone appearance.

Again Richard explained his hollow cheeks and sunken eyes as the result of a slow fever, and added that never again would he be tempted to expose himself to the treacherous climate of the Mediterranean. For a few moments they talked of Cannes, where he said he had spent the greater part of his period of exile, owing to its already having become a favourite resort of the English; then he remarked.

`From what I hear you do not seem to be making much progress with your Revolution.'

'On the contrary,' replied the Bishop blandly. `The Revolution became an accomplished fact three days ago.'

Richard cocked an eyebrow. 'Are the people then already become bored with politics, that they have accepted their triumph with so little excitement?'

`Nay, 'tis simply that few, even of the deputies themselves, realized the full implication of the momentous step taken by the Third Estate until this morning.'

`I pray you read me this riddle.'

`On Friday the 12th, all efforts of the Third Estate to induce the other two Orders to join them having failed, they decided to proceed with verification on their own. The verification was completed on the 14th. From that Point they could not go backwards, or stand still, so willy-nilly they had to go forward and consider themselves as a duly elected parliament with powers to legislate on behalf of the nation. If the taking of such a step without the consent of the King, clergy or nobles does not constitute a Revolution, tell me what does.'

`You are right. But what has occurred this morning to make people suddenly sensible of this epoch-making development?'

`For the past three days the deputies of the Third Estate have been debating their next move. They sat all through last night until near dawn. After a few hours' sleep they met again and formally announced their decisions. They have assumed the title of National Assembly, promised an immediate enquiry into the reasons for the scarcity of bread, pledged the credit of the nation to honour the public debt and, last but not least, deprived the King of all power to levy future taxes. They have decreed that all existing taxes, although unlawful, not having been sanctioned by the people, should continue to be paid until the day on which the National Assembly separates; after which no taxes not authorized by them should be paid by anybody:

`Strap me!' exclaimed Richard. `This is indeed a revolution. Should the King now force their dissolution he will be left high and dry without a penny. Who were the men that initiated such defiance?'

'Their new title was suggested by Legrand of Berry ; Sieyès drafted many of the minutes; Target and La Chapelier proposed the measures, but the dynamic force of Mirabeau lies behind everything they do. I think him loyal to the Crown but he is determined to humble his own Order.'

`I should much like to meet him.'

`You shall. Come and sup with me one evening at Passy. I can linger no longer now, as I am on my way to a session of my own chamber. Three cura of Poitou went over to the Third Estate on the 12th, and six other clergy joined them the next day. More will follow, without a doubt, so I am watching developments with considerable interest.'

Richard accepted the invitation with alacrity ,and, having said adieu to the cynical Churchman spent an hour or two in casual gossip with various other people. He then returned to Paris, stabled his horse and walked round to the Palais Royal.

The palace had been built by the millionaire minister Cardinal Mazarin, during the minority of Louis XIV. It was a vast edifice enclosing a huge quadrangle in which flourished a number of chestnut trees. The Due d'Orléans' household occupied only the main block and the upper parts of its three other sides. An arcade ran round the latter, beneath which their ground floors had been converted into shops and cafés. The open space under the trees was now what the corner of Hyde Park inside Marble Arch was later to become-the stamping-ground of every crank and soap-box orator who thought he could impart a certain remedy for, the public ills. In recent months, under the protection of M. d'Orléans it had become the central breeding ground of all sedition, and from morning to night agitators were to be seen there openly inciting the mob to resist the edicts of the Government.

At the Café de_Foix Richard had a drink, then strolled across to join the largest group of idlers, who were listening to an attractive looking man of about thirty. He had wild, flowing hair and, despite an impediment in his speech, drove his points home with the utmost violence. An enquiry of a bystander elicited the fact that he was a lawyer from Picardy, named Camille Desmoulins, who held extreme views and was one of the crowd's favourite orators.

Having listened to his diatribes for a while Richard picked ten chestnut leaves and a twig from a low branch of one of the trees, put them in an envelope he had brought for the purpose, and took it along to Monsieur Aubert's. He then returned to his inn and spent the evening writing a report for Mr. Pitt upon the political situation as he had found it in Tuscany, and the personality of its ruler.

Next morning at ten o'clock he met Mr. Daniel Hailes at a small café just round the corner from the Palais Royal, in the Rue Richelieu. After handing over his dispatch he gave a bare account of his journey to Italy, omitting all mention of his love affair with Tansanta, then asked the diplomat what he thought of the present situation.

`This week,' Mr. Hailes replied a trifle ponderously, `we shall witness the crisis in the affairs of France to which events have steadily been leading ever since Louis XVI dismissed Turgot in '76. Had the King had the courage to maintain that wise Minister in office a steady series of Liberal reforms, each initiated before it was demanded, might by now have regenerated the nation and even further increased the stability of the monarchy. But thirteen years of vacillation and futile announcements that reforms were being considered have ended by bringing the monarchy to the brink. If the King accepts the declaration of the self-constituted National Assembly, he will be laying his crown at their feet. But he may not do so. At the moment troops from all parts of the country are being concentrated in the neighborhood of Paris. Having ample forces at his disposal His Majesty may decide to face the people's wrath and send "his loyal commons" packing.'

'One thing is certain,' remarked Richard. `He will do nothing into which he is not forced by some stronger personality.'

Mr. Hailes nodded. `Yes, he is now doubtless tossing like a shuttlecock between Messieurs Necker, Móntmorin and St. Priest on the one hand, and the Queen, the Comte d'Artois, Barentin and d'Espréménil on the other.'

`I thought the latter was the member of the Parliament of Paris who led its violent opposition to the King two years ago.'

'He is, but times have changed. The Parliament now realizes that in having weakened the King's authority it has also weakened its own. Since he was forced to call the States General, the Parliament has become practically an anachronism. All too late it is now trying to get back its prestige by clinging to the coat-tails of the Sovereign. D'Espréménil is one of the few Nobles of the Robe who have secured a seat in the Second Estate, and he has emerged as an ardent champion of the monarchy.'

Leaning forward, Mr. Hailes went on in a lower tone: 'I have much to do, so I must leave you now. But this is for your ear alone, as it is still a closely guarded secret. I have it on good authority that on Monday next, the 22nd, the King intends to hold a Royal Session. At it he will address the Three Estates in person. He is in a corner now and can vacillate no longer. When he has spoken the fate of France will be known.'

The Royal Session did not take place on the 22nd; it was postponed till the 23rd ; but the preparations for it brought about an event of the first importance. The Court not only kept the secret well but committed the stupid blunder of not even communicating the King's intention to Monsieur Bailly, the much-respected scientist whom the National Assembly had appointed as its President.

In consequence, on the morning of Saturday the 20th, the members of the Third Estate arrived at their usual meeting-place to find its doors closed against them. Actually this was in order that workmen could once more erect the throne dais and stands in the hall necessary for a royal appearance there; but the deputies, not unnaturally, jumped to the conclusion that an attempt was being made to prevent their holding further meetings.

Thereupon, they adjourned in an angry crowd to the palace tennis court and, in the presence of numerous members of the public, gave vent to their indignation. Mounier proposed that they should take an oath not to separate until Constitutional Government had been established, and the oath was taken amid scenes of wild enthusiasm, only one solitary member dissenting.

On the Monday the situation was further aggravated by the Comte d'Artois taking possession of the tennis court to play a game there; but the Assembly resumed its sittings in the Church of St. Louis and the day proved one of triumph for it. Already, on the 19th, the clergy, their long indecision resolved by the momentous events of the proceeding days, had voted by 1 49 against 115 for joint verification; and now, headed by the Archbishops of Vienne and Bordeaux, and accompanied by two nobles, the bulk of the First Estate came to sit with the Third in its new temporary quarters.

Richard, meanwhile, had found his plans frustrated by the death of the Dauphin. Normally he would have sought access to the Queen as soon as possible, reported the delivery of her letter, and requested permission to remain at her disposal, as that would have placed him in a good position to find out the intentions of the Court. But he did not feel that he had sufficient excuse to disturb her at Marly, so he remained gloomily in Paris, occupying his mind as well as he could by renewing his acquaintance with various -

people.

However, on Sunday evening he learned that the Court had returned to Versailles; so on the Monday morning he rode out there again, and, after some difficulty, ran de Vaudreuil to earth. His ex-jailor greeted him as an old friend but advised against any attempt to see the Queen for the moment. He said that far from the Sovereigns having been left to their grief while at Marly they had been disturbed almost hourly with fresh advice as to how to deal with the crisis, and were still fully occupied by it. The Royal Council had joined them there, with the addition of the King's two brothers, and the most frightful wrangles had ensued. Monsieur Necker had prepared a speech for the King which Barentin, the Keeper of the Seals, had violently opposed as a complete surrender to the Third Estate. Necker had retired in a dudgeon and the others had altered his speech till it was unrecognizable; but no one yet knew for certain what the unstable Monarch really would say at the Royal Session.

Richard said that he would greatly like to be present at it, so de Vaudreuil obligingly secured him a card of admission to the stand reserved for distinguished foreigners.

In consequence, he was up before dawn the following day and early at Versailles to secure his place in the Salle des Menus Plaisirs. It was raining quite hard and when he arrived he found that although the great hall was already a quarter filled with clergy and nobles, standing about talking in little groups, the Third Estate had been locked outside to wait in the wet until the two senior Orders had taken their seats. Since the hall was so vast that it would hold 2,000 people there seemed no possible excuse for such invidious and flagrant discourtesy.

As an Englishman, he appreciated the great virtues of his own country's political system, by which King, Lords and Commons each enjoyed a degree of power that acted as a protection against dictatorship by either of the other two; so he sympathized with the Court and nobles of France in their endeavor to retain powers which would act as a brake upon any attempt by the representatives of the masses to overturn the whole established order. But the way they were going about it filled him with angry amazement, and the idea of keeping even a deputation of peasants out in the rain unnecessarily showed both their stupidity and heartless lack of concern for anything other than their own interests.

Eventually the Third Estate was let in and in due course the royal party arrived, so Richard was able to let his eye rove over the sea of faces behind which lay the thoughts that would prove the making or marring of the France that was to be. Many of the senior prelates looked fat, self-satisfied and dull. The nobles held themselves arrogantly, but they were mainly narrow-headed and rather vacuous- looking. The faces of the Third Estate were, on average, much sharper-featured than those of the other two, their eyes were keener and many of them possessed fine broad foreheads. Richard decided that in them were concentrated four-fifths of the brains, ability and initiative of the whole assembly.

On the King's appearance many of the nobles and clergy had received him with shouts of 'Vive le Roi!' but the whole of the Third Estate had maintained a hostile silence. A young Bavarian diplomat, who was next to Richard, remarked to him that the gathering had a sadly different atmosphere from that at the opening of the States on the 5th of May, as then everyone had been hopeful and enthusiastic, whereas now, not only good feeling, but the splendid pageantry of the first meeting, was lacking.

From the throne the King made his will known. As he proceeded to reprimand the Third Estate for its recent assumption of powers without his authority, he spoke awkwardly and without conviction. His uneasiness became even more apparent when two secretaries read on his behalf the decisions arrived at, as these

were mainly contrary to his own sentiments and obviously those of the more reactionary members of his Council.

The statements decreed that the three Orders should remain separate as an essential part of the Constitution, but could meet together when they thought it convenient. Revision of taxes was promised, but all feudal rights and privileges were to be maintained. Provincial Estates were to be established throughout the kingdom, but no promise was given that another States General would be summoned on the dissolution of the present one. The creation of the National Assembly and the measures passed by it the preceding week were declared illegal and thereby cancelled.

Finally the King spoke. again, bidding the three Orders to meet again in their respective chambers the next day, and in the meantime to separate.

When the Monarch had retired the majority of the clergy and nobles followed him, but the Third Estate remained where they were. The Marquis de Brézé, who was Grand Master of the Ceremonies, then came forward and said in a loud voice:

'Gentlemen, you have heard His Majesty's commands.'

All eyes turned to the Comte de Mirabeau. Springing to his feet, the great champion of liberty cried:

`If you have been ordered to make us quit this place, you must ask for orders to use force, for we will not stir from our places save at the point of the bayonet.'

The declaration was a bold one, as the town was full of troops, and a company of guards had even been stationed in and about the chamber. But Mirabeau had voiced the feelings of his colleagues, and his words were greeted with a thunder of applause.

De Brézé refused to take an answer from a private member, so Bailly, as President of his Order, announced firmly that he had no power to break up the assembly until it had deliberated upon His Majesty's speech.

On De Brézé withdrawing an angry tumult ensued. The Abbé Sieyés at length got a hearing and with his usual penetrating brevity reminded the deputies that they were today no less than what they were yesterday. Camas followed him with a resolution that the Assembly persisted in its former decrees, which was passed unanimously. Then Mirabeau mounted the tribune and proposed that `This Assembly immediately declare each of its members inviolable, and proclaim that anyone who offers them violence is a traitor, infamous and guilty of a capital crime.'

There were excellent grounds for such a proposal at the moment, as many of the more outspoken deputies now feared that their defiance of the royal command might be used as an excuse for their arrest; so the motion was passed by an overwhelming majority. The Assembly, having assumed this new sovereign power of the sacredness of its persons, then adjourned.

After lingering for an hour or so at Versailles, talking to people whom he knew, Richard returned to Paris to find the city in a state of frantic excitement. The King had that day tacitly acknowledged a Constitution ; but he had given too little and too late. Good solid. citizens as well as the mobs were now alike determined that he should give much more.

It was rumored that Necker had resigned and this caused a panic-stricken run on the banks. Next day it transpired that he

had done so but the King, now scared by such widespread commotions, had humbled himself to the extent of begging the Swiss to continue in office, for a time at least.

On the 25th Richard went again to Versailles and found it as 'agitated as Paris. That morning, to the wild applause of the population, the Due d'Orléans had led 47 nobles to join the National Assembly, and the clergy who had so far stood out were now coming over in little groups hour by hour. Their most obstinate opponent of union was the Archbishop of Paris. During the previous winter he had practically ruined himself in buying food for the starving; but, despite this, he was set upon by a band of ruffians and threatened with death unless he joined the Assembly.

Alternately the streets of the royal town rang with cheers and echoed with shouts of hatred.

Late that afternoon Richard found de Vaudreuil, who agreed to mention his return to the Queen, and asked him to wait in the Galerie des Glaces, from which he could easily be summoned if she had a mind to grant him an audience.

The long gallery was crowded with courtiers and their ladies, and Richard was immediately struck by the contrast of the calm that reigned among them to the commotion going on outside the palace. Faultlessly attired, bowing to each other with urbane grace as they met, parted or offered their snuff-boxes, they were talking of the latest scandals, gaming parties, books, Opera-in fact of everything other than the political upheaval that menaced their privileges, and incomes. Richard did not know whether to admire their well-bred detachment-which was quite possibly assumed so as not to alarm the women-or dub them a pack of idle, irresponsible fools.

An hour later there was a call for silence, the ushers rapped sharply on the parquet with their wands, and the occupants of the gallery formed into two long lines, facing inwards. As the King and Queen entered the women sank to the floor in curtsies and the men behind them bowed low. The Sovereigns then walked slowly down the human lane that had been formed, giving a nod here, a smile there and occasionally pausing to say a word to someone.

Richard had never before seen the King so close, and he was no more impressed than he had been at a distance. Louis XVI was then nearly thirty-five, but owing to his bulk he looked considerably older. He was heavily built and now grossly fat, both in figure and face, from years of overeating. His curved, fleshy nose and full mouth were typical of the Bourbon family; his double chin receded and his mild grey eyes protruded. Even his walk was awkward and he lacked the dignity which might have made a stupid man at least appear kingly.

To Richard's disappointment the Queen did not, apparently, recognize him, and, having reached the end of the human lane, the royal couple passed out of a door at the far end of the gallery ; so he feared that he had had his wait for nothing. But presently de Vaudreuil came to fetch him, and led him to the petit apartments : a series of small, low-ceilinged private rooms adjacent to the Queen's vast State bedchamber. Her waiting woman, Madame Campan, took him into a little boudoir; where Madame Marie Antoinette was sitting reading through some papers.

He thought her looking tired and ill, but she greeted him with her habitual kindness, and obviously made an effort to show interest in the journey he had undertaken for her. When he had given a brief account of it, she expressed concern at his having been wounded, asked after her brother, and then said:

'You find us in a sad state here, Mr. Blane, but that is no reason why I should fail to reward you for the service you have rendered me:

'If that is Your Majesty's gracious pleasure,' he replied at once, 'I have two requests to make, one for myself and one for another.'

As she signed to him to go on, he continued: 'On my first coming to France I sailed in an English smuggler's craft. She was sunk off Le Havre by a French warship and the crew taken prisoner. The captains name was Dan Izzard, and I imagine that he and his men were sent to the galleys. They may be dead or have escaped long ere this, but Dan was a good fellow, and if Your Majesty-'

With a wave of her hand she cut him short. 'At least le bon Dieu still permits the Queen of France to perform an act of mercy at the request of a friend. Give all particulars to Monsieur de Vaudreuil and if these men are still our prisoners I will have them released and repatriated. And for yourself, Monsieur?'

Richard bowed. "Tis only, Madame, your permission to remain unobtrusively about the Court, in the hope that I maybe of some further service to Your Majesty.'

She smiled rather wanly. 'I grant that readily; although I warn you, Mr. Blane, that in these days the Court of Versailles is but a poor place in which to seek advancement.

We are having all we can do to maintain ourselves.'

As Richard was about to reply the door was flung open and the King came lumbering ;n. Ignoring Richard and Madame Campan. he cried.

'What do you think, Madame! D'Espréménil has just been to see me.'

The Queen sighed. 'To offer more advice, I suppose; and no doubt contrary to the innumerable opinions we have heard so far.'

Pulling a large handkerchief from his pocket the King began to mop his red, perspiring face. 'But what do you think he said, Madame; what do you think he said? He wants me to summon the Parliament of Paris, of whose loyalty he now assures me; march on the city with my troops, surround the Palais Royal, seize my cousin of Orléans and his confederates, try them summarily and hang them to the nearest lamp-posts. He says that if I will do that the people will be too stunned to rise against us. That I could then dissolve the National Assembly as unfaithful to its mandates; and that if I will grant by royal edict all reasonable reforms the Parliament will register them, the country be pacified, and the monarchy established on a firm foundation.'

'Worse advice has been offered to other Monarchs who found themselves in similar difficulties,' said the Queen quietly.

'But Madame! the harassed man exclaimed in alarm. 'Because I dislike and distrust my cousin, that would be no excuse for hanging him. Besides, such a tyrannical act could not possibly be carried through without innocent persons becoming embroiled in it. We might even have to fire on the crowds and kill a number of the people. The people love me and in no circumstances will I allow their blood to be shed. They are not disloyal, but simply misguided. No! No! If blood is to be shed I would rather that it were my own. You at least agree with me about that, do you not. Madame?'

The Queen inclined her head. 'Sire, you know well that you have my full understanding. and approval of any measures that you think fit to take. What reply did you make to Monsieur d'Espréménil?'

'I-I thanked him for his advice,' faltered the unhappy King, `and told him that we were opposed to extreme measures; but would think about it. You see Madame, I did not wish to offend him, as I am sure that he meant well. I am much relieved that you feel as I do. I pray you excuse me now, for I am due to listen to a lecture from that depressing Monsieur Necker.'

The King made an awkward bow to his wife, and hurried like a naughty schoolboy from the room. There was silence for a moment, then the Queen said to Richard

`Had you been the King, Mr. Blane, what would you have thought of Monsieur d'Espréménil advice?'

`I would have taken it, Madame, and acted upon it this very night,' replied Richard without hesitation. `But may it please Your Majesty to understand me. I have little sympathy for your nobles, and still less for the majority of your clergy. Both Orders have become parasites, and I believe that the only sound future for France lies in utilizing the brains and initiative of the Third Estate. But it should not be allowed to usurp the royal prerogative. Since things have gone so far, I think His Majesty would be justified in taking any measures-however violent-to silence His Highness of Orléans and restore the authority of the monarchy.'

The Queen nodded noncommittally. `You are not alone in your opinion, Mr. Blane; but His Majesty's feelings are also mine. You may leave me now; and in future I shall see you with pleasure among the gentlemen of our Court:

As Richard rode back to Paris he felt sad for the French nobles; for, although he found little to admire in them as a body, he would have hated to be one of them and have to rely for support on such a sorry King. His pessimistic view of their chances was confirmed the very next day.

Barentin had won the round over the speech at the Royal Session, but Necker got the upper hand in the one that followed. At his insistence the King wrote to the Presidents of the two senior Orders, the Cardinal de la Rochefoucauld and the Duc de Luxembourg, asking them to invite their members to join the Third. Both demurred, so he sent for and pleaded with them. Still they held out, preferring his displeasure, and the howls of execration of the mob wherever they appeared, to a surrender that they considered to be against the true interests of the nation. The King then panicked and resorted to a stratagem which came near to baseness. He ordered his brother, the Comte d'Artois, whom the nobles regarded as the leader of their resistance, to write a letter stating that if they persisted in their refusal His Majesty's life would be in danger from the fury of the populace. The letter was read in the chamber of the nobles on the morning of the 27th. The gallant Marquis de St. Simon instantly sprang to his feet and cried: 'If that be the case, let us go to him and form a rampart round him with our bodies.' But the majority were against provoking an armed conflict; so, although with the greatest reluctance, out of personal loyalty to their Sovereign, the remaining member:; of the two senior Orders were tricked into joining the National Assembly.

That it was a shameful maneuver Richard had no doubt, as he was in Versailles at the time with every opportunity to assess the facts ; and he knew that there was as yet little real strength behind the noisy rabble, whereas the Court still had ample power to suppress any serious disturbance.

For a week past bands of hooligans had been parading the streets creating disorder, and threatening anyone they saw whom they believed to be opposed to the idol, Monsieur Necker. In the neighborhood of the park the peasants now defied the gamekeepers ; three poachers had been brutally butchered, one of them only a few days previously, and the villagers round about were openly shooting the game in the royal forests. The whole country was in a state of extreme agitation, and during the past four months over 300 outbreaks of violence had occurred in different parts of it.

Even the French Royal Guard were no longer to be relied upon, as the agents of the Duc d'Orléans were employing women as well as men to stir up sedition, and great numbers of the prostitutes of Paris were being used to suborn the troops. Both in the capital and at Versailles it was now a common sight to see groups of guardsmen arm-in-arm with girls, drunk in the middle of the day, and shouting obscenities, picked up in the gardens of the Palais Royal, against the Queen. Moreover it was known that a secret society had been formed in the regiment, the members of which had sworn to obey no orders except those emanating from the National Assembly.

But despite all this, not a voice, much less a finger, had as yet been raised against the King. Every time he gave way he won a new, if temporary, popularity, and even when he stood firm there was no decrease in the respect shown to him. He had 40,000 troops within a few hours' march of the capital. The discipline of his Royal Swiss Guards was superb, and he had several other regiments of Swiss and German troops who had long been embodied in the French Army in the immediate vicinity. As they did not speak French they understood little of what was going on, could not be tampered with, and were entirely reliable. He therefore had nothing whatever to fear and must have known it from the fact that whenever he appeared even the rabble still greeted him with shouts of `Vive le Roi!'

So he had betrayed his nobility, and deprived them of all further opportunity to exercise a restraining influence on the extremists of the Third Estate, solely for the sake of escaping a little further badgering from a Minister whom he disliked and distrusted, yet had not the courage to dismiss.

Of his abysmal weakness further evidence was soon forthcoming. The Duc de Châtelet, Colonel of the French Guard, much perturbed by the open disaffection of his regiment, arrested fifteen of the ringleaders and confined them in the prison of l'Abbaye. One of them managed to get a letter smuggled out to the Palais Royal. On its contents becoming public a tumult ensued, the mob marched up the prison, forced its doors, released the offenders and carried them back in triumph.

Since the elections the revolutionary Clubs in Paris had gained enormously in strength, and they used as their mouthpiece a body of the Electors who had made their headquarters at the Hôtel de Ville. Instead of dispersing after having been elected their deputies to the Third Estate these Electors continued to sit, forming an unofficial but most powerful committee, who, every day, deluged their representatives in the National Assembly with a constant spate of requests and orders. The Electors now demanded that the Assembly should use its weight with the King to secure the pardon of the mutinous guardsmen. This the Assembly, now itself frightened of the mobs that the Electors controlled, was sapient enough to do ; and the miserable King acceded to their request, thereby destroying at a stroke the authority of the officers of his own regiment of guards.

Richard now went daily to Versailles. He would have moved to lodgings there if he could, but ever -since the assembling of the States General the town had been packed to capacity and every garret in it occupied ; so he often had to ride back to Paris in the small hours of the morning.

His temporary captivity at Fontainebleau now stood him in good stead, as the courtiers he had met through de Vaudreuil extended their friendship to him, introduced him to their families, and invited him to their parties. For, in spite of the 'troubled times, life within the palace went on as usual, except that there were no public entertainers owing to the Court being in mourning for the

Dauphin. Twice the Duchesse de Polignac invited him to musical evenings in her suite, and on both occasions the Queen spoke kindly to him. He now saw her, although not to speak to, several times a day, and his affable manners rapidly gained him an accepted place among the fifty or sixty people whom she regarded as her personal friends.

In consequence, he was now admirably placed for learning what was going on, and he soon became aware that the Court party was by no means yet prepared to knuckle under to the National Assembly. The Marshal de Broglie, a stout-hearted veteran of the Seven Years' War, had been appointed to the supreme command of the Army, and he meant to stand no nonsense if the mobs of Paris took up arms against the King. The Queen's old friend, de Besenval, had been selected to command the troops in the capital, and between them they now had 50,000 men concentrated in and around it.

Most people at the Court now felt that, unless the King's timidity led him to an abject surrender of every right still vested in the Crown, civil war must soon break out. They also believed that, although he might be prepared to do so on his own account, his jelly-like back would be stiffened for once at the thought that his powers did not belong to himself alone, but were held by him in trust for transmission to his children and future heirs as yet unborn.

De Broglie and his staff were therefore preparing against all emergencies with the utmost activity. The palace and its grounds were now an armed camp. Batteries were being erected to cover the bridges over the Seine and thousands of men were laboring to throw up a vast system of earthworks on the slopes of Montmartre, from which guns could bombard rebellious Paris.

Richard kept Mr. Hailes informed of all the details he could gather, but the main facts were common knowledge and, not unnaturally, the National Assembly took alarm at these military measures, believing their purpose to be the intimidation of themselves. De Mirabeau voted an address to the King asking that the troops be withdrawn.

On July 10th the Monarch replied that the troops had been assembled only for the purpose of preventing further disorders, and that if the Assembly had any fears for its security it had his permission to remove to Noyon or Soissons. Then on the night

of the 11th, he at last plucked up the courage to dismiss Necker. When the news reached the Palais Royal next day pandemonium broke loose. Fuel was added to the fire by the tidings that Montmorin, St. Priest and other Ministers who had supported Necker's policy had been dismissed with him; and that the Baron do Breteuil, one of the Queen's intimates, had been appointed principal Minister in his place.

Leaping on to a table, with a brace of pistols in his hands, Camille Desmoulins harangued the crowd, inciting them to insurrection. D'Orléans' swarthy ruffians from the South and a number of deserters from the Gardes Frangais reinforced the mob, which surged through the streets, burst into the Hôtel de Ville and seized all the arms there. For the rest of the day and tar into the night anarchy reigned in Paris. The lawless multitude broke open the prisons, looted the shops and burnt the hated customs barriers at all the entrances to the city.

De Besenval, believing that he would pay for it with his own head if he ordered his troops to attack the people without the royal authority, sent courier after courier to Versailles for instructions. But the King was out hunting and, even when he did return, could not be prevailed upon to give any. Meanwhile de Besenval's men had begun to fraternize with the rioters and were deserting by the score; so, as the only means of stopping the riot, he withdrew his troops during the night to the open country.

On the morning of the 13th Richard set off as usual for Versailles; but when he reached the last houses of the city he found that the road was blocked by a barricade of overturned carts, looted furniture and paving stones. It was manned by an armed rabble who would allow no one to pass in either direction, and were seizing all would-be travelers to rob them of their valuables. Richard's horse saved him from such treatment, but his fine clothes excited shouts of hatred and he did not get away without a shower of stones being hurled at him.

Returning to his inn he changed into his most sober garments, then went out again to discover what was going forward. He soon learned that every exit of the city was in the hands of the mob and that they now regarded Paris as a beleaguered city. Somewhat uneasily he wondered when the bombardment from the royal artillery on the heights of Montmartre would commence; and cursed the idiocy of the King, who a week before could have put an end to the seditions of the Palais Royal with a company of troops, done so yesterday morning with a battalion, but to achieve the same end now would need to employ an army.

In the gardens of the Palais Royal he saw to his surprise that every chestnut tree was entirely stripped of its leaves; but a waiter at one of the cafés told him that green being the colour of the Duc d'Orléans, Camille Desmoulins had, the day before, plucked a leaf and stuck it in his buttonhole, upon which the crowd had swarmed up the trees and decorated themselves with similar symbols before rushing off to the Hôtel de Ville.

The habitual loungers in the garden being now otherwise occupied, it was almost deserted, so Richard decided to go to the Hôtel de Ville, as the new centre of the mob's inspiration. He found it surrounded by a seething mass of people, and only after two hours of persistent pushing managed to edge his way inside.

From the scraps of conversation that he picked up it emerged that the Electors were no* alarmed both for themselves and the city. Events were taking the course usual in revolutions. The more Liberal nobles, and the aristocratic lawyers of the old Parliament, had first opposed the King: they had been pushed aside by the more advanced reformers of the Third Estate; in its turn the Third Estate had recently shown signs of becoming dominated by the Left-wing element of the Clubs and Electors; and now the Electors found themselves at the mercy of the mob.

However, the Electors were mostly men of some substance, and they were determined not to allow further property to be destroyed if they could possibly prevent it. Quite arbitrarily they had virtually taken over the functions of the Municipality of Paris, but they now sought the aid of Monsieur de Flesselles, the Provost of Merchants, and other officials of the city. De Flesselles, with a bravery that was soon to cost him dear, succeeded in getting rid of the major portion of the rioters by telling them that large quantities of arms were to be had for the taking in various places, where in fact, no arms were stored; and, in the meantime, the Electors hurriedly pushed forward a project upon which they had agreed two days earlier.

This was the formation of a Civic Guard, to consist of 200 men per district - 12,000 men in all. The idea had been conceived with the object of creating a counterpoise to the royal troops, and, if necessary, giving armed support to the National Assembly ; but it was now put into operation for the defense of the lives and properties of respectable citizens. By nightfall skeleton companies of the new militia were patrolling the streets in the better quarters, but the mob still reigned supreme in the Faubourgs ; and in the gardens of the Palais Royal a drunken orgy was taking place by the light of thousands of sus' worth of fireworks which d'Orléans' agents were selling to the people at one quarter of their normal cost.

After the better part of two hours in the Hôtel de Ville, Richard had forced his way out of it and returned to his inn. Tired from the press of the crowd and its shouting, much worried by the turn events had taken, and no longer buoyed up by his old love of excitement, he ate a meal in solitary silence, then went up to his room and endeavoured to read a book. He was still wondering when the bombardment would open, but the King had been out hunting again all that day and on his return to the palace declared himself too fatigued to attend to business; so the only explosions that disturbed the stillness in Paris on that summer night were made by the rockets and Roman candles let off by the rowdies at the Palais Royal.

Next day Richard's enquiries produced the information that, although the mobs were still in possession of a large part of the city, the milice bourgeoisie had succeeded in restoring order in its western end and demolished the barricades on the roads leading out of it. So he had his horse saddled and rode to Versailles.

He found the town unexpectedly quiet and, to his amazement, that the occupants of the palace were going about their normal routine as though nothing had occurred to disturb it in the last two days. The people he talked to were aware that there had been riots in the city, but they did not regard them with any more seriousness than they had the minor disturbances that had been taking place there for several months. In vain he endeavored to bring home to several courtiers the imminence of the peril that now threatened the whole structure of the State, but they merely offered him their snuff-boxes and assured him blandly that 'now that vain, blundering fool Necker has gone everything will soon be put to rights'.

Later in the day the sound of cannon could be clearly heard from the direction of Paris. A report came though that the mob were attacking both the

Invalides and the Bastille in the hope of obtaining further supplies of arms and ammunition. The courtiers now smiled a little grimly, and said that a few round shot fired from the towers of the Bastille would soon teach the people better manners.

Early in the evening the usual royal progress was made through the long Hall of Mirrors. It had only just begun when the Due de Laincourt, booted, spurred and covered with dust, arrived on the scene. Thrusting his way through the satin-clad throng lie addressed the King without ceremony:

'Sire! I have to inform you that the people have sacked the Invalides, and with the arms so obtained stormed and captured the Bastille.'

`Bon Dieu!' exclaimed the startled King 'It is then a revolt.'

' 'Tis not a,-revolt, Sire,' retorted the Due acidly. 'It is a revolution.'

De Liancourt was one of the most Liberal-minded nobles, and also suspected of Orleanist tendencies, so the obvious concern with which he announced the news was all the more striking; but he knew little of what had occurred apart from the bare facts.

Hard on his heels came de Besenval, with a more substantial account, which had been furnished by the agents he had left behind him on his withdrawal from the city. The King suggested to the Queen that they should retire with the Ministers to hear the news in private; so, accompanied by de Besenval, de Breteuil, de Broglie and a few others, they withdrew amidst the never-failing ceremonial bows and curtsies that took place at their every movement.

But the details soon leaked out. Having secured a few cannon from the arsenal at the Invalides the mob had marched to the Bastille with the object of obtaining further weapons. The Marquis de Launay, who was governor of the fortress, had refused their demands and threatened to fire upon them. They had then attacked the approaches to the castle with great determination, and succeeded in severing the chains that held up the outer drawbridge. De Launay's garrison consisted of only 32 Swiss and 80 pensioners, and his cannon were ancient pieces no longer of value except for firing salutes; so he offered to admit a deputation to parley provided that they undertook to attempt no violence while within the fortress. This being agreed a group numbering 40 were admitted, and the inner drawbridge drawn up behind them. As to what next occurred, accounts varied widely. Some said that de Launay had massacred the deputation, but as such an act of brutality could have done him little good it seemed most unlikely. The more probable version was that a nervous gunner had allowed his match to get too near the touch. hole of a cannon that was trained on the deputation as an insurance against their possible treachery, and that the piece, fired by accident, killed a number of them.

In any case the mob outside, believing itself to have been deliberately betrayed, placed such cannons as it had against the gates, blew them in, and stormed through the debris with ungovernable fury. At the sight of them de Launay snatched a

lighted match from one of his gunners and ran towards the powder-magazine with the intention of blowing the fortress up; but he was seized by his own men, who then surrendered to the mob on a promise that his life and their own should be respected.

The French Guard deserters who were present, and had done most of the fighting on the side of the attackers, showed great bravery in endeavoring to protect de Launay and carry out the terms of the surrender. But the canaille overcame them, and dragged the Governor to the Place de Greve, where criminals were habitually executed, and murdered him there with great brutality ; afterwards cutting off his head and parading it in triumph on the point of a pike round the gardens of the Palais Royal.

The gunner who had fired upon the deputation, and several of his companions, were also butchered. In addition, that same evening, another mob had called Monsieur de Flesselles to account for sending them on a wild-goose chase when they had been seeking arms the day before. Having hauled him from the Hôtel de V ille, they were marching him away to try him at the Palais Royal when he was shot by an unknown hand. Thereupon they hacked off his head and carried it to join de Launay's in the garden where so much infamy had been plotted.

On hearing of these wild scenes Richard did not feel at all inclined to return to Paris that night, so he gladly accepted the offer of a shakedown in the apartments of the Duc de Coigny. Next morning news came in that the barriers outside Paris had been re-erected, and that the Civic Guard were now refusing anyone entrance. De Coigny then told Richard that he was welcome to occupy his temporary quarters for as long as he liked, so Richard thanked him and went out into the town to buy some toilet articles and fresh linen.

When he returned he heard that the National Assembly had again sent an address to the King, asking him to withdraw his troops from the vicinity of the capital as the only means of restoring order; and that their request had met with a refusal. But later in the day the unstable Monarch changed his mind and gave way. That evening the sang-froid of even the courtiers was shaken and, although they still preserved appearances by talking of idle topics with their ladies, an atmosphere of gloom pervaded the whole Court.

On the 16th the full extent of the Court party's defeat became apparent. The additional regiments that had been brought into Versailles were evacuating the town. The Marshal de Broglie was deprived of his command. De Breteuil, Barentin and other royalist Ministers were dismissed. A courier was dispatched posthaste to Switzerland to recall the now inevitable alternative, Monsieur Necker.

Feeling depressed by the long faces in the palace, Richard went that afternoon to the National Assembly. The scenes he witnessed there appalled him. He realized now how right Monsieur de Perigord's forecast had been that, lacking all experience in parliamentary procedure, when the States General met it would resemble a bear-pit. No rules of conduct for debates had been laid down and none were observed. Often as many as fifty deputies were all on their feet at once endeavoring to shout one another down; and when at last one of them did get a hearing he did not speak as a participator in a prearranged debate; instead he held the floor for as long as he could, pouring out all the ideas for the regeneration of France which were uppermost in his mind at the moment. In consequence his hearers might wish to support some things he said while violently disagreeing with him about others; so that when a division was finally called for, two-thirds of the members were not clear in their minds upon what they were voting.

Still worse, the public galleries were packed with spectators and no attempt whatever was made to keep them in order. They shouted witticisms and gave loud cat-calls ; yelled for deputies to speak who had not risen, cheered their favourites and booed those they suspected of holding reactionary opinions. With such an audience, mainly composed of roughs and agitators, it was clearly impossible for moderate men to state their views without being subject to intimidation.

Horrified as Richard was by this travesty of parliamentary government, he was so . fascinated by the spectacle that he remained watching it much longer than he had intended. When he came out it was getting dark, and the hour for supper in the palace had already passed, so he decided to get a meal in the town before rejoining his friends.

As he walked back to the palace, in the great square upon which it faced, several hundred people, among whom were many French Guards accompanied by loose women, were busy starting bonfires. The fever of revolution, which still gripped Paris, had spread, and groups of drunken roisterers were now singing ribald songs about the Queen under her very windows.

Sadly, Richard went up the great staircase, and made his way to de Vaudreuil's rooms. To his surprise he found his friend throwing books, boots and pistols higgledy-piggledy into a big trunk.

`What in the world are you about?' he asked anxiously.

'Packing my own things, as I have sent my man to get my coach,' replied the Count tersely.

'Indeed! And where are you off to in such a hurry?'

'Germany! Holland I England! Heaven knows, for I do not.'

`Come,' Richard insisted. `I beg you make yourself plain:

`I thought that I had done so. I am going into exile.'

'Exile!'

`Yes. I have been banished. An hour since Her Majesty told me to pack this very night and leave the country.'

`But you are one of her oldest friends. How could you possibly have offended her to such a degree?'

'I spoke my mind too freely. For weeks past her brother, the Emperor Joseph, has sent letter after letter, urging her to take refuge with him in Vienna from the hatred of the people. This evening I told her plainly that it was useless to rely further upon the King. That he is constitutionally unfitted to cope with the problems with which he is faced. That she must either raise the standard of the monarchy herself and let us draw our swords in its defense, or seek safety in flight. She replied that she had complete faith in His Majesty's

judgment, would never abandon him or the _station to which God had called
her, and would not suffer to remain in her presence anyone who spoke ill of
her husband; therefore I was to proceed abroad immediately.'

`She cannot have meant that!' cried Richard impetuously. `She is
distressed beyond measure by events, and cannot have realized the full import
of what she said. At such a time she more than ever needs her true friends
round her. I beg you to ignore her order; for I vow you will find that she has
repented of it by tomorrow.'

De Vaudreuil frowned, shook his head, and said sadly: `Nay. I have long
been wearied of the Court and its futile ways. I have wasted half a lifetime
bowing and posturing with a lot of other fools who have now brought calamity
upon themselves. I have served her to the best of my ability, and would serve
her still if she ,would but listen to the dictates of her own high courage instead
of playing the loyal, subservient wife to that poor stupid man whom fate has
made our King. But since she will not, did I remain I should only add to her
distress by telling her further truths that she knows already ; so 'tis best that I
should go.'

In vain Richard argued and pleaded, so at length he left the Count to
continue with his packing. Yet he knew that de Vaudreuil loved the Queen
with a selfless devotion, and in recent weeks his own heart had ached so much
for Tansanta, that now, from sympathetic understanding, it ached for his
friend.

He could not bear the thought that the Queen and her faithful knight
should part in anger, so after a while he summoned all his resolution and went
to her apartments.

Madame Campan opened the door of the ante-chamber to his knock. On
his requesting an audience on an urgent matter she looked at him in
astonishment and said that she could not take his name in at that hour, and in
any case the Duchesse de Polignac was closeted with Her Majesty.

At that moment the Duchesse came out. She was holding a handkerchief
to her eyes and weeping bitterly. Richard again urged Madame Campan to beg
the Queen to see him for a moment and at length she reluctantly consented.

She returned after a moment to say that the Queen was about to retire for
the night, and could see no one. With his usual persistence when he had made
up his mind to 'do anything, Richard said that he had been sent on a matter of
the greatest urgency by Monsieur de Vaudreuil. Again Madame Campan
reluctantly gave way. When she came back the second time she opened the
door wide and led him without a word across the room to the great gilded
double doors at its far end. At her touch one of them swung back a few feet,
and he stepped through into the huge, lofty, ornate chamber, in which the
Queen both slept and held her morning receptions.

Madame Marie Antoinette was sitting at her dressing-table, her head
bowed between her hands, crying. As she turned to look at him her blue eyes
were dim and the tears were still running down her checks. In that vast
apartment she now seemed a small pathetic figure. Richard was suddenly
conscious of an extraordinary urge to run to her and put his arms protectively

about her.

Repressing this symptom of madness that she inspired in men, he made her three formal bows and waited to be addressed.

After a moment she said in a low voice: `You-you bring me a message from Monsieur de Vaudreuil.'

`I most humbly beg Your Majesty to pardon me,' he replied. "Tis not Monsieur de Vaudreuil's words I bring, only his thoughts; and those upon my own responsibility. He is distressed beyond measure at your treatment of him.'

The Queen drew herself up. 'Monsieur! How dare you force your way in here. and require me to explain my conduct'

Richard went down on one knee, and bowed his head. `Madame, I come but to implore you to forgive him.'

She put her handkerchief to her eyes, brushed away fresh tears, and said more quietly: 'I did no more than my plain duty in reprimanding him for what he said.'

Throwing discretion to the winds, Richard burst out: `But, Madame! He has been so long in your service. He loves you so dearly. He would, I know, give his life for you without a moment's hesitation. How could you find it in your heart to treat him with such harshness! 'Tis one thing to administer a rebuke, but quite another to send a faithful servant into exile because he has spoken over boldly, and at that solely from his devotion to you.'

For a full minute there was silence, while Richard continued to kneel, his eyes fixed on the floor. Then she said.

`Be pleased to rise, Mr. Blane. I thank you for coming to me. It will enable me to repair a misunderstanding, which I should deeply regret. I spoke to Monsieur de Vaudreuil upon two matters. Firstly in reply to the uncalled-for advice he offered me; secondly regarding his own future. But neither had any connection with the other. I now see that in his distress at having incurred my displeasure, my poor friend must have confused the two. I told him that he must leave my service, only because His Majesty and I have decided that France is no longer safe for anyone who has shown us personal-devotion.'

The Queen choked upon the word and began to weep again; but after a few moments she restrained her tears, and went on: "Tis said that in Paris there are already placards up demanding the head of Monsieur le Comte d'Artois ; so the King has ordered his brother to leave the country. He has done the like with the Prince de Condé, arid the Prince de Conti; with Monsieur de Breteuil, the Marshal de Broglie and a score of others. I have but this moment parted from my dear friend the Duchesse de Polignac.'

Once more her tears checked her speech, but she struggled to continue. `The de Coignys, de Ligne; all those we love we are sending abroad for their own safety. They begged to stay, but the King helped me to persuade a number of them only a few minutes after de Vaudreuil had left me. In the end His Majesty had to command them, and he urged them to depart without losing a moment. You, too, Mr. Blane must go. Short as your time has been here, you are already known as one of those they call "the party of the accursed Queen". Think kindly of me sometimes, I beg, but leave me now and make all speed to

England.' ,

There was nothing Richard could say; and, his own eyes now half blinded by unshed tears, he bowed very low.

As he was about to make his second bow she impulsively, stood up, and thrust her handkerchief into his hand.

'Give this, please to de Vaudreuil,' she stammered. `Tell him that I have shed many tears tonight; but that the first to fall on it were those I shed at the thought of having had to send him away.

The moment Madame Campan had closed the door of the anteroom behind Richard, he hurried back to de Vaudreuil's room. But he was too late. Both the trunk and its owner were gone: A mass óf only partially torn up letters left scattered about the floor told of his hurried departure.

In the hope of catching his friend Richard ran through the long corridors, down the great staircase, and out on to 'the steps at the main entrance of the palace. But the Cour de Nlarbre was empty and no coach in sight.

Beyond the railings the bonfires now brightly lighted the square. Like the nightmare figures at a Witches' Sabbat men and women with linked arms were wildly dancing round them. Their drunken shouts made hideous the summer night.

In his hand Richard still clutched a small, damp handkerchief.

CHAPTER FOURTEEN
UNEASY INTERLUDE

Richard did not even contemplate following the Queen's injunction to set off for England; his duty to his own master quite clearly lay in remaining at the center of events. The problem that exercised him now was, since he could no longer remain in the palace, how was he going to get back to Paris unmolested?

Having decided to sleep upon it he went to his temporary quarters with the de Coignys. The suite of rooms was in disorder and the Duc and Duchesse gone. A footman told him with a pert grin that they had left half an hour before by a side entrance of the palace, as plenty of other fine people were doing that night. Richard worked off a little of his nervy unhappiness by taking the insolent fellow by the scruff of the neck and kicking him out of the room. Then he undressed, got into the Duke's bed and soon fell asleep.

Next morning his problem was solved quite simply for him. The good people of Paris had demanded a sight of their King, and however weak Louis XVI may have been as a Monarch, neither then nor during any of the terrible situations with which he was afterwards faced did he show the smallest lack of physical courage.

To those who sought to dissuade him from such rashness he replied: 'No, no, I will go to Paris; numbers must not be sacrificed to the safety of one. I give myself up. I trust myself to my people and they can do what they like with me.' And that he thought himself probably going to his death was shown by the fact that he made his will and took Holy Communion, before his departure under escort by the new troops of the Revolution.

The Electors had decreed an increase of the Civic Guard to 800 men per district, making a total of 48,000 ; and at the instance of the Marquis de Lafayette, whom they appointed to command it, this milice bourgeoisie had been re-christened the Gardes de la Nation.

As a young man, fired by the thought of adventure, Lafayette had volunteered to go to America and fight for the rebellious Colonists against the British. Although only nineteen at the time, owing to his rank, wealth and connections it was agreed that he should be given the rank of Major-General. Actually he never had any great number of troops under his command, but he fought with gallantry, had received the thanks of Congress, the friendship of Washington, and returned to France a national hero. In the Assembly of Notables, held in '87, he alone had proposed and signed the demand that the King should convene the States General, so in a sense he was the Father of the Revolution. He was now thirty-one; a sharp-featured man with a pointed chin and receding forehead. He was vain, dictatorial and of no great brain, but honest, passionately sincere in his desire to bring a free democracy to his country and immensely popular with both the middle and lower classes.

On the morning of July 17th, therefore, it was into Lafayette's keeping that the King gave himself for his journey to Paris. Only four of his gentlemen and a dozen of his bodyguard accompanied him. Lafayette rode in front of his coach ; the captured flag of the Bastille was carried before it and the captured cannon, with flowers stuffed in their muzzles, were dragged behind. The rest of the long procession consisted of the newly enrolled National Guard, which as yet had neither uniforms nor discipline, so presented the appearance of an armed mob. Thousands of women were mingled with them, and occasional horsemen rode alongside the throng, so it was simple for Richard to ride to Paris as one of the procession.

At the barrier the King was met by the honest and courageous Bailly, who, in addition to his Herculean labours of endeavoring to direct the debates of the National Assembly, had suddenly had the office of Mayor of Paris thrust upon him. He handed the keys of the city to the King with the tactless but well-meant words: 'These are the same that were presented to Henri IV. He had re-conquered the people; now the people have re-conquered their King.'

Once inside the barrier Richard left the procession as soon as he could, so he learned only by hearsay what transpired later. The King was conducted to the Hôtel de Ville, where Badly delivered an address, then offered him the new tricolor cockade. Its adoption as the national colours was an inspiration of Lafayette's, as it combined the red and blue of Paris with the royal white. After a second's hesitation the King took it and put it in his hat; but the poor man was so embarrassed that he could find no words to reply to the address, except the muttered phrase: 'My people can always count on my love.' However, on leaving the building he received some reward for his humiliation.

Lafayette had that morning ordered that in future the people should greet the Monarch only with shouts of 'Vive la Nation!' But on seeing that the King had donned the tricolor, the old shouts of 'Vive le Roi!' rang out ; and he was escorted back to Versailles by a cheering multitude.

During the days that followed it soon became clear that, as was always the case when he gave way to the people, he had won a new lease of popularity; but this time, his surrender having been so complete, it looked as if he would retain the public favour longer than he had on former occasions.

The new National Guard had the Gardes Français incorporated in it, and was taking its duties seriously. Most of the bad elements had been disarmed; and, although the ex-Minister Foulon, and de Sauvigny, the Intendant of Paris, were murdered, relative quiet had been restored in the city.

As Richard moved about it he now began to see the other side of the Revolution, The cutthroats and extremists formed only a small part of the population, and at times of general excitement colored the picture more by their excesses than their numbers.

The great majority of the Parisians were good, honest people, and they now went about their work again with a real happiness and pride in their new-won liberties. By comparison with the idle, arrogant, narrow-minded nobles and the fat, self-indulgent priests, Richard found them, on average, much more genuine and likeable; and he felt every sympathy for their ambition not only to make their country rich again but also to enjoy a fair share of its riches.

Like everyone else in Paris, he went to see the fallen Bastille. A start had already been made at pulling down this symbol of the old tyranny, and some 200 volunteer workmen were tackling the job with a will ; but the fortress consisted of eight massive towers, linked by high curtains, the whole being built of immensely heavy blocks of stone, so it looked as if a considerable time must elapse before these patriotic enthusiasts succeeded in leveling it to the ground. In spite of the excitement at the time, only eight people had lost their lives during its capture, and only seven prisoners were found in it. Of the latter, one, an Englishman named Major White, had been there for thirty years and when released had a beard a yard long; two others were lunatics and the remaining four convicted criminals.

Towards the end of the month it seemed to Richard that the Revolution was virtually over. It still remained to be seen which men would emerge as the permanent leaders of the nation, and what their foreign policy would be; but his visit to the National Assembly had convinced him that, for some time to come, it would remain far too much of a melting-pot for any serious forecast to be made about the deputies who would rise to its surface. In consequence, he decided that, since he could now do little good by staying in Paris, he might as well take a few weeks' leave; and with this in view he set off for England on July 28th.

He slept that night at Amiens, and found the situation there typical of what he had heard reported of the other great cities in France. There had been many disturbances and the old municipal authorities had been overthrown; the most vigorous among the Electors had taken the running of the city on themselves and a local copy of the Parisian National Guard was now keeping the rougher elements in check.

Next morning, on riding through a village, he passed a meeting of yokels who were being brought up to a pitch of angry excitement by an agitator; but he took scant notice of them. f However on seeing a similar scene a few miles farther on, he began to wonder what was afoot. At Abbeville, where he meant to take his midday dinner, he realized that fresh trouble of a very serious nature had broken out.

The town was in an uproar. Armed bands were marching through the streets. In the square the National Guard had been drawn up, but apparently had no intention of interfering with the rioters. From three directions Richard could see columns of smoke swirling above the rooftops, so it looked as if the mobs were already burning the houses of people known to be opposed to the new reign of liberty.

His enquiries elicited the most fantastic rumors. `The Queen had conspired with the nobles throughout the country to kidnap and kill the people's leaders. The royal troops had marched on Paris two days before and were now systematically leveling it to the ground. The Swiss Guards had been sent to massacre the National Assembly. The Comte d'Artois had gone to Germany for the purpose of raising an army there, and he had crossed the Rhine with 100,000 men to conquer France and re-enslave her people.'

In vain Richard assured his informants that there was not one atom of truth in their wild stories; they would not believe him, and said that couriers had arrived from Paris the previous night bearing this terrible news. When he said that he had left Paris himself only the day before, they began to suspect that he was an agent of the Queen sent to lull them into a false sense of security.

Suddenly realizing that he had placed himself in imminent danger he admitted that all these things might have occurred after he had left; then, seeing that there was nothing he could do, he got out of the town as quickly as he could.

A few miles beyond it, he saw a château, some half mile from the road, roaring up in flames, and a little farther on a gibbet with a welldressed man hanging from it and a crowd of villagers dancing round their victim in a circle. It was now clear that the whole countryside had risen and was exacting a centuries-old vengeance on its seigneurs for their past oppressions.

During the afternoon he saw several other burning châteaux in the distance and passed many bands of peasants armed with scythes, pitchforks and old muskets. As far as he could he avoided them by cantering his horse across the fields, and when he had to reply to shouted questions he made it clear that he was an Englishman, speaking only a little bad French.

He was much relieved to reach Calais in safety, but found that, too, in a state of panic and wild disorder, with the same fantastic

rumours flying about. Hungry as he now was he rode straight down to the quay, only to find that the packet-boat sailing that night was already crammed with well-dressed people flying from the Terror. But, luckily for him, the ship was an English one, and after two hours' wait among a crowd of several hundred would-be passengers who could not be taken, he managed to, get hold of one of the ship's officers. Gold would not have done the trick, as it was being offered by the handful, but his nationality secured him three square feet of deck; and the following morning he landed at Dover.

Although he did not realize it at the time, he had witnessed the beginning of the `Great Fear', as it afterwards came to be known; for not only had the peasantry of the Pas de Calais risen on that and the following days; they had done so throughout the whole of France.

The fall of the Bastille on July 14th had unexpectedly precipitated the complete surrender of the King three days later. The Monarch's newly won popularity had upset the calculations of those who were conspiring to force his abdication. Like Richard they had come to the conclusion that the political revolution having been accomplished the country would never settle down; unless steps to create further anarchy were taken. Since they had little more to hope for in that direction from Paris they had turned their attention to the provinces.

On July 28th hundreds of couriers had been dispatched in secret to all parts of France with instructions to disseminate false news of such an alarming nature that the whole country would be set ablaze. The fact that the risings took place simultaneously in every part of the Kingdom proved beyond question that this terrible nation-wide outrage was the result of deliberate organization. Moreover, the general acceptance of these baseless and improbable rumours in every city and town could not possibly have been brought about by the work of a single courier arriving in each. So everyone who knew anything of the inner forces animating the political situation had little doubt that the `Great Fear' was the work of the unscrupulous Duc d'Orléans, operating through the vast spider's web of Masonic Lodges that he controlled.

Its results were beyond belief appalling. Terrified that the hated Queen and arrogant nobles were about to wrest their newly won liberties from them, a madness seized upon the people. In the course of a few days hundreds of châteaux, great and small, were burnt. Thousands of gentry, their womenfolk and even little children, were murdered, in many cases being slowly tortured to death with the most hideous brutality. Many of these petit seigneurs had been bad landlords, but the great majority had already imbibed the new Liberal doctrines, were eager for a Constitution, and anxious to do what they could to improve the lot of their peasantry. Tens of thousands succeeded in escaping abroad, some with such few valuables as they had been able to collect in the haste of a flight for life, but most of the exiles arrived near penniless, so were compelled to live for many years in poverty. Thus in the course of one summer week France was decimated.

Richard had been so absorbed by his own affairs that it had not occurred to him that the London season would be over, but on his arrival he found the West End deserted and Amesbury House closed down except for the skeleton staff always kept there. Donnie Ned had left a week before and was at his father's seat, Shambles, in Wiltshire.

Finding his best friend absent was a sad blow to Richard, as his broken romance with Tansanta still weighed heavily upon him and lie badly wanted to unburden his heart to someone. So far he had said not a word of it to a soul and it gnawed at him so unremittingly that he had come to believe it would always do so until he could ease his pain by talking freely about her. But there were only- two people to whom he would have been willing to do that, Donnie and his dear Melissa; and a letter awaiting him at Amesbury House informed him that the beautiful Lady Etheridge was now upon the Rhine.

In her bold, vigorous scrawl she wrote glowingly of Vienna; telling of balls and receptions at the Hofberg, drives in the Prater, picnics on the Kobentzel, and midnight water parties on the Danube; she declared Viennese music the most haunting, and Viennese society the most gallant, in all Europe. The Emperor Joseph's illness had caused some concern, as had also the unrest in his dominions brought about by the resentment of his subject peoples at the reforms he had endeavored to force upon them. But his health had recently improved and it was still hoped that a settlement might be reached in both Brabant and Hungary without further bloodshed. Such matters had, however, in no way interfered with her own enjoyment, and she could have become an Austrian Countess six times over, had she had a mind to it.

At the invitation of Count Apponyi-a most dashing, handsome man-she and her father had removed for a while to Budapest, and also paid a visit to the Count's Castle, near Lake Balaton.

Budapest had to be lived in to be believed; its nobility were graced with , all the culture of the West, yet lived as though still in the Middle Ages, wore scimitars instead of swords, and clad themselves in all the rich, barbaric trappings of the East. While in the country she had attended a wedding. It had been kept up for three days, a dozen oxen had been roasted whole to feast the local peasantry, and they had danced every night till dawn to a gipsy band that distilled pure romance instead of music.

After a further sojourn in Vienna they were now about to remove to Salzburg and thence to Munich. By August they hoped to reach the neighborhood of the Rhine, as they had accepted an invitation to stay at Darmstadt; and another, later, for September, from Prince Metternich, to be present at the vintage on his estate at Schloss Johannisberg.

,She ended by saying that since a contrary Nature had seemingly made it impossible for her to remain good for any length of time, she was at least trying to be careful;, and urged on Richard the same sisterly precept.

He could not help laughing as he laid the letter down, but lie wondered if Melissa's zest for enjoyment would ever fail her, as his own had done. He sincerely hoped not, as he already knew it to be a terrible thing to be still young yet unable to any longer take pleasure in anything. Moreover, he could not help contrasting her carefree existence with that which now confronted the scared, white-faced young French women who had crossed with him in the packet-boat from Calais. Even if none of them had been blessed with a combination of her abounding health, fine brain and dazzling beauty, many of them had been brought up in the same security and comfort that she had enjoyed as a young girl ; and the thought of their uncertain future saddened him.

Next day he learned that the indefatigable Mr. Pitt was still in London, and managed to secure an interview with him. The tall, lean, young old-looking Prime Minister offered him a glass of Port as usual, and listened with interest to his first-hand account of the last days of the absolute monarchy at Versailles; but the news of the events that had followed was already stale.

Apart from securing the Queen's letter, which was now an old affair, Richard had brought off no considerable coup during his four months abroad; and the Prime Minister suggested, a little coldly, that he might have arranged for the safe delivery of the copy to the Grand Duke through British diplomatic channels, instead of wasting seven weeks in a journey to Italy and back.

Richard thought the comment unfair. He protested that if he had not delivered the letter personally he might have found it impossible to convince the Queen that he had carried out her mission. Or she might later have learned from her brother that he had not done so, which would have proved equally disastrous.

Mr. Pitt admitted that there was something to be said for the points Richard had made, and let him go on to give his impressions of Leopold of Tuscany; but the truth was that he was giving his visitor only half his attention. Had Richard's business been urgent or important he would have got a fair and full hearing, but, as it was neither, the Prime Minister was allowing his mind to roam on a subject that was then giving him much concern.

That summer, inspired by his closest friend, the great humanitarian William Wilberforce, and supported by many Members on both sides of the House, including even his normally most bitter opponent, Charles James Fox, he had made a determined attempt to abolish the Slave Trade. But the vested interests that would have suffered from abolition, particularly in Liverpool, Manchester and Bristol, were enormous, and the anti-abolitionists had enlisted in their aid the crafty and powerful Lord Chancellor Thurlow. It now looked almost certain that the Chancellor would succeed in wrecking the measure, and Mr. Pitt was wondering if he could possibly devise some means of saving it.

However, his brilliant memory had not deserted him, and as Richard was about to take his leave, he said: 'When last we met we talked of the Bourbon Family Compact. Have you, perchance, Mr. Blane, happened upon any circumstances which might be developed as a lever for the breaking of it?'

In spite of his grande affaire de coeur with a beautiful lady of Spain, Richard knew little more of that country's present political relations with France than he had when he left England; and he had to confess as much.

The Prime Minister shrugged his narrow shoulders. 'Ah, well! There is no great urgency about the matter, but I should be glad if you would bear it in mind. I judge you right that the National Assembly will take a month or two to settle down; so you had best enjoy what is left of the summer here, then return to France in the autumn and endeavor to find out what you can of the new Government's intentions.'

After his visit to Mr. Pitt, Richard tried to make up his mind what to do with himself. He did not want to go to his home at Leamington just yet, because he felt certain that his mother would remark upon his moodiness, and, dearly as he loved her, he was averse to giving her a true explanation. Now that he had discharged his responsibilities to the Prime Minister, the impulse came to him again to get drunk and beat up the town. But for that one needed suitable companions, either male or female. During most of the year he could have found some young sparks at his Club with whom to drink and gamble; but it was closed for its August cleaning. He knew a gay and pretty trollop of the more superior kind who was kept by an elderly nobleman in a comfortable apartment off Jermyn. Street. It was most unlikely that her Earl would be visiting her at such a season, and he wondered if a week or so spent in her hilarious company would dispel his misery; but he decided that feminine endearments would only repel him at the moment.

He had had to abandon his horse at Calais, not having had time to sell it, but he had returned from the Continent with more money than he had ever possessed before. Tansanta had refused to allow him to pay for anything on their journey south to Italy, which had meant a considerable saving of his own funds, and the string of animals he had bought in Florence had cost less than an eighth of the hundred pieces of Spanish gold she had given him; so he had on him nearly £600 in bills of exchange on London, and it seemed absurd that with such a sum at his disposal he could not find some means of buying, himself distraction.

For an hour or two he mooned about the art dealers' in the West End, but saw nothing that he really liked in the way of pictures, and even looking at them made him feel the loss of Tansanta more poignantly. Suddenly it occurred to him that -it would be intriguing to lay in a stock of wine; and the idea had to some degree the merit of unselfishness, as he knew that a good addition to the cellar at home would please his father.

Accordingly, having long recognized the wise principle that the best is always the cheapest in the long run, he took a sedan chair along to the King's wine-merchants, Messrs. Justerini and Johnson, at No. 2, Pall Mall.

A scene of desolation met him in the neighborhood, as on July 17th the Royal Opera House in the Haymarket, upon which the wine merchants' shop backed, had been burnt to the ground. But the southern frontage of Sir John Vanbrugh's fine edifice had been saved, and Messrs. Justerini were still carrying on their business among the surrounding debris.

Mr. Augustus Johnson the younger, a pleasant young man of about Richard's own age, received him and pressed upon him a glass of excellent French cognac for the good of his health; then spoke with quiet confidence of his wares. They had just received a particularly good shipment of Constantia from the Cape, and some Canary Sack that would be much improved from having been sent on a voyage round the world. Richard bought some of each, some Port that had been shipped to Newfoundland and back, some Madeira, Coti-Roti, Alicante Rhenish, Bordeaux and sparkling Sillery. To these he added a number of liqueurs to which the firm specialized, many of which were strange to him.

It was this purchase of good liquor that suddenly decided him to go home after all, as he would then have the fun of binning the stuff away himself and trying each of the items out at his leisure. Mr. Johnson agreed that there would be no difficulty about having them packed in wicker hampers to go on a conveyance the following morning; so Richard hired a private coach and set out next day. He spent the night at Watford and on the afternoon of the 3rd of August arrived at Leamington.

He found that his father was at sea as a Rear Admiral with the Mediterranean Squadron, but his mother was there, and her surprise at his unannounced return added to the joy of her welcome. On their first evening together he gave her Madame Marie Antoinette's handkerchief, and on Lady Marie Blane learning how it had come into his possession her tears fell upon the little square of cambric that only eighteen days before had been wet with those of the unhappy Queen.

In making the present to his mother Richard wrought better than he knew, for she at once accepted his sadness as the result of the harrowing scenes through which he had passed, so he was spared any necessity to either tell her about Tansanta or invent some excuse for his acute depression. Yet, after a few days, seeing that he showed no signs of cheering up and did not even go out to see his old friends in the neighborhood, she became worried about him, and with the object of taking him out of himself decided to give a small dance.

From fear that Richard might oppose the idea she told him nothing about it until the servants began to prepare the house on the morning of the party; then she announced with a laugh that it had been planned as a surprise for him, and swiftly began to reel off the names of the twenty-odd young people she had invited. Casually, towards the end of the list, she put in that of Amanda Godfrey, adding that Amanda was staying again for a while with her uncle at Williamston. Although Lady Marie was not supposed to be aware of the fact, she knew quite well that Richard had had a somewhat hectic flirtation with Amanda the preceding Christmas, and she had been greatly disappointed that nothing had come of it.

Lady Marie had little hope that Richard would really settle down, even if he did marry. She had only the vaguest ideas about his work-having been led to believe that he carried information that was considered too confidential to entrust to paper from Mr. Pitt to the British Ambassadors in various capitals, then acted as a liaison officer, as required, between them-and she knew that foreign travel had become the breath of his life, so it was most unlikely that he would be prepared to give it up. She did not even think that it would be a good thing for him to do so. He was much too imaginative and highly-strung to be happy with the humdrum pursuits of a country squire. She supposed that part of his character came from her own West Highland folk, as they had always been mercurial in temper, and better at thinking out a skilful plan for raiding their neighbors' cattle than sticking to the unexciting business of rearing their own. It was just as well that the boy had also inherited some of his father's practical good sense and tenacit f purpose. '

Lady Marie herself had plenty of good sense and knew that it was useless to try to make a silk purse out of a sow's ear. Her son's interests were not in country things. They were in books, pictures, ancient cities and strange foreign customs ; so it was right for him that he should spend a large part of his life in places where he could enjoy such things.

But she did not see that as any bar to Richard marrying. As a sailor, her own husband had often been separated from her for years at a stretch by his duties, and that had not prevented them from being very happy. Such absences often had the effect of making the spiritual tie much deeper; and she felt that the time had come when Richard should get married. His first love, for Athénais de Rochambeau, had kept him out of serious trouble as a youth; but last year there had been that unfortunate episode with the Russian woman; and now it was possible that he might get himself tied up at any time with some other foreigner. Lady Marie felt very strongly that only marriage with the right type of English girl could give him the solid background that he lacked.

Amanda's uncle was Sir Harry Burrard; he was the richest man, and his estate of Williamston the finest property, in the district. But, far more important in Lady Marie's eyes, she thought Amanda just the sort of daughter she herself would have liked to have. It was not that Amanda was especially beautiful, or good or intelligent; but she had a certain something that made women her friends as well as men. She was at times an absurdly vague creature, and often said the most outrageously silly things, but always with such airiness and charm that people loved her for it. When she spoke to anyone she always looked them straight in the eyes and her mouth, which was one of her best features, was always a trifle open, ready to break into laughter. She always behaved with naturalness, and she could afford to, as no one had ever known her to express a mean thought or do an unkind action. But perhaps the real secret of fascination that she exercised over both sexes was that, although she was so vague about mundane matters, she possessed the tolerance and understanding of human frailties, which goes only with real wisdom.

One thing Lady Marie had omitted to mention to Richard was that Amanda, having no male relative of an age suitable to escort her available at Williamston, had asked if she might bring a beau of hers who was a Captain of Dragoons. Naturally Lady Marie had assented, and she had been delighted, as she felt that nothing could be better calculated to arouse Richard from his torpor than the sight of the young woman for whom he had shown an inclination hotly pursued by another admirer.

This time it was Lady Marie who had wrought better than she knew, for had she had the choice of all the men in England she could not have provided Amanda with an escort more certain to electrify her son. As they stood together that evening just inside the drawing-room, receiving their guests, old Ben, the houseman, now raised to the rank of butler by the donning of his black coat, announced: `Miss Amanda Godfrey. Captain George Gunston'

Richard stiffened and the blood drained from his face. Gunston had been at Sherburne with him and had distinguished himself only as the bully of their year. Many a 'time he had taken an oafish delight in tormenting young `Bookworm Blane', as he had dubbed Richard. Since, they had fought a duel with pistols, each wounding the other slightly and, at the insistence of their seconds, afterwards made up their quarrel. But although they had observed the formality of dining together when they had recovered from their wounds they had no single trait in common except courage, and Richard still regarded George with an almost passionate hatred. The very sight of him, therefore, was like that of a red rag to a bull.

Next moment Richard had completely recovered himself, and was welcoming the couple as a well-bred host. Once he had sustained the initial shock he gave Gunston the credit for being less prone to bear rancor than himself. It was, too, much easier to forget having been a bully than having been bullied; so it seemed

only fair to assume that Gunston would never have come to the house had he not regarded the past as over and done with.

But as the party got under way Richard was quick to observe that Gunston adopted a possessive attitude towards Amanda, and, evidently having heard of her affair with his host, was deliberately flaunting her under his nose. The hearty soldier's by-play was of the clumsiest, so it was soon apparent that he had accepted the invitation for the fun of crowing over his old enemy; and that was more than Richard was prepared to stand.

It was not that he was in the least in love with Amanda. They had had only a brief holiday romance of the very lightest kind. He had scarcely given her a thought in the past six months, and now, his heart turned to stone by the loss of Tansanta, seeing Amanda again in any normal circumstances would not have made the least impression on him. Had she produced any other man and introduced him as her fiancé, Richard would have wished her joy with all possible sincerity. But he was certainly not going to let George Gunston pose as a beau of the most sought-after girl in the district. It seemed even possible that Amanda might be thinking of George seriously. That would never do. She was much too nice a person for a lout like that.

Richard let George have his fun for an hour or so, then took an opportunity to go up and talk to him and Amanda just as they were moving off to the buffet after a dance. He could not help noticing that they made a striking couple. George was as tall as and broader than himself; a fine specimen of manhood; handsome in a florid way, with a crop of ginger curls, and he derived an added glamour from his scarlet uniform. Amanda was also redheaded, but her hair was of a much darker shade, which reminded Richard of the Titian locks of Donna Livia. But Donna Livia's hair had been only artificially curled, whereas Amanda's had a natural crinkle, which at times made it almost unruly. She was a little above medium height and had a fine figure; her skin was milk-white but inclined to freckle in the summer. Her features were strong rather than pretty, and it was her laughing mouth that gave her whole face such charm.

It soon emerged that George's regiment was now quartered in Leamington Barracks, for the purpose of readily supporting, whenever called upon, the operations of the Preventive Officers against smuggling. Richard knew quite well that such arrangements were customary, but with an air of complete innocence he suggested that since George had become interested in the suppression of crime he ought to transfer to the Police.

The soldier flushed, and stuttered something to the effect that no gentleman would consider soiling his hands with such dirty work. Upon which Richard blandly apologized for his ignorance and enquired the difference between catching smugglers and cutpurses.

Gunston had never been quick-witted or overburdened by intelligence.

Moreover he had spent the past six years among the provincial society of garrison towns; whereas Richard had been born a man of parts, and since leaving school had walked in Courts and talked with Kings. He could tap his snuff-box with the air of a Prince of the Blood, and launch a sarcasm with the swift acidity of Mr. Pitt. Without ever overstepping the bounds of courtesy imposed upon him by the fact that he was in his own house, ten times in ten minutes, by some subtle inference, he made Gunston look cheap and foolish. Then, with a delicate flutter of his lace handkerchief as he bowed to Amanda, he excused himself to look after his other guests.

He danced with Amanda only once that evening, and afterwards they sat together on the , curved staircase leading up to the first floor. When she charged him with having been unkind to George, he looked at her in feigned astonishment, and said:

'Unkind! My dear Amanda, why in the world should you think that? I regard him as a prodigious fine fellow. He is so indisputably right in his setting-and so very British.'

'You cannot deceive me,' she smiled. `You think him a bore; but he has many qualities that make him at this moment a better man than yourself. I would rather hear him blurt out his honest opinions than listen to you airing the shallow cynicisms you have learnt abroad.'

Richard realized that he had overplayed his hand; but her remark did nothing to lessen his conviction that Gunston was a coarse-grained brute. On the contrary, it determined him to take the implied challenge, so he asked Amanda if she would go for a ride with him the following morning.

From mid-August they went for rides almost daily, and met at every party given in the neighborhood. At Priestlands, Vicar's Hill and Backland Manor they danced half the evening together. But Richard was vaguely conscious that he was not as popular among his old friends as he had been in the past. They could not complain of his manners, but sensed hardness in him that had not been there before. His interests had grown away from theirs, and thinking he had become conceited they openly showed their preference for the simple, boisterous George, who, if he had never graced a Court, was `a darn' good man to hounds'.

And George fought back. He was nothing if not persistent, and Amanda never failed in kindness to him; but Richard's goading at length provoked an open quarrel. When three parts drunk one night, early in September, after a ball at Highcliffe Castle, he challenged Richard to a duel.

It was against the canons of any two men who had already, fought to fight a second time, except in very exceptional circumstances, and Richard knew that if the affair was noised abroad George would risk the loss of his commission. As Richard was the challenged party the choice of weapons and place lay with him, so next morning he sent two friends to tell Gunston's seconds that his choice was swords, but that unless George could obtain his Colonel's permission to fight with naked blades they would settle the matter with buttoned foils in the courtyard at Williamston, under the cover of a fencing tournament, which could easily be arranged for the purpose.

George realized that he had no alternative but to accept these conditions, so a day was fixed and a dozen bouts arranged, with Richard and George as the concluding contest. A numerous company, including Amanda and two-score other ladies, assembled to see the sport, which was just what Richard wanted.

Everyone present was aware of the bitter animosity that lay between the participants in the last bout, so as it began a hushed expectancy fell on the spectators. George was no bad swordsman, but Richard had learned the art in French schools as well as English, and was infinitely his superior. For the first few minutes he merely played with George to amuse the ladies, then he proceeded to whip him round the yard as though he was a novice being given a harsh lesson by a professional. In the bouts that followed Richard was an easy winner, and it was not until the final that he had to extend himself fully against the hard-bitten Major of Hussars, but he won the bout by five points to three.

George Gunston was not the type of man who gives way to tears, but afterwards, had he been able to, he would have done. Yet Richard gained no immediate benefit from his public triumph. Secretly he felt rather ashamed of himself for the way in which he had behaved; so he was not surprised when Amanda told him with, for her, quite unusual sharpness, that it had been ungenerous in him to humiliate his rival to such a degree, or that she had spent the evening consoling George for his defeat. Nevertheless, the affair took the entire swagger out of George, and his mortification was so keen that two days later he left the field clear to Richard by going on leave.

When Richard first heard the news he was delighted; but very soon his victory turned to dust and ashes in his mouth. He realized only too clearly that for the past month his efforts had been directed to ousting George, not winning Amanda, and now -he had her on his hands. He knew, too, that although he had been driven to it by his unhappiness, ever since the night of the dance his mother had given for him he had played a part quite unworthy of himself ; and the thought that he might now cause Amanda pain by having led her on added further to his misery.

A week after the fencing tournament she brought matters to a head herself. She was an unconventionally minded young woman who cared little what servants, or anyone else, thought of her; so on several occasions in the previous winter she had slipped out of her uncle's house after everyone else was in bed to go with Richard for walks round the grounds in the frosty moonlight; and soon after his return they had resumed these clandestine meetings.

Now, on these warm summer nights, if they had not been out dancing, they usually went down to one of Williamston's three lovely wood fringed lakes and, getting out a punt from the Chinese pagoda boathouse, spent an hour or so on the water.

On this occasion they were drifting gently, looking up at the myriad stars, and had been silent for a few minutes when Amanda said quietly.

`Do you not think the time has come when you should ask my uncle for my hand in marriage?'

Richard stiffened on the cushions where he lay. Subconsciously he had recently been dreading such a situation; and although he was extremely fond of Amanda as a companion he still felt that he would never love anyone, apart from Tansanta, sufficiently to want to marry them.

After a moment she gave her low laugh. `Be not distressed, my dear, at the prospect of so awful a fate; for did you ask me I would not have you.'

His relief was mingled with the most acute embarrassment. He could not be certain that she really meant what she had said, and was desperately anxious not to hurt her feelings. But before he could think of anything appropriate to say, she went on:

`You are in love with someone else, are you not?'

'I'll not deny it,' he confessed. `And if I have led you to think otherwise my only excuse is a genuine fondness for you. Yet that is no real excuse and I feel so meanly about it now that I could throw myself in the lake from shame.'

`Do nothing so desperate, I beg,' she smiled ; `for the resulting scandal would prove my utter ruin. But I knew it all along from your kisses. Your heart does not lie in them. Tell me about her.'

Richard shrugged unhappily. `I will spare you the harrowing details. She is a Spanish lady that I met abroad. Although she is of the Popish faith we had plighted our troth; but her family intervened, and she is now married to another; so my case is hopeless.'

`That accounts, then for the new bitterness that all your friends have observed in you since your return. But it will pass. You must occupy your mind, Richard, and with something of more worth than making a fool out of a poor booby like George Gunston.'

`You are right,' he sighed, `and prodigious generous to me in taking my ill conduct to you so well.'

'Think no more of that,' she said after a moment. `I have derived much pleasure from your company, and shall ever think of you with kindness; though we can no longer continue as at present. As long as George was dancing attendance on me I could afford to let you do so too; for it was assumed that I was hesitating as to which of you I would take. But by driving him away you have put a period upon our intimacy. All south Hampshire will now expect to hear of our engagement, and if they do not, malicious tongues will begin to wag. That I may be spared such unpleasantness either you or I must shortly take coach and leave Leamington to think what it will.'

Full of contrition at the awkward situation in which he had placed her, Richard immediately volunteered to leave the next day. But, on second thoughts, he suggested that, if it would not too seriously interfere with her plans, it would be better for her to leave first, as that would give the impression that it was she who had broken off their affair.

As it was now mid-September, and a few people would be drifting back to London, Amanda agreed that his idea was a sound one. Kissing him lightly on the cheek she declared that she would announce her departure for the end of the week. He, rather shamefacedly, returned her caress and said that until she went he would press his attentions more assiduously than ever. then shut himself up at home as though broken-hearted at losing her. A moment later they saw the funny side of the little comedy they proposed to play for the benefit of their acquaintances, and were laughing over it.

So Richard got out of the mess in which he had landed himself far easier than he deserved, and he was genuinely sorry when, with the longest face he could pull, he watched her coach drive away to London. Her going left him lonely once more and even his disappointed mother was taken in by the return of his moodiness. He had no need to act a part, as with lack of companionship his thoughts turned inwards again and with the loss of Amanda he felt more bitterly than ever the, to him, infinitely greater loss of Tansanta.

In consequence, Lady Marie was not surprised when, three days after Amanda's departure, he announced that he would shortly be returning to France. The following Wednesday he took passage in a brig sailing with a cargo of salt from Leamington, and on the evening of Thursday September the 24th landed at Le Havre.

CHAPTER FIFTEEN
THE ASSASSINS

The upheavals that had shaken France only two months earlier were of such magnitude that Richard expected many signs of their repercussion to be visible in so large a city as Le Havre; so he was somewhat surprised to find that, apart from the new uniforms of the National Guard, there was little overt evidence to show that the Revolution had ever taken place. The town was orderly and people going about their business in a normal fashion.

There being nothing to detain him there, next morning he bought a bay mare with a white star on her forehead, and set out for Paris. Inland, just as in the Pas de Calais, here and there the blackened walls of roofless chateaux told their horrifying tale ; but others that had escaped the holocaust still dignified the countryside, and within sight of them the peasants were placidly working in the fields as they had done for generations.

Paris, too, showed little outward change, except that fewer private equipages with footmen in attendance were to be seen in the streets than formerly ; so it seemed at first sight that France had come through the birth-pangs of her regeneration surprisingly quickly.

But Richard soon learned that all was far from well beneath the *surface. At La Belle Etoile,* his landlord answered an enquiry as to how he did with a glum shake of the head. Business had never been so bad as during the past month. Every man now considered himself as good as his master, which was foolish because the world could not go on that way; and what good did it do anyone to assume such superior airs if it brought no money into their pockets? The workpeople now had to be asked to do every little tiring instead of accepting an order, and they did it or not as they felt inclined. Most of them idled away half the day, but they expected their wages just the same at the end of the week. In fact they were demanding more. In that Monsieur Blanchard would have sympathized with them, had they been willing to do an honest day's work ; as corn was still terribly scarce and the cost of living higher than ever. But one could not pay people higher wages when one's own takings had fallen by more than 50 per *cent. That* stood to reason. Where all the money had gone he did not know. It was said that the thousands of aristocrats who had emigrated at the beginning of August had taken it all with them. There might be some truth in that. It was certainly no longer in Paris.

Wherever Richard went he heard the same gloomy story, and he soon became aware of the reason that lay behind it. On the 4th of August an extraordinary scene had taken place in the National Assembly. A report on the disorders in the Provinces had been presented the previous day and the deputies were considering how to produce some measure which would appease the fury of the peasants.

Two noblemen, the Vicomte de Noailles and the young Duc d'Aiguillon, came forward and proposed that a solemn declaration should be made assuring future equality of taxation for all and the suppression of feudal burdens, except in certain cases where they should be redeemable by long-term purchase. Others rose to support the motion and there followed a stampede of self-denial which afterwards earned the session the name of `The Night of Sacrifices'.

The Bishop of Chartres proposed the abolition of the game laws; de Beauharnais that punishment for crime should be the same for all classes, and that all ranks in the Public Services should be thrown open to everyone; de la Rochefoucauld that the vote be given to all serfs remaining in the Kingdom. The Archbishop of Aix moved the abolition of the salt tax, the Duc de Chatelet that tithes in kind should be commuted, and the Bishop of Uzes recognized the right of the nation to dispose of the property of the Church. The deputies of the Third Estate, not to be outdone, then tumbled over themselves in their eagerness to renounce the privileges of the Provinces and cities they represented.

The renowned economist, Dupont de Nemours, was one of the very few to throw some doubt on the wisdom of this wholesale wrecking of the ancient order, and Count Lally-Tollendal, the foremost Liberal of all the nobles, the only man to keep his head. He sent a note up to the President that read `Nobody any longer has any self-control ; break up the sitting.' But a positive madness had seized upon the assembly. Before dawn it had passed every motion; and since there was no Upper House to send back the bills for reconsideration, they became forthwith the law of France.

The result was catastrophic. In a single night the whole economy of the nation had been destroyed. Already, for a year past, or more, there had been increasing difficulty in collecting taxes; now the people refused to pay any at all. The old courts of justice had continued to function, although with decreasing efficiency; now all feudal courts and many superior ones were wiped out entirely. Overnight the Assembly had destroyed the very foundations of French society without any attempt to create even a vestige of a new system.

It was no wonder that money was scarce. Everyone who had any was now clinging to it from fear that once it was gone they would not be able to get any more. The treasury was empty, the Army and the public services unpaid. And the King could not help, as he had given all his gold plate to the nation as a means of reducing the national debt. What the colossal extravagance of Louis XIV and XV had failed to achieve the National Assembly had accomplished. France was bankrupt.

From Monsieur Aubert Richard learned that there had been changes at the British Embassy in recent months. His last contact with it had been soon after is return from Italy, so he was unaware that early in July Mr. Daniel Hailes had left on a visit to Berlin, as a prelude to becoming Minister Plenipotentiary in Warsaw, and that early in August the Duke of Dorset had gone on leave from which he would not be returning. Lord Robert Fitzgerald had joined the Embassy as First Secretary, in the spring, and vas in charge pending the appointment of a new Ambassador. Richard could well understand that His Grace would have little taste for Paris now that so many of his friends there lead gone into exile, and he was glad to hear of the worthy Mr. Hailes promotion ; but he did not feel that the departure of the latter would greatly affect him, as at their meetings he had generally been the giver, rather than the receiver, of information.

To acquaint oneself with the proceedings of the National Assembly it was no longer necessary to go there, or rely on the often garbled third and fourth-hand accounts of others. After the July insurrections the Press was freed from. all restraint and a number of newspapers, independent of the Government, were now appearing in Paris. They were small in size and more on the lines of political essays than newssheets, but their circulation, particularly that of the more violent ones, soon became immense. Loustallot's The *Revolutions of Paris* reached a sale of 200,000 copies, and a paper called *The Friend of the People,* first issued in mid-September, bid fair to rival it as the organ of the extreme Left. The latter was the work of a doctor of forty-seven, named Marat, a man embittered by ill-success and diseased in body and mind, and his violent diatribes against the rich did more than any other single factor to inspire the bestial excesses later committed by the mobs.

But whatever their shade of opinion, these journals gave the gist of the problems with which the Assembly was concerning itself, so by obtaining a collection of back numbers Richard quickly acquired a general view of the present situation.

Having done so he pondered the problem of whether he should go to Versailles and present himself to the Queen. Now that so many of her friends had gone into exile, and small fry like himself were no longer likely to incur danger from associating with her, he felt confident that she would be pleased to see him. But he decided against it. Power to govern future events did not lie in the royal circle any longer. It was now vested in the leaders of the National Assembly, and a few outstanding men in Paris. Therefore, he felt, little of advantage was to be gained by dancing attendance at the emasculated Court; and, moreover, his hopeless longing for Tansanta still made ~ him so misanthropic that he shunned the thought of engaging again in the light social life he would find there.

This time he had brought with him a few old suits. They were serviceable garments that he wore during the day when at home at Lemington, and in them he could pass easily as a small property owner or respectable business man. So, eschewing his silks and satins, he now went about in honest broadcloth, intent on finding out what His Highness of Orleans was up to, and what was likely to be the outcome of the near-desperate depression in Paris.

As everyone was now equal a man could walk into any public building he liked without let or hindrance, and every committee in the city had its daily crowd of idlers overseeing its proceedings ; so Richard found no difficulty at all in penetrating to the committee rooms of the *Hotel de Ville.*

There, he spent a morning watching the unfortunate Bailly grappling with the problems of feeding the capital. As Mayor it was his duty to ensure the daily bread of 700,000 people, and with commerce breaking down in all directions he could never be sure of more than a forty-eight hours' supply.

Richard left the harassed man with deep sympathy for his unfortunate lot and a great admiration for the way in which he managed to keep a clear head during the often ill-informed digressions of his colleagues, and the frequent interruptions of the still less well-informed onlookers.

Next morning he went to have a look at General Lafayette, and was by no means so impressed. Lafayette was now responsible for the safety of Paris, and the job was clearly beyond his capabilities. His task was, admittedly, a superhuman one, as his troops, apart from the old *Gardes Français,* were all volunteers, and imbued with the new idea that the opinion of a private was as good as, or better than, that of a Colonel. But the orders he issued often appeared contradictory, and he showed great weakness in giving way to the wishes of deputations of the rank and file who presented themselves to him almost hour by hour, without any previous intimation of their coming.

It remained for Richard to see if he could get a dress-circle view of the Duc d'Orléans, and that, too, proved easy, as the Prince, anxious to court the maximum possible popularity, had now opened practically every room in the Palais Royal to the public. That evening, Richard found him in one of the larger salons, surrounded by a crowd of sycophants and being watched by groups of people, apparently composed of both obvious riot-raisers and and casual spectators, who stood round the walls.

Louis-Philippe d'Orléans was then forty-two years old. He had the Bourbon cast of countenance, but his features were not so gross as those of the King, and his manner, in contrast to that of his awkward cousin, was gay, easy and affable. As Duc de Chartres, before the death of his father, he had already acquired the reputation of a rather stupid and very dissipated young man. He was a close friend of the equally dissipated Prince of Wales and often stayed with him in England.

D'Orléans was not distinguished for his courage. With the prospect of succeeding his father-in-law, the Duc de Penthiévre, had decided that as a Lieutenant-General of Marine it was his duty to return. He had done so three weeks earlier ; the Queen had received him most graciously, and told him of Richard's generous but abortive attempt to clear up this misunderstanding on the night that she had sent so many of her best friends abroad.

De !a Marck joined them at that moment. It appeared that the *poissardes* had left the Assembly and were now gathered outside the palace demanding to see the King. The Comte de St. Priest had sent messengers to find His

Majesty, the Queen and also Monsieur Necker; but he was not in the least perturbed, and insisted that the trouble amounted to nothing graver than a bread riot.

Richard joined de la Marck in protesting. Both averred that they had passed armed bands advancing on Versailles. The young Austrian went further and declared that his Embassy had received intelligence that there was a plot on foot to assassinate the Queen, as the only person who had the courage to order armed resistance to the extremists.

The Minister still refused to be convinced, and he was now supported by his colleague the Comte de Montmorin, who had jot-ned the party a few moments earlier.

With de la Marck, de Vaudreuil, the Marshal de Beauveau, the Duc de Luxembourg and the Comte de la Tour du Pin, Richard withdrew to a corner of the room. There they remained for a few moments muttering angrily together. The Foreign Minister, Montmorin, was known to be a creature of the weak-kneed "-Tecker, and St. Priest had also fallen and risen again with the Swiss, so the Queen's friends had good reason to suspect a policy of `better that the King should grovel than we should lose favour with the mob'; but they were powerless to take any .steps for the defense of the palace without the Minister's authority.

At last the King arrived and the Queen appeared shortly after him. The Council chamber was cleared and he agreed to receive a deputation of *poissardes*. The deputy Mounier presented six women, and the King told them that if he had had any bread to give they would not have had to walk to Versailles to ask for it, for he would have sent it to Paris already. Much affected by his sincerity they rejoined their companions outside and endeavored to pacify them ; but they were mobbed and narrowly escaped being hanged from lamp-posts as a result of their sudden change of heart.

The original crowd of women had now been reinforced by hundreds of armed roughs ; but the lattice gates in the iron railings that separated the *Place d'Armes-as* the great square of the town was called-from the courtyards of the palace had been closed against the first arrivals ; and the courts were now manned by the *Regiment de Flandres* and the *Garde du Corps*. The Duc de. Luxembourg, fearing that the gates would be forced, and having standing orders that without the King's authority the people were never to be fired upon, went to the Monarch and asked for emergency orders.

'Orders!' laughed the King, who knew only what his Ministers had told him. `Orders for war against women! You must be joking, Monsieur de Luxembourg.'

Darkness fell and several times the mob attacked the gates. A number of skirmishes occurred with the more audacious who scaled the railings, but the troops succeeded in repelling the assaults without firing on the crowd. It was still pouring with rain, but the angry multitude would not disperse, and continued to howl without while the King held a series of Councils within.

The deputy Mounier had remained, and he importuned the King to sign a *carte-blanche* approval of the new Constitution, as a means of pacifying the people. The King protested against giving his consent to a Constitution that had not yet been formulated, but Necker was now present and urged him to, so eventually he gave way. His complaisance effected nothing, as the mob booed Mounier when he announced this triumph for democracy snatched in an emergency, and roared at him that it was not interested in political rights for tomorrow; it wanted bread today.

The Queen paid several visits to the Council Chamber and at other times paced restlessly up and down the long gallery; but even in her extreme agitation she gave smiles and a few words of recognition to de la Marck, Richard, and a number of other gentlemen who had arrived from Paris to offer their services.

From the scraps about the Council's deliberations that leaked out, it appeared that Monsieur de St. Priest now, belatedly, realized that the lives of the Royal Family were actually in danger; so he and several other Ministers advised an immediate flight to Rambouillet and that the troops should be ordered into action against the insurgents. But the King's evil genius, Necker, and Montmorin, opposed the plan; and by insisting to the Monarch that it must lead to civil war persuaded him to reject it.

At eleven o'clock news came in that Lafayette was advancing from Paris with the National Guard, and that their intention was to take the King forcibly to Paris. Only then did the irresolute man give way to the prayers of those who were begging him to save himself while there was still time. Six carriages were ordered and the Queen, courageously endeavoring to prevent a panic, quietly told her ladies to pack their immediate requirements as they would be leaving in half an hour's time.

But, either through stupidity or treachery, the carriages were ordered round to the gate of the *Orangerie,* to reach which they had to cross the *Place d'Armes.* The crowd, determined to remain where they were until morning despite the rain and wind, had now lit bonfires in the square and were erecting rough bivouacs under the trees for the night. On seeing the carriages they at once guessed the King's intention and rushed upon them. Four were instantly seized and stopped ; the two leading ones, driven at greater speed, succeeded in reaching the *Orangerie,* but again, probably through treachery, the gates were found to be locked. *The mob* caught them up, cut the traces of the horses, and smashed the carriages to matchwood.

St. Priest and de la Tour du Pin then offered their carriages, which were round at a back entrance. In them the Royal Family might yet have escaped. The Queen urged the King to take this last chance ; but once again the malignant Necker intervened, arguing that such an attempt was now too dangerous. The foolish King took the advice of the Minister who had done more to bring about his ruin than any other man, instead of that of his courageous wife. Again deferring to her husband's judgment Madame Marie Antoinette made no further protest, nor did she suggest that she should seek safety with her children. With tears streaming down her face she rejoined her ladies, saying simply

`All is over; we are staying.'

At midnight Lafayette arrived. In one breath he assured the King that he would rather have died than appear before him in such circumstances as the present ; but he had been forced to it and had covered the last few miles only because his men were pushing their bayonets into his back. In the next he said that all his men wanted was to see the King, vouched for their complete loyalty, and offered to be personally responsible for the safety of the Royal Family and everyone within the palace.

The King listened without comment to these heroics, and accepted the guarantee of protection for himself, his family and his servants. Others were not so sanguine. Their Majesties then retired. Lafayette posted detachments of his men round the palace ; then went to bed and to sleep.

Meanwhile de Vaudreuil collected Monsieur de Beauveau, de la Marck, Monsieur de Chevenne, Richard and several other gentlemen, and said to them that he believed the Queen's life to be in extreme danger. The Marquise to Tourzel, who had succeeded Madame de Polignac as governess to the royal children, had told him that during the course of the evening Her Majesty had received not one but several warnings.

One note, from a Minister of the Crown, had contained the words: `Madame, make your plans; or tomorrow morning. at six o'clock you will be murdered.'

A group of loyal deputies from the National Assembly had sought an audience, and assured her that she would be murdered during the night unless she saved herself by immediate flight. She had replied: `If the Parisians have come here to assassinate me it shall be at the feet of my husband. I will not fly.'

They had then asked permission to remain with her; but she said that they needed rest more than she did, and giving them her hand to kiss, had bid them leave her.

As a last resort they had begged her to pass the night with the King; but, knowing that the plot was directed against herself, she refused and ordered Madame de Tourzel, in the event of trouble, to take the children to the King, in order that she might face the danger alone, and keep it away from those she loved.

Finally, when her women besought her to take heed of these warnings, she had said: `I learned f rom my mother not to fear death. I shall await it with firmness.'

When de Vaudreuil had finished telling of these sinister threats and superb courage, none of his hearers had a thought of sleep, in spite of the long day they had been through, and they arranged to post themselves in the various apartments which led to that of the Queen.

Richard was allotted the *(Ell de Bœuf,)* one of the principal salons of the palace, so named from being lit by one large circular window. If the mob did break in it was most unlikely that they would come that way, as it did not contain any of the regularly used approaches to the Queen's apartments; but it was a good central post from which he could be called on for help from two directions.

It was now getting on for two o'clock in the morning. Most of the candles in the big room had been doused and the wood-fires flickered fitfully on the gilded carving of panel surrounds and door pediments. As Richard threw some more logs on one of the fires it flared up, lighting for a moment the pictures in the nearest panels, but the lights in the great crystal chandeliers had been put out and the painted ceiling was lost in shadow.

For a time he sat by the fire and idly followed the chain of events that had led to his being there. This was not his quarrel, and he wondered now at the impulse that had sent him galloping to Versailles in the middle of the day. In part it had been curiosity to see at first hand the outcome of this new crisis ; but it had also been something more than that. He recognised that as a class the nobles and prelates were now getting no more than they deserved as a result of generations of indolence and avarice, but many of the present generation were liberal-minded men and quite a number of them had shown him friendship. The cause of the people might be just, but the great bulk of them would also become sufferers in the long run unless order could be maintained; so it was fitting that every man, whatever his nationality, should lend his hand to resist violence.

Above all there was the Queen. As he thought of her innocence, kindheartedness and courage, he was glad to be sitting there; and knew that if the attack matured, and he lived *through it,* he would always feel proud and honored at having drawn his sword in her defense.

Each time he found his thoughts drifting he stood up and walked about for a little to keep himself awake. An officer and two gentlemen of the bodyguard came through the apartment on their rounds every hour, otherwise the palace now seemed sunk in exhausted sleep. But it was not so with a large part of the 30,000 troops and 10,000 brigands massed outside. The drums beat all-night and, sodden with the rain, gave out a hollow, menacing note.

It was half-past four in the morning when Richard started up from his reverie at the sound of a musket-shot. There followed a dull clamor pierced with yells and more firing, but muffled by the passages and walls. Richard had been asked to remain at his post, unless called on for help, so he eased his sword in its scabbard and with straining ears listened to the tumult that had broken out somewhere on the ground floor of the palace.

After a few minutes there suddenly came a sharp rapping on the wall near which he stood, and a voice cried: 'Open! Open! Let us through! Let us through!'

Moving quickly to the place from which the sounds were coming, he stared at it. Only then, in the dim light, did he perceive the crack of a small doorway, which had been skillfully concealed. It was barely five feet high and two and a half across; the upper part of it cut through the corner of a panel that contained a picture, and it followed so exactly the molding of the wall as to be imperceptible to the casual glance. De Vaudreuil had not told him of its existence when posting him in the Æil *de Bœuf, f,* and he had no idea where it led.

The banging and shouts on the far side of the door had now reached a crescendo. Richard thought that it was the mob who were trying to break through, and he hastily looked to either side along the dim passages for help to defend it when it gave way. But both the long corridors leading from the room were deserted. From the distance, shouts, shrieks and the trampling of many feet could be heard.

Suddenly he realized that the voices beyond the panel held an imploring note and were those of women. It was possible that some of the inmates of the palace were endeavoring to escape that way from an attack on a range of apartments that lay beyond the door. Yet he could not be certain, and if he opened it he might be overwhelmed by the mob in a matter of seconds.

Still he stared at the door, desperately uncertain what to do ; then he caught a cry above the rest: *'Mon Dieu! Mon Dieu! Ouvre la porte ou nous sommes mortes!'*

Hesitating no longer, he found the small catch lock and, inserting his finger in the shallow slot, pulled it back. The door burst open, and the Queen almost fell into his arms.

She was in her nightdress with only a petticoat pulled loosely over it, and clutched her stockings in her hand. Stumbling past him, and followed by two of her women, she ran across the wide parquet of the Æil *de Bœuf, f* , wrenched open another low, concealed door on the far side of it and disappeared.

Later Richard learned that the door he had opened gave on to her dressing room, and was used only as a private means of communication between her and the King, the similar door through which she had disappeared giving on to his apartments. And that normally the little door was kept locked only on her side of it, so that night some murderous hand must have locked it on the side of the Æil de Bæuf to prevent her escaping that way from her assassins.

He learnt too that had it not been for the loyalty of her women she would certainly have been murdered. Madame Auguié and Madame Thibaut, with their two *femmes de chambre,* had ignored her orders to go to bed, and the four of them had sat up with their backs against her bedroom door. At the first sounds of com- motion Madame Auguié had run to the door of the ante-chamber and found one of the bodyguard, Monsieur de St. Marie, his face covered with blood, defending it against a horde of *poissardes,* who were screaming: 'We have come in our white aprons to get the Queen's bowels, that we may make red cockades out of them!'

Slamming and relocking the door Madame Auguié had rushed back to the bedroom. Madame Thibaut had in those few seconds roused the Queen; and they had succeeded in getting her away before the doors of the ante-room were broken in.

The Queen had hardly entered the King's apartments when a dozen *Guarde du Corps* and other gentlemen came running into *the Æil de* Bæuf f with drawn swords. Among them was Madame de Tourzel with the Royal children. When they had followed the Queen, their escort drew themselves up in front of the door, ready to defend it with their lives.

Pandemonium had now broken loose in the Queen's apartments. Drawing his sword Richard ran through the dressing room. He found the bedroom empty, but in the antechamber beyond it a fierce struggle was taking place. Some of Lafayette's National Guard had arrived upon the scene and were fighting with the members of the bodyguard, whom they had been told were plotting to surprise and massacre them.

De Vaudreuil was there standing on a table, shouting that they had been told a pack of lies, and begging both sides to put up their weapons. His Liberal sentiments were known, so some notice was taken of him. Then Monsieur de Chevanne ran forward and, baring his breast, offered himself as a victim if the citizen soldiers demanded one. With the swift change of sentiment so typical of the French the attackers immediately acclaimed him a hero, embraced the members of the bodyguard and swore to defend them from their comrades.

But all was not yet over. The mob had fought its way up the great marble staircase and penetrated to the Æil Æil de *Bœuf. f* . *By* another entrance Lafayette had arrived and reached the King, whose only reproach to him was: `Monsieur, had I foreseen that you would be obliged to sleep, I should have remained awake.'

Although belatedly, Lafayette now showed both loyalty and considerable courage. Out in the courtyard he saved the lives of ten bodyguards by offering his life for theirs ; then declared that he would no longer command cannibals, and would resign his post unless his men would accept his orders. This turned the tide and his troops began to clear the place of the *sans-culottes.*

They were assisted in their task by the bodyguards and courtiers. In a hundred rooms, scores of corridors and on a dozen staircases, altercations and scuffles were going on. The majority of the rabble, now finding the National Guards against them, offered no resistance and slouched off, hurling curses over their shoulders ; but, here and there, groups put up a fight and could not be turned out without bloodshed. In one such group, Richard saw a tall fishwife slash at a soldier with a hatchet, wound him in the arm, duck under the guard of another and run from the room. Sword in hand, he went after her.

The clothes of the *poissardes* amounted almost to a uniform, so it was easy to distinguish them. Most of the women were great muscular creatures, coarse-mouthed and brutal-faced; but Richard had been surprised to see that many of them were much above the average height. The one that he was chasing looked as tall as himself.

Seeing two Swiss guards approaching along the corridor, she darted up a service staircase. Richard dashed after her and caught sight of her again on the next floor. Shouting at her that if she halted and agreed to leave the palace quietly he would not harm her, he pursued her down the passage. At its end she came to a door and, finding it locked, turned at bay.

As Richard came pounding up he saw her face clearly for the first time. It was not that of a woman, but of a man. Next second he realized that his quarry was de Roubec.

Instantly there recurred to his mind the words he had overheard in the Palais Royal a few nights before--about not giving out the women's clothes until a first-class opportunity presented itself. This, then, explained why so many of the *poissardes* were much taller than the average woman. The Orleanists had taken advantage of the ancient liberty accorded to the fishwives of Paris to approach the King and Queen without formality, to disguise a number of assassins in the type of garments the poissardes always wore, so that they could mingle with the real *poissardes* and under that cover commit the heinous task they had been given.

The revelation of this new piece of treachery added fuel to Richard's wrath. He had no thought now of settling his old score by slicing off the villain's ears and nose. With a cry of rage he rushed forward, intent to kill. De Roubec was half-crouching against the locked door with his hatchet raised to strike, but he never delivered the blow. It had been only a second before that he had recognized his pursuer. The knowledge that it was Richard now seemed to paralyze him with fear. The blood drained from his face. His unshaven chin showed blue in the early-morning light, making his lean visage more than ever incongruous under its woman's bonnet. His mouth dropped open, showing his yellowed teeth. It seemed that he was about to scream for mercy; but there was time neither for him to ask nor receive it. Richard leapt the last few paces that separated them. His feet landed with a thud upon the floor. At the same instant he drove his sword through the cowering man's body.

De Roubec's eyes started from his head, a long low moan issued from his lips; suddenly he slid sideways and collapsed in a heap. Richard put his foot on the torso, gave his sword a twist, drew it out, and wiped it on the hem of the dark skirt beneath the *poissardes* white apron. .

For a moment he stood there frowning down upon the man who had caused Tansanta and himself so much misery. They might by now be married and gloriously happy together in England had it not been for de Roubec's evil activities in Florence. Richard felt not an atom of compunction at having struck him down like a rat in a corner. To his mind the self-styled Chevalier had earned dearth thrice over; twice for having wrecked Tansanta's life; and his own, by bringing about their separation, and a third time for having participated in the attempt to assassinate the Queen.

The sound of more firing and fresh tumult down below recalled Richard to the present, and while he was still staring at de Roubec's body an idea flashed into his mind.

It was by no means certain yet that Lafayette would succeed in clearing the palace of the insurgents. The National Guards were not to be relied on; at any moment some incident might turn them from , their grudging obedience to renewed fraternization with the mob, then support of it. Should that happen the bodyguard would be overwhelmed and the Royal Family again in dire peril. Even if Lafayette's men did continue to obey him for the next few hours there was still the persistent rumor that they meant to take the King to Paris, and if they did it was certain that the Queen would refuse to be separated from him. In either case, it seemed to Richard, if things went well his presence would be redundant, but if they went badly he would stand a better chance of keeping near the Queen and, perhaps, being able to defend her in an emergency, if he disguised himself as a *poissardes* than if he remained in his ordinary clothes.

Hastily pulling off his coat and unbuckling his sword-belt, he began to strip de Roubec of the coarse female garments he was wearing. On stepping into the petticoats and ragged skirt he found that they came to within an inch of the floor, hiding his riding boots. Untying the queue at the back of his neck he shook his head hard,. and ran his fingers through his *medium-long* brown hair until it was sticking *out wildly in all* directions; then he put on the bonnet and pulled its frill low down over his forehead. To his grim amusement he found that de Roubec had been wearing breast pads, so he put on this false bosom and over it the high-necked cotton blouse. His sword he picked up to carry in his hand, as most of the *poissardes* were armed and one of them might easily have taken it from a fallen bodyguard.

Looking out of a window he saw that the mob was now steadily being ejected from the front entrance of the palace, and decided that he had better join it ; but in his new role he knew it might go hard with him if he fell foul of a group of angry Loyalists, so, hiding from time to time, he cautiously made his way down a back staircase and out through a side entrance.

As he mingled with the mob no one took any notice of him, and he gradually worked through the crush till he got to its densest part, which was swaying in a tightly packed mass that jammed the whole of the Cour *de Marbre.* From time to time there were sporadic shouts for the King, and in the course of an hour they steadily increased till they became a loud, imperative demand to see him.

At length he came out on the balcony, and the fickle populace cheered him ; but after a few moments the cries of *Vive lc Roi!'* died away and the crowd began to call for the Queen.

The King retired and the Queen appeared; she led Madame Royale by the hand and carried the Dauphin in her arms. The crowd hissed and booed, then a shout went up: `We want you without your children! No children! No children!'

Madame Marie Antoinette withdrew. A moment later she reappeared on the balcony alone. Her eyes were lifted to Heaven and she held her beautiful hands shoulder high, in an attitude of surrender.

Richard's heart missed a beat and he closed his eyes. The same thought had leapt into his mind as was already in hers. The conspirators had demanded her presence alone because they did not wish to risk harming the children, but intended to shoot her.

She was standing no more than twenty feet above the crowd, so an easy target, even for a pistol-shot ; but her extraordinary courage seemed to stun her enemies. The vast crowd suddenly fell completely silent, then, forced to it by admiration, they began to cry, Wive *la Reine!'*

After the Queen had gone in, the crowd called for the King again. When he came out there were more cheers, but a few voices started up the cry: 'To Paris! To Paris!'

He went in, but they had him out again, a dozen times in the next hour ; and every time the voices grew more insistent, until the cry became a chant:

`To Paris! To Paris! To Paris!'

Afterwards Richard heard from de la M Marck that each time the King had gone in, he had flung himself down in an elbow-chair, moaning: `I know not what to do! I know not what to do!'

Lafayette asked the Queen her intentions, and she replied coldly: `I know the fate that awaits me in Paris, but my duty is to die protecting my children at the feet of the King.'

Eventually Lafayette came out on the balcony and announced that the King and his family would accompany the National Guard back to Paris at midday.

Expecting the royal party to catch up with them, a part of the mob left at once, bearing on poles the heads of Messieurs Deshuttes and de Varicourt, two of the bodyguard whom they had murdered. At Sevres they halted, and seizing upon a wretched barber compelled him to undertake the gruesome task of dressing the hair on the dead heads.

By one o'clock the main contingent began to follow them to Paris. Several battalions of the National Guard, and another section of the mob, led the miles-long procession. Then came the royal coach, containing the King, Queen, Dauphin, Madame Royale, the King's young sister Madame Elizabeth, the Comte and Comtesse de Provence, and Madame de Tourzel. There followed carriages containing the royal household and then, since the National Assembly had declared its inseparability from the neighborhood of the King, more than a hundred additional carriages filled with the deputies. The rear was brought up by sixty wagon-loads of grain seized from the municipality of Versailles, and more National Guards mingled with the last of the rioters.

Richard was now both very tired and very hungry. He had not slept for thirty hours and had had nothing to eat since a light snack taken in the palace the previous evening at a hastily arranged buffet. But as the procession moved off he elbowed, cursed, jostled and joked his way through the crush until he was within twenty feet of the royal carriage. He could get no nearer as the press was so great that it appeared to be borne on the shoulders of the sea of poissardes that surrounded it.

Craning his head above the crowd now and then, he kept as constant a look-out as lie could. He had thrust his sword through a hip-high hole in his skirt, and had his pistols stuffed into his false bosom ;but he realized now that though his having dressed as a poissardes had secured him a place within sight of the Queen, there was very little chance of his being able to intervene if any of the canaille attempted to harm her. Several times while the procession had been forming up lank-haired, brutal-faced ruffians had screamed out: `Death to the Austrian harlot!' leveled their muskets at her and fired them off. Whether their aim had been bad, or others nearby had knocked their muskets up, Richard could not tell, but each time the bullets had whizzed harmlessly over her head. In no instance had he been near enough to grapple with her attacker, and he knew now that if she was shot all he could hope to do was to endeavor to mark her murderer down and later exact vengeance.

The King, with his usual bravery in the face of personal danger, had sought to shield her with his body, then, placing a hand on her shoulder, forced her to kneel down in the bottom of the carriage until the procession got under way. His complaisance in agreeing to go to Paris had once again brought him a wave of. false popularity, and the firing ceased. Since their fat puppet had done as they wished the mob were pleased with him. Their mood became jocular, and they began to shout: `We've got the baker, the baker s wife and the baker's boy, so now we shall have bread.' But they still took delight in insulting the Queen; the whole way to Paris they sang the filthiest songs and threw the most obscene epithets at her.

The march seemed never-ending. Actually, owing to the slow pace of the multitude, and the frequent halts caused by lack of march discipline in the long column, it occupied seven hours. At long last Paris was reached, and Bailly, with more fulsomeness than tact, greeted the King with the words: `What a beautiful day this is, when the Parisians are to possess Your Majesty and your family in their town.'

Night had fallen, but the ordeal was not yet. over. The Royal Family was dragged to the *Hotel de Ville,* and there compelled to listen for nearly two hours longer to windy speeches. Bailly again spoke of `this beautiful day' and the King replied that he came with joy and confidence into his good town of Paris.

His voice was so low that Bailly shouted in order that the people could hear. `His Majesty wishes me to tell you that he comes with joy into his good town of Paris.'

At that the exhausted but still defiant Queen roused herself and cried: `Monsieur, you omitted to say "with confidence".'

When these grueling proceedings had at last concluded the royal party were allowed to get back into their carriages and, among further scenes of uproar, driven to the *Palais des Tuileries.* There, nothing had been prepared for their reception ; all the living-rooms had either been granted to poor pensioners of the Court or long remained unoccupied. They were damp and dirty and, as it was now ten o'clock, pitch dark. With the few candles that could be found, the Royal Family started to settle themselves in, as well as circumstances permitted, for the night. While the few available beds were being made up the bewildered little Dauphin remarked to his mother: `Everything is very ugly here, Madame.'

`My son,' replied Madame Marie Antoinette, `Louis XIV lodged here and found it very comfortable; we must not be more particular than he was.'

Seeing her utter exhaustion, Madame de Tourzel then took the child from her and to the room which someone had hastily allotted them. It contained only one small bed, had entrances on three sides, and all of the doors having warped none of them would shut. She put the Dauphin to bed, barricaded the doors with alt the movable furniture, and spent the night in a chair at his bedside.

After seeing the Queen enter the *Tuileries,* Richard had staggered back to La *Belle* Etoile. At first, not recognizing him in his strange garments, Monsieur Blanchard refused to let him in. But, croaking out who he was,

Richard pushed past him and swayed, drunk with fatigue, up to his room. He was now long past hunger. He had not closed his eyes for two days and a night. Flinging himself down on his bed still dressed in his woman's clothes, he slept the round.

In that he was luckier than the Queen. Next morning thousands of Parisians, who had not seen the Sovereigns during the recent crisis, surrounded the Tuileries and called on them to show themselves. They spent most of the day in satisfying the demands of an ever-changing crowd.

The King's arrival in Paris temporarily quelled the more general discontent. Although bread was as scarce as ever it was felt that by some miracle.he would now soon ensure an ample supply of it. Whenever he appeared shouts of Wive *le Roi!'* rent the air, and even the Queen reaped a little of his reflected popularity.

But all this was on the surface, and no more than the natural expression of a loyalty to the throne which still animated a great part of the people. The real fact was that on July 16th the King had lost his power to continue as an absolute Monarch, and or. October 6th he had lost his personal liberty. National Guard sentries now stood on duty at all the exits of his palace, in the corridors, and even along the walls of the room in which he fed.

It was no longer easy for the Royal Family even to converse in private.

Such was already the situation when, on the morning of October 8th, clad once more in a quiet suit of his own, Richard went to the . *Tuileries to* pay his respects to the Queen.

He thought that she had aged a lot in the past few days, but she received him with her unfailing courtesy, charm and awareness. She at once recalled his having come to Versailles on the 5th to offer his services, and thanked him on behalf of the King and herself.

. When he asked if there was any further way in which he could be of service to her, she replied: `Our friends are all too few in these days, Mr. Blane. If, without danger to yourself, you feel that you can come here from time to time, I shall always be pleased to see you.'

One good thing at least resulted from the terrible scenes at Versailles on the 5th and 6th of October. Many people averred that they had actually seen the Duc d'Orléans, wearing a heavy great-coat and with a broad brimmed hat pulled well down over his eyes, standing at the top of the marble staircase, pointing out to his assassins the way to the Queen's apartments. In any case it was universally accepted that His Highness had organized the attack on the palace. In consequence he had lost overnight the support of all but the vilest of the mob and a few personal adherents.

There was good reason to believe that men of such diverse views as Necker, Mirabeau, St. Priest, Montmorin, de Périgord and the Duc de Liancourt had all been involved to a greater or lesser degree in a conspiracy to force Louis XVI to abdicate and make d'Orléans Regent. But none of these leaders was prepared to countenance murder as a means of achieving that end, and all of. them realized the danger of inciting the mob to such acts of violence. They condemned the outbreak in the strongest terms and insisted that a public inquiry should be set on foot to investigate its origins.

The Marquis de St. Huruge, who had been definitely identified as one of the men dressed up as *poissardes,* and several others of d'Orléans' intimates, were arrested and, to the consternation of his remaining supporters, on October 14th the Duke left Paris without warning. It later transpired that he had had a brief, frigid interview with the King, and accepted a mission to England; and it was generally assumed that since he dared not face a public enquiry the King had sent him away rather than have a member of his own family exposed as a potential murderer.

During the few weeks that followed the installation of the Royal Family at the *Tuileries,* Richard took the Queen at her word, although, as things seemed to be settling down again, he made no further attempt to play the part of watchdog. He still could not rid himself of his heartache, and the tormenting thoughts of Tansanta, so far away in Naples, that harassed him each night continued to rob him of all joy in life by day ; but he did not allow that to interfere with his work, and stuck to it with dogged, if somewhat gloomy, persistence. The National Assembly now met in the Riding School of the *Tuileries,* and he spent most of his time in its vicinity, cultivating as many as possible of its members in order to gather material for his reports to Mr. Pitt; and every few days he made one of the little group of gentlemen who continued to wait upon the Queen.

It was on November 3rd, while he was attending one of these small gatherings, that Madame de Tourzel came up to him and said in a low voice : `Please to remain, Monsieur, until Her Majesty's visitors have gone. She wishes to speak with you in private.'

Richard obediently outstayed the other ladies and gentlemen who were present, and when they had taken their leave the Queen beckoned him to follow her into a smaller room. Two National Guards had been posted inside the door of the salon. There were none here, but evidently she feared that one of the many spies who were set about her might walk in without permission-as now often happened-for she gave Richard a skein of silk to hold, motioned him to sit down on a stool near her embroidery frame, and sitting down herself, began to wind the silk into a ball. Without raising her eyes from the work, she said in a whisper.

'Mr. Blane, six months ago you undertook a dangerous mission for me, and executed it with skill and courage. I am now in an even more difficult position than I was then, and in much greater need. Nearly everyone who comes here is suspect, but you are less so than most because you are an Englishman; and also because you have been sufficiently discreet not to show the sympathy I know you bear us, by daily attendance at this mockery of a Court to which we have now been reduced. Would you be willing to serve me again by going on another journey?'

Richard felt that the chances were all against his gaining anything by undertaking another mission for her. He had already won as much of her confidence as it was possible for any man in his circumstances to obtain. Moreover another mission would mean his leaving Paris to the detriment of his secret work, and this time there would be no adequate excuse for his doing so which he could give to Mr. Pitt.

Nevertheless, he was not at present involved in any particular undertaking of great moment to his country, and he felt that any displeasure he might incur for having temporarily abandoned his post must not be allowed to weigh against the urgent need of this unfortunate but courageous woman. Better men than himself had jeopardized their careers in causes far less deserving, and he knew that if he refused he would feel ashamed at having done so for the rest of his life. So, loath as he was to risk possible dismissal by his own master, after only a moment's hesitation, he said

`Madame, I will serve you willingly, in any way I can. Pray give me your orders.'

She smiled her thanks, and said with tears in her voice : `It is my son. How I will bring myself to part with him, I cannot think. But I have reached the conclusion that it is my duty to do so. He is France-the France of the future-and it is my belief that if lie remains here he will be murdered with the rest of us.'

`No, Madame, no!' Richard protested. `The situation is now becoming more tranquil every day.'

Impatiently, she shook her head. `Do not be deceived, Mr. Blane. This quiet is but the lull before another and greater storm. Yet I think we may be granted a few months in which to take such measures as we may; and it is my dearest wish that before the tempest breaks the Dauphin should be conveyed to a place of safety. More, if 'tis known that he is beyond the power of our enemies, and in a situation to continue the royal line, that might well prove an additional safeguard to the King, his father.'

Richard nodded. `There is much in that, Madame, and your personal sacrifice may prove to have been well worth while in the long run.'

`But my problem has been where to send him,' she went on. `The people will be furious when they learn that he has been sent abroad, and the National Assembly may demand his return; so it must be to some country which would be prepared to reject such a demand, and if need be incur the ill will of France on that account: I had at first thought of my brother, the Emperor Joseph, but he is again too ill, and his dominions in too great disorder, for me to burden him with such an additional care.'

She was crying now, and as she paused to dab her eyes with a handkerchief, Richard threw a quick glance of apprehension at her.

The obvious alternative seemed her other brother, Leopold of Tuscany, and Florence was the one city 'in Europe to which he could not go without exposing himself to very considerable danger.

After a moment she went on: `The Grand Duke Leopold would, I am sure, take M . le Dauphin at my request ; but he needs a mother's care, and I feel that my sister is more to be relied upon to bring him up as I would wish. First, though, she will have to obtain her husband's consent to receiving a guest whose presence may embroil his Kingdom with France. Will you go for me, Mr. Blane, on a mission to Queen Caroline, and bring me back word whether King Ferdinand is willing to give my son asylum at the Court of Naples?'

CHAPTER SIXTEEN
A NIGHT IN NAPLES

I n an instant Richard's whole outlook on life was changed. For the past five months he had been a misanthrope; bitter, cynical, engaging himself from hour to hour in the first thing that offered, but unable to take a real joy or interest in either pleasure or work. Now, as by the waving of a fairy wand, all his old youth, vigor and enthusiasm flooded back to him.

He had not sought this mission of the Queen. On the contrary, he had agreed to undertake it out of chivalry. And now, accepting this task that had seemed so much against his own interests was to bring him a great reward. The magic word `Naples' meant that he would see Tansanta again.

The thought that she might no longer be there did not even occur to him. The fact that she must now be married cast no shadow on the dawn of his renewed zest for life. Of his own volition he would never have gone to Naples and deliberately risked jeopardizing her relations with her husband; but now, he was being sent there. Fate had relented, and, it seemed clear to him, ordained that they were once more to breathe the same air, watch the stars hand in hand, and listen to one another's happy sighs. For many months his hopeless longing for her had been well-nigh intolerable, and now he had no doubt whatever that it was soon to be satisfied.

As in a dream, he took in the remainder of what the Queen had to say and received from her a locket, containing a miniature of the Dauphin, copied from a recent painting by Madame Vigée le Brun. It was to serve a dual purpose. Firstly, as the frame was set in brilliants in a curious design, and Madame Marie Antoinette had often worn it herself when a child, Queen Caroline would be certain to recognize it; so it would serve as a passport to her and make it unnecessary for Richard to carry any letter of introduction, which might have proved a danger to him. Secondly, the picture it now contained would show Queen Caroline what a charming little boy the nephew was, whom she was being asked to receive and mother.

A dozen times that evening Richard surreptitiously felt the locket, where he had concealed it under the frill of his shirt, to make quite certain that he had not imagined his interview at the *Tuileries* that afternoon. But there it was, the light but solid and slightly scratchy proof that next day he would be on his way to Tansanta. Hardly able to contain himself for joy he packed his gayest clothes in a valise and dashed off a note to Lord Robert Fitz-Gerald, simply stating that urgent business necessitated his absenting himself from Paris for about a month, and asking for that information to be conveyed to Whitehall.

The only cloud on his horizon was the small but very dark one that when he got to Naples his stay there could be only of very brief duration. Madame Marie Antoinette's letter to the Grand Duke Leopold had been a highly private assessment of the leading figures in French politics, -and had called for no reply, so its delivery had not been a matter of any great urgency. But his present task was one of a very different nature. If he delayed in Naples overlong his whole mission might be rendered abortive by some new development in Paris during his absence. In any case poor Madame Marie Antoinette would be on tenterhooks until she received her sister's answer. So it was clearly his duty to get to Naples and return as swiftly as he possibly could.

In consequence, he decided that the only way in which he could square it with his conscience to remain a few days there was to travel with a speed beyond anything that even a fast courier would normally have accomplished. There were post houses every five miles along the main roads, so by changing horses every time he reached one a courier could make the journey to Marseilles in about six days, but such hard riding demanded a good night's sleep at an inn each night. On the other hand a post chaise could travel nearly as fast as relays of riding horses and, with changes of postilians as well as animals, it could continue on its way both day and night. Such a mode of travel was expensive, for it cost *a shilling* a mile; it also entailed great discomfort on the occupant of the post chaise as, after a day or two, its continuous jolting became almost intolerable, quite apart from the fact that it deprived him of all proper sleep. Nevertheless Richard adopted this course without a moment's hesitation, considering it a small price to pay for a few days in which to do as he would, with a quiet mind, at the other end of his journey.

He ordered the post chaise to be at *La Belle Etoile at four* o'clock next morning, and before dawn on November 4th he was out of Paris. There was hardly a stage on his way south that did not bring him vivid memories of Tansanta.

By midmorning he was being driven at a swift trot through the eastern edge of the forest of Fontainebleau, and it was in the forest that he had first met her. Many hours passed and the night was nearly gone when he reached the spot where he had come upon her coach being attacked; but dawn was breaking again as he entered Nevers, and he had a meal at the inn to which she had carried him bleeding from his wounds and sweating with pain; and at which, on a Sunday while the Señora Poeblar and the others were at church, Tansanta had persuaded him to accompany her to Marseilles instead of going to Florence via Chambery and Turin.

It was late that afternoon when, just on the far side of St. Pourcain, he traversed the place where some baggage had nearly fallen on his injured foot, and he and Tansanta had first called one another by their Christian names; and it was the middle of the second night when the chaise mounted the hill beyond Lempdes where, in the close, warm semidarkness of the coach, they had first kissed.

Evening had come again when he pulled up to sup at Orange, where Quetzal had had his encounter with the goat; and it was midnight when the chaise passed through the silent streets of Avignon, recalling to Richard the Senora's death, her dying plea to him to respect Tansanta's chastity and, two days later, the plighting of their troth.

At ten o'clock the following morning the chaise was rattling over the cobbles of Marseilles. He was incredibly tired, had a three days' beard on his chin and was covered with dust, but he had done the journey in three and a quarter days. He had already ordered his leading postilian to take him straight to the *Cafe" d'Acajon,* and as they drove up to it he saw that his luck was in ; Monsieur Golard was quietly taking his morning repast there.

Climbing out of the chaise, Richard stretched his aching limbs; then, apologizing for his disheveled appearance, accosted his old acquaintance. The ship owner recalled their- previous meeting with pleasure, and at once pressed him to take spine refreshment after his journey. To help keep himself awake for a few hours longer Richard ordered black coffee laced d with brandy, and while it was being fetched enquired about sailings for Naples. Monsieur Golard said that he knew of no bottoms due to leave under three days ; but on being pressed, he added that if speed was a greater consideration than either money or comfort, he thought he could arrange for a *felucca to* do the trip by private charter at a cost of about twenty-five Louis.

Richard considered the saving of time well worth the money, and by midday he was aboard a low, lateen sailed craft that had a Corsican captain and a crew of four, all of whom looked like pirates. His main anxiety was that the weather should hold, as he was by no means a good sailor, and feared that if a storm arose such a light barque would receive a most frightful buffeting. On his journey south he had hardly given a thought to the weather, but he realized now that when he left Paris it had been cold, dreary and raining, whereas here in Marseilles it was still as warm as late summer in England, and the midday sun made the low gunnels of the felucca hot to the. touch.

But he was far too tired to take pleasure in the balmy Mediterranean climate at the moment, or even worry very much at the prospect of being seasick if they struck one of the storms to which that treacherous sea is liable in all seasons. No sooner had the vessel cast off from the pier than he dropped down her deck hatch, 'stumbled to the berth that had been made up for him, lay down on his face to spare his aching backside, and fell into a sleep of exhaustion.

During the voyage Fortune continued to favour him. No ominous cloud darkened the horizon and a moderate wind enabled the *felucca* to make good headway. On the second evening out from Marseilles they cleared safely the tricky passage between the islands of Corsica and Sardinia ; and later, looking astern, he enjoyed one of the loveliest sunsets he had ever seen. A sky of salmon, orange and gold threw up into sharp relief the dark outline of the two islands, giving their crags and forests an air of enchanted mystery. Yet even this scene of beauty took second place in his mind to that which unfolded before him the following afternoon.

Soon after midday they raised the island of Ischia, with beyond his beloved's beauty was driven from his mind by an older man remarking 'l f you carry a letter of introduction to Don Diego I fear that you will have no chance of presenting it as yet. He is one of the Court Chamberlains, so from home at the moment, attending, Their Majesties in Palermo.'

Instantly Richard's spirits soared up like a rocket. The statement surely implied that, of all the times in the year that he might have come to Naples, on just these few days he had earned so hardly he would find Tansanta alone, unhampered by a jealous husband. Next second, his spirits fell like lead to his boots. It might equally well, or even better, be implied that she had accompanied her husband to Palermo; in which case those desperately won days would be utterly wasted, and from lack of even a sight of her become as gall and wormwood in his mouth.

From fear of compromising her, he could not possibly ask the all-important question that itched upon the tip of his tongue; so as soon as he could he excused himself, and next had a word with the hall porter.

A straight question elicited the fact that the Sidonia y Ulloas lived in a big villa half a mile further up the hill, and the man described its situation so clearly that it would have been difficult for a stranger to fail to find it, even at night. Then he added as an afterthought: 'The Conde Diego is at present in Sicily with Their Majesties; but I saw the Condesa drive past in her carriage this morning.'

Just as Richard could have slain the wit a few minutes earlier, he could now have kissed the porter. Fortune seemed to be wafting him on 'a magic carpet towards his dearest desires. Yet he did his utmost to conceal his elation, and remarked that, in that case, he must postpone his call.

Exercising an iron control over feet that itched to run, he sauntered slowly across the hall and upstairs to his room. Having collected his cloak he slipped quickly down a flight of back stairs to a side entrance, and so out into the garden. Darkness had come, and despite the warmth of the day the November night was chilly. Drawing his cloak about him, he slid like a shadow between the oleanders along a path to the road, then turning, he set off in yard long strides up the hill.

Within a quarter of an hour he found the villa. It was a big house standing in about three acres of its own grounds. Its front façade was in complete darkness, except for a lantern above the porch. He walked some way round the wall that encircled the garden, hoping to get a full view of the back of the house; but that proved impossible, owing to intervening trees. As far he could see there were no lights in the upper windows. A sudden depression descended on his mind like a damp, cold hand, as it occurred to him that Tansanta might be out at some party and not be returning until the small hours of the morning.

To find out if she was or was not there now seemed more than ever a matter of desperate urgency. Feverishly he began to hunt for a foothold in the wall. After a few minutes' search he found one, stuck the toe of his boot in it, kicked off hard with his other foot, grabbed the top of the wall and hauled himself up till he was astride its coping.

He could see better now. There were lights in three of the downstairs windows. Instantly his depression lifted. Dropping down on the far side of the wall, he thrust his way through a screen of bushes and emerged on to a path. Treading gently now he advanced towards the house. The path ran round a fishpond, and as he skirted it he could see the lighted windows only from an oblique angle. It was not until the path turned inward again, quite near the house, that he could see into the room on to which the three tall windows gave.

His view was partially obscured by muslin drapes, but the heavy brocade curtains behind them had not been drawn, so between the drapes three diamond shaped sections of the interior Were visible. The room was long but of only medium height; the windows ran almost up to its ceiling, and Richard now saw that the canter one was really a pair of narrow double doors that opened on to the garden. He took another few paces forward to get a more direct view of the room. As he did so a section of a woman's skirt, beyond the nearest muslin drape, came into his line of vision. Next moment he could see the whole figure. It was Tansanta.

She was sitting in a low chair reading a book, and as she read she occasionally took a puff at a long cheroot. Richard knew that many Spanish ladies smoked. He had never seen Tansanta do so before, but it occurred to him that perhaps she had been unable to obtain tobacco in that form in France.

His heart was pounding like a sledgehammer in his chest. Had he, six nights before in Paris, been presented with a djinn out of the Arabian Nights to do his bidding, it could not have served him better than his own endurance and luck. He could hardly believe it to be true that he had really found his adorable Tansanta again and found her alone. But there she was, within a dozen yards of him. He had only to open the French window and walk through it to hold her in his arms.

It remained only to let her know of his presence without frightening her and causing her to alarm her household. Stooping, he picked up a few little pieces of lava, from which the path he was standing on was made; then he threw one gently at the window.

At the faint tap it made she looked up, but after a second reverted to her reading. He threw two more in quick succession. She looked up again, staring straight towards him now, yet not seeing him outside in the dark. He threw another. She closed her book, put down her cheroot, stood up, came over to the window, and opening, it a little, called in Spanish: `Who is there?'

Richard's voice came in a whisper: ` 'Tis I, dear heart.'

Tansanta stiffened as though she had been struck with a whip; then her hands began to tremble violently, and she almost whimpered: *'Riché!* It cannot be true! It cannot be true!'

He too was quivering as he stepped out of the shadows. She swayed towards him, her arms outstretched. He sprang to meet her, and drew her into an embrace so fierce that it threatened to crush the very bones of her body. Her mouth found his, and melted under it in a delirious, half swooning kiss.

Nine hours later, just as dawn was breaking, she let him out of the french window, and he stole across the silent garden to the place where he had entered it over the wall. As he straddled it and dropped down on the far side he could well have exclaimed with joy as did Henry VIII on greeting his courtiers the morning after he had been married to Catherine of Aragon Gentlemen, this night I have been in the midst of Spain.'

CHAPTER SEVENTEEN
THE EARTHLY PARADISE

Those nine hours that Richard spent with Tansanta in her great-canopied bed passed for the reunited lovers as though they had been no more than ninety minutes. Neither closed an eye except momentarily to savor better the cup of pleasure, and they were not even called upon to control their transports from fear of being overheard. Tansanta's bedroom lay above the garden room where Richard had found her, and the previous owner of the villa beautiful Neapolitan who had been notorious for her amours had had a narrow staircase connecting the two cut in the end wall of the house, so that whenever she wished she could receive her lovers in secrecy.

The only other entrance to the bedroom lay through an antechamber in which Maria slept at night. She was in Tansanta's confidence and entirely to be trusted. When Tansanta had called her in, and she saw Richard, her fat, honest face had glowed with delight, and she ran to kiss his *hand*. Now that her mistress was married she would have thought her mind unhinged by shock had she failed to reward her lover for his faithfulness *and* restraint while she was still unwed. She had gone downstairs and smuggled them up a supper of oysters, cold truffled pheasant pie, tartlets, fruit and wine; then left them to take their joy of one another. So, at long last, when the gods had decided to be kind to these two young people they had grudged them nothing.

Although the lovers had so much to say to one another, the golden hours sped by so swiftly that when they exchanged their parting kiss it seemed they had said almost nothing. Yet, as Richard made his way, feeling as though he walked on air, back to his hotel, he realized that they had talked of many things.

First, and most important, there were the arrangements for their meeting again. To his unbounded joy there was no impediment to his passing every night with Tansanta until her husband returned with Their Majesties from Sicily. But that was not enough; they were greedy for every hour, for every moment that they could spend in one another's company, and Tansanta had declared that the solution to their problem lay in Richard's immediate introduction to Neapolitan society.

Her grief at losing him had equaled his at losing her, but she had found some consolation in life at Naples. She had expected to find herself virtually a prisoner, hedged about with the same restraints and wearisome etiquette that made existence so dreary for ladies of high rank at the Court of Madrid; but that had not proved the case.

Although King Ferdinand was a Spaniard, during his reign of thirty years various causes had gradually whittled away the Spanish influence in his Kingdom. His father, Don Carlos, while still once removed from the Spanish throne, had conquered Naples and made himself its King; but to win the goodwill of the Neapolitans he had given them a treaty guaranteeing that the crowns of Spain and Naples should never 6e merged upon one head. So, when his half brother died in 1759, and he ascended the throne of Spain his eldest son, Phillip, being an idio he had made his second son, Carlos, Prince of the Asturias and heir to the Spanish crown, and given his third son, Ferdinand, Naples as an independent Kingdom.

Ferdinand, then only a boy of eight, had ruled by a Council of Regency, dominated by his tutor Tanucci ; but a year after Ferdinand attained his majority he had married the Archduchess *Maria Carolina of* Austria. The marriage treaty had stipulated that she should have a say in all affairs of State; and, being a strong willed young woman, she soon got him under her thumb. She had allied herself with the Neapolitan nobility, succeeded in getting Tanucci dismissed, and reversed his policy. Queen Caroline had not gone to the length of attempting to break the Bourbon Family Compact, so Naples was still allied to France and Spain; but in the twenty-one years that she had now been Ferdinand's consort she had modeled his Court on that of Vienna, instead of Madrid, and done away with all the hidebound etiquette with which the Spaniards surrounded royalty.

There were still several great Spanish families, such as the Novinos, Santa Marias and d'Avilas, living in Naples; but they had intermarried with the Sambucas, Monteliones, della Roccas, and other ancient Neapolitan houses; so now formed part of one aristocracy.

Tansanta said that after the glittering Court of Versailles she found these petty princes and their ladies very provincial, but far nicer than the French. As Sovereigns, King Ferdinand and Queen Caroline left much to be desired. Naples was one of the most backward States in Europe, and its peasantry still groaned under the burdens of a feudal tyranny while its rulers concerned themselves with little except their own pleasure. But they mingled freely with their nobility, often in an almost bohemian manner, and this gave an air of spontaneous gaiety to life in their capital.

Everyone of importance in Naples owned one or more villas with lovely gardens, within an easy drive of the city, at Posilipo, Portici or Sorrento; and even in winter the mildness of the climate enabled them to enjoy these properties. Almost every day one or other of Tansanta's friends made up a little party of eight or ten people, to lunch informally and spend the afternoon at a villa along the coast; so while she could not invite Richard openly to her own house, she could get her friends to include him in these parties, and thus spend most of each day with him.

In the Princess Francavilla she had found such a sweet and sympathetic friend that she had confided to her the story of her love affair with Richard; so it would be easy to send the Princess a note that morning and have him invited for the afternoon. After that the Princess would take charge of matters and, without Tansanta being compromised, arrange for him to, be asked by mutual friends to every party where she herself would be.

When he had enquired after Quetzal Tansanta told him that her Indian was well, as devoted to her as ever, and showed great intelligence over his lessons, which now occupied most of his time ; but, unfortunately, had taken an intense dislike to her husband. Feeling that he must find out where he stood, in case Don Diego returned from Sicily earlier than was expected, Richard had then asked, as casually as he could, if she found her husband tolerant to live with, and she had replied.

`I have no reason to complain of him. We were married almost immediately after my arrival here, and I had no option but to submit to his will. As my heart was, and is, yours, 'tis hardly to be wondered at if he found me cold. After the first few weeks he ceased to exercise his rights and openly returned to his mistress. In Naples it is the fashion for every man of quality to keep a mistress, whether he has a use for her or not. He had retained a pretty young thing of seventeen, whom he had been keeping before my arrival ; so my failure to provide a counterattraction caused him no inconvenience.

`For a man of only thirty he is very old-fashioned, and if he could, he would, I am sure, make me live the type of life to which women are condemned in Spain; but fortunately he dare not, for any husband who attempted to put his wife behind bars here would be the laughingstock of Naples. He treats me with grave courtesy and is at most times of a pleasant temper; but now and then he is subject to very black moods. I soon learned their cause. It is not the custom here for men to remain faithful to their mistresses any more than to their wives, and these moods arise each time he had set his mind on some new charmer. They last as long as she rejects him ; but as chastity is the exception rather than the rule among the fair of Naples his black moods are rarely of lengthy duration.'

When Richard asked if Don Diego knew of their own affair, Tansanta had shaken her head. `Had he heard anything of it, I feel sure he would have questioned me; but he has never done so. Fortunately there is little communication between this Court and that of Tuscany, and my cousin, who escorted me hither.

He naturally kept a still tongue for the family's sake. My aunt, of course, wrote to my mother of it, and it was from fear that someone who knew about my clandestine stay in Florence should arrive here that she hurried my marriage forward; but the fact that I had retained my virginity saved me from all but mild reproaches at having been most foolishly indiscreet. She and my father have since returned to Spain; so I do not think anyone here, except my friend Dorian Francavilla, will realize that we have even met before.!

'There could be no harm in letting it be known that we met at

Fontainebleau,' Richard hazarded.

To that she had agreed, and added: `I think it might be well to do so. If we are to meet frequently in company a common interest in the Court of France will provide good grounds for our having a lot to say to one another.'

During his walk down the hill Richard turned these matters over in his mind, and found them all extremely satisfactory. On arriving at *Croeielles* he ordered cans of water to be brought up to his room so that he could have a bath, and while he was having it contemplated his next move.

On his voyage from Marseilles he had decided to make capital out of what he felt to be Mr. Pitt's unmerited rebuke regarding his earlier mission. The Prime Minister had tentatively suggested that he might have sent Madame Marie Antoinette's letter by way of the British Embassy bag, and Richard still felt that to have done so would seriously have jeopardized the credit he was then hoping to gain with her. But he saw now that where he had been at fault was in not making use of British diplomatic facilities when he had arrived in Florence. He could easily have gone to the Ambassador, Lord Hervey, told him the facts, and got him to arrange a private audience with the Grand Duke.

At the time the idea had never occurred to him, but had it done so he could have saved himself a vast amount of trouble, considerable danger, and probably the loss of Tansanta. Now, profiting by his previous shortsightedness, he had made up his mind to wait upon Sir William Hamilton, the British Envoy in Naples, as the best and simplest means of securing an audience with Queen Caroline.

When *he* had told Tansanta his intention during *the past* night, she agreed to its wisdom, and pointed out that as they planned for him to enter Neapolitan society at once, the sooner he waited upon Sir William the better; for if he delayed it might later be thought strange that he had failed to present himself on his arrival. Then she asked him if he knew anything about the diplomat.

When Richard replied that he knew him only by name, she said

`He is a cousin of the Duke of Hamilton, and must now be a man of about sixty. 'Tis said that when he first entered your diplomatic service he had ambitions, but he has been *en post* here for over a quarter of a century, and the *laissez-faire* atmosphere of the city of the bay has now no doubt reconciled him to remaining in this backwater until his career is terminated. He has the bearing of a true aristocrat and is intelligent beyond most. Moreover, he is a man of great taste. His collection of Roman antiques can scarcely be rivaled, and his mistress, although a flamboyant creature, is one of the most beautiful women I have ever met.'

`You know her, then?' Richard exclaimed in some surprise.

`Everybody does,' had come the quick reply. `She lives with h him m at the Palazzo Sessa, but the affaire is conducted very discreetly. His wife, who brought him his fine fortune, died in '82 ; and evidently after a few years of widowhood he found casual amours unsatisfactory to a man of his age and quiet tastes. Three seasons ago he brought out two ladies from England to winter with him in Naples. The elder, a Mrs. Cadogan, he installed as his housekeeper, and it was said that the younger, a Miss Amy Hart, had come here to study art and music. They repeated the visit last year, and are here again now. But there are so many English visitors to Naples that the truth of the matter soon leaked out. Miss Hart, or 'Emma', as he calls her, is Mrs. Cadogan's daughter, and was an artist's model. She sat, I am told, for several paintings by your great artist Romney. Meanwhile she was kept and educated by Sir William's nephew, Charles Hamilton; but he became heavily in debt, so his uncle struck a bargain with him. He paid off his debts in exchange for his beautiful mistress.!'

'Since all this is known, I find it more surprising than ever that she should be received into society.'

`You would not think so if you knew Naples better. The people here count sweetness of disposition as of greater worth than virtue. She is well behaved and does the honours of the Palazzo Sessa charmingly. 'Tis believed by many that they are secretly married and that in reality she is Lady Hamilton. In any case Queen Caroline, whose own morals are not beyond reproach, has made a friend of her, although, of course, she is not officially received at Court.'

A few hours later Richard was still pondering the information Tansanta had given him about this interesting *menage,* when he drove up to the Palazzo Sessa. Sir William was at home, and, after only a short wait, received him.

The elderly diplomat's aquiline features were bronzed by the sun of many Neapolitan summers, but its enervating climate did not seem to have undermined his quick perception, and Richard took an immediate liking to him. As soon as he had disclosed his business, and produced the miniature of the Dauphin, Sir William said. `Although you tell me that you are acting privately on behalf of Madame Marie Antoinette, and Whitehall has no cognizance of your mission, I see great possibilities in turning it to the advantage of Britain, so will willingly do all I can to assist you.'

As Richard thanked him, he went on: `You will no doubt be aware that Naples is still tied to France by the Bourbon Family Compact. For many years it has been my principal task to loosen that tie, and my efforts have not been altogether unsuccessful. In that, of course, I have been much assisted by the attitude of Queen Caroline, and the friendship of General Acton.'

Richard knew that Sir William referred to the Neapolitan Prime Minister, but knowing nothing of the General's history, he committed the faux pas of remarking: `It must certainly have been a great asset to you, sir, that King Ferdinand should have chosen an Englishman for his principal councilor.'

Sir William raised a humorous gray eyebrow. "Tis stretching something of a long bow to term him that; for he is half French, was born in France, educated there, and has spent the whole of his adult life in Italy.'

`I pray you forgive me, sir,' Richard said, with a slight flush. `But this is my first visit to Naples and I am abysmally ignorant of Neapolitan affairs.'

`Then I had best tell you something of them,' smiled Sir William; `at least to the extent of a few brief details about the people you will have to meet, and on whom the success or failure of your mission hinges. John Acton has carved out a fine career for himself, as his father was no more than a physician. He was traveling in France with the father of Mr. Edward Gibbon and on their coming to Besancon he decided that it would be a good place in which to settle and establish a practice. He married a French lady, and John was born a year or so afterwards. John's uncle had some influence at the Court of Florence, and at his suggestion the boy entered the Tuscan navy. His big chance did not come until he was nearly forty. It was in '75. Spain and Tuscany sent a joint expedition against the pirates of Algiers and the affair proved a serious disaster; but John who had command of a frigate, performed prodigies of valor in the retreat and from that point received rapid promotion.'

Sir William paused a moment, before going on: `You should also know that Queen Caroline has a very strong personality. She is extremely ambitious and by no means non-inclined to gallantry. At that time her favorite was Prince Caramanico, and knowing her desire to make Naples a stronger power the Prince suggested to her that she should get John Acton to reorganize the Neapolitan navy. The Queen induced her brother, the Grand Duke, to part with his most promising sailor, and Acton was made King Ferdinand's Minister of Marine. He achieved such rapid progress in his task that he was asked to also undertake the reorganization of the army, and given a second portfolio as Minister of War.

`He has, of course performed miracles. When he came here ten years ago the Neapolitan navy was practically nonexistent and the army numbered less than fifteen thousand men; whereas now Naples can send a fleet of one hundred and twenty sail to sea and put sixty thousand men in the field. But such feats cost money and quite early in the game John's demands practically emptied the Neapolitan treasury. To that only one answer could be found; they gave him a third portfolio and made him Minister of Finance.'

Richard began to laugh, and Sir William smiled back at him. `By that time Prince Caramanico was in something of the position of a bird that has inadvertently imported a cuckoo's egg into its own nest. But the little monster had hatched out, so it was too late to do anything about it. However, Acton pushed him out of the nest quite gently. He got him sent as Ambassador to London. Then he had himself appointed Commander-in-Chief of the Neapolitan Forces by Land and Sea, and Prime Minister.'

`All that, I take it, sir, was by favor of the Queen?' Richard enquired.

`By that and his own great abilities. It has always been her ambition to have a voice in the councils of Europe; but a voice not backed by force is as one crying in the wilderness. Naples is by nature a small and poor State. When she came here it was accounted insignificant. But in General Acton she found a man who could make Naples, if not feared, at least well worth courting. So they have good reason to be pleased with one another.'

`Am I right in supposing, sir, that His Majesty concerns himself only with his own pleasures?'

Sir William nodded. `His tutor, Bernardo Tanucci, sought to gain a permanent hold over him by initiating him into vice while he was still a boy; and even took him to such low haunts as the public stews. Queen

Caroline soon got rid of Tanucci, but the King has never lost his taste for low company. Although he is now thirty-eight his mentality is still that of a boy of fourteen. He likes to think of himself as an Haroun al Raschid, and often goes about the city with a few of his cronies in disguise; but disguised so thinly as to ensure recognition, so that he may enjoy his favourite sport of playing the King among the beggars.'

Richard recalled that Tansanta had said something about Ferdinand having been nicknamed *El Rey de Lazzarone.* He had not understood the inference at the time, but Sir William was continuing

`As you must have seen, there are thousands of idle vagabonds about the city. They are known as the *Lazzarone,* and live almost entirely by petty crime; but they enjoy extraordinary license, and no official dare bring them to book, as the King himself is the chief of their Guild, and they enjoy his special protection. When he is not clowning with them, he is either making childish attempts to deceive the Queen while pursuing some woman,, or engaged in "Nimrodical expeditions", as he terms the big shooting parties that are another passion of his, from his country palace at Caserta.'

`It seems then, from what you tell me, sir, unlikely that His Majesty will have much say in the deciding of my business.'

`If the Queen and General Acton are favorably inclined you may count it as good as done. But the King will have to be consulted; as, in the last event, should they receive the Dauphin ::here,, and later refuse a peremptory demand for his return by the new National Government of France, that might involve Naples in war.'

`Think you the French would really go to such lengths, sir?'

`They might; although the greater probability is that it would beget *no* more than ill feeling between the two States. But 'tis that which interests me so greatly in your project. General Acton quite rightly -laces the interests of Naples before all else, although his English .Mood naturally inclines him favorably towards us. The Queen, as a daughter of Maria Theresa, has a natural bias toward Austria. So the present alliance of Naples with France and Spain is in opposition to the sentiments of both. Moreover, I am in the happy position. of enjoying a far greater degree of their confidence -e than are the Ambassadors of France and Spain, so able to take the best advantage of any new turn in the diplomatic situation which may offer. If your mission is successful it may well create one, and give me just the chance I need. On grounds of sentiment alone, it should not be difficult to persuade Queen Caroline to give asylum to her nephew, and if she once does so she is far too proud and stubborn a woman ever to give him up. Should serious friction with France result on that account I feel confident that I could detach Naples from her old alliance and bring about a new one between her, Austria and Britain.'

`I pray that events may enable you to do so, sir,' Richard said smiling.

Sir William stood up, beckoned him across to the big window, and waved a well manicured hand towards the magnificent panorama of the bay.

`Let your eyes dwell there, Mr. Blane,' he said with sudden seriousness. `As mine have done for twenty-five long years. You can forget John Acton's army and navy. In creating them he has served his mistress to the best of his ability; but the army is a rabble that would run at the very sight of my old regiment of Foot Guards, and it needs more than fisher folk dressed as tars to make a navy. But the bay's the thing.'

The elderly dilettante laid a friendly hand on Richard's shoulder, and went on: `You are too young to have played a part in the wars that near destroyed us in the '70s. and you were still in your cradle when Clive won Plassey and Wolfe Quebec. But for fourteen of the best years of my life we have been at war with the French, and I've not a doubt that we've yet to fight them again. M Amesbury, Ewart, Murray Keith, Eden, Dorset, Elliot, all my colleagues who have had the luck to represent their King in more important capitals than myself, think the same. And when it comes Britain must stand or fall, as she has always done, by sea power. If war broke out next week Naples would become a French fleet base. Just look at it. 'Tis the finest harbor in the Mediterranean ---nay, 'tis the finest harbor in the world. But if we could stymie the French! If we could break their hold by a piece of skilful diplomacy, eh? Think of an English squadron lying there! It would dominate the whole of the western Mediterranean. Britain needs that bay. God grant me a few years yet to conclude the task my heart has so long been set upon. Britain has got to have that bay.'

For a moment they stood there in silence, looking down ors the vast lagoon. In four more years, almost to the day, Sir William Hamilton the man whom Whitehall had forgotten for so long was to see his heart's desire reaped. He was to stand at that very window, with a promising young Captain named Nelson beside him, gazing with pride and joy at a British squadron being revictualled by the ally he had won for his country.

But his triumph was still part of the unknown future, and with a sudden return to his light, affable manner, he said: `I trust you'll join me in a glass of wine, Mr. Blane, and tell me the latest news of the terrible disturbances that now convulse France.'

Richard spent a further hour with him, then as he rose to take his leave Sir William said: `It is my loss that you have friends in Naples to whom you have already engaged yourself to dine; but I must insist that you have your things sent round from *Crocielles* and make the Palazzo Sessa your home during your stay in Naples.'

The very last thing that Richard wanted was to tie himself up as a guest in a private house ; so as he stammered his thanks he sought desperately for some way to excuse himself, and went on to murmur that, while he would be most happy to dire one evening, he could not dream of imposing further on Sir William's kindness.

Catching the note of perturbation in his voice the diplomat replied with a twinkle in his eye: `Please have no fear that I will seek to keep you from your other friends, Mr. Blane. Besides, at your age you will naturally wish to see something of the gaieties of the town. I have long nicknamed my home "The Royal Arms", as I encourage my guests to treat it as an hotel. There is a night porter on the gate who will let you in at any hour you wish, and I will only add that when you have no other engagements we shall be delighted to have you with us.'

To such true hospitality there could be only one answer. Having thanked Sir William again Richard returned to *Crocielles,* settled his bill and had his valise sent along to the Palazzo Sessa.

At Crocielles. he found a note awaiting him from the Princess Francavilla. It requested his company at her town house at one o'clock, to join a party for a drive out to her villa at Posilipo, where they would spend the afternoon. As it was still only a little after twelve he had ample leeway to get there at the time for which he was asked, so decided to walk to see something more of the city.

Naples, he found, could not approach Florence for the grandeur of its buildings; neither had it the cleanliness that the reforming Grand Duke had imposed upon the Tuscan capital. It' beauty lay in its rnarvelous, setting, and a distant view was nee led to savor its full enchantment. The streets were narrow, their smells noisome and the swarms of people in them, for the most part, indescribably ill clad and dirty. Yet they seemed far from unhappy, and the beneficent climate they enjoyed for so many months of the year was clearly a great offset to their poverty.

They were going about their work as though it did not matter in the least if it got done that day or next week, and half of them were gossiping' idly or playing games of chance in the gutters. The rags they wore were the only visible sign of hardship, for their bronzed faces were healthy, their black hair lustrous and curly and their dark eyes sparkling with vitality. In the better part of the town there were many black-coated abbés, brown-robed friars, and nuns wearing various types of headdress. Every street had its quota of mendicants, who often displayed repulsive deformities while calling on the passersby for alms; and Richard noted with interest that, poor as the crowd appeared, they gave freely of little copper coins.

At the Francavilla mansion, on the Chiaia, he was shown up to a salon on the first floor, where he found both the Princess and Tansanta awaiting him. Dorina Francavilla was a Spaniard, her grandfather having been one of Don Carlos' captains at the time of the conquest of Naples; but she had f air hair and gray eyes. She spoke French fluently and told Richard that having heard so much about him she was enchanted to meet him. As Tansanta's confidante her pleasure was unbounded at this unforeseen resumption of her friend's broken romance. She said that he was lucky indeed to love such a pearl among women, as all her efforts to persuade Tansanta to console herself for his loss by taking a lover had proved in vain ; so that after five months in Naples she was near acquiring the horrid reputation of a prude ; and that now they were together again she meant to see to it that they made up for lost time, by not losing an hour of one another's company.

Richard thanked her with a grace that came naturally to him, and she gaily declared that she liked him so well that if Tansanta did not look to her laurels she would snatch him for herself. Soon afterwards her husband came in, a portly middle-aged man of jovial countenance, who gave Richard an equally pleasant welcome. While they were taking a glass of wine the other guests arrived two cavaliers, a handsome Abbe, and three ladies. When they were all assembled they went downstairs to a line of waiting carriages, and were driven for three miles west, along the waterfront, to Posilipo.

The Francavilla' country house was situated on the point looking due south across twenty miles of water to the isthmus of Sorrento. Below the great cone of Vesuvius it looked as if Naples stretched as far as the eye could see, but actually the distant clusters of buildings fringing the shore were those of towns and villages linked by country villas in an almost continuous chain. In the gardens of the villa there were palm trees, cypresses, magnolias, camellias and oleanders, making shady walks, each terminating in arbors, stone seats, or fine pieces of ancient statuary.

It was, as Richard soon found after an excellent repast, a paradise for lovers. Without the least suggestion of indecorum the five couples paired off and strolled at their leisure through the green alleyways, to settle themselves for the rest of the afternoon in some of the many retreats where there was no likelihood whatever of their being disturbed.

At five o'clock they reassembled on the terrace, and shortly afterwards drove back to Naples. Before they separated the Marchesa di Santa Marco asked Richard to join a party for a visit to her villa at Resina the following afternoon, and at a flutter of the eyelid from Tansanta he readily accepted.

Soon after six he was back at the Palazzo Sessa. There, a middle-aged lady with a quiet, self-effacing manner introduced herself to him as Mrs. Cadogan, Sir William's housekeeper. She showed him up to his room, summoned a footman to act as his valet and told him that Sir William had a small company coming that evening f - - whom supper would be served at nine. As Richard was now have difficulty in suppressing his yawns, he asked that the footman should call him at eight thirty ; then, after one of the happiest twenty hours he had spent in his life, he enjoyed two hours' refreshing sleep.

At a little before nine he presented himself to his host's fine range of reception rooms, where he was introduced to some three dozen guests, among them the beautiful Emma. His first impression was that she was a little overwhelming, as the robust health she enjoyed manifested itself in her almost unnaturally brilliant coloring and extraordinary vivacity, added to which her magnificently proportioned figure was so large that Sir William, although a man of medium height, looked quite small beside her. But Richard quickly fell under her spell, and later he realized that it was her genuine interest in everyone she met and her inexhaustible kindness, far more than her decorative effect, which made her so universally popular.

Mainly for the benefit of Richard as a newcomer to Naples, after they had partaken of a buffet supper, Emma was persuaded to give an exhibition of her `attitudes'; and for this unusual entertainment the whole company adjourned to one of the smaller salons at one end of which there was a little curtained stage. Emma went behind the scenes while Sir William busied himself arranging the lighting effects; after which the curtains were withdrawn every few moments to display the ex-artist's model posing to represent various

Emotions or Mythological characters. Had Richard been forced to sit through a similar performance by a hostess less well endowed with charms, he might have found it distinctly wearisome; but as Emma was then twenty-four, and at the height of her Junoesque beauty, he derived genuine artistic enjoyment from it.

When she had exhausted her repertoire some tables for cards were made up and such guests as did not wish to play settled themselves for a *con versazione* ; so at half past eleven it was easy for Richard to excuse himself on the plea of having had a long day, and by midnight he was again climbing over the wall of Tansanta's villa.

He got home only a little before dawn, then slept late; but on getting up he found he had an hour to kill before he was due to wait upon the Marchesa di Santa Marco, so he set about exploring the ground floor of the Palazzo Sessa. To his surprise the whole of the south frontage and both wings consisted of one great suite of lofty chambers housing Sir William's collection of antiques. The place was a veritable Aladdin's cave, and he determined that he must ask his host if he could spare the time to tell him about some of the treasures it contained.

The Santo Marco villa, where he spent the afternoon, was on the slope immediately below the western side of Vesuvius, and within a stone's throw of Herculaneum. Forty years earlier the systematic excavation of the buried Roman town had been begun by Don Carlos, and Richard would greatly have liked to see the remains; but his hostess, a large, lazy sloe-eyed woman in her early thirties, was evidently looking forward to spending the next couple of hours with her cavalier in the garden, as she quickly turned the conversation, and, even in this tolerant society, it would have looked too pointed had Richard and Tansanta left her grounds on their own.

Nevertheless he saw Herculaneum, and also as much as had been excavated of Pompeii, later in the week under the most favourable circumstances. Sir William had willingly agreed to show him what he called `his lumber' and they spent the following morning together admiring bronze statuettes, graceful painted vases, curious amulets, mosaics, cameos and fragments of frescoes depicting life as it had been lived under the sway of Imperial Rome. It was while they were in the room that the Brothers Adam had specially designed to contain some of Sir William's most precious treasures that he said

. `In view of your interest, Mr. Blane, in this gracious civilization which so far surpasses anything that Christian nations have yet achieved, you must certainly devote a day to allowing me to show you the buried cities.'

For Richard it was an awful moment; as he was torn between a longing not to miss such a chance, added to the difficulty of refusing Sir William's offer without rudeness and the appalling thought that acceptance would mean the loss of one of his few precious days with Tansanta. But to such an old hand as Sir William the workings of Richard''s young mind were transparent as glass, and while fingering some long gold pins that had once held up a Roman lady's hair, he went on casually

`No doubt you have made some friends in Naples to whom you would like to return hospitality. Allow me to do so on your behalf. We will make up a party and I leave it to you to invite anyone you wish.'

`"bb are too good to me, sir,' Richard exclaimed with heartfelt gratitude. `The Prince and Princess Francavilla have shown me much kindness, and there is the Condesa Sidonia y Ulloa, with whom I was acquainted at the Court of France . . . .'

Sir William nodded. `So you met the dark-browed daughter of Conde d'Aranda there, eh? It increases my esteem for you, Mr. Blane, that you prefer the companionship of intelligent women. Pray ask her, then, and those charming Francavillas, and anyone else to whom you have a mind. Emma, I am sure, will be delighted to have their company.'

Then, to this delightful invitation, Sir William added what was to Richard a magnificent bonus. `A sloop arrived from Palermo late last night, bringing the news that instead of Their Majesties getting back here on Saturday, as we expected, they have decided to stay on over the weekend, so they will not now reach Naples until Tuesday. In view of the extra time this gives you, if your friends are agreeable, we might make our visit to Herculaneum and Pompeii on Sunday.'

So on the Sunday a party of eight made an early start in two carriages with well filled picnic baskets and the erudite Sir William as their cicerone. In vivid phrases he made live for them again the terrified ,inhabitants of the cities of the bay on the night of August 23rd, A.D. 79. Vesuvius had then been known as Mount La Somma and was less than half its present height. There had been earthquakes in the neighborhood before, and a severe one sixteen years earlier which had thrown down some of the buildings in Pompeii; but they had since been rebuilt with greater beauty, and the 22,000 people who lived in the busy port had almost forgotten the occurrence.

At two o'clock in the morning everyone in the towns for miles along the coast had been alarmed by a terrible growling sound coming from underground. The sky was serene and sea calm, but by dawn it was seen that an enormous column of watery vapor was steaming up like a vast pine tree from the top of the mountain. As the morning advanced it grew and spread, assuming the form of a huge mushroom. For some time it remained suspended motionless in the air, a strange and terrifying sight, but endangering no one. Suddenly it burst and descended on the mountain sides in torrents of boiling rain. Gathering the soil in its progress it rushed down the slope towards the sea in the form of scalding mud and totally engulfed Herculaneum.

In a few hours the town had not only disappeared from the face of the earth, but was buried sixty feet below it. Such of the inhabitants as got away in time fled either to the little town of Neapolis, as Naples was then called, or to Pompeii. The former were inspired by the gods, as Neapolis sustained little damage, and up to eight o'clock in the evening it was thought that Pompeii would also be spared. But at that hour the eruption redoubled in violence, and the volcano began to throw up masses of molten stones. They struck against each other as they were vomited into the air with the roar of continuous thunder, and breaking into small fragments descended on the doomed city.

By two hours after midnight a mineral rain of red-hot stones, each no bigger than a pea, but in effect like a fiery hailstorm, was descending steadily on Pompeii, burning and blistering everything it touched. Then after it, for hours on end, there fell hundreds of thousands of tons of claimed earth in the form of dust, and a black snow composed of ashes. The clouds laden with these suffocating components had spread far and wide, so that the whole terror occurred in pitch darkness. There now seemed no greater hope of safety in taking one way rather than another.

In wild confusion, patricians and plebeians, freedmen and slaves, priests, foreign traders, gladiators and courtesans ran backwards and forwards in frantic efforts to save themselves. Blindly they rushed into one another and into the walls of the houses they could no longer see. The heat was so stifling they could not get their breath. The sulphur fumes got into their eyes and longs ; the falling dust suffocated them, and thousands of them choked out their lives in agony.

The air for many hundreds of feet up was so thick with particles that the night seemed eternal. On the day that followed, the distraught people who had escaped with their lives did not even know that the sun had risen, and thought that it had been blotted out forever. Even as far away as Rome day was turned into night, and the crowds wailed to the gods in panic, believing that the end of the world had come.

`That,' Sir William told his guests, `is no figment of my own imagination, but almost the words in which this appalling catastrophe was described by cultured Roman men of letters, such as Plinhy the Younger, who were actual eyewitnesses to these ghastly scenes.'

Then he took them to the Forum, the Temples, the Theatre, the Baths, the houses and the shops, showing them the amenities the Romans had enjoyed. And as they ate their picnic lunch he smilingly apologized that he could give them only Lachrima Christi to wash it down, instead of Falernian, as he did not doubt that just as the Roman way of life had reached the peak of civilization still unrealized by themselves, so had the wines of those times been proportionately better drinking.

The following morning it was with something of a shock that Richard realized that it was Monday, and that he had been a week in Naples. It had been a marvelous week, unforgettable as one of unalloyed enjoyment. He had spent every night of it in Tansanta's arms and the greater part of each day with her beside him.

Every afternoon had brought a renewal of this lovely carefree existence, where with a little group of charming, laughing companions they had eaten of all the delicacies that sea and land provided, then wandered hand in hand through enchanted gardens.

None of the country villas compared with most of the chateaux he had seen in France. Their furnishings were usually either very old or else tawdry; grass grew between the paving stones of the terraces and moss upon their steps. The liveries of the footmen were often worn and shabby; but they showed no servility, and seemed as happy to serve a meal as their masters and mistresses were to eat it. Everyone laughed at the most stupid things, and the servants joined in the jokes that were made at table. They gathered round too afterwards, when to a highly appreciative audience the cavaliers read aloud to the assembled company poems that they had written in praise of the charms of their respective ladies.

Sometimes there had been older people in the parties, but never by a word or look had they suggested that there was anything improper in their juniors pairing off to spend the latter part of the afternoons in amorous dalliance. They had remained, dozing or playing a quiet game of cards up in a sunny, sheltered angle of the house, while the younger people wandered down on to the lower terraces until the colors of the gay silks and satins that they wore disappeared among the greenery of the gardens.

And what wonderful gardens they were! Richard knew that he would never forget their flights of old stone steps, tall, candle like cypresses, ilexes gently whispering in the breeze, miniature cascades, fountains with naiads, tritons and dolphins whose jets of water softly plashed into marble basins; their busts of long dead Roman Emperors posed on pedestals in bays of clipped yew; their temples to Flora, Diana and Apollo; arbors, rockeries and grottos; their little pavilions, belvederes and semicircular balustraded viewpoints, from which lovely vistas opened on to the tranquil bay.

In each there had been a hundred places in which to steal a kiss, or more; and about the light, ethereal loves of these friends of Tansanta there had seemed not the least suggestion of sordidness. They gave the impression that they were living again the pastoral loves of shepherds and shepherdesses from the writings of the ancient Greeks; and had created here a new Olympus.

Richard recalled a morning, now over two years ago, when he had gone to call on his clever friend Monsieur de Talleyrand Perigord. The Abbe, as he was then, had just returned from dinner, followed by an all night entertainment, given by Madame du Barri at her chateau at Luciens, where, in her retirement, she lived in almost fabulous luxury. De Périgord had that day predicted the upheavals that had since occurred in France, and were now sweeping all culture, beauty and lightheartedness away; and, with a sad shake of his handsome head, he had remarked: '*Mon* ami. Those who have not had the good fortune to have lived in Paris before the Revolution will never know what it is like to have lived at all.' Yet Richard felt that could the cynical Bishop have spent a week in Naples he would have been compelled to alter his opinion.

But his own week was up. It had gone with incredible rapidity. Tomorrow Their Majesties would be back *in Naples.* Then, within a few hours, he would be forced to leave this earthly paradise.

CHAPTER EIGHTEEN
DESPERATE MEASURES

Now that Richard faced the issue, he knew that it would be futile to buoy himself up with false hopes of further delays. His mission was an urgent one, so it would receive prompt consideration; and immediately a decision upon it was taken he must return to France. Even should circumstances postpone his actual departure for a day or two, the gates of paradise were now closing against him with a terrifying rapidity. When Their Majesties landed tomorrow Don Diego would land with them. Tonight was the last he would be able to spend with Tansanta.

In the morning he must give her back the key she had lent him to the garden gate, to save him having to climb over the wall. Don Diego used that key and gate. He was in the habit of coming in at all hours of the night by it; and Tansanta had said that after his return nothing would induce her to receive her lover in the house, from fear that they might meet going or coming in the garden.

The more Richard thought of his approaching departure the deeper his gloom became. Now that he had lived with Tansanta she meant even more to him than she had before. To give her up would be worse than tearing off one of his own limbs. He felt that he positively could not bring himself to do it. Yet there seemed no other alternative.

The gods, too, seemed suddenly to have deserted him. He had been blessed with a week of marvelous sunshine, but at last the weather had broken, and it had turned to rain. They had for that day accepted an invitation from the Prince and Princess Siglio to join a party going out to Lake Agnano. The Princess's younger sister had recently entered a convent in that neighborhood; so they were to lunch at the Convent, then spend the afternoon in the gardens of the Prince's villa, which stood perched on the cliff that separated the lake from the sea.

Now that it was raining Richard feared that the party might be put off or, almost as bad from his point of view, they would have to spend the afternoon indoors. To his great relief, a messenger arrived in the middle of the morning with a note from the Princess to let him know that as lunch had been arranged for them at the Convent they would go there in any case; and they could then see if an improvement in the weather made it worth while to go on to the villa.

To Richard the lunch party was a strange experience. On arriving at the Convent he and his friends were conducted to a big room which was divided in two by a partition wall ; but in the center of the wall there was a fifteen foot wide archway, from the top of which a grille of iron bars, about ten inches apart, ran right down to the floor. In both halves of the room tables had been laid for a dozen people, and one end of each was separated from the other only by the grille, so that the two tables had the effect of one long one. The visitors sat on one side and on the other the Mother Superior, several pretty young nuns, and three jolly looking priests. Both parties were served with the same rich food and wines, made merry with the same zest, and unblushingly exchanged the latest scandals and *risque'* stories.

Tansanta told Richard afterwards that many young women preferred going into a nunnery to marriage, as it relieved them of all responsibility; and in the Kingdom of Naples these girls still enjoyed the great degree of freedom which, until comparatively recently, had for many centuries been customary in all Catholic countries. They had their love affairs with their confessors, and sometimes even secret ones with laymen who managed to smuggle themselves into the convents disguised as gardeners, friars and workmen. But they were never burdened with the cares of rearing children, as their infants were taken from them at birth. If the mother was rich her child was put out to nurse; if not it was quietly strangled and buried in the garden. Richard considered himself broadminded but, for once, he found himself shocked.

By three o'clock the weather had cleared a little, so it was decided to go on to the villa. From it the views both to seaward and inland were beautiful beyond expression. In the clear water of the lake deer were drinking, and bright kingfishers skimmed through the reeds on its shore. But to Richard"s intense annoyance it came on to rain again, so lovemaking in the garden was out of the question ; a card party was made up, and he and Tansanta had no option bat to join it.

That night, for the first hour or two, they said little, but their embraces took on an almost desperate fervor. Then, towards morning, Richard suddenly made up his mind to commit himself to a course of action with which he had been toying, on and off, all day.

'Tansanta!' he cried at last, in an agony of passion. `I cannot give you up ! I cannot! Not for good! 'Tis too much to be required of any human being. I must return to France, I know. But as soon as I have concluded my mission I mean to come back to Naples and settle here.'

He knew that to do so meant the end of his career, and that his private means were far from adequate to support the expensive tastes he had acquired in the past few years ; but he felt sure that he could count on Sir William to find him some sort of post in Naples, and he was prepared to tackle any job provided it enabled him to remain near Tansanta.

For a moment she remained silent, then she said sadly: 'Nay, *Riche.* You must not do that. My hart is aching as much as yours; but at least we have been blessed with this wonderful week to look back upon; and now we must face our cruel separation bravely. I forbid you to return. Your doing so would create a situation that I shudder to think of.'

'Why should it?' he burst out. `Every woman here has her lover; more, most of them give themselves to one plan after another as they list, yet none of their husbands takes serious notice of their infidelities.'

She shook her head. `My husband is not like the rest. If he found out that you were my lover, he would kill you.'

'Nay, sweet. You are allowing your fears to run away with your imagination.'

'I am not, *Riché!* ! I am not! Remember he is a Spaniard; and not even one who was brought up here. True Spaniards hold the honor of their wives more precious than their own lives. Don Diego despises the Neapolitan gentlemen for their laxness. I have heard him voice that opinion. If he found us out I swear that he would kill you.'

Tansanta's unexpected opposition had only the effect of making Richard more set than ever in his resolve to make her the be-all and end-all of his future. In the past week a score of people had told him how lovely Naples was in the spring, with its almond and peach blossom, its fields gay with crocuses, its gardens scented with magnolias and stephanotis; and how joyous the nights could be during the heat of summer, with dancing in the open under the stars, moonlight bathing parties, and trips across the phosphorescent water to Ischia and Capri. It seemed to him at the moment that only a fool would wear himself out intriguing to obtain information in the cold northern Courts if, instead, he was capable of earning the modest competence which would enable him to live as Tansanta's lover in this lotus land. Turning towards her, he said earnestly

'Listen, my love. Even though I think your fears to be exaggerated, I will take your word for it that should Don Diego believe his honour touched upon he will prove dangerous. We will, then, deny him, all chance of proving that we have given him a pair of horns. I promise you that I will make no attempt to come to you in secret here. Quetzal can act as our confidential messenger, and I will content myself with such opportunities as are bound to offer from our meeting several times a week at the houses of our friends. To that your husband can raise no objection.'

`Oh, *Riché!* ! Riché!' Tansanta sighed. `How can you be so blind to the inevitable result of this course that you propose? 'Tis an old saying that there is safety in numbers; and that is the protection of most of these Neapolitan ladies. They change their beaux so lightheartedly that no one is ever certain if any one of their affairs has ever reached its logical conclusion. On that account 'tis near impossible for even a jealous husband actually to pin anything upon them. But I could not bring myself to flirt with other men, neither could I support the thought of your making love to other women, even as a cover. In a few weeks our fidelity would become conspicuous and my husband would have only to watch us for a little while when together to realize our love, and be certain that we were deceiving him. His Spanish pride would never stomach the thought that other men might be laughing at him, and in the , end your life would prove the forfeit for your attachment to me.'

`Be not too certain of that,' Richard murmured truculently. `I am accounted no bad swordsman, and did he challenge me I would be most happy to meet him. Such a conversation might well prove a swift way out of all our difficulties.'

Tansanta flung her arms about his neck, and began to sob. `My own I My loved one! 'Tis clear you have not the understanding of a child upon such matters. In Spain, a husband who believes he has been wronged does not consider himself called upon to expose himself to the blade of his wife's lover. He hires others to do his business. To return here as you suggest would be to expose yourself to the dagger of an assassin.'

Richard was no coward; but her tearful words shook him badly, and conjured up the most horrid visions. For weeks, and perhaps months, all might go well; he would lead that carefree sybaritic life he had visualized and discreetly enjoy Tansanta's favors ; then one dark night when he least expected it he would be caught off his guard, and die in the gutter with a bravo's stiletto plunged to its hilt between his shoulder blades.

Yet his pride would not let him give way altogether, and they parted in the dawn, knowing that they would meet the following afternoon, but with nothing settled.

On the Tuesday it rained again; but not sufficiently heavily for King Ferdinand to forego the public welcome that it had been arranged for him to receive on his return; and *by eleven o'clock* the clouds dispersed to let the sun come through. The streets were decked with flags; carpets, tapestries and gaily colored rugs were hung over balconies and from windows. Just before midday Richard and Tansanta met at the Francavilla mansion, to which a party had been invited to witness the procession.

Both the Neapolitans and their King loved a show, so half the army had been turned out to line the route; and, to keep the populace amused while they waited for the Sovereigns, a score or more of Triumphal cars had been decorated and manned to drive up and down the main thoroughfares. These cars were a feature of Neapolitan public holidays and were always brought out in different guises for the great pre-Lenten Carnival, the summer Battle of Flowers, and other festivities. Most of them were huge vehicles drawn by as many as twenty oxen, and they now moved up and down with their loads of bacchantes, mermaids and acrobats escorted by groups of absurd masked figures on enormous stilts. Meanwhile, bands played, cannon thundered and salvoes of musketry crashed out from the port.

At length the cavalcade came in view; trumpeters, outriders, cavalry; the King's favourite regiment, the *Volontari delta Marina,* in their uniforms of green with scarlet facings and yellow buttons ; then the great gilded coach of the Sovereigns, surrounded by the *Guardia del Corpo.*

As soon as Richard saw it in the distance he drew Tansanta back from the balcony into the room. He had been waiting impatiently for that moment, knowing that his one chance to get a few words alone with her would be while the attention of the rest of the party was held by the highlight of the procession. Without wasting an instant, he said

'If you are still unshakable in your refusal to allow me to return to Naples, will you, instead, elope with me?'

She drew in a sharp breath; then exclaimed: 'No, *Riche!* No What you ask is impossible!'

He had gone very white, but he tried to control his voice, and he carried on: 'I know that it is much to ask ; but there is nothing impossible about it. You know that you can trust yourself to me, and that I would never desert you. When we reached England we could say that we have been married abroad. I swear that in all things I would treat you as my wife; and no one would ever know that we had not been joined in wedlock.'

'In time it would leak out,' she quavered. 'The Spanish and Neapolitan Ambassadors at the Court of St. .James would be certain to hear the story of our elopement. I love you, *Riché!* ! Oh, I love you dearly! But to do as you wish would bring public shame on me, and mar your own future. We could not be received anywhere together once it became known that I .was living with you as your mistress.'

'We would live very quietly in the country for a time, until . . .'

The cheers on the balcony had died away, *and* the guests were beginning to drift in to the refreshment buffet. Richard's last sentence was cut short by a fat, garrulous Abbé coming up to them and interrupting their conversation with platitudes about how fortunate it was that the rain had cleared off for the procession. Two ladies joined their group, and in the half-hour that followed it proved impossible to resume their conversation. It was not until just as Tansanta was leaving that Richard managed to get another few swift words alone with her.

'When shall I see you again?' he whispered.

'Tonight at the Opera. There is a gala performance. Everyone i s going.'

'There will be no chance for us to talk in private. I beg you to come here again, later this afternoon.'

'I cannot. I have not seen my husband yet. He will expect me to be at home, so that he can tell me all that occurred during the royal visit to Sicily.'

'Tomorrow morning, then?'

'Yes, at twelve o'clock.'

'Can you not make it earlier? I may have to attend upon Their Majesties.'

'Nay! I dare not. There is no possible excuse that I could give *for* leaving the *house* appreciably in advance *of my usual hour.'*

There was no time to argue, as neighbours of Tansanta, who had brought her and were carrying her home in their coach, were already waiting for her on the stairs. So he could only kiss her hand and murmur: 'So be it, then. Here, at midday tomorrow.'

That evening lie accompanied Sir William Hamilton to the fine new San Carlo Theatre, for the gala performance. The diplomat had his own box and he remarked to Richard that, *much as* he enjoyed his rolls in the Mediterranean and climbs up Vesuvius in summer, it made a pleasant change of diversion to come there any night he felt inclined when the real winter had set in, and there was ice in the streets of Naples. Richard found it difficult to imagine Naples under snow, but gave the matter little thought as he was anxiously scanning the other boxes for Tansanta and her husband.

When he did catch sight of them he was disappointed, as the man he took to be Don Diego was seated towards the back of the box, and it was difficult to make out his features.

Soon afterwards the Sovereigns appeared in the royal box; there was a great shouting and clapping of hands, the flambeaux were doused and the show began.

However, ample opportunity was afforded Richard later that evening of seeing. the man he instinctively hated, as the performance occupied five hours, including two intervals of nearly an hour each, during which the audience either strolled up and down in the foyer, or called upon their acquaintances in the boxes.

During the first interval Sir William went to make his service to the Queen, and Richard decided to make his first call on the beautiful Duchesa di Lucciana, who had given him a gracious smile from a box nearby. Having spent ten minutes with her party, lie felt he might now pay his respects to Tansanta, without having appeared overeager to do so.

In her box he found the di Jaccis, the Ottobonis and the Abbe Guarini, so for a moment his entrance was not even noticed by Don Diego. He kissed Tansanta's hand and with perfect aplomb she then presented him to her husband. The two men bowed formally and exchanged a few well turned compliments; after which the Princess di Jacci reclaimed Don Diego's attention, so Richard discussed the performance with Tansanta and the Abbe for six or seven minutes, then bowed his way out.

As he made his way slowly towards the Sambucas' box for his next call he tried to sort out his impressions of El Conde Sidonia y Ulloa. Richard had in no circumstances been prepared to like the man but he had to admit that he was both handsome and possessed of a striking presence. Don Diego was slightly taller than himself, or perhaps only seemed so from his exceptionally upright carriage. He was very dark, with an olive skin and sparkling black eyes. His most outstanding feature was an aquiline nose so thin as to be almost knifelike. His mouth, too, was thin-lipped, but well formed, and when he smiled he showed excellent teeth. His face was narrow and his firm chin seemed to be permanently tilted up, which gave him an expression of extreme hauteur. Richard decided that, his own prejudices apart, Don Diego was not a particularly lovable person, and that his main preoccupation in life was to impress other people with the blueness of his blood and the ultra aristocratic good looks with which nature had endowed him. When Richard rejoined Sir William *the diplomat* said: `I have spoken to Her Majesty of you and she wishes me to bring you to her in the second *entr'acte.'*

Richard endeavored to show suitable gratification at the announcement, but actually found difficulty in concealing his distress. His brain was now almost bursting with wild prospects concerning Tansanta, and so far he had failed to concert with her on even the basis of a plan for their future. He had been hoping that *he* would at least be granted until the next day before being called on to discuss his mission with the Queen; but here was the matter being hurried forward without the loss of a moment, and he knew that once the affair was broached his remaining time in Naples might be reduced to a few hours. In a state of nervous anxiety he sat through another hour of the performance, then accompanied Sir William to the royal box.

King Ferdinand had already left it to go out on to the steps of the theatre and accept the homage of the crowd. His hordes of privileged beggars called him Lou Pasco the madcap and their cheers showed how pleased they were to have him back in his capital. So when Richard was ushered into the presence he made his bow to the Queen alone. She was, he knew, several years older than the Queen of France, and he found that although the sisters shared a family likeness, Maria Carolina had little of Marie Antoinette's beauty. Her figure had suffered from having borne thirteen children, her shoulders were rounded and her neck overlong. She also had something disagreeable in her manner of speaking, moving her whole face when she talked, and gesticulating violently. Her voice was hoarse and her eyes goggled. But she impressed him at once as having a strong mind, and her reception of him could not have been kinder.

She expressed the greatest affection and concern for her sister, said she could hardly bear to wait to hear the latest news of her, and asked Sir William to bring Richard to the State Ball at the Palazzo *Reale* as soon as the performance was over. In consequence, his last hopes of a postponement of his business till the following day went by the board, and an hour and a half later he was making his bow to her again.

He had known that the gala at the San Carlo was to be followed by a ball, but had not expected to be invited to it. Now, for the first time, he saw Neapolitan society at Court, and was interested to note that, in sharp contrast to Versailles, little formality was observed. The King was already mixing familiarly with his guests, slapping the men on - their backs and patting the cheeks of the prettier women with a heavy gallantry which, under the eye of his jealous Queen, might have passed for no more than fatherly license.

For years the two of them had continually deceived one another, each conducting a series of shallow amours typical of the Court over which they ruled. The Queen indulged herself with handsome young men whom she raised to positions of wealth and influence according to their potential abilities; and, being a clever woman, she managed her affairs so skillfully that the King seldom found her out. On the rare occasions when he did he was pleased as punch about it, for it enabled him to do as he liked for a week or two, on the principle that what was sauce for the goose was sauce for the gander. But she was such a much stronger personality that she soon overawed him again, and she was so greedy of attention that she grudged him every flutter.

Like her brother Leopold she was intensely suspicious, and she maintained a very efficient spy system among the personnel of her Court; moreover the King was such a simpleton that he was constantlyb giving away his own secrets, so she nearly always knew of it soon after he started an intrigue with some new charmer. She then treated him to scenes of the most violent jealousy and nipped the affair in the bud by sending his flame into exile. Once, when she had caught him kissing a lady at a Court ball, her rage had been so great that she had called a halt to the function there and then, and sent everyone home without their supper.

But tonight she was giving little thought to her wayward spouse. Within a few moments of Richard's arrival she made him give her his arm, and walked up and down one of the side galleries with him for over an hour. She listened to all he had to say, admired the miniature of her nephew, and asked innumerable questions about the state of things in France. Like her brothers the Emperor and the Grand Duke, she had a positive conviction of the divine right of hereditary Sovereigns to rule their peoples as they thought fit. But, unlike them, she was opposed to all innovation. As a woman, in spite of her unattractive manner and appearance, Richard found her likeable and kind; but as a Queen he deplored her reactionary sentiments, and he thought there was something both pathetic and shocking in the fear and hatred she displayed for the common people.

She said at once that, although she regretted the necessity for her sister's sake, she would willingly receive the Dauphin. The King's consent would have to be obtained, but the getting of it was a mere formality. She and General Acton would arrange that between them. Then, of ter her long talk with Richard, she sent a page to find the General and request him to join them.

The half French, half British Neapolitan Prime Minister was a fine-looking man in his early fifties. His manner was firm but courtly, and it was clear that he knew just how to handle his royal mistress. Although he made no direct mention of it, after a few minutes' conversation it was also clear to Richard that he had already been primed on the subject in hand by Sir William. He was entirely at one with the Queen in her wish to receive the Dauphin, but he tactfully overruled her impulsive wish to speak to the King about it there and then.

He shrewdly pointed out that at this hour of night His Majesty might resent being worried with business, whereas tomorrow there would be an excellent opportunity for catching him in just the right humor. As the forest at Caserta had not been disturbed for over three weeks the King was assured of a good hunt in the morning, so if they asked him to attend a short counsel in the afternoon he would then be in a mood to agree to anything without argument.

Richard mentally sighed with relief, as these tactics meant that even if a northward bound ship happened to be sailing next day they could hardly now attempt to pack him off back to France in her. Having come to the ball would give him an unforeseen chance of attempting to bring Tansanta to a decision during a dance that night, and, if he were successful, their meeting at midday next day could then be devoted to arranging final plans. So, as soon as the Queen dismissed him, he made his way to the ballroom and began to search anxiously for his beloved.

He had seen both her and Don Diego several times in the distance, but now could not find either them. While he was still hunting frantically for her in the anterooms he ran into Dorina Francavilla, from whom he learned to his dismay that Tansanta had been feeling ill, so the Sidonia y Ulloas had already gone home on that account.

Richard was both distressed and furious. Tansanta had told him that she was going to the ball, so if only he had known earlier that he would be bidden to it himself he could have arranged for her to keep an assignation with him there; but now, owing to the Queen having kept him for so long, this excellent opportunity of thrashing matters out with Tansanta had escaped him.

He was still standing, angry and disconsolate, where the Princess and her partner had left him, when a tall, thinnish, middle aged man came hurrying round the corner. His powdered hair was a little untidy and his waistcoat was buttoned up unevenly, but he was covered in stars and orders, and Richard instantly recognized him as the King.

Quickly he drew himself up to bow, but the boisterous Monarch suddenly halted opposite him, grinned, clapped him heartily on the shoulder and said something in Italian.

Not understanding what he said, Richard swiftly excused himself in French; upon which King Ferdinand gaily broke into that language.

'I don't know who you are, young man,' he cried with a laugh, 'but you're very welcome here. You've kept that wife of mine busy the whole evening. Each time I've passed the gallery I've seen her talking her tongue off to you out there. You must come here again. Nay, better still, stay here. I'll make you an officer in *my Volontari della Marina.'*

A sly look came over his oafish face, and he added in a lower tone: 'It gave me just the chance I needed with the Marchesa. But say nothing of that, or I will have you clapped into St. Elmo.' Then, with another grin, he turned to hurry away.

'Sire! One moment, I beg,' Richard called after him.

'What is it, eh?' The King glanced over his shoulder, with a suspicious frown. "Tis no use asking me for money. I cannot spare any.'

'Nay, Sire,' Richard smiled. 'But permit me to draw Your Majesty's attention to your waistcoat.'

King Ferdinand looked down, adjusted the giveaway buttons and exclaimed gratefully: *'Dio mio! What* an escape I Had the Queen seen that she would have cancelled my hunt tomorrow.' Then, grabbing Richard by the arm, he added: 'You must certainly stay with us. Come along now, and have some supper.'

In the supper room a meal was being served in what seemed to Richard novel and uncomfortable conditions. There was an abundance of food on tables ranged round the walls but no table in the centre of the room. Instead there were four rows of gilt chairs formed into a square and facing inward. On these a number of the guests were sitting, eating from plates balanced on their knees.

'Look!' said the King. 'Are not their struggles to cut things up amusing to watch? And now and then one of them drops a plate, which makes everyone laugh. Go now and try your luck.'

As Richard struggled with the half of crayfish, he sighed at the thought of the King's offer of a commission in his crack regiment of Sea Cadets. If only he could have accepted it and remained on in Naples ! But he knew only too well that even were the offer to be renewed tomorrow in all seriousness, he would have to refuse it.

By the time he had supped it was getting on for one in the morning, and soon afterwards he ran into Sir William, who asked u *he felt* like going home. Richard agreed at once, so they went down to the diplomat's carriage and set off for the Palazzo Sessa.

The carriage had hardly turned into the *Calle Toledo* when Sir William said: 'The Royal Family will be taking up their residence at Caserta tomorrow, and I have been ordered to take you out there. It is a drive of about sixteen miles, so we had better start at ten o'clock.'

'Then I must beg you to excuse me, sir,' Richard said firmly. 'I have an appointment here in Naples at midday which it is impossible for tie to cancel.'

Sir William raised an eyebrow. 'Really, Mr. Blane! I should hardly have thought it necessary to remind you that the orders of Her Majesty take precedence of all private matters.'

Richard bit his lip for a second, then exclaimed: 'That, sir, obviously applies to everyone who is in the service of the Queen of Naples; but I am not.'

'You are, however, in that of His Britannic Majesty,' Sir William replied coldly, 'and I regard this as His Majesty's business.'

'Indeed, sir, I pray you pardon me.' Richard's voice was desperate. 'After all your kindness to me my behavior must seem monstrous churlish. But this matter is to me one of life and death. Could I not follow you on horseback and still arrive in time? What is the latest possible hour at which it is imperative that I should be at Caserta?'

Seeing his distress, the elderly diplomat said kindly: 'I do not think the Queen and General Acton will tackle the King until the afternoon; but if a particularly favourable opportunity offered they might decide to do so any time after he returns from hunting, and that should be between twelve and one.'

'If you could furnish me with a mount, sir, I could make the journey in an hour.'

'How long will your appointment detain you?'

'I had hoped for half an hour at least.'

'Then I fear it is out of the question. Too much hangs upon the matter for us to jeopardize the issue.'

'Will it satisfy you, sir, if I give you my word to be at Caserta by one o'clock? If I ride all out I can do the sixteen miles well under the .hour, so that would give me five or ten minutes with. . So be it then, Sir William covered Richard's hesitation. 'But remember that I shall count upon you.'

At twenty to twelve next day Richard was at the Francavillas'. He had come early, praying that Tansanta would be early too, and down in the street a groom was holding Sir William's fastest riding horse ready for him. But

Tansanta did not come early, and when midday chimed out he was still waiting for her in a fury of impatience, up in Dorina Francavillas boudoir. It was already seven minutes past twelve when Tansanta arrived looking pale and wan.

Knowing the situation the Princess left them together at once ; and Richard, seizing Tansanta in his arms, told her that they had only a bare few minutes before he must take the road.

A couple of those precious minutes went in kisses, and his asking her if it was really illness that had caused her to leave the ball early the preceding night; but she assured him that she had done so only on account of the strain she had been under, and that she had not seen him, or known that he was there, otherwise she would have remained.

He then plunged into the matter that concerned them so desperately ; swore that he could not live without her, and urged her again either to agree to his returning to Naples or to elope with him.

Wringing her hands she declared that in no circumstances must he return, as if he did he would be dead within three months; then tearfully advanced the arguments she had used the day before against an elopement.

Hurriedly he cut her short. `Yes, yes, my sweet! But what I had no chance to say yesterday was this. We should have to live quietly in the country only for a time, as in due course we could regularize our union. You could get an annulment of your present marriage.'

She sadly shook her head. `Nay, *Riche*. The Catholic Church would never grant an annulment to a woman who had left her husband and was living in sin, for the purpose of enabling her to marry again.'

`But what of Don Diego?' he exclaimed. `Should you leave him, will the Church condemn him to remain wifeless for life through no fault of his own? He is rich and influential; moreover, he is barely thirty and will not wish to spend the rest of his days like a widower. Surely the Church would not refuse an annulment to him?'

Tansanta sharply drew in her breath. `Perhaps you are right. Yes,I cannot think they would refuse him. But how long will it be before he meets someone that he wants to make his wife? And we cannot even be certain that he will wish to marry again. We should be pledging our lives on a desperate gamble. *Riché,* you must give me time to think! I must have time to think!'

`God forbid that I should hurry you in taking such a decision; but 'tis as good as certain now that I shall be leaving Naples tomorrow. I will come to the house for your answer tonight.'

`Nay, *Riché!* ! I implore you not to! I forbid it !'

`I must! I shall be held at Caserta all this afternoon. Tis our only chance for a last meeting ; and if I die for it I must hold you in my arms again.'

As he finished speaking a nearby clock chimed the. quarter after twelve, and he cried desperately: `My poor sweet, I positively must leave you now. I will come for your decision tonight.'

Suddenly she seized and clung to him. `One moment! Listen, I beg, or you will get us both killed. Diego is in one of his black moods. Before he left for Sicily he had fixed his eye on a Signora Goudar. She is little better than a courtesan, but difficult in spite of that; and so far she has rejected his advances. His unsatisfied passions disturb him to such a pitch that when one of them has gripped him he often paces up and down for hours at a stretch by night, in the garden. Should you enter it tonight I vow there will be murder done.'

Richard was silent for a moment, then he said: `I care naught for an encounter with him; but if you fear he would attempt your life as well, I dare not risk it.'

`He would! I know it! Did he surprise us together he would do his utmost to kill the two of us.'

`Then I'll not come tonight. Somehow I will get my departure postponed for twenty-four hours. And in some way I'll lure Don Diego from the house tomorrow night. I'll come to you then and bring a carriage with me. That will give you ample time to decide upon our future. If 'tis favourable to me, I beg you have your things packed and Maria and Quetzal ready to leave with you; for we must take advantage of the night to get away unseen.'

With the tears streaming down her face Tansanta nodded dumbly. Then, as he released her, she swayed and fainted. Catching her in his arms again, he laid her on to a couch, and dashed out of the room.

At breakneck speed he rode out to Caserta; and, as he entered the fine avenue of elms that led to the palace, the clear single note of one came to him from a clock in the stables behind it.

In view of the comparative smallness of the Kingdom of Naples the size of the palace astonished him, for, as he galloped up the straight towards its thousand-foot-long façade, the building seemed positively immense. But the thought was only a passing one. Leaving his sweating mount with one of the grooms at the main entrance, he mopped the sweat from his own brow and hurried inside.

The entrance hall, great staircase and galleries around it were even more astonishing than the exterior, as they were entirely fashioned from the most rare and costly marbles, but his surprise was still further added to by the fact that there was hardly anybody about. A swift enquiry from a portly factotum produced the laconic reply that His Majesty was out hunting and might not yet be back for some time. Richard was furious. He had curtailed his all-important interview with Tansanta, winded Sir William's best horse, and had his grueling ride, all quite unnecessarily.

The official pointed through the open door to an upward slope of the park beyond which he said the royal party would be found; so, having given his horse a good breather, Richard mounted again and set off in that direction. On the far side of the hill he arrived at a big enclosure with rustic arbors for protection from the rain, and in it was the Queen surrounded by most of her Court. The enclosure faced towards a natural amphitheatre of woods so that the spectators had a fine view of the sport which was in progress. In the woods hundreds of beaters were banging kettles and firing off petards so that the game, which consisted of deer, boar, hares and foxes, should be driven out into the open for the King to shoot at.

After watching for a few moments Richard found Sir William, who apologized with a wry smile for having caused him to hurry his departure from Naples unnecessarily, and explained the present situation by adding that the King had found the sport so good that he had sent a message at midday saying that he intended to prolong his shoot for an hour longer than usual. He then took over to the Queen, who had General Acton beside her, and they both received him with marked kindness.

Half an hour later King Ferdinand reached the enclosure. His hair was tousled and he was dressed so like a peasant that he could easily have been mistaken for one. When Richard commented in a low voce to Sir William on the Sovereign's strange choice of costume, the diplomat laughed and replied

`Nothing delights him more than to be taken by some young beater who does not know him for one of themselves, and egging the poor fool on to grumble to him about what a bad King he is. But such episodes do not cause him to become a better ruler. He regards the matter as a joke, and does not even give the fellow who has amused him a sixpence. He is much too mean for that.'

In a fine good humour the boorish King watched the big bag of mixed game he had shot piled in a small mountain at the Queen's feet. Then, when this ceremony was over, the company entered a row of waiting carriages and was driven back to the palace.

A huge meal followed the hunt and when everyone had eaten their fill the ,King sent for a blanket. On seeing it brought in Sir William tapped Richard on the arm and whispered: 'Quick! Follow me, or you'll rue it.'

Much mystified Richard got up, and slipped after his mentor to the nearest doorway. As he did so he noticed that quite a number of other courtiers who had been standing about were making unostentatiously for the entrances, and on catching Sir William up he asked what was afoot.

`Watch from here and you will see,' replied the diplomat, entrenching himself behind one of the great marble pillars that flanked the door. `I have seen him play this game before, and know its sequel.'

As Richard watched, the King began to undress himself, and although the ladies pretended to hide their blushes behind their fans they were clearly much amused. When His Majesty was stark naked, he stepped on to the middle of the blanket, which had been spread out on the floor, and, at his order, twelve lusty footmen began to toss him in it. 'One! Two! Three!' chanted the footmen, and up towards the ceiling sailed the nude monarch.

A dozen times he was shot into the air, amidst clapping of hands and shouts of applause. Then, having ordered a halt, he scrambled out of the blanket, pointed at a fat man nearby who had been laughing heartily, and cried: `You next! Your turn next.'

In vain the fat man protested. He had to submit to the King's will, undress himself and be tossed in the blanket.

`You see,' remarked Sir William to Richard, `from what I have saved you. That unfortunate is a German diplomat but recently arrived here; and as you are also a stranger His Majesty would certainly have had you tossed had his eye lighted on you.'

Richard was quick to voice his thanks, and they remained carefully concealed from the royal buffoon's eye while half a dozen other victims suffered a similar indignity to that undergone by the German. At length the Queen persuaded his Neapolitan Majesty to dress, and with tears of mirth still streaming from his eyes he was led away between her and General Acton to the council chamber.

They remained in council only half an hour, then General Acton came out to Sir William and Richard, and told them that King Ferdinand had formally consented to receive the Dauphin in his realm. He added that it was Her Majesty's wish that a sloop of the Royal Neapolitan Navy should be placed at Richard's disposal to carry him back to France as soon as possible; but that she wished him to bear a letter for her to Madame Marie Antoinette, which she would write that night, so he was to wait upon her to receive it the following morning.

At the mention of the sloop Richard's heart had gone down into his boots, as he had feared to receive an order for his instant departure; but the codicil about carrying the letter restored his equilibrium, and he breathed again.

When the Prime Minister had left them, Sir William said: `I keep up a small villa just outside the park, to spare myself the inconvenience of having to return to Naples every night when the Court is resident at Caserta. I shall be happy to offer you a bed there.'

. `I thank you, sir, but I beg you to excuse me,' Richard replied. `Owing to my hasty departure from the capital this morning, my business there is not yet concluded. Fortunately I have not been bidden to attend the Court this evening, so with your leave I propose to return to Naples.'

Sir William gave an understanding nod. "Tis certain that Her Majesty will expect to see you at supper; but since she has issued no command for your appearance, you are free to do as you wish. She will have ample time to talk further with you in the morning. I suggest that you should be here not later than eleven o'clock, as she does her business from that hour onwards.'

`I will be on hand at that hour without fail, sir.' Richard paused a moment, then went on: `My business tonight concerns a Nignora Goudar. I wonder if you can tell me anything of her?'

`I can tell you that she is plaguey expensive.' Sir William eyed Richard speculatively through his quizzing glass. `Unless you have five hundred guineas to throw away, and are more of a fool than I take you to be, you will find a less ruinous wanton with whom to post, the night.'

'Five hundred guineas 1' repeated Richard, shocked into a vulgar whistle. `Strap me, sir. But she must be the eighth wonder of the world to demand such a sum for her favors.'

`She is not far from it,' came the quiet murmur. `Few women that I have met are more beautiful, her conversation is delightful, and her career at least unusual.'

`I pray you to inform me of it, sir; though I assure you that I wish to meet the lady only on a matter of business.'

`Then I must give you another warning. Her husband is a rogue of the first water and she is his willing accomplice. As you may know, gambling is forbidden by law in Naples; with the inevitable result that even the beggars gamble in the gutters, and the rich, having no public casinos to go to, feel the greater itch to stake their money, so get themselves fleeced nightly in private houses where professional games are run. Goudar is the proprietor of the establishment most frequented by Neapolitan society. Thousands of guineas are often won or lost there at a single sitting, and Madame Goudar acts as the lure to draw rich foreigners into this gilded thieves'-kitchen.'

`*I had no* thought to gamble either, sir. 'Tis another person"s business upon which I wish to see the lady.'

`Even so you may burn your fingers unless you have a care. A combination of brains and beauty make the Goudars a pair of cheats *second* to none in my experience.'

Richard fingered the lace at his throat. `I will heed your warning well, Sir William. But you intrigue me mightily. I pray you will tell me Madame Goudar's history.'

`Some sixteen years ago the lovely Sara was a little slut serving in a London tavern. She had hardly a rag to her back and could neither read nor write. Goudar saw her there and with the eye of a connoisseur appreciated the fact that one day she would be a remarkable beauty. He took the child away, made her his mistress, and spent six years in educating her. He was abundantly repaid for his trouble, for she proved quick to learn, and now, or even when he first brought her to Naples, I would defy you to detect that she had not been brought up among people of the first quality. On arriving here he devised -, most skilful expedient for drawing attention to this beautiful little stool pigeon, that he had reared with such care; he made her appear in sackcloth and publicly renounce the Protestant religion as the work of the Devil.'

`What a monstrous thing to do!' exclaimed Richard.

`Nat at all,' laughed Sir William, `for she was of Irish descent and *birth,* had been baptized into the Catholic faith as an infant, and had never subscribed to any other.'

Richard joined in the laugh. `What a delightful cheat! They certainly deserved to do well for themselves.'

`And they did!' Sir William rejoined. `The Neapolitan nobility flocked to Goudar's house to make the acquaintance of the beautiful apostate, and their gaming-room prospered exceedingly. But more, the ladies were so intrigued that they wanted to know her too; and her manners were so charming, her taste so exquisite, her ton so exactly right, that she acquired the friendship of many of the best-born women in Naples, including even that of the Queen. She does not, of course, visit them, owing to the anomaly of her position, but they visit her ; and in the afternoons there are often half a dozen titled ladies to be found taking a dish of tea with her in her apartment.'

'Tis an amazing achievement for one of such lowly beginnings,' Richard murmured, `and makes me all the more eager to meet her.'

`They had one setback,' Sir William remarked. `It was several years ago, round about '82, I think, as it was at the time that a notorious rogue called Giacomo Casanova was living in Naples, and held a partnership in Goudar's crooked bank. King Ferdinand took a fancy to the lovely Sara Goudar, and rumour has it that she was not unkind to His Majesty. In any case, the Queen found a *billet-doux* from her in the King's pocket, with the result that the Goudars were promptly sent into exile. But after eighteen months they returned, and ever since have enjoyed such an admirable prosperity that Sara will not even consider an offer for a single night with her if it be less than five hundred guineas.'

It was now getting on for seven o'clock, so Richard thanked Sir William for his valuable information and excused himself to return to Naples. By half-past eight he arrived at *Crocielles,* supped there and secured the address of the G oudars' house. After what he had heard from Sir William of Madame Goudar's firm adherence to her enormous fee he was far from sanguine about his chances of bringing to fruition the plot he had hatched ; but he could think of no other way of securing his own ends, so desperation drove him on to attempt it, and soon after ten he knocked at the Goudars' front door.

A negro porter dressed in scarlet livery opened it. On seeing Richard's well-groomed appearance and learning that he was an Englishman who had come from *Crocielles the* porter made no difficulty about letting him in. A footman took his cloak and hat, asked him to be good enough to leave his sword in the sword rack, and conducted him upstairs.

He was ushered into a big, comfortably furnished salon. It contained only one large table at its far end, and at that, owing to the early hours which were kept in Naples, the game was already in full swing. About a dozen men were seated at it and most- of them wore broad-brimmed straw hats, which looked incongruous in conjunction with their satin clothes, but were part of the stock in-trade of such places, as they shaded the eyes of the gamblers from the strong light thrown from the multi-branched pair of candelabra on the table. On a sofa at the end of the room nearest the door a lady was sitting, holding a small court of four cavaliers, but as Richard entered she at once stood up, left them and came over to greet him.

She curtsied; he made a leg, then introduced himself. As he did so he had no doubt at all that he was addressing the remarkable Sara. Her hair was beautifully coiffured and powdered, so he could not tell if it was black, but in all other respects she possessed the typical coloring of an Irish colleen. Her eyes were a midnight blue, her lips cherry red, her brows arched and dark, her skin f resh, and her cheeks held a rosy flush that art might have added to but could not have simulated. Her figure was well rounded; and if she was on the wrong side of thirty, as from what Sir William had said she must be, she certainly did not look it. Richard agreed with the diplomat's estimate that she was an outstandingly handsome woman.

She had greeted him in French, which she spoke almost as fluently as himself, so for a few minutes he conversed with her in that language. With long-practised skill she plumbed him with the utmost discretion on his visit to Naples and his acquaintances there. Then, quickly satisfied by his air of breeding and casual mention of a few of the leading families, she led him over to the gaming table and introduced him to her husband.

Goudar was holding the bank. He was a small, sharp-featured man, with a guilelessly innocent expression. After bowing politely to Richard he gave him a swift appraising glance, then waved him to a chair. Richard pulled out a fistful of golden ducats, put them on the table and was dealt a hand of cards in the next round. He had not the least desire to play, but felt that to win the goodwill that was so imperative to the success of his plan he must lose a certain amount for the good of the house.

As so frequently happens in such cases, he positively could not lose. He was very far from being one of the highest players at the table, so Goudar showed no particular interest in him, obviously regarding him as one of the casual visitors to Naples who was no true gambler but just liked an occasional flutter, and normally left a score or so of ducats behind which helped to pay the running expenses of the establishment. When such people went away in pocket they usually came another night and lost their winnings with a bit more in addition. When they did not they were a good advertisement to the place and its proprietor's apparent honesty.

After an hour's play Richard found himself nearly forty ducats to the good, so deciding not to waste any more time he picked up his winnings and left the table.

Madame Goudar had from time to time been over to see how Fortune was treating the gamblers. She now got up at once and came to meet Richard. With a charming smile she said: `Monsieur is in luck tonight. But he will come again to give my husband his revenge ; is it not so?'

Richard returned the smile, but shook his head. `Alas, Madame, my time in Naples is short ; yet, all the same, I would not have you be the loser by my visit.' Then, taking her hand, he poured the fistful of gold that he had won into it, and added: `These are to buy roses for you, Madame; but no roses that you can buy will equal those you already carry in your cheeks.'

Her blue eyes lit with swift appreciation of his gesture and compliment; then with a modesty all the more fascinating from being unexpected, she veiled them with her long, dark, curling lashes, and murmured: `Ca c'est tres gentill, Monsieur.'

`Non, Madame; c'est une tribute juste,' replied Richard.

Suddenly she lifted her eyes and asked shrewdly: `Why do you do this, Monsieur? You are both young and handsome, and men who are that are rarely rich.'

`Because I would crave a few words with you apart, Madame.'

She smiled again, and beckoned him to a smaller settee, out of earshot of both the gaming table and the big sofa round which she had been holding her little court of changing 'men ever since Richard had arrived. As they sat down she said quite simply. `You wish to make your suit with me?'

`Nay, Madame,' he replied frankly. `Were I to be longer in Naples I would be greatly tempted to haunt your doorstep until you either gave in or drove me from it ; but tonight I come to plead the suit of another.'

He caught her glance of surprise, but went on quickly: `I have reason to believe that Don Diego de Sidonia y Ulloa is quite mad about you, yet you are so stony-hearted as to treat him with disdain.' Instantly she stiffened, and asked: `Is he, then, a friend of yours?'

'Hardly that, Madame. No more than an acquaintance; yet I am vastly concerned that you should regard his suit with greater kindness.'

`Why should I?' she replied, with a hard note in her voice. `I am no ordinary courtesan, to jump into bed at any man's bidding. Time was when I had to oblige certain of our best patrons, but thank God 'tis no longer so. At a price I am still willing to consider giving myself to a man from whom I shall derive little pleasure, providing he be reasonably personable. Don Diego fails to raise a flicker in me, *and so* far he has come up to only half the price I ask. Why should I put myself out to oblige that stiff-necked Spaniard?'

`Madame, I have a genuine appreciation of your feelings,' Richard murmured tactfully. `As you have guessed, I am unfortunately by no means rich myself. Otherwise I would offer to make up the price you demand. As it is I can only cast myself on your good nature. I beg you, as the greatest possible favour to myself, to accept the sum he offers, and give him an assignation for tomorrow night.'

She gave him a cynical little smile, and then began to laugh. `I see it now. You are in love with the equally stiff-necked black-browed wife of his, and want me to take care of him so that the coast is clear for you to get into his house.'

Richard grinned at her. `Madame, it would ill become me to admit it; but if you choose to think that the reason for my request, I should be hard put to it to prove you wrong.'

Sara Goudar shook her head. `Nay, Monsieur. You have afforded me much amusement, but I am no philanthropist. The Spaniard can well afford to pay, so if he wants me let him disgorge his ducats. As for yourself, love is the best of locksmiths and time brings opportunity. If you have an urge to enjoy his wife, good fortune to you.'

`Alas, you have named my trouble,' Richard said sadly. `I am debarred the benefits with which time so often rewards her patient votaries. I am under orders to leave Naples within thirty hours, and 'tis tomorrow night or never.'

Again she shook her head, now a little impatiently: ' 'Tis my time and your own that you are wasting, Monsieur, in this profitless conversation. I see no reason whatever why I should incommode myself to further the amours of people who are of no account to me.'

Richard now feared that he was bowling against an impregnable wicket, but he pulled his last trick. Taking her hand he suddenly changed from French to English; and, gambling on the fact that as far as he knew she had not been in Ireland since her childhood, he said with the best imitation of an Irish brogue that he could muster

`Ach, come now! Ye'll do it fer the sake of ould Ireland?'

Her blue eyes lit up again as she stared at him in surprise. `Are ye tellin' me you're Irish then?'

`Bejabbers, I am! Now wasn't I born no more than five miles from Limerick town?'

`Ach well now, to be sure.' She clasped his hand and put her other upon it. ` 'Tis all the difference in the wide world that's making'. An' how could I bring myself to refuse such a broth of a buoy? It's an ould hack I am if the truth be known, for all the blessed Saints have preserved me looks. What's a night in a lifetime to such as meself ? Sure an' I'll give that tailor's dummy of a Spaniard an assignation just as yourself is wishin'. Though I'd leifer 'twas you than he that had designs on this bit of a woman that I am.'

So Richard and Sara parted the best of friends, and with a firm understanding that she should send a *billet-doux* to Don Diego saying that she had relented, and was prepared to receive him at midnight the following night.

Richard slept at the Palazzo *Sessa*. In the morning he made his adieux to Mrs. Cadogan and the Junoesque Emma, thanked them for the hospitality that they had afforded him, and said he hoped that the future might bring him some opportunity of being of service to them. Then he rode out to Caserta.

Queen Caroline received him a little before midday. TheY had another long talk about the difficulties of Madame Marie Antoinette, then the Queen gave him her letter, told him that he would always be welcome at the Court of Naples, and bade him godspeed.

Afterwards General Acton gave him another letter. It was addressed to the *Tenente* Umberto Godolfo, of the sloop *Aspide*. The Prime Minister said that it contained instructions for the sloop to put to sea at the earliest possible moment and convey Richard to Marseilles, or the nearest French port to which contrary winds might bring her. He added that he had selected Lieutenant Godolfo for this task because he spoke French well and could readily be made aware of the wishes of his passenger.

Richard thanked the General, took leave of him, then said goodbye to Sir William Hamilton with real affection and regret. By half-past two he was back in Naples. Having stabled Sir William's horse, he had a quick meal, then took a carozza down to the harbour, where enquiries at the *Castello dell'Ovo* soon enabled him to run Lieutenant Godolfo to earth.

The *Tenente* proved to be a tall, dark young man of about the same age as Richard. On reading the Prime Minister's order he said that he was delighted with his mission, and would be most happy to serve the Chevalier Blane to the best of his ability.

Richard then asked him how long it would take to prepare the sloop for sea.

`We have first to water and provision her,' replied the *Tenente ;* 'that will take some six hours; but I will hasten matters all I can to meet the wishes of the distinguished passenger that the *Aspide* is to have the honour of carrying.'

Having seen a crew of Corsican fishermen do a similar job in two hours, on the *felucca* that had brought him from Marseilles, Richard was not impressed; but, in view of all he had heard of the Royal Neapolitan Navy's shortcomings, he was not surprised, and he would not have minded if the *Tenente* had required double the time. So he said

`That is excellent, *Tenente mio. But* I beg you, do not work yourself or your men too harshly, as the lady is unlikely to come aboard before midnight. In fact I doubt if she will have completed her packing by then, so I may have to kick my heels far her till one or two in the morning.'

`The lady?' exclaimed the young officer, giving him a puzzled look.

`Yes,' Richard replied with a frown. `A lady, her maid and page are making the voyage with us.'

The *Tenente* glanced again at General Acton's letter. `His Excellency the Prime Minister says nothing about a lady here.'

`Does he not!' Richard shrugged. 'Ah well! *Excellentissimo* Acton is a busier man than you or I, *Tenente,* and has little time for making his letters longer than they need be. No doubt he thought it unnecessary to mention the matter, and considered it quite sufficient to order you to place yourself at my disposal.'

`Indeed, *Monsieur le Chevalier,'* the *Tenente* agreed eagerly. `I feel sure you must be right. You have only to tell me your wishes. The lady will not be as comfortable as I would like on board my little ship ; but I will make the best possible preparations for her reception.'

Richard thanked him graciously, said that he hoped to bring the lady and her attendants down to the quay at about one in the morning, and, returning to his carozza, ordered its driver to take him straight to Crocielles.

There he booked a room, said that he was going straight to bed, asked to be called at ten o'clock that night with a light meal, and at-ranged for a coach with a reliable driver to call for him at a quarter to eleven.

When he was woken after his six hours' sleep he felt fit for anything and extraordinarily confident of success. He was sure that he could count on lovely Irish Sara to do her part, and that Tansanta, having had nearly thirty-six hours for refection, would have decided to come with him.

To his mind it was unthinkable that the proud Don Diego should take any course other than that of repudiating a wife who left him. A noble Spaniard of such ancient lineage would naturally wish to have an heir to succeed to his titles and estates, and he could not beget a legal one without a wife. For that, if for no other reason, he would obviously set about getting an annulment of his first marriage without delay, thus leaving Tansanta free to marry again. Richard felt certain that after a little thought she would see that for herself; so he was now untroubled by any further doubts about the issue. Since she loved him, had abundant courage and could rest assured of reassuming an honorable status within a comparatively short time, he would find her packed and ready to enter on a new and happier future as his wife-to-be.

Having eaten his meal, washed, dressed and scented himself, he came downstairs, settled his reckoning and, going outside, gave the driver of the coach careful instructions. He then had himself driven to within a few hundred yards of Tansanta's home, got out and walked to a spot near the garden gate where he could keep it under observation without being seen.

To his great satisfaction, shortly after eleven o'clock, Don Diego's tall figure emerged, and the Spaniard's jaunty step was sufficient to indicate the happy errand on which he was bent. Richard watched him disappear from view, allowed a safety margin of ten minutes, then went in over the wall.

A light was burning in Tansanta's bedroom, so he advanced boldly across the garden and called softly up to her. After a moment she appeared darkly silhouetted against the partly open, lighted window.

`All is well, my sweet,' he said in a low voice. `Don Diego went off a quarter of an hour ago to rendezvous with Madame Goudar. I arranged the matter with him myself, so I am certain of it; you have nothing to fear. Are Maria and Quetzal ready? I have a coach waiting. Shall I come up and help carry down your boxes?'

She shook her head and began to sob.

`What is it? Surely you are not still hesitating?' he asked in a slightly louder voice that held a tremor of uneasiness. ` 'Tis as certain as that tomorrow's sun will rise that Don Diego will ask for an annulment. He must! And the Church could not refuse to grant it to him. 'Tis the only way in which he can beget himself an heir.'

`I cannot come with you, *Riché!'* !' she sobbed. `I cannot!'

`Why?' he cried sharply, made terse by sudden desperation. `Why not?'

`I I cannot!' she choked out. `I love you! I would remain your mistress all my life. I would be your slave! There is nothing I would not do for you, except this. I already carry his child! I shall be the mother of his heir and 'twould be unforgivable to deprive him of it. I cannot go with you.'

Turning suddenly, she fled back into her room. Stunned for a while, Richard stared up at the lighted oblong of the window. For him, those words of hers, `I already carry his child', conveyed a terrible finality. He knew now instinctively that no threats, arguments or prayers could prevail. Slowly he turned about, stumbled across the garden and climbed over its wall.

Half an hour later Lieutenant Umberto Godolfo received him aboard the sloop *Aspide*. Advancing across the narrow deck the young Neapolitan spread out his hands and asked in surprise

`But, *Monsieur le Chevalier,* where is the lady you were to bring with you?'

`As far as I am concerned she is dead,' replied Richard tonelessly. Then, with a touch of his father the Admiral, he added in a voice that Blaneed no reply

`*Tenente.* Be good enough to order your ship to sea.'

CHAPTER NINETEEN
THE GATHERING STORM

Richard had spent nine days and nights in Naples. During that time he believed himself to have been carried up to the highest peaks of human happiness and dashed down to the lowest depths of human misery. He had not only burnt the candle at both ends, but also burnt himself. For a week, lack of sleep, except for a few hours a day snatched when most other people were getting up, had made no impression on him. He splendid youth, fortified by love as by draughts of some Olympian nectar, had given him temporarily the buoyancy of a demigod. But the past forty-eight hours of uncertainty, strain and desperation had done what his physical excesses had failed to accomplish. His nerves were in shreds; he felt empty as a drum, mentally exhausted and absolutely at the end of his tether.

Yet, as he drove down to the harbor, the core of sound common sense, that acted as a balance to his highly-strung nature, had enabled him to take stock of his position clearly.

It was seven months since he had first met Tansanta. For one month of that time he had enjoyed a love idyll with her, and for one week a tornado of passion; but for close on half a year his love for her had deprived him of all his normal zest for life. The future offered no hope of a higher proportion of happiness against misery either for her or him. Therefore, it seemed, there was only one sensible thing to do. If he wished for any contentment in the future he must exercise his willpower as he had never done before. Each time he thought of Tansanta, instead of letting his mind dwell upon her, as he had previously, he must force himself to think of something else. He must cut her right out of his life, and henceforth regard her as though she had died that night.

On his return voyage to Marseilles the weather did not favour him as it had on his outward trip. For a good part of the time it rained and blew, but not sufficiently to make him seasick; and so that he should not have time to brood he spent all his waking hours helping the crew with the sails and winches. On the evening of Tuesday, November 24th, after six days at sea, he said goodbye to Lieutenant Godolfo and stepped ashore. Then, knowing how anxious Madame Marie Antoinette would be to learn the result of his mission, he took post chaise first thing next morning,

Having sustained three days and nights of appalling jolting, and arrived in Paris at midday on the 28th.

He was, once more, incredibly tired from his arduous journey and, feeling that his reappearance at the *Tuileries* might arouse comment, he wished to make it at a time when it was least likely to attract attention. The next day was a Sunday, and knowing that the Sovereigns received the Foreign Ministers on that day, he felt that it would offer as good an opportunity as any ; so he slept the clock round at *La Belle Étoile,* and made his way to the palace on the following afternoon.

There he found things much as he had left them. The Royal Family had practically no privacy. The garden was full of idlers staring in at the windows, and 800 National Guards were. posted in and about the building; there were groups of them lounging in all the halls and principal rooms, and sentries on the staircases and at almost every door.

Mingling with the crowd of diplomats and such courtiers as continued to attend the royal receptions, he made his way upstairs. Most of the Ambassadors were known to him by sight, but there were not many people there with whom he had ever exchanged more than a few words, and, with one exception, to those who addressed him he mentioned casually that for the past three weeks he had been absent from Paris on a trip to England.

The exception was Lord Robert Fitzgerald, who was still acting as the British *Charge d' Affaires* pending the appointment of a new Ambassador. They had met several times at the far more brilliant receptions of a similar nature held at Versailles, and Lord Robert knew from Mr. Hailes of Richard's secret activities. Richard was responsible only to Mr. Pitt, and his connection with the Embassy was limited to using it as a post office and a bank; but, as a matter of courtesy, he thought it proper to inform Lord Robert where he had actually been; and, having done so in a low voice, he added that he would be making a full report of his journey direct to the Prime Minister.

At the entry of the Sovereigns a human lane was formed and the usual procedure gone through. Richard had placed himself in a position where the Queen could hardly fail to see him, and on doing so, she gave a faint start, then a little nod of recognition ; but she did not beckon him towards her. For the better part of an hour the King and Queen talked to various people each for a few moments, then they withdrew.

The company did not disperse at once, as these biweekly receptions of the *Corps Diplomatique* were a good opportunity for the representatives of the foreign, powers to exchange news and conduct informal business; so Richard was able to remain among them inconspicuously while waiting to be sent for, as he felt sure he would be in due course.

Presently a fair woman, some five or six years older than the Queen, paused near him. As he took in her large gentle eyes and air of tender melancholy, she gave him a faint smile. He was somewhat surprised, as, although he recalled having seen her at the *Tuileries* before his departure for Naples, he did not know her; but he at once returned her smile and made her a bow.

She sank in a curtsy and, as she rose from it, murmured: `*Monsieur. Je suis la Princess de Lamballe.'*

Her whispered introduction at once recalled to Richard all he had heard about her. She was said to be not overburdened with brains, but very pious and extremely charitable. She had married the only son of the immensely rich Duc de Penthièvre, so was the sister in-law of the Duc de Orleans, but, unlike him, she was wholly attached to the Queen. After only a year of marriage her husband died, so she had devoted herself to good works on her father-in-law's estates; but on coming to Court for the wedding celebrations of Madame Marie Antoinette, the young Dauphine had taken a great fancy to her, begged her to remain and made her Superintendent of her Household.

For some six years she had remained the Queen's closest friend ; until the latter began to frequent the gayer company of Madame de Polignac. Then, for ten years that followed, the Princess had again given most of her time to improving the conditions of the peasants on her father-in-law's estates, so .that she had become known throughout the Province as `the good angel'. During the terrible events that had taken place at Versailles early in October she had been at Rambouillet ; but, immediately on hearing of them, she had courageously driven through the night to Paris, arrived at the *Tuileries* on the morning of the 8th, and at once resumed her old place as the Queen's first lady and *confidante.*

For a few minutes Richard exchanged the type of banalities with her that might have passed between two acquaintances who had not met for a few weeks; then she dropped her handkerchief. As he picked it up he felt the stiffness of a piece of paper in its folds. Guessing it to be a note for him, he swiftly palmed the paper before handing the handkerchief back to her. After a few more airy exchanges she left him; then he strolled out of the room, and as soon as he could find a corridor in which he would be unobserved, read the note. It ran *My apartments are above these. Please go to them. Show this note to my maid and she will let you in. Wait there until I can join you.*

Unhurriedly, so as not to attract attention, he followed the directions he had been given. In the anteroom he found an elderly maid busy with some mending. At the sight of the note she let him through to a salon, and asked him to take a seat by the fire.

After about ten minutes the Princess de Lamballe came in, and locked the door of the anteroom chamber behind her. With no more than a smile in response to Richard's bow, she walked across the salon to a door at its far end, and disappeared through it. Wondering what these mystifications portended, Richard sat down again. He had not long to wait for an answer. Within two minutes the door opened and the Princess came out, but this time she was preceded by the Queen. Evidently the two sets of apartments were connected by a secret staircase in the thickness of the wall, and the Queen was now coming up to Madame de Lamballe's rooms whenever she wanted to prevent it becoming known that she was giving anyone a private audience.

Richard thought her looking somewhat better than when he had last spoken to her; but she had aged a lot in the past few months, and he noticed a slight nervous twitching of her hands as she asked him about his mission.

With a cheerful smile he at once assured her that it had been successful and presented the letter he had brought her from her sister; so he felt a natural disappointment when she said, with a sad shake of her head.

`Alas, Monsieur, I fear you have had your long journey to no purpose. At first the King was in favour of my idea, but he has since decided against it, and now feels that it would be both impolitic and wrong to send the Dauphin from us.'

Richard was silent for a moment, then he said: `Forgive me, Madame, but His Majesty has frequently been known to change his mind on other matters; is there not a possibility that he will do so on this?'

`I fear not,' she replied unhappily. `Since your departure we have enjoyed a reasonable tranquility. How long it will last it is impossible to say; but His Majesty fears that the moment it became known that we had smuggled the Dauphin out of the country another outbreak of violence would result.'

"Tis a risk, Madame, but one that I should have thought well worth taking,' put in the Princess. `Further outbreaks may occur *in any case,* and if you take this chance you would at least have the satisfaction of knowing His Highness to be safe; whereas, if you do riot send him away now it may prove impossible to do so later.'

`Oh, dear Lamballe, how I agree!' exclaimed the Queen. "Tis my worse nightmare that a time may come when we shall be still more closely guarded, and those furies breaking in again will do my son a violence. But His Majesty has ruled that even our child is no longer our own to do with as we will. Like everything else I once thought was ours, he maintains that. we hold the Dauphin in trust for the Nation, and that to send him away would be to wrong the people. If there be reason in that, then my mother's heart makes me blind to it ; yet the King has so many cares that, even in this, I could not bring myself to argue with him.'

Richard would have liked to suggest to the Queen that the best thing she could do was to box her stupid husband's ears, and tell him that when it came to the safety of her son she would not stand for any more of his pathetic daydreaming ; but, since such sound comment was impossible, he remained silent until she asked him how he found Queen Caroline.

For some twenty minutes he gave her the news from Naples, then she took a paper from her pocket and, handing it to him, said

`This, Mr. Blane, is to cover the expenses of your journey. And, believe me, because it can have no sequel, I am none the less grateful to you for undertaking it. For what little it is worth in these sad times you may always count upon my friendship.'

Having murmured his thanks and kissed her hand, he watched her leave the room by its far doorway with the Princess, then, a few minutes later, Madame de Lamballe returned and let him out into the anteroom. He did not look at the paper the Queen had given him until he was outside the palace, but when he did he was pleasantly surprised. It was a draft on Thellusson's Bank for 500 Louis, and his journey to Naples had cost him barely a third of that sum.

Now that Richard was once more free of the Queen's business he felt that he must try to make up for lost time in cultivating the most prominent figures in the National Assembly; so he began to spend several hours each day in the Riding School of the *Tuileries,* where it now met. As he already knew quite a number of the deputies it was not difficult for him to get himself introduced to others that he wished to meet, and he soon had acquaintances in all parties.

In the late summer, during the first few weeks that the Three Estates had sat as one body, the Assembly had naturally resolved itself into two parties: those who had been in favour of joint sittings and those who had opposed them. The more reactionary nobles and clergy, who composed the latter, had taken little part in the debates, treated the deliberations with cynical contempt and, wherever possible, sabotaged the proceedings. But in the autumn, realizing the futility of such a policy, the more sensible among them had begun to play a more constructive part, and this had resulted in the whole body splitting into a great number of small parties, all varying slightly in their views and ranging from absolutists to outright republicans.

The Extreme Right was led by d'Espréménil and the Vicomte de Mirabeau, brother of the great orator. The Main Right was a slightly larger body and possessed two of the best statesmen in the Assembly: the Vicomte de Cazalès, a young Captain in the Queen's Dragoons who had emerged as a clear thinking and lucid speaker; and the Abbé Maury, an extraordinary skilful and subtle debator. The Right Center, which aimed at Constitutional Monarchy on English lines, was a loose but still more numerous party. It included many of the most respected members of the original Third Estate, Mounier and Malouet among them; also the Counts Lally Tollendal and Clermont-Tonnerre, with most of. the other Liberal nobles.

The Left, which desired a strictly limited monarchy, was nebulous but powerful in numbers, as it consisted of the larger part of the deputies elected to the Third Estate and the majority of the curs who had been elected to the First. The Protestant pastor, Rabaut-Saint-Étienne, Duport, Alexander Lameth, Barnave, Camas, Le Chapelier, Lafayette, Bailly and the Abbe Sieyès were all members of it, but a number of them were now gravitating towards the Extreme Left, which consisted of a small group *of enrages,* as they were called, led by Petion and a dry little lawyer from Arras named Maximilien Robespierre.

Richard found that even his three weeks' absence from Paris had brought about a marked change in the character of the Assembly. As early as August, the surrender of the King after the taking of the Bastille and the `Great Fear' had led to a number of the most reactionary among the nobles who sat for the Second Estate following the Comte d'Artois, and other Princes, into exile. The attack on Versailles and removal of the Royal Family to Paris in October had greatly accentuated the movement, so that over two hundred deputies, all of whom were strongly Monarchist in principle, had now abandoned their seats and gone abroad, thus enormously weakening the Right and Right Center.

Moreover it was apparent that the mob that daily filled the public galleries of the Assembly now exercised an even greater influence on its deliberations than before. The Riding School was a somewhat smaller chamber than the Salle *des Menus Plaisirs* in which the Assembly had sat while at Versailles, but, owing to the decrease in the number of deputies that now attended, the accommodation for the public was as commodious as before. In consequence, the deputies of the Right were constantly exposed to methodical terrorism from the supporters of the Left, both in tile chamber and out of it. In several instances members who spoke strongly in support of the monarchy were threatened with having their houses burnt down, and all those who held moderate opinions found it necessary to go about armed. Even the highly respected Malouet never attended a sitting without a brace of pistols in his belt; and Mounier, wearied out with the threats and heckling of the people to secure whose liberties he had done so much, had resigned in disgust and joined the exiles abroad.

This recent abandonment of the struggle by Mounier struck Richard as a particularly alarming portent, as the deputy for Grenoble could be considered, even more than Lafayette, Bailly or Mirabeau, as the Father of the Revolution. As far back as June, 1788, the *noblesse* of Grenoble had held a consultation with local representatives of the other Orders and decided that, in view of the troubled state of the country, the ancient Estates of Dauphine should be revived. Without the royal consent elections had been held, and deputies nominated to sit in a Provincial Assembly to consist of the Three Estates deliberating together, and in which the representatives of the Third Estate equaled the total of the other two.

The Government had sent the Marshal de Vaux with troops to put a stop to these unorthodox proceedings, but he had found opinion in the Province so firmly united that he had been forced to compromise, exacting only the concession that, instead of the Assembly sitting in the Provincial capital, it should meet at the nearby town of Vizille. And there it had met, ten months before the States General assembled at Versailles, and already constituted on a basis that it later took the States General two months to achieve. The mainspring of this extraordinary innovation in the Government of the ancient Monarchy of France had been the young and energetic lawyer Jean Joseph Mounier, who was chosen Secretary to the Assembly and drafted most of its resolutions. Moreover, when the States General met in the following year it had naturally adopted most of the precedents set by the Assembly of Vizille as the . only example of democratic government then existing in the country, and recognized Mounier as the leading authority on parliamentary procedure.

Yet now, only seven months after the States General had assembled, such an iconoclastic fervor had seized on the mentality of the people, and so intolerant had they become of all moderate opinion, that this great champion of democracy had despaired of seeing a stable Constitution emerge from the state of semi anarchy to which the surrender of the royal authority had reduced France. He had been driven into exile amidst the hoots and menaces of the scum of the *Faubourgs,* who used the cry of 'liberty' as an excuse to set all law at defiance, and whose sole object was to raise riots which would enable them to plunder the houses of the richer citizens.

This question of formulating a Constitution had naturally been one of the first matters with which the Assembly had concerned itself. The King had long been willing to grant one and, if he had had the courage of his convictions, he could have saved himself infinite trouble by doing so in '87 or '88. Then, practically any Charter ensuring the people reasonable liberties would have put an end to all serious agitations for reform. Even after the States General met, had he possessed an ounce of resolution he could still have taken matters out of their hands, and by giving the people a permanent voice in the government of the country retained the whole executive power himself. But his policy of drift had now landed him in a situation where he was not to be *allowed any* say in the matter at all ; and as the year '89 drew to a close a succession of debates in the Assembly showed an ever increasing tendency to leave the King as nothing but a puppet to be paraded for the amusement of the people on State occasions.

Owing to the innumerable problems that confronted the Assembly, and the impossibility of its hearing all the deputies who wished to speak, it had adopted the wise course of appointing a number of Committees to look into various matters and report upon them. On the very day of the fall of the *Bastille,* a Committee had been set up to draft the Constitution, its members being: the Archbishop of Bordeaux, the Bishop of Autun, Counts Lally Tollendal and Clermont-Tonnerre ; Mounier, Sieyès, Le Chapetier and Bergasse. They had laboured for two months, but by the time they produced their recommendations public opinion had so far outstripped them that all the most important clauses in their draft were rejected. Another Committee had then been appointed, this time consisting entirely of members of the Third Estate with the one exception of the Bishop and, gifted as Monsieur de Talleyrand Périgord might be, lie could hardly be considered as a typical representative of the clergy. He had in fact, two days before Richard left for Naples, actually proposed and carried through the Assembly a motion that all Church property *should* be confiscated and sold for the benefit of the State.

Richard was greatly interested in this question of the Constitution, because he was shrewd enough to see that, in its final form, it would decree the manner in which all vital decisions were to be taken by the French Government in future. If France was to continue as a monarchy and that was clearly still the wish of 95 per cent of her population the King must be left with some functions, otherwise it was pointless to retain him. But would he, be left, for example, with the power to make war or peace without the consent of the Assembly? That was the type of knowledge which, should a sudden international crisis arise, would prove invaluable to Mr. Pitt; and it was Richard's business to obtain it.

In the last days of November and the first half of December Richard dined or supped with a number of interesting peoples the Monarchist leader Cazales, the clever antimonarchist lawyer Barnave and the fiery young journalist Camille Desmouhns among them but he had been disappointed in his efforts to secure more than a few words at any one time with his old friend, the now extremely busy Bishop of Autun. As de Périgord was one of the only three men who had served on the Committee of the Constitution since its inception, and therefore in an almost unique position to talk about it with authority, Richard decided that he must somehow get him to give him an evening. So one morning he tackled the lame prelate as he was about to enter the Chamber, and said with a smile *'Monsieur L'Evéque,* I never thought I would have to reproach you on the score of hospitality; yet I feel the time has come when I have some right to do so.'

'Indeed!' exclaimed the Bishop, raising a *quizzical eyebrow.* `And why, pray, may I ask?'

`It was June when you promised to arrange for me to meet Monsieur de Mirabeau at dinner, and here we are in December; but you have not done so yet.'

`Well, well!' De Perigord murmured. `The distractions of a changing world must serve as the excuse for my forgetfulness. But by a lucky chance de Mirabeau is pledged to dine with me on Saturday next. We have some private business we wish to discuss after dinner; but if you would not take it ill of me in asking you to make some excuse to leave us early I should be delighted if you will join us for the meal.'

Richard was enchanted with this opportunity to kill two birds with one stone. He had met the Comte de Mirabeau several times in '87, at the famous breakfasts that De Perigord used to give for talented men of Liberal views; but in the present year he had found the now famous deputy much too occupied to acknowledge their acquaintance when they met by more than a smile and a brief greeting. It had been only as an excuse to secure a good long talk with de Périgord that he had mentioned de Mirabeau's name, but Fortune was now favoring him with the chance to talk on terms of *intimacy with* both *these* intellectual giants at the same sitting.

On the Saturday, feeling that his promise to leave soon after dinner justified his arriving early, he was at the wicket gate of the charming little house at Passy by a quarter to four. The first snow of the year had fallen, but the garden path was neatly swept; and within a few moments of knocking on the door he was standing in front of the bright wood fire in the sitting room.

Having greeted his host he remarked: `Is it not positively fantastic to consider the changes that have occurred in France since I was last in this room; and that less than eight months ago?'

De Périgord smiled. `At least there no longer exists a *Bastille* for the Queen to pop you into, and *lettres de cachet* are quite gone out of fashion.'

Richard suppressed a start. He had completely forgotten the lie he had told on his last visit there ; but fortunately the Bishop failed to notice his guilty flush, as he was fiddling with his snuffbox before offering it. As he did so, he went on: `Joking apart, though, there have been changes enough, and in my opinion far too many.'

`It surprises me to hear you say so,' Richard replied, accepting a pinch with a little bow. `I thought you firmly set upon overturning the old order.'

`Rehabilitating rather than overturning,' corrected de Périgord mildly. `I pride myself somewhat upon being a realist; and it was clear to most of us who used to meet here at my little breakfasts in the old days that the Court were living in a land of make-believe. I wished to bring them down to earth with a full realization of their responsibilities ; but it was far from my desire to witness the degradation to which the monarchy has been subject in these past few months.'

`Since we have always spoken frankly,' Richard said a little diffidently, `you will forgive me if I remark that Your Grace's name ranks high among those who have brought the degradation of the Monarch about.'

De Périgord gave him a swift calculating look. `That is fair comment upon my public acts. My only desire is to serve France, and if I am to do so I must continue to swim with the tide. But my private hopes for the outcome of events in this momentous year were very different. As far back as last July, on the day the *Bastille* fell, so perturbed was I by the course matters were taking that I went secretly, in the middle of the night, to the Comte d'Artois and woke him in his bed.'

For a moment the Bishop paused, then, with a flutter of his lace handkerchief, he went on: `For the King I have nothing but contempt, and I regard the Comte de Provence as a treacherous and pompous fool; but I am not altogether without respect for the younger of the three brothers. I told His Highness that, in my opinion, owing to the King's mental cowardice, matters had already been allowed to go far beyond the point at which all reasonable reformers aimed, and that the monarchy was in grave danger. I added that the only way to save it was for the King to dissolve the National Assembly by force if need be and to march on Paris with his troops. I implored him to tell the King that this was his last chance ; and that if he failed to act, in another twenty-four hours it would be too late. His Highness was so impressed with my earnestness that he at once got up, dressed and went to the King. No doubt His Majesty made his usual promise that he would "think it over". In any case, he did not take my advice; but it is not my fault that he is where he is now.'

Richard had been staring at his friend in astonishment, and he exclaimed: 'Knowing as I do your animosity to the Sovereigns, I think the step you took does you great credit.'

'*Mon ami, I do not* care a rap for the Sovereigns, but I did and do care a very great deal for the future of my country.!

'That I have always realized; yet I have always regarded Your Grace as a cautious man, and in this instance you took an extraordinary risk. Were your act to become known your colleagues i n the Assembly would tear you to pieces.'

The Bishop shrugged. `Only one man could prove it, Monsieur d'Artois himself. It may even be that should he ever ascend the throne of France as Charles X he will recall my warning, and in some similar emergency seek my advice with a mind to put it to better account.'

With extraordinary prescience Charles Maurice de Talleyrand Périgord was at that moment looking into the future; for a quarter of a century later, after the Napoleonic Empire had waxed and waned, Charles d'Artois returned to France to take over the Kingdom for his elder brother. In all those years the two had never met; but the Prince at once sent for Talleyrand, recalled their meeting on the night that the *Bastille had* fallen, and sought his counsel; and he became in turn Grand Chamberlain to both Louis XVIII and Charles X.

Richard was still pondering this revelation of the revolutionary Bishop's true feelings when he was almost startled out of his wits by the subtle prelate adding: `However, I should not have told you of the matter had I been averse to your mentioning it in your next report to Mr. Pitt.'

'Eh!' Richard exclaimed. Then he laughed. `Why in the world should you imagine-'

With a wave of his elegant hand, de Périgord cut him short. 'To others you may pass as a rich young man who likes to spend a good part of his time in France; but not to me. I am probably the only person in Paris who knows it, but your family are not of sufficient fortune to keep you in idleness. Someone in Whitehall had the sense to realize that your training here as confidential secretary to Monsieur de Rochambeau fitted you admirably for your present work; and your recent comings and goings this year opened my eyes to it.'

The wily Bishop paused and quizzed Richard through his glass, obviously much amused by his young friend's discomfiture. Then, relenting, he went on with a smile: `But you need have no fear that I shall give you away, unless it comes to my knowledge that your operations are in the long run likely to prove harmful to my own country. On the contrary, I have for some time had it in mind to put a proposal to you. If you will be guided by me I believe that we may both serve our countries well, and be of great use to one another. So I suggest to you that we should agree to work together.'

Richard had to make a quick decision. If he denied de Périgord's assumption the odds were all against his being believed, and there would then be no guarantee that the prelate would keep his shrewd guess to himself. Moreover, to reject the offer might turn a good friend into a dangerous enemy. On the other hand the Bishop was in the position to give him invaluable information f tom tune to time, so a secret alliance with him might prove extraordinarily valuable.

`Since Your Grace has faced me with the matter,' he replied after only the briefest hesitation, `I will admit that I am here as an observer. I am as anxious as yourself to see France in a settled and prosperous state again ; so I willingly accept your proposition.'

De Périgord smiled and held out his hand. `Let us shake hands upon it then. For my part I have always believed that France and Britain should forget their old differences and enter on an alliance. If united they could ensure the permanent peace of Europe, and that should be the first aim of all right-thinking men. De Mirabeau, who should be here shortly believes that, too ; otherwise I would not have asked you here this evening. I shall, of course, make no mention to him of our personal pact. To disclose it to a *single soul* might later jeopardize its usefulness. But we may not now have much time left to talk alone together, so tell me the matter upon which you sought this meeting with a view to pumping me.'

` 'Tis the making of the Constitution,' Richard said frankly. `I have followed the deliberations upon it to the best of my ability, but the subject seems of an incredible complexity. Since you sit on the Committee I was in hopes that you would be able to tell me what shape its final form is likely to take.'

`You ask something that it is beyond my powers to predict,' the Bishop replied with a shake of his head. `Even the declaration of the "Rights of Man", that Lafayette was so anxious we should proclaim in imitation of America, took weeks of work to formulate. Most of my foolish colleagues thought that it could be drafted in a single sitting, bull'. every clause provoked most bitter argument; and now 'tis done 'tis little more than a long hotchpotch of mainly irrelevant aphorisms. As to the Constitution, it would not surprise me in the least if another year or more elapses before the Assembly wilt accept it. And who can tell to what degree its present draft will have had to be twisted to meet with the approval of the men who may then be the masters in that bear pit?" .

'How far has it progressed up to the moment?' Richard enquired.

`To the extent of settling the organization of the legislature; no more. The first Committee recommended that it should consist of three parts, as with you in England ; a Representative Chamber, a Senate, and the King with power to exercise an absolute veto. But the recommendation was rejected. The Assembly would agree neither to the creation of an Upper House nor the King being allowed to quash its measures.'

`So much I gathered from the debates. The last did not surprise me ; but I should have thought the whole of the Center as well as the Right would have supported the project of two Chambers. Is there no hope of its being revived?'

`None ; and it was not killed by the moderates but by the reactionaries. The *grand seigneurs* are so stupidly jealous that they feared the Senatorial dignity, if conferred on men of lesser birth, might create a new nobility with a prestige greater than their own; so they combined with the Left and cut off their noses to spite their faces.'

`What incredible folly to sacrifice the safeguard of an Upper House to such a paltry consideration!'

`It was indeed. And that made it infinitely more important that the right of exercising an absolute veto should be conferred upon the King; for it then became the only safeguard left against the people's representatives running amok, as they did on the famous "Night of Sacrifices". Mirabeau, with his usual sound common sense, saw that, and declared that he would rather live in Constantinople than in France if the legislature were to dispense with the royal sanction. Mounier, Malouet, Lally, Cazales, Maury, all the soundest leaders worked desperately hard to get it through, and we had the backing of every prudent man in the Assembly.'

`What, then, caused your failure to do so?'

De Perigord sighed. `Again, 'twas not the bitter opposition of that monarchy hater Sieyes, and other champions of the mob. 'Twas a combination of ill applied idealism and timidity, in men who should have known better.

That honest fool Lafayette is so imbued with the perfection of all American institutions that he can scarce abide the thought of our having a King at all, and feels impelled to use all the influence he has to reduce the monarchy to a cipher. Apparently, quite forgetting that the United States has a Senate to put a check on any rashness in its Lower House, he wrote to Necker urging him to advise the King to win popularity by voluntarily forgoing an absolute veto and asking only for a suspensive one. Necker, whose object in life now is to regain his own failing popularity, naturally jumped at the chance to get the credit for a further abasement of the Court, so he advised the Council and the King in that sense. I need hardly add that the royal weakling ran true to form ; so that the very ground was cut from beneath our feet, and France is today in all but name a republic.'

'Should a sudden international crisis arise, and the country be threatened from without, what is the King's position? Could he still declare war upon his own authority?'

'At present he could ; for his right to do so has never yet been called in question. But I greatly doubt if he will be allowed to retain that power without certain restrictions. It is one of the many problems involved in the Constitution that the Committee has so far not had time to consider.'

Through the window Richard saw a richly gilt coach drive up, and he said quickly: 'About Monsieur de Mirabeau. From his speeches in the Assembly I have never yet been able to decide to which party he belongs. A word of guidance on that would at the moment be most helpful.'

'He belongs to no party,' de Périgord smiled. 'Whatever he may be in other things he is at least honest in his politics. Being a very clear-sighted man he is quick to see the weakness in the policies of others, so he will tie himself to none. Only so can he retain his liberty to criticize every measure that he feels to be unsound. Like myself, although he frequently supports the Left, he is a convinced Monarchist; and in the Assembly there are many men of a similar disposition. It is that great floating vote that makes Mirabeau such a power in debate. Upon whatever subject he may speak his common sense attaches to him all those who are not committed to a course of action in advance; arid men of the most diverse opinions will rub shoulders in order to follow him into the lobby.'

'Think you, in view of the reduction of the Monarch to near a cipher, that he is likely to emerge as virtually the new ruler of France?'

The Bishop sadly shook his head. 'I fear that things have now gone too far for anyone of such moderate views to long remain master of the situation. Do not be deceived by the present comparative quiet of Paris. Terrible forces have now been set in motion, and no man can gauge the destructive power with which they may yet sweep not only France but the whole world. This year, for the first time in history, the proletariat has become conscious of its power. The fall of the French monarchy is a threat to all others, and a new kind of war may result. Instead of Kings fighting Kings there may be a bloody clash of ideologies in which class will fight class, throughout the length and breadth of Europe. In such a war no true democracy could survive, and the proletarian leaders will inevitably be men of utter ruthlessness; Dictators, driving their peoples on with a tyranny and ferocity greater than they have ever suffered under any King. It is my belief that this year of '89 will be termed by historians that of the gathering storm.'

CHAPTER TWENTY
THE QUEEN'S FRIENDS

As de Talleyrand Périgord ceased speaking the most talked of man in France at that period was shown into the room.

The Comte de Mirabeau was then forty, but years of overwork, anxiety and dissipation had made him look considerably older. He was a giant of a man ; tall, broad shouldered, deep chested; though his huge hands, wide forehead, and the great thane of coarse black hair that swept back from it made him appear even larger than he was in fact. The scars left by the smallpox, which he had contracted at the age of three, made him quite incredibly ugly, but he radiated vitality and good humor.

Most of his adult life had been spent owing in part at least to his own folly and extravagance in abject poverty; but now that France had a free Press, and he was the man of the hour, his pamphlets and journals were bringing him in a huge income. In consequence he was at last able to give f free reign to his flamboyant tastes. At a time when most of the noblemen who had remained in Paris were going about the capital as unostentatiously as possible in hired hackneys, Mirabeau, for the first time in his life, had a coach of his own and it was a vast gilded affair with the arms of his family emblazoned on its panels. His dress, too, was now always of an almost Eastern splendor although the rich fabrics sat ill on his unwieldy person and from his hands and the lace at his neck there flashed diamonds, sapphires and rubies.

The half dozen or so very able secretaries whom he employed no doubt paid for their keep; as, after touching up their work with a few strokes of genius, he published all their writings under his own name. But the establishment he ran, the money he gave away and his personal adornment, ate up such sums that it was hardly to be wondered at that, however big the income he made. he was still always hopelessly in debt.

De Périgord had no need to introduce his two guests ; and immediately Mirabeau set eyes on Richard he said jovially: 'When last we met here. Monsieur Blane. I recall that it was between two of my visits to Berlin. I was very grateful then for the chance our friend the Bishop secured me to earn a few hundred livres acting as his correspondent from Frederick the Great's deathbed.'

`And I was grateful to be invited here to drink His Grace's chocolate,' replied Richard, not to be outdone, `for I had few friends in Paris in those days; and 'twas a great privilege for a youth like myself to meet men like you, Monsieur le Comte, who have since made history.'

The Bishop's manservant had been waiting only for de Mirabeau's arrival to announce dinner; and while they went into the next room, settled themselves at table and tucked their napkins under their chins, Richard thought his fellow guest deserved full credit for his frank, unabashed mention of his visits to Berlin.

Everyone now knew the story, as de Mirabeau had recently published the reports he had sent back to France of his activities and observations while in the Prussian capital. Their publication had created a furor, since the documents were not his to publish but belonged to the French Government, as he had written them while a secret agent in its employ. He had endeavored to exculpate himself by declaring, first that the papers had been published without his authority, then that they had been stolen from him; but it was universally believed that he had connived at the business in order to make some quick money. It was now, in any case, common knowledge that de Périgord, having recognized de Mirabeau's genius from the beginning, had begged the Government to employ him; and that, failing to get him anything better, he had induced Monsieur de Calonne to send him on this secret mission to Berlin.

The thing Richard knew about the original transaction that de Mirabeau did not and Richard's knowledge was in all probability shared only by his old master, Monsieur de Rochambeau was that de Périgord having been instructed to act as a post office for de Mirabeau's secret reports, had, being hard up himself at the time, sold copies of them before passing the originals on to Monsieur de Calonne.

Glancing from one side of the table to the other, Richard wondered which of his two companions was the greater rogue; and decided that there was really little to choose between them. Both were honest according to their lights, and both would not hesitate to cheat if their own well-being or that of their country depended upon it. But if a capacity for unscrupulousness was to be judged in proportion to the strength of character of the two men, Richard had no doubt at all that the Bishop would win at a canter. Mirabeau could dominate the Assembly; he could quell a riot and make a murderous mob whose hands were still dripping blood hang upon his words, but with effortless ease de Perigord dominated him. Beside the slender, elegant Bishop, the bear like Mirabeau was common clay.

Over dinner the talk covered many subjects, and Richard was pleasantly surprised to see his host shine in a new light. He had always found de Perigord a most charming and stimulating companion, but had thought of him as a selfish hedonist whose main aim in life was his own pleasure and advancement; now, he was given a glimpse of the great humanitarian that the `unworthy priest' usually concealed beneath the cynical aristocrat. One after another he spoke of the reforms he wished to have passed by the Assembly, and pressed de Mirabeau for his support.

He wanted the royal lotteries abolished, because they beggared far more people than they enriched; he wanted the Jews emancipated and given equal rights of citizenship; he wanted a Franco British conference arranged to agree on a uniform system of weights and measures; he wanted pressure to be exerted on the Pope to allow the wives of fishermen to presume the death of husbands who had been reported lost at sea, after three years, so that they might marry again; he wanted to revolutionize and coordinate in one national system all the schools and colleges in the country, so that every child in France should receive the benefit of an education.

De Mirabeau was wholeheartedly with him, but said at last

`All these things should be done, and many more. I am impatiently awaiting an opportunity, myself, to introduce a bill for the abolition of slavery in our West Indian islands. The trouble is, as you know well enough, that ninetenths of the Assembly's time is wasted by the windy verbiage of our colleagues. Hardly a man among them can make the simplest statement without employing twice as long in telling us all what mighty fine fellows we "restorers of French liberty" are, and urging us to fresh efforts, instead of sitting down and letting us get to practical reforms such as you suggest. Could he but know it Jean Jacques Rousseau served the cause he had so much at heart ill, instead of well, by his writings; for not a day goes past but an hour or more that should be devoted to business is frittered away by nonentities declaiming long passages from his Contract Social.' `How right you are!' exclaimed de Périgord. And, heretical as it may sound, I would to God that Saint of the Revolution had never been born. 'Tis positively tragic that the Assembly should have taken his sentimental, impractical nonsense for their Bible. At the moment it threatens to force upon us the worst possible solution for some of the most important clauses in the Constitution.'

`You refer to the status of Ministers of the Crown?' said de M Mirabeau.

`I do. The English system by which they are chosen from the members of the National Assembly, sit with it, debate with it and are responsible to it, is so obviously the right one. Any other is sheer madness ; for, if the Ministers are to remain outside it, as at present, they are debarred all opportunity to assess the feeling of the Assembly, and reduced to no more than ill-informed private advisers to the King. Yet an overwhelming majority of the deputies are so hypnotized by the dogmatic doctrines of Montesquieu and Rousseau that the separation of the executive and legislative powers is a first essential for the maintenance of. liberty that I greatly fear we shall have to submit to that farcical form of Government.'

`We will fight it, though!' declared de Mirabeau truculently ; and, although his black eyes were dimmed by ophthalmia from overwork, they flashed as he spoke. `I regard it as imperative that the King's Ministers should be drawn from the Chamber yet retain their seats in it. Where else can he find men capable of governing France? Necker, Montmorin, and the rest of his present crew are all men of straw. In fact the Queen is the only man the King has about him.'

He paused for a moment, then went on to describe in glowing phrases the type of Minister he thought the King should have; naively enumerating one after another all his own qualities. De Périgord caught Richard's eye, waited until de Mirabeau had done, then remarked with gentle irony

'*Mon ami. You* forgot one thing. Such a man should also be marked with the small-pox.'

De Mirabeau took the jest in good part, roared with laughter, and said: `Well, the King might do worse. If he would only give me the chance I would save the monarchy for him.'

All too soon for Richard the coach he had ordered to fetch him was announced; but true to his engagement with de Périgord he excused himself and left the two great men together.

Having had his true business guessed by de Perigord had shaken him badly, and for most of the way back to Paris he took serious thought about the possibility of other people unmasking him. On the whole it seemed unlikely, as not only was the Bishop a man of exceptional shrewdness but he also had had information about `Monsieur le Chevalier de Blanes' antecedents that no one else in Paris possessed. The disquieting episode had, however, served to call Richard's attention to an important development he had overlooked.

Up to the preceding August it had been good enough cover to pose as a young Englishman of means who was travelling for pleasure and liked to spend a good part of his time in Paris, as there had been many such; but it was so no longer. The riots culminating in the fall of the *Bastille,* the `Great Fear', and finally the removal of the Court from Versailles, had driven the rich English milor's to take their pleasures in the German and Italian cities. Most of their friends among the French nobility had fled, and, as the gay Duke of Dorset had gone home, this winter there were not even any elegant *thés-dansant* to attend at the British Embassy.

After some thought, Richard decided to adopt a new line. He would gradually put it about that he was staying on in Paris because he had taken up journalism, and was now writing a weekly newsletter. For the paper in which these mythical articles were to be published he chose the *Morning Chronicle,* as that was the most important Whig organ of the day and would sound well with the majority of his French acquaintances, as most of them were men of Liberal opinions.

However, in spite of that unnerving moment when de Perigord had blandly charged him with being an agent of Mr. Pitt, he felt that he had had an extremely fortunate day; as not only did his secret alliance with the Bishop hold great possibilities for the future, but de Mirabeau had promised to introduce him to a Club called the Jacobins, which was beginning to assume considerable importance on the political stage.

Three nights later Richard dined in very different company. He had continued to see the Comte de la Marck occasionally when visiting the *Tuileries* or about the city, and in the previous week the young Austrian had asked him to dine at his Embassy, where he was still living.

During the past six months fashions in Paris had undergone a greater alteration than in the whole of the preceding sixty years. Silk coats, satin breeches, gold lace and feathers were now regarded as the outward symbols of an inward desire to arrest the march of Liberty ; so few men any longer wore there in the streets or had their hair powdered before going out in the evening. But, realizing that the Embassy was Austrian soil, and that few changes were likely to have occurred there, Richard had his hair powdered for the first time since leaving Naples, put a patch on his chin, and went out to dine clad in his best satins and laces.

When he arrived he was pleased to find that he had done the right thing, as the party consisted of a dozen people and it was being conducted with all the courtly formality that only such a little time ago had been the fashion, yet in Paris already seemed of a bygone age. Even for this small gathering, hundreds of candles lit the great chandeliers in the hall and above the staircase; a string band played softly behind a screen of palms; black clad majordomos, with silver chains about their necks, and a line of rigid footmen stood ready on either side of the entrance doors to take the wraps of the guests.

The Ambassador, Count Florimond de Mercy-Argenteau, was himself receiving. Richard knew him well by sight but had never before spoken to him, so he was pleasurably surprised when the elderly diplomat returned his bow with the words: `Monsieur le Chevalier, I know you to be a friend of the Queen; so I hope you will permit me to make you one of mine, and to assure you that you will always find a very warm welcome here.'

As Richard thanked him and turned to greet de la Marck, he wondered if the Queen had told Mercy-Argenteau of his journeys on her behalf to Florence and Naples, and thought it highly probable that she had. The Ambassador had represented Austria at the Court of Versailles for over twenty years; so from Madame Marie Antoinette's arrival there as a child bride of fourteen he had been her counselor and champion, and had come to be regarded by her almost as though he was a favourite uncle.

De la Marck presented Richard to the Spanish Ambassador, the Conde Fern Nunez and his Condesa ; then to the charming old Abbe de Vermond, who shared with Mercy-Argenteau the distinction of being the Queen's oldest friend in France; for he had been sent to Vienna to teach her French when her marriage had first been mooted and, returning to Versailles, in her entourage, had continued as her preceptor until she left the schoolroom.

But Richard broke away from the group as soon as politeness permitted, for he had seen an old friend on the far side of the room. It was Count Hans Axel Fersen, who had entertained him most hospitably when he was in Sweden two summers earlier.

The Swedish nobleman was a tall good-looking man in his middle thirties, and all the world knew the story of how he met the Queen when she was Dauphine, and they were both still in their teens, at a masked ball at the Opera. Fersen had himself. admitted to Richard that he had fallen in love with the beautiful Princess, and later gone to fight in the American War in an endeavor to forget her; but everyone who knew the Queen's character discredited the story that he had actually been her lover, just as they did of those concerning innumerable other men including even the old Abbé de Vermond with whom the gutter pamphleteers never tired of coupling her name.

Fersen was delighted to see Richard again, and when they *compared notes both were a little surprised that they had not run across one another during the past few months, as Count Hans said that after revisiting France in the autumn of '88 he had returned there permanently the previous summer. But that they had not met was explained by Richard's journeys, and the fact that Fersen spent much of his time at Valenciennes with a French regiment of which the Queen had procured him the Colonelcy.

The round dozen in the party was made up by ladies, and Richard was allotted to take in to dinner a niece of the Ambassador who happened to be staying in the Embassy for a few nights on her way through Paris. After he had talked to her for a while he turned to his other neighbor, who was the Condesa Fern Nunez, and she asked him if he numbered any Spaniards among his acquaintances.

For a second he hesitated. Since leaving Naples he had stuck to his resolution to discipline himself against thinking of Tansanta, and although temptation to do so had proved too much for him at times, he had at least succeeded in banishing her image from his brain except when some special occurrence reminded him of her. This was just such a chance occurrence ; and it suddenly struck him that, since the opportunity offered, it would be a test of his progress to talk about her now and see if he could get to sleep that night without suffering his old tormenting longings. So he replied

`I had the good fortune to form a most sincere friendship early last summer with a lady of your country, Madame; and I should be much surprised if you do not know her. She is the daughter of General Count d'Aranda.'

`But of course!' exclaimed the Condesa. `A most charming and Sweet - natured creature. *I knew* her well; for when her father was succeeded as Ambassador here by my husband he left her in my care. Naturally, as she was one of Madame Marie Antoinette's ladies, Her Majesty was formally responsible for her well-being, but I assumed towards her the role of a benevolent aunt. I do not remember, though, her ever mentioning you to me.'

Richard explained that while he had been presented to Tansanta by the Queen at Fontainebleau, he had not come to know her at all well until chance decreed that he should act as her escort on the greater part of her journey south to Marseilles. He refrained from any mention of her having accompanied him to Florence, or their having met again more recently in Naples; but he was under no necessity to pursue the subject himself, as the Condesa proved to be a garrulous lady and talked for quite a time, first in praise of Tansanta, then about her marriage. As a dinner table topic, the subject seemed near exhausted, when she added.

`I heard of her through a mutual friend only last week. It seems that her marriage was swiftly blessed. She is expecting a child towards the end of March, so she and her husband are leaving Naples to return to Spain in the New Year.'

`Why should they do that, Madame?' Richard enquired, not seeing any connection between the two statements.

The Condesa smiled at him. `Naturally they must be hoping that it will be a boy, and whenever an heir is born to a noble Spanish family a great *fiesta* is given on the father's estates. Even if it is a girl many bulls will be slaughtered and casks of wine broached. At such a time the lord and his lady always repair to the family's ancestral home, so that after the lying-in they may witness the rejoicings of their serfs. It will prove a good opportunity, too, for the Sidonia y Ulloas to make their court to our new King and Queen; so no doubt when Tansanta is safely delivered they will spend some months in Madrid. That will be pleasant for her, as she has not been in the capital since she was quite a young girl, and there must be many of her relatives . . .'

For several moments longer the Condesa rattled on, but Richard was listening to her with only half an ear. His hands had gone clammy at the awful thought of Tansanta in the agony of childbirth and he was wishing desperately that he could be near her at the time to give her at least the comfort of his love during her ordeal.

Automatically he continued to make polite conversation until the ladies left the table. When they had gone, the dozen footmen, one of whom had waited behind each chair during the meal, the two wine butlers and the majordomo, silently withdrew. As the doors closed behind the last of the servants the Ambassador beckoned Richard up to a vacant place near the head of the table, and only then did he manage to thrust Tansanta out of his mind.

The conversation of the six men at once turned to politics and, in particular, the situation of the Queen. Richard felt certain now that he had been asked only because de Mercy-Argenteau knew of his journeys and felt that he was entirely to be trusted, as they began to talk with complete frankness of ways and means to save her should another emergency arise in which her life was threatened.

It struck Richard as interesting that the old Abbé was the only Frenchman present; but it occurred to him that, since so many Frenchmen were now being torn between two loyalties, it might have been decided that it was wiser to keep them out of it, and that an exception had been made in the Abbé's case only because, in the role of a father confessor, he would never be denied access to the Queen, however closely she might be guarded. Richard hazarded a guess, too, that de Mercy-Argenteau reluctance to take Frenchmen into his counsels was probably the reason why, on. de la Marck's recommendation, he should have been singled out for the honour of inclusion in such a company.

It soon emerged that although Count Axel Fersen held no official diplomatic status, he had come to France as the secret representative of King Gustavus III, charged to do everything in his power to aid the Queen. The Spanish Ambassador had also been instructed by his King to take all possible steps to succor and protect the French Royal Family. Both were of the opinion that while the prisoners of the *Tuileries* still had some degree of liberty they should leave the capital on the pretext of a Royal Hunt, and when the carriages were well out in the open country order them to be driven to Compiegne, Rheims or Metz, at any one of which they could swiftly surround themselves with the Army.

Richard had naturally refrained from putting any view forward during the early part of the discussion; but now he said: `Such a scheme should be well enough if you could rely upon the loyalty of the Army. But can you do so? From all I hear the rate of desertion has been appallingly high in the past few months, and in many of the regiments the men who remain will no longer take orders from their officers.'

`That is true in many areas,' agreed Count Hans. `But the Army of the East is still mainly loyal. General de Bouille has some good troops under him, and I can vouch for my own regiment. It was in order to make certain of its dependability for just such an emergency that I spent so much time with it this summer and autumn.'

`Messieurs, I too should be in favour of such a plan, did I not know it to be impractical,' announced de Mercy-Argenteau. He spoke with the German accent that he had never quite lost, and went on heavily: `To do as you suggest would mean civil war, and we shall never bring the King to face that. Quite apart from his morbid horror of bloodshed, he is obsessed with the example of the Great Rebellion in England, and he maintains that the unhappy CharlesI would never have lost his head had he not taken up arms against his subjects.'

`There may be some truth in that,' remarked the Spaniard. `In any case there appears to be little danger of Louis XVI losing his head as long as he remains in Paris.!

'I agree, Excellency,' the Austrian nodded. `For the King's life we fortunately have no reason to concern ourselves. It is for the life of the little Archduchess who was entrusted to me as a child that I am so gravely perturbed. The hand of God has already saved her from more than one attempt upon her life, and it is, known to me that others are maturing. Her enemies are well aware that it is her courage alone that stands between them and the achievement of their evil designs, and they are seeking to poison her. She now dare eat nothing but the plainest food prepared for her by her own attendants, and the sugar she keeps in her bedroom to make eau sucré at night has twice been tampered with, so that Madame Campan now has to keep a secret supply for her.'

`Then,' said Fersen, with an anxious frown, `we must get Her Majesty away. And with the minimum possible delay.'

The Abbé Vermond sadly shook his head. `Alas, Monsieur, she will not leave the King. I am convinced of that.'

`Somehow, we must find means to persuade her, She would perhaps if we could bring her to believe that the Dauphin's life was in danger, and that it was essential that she should escape with him.'

De Mercy-Argenteau gave a swift glance under his gray eyebrows at Richard; then, as Richard remained silent, he said: .`Her Majesty made a plan some time ago to send the Dauphin to Naples, but the King refused his consent to the project. She then had no thought of going with her son, and even if the

King changes his mind I greatly doubt if she could be persuaded to do so.'

`I am certain that she could not, Excellency,' declared the Abbé. `She is a convinced fatalist, and with superb courage has already made up her mind to face some tragic end that she believes Fate has in store for her. She is a religious woman as we all know, but even her acceptance of the fundamental goodness of God is insufficient to overcome her conviction that destiny has marked her down. And one cannot deny that there have been portents enough in her life to give her reason for that black thought.'

The Abbé paused for a moment, then went on: `We have but to recall the terrible tempest that raged upon the night of her marriage. A wind so great that the park at Versailles was devastated; mighty oaks rent in twain by lightning; the windows of her bridal chamber blown in, their shutters battered to matchwood, and the gale howling in the room so that the very coverlets were blown from the bed. Then a fortnight later the public celebrations for her marriage in Paris. I shall never forget how we set out from Versailles to witness the great display of fireworks that had been arranged. That beautiful child, so gay, so happy, so excited; and when we arrived the vast sea of people who had assembled to do her homage, cheering and throwing flowers as she smiled and blew kisses to them standing up in her carriage.

'Then the rocket accidentally igniting the pile of wood, the flames reaching the powder barrels before the firemen could get to them ;the terrible explosion, the crowd stampeding, the cheers turning to screams of agony, the hundreds of people trampled to death, and the number of injured so great that it was beyond the capacity of the hospitals to take them.'

Again the Abbé paused, then he looked up at de Mercy-Argenteau. 'And above all, Your Excellency, you and I are old enough to remember the day she was born. November the 2nd, 1755. 4n it there was the most frightful disaster that has afflicted Europe for centuries: the Lisbon earthquake. No Princess has ever had a more inauspicious omen at her birth; so can one wonder that she has always felt the hand of Fate to be upon her?'

Richard was twelve years younger than Madame Marie Antoinette, but he remembered the stories of the earthquake that had still been current in his childhood. The shock had been so terrific that it had been felt at places as far distant as the Baltic, the West Indies, Canada and Algiers. The greater part of Lisbon had been thrown to the ground. The great marble quay sank down with hundreds of people on it; every ship in the harbor was engulfed, and neither wreckage nor bodies ever came to the surface. In six minutes 40,000 people had perished.

For a moment there was silence, then the Conde Fern Nunez spoke. `If she is adamant in her determination not to leave, the only course open to us is to endeavor to concert measures to restore some degree of the royal authority.'

`That is my own view, Excellency,' nodded de Mercy-Argenteau. `And it seems to me that our only hope of doing so lies in winning over to the Court some of the popular leaders.'

`But who?' asked Fersen pessimistically. `All the honest leaders who incline to support the monarchy no longer carry any weight with the masses.

For the rest, the Assembly is made up of little men, who would be useless to us, or rogues.'

`Then let us buy a rogue,' suggested the Spaniard. `What does it matter, provided that he be the man with great enough prestige to sway the people?'

`I believe there is only one man big enough to do this thing,' put in Richard, `and that at heart he is by no means a rogue. The Comte de Mirabeau.'

`I agree with you,' said de la Marck quickly. `He is the very man I have myself long had in mind for such a role.'

Fersen turned and looked at Richard. `Think you he would agree to such a proposal? Are you shooting in the dark, or do you know him personally?'

`I dined with him three nights ago. Like many others who took a hand in stirring up this hornet's nest, he is much perturbed by the way events are trending. He came out most strongly in favour of an absolute veto for the King and deplores the weakness of the present Ministry. One remark he made struck me particularly; he said: "The Queen is the only man the King has about him."'

De Mercy-Argenteau *was now* leaning forward, listening to Richard with the greatest interest. `If de Mirabeau said that,' he murmured, `it is certainly a good indication that he would be willing to serve Her Majesty. But please go on, Mr. Blane.'

`I would only add, Your Excellency, that I believe it would be *a* mistake to *ask* too much of him. I think that he would willingly cooperate with Their Majesties in *an* effort to give the country a sound Liberal Constitution, and enforce the restoration of order in it. But I feel certain that, dubious as his private life may have been, where the welfare of his country is concerned he has a conscience; and neither promises nor bribes would *induce him to* assist the Court in an attempt to reestablish an autocratic Government.'

De la Marck nodded vigorously. `That is exactly my opinion; and I have taken some pains to get to know de Mirabeau well. He is, of course, always in need of money, and under the guise of literary patronage I have allowed him a small monthly pension ever since I came to appreciate his worth. But no amount one could offer him would tempt him to betray his political ideals. If he accepts a salary from the King it will be only on his own conditions. and then because he would feel that he was just as much entitled to it as any other Minister.'

`If the King made him a Minister he would lose his seat in the Assembly,' objected the Conde Fern Nunez. `Then more than half his value would be lost to us. His power to influence the decisions of the Chamber is his main asset.'

`I fear I did not make myself plain, Excellency. I meant the salary he would receive if he were a Minister; not that he should be made one. The suggestion is that he should be asked to formulate a secret policy for Their Majesties and be paid a retainer for advising them on every stage of it; but himself continue as a deputy, and do all he can to forward the programme in the Chamber.'

After some further discussion it was agreed that in a secret alliance such as de la Marck suggested lay the best hope of preventing the extremists from becoming absolute masters of the State, and it was decided that he should sound de Mirabeau upon it. De Mercy-Argenteau then thanked everyone present for the advice they had offered, and asked them to keep in touch with him.

Christmas fell two days later, but as it was not kept up in France with the gaiety and good cheer traditional in England Richard hardly noticed its passing. As he enjoyed full liberty to come and go as he pleased, he had thought of taking ten days' leave to go home for it, but had decided against doing so for a variety of reasons. It was highly probable that Amanda would be at Walhampton and meeting her again at all the local parties would be awkward after their *affaire* in the summer. During his last visit to Lymington he had been driven half crazy by his longings for Tansanta; and, although he was well on the way to freeing his mind of thoughts of her, he feared that such an early return to the scene of his misery might bring them flooding back. But the decisive factor was that lie felt he was now really getting to grips with his mission, and that the reports he was sending to Mr. Pitt must be too valuable for him to be justified in losing touch with his contacts even for a matter of ten days.

On the 10th of December he made his first appearance at the Jacobin Club. It had been started while the National Assembly was still at Versailles by a few Breton deputies who wished to discuss overnight the measures that were to be brought before the Chamber on the following day. Since the removal to Paris it had enormously increased both its membership and its influence. Men of all shades of opinion, other than declared reactionaries, went there, but it was tending more and more to become an unofficial headquarters of the Left. As a clubhouse the ex Convent of the Jacobins, off the *Rue St. Honore* within a hundred yards of the *Place Vendome,* had been taken over, and thus gave the Club the name by which it had now become generally known.

Richard kept de Mirabeau to his promise to take him there and the Count said that there would be no difficulty about his becoming a member of the Club if he wished to do so. Anyone could join provided they were introduced by an existing member and had either published some work expressing Liberal sentiments or were prepared to make a short speech which met with the approval of the members present at the time. Colour; religion and race were no bar to election, as the spirit of the Club was `Liberty, Equality, Fraternity' for all ; and British subjects always received a particularly warm welcome on account of their having been the first people in the world to throw off the `tyranny of the Kings'. The Count added that only a few days before Christmas an English gentleman farmer of Suffolk, named Arthur Young, who was staying in Paris with the Duc de Liancourt, had been elected a member with much enthusiasm.

The great hall of the Convent was already famous in French history, as it was here that the Catholic League had been formed in the reign of Henri III, to resist the armies of insurgent Huguenots. When de Mirabeau led Richard into it a further chapter of French history was being written, but by a very different type of man from the great nobles who had once stuck white crosses in their feathered caps and sworn an oath there with drawn swords. It was crowded with democrats of all classes and over a hundred deputies were present, debating the policy they should pursue in the Assembly the following day. After listening to them for a while it was soon clear to Richard that Barnave, the Lameths, Pètion and other *enrages,* as the most violent revolutionaries were called, were much the most popular speakers.

In due course a halt was called to the debate to elect new members, and de Mirabeau introduced Richard as an English journalist of sound Whig convictions. Richard then spoke briefly, saying several things in which he fully believed, with regard to the liberty of the subject, and ending with a peroration in which he did not, concerning the imperishable glory of Jean Jacques Rousseau. He was elected with acclamation and afterwards signed the book as a member.

On January 1st he celebrated the opening of the year 1790 by buying himself one of the new hats. Three cornered hats were now rapidly going out of fashion and being replaced by two new .types of headgear. The first, now being worn by more sober men of substance, was a round beaver or felt with an in sloping crown, like a steeple that had been cut off short. The second, affected by the fashionable youth of the new era, was a sickle moon shaped cocked hat of moire silk, worn on the back of the head with its points sticking out level with the ears; which could be folded flat for holding under the arm more conveniently than the old three cornered type. Richard chose one of the latter and had just completed his purchase when he ran into de la Marck.

Somewhat to his surprise the young Austrian told him that he had been seeking to use the Comte de Provence as a medium for negotiations between de M Mirabeau and the King. Louis XVI had not considered it necessary to send his younger brother abroad, as, unlike d'Artois, he had not incurred the hatred of the mob. On the contrary, he had pandered to it and, on the removal from Versailles, come to live at the *Palais du Luxembourg,* on the south side of the river, where he now enjoyed a faint replica of the popularity that the Duc d'Orléans had had while living at the Palais Royal.

De la Marck explained that he had been influenced in the course he had taken by knowing that although the Queen had never met de Mirabeau, all she had heard of him had led her to dislike and distrust him intensely; so he had feared that a direct approach to her might result in the project being killed at birth, and had decided to attempt to interest the King in it through his brother.

However, he felt now that he had been something of a simpleton to count on family loyalty, and had probably underestimated de Provence's jealousy of the King and hatred for the Queen, as the pompous Prince had merely temporized, and was proving of very little help.

Richard strongly advised a direct approach to the Queen, and some days later he was gratified to hear from de la Marck that the move had proved successful. At first Madame Marie Antoinette had proved extremely difficult to convince that de Mirabeau would observe any pact loyalty; but in the end she had been won round, and an agreement had been reached by which the King was to pay de Mirabeau's debts and allow him 6,000 livres a month; and the great demagogue was now busy compiling in secret a long paper on innumerable questions, for the future guidance of Their Majesties.

The rest of January and the first half of February passed for Richard in a round of intense activity. There were outbreaks of disorder in Versailles and the Provinces, and rumours of plots of all sorts, to be investigated. He continued to attend the Queen's public receptions occasionally, went frequently to the National Assembly and spent several evenings each week at the Jacobin Club. He kept in close touch with de Périgord and, now fully convinced of his fundamental loyalty to the Crown, confided to him the secret alliance that had been entered into between de Mirabeau and the Sovereigns; in exchange for which he received much valuable information. In turn he dined with de la Marck, Fersen, de Cazalès, Barnave, de Mercy-Argenteau, Desmoulins, and many other men of all shades of opinion.

He was quieter, graver and much more sure of himself than when he had come to Paris in the spring; but he was enormously interested in his work, had regained much of his old natural cheerfulness anti now rarely thought of Tansanta.

It was on the afternoon of February 14th that he received a note by hand from Lord Robert Fitzgerald. It read simply: A *certain person requires your immediate presence in London.*

That night he was in the fast diligence, rumbling along the road ' towards Calais. The weather was filthy and the diligence an icebox, the straw on its floor barely keeping the feet of the passengers from freezing ; and he thanked his stars that he had decided against making the trip home for Christmas, when it had been even colder. But only a moderate sea was running and the wind was favourable, so on the 17th the Dover coach set him down at Charing Cross.

Tired as he was, he went straight to Downing Street; and only ten minutes after he had sent up his name he was ushered into the Prime Minister's room.

After greeting him pleasantly and offering him a glass of Port, Mr. Pitt came to the point with his usual directness. He said

'Mr. Blane, I recalled you from Paris because I wish you to proceed at once to Spain.'

CHAPTER TWENTY-ONE
ON THE BEACH

For a moment Richard was silent. A mission to Spain could only mean that the Prime Minister was sending him to Madrid. It would take him a fortnight or three weeks to get there. Tansanta's baby was due to be born in little over a month. The Condesa Fern Nunez had said that after Tansanta's lying-in the Sidonia y Ulloas would be certain to spend some months in Madrid making their court to the new King and Queen. So if he went there it was a 'virtual certainty that he would see Tansanta again within six or seven weeks.

`I am sorry, sir,' he said. `But I cannot go to Spain.'

'Cannot!' Mr. Pitt repeated, raising his eyebrows in astonishment. `That, Mr. Blane, is a word which I do not permit those I employ to use to me.'

`Nevertheless,' said Richard, `much as I regret to have to do so, I fear I must use it now. I am extremely sorry, but I cannot go to Spain.'

`Why?' asked the Prime Minister coldly. `Have you committed some crime which would make you *non persona grata at* the Court of Madrid?'

`No, sir. It is a purely personal matter. I will willingly go anywhere else that you may choose to send me, but not to Madrid.'

`But I do not wish to send you anywhere else. I have special work of urgent importance that I wish you to undertake for me in the Spanish capital.'

`Then, greatly as it distresses me to refuse you, sir, I fear you must find someone else to do it.'

The Prime Minister's long, thin face paled slightly, and he said with extreme hauteur: `Mr. Blane, your personal affairs cannot be allowed to interfere with the business of. the State. Either you will accept the orders that I give you or find another master.'

Richard's face went whiter than Mr. Pitt's. He had been shocked into an abruptness that he did not intend. `I pray you sir, reconsider this matter,' he faltered. `I now have excellent contacts in Paris, and have good reason to believe that I am serving you well there. I beg you to send somebody else to Spain and allow me to return to France.!

'On the contrary,' replied Mr. Pitt sharply, `I am by no means satisfied with your activities in Paris. In my opinion you have become involved with the wrong type of people. On the one hand you have entered on what may be termed a conspiracy with the Austrian Ambassador to forward the reactionary projects of the Queen in opposition to the new democratic Government; and that is contrary to the interests of this country. On the other you have entered into an alliance with Monsieur de Talleyrand Périgord. Having met him when I was in France I have a great admiration for his intellectual gifts; but he has proved himself to be an iconoclast of the most dangerous description, and as he is completely unscrupulous it is certain that he will use you for his own ends.

`Lastly, there is this story of yours about a rapprochement between Monsieur de Mirabeau and the Queen. One might as well try to mix oil and water, and I do not believe there is one grain of truth in it. Except upon purely general matters the information you have been sending is in complete contradiction to that furnished by the British Embassy, and I can only conclude that you are being made a fool of by de Perigord and your other friends.'

Utterly flabbergasted, Richard stared at him in dismay. Then he burst out angrily: "Tis the British Embassy that is being fooled, not I ; as time will show.'

`You must pardon me if I doubt that. In any case, I have decided to send another man to Paris. But in the past you have shown much courage and initiative, and I had hopes that you would recover them by a change of scene. Are you, or are you not, prepared to receive my instructions for this mission to Madrid?'

'No!' declared Richard firmly. `I am not'

The Prime Minister stood up. `Very well then, Mr. Blane. It only remains for me to thank you for your endeavors in the past, and to wish you success in some other career. This evening I will have a word with His Grace of Leeds and request him to have your accounts looked into. If you will wait upon His Grace some time next week he will see to it that you receive any monies that may be due to you.'

Five minutes later Richard found himself in the street. He was utterly bewildered at the course events had taken, and wondered now if he had acted like a fool in refusing the mission to Spain. But, almost at once, he decided that he had been right to do so. Both Tansanta and he had suffered too much from their affaire for it to be anything but madness to renew it, and that would have been inevitable if he had given way to Mr. Pitt and gone to the court of Madrid. She would soon have her child about which to build her life, and for the past two months the vision of her had ceased to obsess him ; so of two evils he felt sure he *had* chosen the lesser. Yet the price he had *had* to pay filled him with dismay. He could hardly realize it yet, but he was now, as his father the Admiral would have said, `on the beach'. No, worse! For him there was no chance at all of another ship; he was a man without a future.

Mr. Pitt, meanwhile, was much annoyed at Richard's refusal of his mission, as he had counted on him for it. In less than three years Richard had been instrumental in checking two serious foreign aggressions that threatened to lead to war, and the Prime Minister had felt that his peculiar flair for such situations might help in arresting another.

Having become Prime Minister at the age of twenty-four, Mr. Pitt naturally did not share the common belief that a man must reach middle age before he could be entrusted with discretionary powers in matters of high policy. There had been no British Ambassador at Madrid since the previous June, so, until a new one could be appointed, he had intended to send Richard there with Letters of Marque which would have given him wide scope for his talents, and he felt aggrieved both at the upsetting of his own plans and that his young protégé should have missed such an excellent chance to distinguish himself. On the other hand, as he knew much more about Mr. Blane's private affairs than that young man supposed, he was not altogether sorry that his insubordination had offered the opportunity to give him a sharp lesson.

It was not that he wished to reduce Richard to a cautious, humdrum collector of information ; as to have attempted it would have deprived him of the use of his most valuable assets   imagination and initiative but he did want him to develop a greater sense of responsibility regarding his work.

Mr. Pitt had no personal animus against Madame Marie Antoinette, but since her removal to the *Tuileries* he had had no confirmation of Richard's story that her life was in danger, and he saw no reason why he should pay him to further her intrigues.   .

In the matter of de Périgord he had been much influenced by the opinion of his old preceptor and friend Bishop Tomline, and he recalled the positive horror that had shaken the poor Bishop when he had learned of de Perigord's bill to rob the Church of all its property in France. As a fiscal measure there might be sound arguments for such a step ; but for an ordained priest to propose it had seemed to both of them a perfidy which put him for ever outside the pale. As for the story of his midnight visit to the Comte d'Artois, there was no possibility of checking that, as His Highness had taken refuge with his wife's relatives at the Court of Turin, but Mr. Pitt did not believe it for one moment.

The intelligence about de Mirabeau sounded even more improbable. Billy Pitt was of aristocratic descent only on his mother's side, but the truly noble mentality of his great father, and a very unusual upbringing, had combined to make him the most fastidious of aristocrats ; and he regarded de Mirabeau as a renegade to his order. According to British Embassy reports the King and Queen of France continued to hold receptions in the *Tuileries,* to transact business and be advised by the same Ministers as they had had while at Versailles; so, as yet, Mr. Pitt had no true appreciation of their situation. In consequence, to anyone of his haughty nature it was inconceivable that Madame Marie Antoinette could have brought herself to have dealings with any demagogue, let alone one having de Mirabeau's debauched and venal history.

The Prime Minister had always regarded Richard as rather a shrewd young man, so he was somewhat surprised that he should have allowed himself to be taken in to such an extent; and could only account for it by the supposition that outside interests had prevented him giving his full mind to his proper duties. In any case, he had for some time been of the opinion that Richard's talents could be used to better advantage at a Court than in a democratic society; and William Grenville, Mr. Pitt's trusted friend, had suggested that one William Augustus Miles should be sent to Paris to replace him. Mr. Miles had got on very well with the Dutch burghers while acting as a secret diplomatic agent in Holland, so no doubt he would prove equally successful in winning the confidence of the bourgeois politicians from whom the new governing class in France were mainly drawn. He might not have the debonair charm of Mr. Blane, but he was much better qualified to operate in the Paris of the new *régime*

Nevertheless, 'the longsighted Mr. Pitt had no intention of denying himself Richard's services permanently. He considered that the young man had more than proved his value in the past and believed that, given the right opportunities, he might do so many times again. In the meantime it would do him a lot of good, and make him more cautious in the future about cultivating contacts of such dubious value, if. he were left to cool his heels for a little with no prospect of employment. In due course a chastened Mr. Blane, would, no doubt, be very happy at being given another chance to exercise his wits and courage to better purpose.

Mr. Pitt emptied the remaining contents of the decanter of Port into his glass, and having no British Ambassador in Madrid to instruct, began to draft a letter to the Spanish Ambassador in London, to the effect that an insult having been done to the British Flag in distant Nootka Sound, he could not even consider any discussion of the reasons alleged by the Spaniards for their act until the wrong had been acknowledged and full reparation for it made.

Richard, knowing nothing of Mr. Pitt's intentions, walked slowly across the Green Park to Amesbury House. There he found his baggage just being delivered from the coach station, and was roused a fraction from his half stunned state by the welcome news that his friend Lord Edward Fitz-Deverel was in residence.

Ned, as his lordship had been nicknamed at school from the permanent stoop that afflicted his tall, frail figure, spent most of his life cultivating three hobbies: the collection of antique jewellery, experimenting with Eastern drugs, and studying ancient religions. That day he was devoting to the last of these, and on going up to his rooms Richard found him employed in carefully unwinding the hundreds of yards of bandage that encased an Egyptian mummy. On the table beside him there were already over a dozen little amulets that he had found among the successive layers of wrappings, and his long delicate hands were trembling with excitement as he picked out another.

Seeing his friend's absorption in his task, Richard restrained his impatience to begin talking about his woes; and, when they had greeted one another, sat down to watch the completion of the business. At length the brown parchment covered body of a short, slender woman was revealed. Her mummy was in an excellent state of preservation, having a cavity only below the left ribs where the flesh had gone to powder, and when Droopy tapped it on the chest it gave out a hollow note. He remarked that his agent had had to pay an Arab merchant two hundred guineas for it; and that owing to the superstitious fears of sailors at having a corpse on board he had had to pay a Greek captain a further hundred to smuggle it to England for him disguised as a bale of carpets; but he was well satisfied with his purchase. Only then did Richard announce the shattering result of his interview with Mr. Pitt.

Immediately, Droopy was all concern, and they set about discussing Richard's future. Financially he had had an excellent nine months, as with the money Madame Marie Antoinette had given him, the balance of the sum he had received from Tansanta, his accumulated allowance from his father and what was due to him from the Foreign Office, he reckoned that he had the better part of fourteen hundred pounds to his credit. So after they had been talking for a while, -he said

`Fortunately I am well in funds, so in no situation where I must take the first thing that offers from immediate necessity to earn my living. The things that distress me most are the breaking of my association with Mr. Pitt, and the unlikelihood of ever obtaining another opening which would afford me both the means and opportunity to continue my travels.'

Droopy scratched his long nose and said thoughtfully: `It would not surprise me greatly if after a while Mr. Pitt sends for you again. Should you prove right in your contention that the information you have sent from Paris is better founded than that supplied by the British Embassy, the fact will emerge in due course. 'Tis even probable that the Prime Minister repudiated your beliefs simply because they do not fit in with his own preconceptions. I doubt if in recent weeks he can have followed events in France at all closely, as such time as he would devote to foreign affairs must have been occupied with the far more serious developments in Belgium.'

`More serious!' Richard exclaimed. `Oh come, Ned!'

`Egad, man, they are so regarded in England. The fall of the *Bastille* and the attack by the mob on Versailles are now half a year old. The general opinion here is that the most dangerous phase of the French Revolution is over, and that in a few more months the nation will settle down under a Liberal Constitution. But the troubles in Belgium came to a head only just before Christmas, and their outcome still lies in the balance.'

`I had heard that there have been riots in the Low Countries in favour of a Republic, but have been too occupied to acquaint myself with the details. Have the Belgians also established a democratic form of government?'

Droopy's wide mouth opened in a grin. `You are indeed out of touch with what we look on here as the burning question of the moment. I had best give you the gist of it. The revolution in Belgium has been of an entirely different character from that in France, and has sprung from a diametrically opposite cause. For a long time past the Emperor Joseph II has been endeavoring to introduce a great variety of reforms in the Austrian Netherlands; but the people appear to prefer their own time-honored way of life, that has existed almost unchanged since the Middle Ages. The root of the trouble lies in the Emperor's Germanic passion for uniformity. Each Province formed a miniature State differing in its constitution and administration from the others. He wished to do away with all these inconsistencies so that everyone should enjoy the same degree of liberty. He wanted all the priests to be educated in one central Seminary at Louvain; and he wanted the *Kermises as the* great Fairs are called of all the different towns to be held on the same day.'

Blinking his weak blue eyes, Droopy went on: `The edicts from distant Vienna ordering these innovations met with increasing resistance, until last November the Estates of Brabant and Hainault defied the Emperor and refused to vote further taxes. On Joseph resorting to disciplinary measures the normally pacific burghers took up arms against him. In December they threw off the Austrian yoke and proclaimed their country as the Republic of the United States of Belgium. At the moment the Emperor is still in negotiation with his rebellious Netherlanders, but he is known to be mobilizing an army for their suppression. Meanwhile they are endeavoring to secure armed support against him from the Prussians and the Dutch.'

Richard knew that it had for long been a cardinal factor in British Foreign policy that the Low Countries, and particularly the great port of Antwerp, should remain in the hands of a power incapable of using them for offensive purposes; so he felt that Droopy's guess that Mr. Pitt had recently been concentrating his interest on events in Belgium to the exclusion of those in France was very probably right. But, if it were so, that still did not alter the fact that he had been dismissed for refusing to go to Spain; and the problem now uppermost in his mind was whether to start seeking some new permanent career right away or first to take things easy for a while at Lymington.

Knowing his friend's highly strung nature, Droopy was much against his going to the country, as he feared that there he would brood over his dismissal. He urged that, while there was no hurry to settle on anything, Richard ought to remain in London, as only in it was he likely to meet people in a situation to offer him some post suitable to his talents, and that if he could first collect a few ideas to think over he would later enjoy a visit to his home much more.

In consequence, instead of staying at Amesbury House for only a few nights, Richard remained on and, in the company of the foppish, shortsighted, but extremely astute Droopy, once more entered the idle round of pleasure that made up the life of London society.

In the latter half of February fresh impetus was given to interest in the Belgian situation by the arrival of the news of the Emperor Joseph's death; and few vigorous, intelligent, Liberal minded Monarchs have died in such sad circumstances. He had started out with high hopes of consolidating his vast, scattered dominions and bringing liberty to all his subjects. Diplomatic defeats had prevented him from achieving the former and the backwardness of the peoples he governed prevented the latter. At the time of his death Belgium had declared her independence; the nobles of Hungary had forced him to cancel all his reforms with the single exception of the abolition of serfdom; he was at war with Turkey in the south; his only ally, Catherine II of Russia, was in no situation to help him; and the Turks had just concluded an alliance with the Prussians, who, in conjunction with the Poles, were now massing an army with

the intention of invading Austria from the north. So it looked as if the whole
Habsburg Empire was about to fall into ruins.

He was succeeded by his younger brother, Leopold of Tuscany; and
Richard wondered if even the outstanding abilities of the equally Liberal
minded but much more cautious Grand Duke would prove up to pulling the
Empire out of the mess it was in. He wondered, too, if the beautiful Donna
Livia had accompanied Leopold to Vienna; and recalled his brief affaire with
her as one of the most amusing and delightful adventures of its kind that
fortune had ever sent him.

Early in March his memories of another titian haired lady with whom he
had dallied, although in a more discreet manner, were revived with much
greater directness. At a ball at Chandos House he ran into Amanda Godfrey.

Somehow he had never associated her with London, so he was all the
more struck by seeing her for the first time in such a setting and dressed in the
height of fashion. Her tall figure and graceful carriage lent themselves well to
fuller petticoats and a higher headdress than she ever wore in the country; yet
she retained her natural, imperturbable manner, which made her even more
outstanding among the affected young women who were flirting their fans and
sniffing their salts near by.

Richard at once asked her for a dance, and she said with her usual
vagueness that she had no idea if she had any left, but would be enchanted if
he cared to snatch her sometime during the evening ; so snatch her he did, and
to avoid possible trouble with other claimants to her company they sat out
three dances running in an alcove off the refreshment room.

After they had been talking for some twenty minutes she said

`Richard, my dear, you are mightily improved since we last met, and I
am happy indeed to find you so much more like the man you were a
twelvemonth back.'

`That is easy to explain,' he laughed. `I am no longer in love. Except, of
course, in being newly smitten with your fair self.'

`You foolish fellow,' she smiled languidly. `But I am glad to hear it. That
you are no longer in love, I mean. 'Tis a plaguey wearing business.'

He sighed. `There is certainly no other to compare with it for depriving a
man of his normal faculties, and reducing him to a morose, hagridden shadow
of himself.'

`Or a woman either. I pray God that I may never again be afflicted with
the disease in virulent form.!

'so you, too, have known that agony?'

She nodded. `I thought I would ne'er recover when we first met, but your
gallant attentions over that Christmas did much to help me. They were
flattering without being serious enough to cause me any perturbation, so the
very tonic needed to restore my amour propre.'

`I am glad,' said Richard seriously, `that I should have been even the
unconscious means of assisting your recovery.'

`I would that I could have done as much for you,' she replied `but your
amour propre needed no restoring.'

`Your kindness in allowing me the status of a favored beau last summer, while knowing that my heart was set elsewhere, was truly generous, and helped me mightily!

'Nay; not in the healing of your wound.' She shook her head, then went on thoughtfully: `I -had been near desperate with love for a man who would have none of me. H. thought me a fool. Mayhap he is right in that, for I know well that at times I both say and do the most plaguey stupid things. 'Twas my hard lot to have to play gooseberry to a cousin of mine while he courted and married her. She has a bookish cleverness that I shall ever lack; but a mean, petty mind; and that made it all the harder.

`Then there came Christmas at Lymington, and yourself. I knew full well that your intentions were not serious; but you were the handsomest beau in the district, so well enough to flirt with. And it was, I think, the very fact that you were not obsessed with my physical attractions that made you talk to me the more. I mean, apart from the usual persiflage of gallantry. You would not recall it, but you asked my opinion upon a hundred matters, ignored my vagueness about things that are of little account, and showed a genuine interest in all I had to say. On one occasion you said to me: "'Tis the combination of such femininity with so clear and deep a mind as yours, Amanda, that enables great courtesans to rule Empires." Oh Richard, had you been the ugliest man on earth I could have kissed you for that!'

He placed a hand gently over hers. `My dear, I vow to you I meant it.'

She smiled. `The way you said it at the time convinced me of that; and although clever I shall never be, no one will ever again make me believe that at bottom I am a fool. But your case last summer was very different. You were in love with a woman who returned your love, but debarred by circumstances from attaining your mutual desires. Consciously or unconsciously I could do nothing to aid you in such a pass. Yet I find you now recovered. Tell me; how have you managed to free yourself from the grip of this ghastly malady that is praised by poets with such stupendous unreason?'

`I hardly know myself,' Richard confessed. `In part, perhaps, 'tis because when I was last abroad I met the lady of my love again, under unexpected and most favourable conditions. Yet since we were little more than a week together 'tis no case of having satiated our passion on either side. I moved heaven and earth in an attempt to persuade her to fly with me, but she would not ; and her refusal was no slight upon her love, as she considered herself tied from the fact that in a few weeks now she is to bear her husband a child.'

`You could rejoin her later; visit her from time to time and seize such opportunities as offer to renew your transports.'

`Nay. What kind of a life would that be? 'Tis better, far, that she should build a new life round her child ; and that I should consider myself free to marry.'

`If you marry even had you been able to marry her do you believe that you would remain faithful to a wife?'

Richard laughed. `You have me there! I fear 'tis most unlikely.'

`I am glad you have the honesty to admit it.' Amanda smiled, `for all I have ever learnt of men has led me to believe that 'tis against nature in them to be monogamous. Granted then that you would be unfaithful to a wife, why should you not marry if you have a mind to it, and still at intervals indulge your passion for your Spanish mistress, rather than for some other?'

`Your logic is unanswerable,' Richard replied, after a moment. `But recently my circumstances have changed, and in future 'tis probable that my work will lie here in London: Were I to marry, 'tis hardly likely that my wife would be agreeable to my going gallivanting alone on the Continent.'

`Then she would be a ninny,' Amanda declared serenely. `A wife whose husband deceives her only when he is abroad should count herself lucky. At least she is spared the sweet innuendoes of her friends when his latest affaire becomes common knowledge in her own circle. I only pray that I may be sent a husband who betakes himself once or twice a year to foreign parts and confines his infidelities to his absences from England.'

Richard sighed. `How wise you are, my dear Amanda. Yet even had I the good fortune to marry a wife so clear-sighted as yourself I believe it would be a great mistake to follow the course you propose. The nature of my Spanish love is so intense that I feel sure she would consider herself desperately aggrieved did I marry another. And though I am in no situation to marry at the moment I have recently felt more than once that I would like to settle down in a home of my own. So 'tis best for both her and me that we should not meet again.'

`If you now feel that, you are cured.!

'Yes; for I no longer think of her with any frequency, and am able once more to regard life as a joyous adventure.!

'Think you that you are now inoculated of the fell disease?'

`I trust so. It went so deep that 'tis unlikely a similar madness will seize upon me for some other woman, at least for some years to come.'

`I feel that, too ; for my love also was most desperate while it lasted, and I'll not willingly surrender the freedom of my mind again. In that I intend to model myself on Melissa Etheridge ; though I am not of a temperament ever to become quite so reckless a wanton as her hot, half gipsy blood has made her. She has reduced love to a fine art. Whenever she finds herself becoming too deeply attached to a man she dismisses him and takes another!

Richard glanced up in surprise. `I did not know you knew Melissa!

`I met her first when she was married to Humphrey Etheridge, then again on her return to England last October. I stayed with her for a while at Shambles and found her positively enchanting.'

`She is my oldest and dearest friend.!

'I know it; and you had written to her most gloomily from Lymington last summer, mentioning me in your letter. 'Twas the discovery that we were both worried on *your account which* formed a special bond between us; for the ravishing Melissa is not normally given to making women friends.'

`I have not seen her now for close on a year ; and 'twas a sad blow to me to learn on my return from France last month that she had gone abroad again.'

`She and her father left early in December to spend the worst months of the year in Italy; but they should be back soon, as she told me that she could not bear the thought of missing another spring at Shambles.'

Richard nodded. "Tis a heavenly place. When Melissa returns we must arrange a visit to her.'

For the third time since they had been sitting there the violins struck up, so Amanda said: `Richard, my dear, we must dally no longer, or the number of my irate disappointed partners will be greater than even my notoriously poor memory will excuse.'

As he escorted her back to the ballroom he asked if he might call upon her, and she replied: `Do so by all means. I am as usual with my Aunt Marsham in Smith Square; but let it be within the next two days, as we leave on Thursday to stay with friends at Wolverstone Hall in Suffolk.'

On the Wednesday Richard had himself carried in a sedan down to Westminster, and took a dish of tea with Amanda and Lady Marsham. The latter had mothered Amanda ever since she had been orphaned as a child of. four, and Richard had met her on numerous occasions when she was staying with her brother, Sir Harry Burrard, at Walhampton. There was a striking family resemblance between Amanda and her aunt. Age had increased Lady Marsham's figure to august proportions, but she was still a very handsome woman of fine carriage, and she had the same effortless charm of manner. In her vague way she at first took Richard for someone else, but welcomed him none the less heartily when her mistake was discovered.

Nevertheless the visit was not an altogether satisfactory one, as the two ladies were in the midst of packing. Their mutual untidiness had turned Lady Marsham's boudoir, in which they took tea, into a scene of indescribable confusion, and frequent interruptions by the servants to hunt there for articles that had been mislaid played havoc with all attempts to carry on an intelligent conversation.

It was perhaps Amanda's departure for the country that subconsciously decided Richard to pay a visit to his mother. His own enquiries and those of Droopy Ned had so far not produced any suitable opening, and while he was anxious not to waste longer than necessary before starting a new career, he had funds enough to keep him as a modish bachelor for two or three years; so there would have been little sense in his jumping into a blind alley simply to salve his conscience.

4n arriving at Lymington he found, to his distress, that his mother was far from well. Lady Marie had for some months been suffering from pains in her inside, and although the doctors had failed to diagnose the cause of the trouble they feared a tumor. She had not taken to her bed, but tiredness now brought on the pain, and having always led a very active life she naturally found it hard to have to limit herself in the time that she could now spend in her stillroom and garden.

Richard had meant to spend only a few nights at Lymington but. in the circumstances, he prolonged his visit to a fortnight; and, seeing his solicitousness for her, she took occasion one evening to speak to him more seriously than she had done for a long time past.

She disclosed how worried she had been about him in the summer, so he told her about his *aff* afire with Tansanta; and also that it was unlikely that he would be going abroad again, as his work for the Government had been terminated. With her usual tact she refrained from telling him that she had guessed him to be involved in some foreign entanglement, or remarking how pleased she was to hear that he was now free of it; but she expressed considerable concern about his future, and discussed various possibilities with him. However, the trouble as had been the case with Richard on his first return from France two and a half years before was that the combination of qualities he possessed did not particularly fit him for any career outside the fighting services.

(t was not until he kissed her good night that she said quietly

`I do not wish to alarm you; Richard; and when next you write to your father in no circumstances are you to put ideas into the dear man's head. But I do not think I shall live to make old bones.'

He knew that she was confirming his own half formed fears, that her illness was serious; so in a swift effort to comfort her he kissed her again and pressed her very tightly in his arms. She smiled up at him, patted his cheek and murmured

`Don't worry, my lamb. I feel sure God will spare me to you for a year or two yet. But before I go I would like to see you happily settled, if that be possible. Mind, I would not for the world have my wish overweigh your own judgment in any case where you feel an inclination, yet have doubts. I mean only that should you find the right girl, I beg you not to hesitate on account of your present lack of employment, or the smallness of your income. A man of your parts cannot fail to climb high, so 'tis but a matter of. finding a good ladder; and I can vouch for it that in the meantime your father would see to it that you did not lack for money.'

when, a few minutes later, Richard reached his own room, his thoughts turned to Amanda. If he married her, how overjoyed his mother would be! But would Amanda be willing to marry him? In view of their conversation a fortnight back he thought she probably would. Neither of them had any illusions left about unreasoning passion; both had been burnt by it too badly. She did not wish to experience that kind of love again ; nor did he. Both of them wanted something more gentle but more enduring. Melissa held a special place in his life that no one else could ever fill; but, Melissa apart, he liked Amanda as a person better than any other woman he had ever met. Mentally they had been attracted to one another from the beginning; quite early in their game of make-believe they had toyed with passion just enough to know that each was capable of raising in the other swift desire, and between them, like two sturdy trees, there had grown up trust and genuine affection.

Before he went to sleep, Richard decided that if Amanda felt the same way about him as he did about her, they would have a far better prospect of enjoying many years of happiness together than the great majority of couples that got married. Yet he refrained from committing himself to any definite course of action. Amanda was due back from Suffolk at the, end of the month.

He would take an early opportunity to see her again and unostentatiously reclaim his position as one of her beaux. After that he would leave the development of matters on the knees of the gods and to Amanda.

But, as always happened when a fresh line of thought came to him, his mind gripped, exploited and would not let it go ; so by the time he arrived in London, on the night of March 20th, he was looking forward to Amanda's return with the utmost eagerness, and was highly conscious that in the next few weeks life might hold a new excitement and a new meaning for him.

Then, on the morning of the 22nd, a letter was delivered to him at Amesbury House. He saw by the franking that it came from Portugal; next second he recognized the careful, angular writing as Tansanta's.

With unsteady hands he opened it, and with eyes jumping from line to line swiftly took in its contents. The paragraphs were not many, but every one of. them aroused his deepest emotions.

She loved him more than all the world. She was desperately unhappy. She believed her life to be in danger. Would he endeavor to reach Madrid by mid-April and snatch her from hell to the paradise of his protection?

CHAPTER TWENTY-TWO
THE KING'S BUSINESS

With his heart hammering in his chest, Richard read the letter through again more carefully. It had been written as recently as the 4th of the month, and Tansanta having sent it by fast personal courier as far as Lisbon explained its swift transit. She added that she had sent a duplicate of it *to La Belle toile* in Paris, with her prayers that one or the other would reach him in time for him to save her.

She and her husband had left Naples at the end of January in order that she might have her baby in the traditional manner at the castle from which he took his title. She expected the event in the latter part of March. She still felt that she had been right in her decision not to elope with Richard from Naples, and that he could not love her less on that account. To have done otherwise would have been shameful. She had intended to resign herself to a life without love except that for her child. But she had discovered that her husband was a monster.

Little Quetzal was one of the very few people *who* did not shun the village witch, so the old crone doted on the boy. She had told him that Don Diego had bought poison from her, and that from her private reading of his horoscope he intended to use it on *his* wife. The motive for such a frightful act was, alas, all too plain. Some weeks previously he had conceived one of his uncontrollable passions for an Englishwoman. She was a beautiful creature, but cold, designing and ambitious.

Like other Spanish noblemen Don Diego never stooped to conceal his infidelities from his wife; and, in one of *his* black, morbid fits, he had told Tansanta frankly that the cause of his distress was that their beautiful visitor would not give in to him or any other man for either love or money; she wanted both a title and a fortune, and her price was marriage. A week later Quetzal's terrible discovery had disclosed the way Don Diego's mind was now working. Since he was in no situation to pay the Englishwoman's price without first getting rid of Tansanta, his wild obsession was such that he had determined to take the step which would enable him to pay it.

Tansanta felt confident that she would be safe until she had had tier child. Afterwards, she meant to exercise the utmost caution and keep to her bed for a fortnight, as there she need eat nothing but food that had been specially prepared for her by Maria. But by mid-April, or possibly earlier, it was certain that the doctor would declare her well enough to leave for Madrid. From then on she would be in extreme danger, but fit to travel. So she begged Richard to hasten to Madrid at the earliest possible moment and carry her off back to England with him.

Richard noted that it did not seem to have even entered her head that since she had refused to leave Naples with him his passion for her might have cooled. It was clear that her love for him had not abated one iota ; and obviously she assumed that his love for her had equally sustained no diminution. Now that her letter, with her desperate plea, raised her image so clearly in his mind again it seemed as if for the past four months he had been boxed up in an airtight compartment, and that its walls had *suddenly* been whipped away like paper in a gale.

Melissa Etheredge was a case apart, and with the possible exception of his calf love for Athenais de Rochambeau-he knew that he had never felt so deeply for any woman as he had for Tansanta. The idea that her life was in danger made his throat contract; yet he caught himself wondering if he would ever quite recover the wild passion for her that had obsessed him in Naples, and that he had since striven so successfully to kill.

The thought of Amanda gave him pause for a moment. He was not committed to her in any way; yet for these past few days he had been envisaging the seductive possibilities of married life with her. If she felt as he did, everything could be so simple and so suitable. The wedding would be from Walhampton, the ceremony in the old parish church at Lymington, blessings and good wishes would ' be showered on them by all their friends. They would have only themselves to blame if they were not happy; and his poor, darling mother would be overjoyed in seeing her dearest wish come true.

In contrast to that picture Tansanta did not even mention the prospects of an annulment, and he could not possibly expose her to the risk of insult, as his kept woman, in London; neither could he take her to Lymington. During his fit of madness in Naples he had had vague thoughts of taking her down to Hampshire and passing her off as his wife, but he knew that he would never be able to bring himself to do that now. Should some ill chance reveal such a deception, in his mother's present state the shock arid shah shame involved might prove so great a blow that it would aggravate her illness and send her into a swift decline.

Yet Tansanta was asking no more of him than he had asked of her four months ago, and in her case with far greater reason. From the moment he had first skimmed through her letter there had been no real doubt in his mind. He knew that he must go to Spain, if only to save her from becoming the victim of Don Diego's ungovernable passion. As there were no other possible means of doing so than eloping with her, it followed that Fate had, after all, decreed that their lives were to be permanently united.

It struck him that the blind goddess had behaved with a certain *cynicism, in first causing him* to wreck his professional career by refusing a journey to

Spain that would have led to reopening his nerveracking affaire and now compelling him to go there at the price of his new prospects of quiet, domestic happiness. But he swiftly upbraided himself for a thought so disloyal to the woman whom only four months before he had loved so desperately. That love would blossom anew once he was with Tansanta again and prove a buckler to them against all the difficulties they might meet with when he got her to England.

Fortunately he had ample money to keep them in modest comfort for a long time to come. They could live very quietly somewhere in the country under an assumed name; perhaps in Kent or Sussex, as in both counties there were now many French exiles, so Tansanta being a foreigner would not arouse unwelcome interest in either of them. He would give out in London that he had been, sent abroad again ; and could only pray that the Catholic Church would allow Don Diego to repudiate Tansanta so that they could regularize their union While his mother was still able to give them her blessing. There was, too, always just a chance that Fate might intervene again, and give Tansanta her freedom through her husband's death.

Swiftly upon these thoughts another came to Richard. Since he was going to Spain, both courtesy and his own interests suggested that he ought to offer himself to Mr. Pitt to carry any dispatches that were awaiting transit to Madrid. At least by doing so he could show that he bore no rancor against the Prime Minister, and was still willing to serve him in any way he could. It was possible, too, that by this time Mr. Pitt had had confirmation of de Mirabeau's alliance with the Court, and so took a better view of his ex-agent's last activities in Paris. If so, Richard felt, there was just a chance that he might be forgiven his insubordination, and entrusted with a new mission on his return from Spain.

At even this slender prospect of reinstatement his spirits went up with a bound. He had felt all along that no opening he could find would prove so congenial to him as his old work and, with luck, a resumption of it would enable him to live abroad with Tansanta as Madame de Blane, which would solve a multitude of problems for them.

At once he hurried off to Downing Street; but it was a Monday, and he learned that the Prime Minister, having as usual spent Sunday at Holyrood, was not expected back until it was time for him to take his place in the House of Commons that evening.

Richard knew it would be useless to leave a note, as M r. Pitt was too poor to be able to afford a private secretary and very often left his letters lying unopened for weeks.

It was one of the strangest anomalies that by his financial genius Mr. Pitt should have brought Britain, in the space of a few years, from the verge of bankruptcy to a wonderful prosperity, yet be quite incapable of managing his own affairs; and another that, while he was incredibly hardworking and extremely punctilious about the discharge of all business that could be transacted verbally, he was one of the worst correspondents in the world. He was shamefully robbed by his servants and hopelessly in debt; but, maintaining that the nation's affairs must come before his own, he refused to open letters from fear they would be bills, which would distract his attention from more important matters; and he never answered a letter unless he thought it absolutely imperative to do so.

In consequence, Richard, being reluctant to waste a whole day, decided that the best course was to go down to see him in the country. So, returning to Amesbury House, he had a horse saddled and rode through Southwark, down the Old Kent Road, to Bromley. A few miles beyond the village he came to Mr. Pitt's country home and, having had himself announced, was shown through into the garden.

There he found the tall, lean, worn looking Prime Minister admiring his crocuses and daffodils. He smiled as Richard approached and asked: `Well, Mr. Blane, am I to take this as a social call?'

Richard bowed. `Nay, sir. I would not be guilty of such boldness. It is that I am about to set out for Spain.'

Mr. Pitt raised his eyebrows. `Is it not a little much to assume my forgiveness; and by so bald an announcement take it for granted that although a month has elapsed since we last met, I am still willing to give you my instructions?'

'I made no such assumption, sir; and while I should be delighted to be received back into your good graces, I did not come here to ask forgiveness.'

Giving him an amused look, the Prime Minister remarked

`Humility has never been one of your outstanding attributes, Mr. Blane; but as I have little use for that quality myself I do not think the less of you for that. Since we are such a. stiff-necked pair, I will for once incline my own head a tree. Your reports from Paris have turned out considerably better fir than I had any reason to suppose would be the case. Mark you, I still most strongly disapprove of the manner in which you involved yourself with the Queen and her Austrian friends. And I equally disapprove your secret understanding with that rogue de Talleyrand Périgord. But your information about de Mirabeau was correct, and your general assessment upon numerous other matters shows that you did not allow yourself to be fooled. In view of that, and your having thought better of the pigheadedness you displayed in February, we will let bygones be bygones.'

Richard's hopes first thing that morning for such an outcome to this interview had been only slender ones, and the nearer he got to Bromley the more they had tended to decrease ; so his reaction was all the greater and, being no more given to hypocrisy than to humility, he expressed his gratitude and pleasure in no uncertain terms.

Waving aside his thanks, Mr. Pitt went on: `Owing to the Don's natural dilatoriness where business is concerned, little has been lost by your delay in setting out. They made their *démarche on* February 10th, and I sent for you at once to take our reply. Since you failed me, I had it handed to del Campo, the Spanish Ambassador here ; but so far no answer to it has arrived. It fits in well, therefore, that I should now follow up my letter by sending you to Madrid as my personal emissary, to protest at their delay and demand full satisfaction.'

The Prime Minister's words simultaneously delighted and alarmed Richard. He was still completely in the dark as to the nature of this trouble with the Spaniards, but it was clear that Mr. Pitt meant to send him to Spain with some form of diplomatic status; and that would be not only reinstatement but promotion. On the other hand, Mr. Pitt was obviously under the impression that, however awkwardly he might have put it, he had repented his refusal to go to Spain and had come there in the hope that it might not yet be too late for him to be given this mission. With an effort he brought himself to say

' Tis only proper to inform you, sir, that I am about to proceed to Madrid because my private affairs require my presence there. I came here only to offer my services in case you had dispatches that you wished conveyed thither.'

`I thank you for your candor, Mr. Blane,' came the reply. with a slight frown. `But I trust this does not mean that you are still unwilling to serve me in the more important matter?'

Richard's mind hovered with frightful uncertainty for a moment on the horns of a dilemma. If he accepted, he would be tied by his country's interests and might find them come in direct conflict with plans for his elopement with Tansanta. As against that, should he refuse this chance of getting back into the old work that meant so much to him he felt certain ,4 would never be given another. Mr. Pitt was far too intolerant of halfhearted, undependable people; and, as though he read Richard's thoughts, he remarked now with some asperity

`I need hardly stress that should you accept my instructions they must take precedence of all else. You have already, more than once allowed *other* interests to distract you from the King's business, anti we had best part company for good if that is likely to occur again.'

Those words `the King's business' rang a sudden bell in Richard's mind. They recalled to him his mother down at Lymington with, he feared, only a limited time to live, while duty kept his father tied to his flagship, far away at sea. It was the King's business that separated them and, of necessity, called for sacrifices in thousands of other people's lives. For the first time he acknowledged to himself that Mr. Pitt had been justified in censuring him for devoting so much of his energies to Madame Marie Antoinette's affairs, and that during the past year he had, all too frequently, allowed influences that touched his sentiments to interfere with strict concentration on his duties.

With swift contrition he said: `I am truly sorry, sir, that in my last mission I did not give you full satisfaction; but if you will entrust me with this affair in Spain I give you my word that I will not allow the private business that takes me to Madrid to interfere with its execution.'

Mr. Pitt nodded approval, and his thin face broke into a smile. He felt that Richard had had his lesson and would prove more conscientious in future. `Let us go into the house, then,' he said ; and as they walked towards it across the lawn he added: `You will, no doubt, have seen the reference in His Majesty's speech on opening Parliament to this difference of ours with Spain?'

`No, sir. I have this past fortnight been in the country with my mother at Lymington, so I fear I am somewhat out of touch with affairs.'

`It has aroused little comment as yet, owing to public interest being concentrated on events in Austria and Belgium; but unless we can curb the Don's pretensions promptly, it may well lead to a dangerous situation.'

As they entered the house by a pair of french windows and settled themselves in the Prime Minister's library, he went on

`This then is the issue. As a result of their early explorations the Spaniards have long claimed suzerainty over the whole of the North American Pacific coast right up to Alaska; but they have never troubled to establish trading posts much further north than San Francisco. However, in '74, one of their captains discovered an exceptionally fine natural harbor in the neighborhood of the island of Vancouver, and adopted the local Indian name for the place: Nootka Sound.

`Four years later Captain Cook also came upon it, and used it for some months as a base during one of his voyages of discovery. His report upon it as a valuable anchorage was duly filed, and when the cessation of the American War enabled commerce to expand again some of our traders began to use it. Apparently the Indian trappers bring their skins there to a market at certain seasons of the year, and the Chinese pay very high prices for rare furs, so a new trade in such commodities arose across the North Pacific, between Nootka Sound and China.

`In '88 several merchants of the British East India Company decided to form an Association of their own for the development of this profitable business; so they sent out one John Mears, an ex-lieutenant of the Royal Navy, with orders to establish a permanent trading post at Nootka. Mears bought a piece of land from the Indian Chief, Macquilla, and the exclusive right to trade with his subjects; then he built a small settlement on the land he had acquired, fortified it and hoisted the British flag.

`Last summer it seems that Flores, the Viceroy of Mexico-, became alarmed at rumours that the Russians were *establishing* themselves on the North American seaboard, so he sent two warships under the command of a Captain Martinez *north* to investigate. To his surprise Martinez found Nootka occupied by the British. He destroyed the settlement, seized two ships that we had there, and carried Mears and his men back as prisoners to Mexico.

`We have had no Ambassador in Madrid since the recall of Mr. William Eden last June; and Mr. Anthony Merry, our Consul, whom you will meet there, has since been acting as Chargé . d'Affaires. I had the first rumours of this matter from Mr. Merry in the latter part of January. Then, on February 10th, the Conde del Campo, who is the Spanish Ambassador at the Court of St. James, presented a formal note upon it.

`The note stated that out of His Most Catholic Majesty's consideration for His Britannic Majesty, the prisoners have since been liberated ; but it asserted the right of Spain to absolute sovereignty in those districts "which have been occupied and frequented by Spaniards for so many years". Further, it called upon us to punish those responsible for the undertaking and to prohibit future ones of a similar nature.

`The statement that the Spaniards have occupied these districts for many years is entirely without foundation, and I will never submit to such unprovoked insult to the British flag. Having no Ambassador in Madrid to instruct, I took the matter in hand myself. After consultation with the Cabinet I replied to del Campo through His Grace of Leeds that an act of violence having been committed made it necessary to suspend all discussion on the pretensions set forth in his note until just and adequate satisfaction should have been made for a proceeding so injurious to Great Britain.'

Mr. Pitt stood up and, walking over to a big globe map of the world that occupied a corner of the room, added: 'There the matter rests. But I wish you to see what this strangely named harbor on a far distant shore may mean to us in the future.'

With his long, sensitive forefinger he pointed first to the United States. 'See, here are England's first Colonies in the Americas. A hundred years ago they were no more than a number of small widely scattered settlements; today they form an independent nation whose wealth, population and power already exceeds that of many States in Europe.'

His finger moved north. 'And here are our Canadian territories, with their flourishing communities at Quebec, Three Rivers, Montreal and Williamsburg. In another two generations those towns may be fine cities having populations as large as Boston, New York and Philadelphia have today; and in the same area hundreds of smaller towns and villages may have sprung up.'

Richard nodded. 'You mean, sir, that now the hatchet has been buried between the Canadian French and our own settlers, the population will increase much faster from both families enjoying greater security to develop their properties and rear families on them?'

'I do indeed; but it is not that alone I have in mind. For many centuries the land of England has sufficed to support her population, but the time is fast approaching when it will do so no longer. Only last summer, when the famine in France was nearing its worst, Monsieur Necker wrote to me begging that I would help him avert the crisis by allowing a large quantity of grain to be sent from Britain ; yet, to my regret, I had to refuse him ; for the safety margin here was so narrow that to have done so would have meant acute shortage among our own people.

'With the great increase of factories in our towns a new age is dawning and I foresee a not-far-distant time when we shall have both to import large quantities of grain ourselves and also encourage the most hardy and adventurous among our people to emigrate. Therefore, both through natural causes and a great influx of new settlers, we are justified in anticipating a very large increase in the inhabitants of Canada. Should that come to pass, as it must short of some unforeseen catastrophe, in another few decades the Canadians will be a great people, and they will require a far larger domain than they have at present on which to support themselves.'

Once more Mr. Pitt put his finger on the globe, and its tip rested in the center of the big blank space, eight times as wide as Canada was then, between the eastern end of Lake Ontario and the Pacific coast.

'Look, now, at that vast unknown territory east of Lake Simco and Fort Toronto. 'Tis into its endless miles of forests, plains and rivers that the Canadians must spread, and from them draw their future sustenance. But look again at its far extremity ; there are Vancouver Island and Nootka Sound. If we allow the Spaniards to maintain their title to Nootka they will spread westward from it, and in a few years claim the half of this splendid northern Empire for their own. That I will not suffer. I want it all. Our Canadians will find a good use for it in the future, and I will fight Spain now if need be so that they may have it when we are dead and gone. I will make no compromise, but am determined to have every square mile of it; so that in course of time Canada may become the mighty child of Britain that I would have her be.'

For a moment Richard remained looking at his great master in silent admiration, then he said. 'What think you, sir, are the chances that we shall have to fight the Dons, in order to make possible this splendid vision of yours?'

Mr. Pitt turned and walked back to his desk. 'I think everything hangs upon our forcing them to take a prompt decision in the matter. As I see it our present case is very similar to that with which we were faced in '61. The late Don Carlos had then been but two years on the throne of Spain. As a young Prince, while Duke of Parma, he had conquered Naples and afterwards reigned there for twenty-five years, doing much to improve the condition of that country. But on his succeeding his father as King of Spain he found his own country ill prepared for war. Even so, his ambitions led him to enter into a secret pact with France, in which it was agreed that lie should make certain demands of its and, if we failed to satisfy them, join France in the war she was then waging against us.

'My father was then Prime Minister. He saw at once the danger of the situation, and that the only way to meet it was to employ highhanded measures. He urged very strongly that His Most Catholic Majesty should be told that either he must withdraw his demands forthwith or we would instantly declare war upon him. Don Carlos' navy and army were then in no state to commence hostilities, moreover his money chest was near empty and he was dependent for paying his forces upon the arrival of a great treasure fleet that had not yet set sail from Peru. Therefore, had my father's advice been taken, the Spaniards would either have been forced to climb down and war with them been averted, or we should have caught them at a grave disadvantage.

'Unfortunately King George III was then very young, and had only the previous year ascended the throne. He placed more reliance on my Lord Bute, who had been his tutor, than he did upon my father, with the result that my father resigned the seals of office. In his place my Lord Bute was appointed principal Minister. He proceeded to temporize with the Spaniards and a long exchange of notes ensued, which achieved nothing. Don Carlos was given time to organize his forces and get his treasure fleet safely across the Atlantic, instead of its being sunk or captured. When he was ready he declared war upon us, and although we defeated him in the end, he inflicted grave damage on us before we succeeded in doing so.'

Richard smiled. 'That certainly is a lesson, sir. Am I to take it, then, that Spain is again unprepared today?'

'Not to the extent she was in '61. The new King, Carlos IV, is, I believe, a weak and inept ruler; but he still enjoys the benefit of his father's endeavors to raise Spain to her former greatness. After his apprenticeship of a quarter of a century as King of Naples, Carlos III reigned for nearly thirty years *in Spain.* He was therefore no novice *in* the art of Kingship, and being a hard*working,* intelligent, conscientious man in fact the best King that Spain has had for many generation s----.Iie did a great deal for his country. Moreover, :n the Counts d'Aranda and Florida Blanca he had two great Prime Ministers to assist him. The latter is still in office, and in the event of war will undoubtedly follow a policy which would have been approved by his late master. Therefore, it we have to tight it will not be against the weak Spain of Carlos IV but the relatively strong Spain created by Carlos III.'

Mr. Pitt stood up, walked over to a side table, poured out two glasses of Port, handed one to Richard, took a drink himself, and went on: 'In spite of what I have just said, in the event of war with Spain with Spain alone, mark you I have no fears whatever regarding its outcome. We can beat the Dons with ease. But this is where the lesson of my father's policy towards them comes in. They know that they dare not fight us single handed, so they are now endeavoring to postpone further discussion on this matter until they have made certain of securing an ally. The ally they hope to win is, of course, France.'

'You mean, sir, that they will invoke the Family Compact?' Richard murmured.

'Precisely. As you must know, King Carlos III fought us a second time during his reign. He was then most reluctant to .do so, but in '79 the French called on him to honour his treaty with them, and at great cost to himself he did so. Now it is France's turn to help Spain, and it is difficult to see how she can refuse to pay her debt. But in view of her recent internal troubles it is certain that she will procrastinate, and urge the Dons to settle their dispute with us without resorting to war. That should give us the time we need. If we can force them into a corner while they are still uncertain whether they can place definite reliance on French support, I feel convinced that they will climb down.'

'You are then, sir, prepared to threaten them with war?'

'I am. If their stomachs are so high that they feel compelled to accept our challenge, that will be regrettable, but by no means catastrophic ; for if they go to war with us on their own 'tis as good as certain that France will refuse to honour her obligations, on the plea that hostilities were entered into without sufficient consultation with her. War with Spain presents no serious danger to us, so 'tis far wiser to risk it than the possibility that we may later be called on to fight Spain and France together. Your task, therefore, is to browbeat the Spaniards into a settlement before they have time to shame their ally into a definite undertaking to fight beside them.'

Richard could hardly believe his ears, but a few moments later he had the evidence of his eyes to support them. The Prime Minister had drawn a sheet of notepaper towards him and was writing on it. When he had done he sanded it carefully and handed it across. It was a Letter of Marque consisting of a single potent sentence.

Mr. Richard Blane knows my mind upon the matter of Nootka Sound, and is commissioned by me to speak upon it.

                                                                                    W

                                                                    illia

                                                                    m

                                                                    Pitt.

As Richard folded it and tucked it into his inner pocket, Mr. Pitt said: `I shall be seeing His Grace of Leeds tonight and also my brother, Chatham. If you will wait upon the former at the Foreign Office tomorrow morning he will furnish you with such funds as you may require, and papers ensuring that all diplomatic facilities will be afforded to you. When you have finished with His Grace go to the Admiralty and send your name up to the First Lord. I will ask my brother this evening to give orders for a frigate to carry you to Lisbon, and when you see him tomorrow he will inform you of the name and port of sailing of the ship selected. Now; are there any questions you would like to ask me?'

`Yes, sir. In the event of the Dons climbing down, have you any instructions for me with regard to terms? I do not infer the giving way by a hairsbreadth over Nootka ; but they are a proud people, and did you see your way to offer them something to salve their pride it might make the difference between peace and war.'

The Prime Minister smiled. `Mr. Blane, I approve your language. 'Tis a pleasure to see how readily you slip into the role of a budding Ambassador; but I think we must leave the discussion of terms to a fully accredited envoy. Mr. Alleyne Fitzherbert has been sent his recall from the Court of The Hague, and should peace continue I have it in mind to send him out to fill the vacant post of Ambassador in Madrid; but another month or so must elapse before he would be ready to proceed there. When he arrives in London His Grace of Leeds and I will discuss with him how far we are prepared to meet the Dons should your own mission prove successful. They have long complained of infringements by our adventurous merchants of their rights in South American waters and of British smuggling activities between our islands in the West Indies and the Spanish Main. We could, if we would, give a formal undertaking to check these interferences with their commerce; but it will be time enough to go into details about such matters if your report of their attitude proves favourable.'

`My function then, sir, is solely to threaten war?'

'Yes. You will not, of course, actually declare it, but are to make it plain that we mean war unless the Spaniards are willing to give us full satisfaction without further delay. If they consent to do so, you may indicate that they would find me not unwilling to give favourable consideration to steps for removing their commercial grievances against us. But before I am prepared to talk at all, I must have their assurance that the North American Pacific coast from parallel forty-five degrees northward to Alaska, and all its hinterland as far east as the St. Lawrence river, will be recognized in a formal treaty as part of His Britannic Majesty's dominions.'

As Richard rode back to London he could still hardly believe it true that he had been entrusted with such a weighty matter. But as he thought it over he saw that his mission was actually a very straightforward one. He was being sent to Madrid as a herald to throw down the gauntlet, and the possible results of his action had been well weighed beforehand. If the Spaniards failed to pick it up, that would stop a war, but even if they accepted the challenge, that should prevent a war of much greater magnitude with real menace to the security of Britain.

Nevertheless, having been given such a task showed that Mr. Pitt could not think too ill of him, in spite of the recent differences that had occurred between them, and his reinstatement in the great man's service filled him with elation. He was still somewhat perturbed at the thought of Tansanta, as he realized very plainly that he was now no longer in a position simply to go out to Madrid and abduct her. But, as an offset to that, now that a frigate was to carry him to Lisbon he would reach Madrid considerably earlier than he could otherwise have done; and once there he felt confident that he would find some means of protecting her. The whole essence of his mission was to obtain a plain answer swiftly, so it could not detain him in the Spanish capital for long. If Tansanta was really in imminent danger she could run away from her husband and somehow he would arrange for her to hide in the city until he was ready to leave it.

Next day he waited upon the Duke of Leeds at the Foreign Office. His Grace proved as charming and friendly as ever. He congratulated Richard on his reinstatement, and further increased his elation by saying that he had found much valuable information in his reports from Paris, which were now proving to have contained more accurate forecasts on some aspects of the situation than those sent by the British Embassy.

He added that, in his view, Richard had been right to go to Florence and Naples on behalf of Madame Marie Antoinette, as they had plenty of people who could collect information about the deputies, but no other who was now so well placed as himself to inform them of the intentions of the Queen; and that he knew Mr. Pitt's strictures on the matter to have been governed, not by disapproval of Richard's initiative, but by his strong feeling that no servant of the British Crown should involve himself in anything which might weaken the new democratic Government of France.

Much heartened to find he had such a champion in His Grace, Richard received from him bills of exchange on Lisbon and Madrid, a diplomatic passport, and a letter of introduction to Mr. Anthony Merry instructing the Consul to render all possible assistance. He then walked on up Whitehall to the Admiralty.

After a wait of an hour he was shown in to the First Lord. It was the first time that Richard had met Mr. Pitt's elder brother, so he had been looking forward to the interview with interest. The second Earl of Chatham was then thirty-three, so some two and a half years older than the Prime Minister. He had started life as an Army officer and had served both at the siege of Gibraltar and in the American War. It was said that his appointment to the Admiralty, eighteen months earlier, had not been altogether due to nepotism, as he was held in high personal regard by the King; *but he* was far from generally popular and entirely lacked both the wit and energy of the brilliant Billy. He was of heavier build, lethargic by nature, and affected with the same nervous frigidity in the presence of strangers.

As Lord *Chatham* expressed no interest whatever in his visitor, the interview was limited to a formal exchange of compliments and the handing over of a letter; so within a minute Richard was out of the First Lord's room, and prepared to agree with the general opinion that he was cold, ponderous and haughty.

Richard had already noted that the letter was addressed to `Captain G. B. Harcourt, H.M.S. *Amazon, Lying* in Portsmouth Roads'; so he walked over to Charing Cross and booked a seat in the night coach for Portsmouth. He then returned to Amesbury House, wrote to his mother, finished his packing and spent his last few hours in London in the company of the amiable Droopy Ned. By eight o'clock the following morning he was on Portsmouth Hard.

A bumboat took him off *to H.M.S. Amazon;* and when introducing himself to her Captain he mentioned that it was in her that his father had returned to England on being recalled from the West Indian Squadron in the summer of '83. As that was nearly seven years ago Richard was surprised *to* hear that Captain Harcourt had the Amazon then, and well remembered carrying his father home with dispatches.

The Captain remarked that as he was a long way down the list, far from expecting promotion to the command of a ship-of-the-line, he was very lucky to have retained a ship at all in times of peace, as after the late war scores of fighting vessels had been scrapped. When serving in the West Indies he had known a dozen promising junior captains who had since been high and dry for years. For instance, one youngster of extraordinary dash and brilliance named Nelson ; but he had been on the beach for a long time past, and it was now doubtful if he would ever get another ship unless Britain again went to war.

Richard naturally said nothing of the business that was carrying him to Lisbon; but he wondered if it would result in Captain Nelson, and those other frustrated young seadogs, being recalled from their quiet farms to once more pace a quarterdeck and order their ships to close upon the enemy. He sincerely hoped not; for if shaking a fist in the face of the Spaniards could prevent it, the fault would not lie with him if Britain had to draw the sword again.

H.M.S. Amazon was that month the duty frigate which was always kept in readiness for special service, so within an hour of Richard coming aboard she put to sea. Off Ushant they struck bad weather, but in spite of that, owing to good handling, the ship put in to Lisbon on the afternoon of Sunday, March 28th.

On landing Richard went straight to the Embassy, where Mr. Robert

Walpole, who had been British Minister to Portugal for nearly eighteen years, gave him an excellent dinner, put him up for the night and made arrangements for him to proceed on his journey to Madrid the following morning.

Only then did Richard's troubles begin. The Portuguese roads proved abominable and those in Spain, if possible, worse. Mr. Walpole had provided him with a Portuguese courier who spoke enough French to act as interpreter, but neither bribes nor threats delivered through him seemed to hurry the personnel that accompanied Richard's coach. It was drawn by eight mules, while an additional team of six ambled along behind, as a reserve which could be hooked on in front of the others to help pull the coach up hills, or out of boggy patches, when it got stuck which seemed to happen with maddening regularity every three quarters of an hour. The muleteers proved more mulish than the mules; and the six armed guards, which Mr. Walpole had insisted on his hiring to protect him from bandits, apparently hoped that the journey would last a month, as they refused to lift a finger to help even when the coach had to be dragged across the worst of the stony watercourses. that severed the road at the bottom of every valley.

The inns in France that Richard had regarded as such miserable places were, he now found, mansions by comparison with those in the Peninsula. Most of them consisted only of a single bare room, with a lean-to behind it in which the innkeeper and his family huddled in appalling squalor. Few of them could even boast a chimney stack, so that the smoke that failed to find its way out through a hole in the roof filled the soot blackened common room where occasional travelers both ate and slept. Every one of them was so alive with bugs that he was soon red from head to foot with bites, and in an endeavor to escape further torment took to sleeping in his coach. Such food as he could get was brought to him half raw, half cold and smothered in garlic ; so that he was near sick every time he forced himself to swallow a mouthful. And the journey seemed never-ending.

Actually, although it did not appear so to him at the time, his lavish offers of largesse for increased speed did have considerable effect, as the coach covered the 400 miles in twelve days, instead of the three weeks that he was assured it would normally have taken. On Friday the 9th of April he arrived in Madrid, itching all over, half famished from lack of decent food, and cursing Spain for the lousiest country that he had ever had the ill fortune to enter.

To add to his fury he found the British Embassy shut up; but, to his relief, it soon transpired that Mr. Anthony Merry was living in a smaller house nearby. The Consul turned out to be a youngish plan of not very enterprising disposition. Madrid was his first post and he had not been there many months when the Ambassador had been recalled, leaving him as Charge *d'Affaires;* and it was soon clear to Richard that he did not care for the responsibility, particularly now that serious trouble was brewing with the Spaniards. It was perhaps this, added to a natural politeness, which accounted for the particular warmth of the welcome he extended to Mr. Pitt's personal representative. '

He said a little plaintively that it was all very well for Whitehall to complain about delays; they did not realize there how hopeless it was for anyone of his junior rank to compel the attention of a Spanish Hidalgo like Count Florida Blanca, but perhaps the Prime Minister would be more impressed by a special envoy, even if Richard did not carry the powers of a Minister Plenipotentiary.

Richard had a good mind to tell him that rank had nothing to do with the matter, and that he ought to be ashamed of himself. For ten months he had been the sole representative of His Britannic Majesty at the Court of Madrid, and that was status enough for any man to demand an audience of the King of Spain himself, if need be. But Mr. Merry's lack of initiative was not his affair, and, even tired and irritable as he was, he was much too tactful to give gratuitous offence to a man upon whom he would have to depend for all sorts of trivial services. So he gratefully accepted Mr. Merry's offer of a bath, put on clean linen and rejoined him for dinner.

Mr. Merry was naturally anxious to hear all the news from home and would have liked to spend the evening enjoying an account of the latest gossip in London, but Richard had no mind to let the grass grow under his feet. While the servants remained in the room he did his best to satisfy the craving of his host, but directly they had gone, he said

`I expect to be here only a few days, so I have no time to waste, and I would be greatly obliged if you would tell me all you can of the Court of Madrid.'

Mr. Merry laughed. `I think, sir, you would be well advised to count your days as weeks while you are in this country; for it is the immemorial custom here.'

'That we shall see, sir,' replied Richard with a hard note in his voice. `In any case, I should be glad if you would accede to my request.'

His host shrugged. `Let us start then with King Carlos. He is a typical Bourbon. both physically and mentally. His muscular strength is quite exceptional, he is entirely devoted to sport and enjoys only the simplest amusements. He is religious, good-tempered, believes implicitly in the Divine Right of Kings, and is one of the stupidest men you could meet in a long day's march. It is Queen Maria Luisa who wears the breeches. You must have heard the classic story of her as a little girl?'

As Richard shook his head Mr. Merry went on: `She was a daughter of Parma, and married at the age of twelve. The very day she heard that her marriage contract with the Prince of the Asturias had been signed, she became so puffed up that she said to her brother, Ferdinand: "You must learn to treat me with more respect, because I'm going to be the Queen of Spain, whiie you'll never be anything but the little Duke of Parma." To which lie replied: "If that's the case, the little Duke of Parma will now have the honour of boxing the Queen of Spain's ears." And he did.'

Richard laughed. "Tis a delightful anecdote. Does she still ride so high a horse?'

`Yes. For all the years her husband was heir apparent she kept him under her thumb; and on his succeeding to the throne in '88 it was she, not he, who called the first Council of Ministers in the new reign. She is a ghoul to look at, with small, pig like black eyes, no teeth of her own but false ones that fit badly, and a greenish, withered skin. Yet from her teens she has never ceased to command lovers to her bed, and woe betide any handsome fellow of the Bodyguard who has the courage to refuse her.'

`Has she any special favourite at the moment?'

`There is a young man of about twenty-three, named Manuel Godoy, who bids fair to become a permanency. He was a Lieutenant in the Flemish Guard at the time Maria Luisa first singled him out for her favors. She was then still Princess of the Asturias, and from fear of her father-in-law kept her liaisons as quiet as possible, but since his death she has made no secret of them, and has showered honours on this handsome paramour of hers. Since he has stayed the pace for nearly three years now, it seems likely that he has acquired a certain influence over *her* other than by merely satisfying her passions.'

`Think you, sir, that it might repay us to court this Señor Godoy, and promise hire some substantial reward if he is willing to use his influence with the Queen in our favour?'

Mr. Merry shook his head. `No, sir. I fear you would find such a course a waste of time. 'Tis not that Godoy would refuse your presents. It is said that he was so poor when he first became the Queen's lover that he had to spend every other day in bed in order to *have his* only shirt washed; so he is now seeking. by every possible means to amass a fortune while his star is in the ascendant. But I greatly doubt if he has the power to be of the least service to you in any political matter. It is believed that on King Carlos IV coming to the throne the Queen made a secret pact with Count Florida Blanca, by which he was to be left in control of all affairs of State while she should be allowed a free hand in the disposal of offices and honours. So 'tis to the Prime Minister that I advise you to address yourself.'

`He has held sway at this Court for many years, has he not?' Richard asked.

`For the best part of thirteen, sir. He came to power as the result of the resignation of Grimaldo and General O'Reilly, following the disastrous joint attack by Spanish and Tuscan forces on the Moors of Algiers. His only serious rival for power has been the famous General Conde d'Aranda, who was King Carlos III's first great Minister. He lost his place in '73, owing to the humiliation Spain suffered at our hands in her abortive attempt to deprive Britain of the Falkland Islands. He was sent as Ambassador to Paris and remained there fifteen years; but his personal prestige continued to be so great, and he is such a forceful personality, that a slip on Florida Blanca's part at any time might well have led to d'Aranda being recalled to replace him as Prime Minister. Even now, although d'Aranda has been living in retirement for the past few years, his recall is not beyond the bounds of possibility.'

Richard asked if Mr. Merry knew the Sidonia y Ulloas, but he did not, and had heard the name only as that of one of the great Spanish families. For a further hour they talked on while Richard absorbed as much information as he could about the Spanish Court ; then, just as they were about to go to bed, he said.

`Since Count Florida Blanca is his own Foreign Minister we shall be spared the formality of first submitting our business through a third party. I should be glad therefore, sir, if you would make the necessary arrangements to present me to him tomorrow.'

Mr. Merry smiled. `You will be fortunate, sir, if you succeed in obtaining an audience with the Prime Minister under two weeks. The best I can do is to take you out to Aranjuez, where the Court is now in residence, and make you known to one of his secretaries.'

`How far is Aranjuez?' Richard enquired.

`It lies about thirty miles to the south of the capital. 'Tis the Versailles of Spain and the Court spends a good part of each year there. For convenience the Embassy owns a villa in the neighborhood. If you wish I will have it opened up, and you can stay there.'

`I would be obliged, sir, *if you will. And thirty miles* being a long day's journey in Spain, I trust it will be convenient to you to make an early start, in order that we may not arrive too late for me to make my first contact with the Court tomorrow evening.'

`..As you will, sir.' Mr. Merry bowed. `But unlike the sandy tracks over which you have been struggling in your journey across Estramadura and Castile, the road between the capital and the King's country home is a fine one; so if we leave at eight we should be there early in the afternoon.'

Although it was only April, when Richard arrived in Madrid he had found it sizzling with a heat that is rarely experienced in England except during the height of summer, yet on the following morning it was near freezing. As he stood shivering in his cloak, Mr. Merry told him that these extremes of temperature occurred daily and were due to Madrid being over 2,000 feet above sea level ; then as they drove through the city he pointed out such few buildings as were of interest. Richard knew that it was far from old, as capitals go, and he found little to admire in it, apart from one broad modern boulevard called the Prado which had been constructed by the Conde d'Aranda and the situation of the city, with the snowcapped peaks of the Sierra de Guadarrama outlined against a blue sky in the distance to the northward.

Aranjuez had been selected as the site of a royal residence from its very peasant surroundings, as it lies in the middle of a fertile plain where the river Jarama joins the upper Tagus, and the country round about forms the principle market garden for Madrid. The little town was the most modern in Spain, as it had been built to a definite plan only forty years earlier, and the Palace was a large late Renaissance building erected twenty-five years before the town.

As they arrived before three o'clock they found the whole place deserted, for the midday siesta was not yet over; but by the time the servants they had brought with them had opened up the villa, the same types of cloaked, sombrero hatted men, and gaily shawled, mantillaed women as Richard had seen in Madrid, began to appear in the streets.

All through his long journey across Portugal and Spain he had been harassed by a double anxiety about Tansanta. She had been due to have her baby in the latter part of March, and it was now April 10th. Yet he still did not know if all had gone well with her, and she had come safely through the ordeal. Then, if she had, there was still the awful thought that during the past fortnight her husband might have poisoned her. I n consequence, now that he was at last within an ace of obtaining news that would either still or confirm his fears, he could hardly contain his impatience to get to the Palace.

Mr. Merry had declared that five o'clock was the earliest hour at which a noble Spaniard could possibly be expected to do business, so at a few minutes to the hour their carriage carried them down a fine avenue and through the formal gardens with which the Palace was surrounded to the wing of it which was occupied by the Prime Minister.

In due course they were received by one of the gentlemen who assisted Count Florida Blanca in the transaction of foreign business: the Caballero Heredia. It transpired that the Caballero had served for some time in the Spanish Embassy in Paris, so he spoke fluent French. He made Richard gravely welcome, examined his credentials and assured him blandly that the Prime Minister would be most happy to grant him an audience at an early date. He added that he hoped that in the meantime Richard would avail himself of the amenities of the Palace, and that the next day being Sunday there was a Court, at which no doubt he could arrange to be presented.

Having thanked him, Richard said: `It is my misfortune, Señor Caballero, to have few Spanish friends, but while in Naples 1 made the acquaintance of a charming couple, the Conde and Condesa Sidonia y Ulloa ; and they are, I think, now in Span. I wonder if you can tell me anything of them?'

`Why, yes,' replied the Caballero, with a smile. `I knew tile Condesa when she lived at the Court of France, before her marriage; and I am happy to be able to give you good news of her. She presented her husband with an heir some three weeks back, and they arrived here to pay their court to Their Majesties only two days ago. No doubt you will see your friends tomorrow night.'

Enormously relieved, Richard said how pleased he would be to see them again ; then, after some further polite conversation with the Caballero Her edia, the two Englishmen withdrew.

Relieved as Richard was he found the next twenty-four hours drag interminably. For a while he occupied himself with an evening walk round Aranjuez with Mr. Merry, but there was nothing to see there except the people. There were few women in the streets; they sat in the deep embrasures of open ground floor windows which were raised some feet above the street level. Every window was heavily barred; in the better houses with an elaborate iron scrollwork that bellied outward in a graceful curve. The men lounged in the street outside. The smarter of them were most colorfully clad, with bright sashes round their waists and scarves round their necks, tight trousers, short jackets and little black hats with pom-poms, beneath which their dark hair was caught up in a net. Many of them carried guitars, and strummed upon them as they softly serenaded their favourite señoritas.

As the season of the Sunday bullfights did not begin till May, Richard whiled away most of the day as best he could, thinking over what he would say to Count Florida Blanca when he obtained an audience. The mission he had been given was, he felt, his great chance; but it was no easy one, for if the Spaniards attempted to procrastinate, as they almost certainly would, he had strict instructions to stand no nonsense from them. So peace or war hung by a thread, and his triumph would be all the greater if lie could maintain the high tone required by Mr. Pitt and yet prevent war breaking out.

At last it was time to go to the Palace ; and at six o'clock he was ushered with Mr. Merry into a vast reception room on its first floor. There were already some hundred ladies and gentlemen present and Richard knew that the same formality would be gone through as he had witnessed at Versailles. When the whole Court was assembled the approach of Their Majesties would be announced, the company would form into a human lane, and the Sovereigns would slowly pass down it. In this case, however, Mr. Merry having been to see the Grand Chamberlain earlier in the day, that functionary would attract the Monarchs' attention to them. and he would be given the opportunity to present his new colleague.

But Richard had no thought for his coming presentation; he was swiftly scanning the crowd for Tansanta. After a moment he caught sight of Don Diego, and then of Tansanta beside him. With a murmured apology to Mr. Merry, he quickly made his way towards the couple.

At sight of him Tansanta's tanned face paled, but she covered her confusion by dropping him a low curtsy in response to his bow. Don Diego also recognized him at once and greeted him very civilly. Richard said that he had heard of their happy event and was delighted to congratulate them upon it; then they began to talk of their mutual friends in Naples.

After a few moments another gentleman claimed Don Diego's attention, so Richard was able to move a little apart with Tansanta. `My love,' she breathed, `My love, I can hardly believe it true that it is really you I see.' .

`Or I, that I am with you again, my own,' he whispered, as he took in all the detail of the thin, fine, dark browed face that had caused him such an agony of love those last days in Naples.

They were standing opposite the main doorway and some distance from it. People were still arriving and at that moment a couple entered. The man was in his sixties, of medium height, and with a thinnish, clever face. The woman was in her early twenties. She had dark hair, black eyes, a faultless complexion, a determined chin and a full, red mouth. Her figure was well rounded for her height and in perfect proportion; her beauty was so dazzling that she eclipsed every other woman in the room.

Tansanta touched Richard on the arm, and her whisper came almost in a hiss. "Look! That is the English woman to marry whom my husband plans to poison me !'

Richard's only reply was a gasp. The superbly beautiful creature round whom a court of bowing men had instantly gathered, was the woman he counted dearer than any other in the world Melissa Etheridge.

CHAPTER TWENTY-THREE
INTRIGUE AT ARANJUEZ

Tansanta half turned to whisper behind her fan to Richard; but, seeing the expression of astonishment on his face as he stared at Melissa, she exclaimed: `Why do you look so surprised? Is it that you know her?'

`Why, yes,' Richard answered in a low voice. `She is my dearest my oldest friend.'

`*Madonna mia!*' Tansanta passed the tip of her tongue over her suddenly *dry lips. 'Role'! You* cannot mean that you, too, have been ensnared by her? Yet from the way you speak . . .'

`No, no! I mean only that we have known one another since childhood. I regard her as a sister.'

Tansanta's dark brows drew together. 'A sister! Only as a sister? Do you swear to me she has never been more to you than that?'

'Hush!' whispered Richard. 'I beg you to control yourself. We are observed. But I can assure you of one thing. You are entirely mistaken in your estimate of her character. She is the kindest and sweetest creature; she would harm no one willingly.'

`Yet she would have me poisoned, so that she may marry one of the greatest fortunes and titles in Spain.'

Richard turned and looked straight into Tansanta's eyes. His voice was suddenly hard. 'Have you one scrap of evidence that Lady Etheredge has knowledge of this fell design of which you accuse your husband?'

'No,' Tansanta faltered. 'No. Yet 'tis rumored here that she killed her own husband some two years ago and narrowly escaped hanging for it.'

' "Tis true that she killed him; but by accident. I was a party to the matter and know every detail of it. Her innocence was vindicated at the trial.' His voice took on a more gentle note. 'I see now how it is that you have been led to think such ill of her; but I swear to you that you do her an injustice. I beg you, too, to believe that my love is entirely yours, and that now I am here I would die rather than let harm befall you.'

Melissa had just caught sight of Richard. Excusing herself from the gentlemen who surrounded her, she waved her fan in delighted recognition, then took her father's arm, and they came through the crowd towards him. When the two women had exchanged curtsies Richard kissed Melissa's hand and shook that of Colonel Thursby heartily.

They .exclaimed with surprise at seeing him in Spain, and he explained his presence by saying that he had been asked to negotiate some questions regarding shipping with the Spanish Government. He then learnt how they came to be at the Court of Madrid. They had meant to spend two months in Naples, but they met the Sidonia y Ulloas there and Don Diego had persuaded them to be his guests in Spain for a few weeks before returning to England.

Don Diego had by that time rejoined the group. He clearly found it difficult to conceal his displeasure at *finding* Melissa talking in English with such animation to Richard, evidently fearing in him a possible rival. His dark eyes never left her face, and Tansanta had fallen ominously silent; but Melissa did not appear to notice the electric atmosphere, and with her usual gaiety she rattled on until an usher called for silence.

Mr. Merry appeared at Richard's side as the Court formed up to do homage to the Sovereigns, and a few minutes later King Carlos and Queen Maria Luisa entered the lofty chamber. In due course the Grand Chamberlain drew Their Majesties' attention to the two Englishmen, and when they had made their bow the King said to Richard, in French

`You are welcome to my Court, Monsieur Blane. Have you ever been to Spain before?'

'No, Your Majesty,' Richard replied. `I have traveled considerably in numerous other countries, but this is the first time I have had the pleasure of visiting your dominions.'

`In which countries have you traveled, Monsieur?'

`Mostly in France, Sire. I have visited Holland, Denmark, Sweden, Russia and Italy, but during the past year I have spent more time in Paris than elsewhere.'

Queen Maria Luisa was regarding Richard intently with her small black eyes. She was, he thought, of *an* incredible ugliness. Her mouth was huge and her false teeth rattled in it as she addressed him

`Were you, Monsieur, a witness to the deplorable events which have shaken the foundations of the French throne?'

He bowed. `I was at Versailles, Your Majesty, both on the night of the taking of the *Bastille* and of the mob's attack upon the Palace. Madame Marie Antoinette has for many months been gracious enough to number me among her gentlemen, so I was in consequence privy to all that passed at Court on those terrible occasions.'

The Queen turned to a fine strapping fellow in a splendid uniform who, with other members of the royal suite, was standing just behind her. `We should be interested to hear at first hand an account of these monstrous proceedings by the French people. Be pleased to bring Monsieur Blane to us tomorrow evening.'

Richard bowed again; then, just as the Queen was moving on, her eye fell upon Tansanta. 'Condesa,' she added kindly. `You were in the service of

Madame Marie Antoinette for some years, were you not? No doubt you too
would be interested to hear news of your old mistress. You and your husband
may wait upon us tomorrow night with Monsieur Blane.'

The reception lasted for about half an hour and during it Richard had no
opportunity to speak further with Tansanta in private, or with Melissa; but he
managed to get a word with Colonel Thursby, just as the King and Queen were
withdrawing.

`Sir,' he said, in a low voice. 'I find that the business I am come to Spain
upon intimately concerns Melissa, and must see her alone at the earliest
possible moment. I pray you to help me in this matter if you can.'

"There is nothing to prevent you calling upon me at any hour of the day
or night,' replied the Colonel with his quiet smile. 'We are staying with the
Sidonia y Ulloas ; but as the Condesa was confined in the country, and arrived
in Aranjuez only three days ago, it would not have been fitting for Don Diego
to receive Melissa into his house in the absence of his wife; so he
accommodated us very pleasantly in a pavilion in his garden. 'is on the left-
hand side of the entrance drive, so you cannot fail to find it. If your business is
urgent you had best come there an hour or so after this party breaks up; but I
do not advise your doing so earlier. You may, perhaps, have observed that our
host is strongly attracted to Melissa, and it might be unfortunate if he got the
impression that you were paying her a midnight visit.'

Richard had hardly thanked him when the fine young man in the
splendid uniform emerged from the crowd. As Richard *had* guessed, he proved
to be Manuel Godoy, the Queen's favourite. Having introduced himself he
asked Richard where he was staying, then requested him to wait upon him in
his apartments at the Palace at seven o'clock the following evening.

In addition to an elegant figure and handsome face, Godoy had an
unusually attractive voice, although he spoke French with a heavy accent. He
also had great charm of manner and an enthusiastic spontaneity in his
conversation rarely found in Spaniards; so Richard took an immediate liking to
him.

A band of violins was now playing indifferent music in one adjoining
salon and a refreshment buffet was spread in another; so the guests had broken
up into little groups and for about an hour continued to exchange politeness
and gossip. Don Diego stuck to Melissa like a leech, but Tansanta was never
alone for a moment, so Richard had to content himself with joining in the
general conversation of the group from which she could not succeed in freeing
herself.

About nine o'clock the guests began to leave, and shortly afterwards
Tansanta, Melissa, Don Diego and Colonel Thursby all went off together.
Richard had asked formal permission to call upon them and received the civil
reply that they hoped to see a lot of rim while he was in Aranjuez, so he had
been able to take the opportunity of finding out the situation of the Sidonia y
Ulloa mansion. Then he, too, left with Mr. Merry and they drove back to the
Embassy villa.

On their arrival Richard announced that, the night being fire, he intended to go for a walk. Mr. Merry, anxious to oblige in every way, offered to go with him, but he excused himself from accepting the offer on the plea that he had certain problems to think out ; then he set off back in the direction of the Palace. His latter statement had at least been true, as he was still trying to adjust his mind to the extraordinary situation with which he had been confronted that evening; but he had some time to kill before he could make his visit to Melissa, so, checking the impulse of his long legs to set off at a stride in pace with his mind, he forced himself to saunter.

There were several things he could not understand. How could his dear, gay Melissa possibly be in love with that dull, conceited stick of a Spaniard? Even if she were, as it was impossible for her to marry him, why, seeing that the wicked darling had indulged herself with a succession of lovers ever since she was sixteen, did she refuse her favors to Don Diego? And why, even were he free to marry her, since she was already rich and titled, should she consider for one moment giving up the carefree life she led in places like London and Vienna to settle in dull, etiquette .ridden Spain?

But of two things Richard was positive: Melissa could not conceivably be concerned in any plot to murder Tansanta, and would give him all the help she possibly could to elope with her. He then began to wonder if there was any real foundation for the plot at all. Had Don Diego's English siren proved to be the hard, fortune hunting adventuress he had expected, his belief in the plot would not have been shaken, but Melissa being the lady in question made it far less probable; and he now recalled that the only evidence for its existence lay in the word of little Quetzal.

That led to another thought. Would Tansanta insist on taking Maria and Quetzal with her? If so it was going to prove next to impossible to bring off a successful elopement. On leaving London Richard's plans for running away with Tansanta had beer of the vaguest, but he had had reasonable confidence in his ability to arrange matters on the lines such affairs usually took in England and France. In either, or most other countries, there would have been nothing to prevent their getting away in a coach with well paid servants and relays of fast horses arranged for in advance.

But he had counted without the special difficulties which confronted travelers in Spain.

The coaches were drawn by mules and the state of the roads was so appalling that it was impossible to travel anywhere with a woman and baggage at any speed. Moreover Madrid was in the very center of the country, four hundred miles from the nearest port. So if they went by coach and Don Diego decided to pursue them they would have little hope of reaching the coast without being overtaken. *On his* journey to Madrid Richard had had ample opportunity to revise his ideas, and decided that he must persuade Tansanta to come with him on horseback; but he had overlooked the fact that a boy of Quetzal's age would never be able to stay the pace required to keep a lead on such a long journey.

He was still wrestling unsuccessfully with this problem when he decided that the time had come at which he might make his call; and *having* already located the long treelined avenue where he had been told that the Sidonia y Ulloa mansion lay, he turned down it. When he came to two tall pillars with stone eagles mounted on them, which had been described to him, he found that the iron gates which they supported were on the latch. There was no lodge; bushes *and* cactus fringed the drive, and obliquely through them he could see lights, showing that the house lay some distance away. Slipping inside he walked cautiously along the drive until, on the left, about a hundred yards from the entrance, the bushes gave way to a group of palms, in the centre of which stood the pavilion.

It was a small, single storied Moorish building with a miniature, tiled court and fountain to one side of it, and in the faint moonlight it looked just the sort of romantic setting to appeal to the impressionable Melissa. Stepping up to the low door Richard knocked, and it was opened almost instantly by his old friend 'Porn, Colonel Thursby's valet, who said he had been warned to expect him. After they had greeted one another warmly Tom showed him *into a pleasant room* with windows of arabesque latticework that looked out on the fountain court. There was too European furniture in it, only chests, stools, vases and brasses of Eastern design; and Melissa, now clad in a becoming negligee, was reclining gracefully against a pile of cushions on a low divan.

`Richard, how truly marvelous this is!' she exclaimed, as he hurried smiling towards her. Then, as he made to kiss her hand she flung a bare arm round his neck and, pulling his head down, kissed him on both cheeks.

Ring him after a moment, she hurried on: "Tis now over a year since we met, and I declare you are grown more monstrous handsome than ever. For two pins I would throw away my Spanish Count for you, and seduce you anew, even if in the meantime you have gotten yourself a wife. But you must tell me all everything.'

Sitting down beside her, he shook his head. `Nay I am not married yet. Whether it will be even possible for me ever to be so to the lady of my choice seems doubtful. But we are fully committed to one another, and 'tis about the matter that I have come here tonight to see you.'

Melissa pulled a rueful face. 'Fie, sir! And shame upon you! When Papa told me of your projected visit he winked an eye *and* said he knew us far too well to think that in any attempt to play gooseberry he could outsit you. Do you tell me now that the poor man has sought his bed thus early for no good reason?'

Knowing she was not speaking seriously, Richard grinned at her. `Could I but die tomorrow I would glory in my last act having been to make love to you ; for you have grown to a beauty that positively takes the breath away. But since I cannot, and have now developed a conscience in such matters, I beg you spare me the terrible temptation that your words suggest.'

`So you have developed a conscience?' She gave him a mocking smile. `Poor fellow! But you'll recover from it, I have no doubt. To be honest, though, I understand that better than I would have done a year ago ; for I, too, have one now. Or shall we say that for a time it pleases me to be chaste? In Vienna, in Budapest, on the Rhine! Ah me! Even my zest for that type of entertainment became a trifle jaded ; so for this winter at least I decided to become a prude. I am discovering a new pleasure in turning over in my bed in the morning and not having to argue with myself whom I will or will not allow to tumble me in it during the coming night. But perhaps that is a sign that I am growing old.'

Richard threw his head back and laughed aloud again. 'Old! Why, you are not yet twenty-four, and with a face and figure unrivalled since Helen of Troy. What you really mean, my sweet, is that you are growing up. But seriously; it must be this new phase upon which you have entered that accounts for your steadfastly refusing your favors to Don Diego.'

She frowned. "Tis true enough. But how comes it, sir, that you should be so well versed in my most intimate affairs?'

`Ah ! I have my spies. Yet I am come here to beg you tell me if you have any interest in this Spanish Grandee, other than to amuse yourself by leading him on a string?'

Melissa's face took on a thoughtful look, then she sighed

`From you, my dearest Richard, I would never seek to conceal the truth. I am mightily smitten with him. He is a very serious person, and though there must be many such, no other of the type has ever held my interest long enough for me to get to know him well. But I will admit that 'tis unlikely I would ever have come to do so had I not first been attracted by his physical attributes. I could gaze upon that profile of his for hours. 'Tis a more lovely, perfect thing than any cameo ever carved by an ancient master.'

`Do you mean,' Richard asked a shade uneasily, `that if he were free to offer you his hand you would accept it?'

`I might. I have a great respect for him; and that at least would be a pleasant change from the contempt with which I was forced to regard poor Humphrey. The castle to which Papa and I accompanied him for a few days for the birth of the Condesa's child, and the celebrations in honour of its arrival, is quite impossible. 'Tis cold as an icebox and draughty as a barn ; but 'twould be amusing to make it habitable as a new background for myself. I I doubt, though, if we should visit it more than once every few years, as I would never give up Shambles ; and whoever I married would first have to agree to allowing me to live where I would as the spirit moved me.'

Richard quickly looked away from her, as he said: `Do you sometimes share these daydreams with the Count?'

`Sometimes,' she murmured; then she laughed. ` 'Tis a most efficient panacea to divert him from becoming troublesome whenever he is more pressing than usual that I should let him lie with me.'

`Have you no thought at all for his unfortunate wife?'

Melissa's big eyes opened to their maximum extent. `His wife! And why, pray, should I have? My faults are many, but at least you should know that I would never be guilty of breaking up a romantic marriage. This was as frigid an example as ever you will meet of an alliance between two great houses. The pulses of neither of them have quickened by a beat since the day they first set eyes on one another.'

`I am aware of that. Yet your encouragement of Don Diego may have terrible results for her.'

`Nonsense, my dear! Do you think that she still has idealistic yearnings for him, and that I have come between her and their realization? If you do, pray disabuse yourself of the notion. Quiet she may be; and sanctimonious, with her long thin face. But, all the same, the sly little cat has consoled herself with at least one lover.'

Richard swiftly suppressed the impulse categorically to deny this imputation against Tansanta; but, controlling his voice as well as he could, he said: `What reason have you for assuming that?'

'My poor Don Diego does not know it,' Melissa burbled, with sudden merriment in her eyes, `but this winter he was still the laughingstock of Naples. It seems that in the autumn an English visitor there became enamored of the Condesa's charms, and at that time Diego had cast his eye upon a notorious gambler's moll, named Sara Goudar ; but she demanded an excessive price. The rich English milor's' paid up for Diego to enjoy the harlot, so that he might have a clear field to enjoy Diego's wife.'

Richard's eyes met Melissa's with no less wicked mirth, as he murmured: `So the pretty Sara told the story to her gossips afterwards, eh! Well, I can show you the reverse of that medal. I was in Naples last November. The story is true enough in essence, though I won Madame Goudar to the project without paying her anything for her trouble; but I was the Englishman concerned.'

All the laughter left Melissa's face. `Richard!' she exclaimed. `You do not mean . . . you *cannot* mean that you are in love with the Condesa! 'Tis impossible to believe that morose, black browed sack of bones to be the Spanish beauty of whom you wrote to me last summer. I pray you assure me swiftly that it is not of her that you have come to speak to me tonight.'

`It is of her ; and I consider your description of her most ungenerous,' Richard said stiffly. `If we are to criticize one another's taste I will frankly express my amazement that you should have set your heart upon a woodenheaded barber's block. Aye, *and* far worse, a potential murderer.'

`Richard! What are you saying? I was indeed at fault in disparaging your lady's looks; but you must be out of your senses to make such an accusation against an honorable gentleman.'

Fishing the letter from Tansanta, that had reached him in London, out of his inner pocket, Richard handed it to Melissa. `I pray you read that. 'Tis the prime reason for my coming to Spain.'

Melissa read the letter through carefully, *then* she said: `From this I gather that you asked her to run away with you when you where in Naples, and she refused to do so because she was carrying Diego's child. That does her credit; but 'tis my opinion that she repented of it afterwards and . . .'

`Go on,' he prompted.

`You will not take offence at what I am about to say?'

`Nay. You know well that no honest opinion of yours could ever offend me seriously.'

`Then 'tis my belief that, having repented her decision, she feared that after four months your ardor might have cooled ; so invented this preposterous story of the poison, as a certain means of bringing you back to her side through its appeal to your chivalry.'

He nodded. `You may be right; or it may be that young Quetzal misunderstood something said to him by his friend the witch. It may even be that the boy is lying, for I know that he greatly dislikes Don Diego; but I doubt that from all I know of him. I admit that discovering you to be the Englishwoman referred to instantly shook my own belief. But tell me this. Have you at any time given Don Diego reason to suppose that you would marry him if he were free?

`Never. Though 'tis possible that he may have put a wrong construction on remarks that I have made as to thoughts about my own future. You know of old how ambitious I have always been; and how I vowed as a girl that I'd be a Duchess before my hair turned grey. 'Tis now two years since Humphrey's death, and I have recently felt that I would like to marry again. If I do it shall be nothing less than an Earl this time, and one with prospects sufficient for me to have good hopes of raising him to higher rank through my powerful political connections. Diego naturally takes it ill that, being a widow, I will not grant him his desires. So I have fobbed him off by telling him of my ambitions, and vowing that I will lie with no man again until I once more enter a marriage bed. That would give a possible -basis for this story; but, even so, I cannot bring myself to believe it.'

`I now doubt it, too. Yet for Tansanta's sake I must act as though I thought her right, and take steps to prevent any possibility of so ghastly an outcome to her fears.'

`You feel, then, definitely committed to elope with her?'

`In view of all that lies between tis, I am resolved upon it.'

`Oh, Richard! I know well the mad acts that love at times impels us to. But is there no other way

for you in this" Think. dearest! In these Catholic countries there is no divorce ; and 1 greatly doubt her ever getting an annulment of her marriage. She might have had she eloped with you in Naples and later concealed the birth of her child. But since she had had her infant here it can nil longer be pleaded that the marriage was never consummated. Think of your future. A man of your parts might rise to any height ; but what future can there be for you if you are tied for life to a woman who is not your wife?'

`I know it, and am resigned to that. We shall have to live quietly -under an assumed name perhaps. But we love one *another, so we* shall be happy.'

Melissa sighed. `I wish that I could *think* it. But passion is not enough ; not even if the bond of intellect goes with it. She has a kind of bookish cleverness, but not a spark of humor. And, Richard dear, I know you so well. After a twelvemonth you would be desperate miserable *with any woman* who could *not laugh* with you over the silly, stupid sort of things that cause so much merriment to happy baggages like myself.'

The thought of Amanda Godfrey suddenly came into his mind. She, too, was a `happy baggage' who would never lack things in life at which to laugh.

Then he realized that the thought of her had cone to him owing to Melissa's use of the phrase `a bookish cleverness'. Amanda had used it in describing to him the mentality of the cousin whom she had no cause to love. After a second, he replied

`Making every allowance for my predilection where Tansanta is concerned, I think you unjust in your estimate of her. The fact that she is exceptionally well educated for a woman is no demerit. That she is serious-minded by nature, I grant you; but she has great integrity and a most sweet and charming disposition.'

'Mayhap you are right.' The splendid rings on Melissa's hands glittered as she fluttered them in a little, helpless gesture. `I hardly know her, so am not properly qualified to judge.'

Richard looked puzzled. `But did I not understand that you accompanied the Sidonia y Ulloas from Naples? If so you must have been in their intimate company during a journey occupying the best part of a month.'

'Nay; you are wrong in that. Papa and I met them in Naples and Don Diego began to pay his court to me at once. Naturally I met his Condesa in society, but saw no more of her than I would have of any other wife in similar circumstances. When Diego asked us to visit them in Spain she joined her formal invitation to his pressing one; but we journeyed by different routes. Papa wished to visit Gibraltar, so we arrived here from the South, whereas they came the shorter way via Valencia, and reached Madrid a fortnight before us. On our arrival the Condesa had already left for the country and Don Diego installed us in this charming pavilion, so we did not see her again until we accompanied him to his castle for the birth and celebrations. But tell me, Richard, about the origin of your affaire with her.'

'It was just a year ago at Fontainebleau . . .' he began; and when lie had told the tale their talk led from one thing to another ranging over their experiences in the past year, so it was three o'clock in the morning before they parted.

When they did so Richard was convinced that although Melissa had no thought at all of devoting her future to Don Diego her feeling for him was deeper than most that she experienced; since, much as she wanted to get back to Shambles, she had already lingered in Spain on his account longer than she had at first intended, and was still putting off the date of her return from reluctance to break with him. And it was very unlike the strong-minded Melissa to allow her plans to be upset by her love affairs.

Melissa was equally convinced that Richard was caught up in *a grande passion* for Tansanta, and that nothing would now deter him from going through with their elopement. Much as she deplored it as ruinous to his future prospects, she had, out of loyalty, agreed to do everything she could to help him, and she was admirably situated to do so. Richard's first fence was the difficulty of securing a meeting with Tansanta alone, so that they could concert a plan, and Melissa had agreed to bring her to the pavilion at the siesta hour the following day, which would enable the two lovers to spend the whole afternoon together.

In consequence, in the broiling midday sunshine Richard once more arrived at the little Moorish building and, to his delight, he found Tansanta already there, alone in the tiled lounge.

They embraced with all their old fervor, and it was several minutes before they were in any state to talk coherently. When, at length, they had regained their breath a little and settled themselves on the divan that G Melissa had graced the previous night, Tansanta said

`Let me at once confess myself wrong about Lady Etheredge. I feel convinced now that she has all along been completely innocent of any evil I design; and this morning she could not have been sweeter to me. She frankly confesses a great fondness for Diego, and says that in view of my love for you she does not see why she should give him up until she has a mind to return to England. But she will aid us all she can, and assures me that for the whole of this afternoon she will guarantee our remaining undisturbed here.'

`f knew we could count upon her,' Richard smiled, `and I am more glad than I can say that you now recognize her for the dear, sweet creature that she is.'

Tansanta nodded. `I have had little chance to do so before, as this morning was the first time we have ever been alone together for more than a few moments. Yet though she be innocent and despite all she urges to the contrary. I am still convinced that nay husband plans to do away with me on her account.'

`Have you, sweet, any fresh evidence of that?'

`None, other than the looks of deadly hatred that he casts at me when he thinks himself unobserved. But Quetzal was so very definite. He is outside now, keeping a watch lest Diego should take it into his head to pay a call upon Lady Etheredge, although that is most unlikely at this hour. I will have the boy in, and you can question him yourself if you wish.'

`If you are yourself convinced upon the matter, that is enough. I will take you away immediately I have completed my arrangements. What, though, of the interim? I had been counting, if pushed to it by dire necessity, on hiding you in Madrid till we could start; but Aranjuez is too small a place to offer any concealment, and the moment you leave your husband a hue and cry will break out. Can you yet guard yourself for a few days?'

'I trust so. I have put myself on a most careful diet, and I doubt if. Diego's somber thoughts will actually key him up to an attempt until he is driven desperate by Lady Etheredge announcing her intention to return home.!

'Even so, I shall be anxious for you every moment until we can get away. But once we are in England I swear I will do my utmost to make you happy.'

`Life will be far from easy for us,' she murmured. `Diego is a good Catholic and has much influence with the Church; so I am in hopes that he will succeed in putting me from him after a time. But now that I have borne him a child the easiest means of securing an annulment are barred to him.'

`Let us not think of that. The essential thing is to place you beyond reach of danger as swiftly as possible. Tell me; do you regard it as essential to take Quetzal and Maria with us?'

`Naturally I would wish to do so. But in that I am in your hands, my love. 'Tis for you to decide if I may.'

`I should be most loath to deprive you of them. 'Tis bad enough that you should be forced to abandon your infant.'

She shook her head. `I have not had it long enough to acquire a mother's fondness for the poor little thing; and the fact that it is Diego's instead of yours has put a check upon the warmth of the feeling which I would normally have for it. My mother and father were at the castle for its birth. She, I know, will give it the tenderest care, unless Diego decides that one of his sisters shall bring it up, and both of them are kindly women.'

'That, at least, is a comfort,' Richard agreed. `The difficulty about our taking Maria and the boy lies in the long journey we must make over bad roads before we can reach a port; and I am much perturbed by it. Your disappearance and mine cannot possibly be concealed for more than a few hours, and in such a small place as Aranjuez everyone will swiftly learn of our going. Whether Don Diego has any genuine desire to reclaim you or nay, 'tis certain that, regarding his honour as touched, he will feel compelled to set off in pursuit ; so unless we leave on fast horses and without encumbrances of any kind I greatly fear we shall be overtaken.'

`My clever love, you are right in that; and, knowing in my heart that you would not fail to come for me, 'tis a matter that I have been pondering over ever since I wrote my letter to you.'

`Have you then devised some plan?' Richard asked with quick interest.

`Yes. 'Tis to get my husband sent away on a mission, so that once he has left Aranjuez we will have a clear field.'

`The idea is an excellent one, but are you in any position to carry it out? I gather you have been here only four days, so can know hardly anyone at Court.!

'I was here for a fortnight before going to the castle to have my child, and during that time made at least one powerful friend. I took special pains to cultivate the Queen's favourite, Manuel Godoy.'

`I was informed that he played no part in State affairs, and that all such matters still lay in the hands of Count Florida Blanca-.'

That is true in the main, but may not continue to be so for long. Tansanta leaned towards him intently. `This is the present situation. Florida Blanca ousted my father from office sixteen years ago and remained supreme in the Councils of Carlos III until the late King's death: but since the opening of the new reign his position has been by no means so secure. My father, both during his long Ambassadorship in Paris and since his retirement, has always remained the leader of a powerful Opposition. He and Godoy have now formed a secret alliance to oust Florida Blanca.'

- Her mouth twitched in a subtle smile, as she went on: `The mission I have in mind is one to France. Their Majesties have for some time been contemplating sending a special envoy there to consult with Louis XVI. As members of his family they are naturally much concerned by the weakening of his power, and are anxious to do anything they can to infuse new strength into the French monarchy. Florida Blanca maintains that our Ambassador, Count Fernanunez, is already doing all that can be done. The Queen, on the other hand, favors sending one of our great nobles to reinforce him. My father was suggested, but he is set upon remaining here, so that should Florida Blanca make a false step he will be at hand to take advantage of it. But any father and Godoy are anxious that whoever is sent to Paris should be pledged to their interests ; and Diego possesses all the necessary qualifications. I suggested him to my father, and having obtained his consent put the idea to Manuel Godoy three evenings ago. He thought it admirable, and is at present working on the Queen with that in view.'

Richard looked at her a shade apprehensively. 'But if they settle upon Don Diego for this task, would not you, as his wife, have to go with him?'

`Normally I should be expected to do so; but not in my present circumstances. My recent delivery, and the care so young a child still requires, will serve as an admirable excuse for me to remain behind, for a few weeks at least. And I should give out that I intended to follow him later'

'What view does Don Diego take of this proposal?'

'As yet he is unaware of it. I asked Godoy to make no mention of it to him. I said that should the matter be settled favorably I would like to tell him of it myself, as it is a considerable honour and would prove a pleasant surprise. The truth is I feared that, did he become aware of what was afoot before the Queen's choice was fixed, he *would* seek to oppose the plan *on account of its* separating him from Lady Etheredge.'

'Think you, should he be nominated, that he will go without protest?'

'If 'tis the King's order he will not dream of questioning it. *No Hidalgo* of Spain would even contemplate refusing a mission from his Sovereign.' Tansanta was smiling a little grimly as she spoke, but after a moment she added with less confidence: 'We can count on nothing yet, though. Everything still hangs upon Godoy persuading the Queen of Diego's suitability for the mission.!

'I would that I could forward this excellent project in some way,' Richard said, with a thoughtful smile. 'Tonight, you, I and Don Diego are to have audience of Their Majesties while I recount to them something of my experiences in France. It is just possible that the question of sending a special envoy to Paris may crop up then.'

Tansanta's dark eyes sparkled. `You are right. A word in season is just what is required to decide the Queen, and this may prove the very opportunity to speak it. Could you insert into your discourse some mention of the high regard in which King Louis and Madame Marie Antoinette still hold the d'Aranda, and how they still speak with affection of both him and myself, I pray you, as you love me, do not neglect the chance.!

'On the contrary, I shall seize upon it,' Richard assured her quickly. `And I am filled with admiration for the way in which you, my own, have thought this out and paved the way so skilfully. Should your clever plan succeed, we'll be spared all the nerve-racking anxiety of a pursued elopement. About mid-May you could announce that you felt your child strong enough to permit of your following your husband, and set *out with Maria.* Quetzal and a whole coach-load of luggage. I would leave a few days in advance of you, and in a different direction, so that none of Don Diego's relatives could form the least suspicion that there was any connection between our departures. Then we would meet at a pre-arranged rendezvous, make our way to Lisbon and be safe aboard a ship before our elopement was even guessed at.. Oh, what a blessed relief it will be if only things are made so easy for us 1'

Simultaneously, they sighed in happy anticipation of such a fortunate solution to their difficulties and slid once more into one another's arms.

Nearly three hours later they were still embraced, when there came a discreet knock on the door. They had no idea that the time had passed so swiftly, but it was Melissa who had come to warn them that they ought not to linger for much longer.

When she joined them a few minutes later, Tansanta thanked her with special warmth for having arranged the rendezvous, and it was only then that Richard learned how fraught with difficulties their intrigue would have been without her. For it transpired that although Tansanta was married, as she was under thirty Spanish etiquette still required that she should have a duenna, and she was never allowed to go outside the grounds of her house without being accompanied by this dragon.

Before Tansanta left them she told Richard that she had suggested to her husband that he should dine with them that evening, as the three of them could then go on afterwards to the Palace together ; so he would find a note inviting him, at the Embassy villa. Then, when she had gone Richard and Melissa settled down for another talk and a few minutes later Colonel Thursby joined them.

Melissa had no secrets from her fond, indulgent father, and knew that Richard had none either as far as his love affairs were concerned so she had told the Colonel that morning of the projected elopement. He had been greatly distressed on hearing of it, and, standing as he did almost as a second father to Richard, he now did his utmost to dissuade him from making an alliance that must prove so disadvantageous to his future. But Richard's three hours with Tansanta had revived much of his old feeling for her, and in the three weeks since hr had received her letter he had come to accept it as a fact beyond all argument that, cost what it might in worldly prospects, his life was now irrevocably linked with hers.

At live o'clock, now dressed for the Court, Richard presented himself at the Sidonia y Ulloa mansion, where he found that the party consisted only of his host and hostess, G Melissa, Colonel Thursby and Tansanta's duenna. Don Diego received him with extreme politeness and he took special care not to arouse the Count's jealousy by showing too great a familiarity with Melissa; moreover, knowing that Spanish gentlemen did not even allow their wives to tread a minuet in public with another man, unless they had first received permission to do so, he treated Tansanta with the utmost formality, speaking to her only when she addressed a question to him.

Even Melissa showed an unusual restraint in this frigid atmosphere, and the dinner would have proved an exceptionally dull one had it not been for Colonel Thursby. Although he was well aware of the tempestuous undercurrents that lay beneath the restraint of four out of five of his companions, he showed no sign of it. With the ease and polish of a highly cultured man who had spent half a lifetime moving in the best society of the European capitals he opened up a dozen subjects, drawing first one and then another of them into the conversation.

As they rose from the table at the end of the meal, Melissa asked Don Diego how a portrait that he was having painted of himself was progressing. He replied that the Court painter, Goya, seemed quite a talented fellow and bade fair to produce a reasonable likeness ; but as to that he would value her opinion. He did not include anyone else in his invitation to see the picture, and as Melissa took his arm Tansanta tactfully showed that she had no intention of following them, by drawing Richard's attention to a fine Velasquez over the mantelpiece in the dining room.

Out of the corner of his eye Richard caught sight of the old duenna's face, and was amused to see her give a shocked glance first at Melissa's back, then in Tansanta's direction. Obviously she was highly scandalized both by the brazen behavior of the one in going off alone with her host and at the other's breach of convention in failing to give her guest the protection of her company. As clearly as if the old woman's skull had been made of glass he could see the thought agitating it, that the moment Don Diego had Melissa outside the door he would commit an assault upon her. Knowing his Melissa so well he was quite certain that Don Diego would get no more than a few kisses, unless she chose to let him ;but he thanked his stars that he was not forced to live in a country such as Spain, where a man and woman could not walk down a corridor alone without being suspected of the grossest immorality.

After only about ten minutes the truant pair joined the rest of the party in the salon, and Richard was intrigued to see that, while Melissa appeared completely at her ease, Don Diego could not conceal traces of the most violent emotion. His handsome face had gone quite gray, causing his knife-like nose to stand out grotesquely from it, and his big dark eyes were so limpid that it looked as if tears were likely to roll down his pale checks at any moment. His distress was such that he could not speak, and only nodded, when Colonel Thursby reminded him that it was time for those of them who were going to the Palace to start; but Melissa gave him a chance to pull himself together by launching out on a lively appreciation of Senor Goya's painting.

As soon as Don Diego had somewhat recovered, he, Tansanta and Richard said good night to the others and went downstairs to a waiting coach. On the short drive to the Palace Don Diego sat hunched in gloomy silence, and Tansanta was greatly puzzled as to what had come over her husband; but Richard was delighted to see him so suddenly and completely overwhelmed. He felt confident that it was due to a measure that he had concerted with Melissa that afternoon, after Tansanta had left them, and he could now only pray that the other half of the plot he had contrived would prove equally successful.

On arriving at the Palace they went first to Manuel Godoy's apartments. The young courtier received them with the usual ceremonious compliments, and then led them through several lofty, vaulted corridors to the presence chamber. It was a square room, painted white and gold and hung with tapestries depicting the life of John the Baptist; but it was very sparsely furnished. There were no settees, chests or side tables round its walls; only two *high,* stiff-backed elbow chairs with footrests in front of them stood in the center, and grouped in a semicircle before them half a dozen low, upholstered stools. King Carlos and Queen Maria Luisa occupied the chairs, behind them respectively stood two gentlemen and two ladies, and two of the royal children were seated on the stools nearest to their parents.

After the ritual of reception had been observed the Sidonia y Ulloas, being of sufficient rank to enjoy the honour of the *tabouret,* as the stools were called, sat down on two of them; but Richard was not invited to sit, and during the entire audience he remained standing, a distinction he shared with Manuel Godoy, who, father and grandfather of Kings and Queens as he was later to become, was as yet also considered as too lowly a person to be permitted to ease his feet in the presence of the Sovereigns.

But Richard did not regard this marked discrimination in accordance with birth as strange. He had been privileged to sit on several informal occasions when talking to crowned heads; but the Spanish Court was notoriously rigorous in the maintenance of strict etiquette, and even in England such distinctions were still carefully observed. He remembered once when at Holwood House he had heard Mr. Pitt remark to the company *that* at official interviews King George III always received him standing, because *the* Monarch was too polite to sit down while keeping his Prime Minister on his feet, yet felt that he could not possibly allow a Minister who was a Commoner to be seated; and that on one occasion, although at the time the King was seriously ill, the two of them had discussed business for over four hours while remaining the whole time standing one on either side of a table.

The fat faced, hook nosed King Carlos opened the conversation in French as Richard knew only a few words of Spanish by enquiring after the health of his cousins Their Majesties of France. Richard replied that when he had last seen them, two months previously, they were both much worried but otherwise in as good health as could be expected. He added that now King *Louis was virtually* a prisoner in the *Tuileries* he greatly missed his hurting. but got such exercise as he could by wielding a hammer at his locksmith's anvil, and also consoled himself to some extent by spending a good part of his time at his other hobby of making clocks. Queen Maria Luisa then took charge of the proceedings and during the next hour and a half plied Richard with scores of questions.

Among other things she asked him if he had met the Spanish Ambassador; so, while not unduly depreciating the qualities of the Conde Fernanunez, he had an excellent opportunity for saying how highly the Conde d'Aranda and his family were still esteemed at the Court of France. But most of her questions concerned the new powers assumed by the National Assembly and the scenes of violence that had taken place.

The Spanish Sovereigns were incredibly shocked by his description of the attack on Versailles and the events that had followed it; as, although they had had numerous written accounts of these matters from various sources, they had never before heard them described by an eyewitness, and had little idea of the indignities to which the Royal Family of France had been subjected.

When the Queen could think of no more questions to ask she turned her beady little eyes on the King and said something to him in Spanish.

Up to then Don Diego, evidently occupied with his own somber thoughts, had paid only the attention demanded by politeness to what was going on; but at the Queen's words Richard saw him give a violent start.

After a moment the dull-witted King nodded his head and, still speaking in French, replied: 'Yes, we must certainly send a special envoy, if only to show our sympathy. He could, at the same time, press them on that other matter.'

Suddenly Don Diego jumped to his feet, threw himself on one knee before his Sovereigns, and began to gabble away in Spanish at nineteen to the dozen.

Richard glanced at Tansanta; her face was flushed and her eyes were shining with excitement. He looked at Godoy ; the favorite's well modeled mouth was curved in a pleased smile. He knew then that the plot he had hatched with Melissa that afternoon was working.

In Don Diego's pleading he caught the word 'Neapoli', then the name 'd'Aranda' several times repeated, so he was able to guess the gist of what the Count was saying to be: 'As I have lived in Naples since the beginning of Your Majesty's reign, I have so far had little opportunity to be of service to you. I beg you now to allow me to show my devotion as your envoy to Paris, and as the son-in-law of the Conde d'Aranda utilize the prestige his name still carries there.'

The Queen spoke to the King; the heavy Monarch nodded; Don Diego jumped up with a delighted cry and kissed the hands of first one then the other; Tansanta joined her thanks to those of her husband by throwing herself at the feet of the Queen, and received a friendly pat on the head. The two I *Infantes, Godoy and* the ladies- and gentlemen-inwaiting all exclaimed with pleasure and offered Don Diego their congratulations.

The little scene was a revelation to Richard that the Spanish did, on occasion, show spontaneous emotion; but it was soon over, for, as though ashamed of having done so, they swiftly resumed their formal dignity, and in that atmosphere the audience was terminated. Godoy alone continued to give free rein to his exuberance, and when he had escorted the visitors from the presence chamber he at once insisted that before going home they should take a glass of wine with him to the success *of the mission.*

In his apartment a fine old Malaga was produced, and when the toast had been drunk the handsome favourite courteously asked Richard if he would permit him to speak in Spanish with Don Diego for a few moments. Richard only too willingly consented, as it gave him an opportunity to offer his arm to Tansanta, and lead her to the other side of the room on the pretext of admiring a fine collection of bullfighting swords that hung on the wall there.

As they stood looking at the beautifully chased blades of blue Toledo steel, she whispered with a little catch in her voice: `What marvelous fortune, my love! For him to request this mission himself was more than I could possibly have hoped for. But why he should wish to go to Paris I cannot think.'

`I can,' Richard whispered back. `We owe this to Lady Etheredge. She intended to stay on here for some time, and when at length she could bring herself to break with him, to hurry back to England. But out of fondness for me she agreed instead to tell him that she means to spend some time in Paris on her way home, and had decided to set out next week. It was her telling him so after dinner that caused his desperate agitation, and what followed was the result of it.'

Tansanta squeezed his arm. 'Oh I Riche, what a brilliant stroke of yours ; and how grateful I am to her.'

`But in this we have courted a great risk,' he warned her gravely. `With time before him Don Diego may well have been putting off so terrible a decision as to make a definite attempt upon your life. Now his coming departure will force him to face the issue. Either he must abandon his awful thought and go to Paris still tied to you, or seek to gain his freedom by using the poison before he sets out. You could still slip away tonight and I could meet you to escort you to some place of hiding ; but otherwise I beg you not to relax your watchfulness for a single moment.'

She turned a trifle pale, but her low voice was firm. `You are right. Only now has my danger become acute. Yet to leave home prematurely would be to throw away all that we have gained. On the plea of health I shall drink naught but water and place myself on an even stricter diet.'

A few minutes later they were in the coach on their way to the Embassy villa, with the intention of dropping Richard there. It had not proceeded fifty yards before Don Diego said to his wife

'Señor Godoy has warned me that this mission has been under consideration for some time; so Her Majesty now wishes it to leave with a minimum of delay. We are to set out next week, so it would be well for you to start tomorrow on your preparations for our departure.'

Richard was filled with admiration for the steadiness of Tansanta''s voice, as she replied: `If that is your wish it is for me to obey you. But have you as yet given full thought to our child? He is not yet a month old and we could not possibly expose him at so tender an age to the hazards of the journey. For another month at least he should have my personal care. Would it not be best if I remain with him till mid-May, then follow you to Paris?'

For a moment Don Diego remained silent. Richard and Tansanta hardly dared to breathe. For them everything now hung on this decision, and they both knew that should it prove unfavourable to them she could not possibly disobey her husband.

After what seemed an eternity Don Diego said: `I judge you right,

Madame. You had best remain here with our son for another month or so.'

When they dropped Richard at the villa he waited there for half an hour to give ample time for the coast to be clear, then walked round to see Melissa and the Colonel in their Moorish pavilion.

As soon as he told them how perfectly the plot had worked they both expressed their pleasure for him, but Melissa was very far from being in her usual good humour.'

`Oh, damn you, Richard!' she exclaimed, after a moment. `Paris is the very last place to which I would wish to go, now 'tis in the hands of those vile revolutionaries. Yet on your account I am committed to it.'

'Knowing your reluctance to do so, I am all the more grateful,' he said gently. 'But you have said several times that you are not yet disposed to break with Don Diego, and now you can both travel with him on the greater part of your journey home and remain in Paris with him as long as you wish.'

'But now that spring is here, 'tis at Shambles I wish to be,' she murmured petulantly.

He smiled. 'It has ever been your nature to wish to have your cake and eat it too ; but you cannot both be soon at "Shambles" and keep Don Diego. You told me last night that rather than give him up you meant to stay on here for some time.'

'I did indeed. The dratted man holds some special fascination for me. Yet I think by the end of the month I might have worked myself free of it. And you know well my habit of letting things slide until some incident causes me to take a sudden decision. As long as Papa and I remained here we could at any time by way of Lisbon have got home in a month; whereas now it will take us much more than that to get to Paris ; so I'll be lucky if I see Shambles before June is gone.'

'Come, my dear,' Colonel Thursby said quietly. "Tis not like you to grudge some upsetting of plans for your own pleasure in the urgent service of so old a friend as Richard'

'Nay,' she replied, with a sudden smile. 'I fear I am being plaguey churlish, Richard dear. I beg you to forgive me.'

'There is naught to forgive.' He took her hand and kissed it. 'I am beyond expression grateful for all you have done and are about to do.'

They arranged that Melissa should again contrive for Tansanta -to come to the pavilion on the following day; then Richard took his leave.

The demands of his own affairs during the past thirty hours had by no means put out of his mind Mr. Pitt's business; so next day, in the cool. of the morning, he went to the Palace *and* waited upon the Caballero Heredia.

The Spaniard expressed courteous surprise at receiving a second visit from him after a lapse of only two days ; but Richard again stressed the urgency of the matter upon which he had been sent to Spain, and asked when he was to have his audience with the Count Florida Blanca.

'I fear, Monsieur, that you have failed to take into account the fact that many urgent matters must always claim the attention of a Prime Minister,' the Caballero replied blandly. 'And at present His Excellency happens to be particularly heavily engaged. I have no doubt that he will make time to receive you in the course of the next few days, or early next week at the latest. In the meantime perhaps you will permit me *to show you* something of our beautiful Spain. Have you yet visited Toledo?'

Richard had to admit that he had not; and, *although* he was most loath to leave Aranjuez even for a night, when the diplomat offered to take him there he felt that he could not possibly refuse the invitation. So it was arranged that the Caballero should call for him next morning in a carriage, then they would spend Wednesday night in Toledo and make the return drive on Thursday morning.

As Richard strolled back along the leafy avenues leading from the Palace, he decided that, although diplomatic politeness had forced him to accept this first invitation, it did not require him to suffer any further attempts on Heredia's part to gain time by taking him on such expeditions. Before leaving he had again pressed most strongly for an early audience with the Prime Minister, and if it was not granted by the end of the week he meant to begin making Heredia's life a misery by going to badger him every day.

King Carlos' words `He could, at the same time, press them on that other matter', when referring to the envoy he was sending to condole with the French Sovereigns on their misfortunes had not escaped Richard; and he felt certain the `other matter' was to secure a definite promise from the French that they would honour the Family Compact in the event of Spain going to war with Britain over Nootka Sound. Although there was no outward sign of it he knew that the arrival of a personal representative from Mr. Pitt must have set the Court of Spain in a fine flutter. And that, he guessed, was the reason why Don Diego was being hurried off to France with barely a week's notice instead of being allowed to set out at his leisure.

When Richard met Tansanta in the afternoon he had from her an exciting confirmation of his suppositions. At eleven o'clock that morning her husband had received an order to wait upon Count Florida Blanca in the evening to receive his instructions. The note had further stated that Don Diego was now to be ready to leave Aranjuez not later than Thursday morning, and to make arrangements for the bulk of his baggage to follow him, as he was to proceed to Paris with all possible speed.

Richard had no doubt at all that this un Spanish haste was the direct result of his call on Heredia some two hours before Don Diego had received the order; and was overjoyed by it. Actually.

like Melissa, he was still far from convinced that Tansanta's husband had ever had any intention of poisoning her; but the possibility that there might be real grounds for her suspicions was quite enough to cause him incessant anxiety. And now, the putting forward of Don Diego's departure reduced the time left him in which to make an attempt on her to less than two days.

For three happy hours they managed to put her danger out of their minds. When they parted it was with the terribly exciting thought that although, owing to Richard's trip to Toledo, they must somehow get through the awful strain of Wednesday without meeting, by Thursday afternoon Don Diego would be gone. The cover provided by Melissa would no longer be necessary. Richard would have only to slip through the gate for them to continue to meet in secret with little risk in the pavilion; and that when they next did so, in forty-eight hours' time, Tansanta would be safe and free.

Having installed Richard in the villa, Mr. Merry, on the plea that his Consular duties required his attention in the capital, had returned to Madrid the previous afternoon ; so that night Richard dined alone. After the meal he could not get his mind off the subject of poison, so spent. a very bad four hours until it was dark enough for him to go round to the Moorish pavilion without risk of running into Don Diego.

He found Melissa in greatly improved spirits. First thing that morning Don Diego had called, told her with delight of his mission to Paris and begged that she and her father would travel in his company. Then, a few hours later, he had informed them that he would be leaving early on Thursday, and asked that they would leave all arrangements about sleeping coaches, a travelling kitchen and provisions to him. Her reluctance to go to Paris at all had been considerably mollified by a start being possible much earlier than she had expected, and Don Diego's intention of travelling at a speed which should get them there in a month, as the two factors combined might yet enable her to be at Shambles by the end of May.

As they would now be leaving before Richard's return from Toledo it was his last chance to talk to them about his own plans. Colonel Thursby, with a kindness typical of him, said that when Richard and Tansanta reached London they were welcome to occupy his house in Bedford Square until they could find a place to live permanently, and Melissa said that Shambles would always beat their disposal. But suddenly, just as Richard was about to take his leave, she stood up, faced him squarely, and said:

`I still cannot bring myself to believe in the poison plot. I beg you, Richard, to give me your assurance that had you not been informed of it, and had some earlier opportunity occurred to revive your intimacy with the Condesa, you would still have formed this determination of eloping with her as soon as she had been delivered of her child?'

Richard had never told Melissa a lie in his life, and he could not bring himself to do so now.

. `Nay,' he said quietly. 'I fear I cannot give you that assurance. After I left Naples I counted the matter as a chapter in my life that was closed. But I am deeply attached to Tansanta and believe that we shall be happy. In any case, my honour is now involved 'in it, and nothing would induce me to draw back.'

Feeling there was no more that she could say, she let him go. But no sooner was he outside the door than she burst into tears at the thought of the trouble she believed him to be laying up for himself ; and her wise, adoring father could think of little to say to bring her comfort as she sobbed again and again

` "Tis a tragedy, a tragedy ! I would give ten years of my own life could I but think of some way to prevent it.'

Richard slept ill on account of his anxiety for Tansanta, and he had puzzled his wits in vain for some way of assuring himself that no ill had befallen her before he set off for Toledo; so, when the Caballero Heredia called for him at eight o'clock, he had to start on his trip still ignorant whether Don Diego had utilized his last night but one in Aranjuez to attempt her murder.

The day was fine and the drive pleasant, as the road lay for the whole thirty miles they had to cover along the banks of the Tagus, and the tortuous course of the river provided variety in an otherwise flattish landscape. Had Richard not been so worried for Tansanta he would have thought even the distant sight of the ancient capital of Spain well worth the long drive, as it was set on a rugged pinnacle of granite, the foot of which was washed on three sides by a great bend in the river, and its towers, battlements and spires rising tier after tier against the blue sky made it look like a fairy city.

After the siesta they visited the Cathedral and in its treasury saw the image of the Virgin, roped with millions of *doubloons'* worth of pearls and other gems, that is carried in procession through the streets on feast days; but Richard was more interested in the strange, distorted, greenish hued paintings by El Greco that hung in the chapels of many of the lesser churches. He was, too, fascinated by the unusual silence that pervaded so large a city, on account of the cobbled ways between its old Moorish buildings being mostly too steep and narrow to permit the passage of traffic. In the evening they went to the fortress palace of the Alcazar, where the Governor entertained them to a meal and provided them with accommodation for the night.

On the Thursday morning they set off early on the return journey and were back in Aranjuez just before midday. In normal circumstances Richard would have enjoyed the excursion enormously, and he did his best to show his appreciation to Heredia ; but he got rid of the Caballero at the earliest possible moment in order to hurry round to the Sidonia y Ulloa mansion.

When visiting the pavilion earlier in the week he had never seen anyone about the grounds during the siesta hour and, had he done so, he could have said that he was calling on his compatriot, Colonel Thursby. Now he no longer had that excuse he wondered a little anxiously if his luck would hold, and he would continue to escape observation. But that anxiety was a small matter compared with the acute one to reassure him that Tansanta had come unharmed through her husband's last two days in Aranjuez.

As he hurried down the avenue he saw Quetzal standing outside the gate. An awful doubt seized upon his mind. Had Tansanta stationed the boy there to warn him that there was someone in the grounds or was he, knowing that she expected her lover, waiting there to break some ghastly news?

A moment later Quetzal caught sight of him and began to run in his direction. During his visit to Naples, and while in Aranjuez, Richard had not seen the little Indian, so it was over ten months since they had met. He thought the youngster had grown considerably, and his education had evidently progressed; as, when he was still some twenty yards off, he broke out into heavily accented but quite understandable French

`Monsieur le Chevalier! I have a carriage waiting. We are to collect your things and set out at once for Madrid.'

`For Madrid!' echoed Richard. `In God's name, why?'

`Yes. They will sup and rest there before proceeding further. If we start at once we can catch them up by nightfall. My mistress said you could give as an excuse for joining them a belated thought that you would like to make the journey to Paris in the company of your English friends.'

`What the devil are you talking about?' Richard exclaimed. `I have no wish to go to Paris. I could not, even if I had, as important matters detain me here. Tell me at once!

'But you must! You must!' the boy broke in. `Did you not come to Spain to save my mistress?'

`Indeed I did!'

`Then how can you allow ought else to detain you?'

Quetzal's black eyes were now *flashing* angrily, and Richard, still at a loss to understand what lay behind his excited words, cried with puzzled impatience *'Mort Dieu!* Be plain with me. Is your mistress still alive and well?'

`Would I be here if she were not?'

`Thank God for that! Then take me to her.'

`Am I not begging to do so? The carriage waits.'

'What! Mean you that she had gone to Madrid?'

`Have I not said so, Monsieur?'

`You had not! But why? Why has she gone? Is it that she has accompanied them on the first stage of the journey, and means to see them off from the capital?'

`It was the Queen, Monsieur. Yesterday Her Majesty learned of my mistress's decision to remain here with her baby. She was angry. She said that the name Sidonia y Ulloa means nothing in Paris; but that of d'Aranda everything. That 'tis not Don Diego, but my mistress, who is the friend of Madame Marie Antoinette, and so can help to win her support for the cause of Spain Last night there came with all this an imperative order from the Queen. So my mistress is still with that fiend who would murder her, and now on her way to Paris.'

CHAPTER TWENTY-FOUR
THE OUTCOME OF THE MISSION

Richard stood aghast, staring in dismay at the young, brown faced Aztec Prince with the beautifully embroidered clothes and gaily feathered headdress. The plot that he and Tansanta had hatched for getting Don Diego sent to Paris had recoiled on their own heads. They had been too clever, and were now hoist with their own petard; or at least separated by it more effectually than they could have been by anything else short of death or prison.

`For what are you waiting, Monsieur?' The little Indian grasped his sleeve and pulled at it impatiently. `Every moment is precious!'

`I have told you,' Richard muttered, shaking off his hold. `I cannot go to Paris.'

`*Cannot go* to Paris?' Quetzal repeated in astonishment. 'Do you mean that you abandon my mistress?'

Richard bit his lip, then burst out: `God knows I have no wish to! But 'tis impossible for me to leave Aranjuez. I have business here that no other person can handle for me.'

The boy's eyes suddenly filled with hate. 'Business!' he cried. `How can you mention it in the same breath with my mistress? I had believed you loved her. Yet you are willing to leave her to be poisoned by that fiend rather than sacrifice some interest of your own.'

The midday sun was glaring down. Richard pulled out his handkerchief and mopped his perspiring face ; then he said firmly: `Listen, Quetzal. I swear to you that I am no less devoted to your mistress than yourself. But there is a thing called duty as well as one called love; and sometimes they conflict. Mine, for the moment, is to remain here. Yours is to catch the Condesa up as swiftly as you can, and do your utmost to protect her while on the road to Paris. Tell her, I beg, that my business here should not take long, and that the instant it is concluded I shall follow her. And that I love her more than anything in the world. Will you do that for me?'

Impressed by Richard's evident earnestness and emotion, the boy nodded. `So be it, then. I will give her your message.'

Without another word he turned and ran back to the gates outside which he had been standing. Richard, too, turned and, shaken to the depths by his recent encounter, walked slowly away. He had not covered fifty paces before the carriage that Quetzal had had waiting to take them to Madrid issued from the gates, its horses moving at a gallop, and *passed him,* covering him in a cloud of dust.

As he watched it disappear his thoughts were chaotic. Tansanta had no idea of the importance of the mission he had been given, so what would she think of him? How soon could he follow her? He could not force Count Florida Blanca to give him an audience immediately. It was unlikely that he would be able to get away from Aranjuez for at least anther week. And Don Diego intended to travel at high speed. They would be halfway to Paris, or further, before he could catch them up.

But of what was he thinking? Even when he had seen Count Florida Blanca he would not be free to go to Paris. His mission would still tie him. Mr. Pitt was anxiously awaiting the decision he had been sent to force. Whether it was for peace or war, he must carry it without an hour's delay back to London. In his shock and distress at finding Tansanta gone he had promised to follow her; but he could do so only by breaking his promise to his master.

He had also told Quetzal that he loved her better than anything in the world. Was that really true? If it was he would be with Quetzal in the carriage on his way to Madrid at this moment. The fact that her life was in danger should have counted more with him than even Mr. Pitt's business. But was it? If Don Diego had really intended to poison her surely he would have done so before leaving for Paris, so that he would be free to make his bid for Melissa's hand on the journey.

If only their plan had worked everything would have been so simple. They could have waited in Aranjuez until he had his answer from Florida Blanca, then gone straight to London. But now! What was to be done? What could be done? He could only hope and pray that his poor Tansanta would survive the journey to Paris. If. she did it would go a long way to show that her fears of being poisoned had no real foundation. As soon as he was through with his mission he could go to Paris, and to elope with her from there should not be difficult. What, though, if she never reached Paris? He could still go there, call Don Diego out and do hi; damnedest to kill him in a duel. But that would not bring Tansanta back. Would he ever get over her loss? Yes, he had counted her as dead before and got over it, so he would do so again. Yet the thought of her dying in agony was unbearable.

Fears for her safety, distress that she would think he had abandoned her quite callously, and black frustration obsessed his thoughts for the rest of the day and most of the night. But on the Friday morning he got a grip of himself again.

He began to see things from a different angle. Fate had played such an extraordinary part in dictating the makes and breaks of his romance with Tansanta, and now the blind goddess had intervened between them yet again. Perhaps, after all, Destiny did not intend their union. On the long journey to Paris Tansanta would not be able to guard herself so carefully as she had while at home, and there would be many opportunities for Don Diego to put poison in her food. Therefore, if she survived the journey it could be taken as fair proof that Melissa was right, and that Tansanta's husband had no intention of killing her.

Suddenly it occurred [o him that, if that proved the case, he would no longer be committed to elope with her. She had refused to leave Naples -with him when his passion was at its height; and, although it had since cooled, he had instantly responded to leer appeal to come to Spain. It was no fault of his that their elopement had fallen through. So, since only her danger had brought him to Spain, if it emerged that she had never really been in danger, why should he, the moment he was free, dash off to Paris and enter on fresh plans to tie her life with his?

He had forced himself to close his mind against all the arguments that Melissa and her father had used in their attempts to dissuade him from running away with Tansanta; but now he felt free to contemplate them in all seriousness and, as he had really known from the beginning, life with her unmarried to him in England would have been one long fight against difficulties and distresses. He had been willing to pay that price, but Fate had relented at the last moment and, it seemed now, still held for him a happier future.

. Nevertheless, illogical as he knew it to be, he still felt a sense of guilt towards Tansanta ; and his anxiety for her safety continued to harass him to such an extent that, as the only means of temporarily freeing his mind from it, he decided that he must endeavor to concentrate all his thoughts on *his mission. So at* an early hour he went to the Palace and called upon Heredia.

The Caballero expressed pleasure but mild surprise at seeing him again so soon, and said that since returning from Toledo he had had no opportunity to discuss Richard's matter with the Prime Minister; however, he hoped to be able to arrange something for him by Sunday.

When Sunday came Heredia was urbane and courteous as ever, but still could give no definite date for an audience. He suggested that, while Count Florida Blanca disposed of other most pressing affairs, Richard might spend a few nights in Madrid with profit, and offered to do the honours of the capital for him.

Richard politely declined the invitation, then added coldly: 'I am much surprised, Señor Caballero, at the little weight that His Excellency the Prime Minister appears to attach to the fact that His Britannic Majesty's Prime Minister had sent a personal envoy to him. It is the desire of my master to settle the matters that lie between our countries amicably; but I have now been here a week and your master has not yet even found time to hear what I have to say. Should His Excellency continue to find himself too occupied to receive me during the course of the next three days, I shall be compelled to assume that it is because he has no wish to do so. My duty then will plainly be to return to England at once, and report His Excellency's attitude.'

At this, the Caballero appeared much pained, and pretended that ha thought Richard's behavior most unreasonable. But he promised once more to do his best, and the following day the ultimatum produced the required result; Richard received a note stating that the Prime Minister would. see him on Thursday, April 22nd, at four o'clock in, the afternoon.

Heredia performed the ceremony of presentation, and Richard found himself bowing to an elderly man with good eyes but a lined, tired looking face. Count Florida Blanca received his visitor with much politeness, but standing, and he did not invite him to sit down, so Richard was reminded of the interviews between King George III and Mr. Pitt.

He produced his letter, expressed Mr. Pitt's surprise at having received no reply of *his* note of February 26th, and went on to say: `His Britannic Majesty's Government is anxious to remain on terms of the utmost amity with that of His Most Catholic Majesty; but Your Excellency must appreciate that the highhanded action of certain Spanish ships last June in Nootka Sound was most prejudicial to *the* maintenance of such happy relations; and the dilatoriness of His Most Catholic Majesty's Government in giving satisfaction in the matter has given my master good grounds for supposing that they have no intention of doing so.'

`Oh, come, Monsieur, come protested the Count. `That is to :.assume far too much.'

`What other interpretation can be put upon your Government's continued silence, sir?' Richard enquired.

`We have been seeking ways that we trust may lead to a suitable accommodation.'

Richard bowed. `Your Excellency, I am delighted to hear it. In that case my coming will I hope prove of assistance to- you, as I am empowered to inform you of the terms upon which His Britannic Majesty's Government . . .'

`Terms!' exclaimed the Spaniard haughtily. `I pray you, Monsieur, be pleased to withdraw such an offensive expression.'

`If Your Excellency prefers we will call it a basis of agreement. The first clause of any treaty between our two countries would be the acknowledgment by Spain that the whole North American Pacific coastline from parallel forty-five degrees north to Alaska, together with the hinterland as far east as the St. Lawrence river, form part of His Britannic Majesty's dominions.'

Count Florida Blanca stared at Richard in angry astonishment. `You cannot mean this, Monsieur? Such a proposal is preposterous!'

`So definitely do I mean it, Your Excellency,' Richard replied firmly, `that I am instructed to inform you that it is the only basis upon which His Britannic Majesty's Government will consider the negotiation of a peaceful settlement.'

`A peaceful settlement! What are you saying? Surely you do not infer that upon this matter England would proceed to extremities?'

Richard bowed again. `I should be failing in my duty if I left Your Excellency under the impression that this is a question of anything less than peace or war.'

At this calling of a spade a spade the Spanish Prime Minister's mental shudder was almost perceptible. He felt that the young man who had been sent to see him was the representative of a new and horrible age. The diplomats to whom he was accustomed were of the old-fashioned sort, who would have been perfectly happy to amuse themselves with the ladies of Madrid for a month or two before, with great reluctance, bringing themselves to use some term even vaguely implying the possibility of hostilities. After a moment, he said:

`This matter is one of the utmost gravity, and will require my most careful consideration.'

`As I see it, sir,' replied Richard promptly, `the issue is a perfectly simple one. Does or does not His Most Catholic Majesty's Government desire to negotiate on the basis that I have stated? But if Your Excellency is troubled with any doubts upon that score, I will present myself to receive your answer at this hour tomorrow.'

Count Florida Blanca found it difficult to conceal his anger. He had counted on being able to evade any definite pronouncement on the Nootka question until he had further information on the likelihood of French support. Only a week had elapsed since Don Diego had been dispatched to press the matter, so, apart from the unlikely chance that a favourable answer was already on the way, a considerable time must elapse before he could hope to hear anything definite ; and here was this young cub of an Englishman endeavoring to force him to a decision within a matter of hours. With a sudden display of haughtiness he attempted to overawe his visitor.

`Indeed, Monsieur! Either I cannot have heard aright, or your youth must excuse your ignorance of diplomatic usage. Responsible Ministers do not take such momentous decisions overnight.'

'I am, sir,' Richard said, in a quiet but telling voice, `just nine months younger than was my master when he first became a Minister of the Crown. While I have no pretensions to his gifts I can at least endeavor to emulate his dispatch when dealing with urgent matters of business. On his behalf I must request a prompt reply.'

Swiftly the Spaniard made amends for his impoliteness. `My reference to your age was not intended as any reflection on your abilities, Monsieur. But you cannot reasonably expect a reply to such a sweeping demand in less than a matter of weeks.'

Richard saw that he had got the tired old Prime Minister on the run, and decided to hit him hard again. `Your Excellency ; I had, myself, thought that a week would be enough in which to settle our business, so promised my master that I would not linger much beyond ten days. Yet, owing to your other occupations, I have already been compelled to kick my heels in Aranjuez for twelve days with nothing done. 'Tis no fault of mine that I must now press you for a prompt decision. The issue is a straightforward one. I must ask you to let me have your answer to it within forty-eight hours.'

Ten minutes later, as Richard walked away from the Palace, he felt that he had nor played his part too badly. However shocked, hurt, or offended the Spaniards might appear to be at his insistence on getting down to business, the truth was that they were only seeking to gain time; and the whole purpose of his mission was to bring them to book with a minimum of delay. Had he believed that it would serve any useful purpose he would have been far more tactful; but his instructions were definite so he could only hope that his firmness would have the result that he so anxiously desired.

Hearing nothing further, on the Saturday morning he went to see Heredia, in order to, confirm that Florida Blanca meant to receive him again that afternoon. It was as well he did so, as the Caballero pretended not to know anything about the arrangement, and said he feared that Count Florida Blanca had to attend a Royal Council which would keep him occupied for some hours after the siesta.

Richard announced calmly that it was all one to him at what hour His Excellency chose to summon him, but that he had ordered his horses for dawn next day; and that if he received no summons before that hour he would know what answer to carry back to England.

Again the ultimatum worked. Heredia, having excused himself for a few minutes, returned to say that the Prime Minister would look forward to a further talk if Richard would wait upon him at five o'clock the following afternoon; he could find time to give him half an hour before the Sunday Court.

As on the previous occasion, they remained standing for the duration of the interview; but this time the Spaniard greeted his visitor with apparent pleasure, as well as politeness. Richard, being still a child in such matters, thought that a good omen; and an indication that, after some face saving remarks, Florida Blanca meant to give in.

The Prime Minister appeared to come to the point swiftly, with the genial announcement: `In the matter of the Americas, Monsieur, I now feel confident that Spain can meet the wishes of Britain; but naturally His Most Catholic Majesty would expect some practical acknowledgment of this friendly gesture.'

`I am delighted to hear it, Your Excellency,' Richard smiled, thrilled with the belief that his mission had been successful, and that he would be going home with a territory eight times the size of the Canadian settlements in his pocket. `My master would, I am sure, be willing to give you full satisfaction on all outstanding questions regarding your commerce.!

'That goes without saying,' shrugged the Count, `for 'tis a mere bagatelle. I had in mind a suitable compensation for the sacrifice that His Most Catholic Majesty would be making. There is only one which could be considered in any way adequate, but it would remove the last possible cause for friction between our two countries. I refer, of course, to Gibraltar.'

Richard went white. He felt that the Spaniard had deliberately made a fool of him, and in a way that he would never have dared to do with an older man. He was intensely angry. His eyes narrowed, and he said with quiet insolence.

'I find it amazing that anyone in Your Excellency's position should be so ignorant of history.'

The Count flushed. 'Monsieur! I do not understand . . .'

'Then I will make myself plain. Ten years ago, when my country had been much weakened by three years of exhausting effort to reduce her revolted colonies in the Americas, and in addition had for a year been at death grips with the French, Spain threatened to join her enemies ; but offered to be bought off at the price of Gibraltar. His Britannic Majesty refused to cede the Rock then, so what can possibly lead Your Excellency to suppose that he would do so now?'

'Monsieur, you put a wrong interpretation on that issue. Spain has for long considered that she has a just title to the Rock, and at the time to which you refer made strong representations regarding it ; but His Most Catholic Majesty would have entered the war in any case, since his honour obliged him to do so.'

'You refer to his obligations under the Family Compact, do you not, sir?'

Florida Blanca nodded, then his eyes shifted from Richard's face. The conversation was not taking at all the line he had intended. and the last thing he wished to discuss was the implications of the Compact; but Richard swiftly followed up: his advantage.

'May I ask Your Excellency if that Treaty is still in force?'

'Certainly, Monsieur. Such friendly understandings with France have been a cardinal factor in the policy of Spain for several generations.'

Richard's tone became more genial. 'I thank Your Excellency for your frankness. More, I apologize for wasting your time by idle curiosity regarding a matter that has no concern for me.' He paused, and added quietly: 'Now I have Your Excellency's assurance that His Catholic Majesty is prepared to acknowledge those parts of North America I mentioned to you to be a portion of His Britannic Majesty's dominions.'

'I implied that, but only with certain reservations, Monsieur.'

'I cannot think that Your Excellency was serious in your mention of Gibraltar.'

'Then you were wrong, Monsieur. That is the price set by His Most Catholic Majesty on the transfer of his Sovereign rights in the North Pacific.'

Richard saw that they had reached a dead end, and he was bitterly disappointed. He felt that to take so firm a stand and ask the impossible, the Spaniard must be very confident of receiving help from France. If that was so, then the sooner Britain declared war on Spain the better. But it was still possible that this might be bluff, and that a really high tone would yet produce a decision to give Britain what she asked, rather than face a war ; so he said:

`By this demand for Gibraltar in exchange for a barren shore, to which the claim of Spain is by no means fully established, I fear Your Excellency has seen fit to trifle with me ; but excusably perhaps, through my youth and inexperience giving so poor an impression of that which I represent. Twould remind you now that behind the message I have brought lies the inflexible purpose of the greatest power in the world, and friendship with -'

`The greatest power!' exclaimed Florida Blanca haughtily. `Monsieur, you forget that you address a Spaniard; and that long before your country '

With a swift gesture Richard cut him short. `I speak of the present. No other country than my own has within living memory fought a world in arms and emerged from the conflict unbroken. Friendship with my country would secure Spain her South American Empire; by war with Britain Spain would risk everything. I beg Your Excellency to allow me to return to my master with the happy tidings that you are prepared to enter into a peaceful settlement on the basis I have had the honour to convey to you.'

The Count stubbornly shook his head. `That is impossible, without further consideration.'

`How long does Your Excellency require? Not, permit me to add, before inviting me to discuss this matter again; but to give me a definite reply.'

`How long are you prepared to give me?'

Richard knew that if he named a period of any length it would only be taken advantage of to the disadvantage of his country. If the Count meant to give way at all there was nothing whatever to prevent his doing so after an interval just sufficient to save his face. So he replied firmly

`A further forty-eight hours should be ample for Your Excellency to decide so simple a question, and I cannot go beyond it.'

Florida Blanca knew that it would be the best part of forty-eight days before he could expect a definite assurance of support from Paris, so it seemed pointless to keep this determined young man on the hook for a mere two days. He shrugged and said:

`Then I can only suggest that you should return to Mr. Pitt and tell him that the matter still has our most earnest consideration.'

Richard bowed, turned and walked towards the door. Just before he passed through it he dropped one of the doeskin gloves he was carrying on the floor. It was his last card; the Prime Minister could either appear to think he had performed the act unwittingly and send it to him with a suggestion that, after all, it might be worth their having a further talk next day, or accept it as a symbol that Mr. Pitt really did intend to go to war.

As he left the Palace the thought that he had failed in his mission filled him with distress. He wondered if he had made too little allowance for Spanish pride, and acted too precipitately. Yet, on going over his two interviews with Count Florida Blanca again in his mind, he could not believe that he had. From his first receiving Mr. Pitt's instructions he had frequently thought of the conduct of his earliest friend in the diplomatic service, Lord Malmesbury, in very similar circumstances, twenty years earlier.

His Lordship had then been Mr. James Harris and a very junior official in the British Embassy at Madrid. In the summer heats of 1770 he had been temporarily left there as Charge d'Affaires. It had come to his knowledge that the Spaniards in Buenos Aires had secretly fitted out an expedition against the Falkland Islands, captured them, and expelled the British colonists. On his own responsibility he had, instantly gone to the Spanish Prime Minister and threatened war unless the Falkland Islands were evacuated and full satisfaction for this unprovoked assault afforded. The Spaniards had swallowed their pride then and acceded to his demands before the big guns of Whitehall had even been drawn into the matter. Richard felt that his language could have been no higher than that the now famous diplomat must have used, and in his case he had done no more than carry out very definite instructions. It was simply bad luck that the Spaniards felt either full confidence in French support, or that they could afford to ignore his challenge and still gain a little time before having to burn their boats.

Nevertheless, the thought that he had suffered defeat in the first diplomatic mission entrusted to him was extremely galling. He was, moreover, very conscious that far greater issues than his own prestige were involved, for his inability to carry home a satisfactory answer now meant that war was almost inevitable.

That night he sat up very late, hoping against hope that Florida Blanca might yet send his glove back with an invitation to another audience. But no messenger came, and as he still sat on he began to think of the dreary, hideously uncomfortable journey upon which he must set out next morning back across Spain and Portugal.

It was then that the inspiration came to him. It needed more than a piece of paper to make an alliance of any value. In the event of its terms becoming operative both the countries that had signed it must take steps for active cooperation. In the present case Spain appeared ready to go to war, but France had not yet signified her willingness to do so. If by some means he could prevent France from honoring the Family Compact he would. after all, have succeeded in his mission.

He still had Mr. Pitt's Letter of Marque. He knew very well that it had been intended only as a credential to be used at the Court of Spain, but it was not addressed to anybody in particular. It simply said: *Mr. Richard Blane knows my mind upon the matter of Nootka Sound, and is commissioned by me to speak* upon it. And it was signed by Britain's Prime Minister. It could be used every bit as effectually in Paris as it could in Aranjuez. Richard knew somebody in Paris whom he thought would listen to him on his producing that letter. Somebody who still had very considerable influence, and, by causing France to refuse Spain's request for armed support, might yet prevent a war.

For greater speed he had already decided to face the horror of the Spanish inns and travel on horseback instead of in a coach. First thing next morning he arranged for horses and an interpreter. For full measure he gave Florida Blanca until after the siesta hour, but no messenger came to return his glove.

On April 26th at four o'clock in the afternoon, in a forlorn hope that he may yet save the peace of Europe, he set out for Paris.

CHAPTER TWENTY-FIVE
A LA LANTERNS

Richard reached Paris on May 13th. He had used every means in his power to expedite his journey, but even with hard riding it had taken him eight days to get from Madrid to Pamplona, then another two on mule back, skirting hair-raising precipices through the misty passes of the Pyrenees, before he reached Bayonne. After that his passage had been far swifter, although no less exhausting, as he had traveled night and day by fast post chaise.

He arrived in Paris deadbeat, but vastly cheered by two matters of the greatest importance to him. Although Don Diego's party had left Aranjuez twelve days in advance of himself he had passed it two nights before at Orleans. Tansanta had then still been alive and he had succeeded in stealing forty-eight hours' march on what he now regarded as the rival Embassy.

From Bordeaux onwards he had enquired at every principal inn for news of the travelers ahead, and at six o'clock on the evening of the 11th he had caught up with them. The four coaches that made up their cavalcade were being washed down in the yard of the *Hotel* St. Aegean, and he had learned that they intended to dine and pass the night there. A cautious reconnaissance had given him a glimpse of the party through a downstairs window, and having seen that Tansanta looked perfectly well he had driven on through the night towards Paris.

Had it not been for a breakdown that night outside Toury, which delayed him several hours, he would have been in the capital by the following evening, but as it was his post chaise did not set him down at La *Belle -toile* until the early hours of the Thursday morning. Worn out as he was he knew that he would be fit for nothing that day, so he slept through it, and got up only to have an evening meal.

After it, in order to bring himself up to date with events in France during his three months' absence, he invited his old friend Monsieur Blanchard to join him in a bottle of wine. When they had settled down in the parlor, in reply to Richard's first question the landlord replied

`Alas, Monsieur! Things here are no better than when you left us. Money and bread are scarce, and Monsieur de Lafayette seems quite incapable of keeping order. Not a day passes but there is some disturbance and people killed without the perpetrators of such crimes being brought to justice. Since the execution of the Marquis de Favras the mobs have taken openly to hanging people that they do not like.'

`DeFavras,' murmured Richard. `He was accused of being mixed up in some counterrevolutionary plot with the Comte de Provence last winter, was he not? I recall that his trial was taking place at the time I left for England.'

The Norman nodded. `Whether the King's brother was really involved I know not, but he saved himself from accusation by giving evidence against de Favras ; and under the new law that decrees the same punishment for all classes the Marquis was hanged. 'Twas the first time a nobleman has ever died by the rope, and the sight of his body dangling from a gibbet in the Place *de* Greve seems to have set a fashion for the scum of the Faubourgs to murder their victims in that way. You will know how our lamps in Paris are strung up by ropes to their posts, so that they can be lowered to be lit or put out. 'Tis easy as winking to lower the nearest lantern, detach it, and string up a man in ,its place. Two or three times a week now, when the mob catches some unfortunate whom it does not like, the cry goes up "A la *lanterne! A la lanterne!"* and before the National Guard can come to his rescue he is choking his life out at the top of a pole.'

`And what of the Royal Family?' Richard asked.

`They are still at the *Tuileries.* It is said that many plots have been made to carry them off from Paris, and each time there is a rumor of one the mob threatens to storm the Palace. The nearest they got to doing so was about a month ago. There was some shooting and a few people were killed, but the National Guard succeeded in driving off the rioters.'

`The National Assembly is, then, no nearer achieving a strong and stable Government than when I was here last?'

Monsieur Blanchard shook his head. `Nay. 'Tis if anything more uncertain of itself ; and more than ever dominated by the mobs and what passes at a Club called the Jacobins. Soon after you left us the Assembly elected the Bishop of Autun as its President. He seems a man of sense, but he is greatly hated by his own Order, and all who hold the Church in regard; particularly since his measure last November for confiscating all Church property has been seized upon as an excuse for many outrages. The intention was to sell a great part of the Church lands and fill the empty coffers of the nation with the proceeds; but the *sans culottes* put a different interpretation on it. They say they are the "nation" and that the riches of the Church now belong to them. So there have been numerous cases of mobs breaking into religious institutions to rob them of their altar plate, and any money that is to be found in their treasuries.'

Richard asked many other questions, and although no event of major importance had taken place and no great riots on a scale of those in the preceding year, it was a grim tale of the general dissolution of order and increased lawlessness that the honest Norman had to unfold. In all but name the mob were now the Extreme Left is against war, and although small it represents a considerable part of the nation ; yet by no means its most influential part. The better type of people are more patriotic, although in this case I think their patriotism misguided. They believe that France's ancient enemy is seeking to provoke a war in order that she may take advantage of our present weakness. In consequence, anti-British feeling is now very strong here ; and, out of pride, the bulk of the educated classes would not hesitate to support a war policy rather than see France suffer the least humiliation.'

'What of the Court?'

`The King, as usual, is vacillating. He sees the danger; hence his attempts to mediate and keep Spain and Britain from one another's throats, and thus eliminate all risk of our being drawn into the quarrel. On the other hand he is being hard pressed by the Extreme Right to give full support to Spain.'

'Why should the Right be so belligerent?'

De Perigord gave Richard a wily smile. 'They see in war the one hope left of restoring the monarchy to its ancient power. As I have just said, a great part of the nation, and all its most solid elements, are already spoiling for a fight. A patriotic war would naturally rally them round the throne. The Right argue that with France in danger discipline would at once be restored in the army and marine; and that with a war in progress it would require only a well organized coup d'etat to replace the National Assembly with the old firm of government.'

'Does not the Assembly see its danger?'

'The Left does, but not the Center; and the Right is now intriguing on these lines in hopes of putting an end to the present unhappy state of affairs.'

After a moment, Richard said thoughtfully: 'Even if the power of the monarchy were restored in this way, it could not long exist without granting a Liberal Constitution; and knowing you secretly to be in favour of such a regime, I am somewhat puzzled to find you opposed to the only policy that offers some hope of it.'

The Bishop shook his head. 'Nay. I have but one interest at heart: the future welfare of my country. I am convinced that we could not wage a victorious war, and that defeat would mean our final ruin. Therefore I will be no party to this suicidal gamble.'

`I see your reasoning,' Richard nodded; `and admire your decision. Since that is your view, I take it that de Mirabeau, who thinks so much on the same lines as yourself, is with you?'

'Alas, no! I would to God he were. But he is secretly advising the Court to adopt a policy that will lead to war.'

'Mon Dieu!' exclaimed Richard. `I thought him near as clear-sighted as yourself, and as strongly convinced that a Franco British alliance would prove the greatest blessing that could be granted to Europe.'

`That was his view. It is still, I think, as a long-term policy. But *he is now set upon* taking any step, however desperate, *that might* lead to a restoration of the royal authority.'

The Bishop pulled a stiff parchment from the pocket of his dressing gown, and went on: `I received this no more than half an hour before your arrival. As President it will be my duty to lay it before the National Assembly today; and 'tis certain that its publication. will cause the war fever that is now running through France to become acute. It is a letter from His Majesty in *which* he informs the Assembly that, owing to the menace, which Britain's war preparations hold for France, he has ordered fourteen ship-of-the-line to be got ready for sea. It is signed by the Foreign Secretary, de Montmorin ; but I know it to be the work of de Mirabeau.'

`This is calamitous!' muttered Richard. `Matters have already reached a far worse pass than I had even feared they might assume several weeks hence: Can naught be done to check this influence of de Mirabeau's that has now turned out to be so malign?'

De Perigord shrugged gloomily. `I know of no way to do so. He is a very juggernaut once he has the bit between his teeth. Strange and unpalatable as such an alliance may be, it seems the only people we can count on to work for the same ends as ourselves in this emergency are Barnave, Robespierre, and the other deputies of the Extreme Left.'

`But this matter of war or peace is outside the jurisdiction of the National Assembly,' Richard argued. `So, even had they a majority, they would not have the power to decide the issue. You said yourself that it still lies within the Royal Prerogative. And, frankly, that is what I had hoped. My influence is little enough, but I have some small credit with the Queen. I mean to see Her Majesty, and do my utmost to persuade her to do all she can to prevent a war. 'Twas to attempt it that I returned to Paris.'

`I would I had your youthful optimism,' said the Bishop, with his cynical little smile, `for I would wager that in this you will do nothing with that woman.' Then he added seriously

`Nevertheless, I wish you all good fortune in your efforts to save three countries from the horrors that war must bring.'

For a further hour they talked of more general matters, then Richard returned to his hackney coach and had himself. driven to the *Tuileries.* There, he paid the man off, found his way up to the Princess de Lamballe's apartment, and sent his name in by her woman. A few minutes later the Princess received him in the salon where he had had his secret interview with Madame Marie Antoinette. It was only midmorning, so the Princess had not yet completed her full toilette, and was wearing her beautiful golden hair unpowdered, in loose ringlets falling about her neck.

When they had exchanged greetings, he asked after the health of the Queen, and she replied: `Her Majesty's constitution is fortunately robust, but she shows signs of the great strain she has been under for the whole of the past year. Her only remaining joy lies in her children, and she, gives all the time she can to teaching or playing with them.'

He then asked if the Princess could arrange an audience for him on a secret matter ; and when he stressed its urgency and importance she left him to go down to the floor below by the staircase hidden in the wall of her bedroom. After about ten minutes she rejoined him, and said

`Her Majesty is now so closely watched that she has to be careful to give such audiences only at times when she is unlikely to be missed from her apartments; but she will receive you for a few moments if you will return here at six o'clock tomorrow evening.'

Having thanked her, he left the Palace by its garden entrance. Seeing a small crowd in one corner of it he strolled over to ascertain the .object of their interest. It was the little Dauphin, with Madame de Tourzel, and he was digging in his garden plot.

He was now a handsome, well grown child of five with a gay and friendly nature. His garden -was *his principal joy* and while he worked in it every day he entered into cheerful conversation with the bystanders, always giving away to them his few flowers as they became ready for picking. Madame de Tourzel told Richard that to see him at work had become one of the sights of Paris, and that when the generous child gave away his flowers he of ten apologized to the people that he could not give flowers to them all, as he would have done had he still bad his much larger garden at Versailles.

That night Richard went to the Jacobin Club, and it proved to be a hectic session. The announcement in the National Assembly, earlier in the day, that the King had ordered fourteen ship-of-the-line to be prepared for immediate service had brought sudden realization that France now really stood on the brink of war.

There were bitter denunciations of both England and Spain, but a general determination to fight, although a few speakers expressed the opinion that the King ought not to be allowed to give the word for hostilities to *begin without* first consulting the , National Assembly.

At six o'clock on the Saturday evening Richard, a little nervous at the most unorthodox step he was taking, but feeling it more than ever justified by the rapid and menacing march of events, was in the Princess de Lamballe's apartment bowing over the hand that Madame Marie Antoinette graciously extended to him.

After he had kissed it she sat down in an elbow chair and motioned him to another. `Madame,' he demurred. `You do me too much honour.'

She smiled a little sadly. `Nay, Mr. Blane. The honours we have to bestow in these days are all too few; and we have been learning fast; that friendship deserves them far more than rank. Tell me now, what led you to seek this private conversation?'

Richard produced Mr. Pitt' Letter of Marque, and handed it to her with a bow. She read it, handed it back to him, and gave him a thoughtful glance. `I was not aware that you were in the service of your Government.'

`Madame, I have been so for some time. But may it please Your Majesty to recall that being so has never deterred me from doing my utmost to be of service to you.'

`Monsieur, I recall it well, and my presence here is an earnest of the regard I have for you. I am certain that you would never say or do aught which you did not believe to be in my interest or that of the King ; so you may speak freely of all you have in mind.'

Richard then launched out on the subject he had come upon. Few people were now better acquainted with the genesis and development of the Nootka Sound dispute, and lie had the gift of marshaling facts with point and fluency. He told her frankly that he had just come from Spain, and that in spite of Count Florida Blanca's dismissal of him he was still convinced that the Spaniards would not go to war unless they felt certain that they could rely on French backing; and he assured her that Mr. Pitt's dearest wish was to preserve the peace of Europe.

At that her eyebrows lifted. `Monsieur, your Prime Minister's words and acts do not conform to what you tell me. He is now openly preparing with all speed for war.'

`Madame.' He spread out his hands. `I do give you my most solemn assurance that these preparations are being taken sole]), in answer to those known to be going forward in Spain. We have no wish for war, but cannot allow the insult done to the British flag to pass. All might yet be well, and an accommodation be reached, if only France will stand aside ; but these recent measures of His -Most Christian Majesty can serve only to encourage the Spaniards in their preparations, and if continued must result in an explosion.'

She shook her head. `His Majesty's having yesterday ordered a fleet to sea is the direct outcome of Mr. Pitt having five days ago required your Parliament to vote a million for war purposes.'

`Madame, I beg you to believe me that Mr. Pitt's measure was taken solely in accordance with his policy of showing the Spaniards that we mean business if they force us to it ; and was in no way aimed at France.'

`You seem to forget, Monsieur, that France is Spain's ally and any measure taken against one must equally be a threat to the other.'

Swiftly Richard changed his ground and strove to impress upon her how disastrous a war would prove for France in her present state ; but the Queen replied a trifle haughtily

`You would be very wrong to suppose, Monsieur, that the disturbances of the past year have in any way lessened the courage of the French people, or affected their loyalty to their country.'

Richard quickly agreed with her; then, after a moment, he took his courage in both hands and said: `I trust you will forgive me, Madame, if I remark that certain people, who hold the restoration of His Majesty's authority a matter of more paramount importance than all else, are credited with pressing a war policy upon His Majesty, in the belief that the emergencies of war would enable him to dispense with the National Assembly.'

The Queen stood up. `Monsieur,' she said coldly. `His Majesty and I are well aware of the horrors and distresses that war inflicts upon any people who engage in it. And *never* would we be guilty of plunging France into war for our own selfish interests. At this very moment the King is doing his utmost to mediate between the Courts of London and Madrid, in the hope of arranging a peaceful solution between them.'

Richard had come to his feet with the Queen; now he went down on one knee before her. `I humbly crave Your Majesty's pardon; but what hopes can be placed in such mediation while His Majesty encourages the Spaniards by such acts as ordering a fleet to sea? I implore you, Madame, to use your great influence in the interests of peace, and dissuade His Majesty from all further measures of a provocative nature.!

'Rise, Monsieur,' said the Queen. `I have listened patiently to all you have to say, and I fear that no useful purpose can be served by prolonging this conversation. You may rest assured that the King and I would *never* countenance a war unless we were forced to it; and that the preparations now going forward are no more than reasonable precautions. But we are allied to Spain, and if Spain decides to fight, France must fight too. It is unthinkable that we should do otherwise, for our honour is involved in it.'

With the bitter knowledge that he had failed, Richard bowed very low, and said quietly: `So be it, Your Majesty. I am distressed beyond words to find that I cannot count upon your help; and I can only beg that you will not think too hardly of me, should you learn that in the cause of peace I have sought other allies.'

Five minutes later he was out in the courtyard. The `other allies' to whom he had referred were the deputies of the Extreme Left. But he knew none of them except Barnave ; to them he could not possibly produce Mr. Pitt's Letter of Marque, and even if he got in touch with them he did not feel that either he or they could do very much to influence the situation. The idea was the slenderest of forlorn hopes, and he had been stung into his last words to the Queen owing only to his anger at her blindness, in refusing to see that the best hope of averting war lay in France refraining from further warlike measures.

As he stood on the steps of the court endeavoring to decide on his next move, a coach drove up. The footman jumped down from the box and opened its door. A lady got out. They were face to face. He found himself staring at Tansanta.

When he had decided in Aranjuez to come to Paris he had realized with considerable misgivings that he might meet her again there. But he could not allow that to weigh with him in the scales against the possibility of still being able to prevent a war. Paris was a large city, he had counted on securing an audience with the Queen within a week, and it had seemed then that once he had obtained her answer there would be nothing further to detain him in France; so he had felt reasonably confident that he would escape further entanglement with the lovely Condesa who had once meant so much to him. Now, Fate had brought them together yet again.

'Riché!' her glad cry rang through the court. `When did you reach Paris? How clever of you to guess that I should not waste an hour before coming to the *Tuileries But* to find you here waiting for me! Oh, *Riché,* I am overcome with joy . . . I . . .' Seizing his hands she burst into tears.

Her assumption that he had come hotfoot to Paris for the sole purpose of reuniting with her there was so transparently obvious that he had not the heart to undeceive her, and he took refuge in garbled half-truths mingled with white lies.

`I got here yesterday, thinking you must have already arrived. Today business brought me to the Palace; but I should have come here in any case, as the best place to get news of you. In that I was disappointed, and I could not imagine why you had not yet been to make your service to the Queen. I did my utmost to catch up with you, and 'tis now evident that I must have passed you on the road.'

`No matter,' she sobbed happily. `No matter; we are together again, and 'twill be easy here for us to slip away so that we may be so always.'

He swallowed hard, then muttered: 'Hush! Have a care of what you say; and control yourself, I beg. Your servants are listening.'

She shook her head. `We need take no heed of them. They are not from the Spanish Embassy, but only hired men. Diego is there, and the Lady Melissa and her father with him. But I went straight to the Carmelites. The Mother Superior is an old friend of mine, and I knew that I could count on her to give me refuge.'

`Refuge?' repeated Richard. `But why, having passed a month with your husband on the road, should you feel this sudden need of it?'

'While on the road I was safe; now I am once more in mortal danger. But I must not linger. Her Majesty is expecting me. And I cannot ask you to come to me this evening, for no visitors are' allowed in the Convent after sundown. Come to me at eleven o'clock tomorrow Morning at the Carmelites. Then we can make our plans.'

In a daze, Richard kissed her hand and watched her enter the Palace. Then he slowly turned away, walked back to *La Belle* toile, mechanically ate a solitary evening meal and went early to bed.

For long time he, lay there staring up at the ceiling. He recalled another occasion when he had lain in bed thinking about Tansanta. That had been twelve and a half months ago, at a less comfortable inn, near *Les Gobelins,* on the far side of the Seine. He was then about to set out for Florence with Madame Marie Antoinette's letter, and he had barely made the acquaintance of the dark browed Senorita d'Aranda.

How much had happened since! Then, the States General had not even met. *Lettres de cachet* were still issued for the imprisonment of people during His Majesty's pleasure; and there still existed a *Bastille* in which to confine them. The de Polignac's, the de Coignys ; their Highnesses d'Artois, de Condé, de Conti, and a host of others had still danced and gambled in the splendid salons of Versailles. The treacherous Duc d'Orléans had been the idol of the Paris mob ; and none but a few rough seamen and Red Indians even new of the existence of a place called Nootka Sound.

Richard had never then been to Avignon, Marseilles, Leghorn, Florence, Naples, Lisbon, Madrid or Aranjuez ; and he recalled speculating on whether, had Tansanta been remaining at the Court of France, and they had entered on an affaire, he would have been able to make her his mistress. He had been inclined to think it most unlikely, because he believed her to be a serious, intense girl who, when she gave herself, would do so with great passion, but would bring herself to it only with a man with whom she hoped to share a lifelong love. Now he knew.

There was nothing to stop him leaving Paris next day for England. Mr. Pitt had not sent him to France and would certainly be much annoyed with him for having gone there. He had shot his bolt with the Queen in vain, and if he stayed on to enter into some almost hopeless intrigue with the deputies of the Extreme Left his master would have more cause for anger with him than ever. It would probably wreck his career for the second and last time.

Yet he knew that he was going to stay on ; both because, having already adopted unorthodox means in the hope of being able to fulfill his mission, he would not give up the game as long as there was a card left in the pack; and because, since Tansanta now felt her danger to be so acute as to have left her husband on account of it, and life for her held no future except with him, he could not possibly abandon her.

At eleven o'clock next morning she joined him in the visitors' parlor at the Carmelite Convent. It was a bare, sparsely furnished room, the antithesis of the surroundings that any couple would have chosen to make love in ; and they did not attempt it.

After they had spent a few moments saying how happy they were to be reunited once more, Richard said: `Tell me, my love. why you have sought this retreat. Have you recently had fresh evidence of your husband's intention to poison you?'

`Nay,' she shook her head. `But circumstances have altered. Had I not pretended a sudden fit of religion during the last stages of our journey, and insisted that I must make a novena here immediately on my arrival in Paris, I^ might be dead by now.'

`I must confess to still having doubts that his intentions are so evil,' Richard told her. `For the past month I have been racked with anxiety for your safety. My ultimate reasoning led me to conclude that if Don Diego meant to rid himself of you he would do so while you were travelling, preferably far from a town, at some small inn where the odds would have been all against any serious enquiry into your death being made. Moreover, had he done so he would then have reached Paris a free man, and been able to offer himself to the Lady Melissa before any question could arise of her leaving for England. Whereas now . . .'

`Riche, you do not understand!' she cut him short. `However black any man's thoughts, he would incline to put off so terrible a deed until the last extremity. Diego believed that Lady Etheridge was willing to spend several weeks in Paris. Perhaps she would have been, but for the fact that she is now pursued by a new admirer, and he an Englishman who is pressing her to return home in his company at an early date.'

`Who is he?' asked Richard with quick interest. `And what type of man?'

'He is the Earl of St. Ermines ; and he is young, rich and handsome. We met him at Tours. He was engaged on a leisurely progress round the historic chateaux of the Loire: but he abandoned it, and joining his coach to our cavalcade accompanied us on the last stages to Paris. Each day Diego became more green with jealousy. By the time we reached the capital he was near desperate. Had I lodged with him at the Spanish Embassy, I vow that within the next few days he would have taken any gamble to rid himself of me; so that he might declare himself, rather than see Lady Etheredge leave for England with his rival.'

`I will admit that puts a very different complexion on the matter,' Richard agreed. `But, thank God, you will be safe from him here until I can make arrangements to take you away with me.'

She smiled. `There is naught for which to wait. I saw her Majesty last night, and she gave me every assurance in connection with Diego's mission that I could desire. I wrote him to that effect first thing this morning.; Maria I had to leave behind at the Embassy, but I could send money to her and instructions how to join us later. Quetzal is here with me now, as I arranged for hire to sleep in the gardener's lodge. There is at last, my dearest love, no reason left to prevent us taking the road to happiness together, tomorrow.'

`I fear there is still one,' he demurred. `Having come to Paris, I took the opportunity yesterday to raise certain questions with the Government in connection with work upon which I am engaged; so I could hardly leave now without making some attempt to complete this business satisfactorily.'

`What is this work of yours?' she asked with a frown. 'You made only the vaguest references to it in Aranjuez, so the thought of it, passed entirely from my mind until Quetzal caught us up in Madrid, and gave it as your reason for not joining us on the pretext I had suggested.'

`It is the agreement of certain navigational rights between several countries,' Richard replied quietly. `For some time past I have been asked by my Government, when travelling here and there, to settle such questions to the best of my ability.'

She shrugged. `Surely such matters are of very minor importance. Can you not take me to England without delay, and get your Government to instruct their Consul here to conclude the negotiations in your stead?'

'Seeing that I started the ball rolling myself, I fear that might be taken very ill. But I think my business will be settled one way or the other within the next few days. So we could get away by the end of the week.'

'Ah well,' she sighed. "Tis a disappointment after the happy dreams I had last night; but since we have waited for one another for so long, and you require only so short a period, I will endeavor not to show too great an impatience.'

For the better part of two hours they talked of the retired but happy life they proposed to lead in England ; then, as he was about to leave her, she asked when he would visit her again.

`In view of our projected elopement it might be unwise for us to court suspicion by my coming here too frequently,' he answered cautiously. `Let us leave it till Wednesday. I will come in the morning at ten o'clock and, with luck, by then I shall be in a position to fix a time for our departure.'

When he had left her he was glad that he had not committed himself to a series of visits. He had found their long talk in that bare, cold room a considerable strain; but he hoped and believed that matters would be very different once they could get away, as there would be the excitement of the elopement and the brighter prospect of all the new interests of their life together.

That afternoon he went to the Spanish Embassy to call upon Melissa, but she was out, so he left a message that he would wait upon her the following morning. In the evening he went again to the Jacobins, and listened for four hours to the heated speeches of the members. The immediate crisis now seemed to have become submerged in the general question whether the right to make peace or war at any time should remain in the hands of the King; and the speakers of the Extreme Left were urging that he should be deprived of the power to do so by a clause in the new Constitution.

On' the Monday morning at eleven o'clock Richard was shown up to the salon on the first floor of the Spanish Embassy. He found Melissa with her hostess, the Condesa Fern Nunez, so for a while their conversation had to remain impersonal. The war scare was naturally mentioned and the Condesa complained unhappily about the situation of the Embassy. Unlike most of the great *hotels in* Paris, which were built round a courtyard with gates that could be closed in an emergency, the Spanish Embassy had all its principal rooms facing on the street. As Richard had noticed on his arrival, there was a little group of ugly looking loiterers outside ; and the Condesa said that since the trouble had started such groups had collected each day, often increasing to large proportions whenever the situation appeared to worsen, and sometimes demonstrating in the most threatening fashion against the Embassy and its Spanish inmates.

Richard duly commiserated with her on this unpleasantness and said he hoped the crisis would soon pass; then, after they had touched upon various other matters, the Condesa, seeing that Melissa and her visitor wished to be alone, tactfully made an excuse to leave them.

The moment the door had closed behind her, Melissa burst out: `Oh, Richard, Richard! What madness has possessed you that you are come to Paris? When you did not join us with little Quetzal in Madrid I counted you saved from your own folly, and long since this happily back in England.'

'I had to come here,' he replied, `though I fear *now that I can* do little good. 'Twas work in connection with the crisis that brought me.'

`God be praised for that!' she exclaimed. `I feared that you still felt yourself committed to the Condesa Tansanta. By a merciful providence she has taken herself off to a convent, so 'tis unlikely you will meet her.'

'I have already done so. I came face to face with her on. Saturday evening at the *Tuileries,* as she was about to wait upon the Queen; and I visited her yesterday at the Carmelites.'

`What say you? Oh, Richard!' Melissa's big dark eyes filled with tears. `I would have cut off my right hand rather than that you should have fallen into the clutches of that designing woman yet again.'

'Melissa, you are unjust to her,' he retorted quickly. 'It i9 more than I could hope that you should make a real friend of anyone so intense and serious-minded ; but she is an honest, sweet natured creature, who asks nothing more than to devote her whole life to me. How can I possibly abandon her, when her own life is in such dire jeopardy that she has been forced to take refuge in a convent?'

'Stuff and nonsense!' cried Melissa angrily. `That wicked snare she laid for you concerning Don Diego's intent to poison her was fully exploded by our journey to Paris. I never did believe one word of it. Had he ever had a mind to such a crime he would have rid himself of her in his own country and house, where he would have had a good chance to conceal the manner of her death; or at some lonely inn on the road to Paris; not waited till he arrived here, where 'tis certain that a close enquiry into her sudden death would certainly result.'

`I thought that, too,' Richard agreed more mildly. `But she argues that any man would postpone so terrible an act while he still had hopes of achieving his ends by other means.'

`You infer that had I been willing to let him become my lover he would no longer have had the same motive to wish to rid himself of his wife?'

Richard nodded.

She smiled a little ruefully. 'Then, my dear, disabuse your mind of that idea. I had promised myself to remain chaste until the summer. But I felt that lest there might truly be something in this poison plot, it was little short of my duty to remove the alleged cause for it. I knew that you would never ask me to play the part of Sara Goudar for you, so I did it of my own account. I let Diego have his way with me before we left Aranjuez, and again several times on our journey.'

"Twas prodigious generous of you.'

Melissa shrugged. `Since I have taken lovers before for my `I pray you say no more on this, for it can serve only to distress us both. I think with you that her fears are groundless, but I would swear to it that she honestly believes herself to be in great danger, and things must now take their course for good or ill.' Then he promised to call on Wednesday afternoon to wish her *bon voyage,* and left her.

At the Assembly he learned that the debate on the Spanish alliance had been postponed for two days; but at the Jacobins that night the question of the King's right to enter into treaties without the consent of the nation was the prime subject of the debate.

On the previous evening Richard had asked Barnave to, introduce him to Alexander Lameth, Potion, Robespierre and several other of his colleagues of the Extreme Left; so he was now able to move round among the tables where the members sat drinking as they listened to the orators, and get in conversation with these men again.

Lameth and his brothers were renegades, for they were of gentle birth and had been brought up as proteges of the Queen, at her expense. Potion was a big, coarse, forceful man, and Robespierre a prim little lawyer from Arras. The latter was an out-and-out Republican; and of such rigid principles that on having been appointed a criminal judge, through the influence of a Bishop who was a friend of his family, he had laid down the office rather than pass a death sentence, because it was against his conscience. He had an awkward, provincial manner of speaking and was not at all popular among his colleagues; but he had gained their respect by his integrity and his uncompromising hatred of everything connected with the old order.

Richard was talking to him and Dupont, another prominent deputy of the Left, when a fattish, square faced man of about forty came up, greeted the other two as acquaintances, and asked him if they might have a word apart. Somewhat mystified, Richard left his companions and accompanied the stranger to a quiet corner under the gallery. The fat man then addressed him in English.

`You are Mr. Richard Blane, are you not?'

'I am, sir, Richard replied. `And I judge from your voice that you are a fellow countryman.'

The other bowed. `My name is Miles, sir. William Augustus Miles, at your service. Mayhap the master, whom we both have the honor to serve has mentioned me to you.'

Fearing a trap, Richard answered with a shake of his head: `I fear, sir, you have mistaken me for another. I am a traveling journalist and owe no allegiance to any particular master.'

Mr. Miles nodded sagely. `You are right in exercising caution, but you have no need to do so with myself. I bear a message to you from Lord Robert Fitzgerald.'

Richard's eyes narrowed. `Indeed, sir?'

`Yes. His lordship is much perturbed by your presence and activities in Paris. At the Sunday reception of the Diplomatic Corps the Queen had a word aside with him about your visit to her. His lordship's view is that such an unorthodox approach to the Royal Family is calculated to do the gravest harm. Moreover you have no business to be in Paris at all. I was sent here to replace you. I am instructed to bid you return to England forthwith.'

To Richard, his successor's words were a body blow. He could attach no blame to the Queen for having mentioned the audience she had given him to Lord Robert, as in showing her Mr. Pitt's Letter of Marque he had posed as an official representative of his country. He had let himself in for serious trouble, there was no doubt of that. After a moment he said in a low voice

`Kindly convey my respects to his lordship, sir, and inform him that I shall be leaving for England shortly.' Then he bowed and returned to his table.

Next day he felt more perturbed than ever by the episode. He was not responsible to Lord Robert for his acts, or under the orders of the Embassy. But it was certain now that his unsuccessful attempt to influence the Queen would be reported, and if he ignored the message he had received from Miles to return to England at once, since it came from an official source, that would gravely aggravate his offence. On further consideration he decided that his conduct would in any case determine Mr. Pitt to dispense with his services once and for all, so he might as well be hanged for a sheep as a lamb and stay on a few days longer in Paris.

But when he went to the Jacobin Club that Tuesday evening his heart was heavy as lead. He knew that short of two miracles his career as a secret agent was ended, and that next day he must make arrangements to take Tansanta to England.

The very first person he ran into on entering the Club was William Augustus Miles, who greeted him with a lift of the eyebrows and said

`After conveying Lord Robert's message to you last night, sir, I am much surprised to see you here.'

`I have private business in Paris which still requires my attention,' replied Richard coldly. `So I shall leave when I see fit, sir; and not before.'

`Oh, come!' protested Mr. Miles. `By ignoring his lordship's o: order you will only make worse the difficult situation in which you have placed yourself. On Thursday morning I am returning to England myself, to make a personal report on the situation to you-know-who. Why not come with me?'

As Richard did not immediately reply, he added patronizingly

`He has a very high opinion of my judgment; and if you return under my wing, I will do what I can to mitigate the displeasure with which 'tis certain he will receive you.'

Richard shook his head. `I thank you, sir, for the offer of your good offices. But I will account for my actions to him who gave me my orders alone, and in my own good time.'

On leaving Mr. Miles Richard sought out Barnave, and put to him the project for which he had been endeavoring to lay the groundwork during the past. few nights. He knew that if only he were given the chance to speak upon the Spanish question, he could do so with fluency and point. He had a number of things to say that had not yet been said, which he felt might strongly appeal to the deputies of the Extreme Left, and bring over to them some of their less radical colleagues in their struggle to put a check on the power of the King to declare war.

The good-looking young lawyer listened to his proposal with interest but vetoed it. *'Mon ami,'* he said. `It is true in theory that anyone who has been accepted as a member here has the right to address the meeting ; but in practice they have to get themselves a hearing. I know you as an English journalist of sound Liberal opinions, but that is not enough. You have made no contribution towards the Revolution either by writings published in France or by deeds. Your countrymen were most popular here as speakers up to a month or so ago ; but now, the very fact that you are an Englishman would damn you from the start. You would be howled down for a certainty. It might even be thought that you were a spy of Mr. Pitt's, who was endeavoring to influence us against our true interests, and you would then find yourself in grave danger of a lynching. Since you have no qualifications as a true Revolutionary, what you suggest is absolutely out of the question.'

With his last hope gone, Richard had to sit there listening to Mirabeau arguing in sonorous, well reasoned phrases that popular assemblies were subject to the same passions as Kings, and not subject to any responsibility as were Ministers ; that if one country was preparing fast for war it was madness for another, against whom those preparations were aimed, to waste weeks while hundreds of its citizens of all shades of opinion argued whether counter preparations were to be made or not; that for a country that was attacked, either itself or though its allies, to await the word of the representatives of the whole nation before drawing the sword in its own defense, was suicidal; and that in consequence it was sheer lunacy to suggest that such powers should not remain vested in the King.

At a little before noon next day Richard was hurrying towards the Spanish Embassy. A sullen, muttering crowd of some two hundred people was gathered in the streets in front of it, but he pushed his way through them and ignored the insults they shouted after him as, seeing him run up the steps of its porch, they took him for a Spaniard.

When the door was answered by a footman, he asked gruffly if Don Diego was in. On the man replying that he was not, Richard thrust the astonished servant aside, dashed up the stairs and burst into the salon.

Melissa and the Condesa Fern Nunez were sitting there. Both of them started up from their chairs at his precipitate entrance, and stared at him with startled eyes.

He was white as a sheet, breathless and trembling. After standing rigid for a moment he gasped out

'Where is he? Where is Don Diego? I must see him at once!'

`You know?' Melissa's voice came in a hoarse whisper. 'You have heard?'

He nodded. `Where is he? I tell you I must see him! Don't dare to hide him from me. I want the truth.'

`He ,is not here,' she faltered. `He has gone out. We expect him back at any moment. But Richard; I beg you control yourself. It was no fault of his. 'Twas the mob .'

With a set face he strode past her, through the french windows and out on to the balcony. As he appeared he was greeted with catcalls, hisses and insults from the crowd below.

Melissa ran -after him and clutched his arm from behind. 'Richard! Richard! Are you gone crazy to act like this? 'Tis terrible, I know. Who could guess that such an awful thing would happen; even with Paris in the state it is. But Diego is as innocent in this as myself. I implore you to come in and let me do what I can to calm your distraught mind.'

Without a word in reply he tore his arm from her grasp. He had suddenly seen Don Diego coming up the street and just entering the fringe of the crowd.

He waited for another minute, then, leaning over the ironwork of the balcony, he thrust out his arm. Pointing it at the Spaniard. he cried at the top of his voice

`Seize him! Seize him! That is Don Diego Sidonia y Ulloa! H e is the Spanish Envoy who has been sent from Spain to drag France into war! He is an intriguing aristocrat and the enemy *of* you all! With Spanish soldiers at his back he plans to rebuild the *Bastille! A la Lanterne! A la Lanterne! A la Lanterne!*

For a heartbeat the mob was surprised into complete silence. Then with a howl of hate and rage it flung itself upon the wretched man he had denounced.

'Richard!' Melissa's cry was a wail of mingled amazement, anger and horror. `Richard you are in truth gone mad! Stop them! Stop them! Oh, my God! My God!'

Thrusting her away from him, Richard kept his eyes fixed upon the terrible scene below. For a few moments Don Diego disappeared from view as his body was kicked and trampled on by the bloodthirsty *sans culottes ; then,* torn and bleeding, it was forced up again. Some of the ruffians had run to the nearest lamppost, hauled down the lamp and detached it from the rope. Next minute the rope was about Don Diego's still writhing neck. A score of hands grasped the free end and hauled upon it. The battered body was hoisted high above the crowd for all to see, and a yell of savage glee echoed down the street.

Richard loosened his sword in its scabbard, ready to fight his way, out of the Embassy if the servants attempted to prevent *his* leaving.

Melissa was still standing beside him, frozen dumb with horror. He turned his bloodshot eyes upon her, and said hoarsely

`I deeply regret this on your account. But it was an act of justice.'

Suddenly she clenched her fist. Then she struck him again and again in the face, as she screamed: `I will never forgive you *for* this I Never! Never! You beast! You brute! You swine!"

CHAPTER TWENTY-SIX
THREE KINDS OF WINE

One week later, on Wednesday the 26th of May, at a quarter -past six in the evening, Richard was at No. 10 Downing Street and in the presence of his master.

Mr. Pitt sat behind his table. It was littered with papers and, as usual, there stood on it a decanter of Port with some glasses, from one of which he was drinking. But he had not offered Richard a glass or asked him to sit down; although he was standing there tired, dusty and travel-stained, just as he had come from Dover.

The Prime Minister's thin, worn face was even graver than its wont, and when he spoke his voice held all the chill vigor and cutting scorn with which at times he crushed his opponents in the House.

'Mr. Blane. That you should have the impudence to show your face here, I find a matter for amazement. But your having done so will spare me the necessity of sending for you at some future date, to require you to return to me the Letter of Marque with which I furnished you when last we met; and to inform you that should you at any future time represent yourself as an agent of the British Crown, you will do so at your dire peril.

'Two years ago I believed you to be a young man of great promise, but my judgment was sadly at fault. You must be aware that your reports - are very far from being my only source of information regarding what takes place on the Continent; and when I last had the occasion to reprove you I spared you the full disclosure of my knowledge. For the past thirteen months I have been following your activities with ever-increasing disapproval and ever-decreasing lack of faith in your ability--or even loyalty.

'In the spring of '89 you left your post in Paris ostensibly to get into the good graces of the Queen of France. But I later learned that the prime cause of your departure was to accompany one of her Maids of Honour to Italy. There, only the intervention of the young woman's family prevented your eloping with her and thus provoking a first-class scandal.

'In the autumn you again left your post; this time without even notifying me of your intentions. You simply decamped, leaving me for a month without what I then considered a valuable source of information on events in Paris. In due course I learned that you journeyed to Naples to renew your love affair in the absence of the lady's husband.

`On your belated return you *had* nothing to report but the failure of another mission, which you say you undertook for the Queen of France. You then proceeded to involve yourself with the reactionary intriguers who surround her, and entered into a pact with that dangerous and unscrupulous apostate, Monsieur de Talleyrand Perigord. I recalled you, in order to get you out of the clutches of these most undesirable people, and offered you another mission in a field that I considered might prove more suited to you. But, in the place where I thought I could use you to advantage, you refuse to serve me.

`In March, to seek out the woman who has bedeviled you, as I am now informed, you decide to go off to Madrid; but first you make your peace with me and, when I reinstate you, give me your solemn assurance that you will place the King's, business before all else. Instead, with the object of getting your mistress to Paris, where you could pursue your intrigue with her more easily than in the rigid atmosphere of the Spanish Court, you persuade King Carlos to send her husband on a mission to France-utterly regardless of the fact that the object of that mission was to strengthen the alliance between France and Spain.

`From that point I can only attribute your acts to a lesion of the brain. It is not enough that in the Spanish affair you have betrayed your country's interests for your personal ends. You abuse my confidence in the most-shameful manner, by using the Letter of Marque I gave you in a way that you knew I never had the remotest intention of its being used. Without one tittle of authority you give yourself the pretensions of a Minister Plenipotentiary accredited to the Court of France. Then, some further aberration of the brain leads you to throw away such influence as you have acquired with the Queen of France by openly espousing the cause of the Revolutionaries.

`In defiance of my Lord Robert Fitz-Gerald's order you remain in Paris, and consort with the demagogues at the Jacobin Club. You next bring about the foul and brutal murder of your mistress' husband by the mob. Then you go to the Jacobins and proceed publicly to glorify your abominable act. You proclaim yourself the enemy of all Kings, including your own, and incite these bloodthirsty terrorists to further acts of violence.

`*Had you* committed your crime in England, justice would have seen that you hanged for it; and I warn you, should the French Government ask for your extradition to call you to account for it in Paris, I intend to give you up to them.'

As the cold, hard voice of the Prime Minister ceased, Richard gave a weary shrug, and said

`I admit many things with which you charge me, sir; upon others I am prepared to defend myself. How long is it since you had news out of France?'

Mr. Pitt frowned. `I have heard nothing since Saturday; when my agent arrived with the tale of your infamies. Owing to bad weather in the Channel no packet boat left after his until the one from which you must have landed this morning.'

`Then you will not have heard the result of the sittings of the National Assembly on the twenty-first and twenty-second.'

`No. What of them?'

`Only that another great blow has been struck against the Royal Prerogative, by the passing of a new Revolutionary measure that I inspired.'

`And you have the insolence to announce this to me as a matter of which you can be proud?'

`I do. The manner of Don Diego Sidonia y Ulloa's death is a matter that lies only between God and myself. Let it suffice that by seizing the opportunity to denounce him when I did I gained the end I had in mind. To save myself from arrest I placed myself under the protection of the Jacobin Club. It was voted that he was an enemy of the people, and that by my act I had served their cause in putting a swift end to his intrigues to drag France into war. You need not concern yourself about any request for my extradition. There will be none. No French official would dare to lay a finger on me; for in Paris I am acclaimed a national hero.

`That night I spoke in the Jacobins as has been reported to you by your ineffectual creature Miles. I spoke again the following night, and yet again the night after that. I declared myself the bitter enemy of monarchy in all its forms, and the Jacobins hung upon my words. In the matter of Nootka Sound I urged them to repudiate the Spanish alliance. I said that it was made by two effete Royal Families for their own aggrandizement, without thought of the horrors that war brings to the common people. I argued that no treaty was binding upon a nation unless it had been entered into with the full knowledge and assent of the people's representatives. I demanded that all existing treaties should be declared null and void, and that in future France should consider herself bound only by treaties made by the nation.

'What the Jacobins decide by night now becomes law in the National Assembly the following day. Mirabeau attempted to sway the Club against me, but he was howled down ; Desmoulins, Lameth, Robespierre, Dupont, Pétion, all supported me. And Mirabeau was again defeated in the debates that followed in the Assembly, by Barnave using my arguments against him.

`I have betrayed the Queen and all my better instincts. I caused a man to be done to death in a manner that will trouble my soul for years to come. I brought about the death of a woman who was very dear to me by remaining on in Paris, when I might have come away with her ten days ago. I have lost a friendship that I value more than life itself. And all this as the price of getting a hearing in the Jacobin Club. I have branded myself as a sans culottes brutal murderer from whom all decent people will shrink. But I have served you and England well.

'You can cancel your preparations in the ports and demobilize your levees. On your own word Spain will not fight alone ; so there will be no war. A year ago you asked me to devise means which might assist you to break the Family Compact. I have broken it for you. On Saturday the twenty-second, by the law of France, it was declared null and void. It is as dead as yesterday's sheep that is now mutton. More; without resorting to war, I have made possible your dream, that all Canada, from the Atlantic to the Pacific, should henceforth become a dominion of the British Crown.'

Mr. Pitt remained quite silent for a moment, then he said: `Mr. Blane. I owe you an apology. I er omitted to offer you a glass of Port.'

When Richard left No. 10 Downing Street dusk was falling. A few yards from the entrance a closed carriage was drawn up. As he walked past it a voice that he knew well called *him by* name. Turning he saw Melissa's lovely face framed in the carriage window. Beckoning to him she threw open the door. After only a second's hesitation he got in, slammed it behind him and sat down beside her. As he did so the carriage drove off.

After an awkward pause, he asked: `How comes it that you knew I had returned to London?'

`I had word from Droopy Ned,' she answered in a low voice. `As soon as Papa and I got back I asked Droopy to let me know the instant that you arrived. He sent me a message an hour ago *that you had* dropped your baggage at Amesbury House and *gone on to* Downing Street.'

Again there was a long, strained silence ; then she said with a sob: `Oh, Richard I All this past week I have been near dead of grief.'

He turned away his face. `I know how bitterly you must feel, but I beg you to spare me your reproaches. The memory of that awful scene and the manner in which I brought about his death is as much as I can bear.'

`Nay,' she replied quickly. `Fond as I was of him, it was not his death that has driven me half-crazy. 'Twas the thought of the breach between us. You are so much a part of me that I could not reconcile myself to cutting you from my life without an attempt at explanation. I had to find out if you had some shadow of justification for the awful thing you did, or if I am condemned to regard you henceforth as a monster. Why did you do it, Richard? Why?

`It is a long story,' he murmured. `But I too have been more distressed by your threat never to forgive me than all else put together. Where can we go to talk alone in comfort?'

`I am taking you to my studio on Campden Hill. I must know the truth, and whether after tonight I may ever look you in the face again without a shudder. Let us say no more till we arrive there.'

As they drove on through Hyde Park and down to Kensington village, Richard recalled the many times that they had taken the same drive together in very different circumstances. Melissa had a natural talent for painting, and Gainsborough and Reynolds had entered on a pleasant rivalry in giving such a ravishing pupil lessons, in her studio villa on Campden Hill; but she also used it as a *pent* maison, and when she felt inclined to play the wanton took her most-favored beaux there to sup with her. With a sad pang Richard thought again of the wine, the laughter and the love that had united them when he had last accompanied her there in the early hours of the morning, after a ball.

But that was long ago ; and no hideous Paris street scene centering round a battered, bloody corpse lay between them then.

When they arrived at the quiet villa, secluded among its grove of trees, Jenny, Melissa's faithful maid, who knew all her secrets, let them in. Richard had not seen Jenny in Paris and only once in Aranjuez ; so after she had bobbed him a curtsy he talked to her for a few minutes as an old friend ; and that served to relieve a little the tension between Melissa and himself . Melissa then told Jenny to bring them a bottle of Canary wine and, as the maid left them to fetch it, asked him when he had last fed.

`I have not eaten all day,' he replied ; `but am more tired than hungry. What I need most in all the world, after your forgiveness, are a hot bath and a few hours' sleep.'

She kept her eyes away from his. `The issue cannot now be altered; so I will contain my impatience yet a while that you may have both, and be the better man to justify yourself--if you can. 'Tis not yet eight o'clock. Jenny shall boil some water for you while we drink a glass of wine and you undress. You can sleep in my bed and later I will have some cold food ready for you.'

In silence they drank two glasses each of the Canary, then he had his bath and flopped into Melissa's big square bed. As its black silk sheets caressed his naked limbs he thought of the last time that he had lain there, with her burbling with laughter beside him, and wondered if he would ever again know such perfect contentment. Then he dropped asleep.

At midnight she woke him, and shortly afterwards he joined her in the lofty studio-sitting-room, one end of which was curtained off to conceal all the paraphernalia of her painting. In the other, *in front of* the fireplace, a small table was set far supper. As they sat down to it, she said.

`Tell me now, Richard, what led you to this ghastly act, that must for ever bring the awful vision of his dead body between us, unless you can once and for all dispel it.'

Melissa and Droopy were the only people from whom Richard had never concealed his secret activities, so, as they slowly ate their supper, he told her of his endeavors to break the Family Compact, then of Mr. Pitt's blasting of him that evening, and his reply.

It was the first time that they had ever eaten a meal together without laughter, and now Melissa did not even smile, as she remarked: `You are right in that you have served your country well by these extraordinary means, and risked your life in doing so; for had you not handled matters with great skill and daring the French authorities would have had you tried and executed for murder. What had the Prime Minister to say on your proving to him that you have sacrificed all else in a fanatical devotion to your duty?'

`He asked me for the Letter of Marque I carried ; struck out the words "of Nootka Sound", altered one other, initialed the alterations and handed it back to me ; so that it now reads: "Mr. *Richard Blane knows my mind on this matter, and is commissioned by me to speak upon it.""*

Melissa's unsmiling eyes widened. "Tis then transformed into an open warrant, empowering you during the course of your work to speak in his name on any subject. It shows that you have now won his complete trust in your judgment. 'Tis a remarkable achievement Richard, and I am glad for you in that.'

`I thank you.' He returned her solemn glance. "Tis even more a testimony to the greatness of his own mind, in that he has overlooked my many shortcomings and paid regard only to the final outcome of my mission. But I'll find no joy in his noble gesture to me unless I can convince you too that I played no dishonorable part.'

She continued to regard him dubiously, as she said: `In so grave an affair of State I can understand that the life of a single man could not be allowed to affect the issue; but 'twas the personal relationship you bore him, Richard, that made your crime so peculiarly horrible. Surely, if a man had to die to win your popularity with the mob, you could have played the part of blind Pate and selected a victim at random, instead of seizing on the chance to slake your hatred of the husband of your mistress?'

"Twos no calmly reasoned plan. The thought that I might achieve my country's ends over Don Diego's dead body came to me only as a flash of inspiration while we stood together on that balcony. But had I had time to make deliberate choice of a victim I greatly doubt if I could have brought myself to throw an innocent person to that pack of wolves. I had in any case come there to kill him.'

`I do not understand you, Richard.' Melissa shook her head. `Diego was as innocent as myself of the Condesa Tansanta's death. She did not even die by poison; she was butchered by those cutthroat robbers.'

`Say hired assassins, rather! Don Diego planned her murder. I am convinced of that. When I reached the Embassy, I was still too distraught to do more than imply that I knew him to be guilty, and after-after what then befell I had no opportunity for any explanation with you. Instead of mumming the part of blind Fate, as you suggest, I took the role of blindfold Justice. He raised the mob to kill her. I raised the mob to kill him.'

`What proof have you of this monstrous charge you make against him?'

Richard spread out his hands. "Tis the very lack of it that has filled me with such despondency at the thought of trying to make my case with you. I have naught to offer but the word of another person, now also dead, and that you may well consider prejudiced by hatred and suspicion of Don Diego. If you refuse to believe it there is no more that I can say. I can but vouch for the story as it was told to me, and pray that you may judge, as I did, that 'tis so circumstantial as to have the ring of truth.'

Leaning forward across the table, he went on earnestly: `In recent months there have been numerous attacks on religious institutions in Paris for the purpose of robbery ; and that excuse served for the one which was made on the night of Tuesday the eighteenth, on the Convent of the Carmelites. I had a rendezvous there with Tansanta at ten o'clock the following morning, and knew naught of it till then.

`On my arrival I found National Guard sentries posted on the broken doors, and at first they refused me admittance. But I insisted on seeing the Mother Superior, and when I declared myself a friend of Tansanta this is what she told me.

`Shortly after two in the morning they were aroused and alarmed by a battering on the door. By a previous arrangement made in case of such a q emergency she and her nuns at once gathered in the chapel; but Tansanta, being a lay visitor, did not know of it and remained in her room. The doors were burst in, but the attackers numbered less than a dozen ruffians. They despoiled the sacristy of the sacred vessels, seized all other articles of any value they could find, insulted the nuns and defiled the altar. After some twenty minutes of such excesses they left the Convent with their loot. It was only then that the Mother Superior recalled her visitor. On going to Tansanta's room she found her dead, and little Quetzal lying under her bed grievously wounded.

`The boy was still alive at the time of my visit and the Mother Superior took me to him. This is what he had to tell. He was sleeping in the gardener's lodge, hard by the main entrance to the Convent. He was awakened by the battering upon it, and getting up ran to his mistress. No sooner were the main doors stove in than he heard the rush of trampling feet along the stone corridor ; then the ruffians attacked the door of Tansanta's room. They forced it and four of them made violent entry. Tansanta had sprung from her bed, thrown a robe. about her person and was standing in the middle of the room. That gallant child had *his tomahawk in his* hand and did his best to defend her. In a moment he was struck down and they rushed upon Tansanta. Two of them seized her arms and forced her back against the wall, while the other two thrust their pikes a dozen times through her body.

`Seeing that she was dead, and hoping yet to save himself, Quetzal wriggled beneath the bed. When *they* had left the room he tried to staunch the blood that was flowing from his wound. He was still attempting to do so when the trampling of .feet came again. Peering out from under the valance, he saw a tall man, who had not been there before, and one of Tansanta's murderers. The tall man was masked, wore a cloak, and a soft-brimmed hat pulled well down over *his* face. He stood for a moment looking down at Tansanta's dead body. Then he drew a heavy bag of money from under his cloak and handed it to the leader of the *murderers with* the words: "Yes; this is the woman. Here is the price *on which* we agreed."

`Quetzal knew the tall figure, and he knew the voice. He died of his wound before I left the Convent, and with his last breath he swore to me that it was Don Diego.'

Melissa nodded. `I cannot doubt you, Richard; and I now understand. I can by inference even confirm the *truth of what you* say. That morning Diego was sent for to go to the Convent about seven o'clock. I was up when he returned, and having told me what had occurred he asked me to marry him as soon as his period of mourning was over. Then, I saw no possible connection between him and the attack on the Carmelites. I was only shocked by his flagrantly indecent haste in proposing before his wife's body was even cold. The thought of his callousness in that afterwards did much to lessen the grief I should otherwise have felt at the death of anyone with whom I had been so intimate. But now I see that his proposal to me was the confirmation of his wife's fears, and nails his motive to the mast.'

For a moment she was silent, then she resumed in a low voice

`What you have told me now reveals that I was greatly guilty towards your poor Condesa. I ridiculed her fears and sought to persuade you that she was lying in order to entrap you. Worse - it seems that I was in a large measure responsible for her death.' 'Nay,' Richard protested. `You must not *think that. The* intensity of Don Diego's passion when unsatisfied drove the poor man into morbid fits, during which he was no longer master of himself. Had he not conceived a desperate passion for you he would have done so for some other fair, just as he did in a lesser degree for Sara Goudar. You did all that lay in your power to avert a tragedy; for you gave yourself to him even while unconvinced that by your continuing to refuse him a tragedy might occur.'

She shook her head. `Dear Richard; I was more responsible than you know; but only out of love for you. I could not abide the thought of your ruining your future for her sake. I concocted a plan with Papa by which we hoped to save you. That day on which you were in Toledo he went to Manuel Godoy, and pointed out to him that General Count d'Aranda's daughter would have an influence far greater than her husband with the Queen of France; so that if the mission was to be successful 'twas of the first import that she should leave her child and go with him. Godoy was quick to see the sense *in that* and went to Queen Maria Luisa. The result was the order that ruined your plans for an elopement and sent the Condesa Tansanta to die in Paris.'

'Strap me! I might have guessed it !' he exclaimed: `I knew the way you felt, and that you were capable of taking any -measure that you thought might save me from myself.'

Her dark eyes were shining and she took his hand. `Yes, Richard. And, even could I have foreseen the terrible result of my secret intervention. I would have accepted the guilt and done the same. Your happiness means more to me than the life of any woman.'

'And yours more to me than the life of any man. I thank you, sweet; for had not matters panned out as they have my life could have been only one long tale of misery. I loved poor Tansanta desperately when we were together in Florence and Naples; but' on leaving the latter place I deliberately killed my love for her, and strive as I would afterwards, I could not revive it. She was incredibly possessive; and had I eloped with her I should have been in honor bound to stick by her for good, in fact, far more so than had she been my married spouse. 'Tis now six months since my first striving to cut her image from my heart, and I would be a liar if I did not confess to you that I am mightily relieved to have my freedom.'

For a full moment they were silent, then Melissa said: `No good can come to either them or us from arguing the matter further. I would suggest that we now regard them as other loves of ours that are past and gone ; and seek to forget their double tragedy by never referring to it again.'

`Egad, you're right!' he nodded. "Twould be hypocritical to pretend that either of our hearts is broken. Shall we, would it be too monstrous callous if we cracked another bottle of wine to seal that pact, and toast the future?'

Melissa smiled. `Since Fate has ordained that they should die and we should live, 'twould be an insult to our own protecting gods did we weep crocodile tears instead of rejoicing in our deliverance. Go get a bottle up from the cellar, m'dear. Meanwhile I'll rid me of these plaguey pinching corsets and take my ease in a chamber robe.'

Ten minutes later Richard was pouring the Champagne into tall glasses, and Melissa had installed herself comfortably in a corner of the big settee. As he carried the wine over and sat down beside her, she asked

`Now that you are so firmly re-established in Mr. Pitt's good graces, will you proceed on another mission for him at an early date?'

'Not for a time,' he replied; then added with a sudden gay excitement: `I did not tell you all his kindness to me. He was good enough to say that I had done more to deserve a Knighthood of the Bath than most men who receive it. But 'tis not possible to reward services of a secret nature in that way ; so he asked me what I would have that it was in his power by patronage to bestow. After a moment's thought I said I would like a small house of my own, if it chanced that any of the Crown properties of a moderate size were vacant. By great good fortune Thatched House Lodge in Richmond Park has recently fallen free. He has promised me a life occupation of it, and I can scarce contain my impatience to see my new home.'

`Oh Richard, how truly marvelous!' she exclaimed, her lovely face now glowing with delight. `I know it well, and 'tis the most charming spot imaginable. 'Twill not be too big for you to run, yet large enough for you to put up a few people if you wish and to entertain in. It stands on a rise with a pretty garden at its back and a view that is enchanting. The older part was once a hunting lodge of Charles I. In the garden there is still standing a large, thatched summer-house which he loved to frequent; and some twenty years ago an occupant of the place had Angelica Kaufman paint the most lovely frescoes on its ceiling.'

'Think you this large summer-house would prove suitable for a studio?'

'Why, yes!' Her eyes widened. `But have you then a mind to take up painting?'

He put his arm about her and they snuggled down together.

For the best part of half an hour they talked of Thatched House Lodge, and the, fun they might have in redecorating and furnishing it; then she said: `But Richard, all this by rights is no affair of mine. Now that you have this charming property, 'tis time that you thought seriously of marriage and settling down. You have racketed with all and sundry overlong. Even though you may continue to tumble some pretty baggage now and then during your trips upon the Continent, you should have a home that you can return to in which to find a quiet contentment.'

`Mayhap you're right,' he agreed. `I have often thought that way myself during these past two years.'

She wriggled a little closer to him, and gave a happy sigh. `I am prodigious glad you feel that way,' since I have in mind the very woman for you. 'Tis that dear Amanda Godfrey.'

`Now bless me!' he exclaimed. 'How monstrous strange you should suggest her! I like her greatly and had serious thoughts of proposing to her before Tansanta's letter took me off to Spain. Do you think she'd have me?'

`I've not a doubt of it. In her vague, lazy way she dotes upon you; and she is wise enough to recognize that marriages based only on passion are rarely lasting. My desperate need to attempt to heal the breach between us compelled me to remain in London until you arrived; but I have arranged with her to accompany me to Shambles as soon as I have seen you on your return. I have invited Charles, and with him there, for appearance's sake t thought it proper to have another woman in the house; so she has most sweetly consented to play gooseberry. Now there is naught to prevent your joining us, and what more ideal setting could you have in which to propose to her?'

Richard shook his head. `I'll think of it, but at present I can promise no more; the other matter is still too close to me. Tell me, though, of your Earl. On closer acquaintance does my lord St. Ermines come up to your first estimate of him?'

`Lud, yes ! He is a proper man, and I am certain that you will like him greatly. Yet whether to tie myself again I am still a little in doubt. Apart from Diego, who failed to rouse me and so hardly counted, I have been chaste all through the winter. Now summer is here again; the sap is rising both in the vines and it my gipsy veins, so I must soon make up my mind. It must either be marriage or another lover.'

`Let it be marriage then. From all you have told me of St. Ermines he sounds the very husband for you; and like myself 'tis over-time you gave up racketing and settled down.'

She turned her face up to his with a wicked smile. `Richard, I'll make a bargain with you. If you'll take Amanda I'll take the Earl.'

His eyes twinkled. `I am inclined to take you up on that.'

'Do, Richard, do! And why waste a day longer of your precious youth than need be? I'll give you till tomorrow morning, but no more. We'll strike our bargain then; or should you refuse I wilt strike you as a horrid, ungrateful fellow from my life.'

"Tis morning- now. It must be well after two o'clock. And since from this secret retreat of yours *tis a plaguey long walk back to Arlington Street, I must beg you a shakedown for the night.'

Dear, foolish Richard.' She put up a hand and stroked his cheek. `As though you would ever lack for a bed where I tray be. But lost know that it is all of two years and a month since thou hast kissed me? Kissed me with more ardor than a brother, is what I have in mind.'

Drawing back his encircling arm he looked down into her fair, smiling face, which mingled delight and mirth. Then for the first time in many weeks he really laughed aloud.

`Strap me, Melissa! But thou art incorrigible! Dost realize that thou hast just invited me to make love to thee tonight, and yet would have me get myself engaged to wed Amanda tomorrow?'

She made a face at him. "Twill be time enough for us to attempt to turn over new leaves when we are married. Come, sir! Am I to find that 'twas no more than an empty compliment, when half an hour back thou didst infer that my lips would always hold a magic for thee? If not, thou art monstrous ill mannered to keep a lady waiting.'

THE END
MORE ADVENTURES OF RICHARD BLANE TO FOLLOW.